Neanderthal Return

Neanderthal Return

by

Roger W. Knight

authorHOUSE

AuthorHouse™
1663 Liberty Drive
Bloomington, IN 47403
www.authorhouse.com
Phone: 833-262-8899

Published by AuthorHouse 07/30/2020

ISBN: 978-1-5850-0234-4 (sc)

About the Book

Over the years, novels exploring the interaction between Neanderthal people and Cro-Magnon people (that's us) have been popular. Two examples are Jean Auel's Clan of the Cave Bear and John Darnton's Neanderthal.

In my story, beautiful Neanderthal women visit Earth in a spaceship and knock us out of our complacency!

Background story line is this:

A truly alien species determined that their home star will soon become a red giant and burn their home planet. They searched the Galaxy for suitable planets to relocate to. They found Earth and many other suitable planets.

Needing to learn how to "terraform" a planet, they used Earth as the source planet in an experiment. They marked their base camp on Mars by carving a face on a mountain. They dragged a planet in to an orbit around Alpha Centauri where it receives the same amount of sunlight as Earth, salted its ocean and provided a moon for tides. They transplanted Earth life and built up ecosystems.

They finished the job by transplanting an intelligent species, Neanderthals.

The relocated Neanderthals developed civilization and modern technology. A terrible disaster left them desperate for our help.

Earth developed radio and came in loud and clear! Wars! Nuclear bombs! RACISM! The Nazi Holocaust! We frightened them. They recognized themselves in the televised pictures of Neanderthal skulls. It didn't help that our scientists characterized their ancestors as less intelligent. They TALKED about how we thought they couldn't speak!

But they need our help! They build the starship *Neanderthal Return* and visit the Earth Solar System.

And that's when the fun begins!

A mechanical engineer by training with experience in the aerospace industry, I'm all science and no magic. I don't let their technology be any more advanced than it has to be for the story, and it's at least theoretically possible.

My story has lots of space adventure stuff that should be appreciated by NASA astronauts and Star Trekkies. But this story should also be popular with fans of Art Bell, Jean Auel, Xena the Warrior Princess, Ancient Egypt, Plato's Atlantis, and Michael Crichton stories.

At the end of this book is an appendix titled

Creation Numbers and Units of Measure

It explains their Base Twelve number system and their weights and measures.
It makes a good reference while you are reading.

Chapter One

Every person alive on Earth today is a member of one human Race. The familiar differences in skin color, eye shape, hair, and other features are completely superficial from a biological standpoint. Only an expert, such as a police department's forensic scientist, could tell whether a skull belonged to a white, a black, or a Native American.

We really are of one Race, all of us.

But there was a time, a time lost in the mists of history, when we shared our Planet with another human Race. A Race with large brow ridges, long faces, huge brains and powerful muscles. Their skulls and jawbones are quite distinct from ours.

One such skull was first found in a limestone cave near Dusseldorf, Germany, by a little valley named Neanderthal.

I learned about this in high school and college. Because we knew racism is a bad thing, we objected to unflattering characterizations of Neanderthals. Sure they were powerfully built, both men and women. But they had large brains. They were smart. In Ice Age Europe, they had to be. But such classroom discussion was over many years ago. A lot has happened in my life since.

Marriage. Divorce. Job. Layoff.

I drove Highway 101 along the Hood Canal in the State of Washington. A friend, Len Taylor, asked me to help harvest broccoli on his farm. I accepted because I grew up and went to school with him. I came to the end of a one lane gravel road in the middle of this forest when I realized I took a wrong turn. These dirt roads come complete with chuckholes that drop your car like a linebacker sacking a quarterback! All that work rebuilding this '66 Pontiac, and then take it on this jeep trail! After checking my road map and Len's directions, I knew where I had to backtrack. 20 miles to get back to 101. 5 miles in a straight line but these roads ain't straight!

As I drove back through a clearcut planted with Christmas tree sized Douglas fir, I saw a large, uh, flying saucer? It blocked the road. Soldiers surrounded my car. I shut off my engine in response to their hand signals. Curious looking warriors. Helmets covered their faces with shiny mirror finish visors. The uniforms looked heavily padded with Kevlar or something like that.

They motioned me out of the car. I walked up to one of them. "May I pass, please?" I started out polite. "I just want to get on my way. You can have your war games, but please, let me pass." No response. "All right! Who the Hell are you guys? I gotta get through here! I'm calling my Congressman as soon as I get to a phone! You don't let me pass I'll complain to the general in charge of Fort Lewis!"

Still no response. "Are you Americans? Russians? We're not at war with anybody I know of. So what's going on here?" One of them suddenly jammed something into my rear end. It hurt! I could see that it was a syringe. The soldier pulled the needle out of my butt. "Oh shiiiiiiiiit!"

I fell to the ground, completely unable to move. One of them leaned over me. I could not see the face behind the mirror visor. I don't remember anything after that.

When I came to, I had a nasty headache. It soon went away. I looked around. I was strapped to a bed in a small room under bright lights. Two exotic looking women with heavily muscled arms were in there with me. Their hair was neat and tied into ponytails. One is a strawberry blonde and the other a brunette. Their faces looked weird but not ugly. They are white, but not like any white people I have ever seen! Their huge eyes are Asian shaped, with the upper lid folded over the tear duct. Broad noses, large eyebrows, the forehead looked short.

One of them grabbed my chin, felt it, moved my head from one side to the other. She looked into each of my ears with the thing that doctors use to look into your ears. They spoke in a language I had never heard. They left for a few minutes and came back with a bald woman. Before I could get a good look at her their hands were all over my face, feeling my chin, eyebrows, and forehead. Hands felt the back of my skull. They forced my mouth open and looked at my teeth. Spoke their observations in their language.

They let go. I shook my head and took a breath. The bald woman spoke with her colleagues. I could see her head in profile.

Then it clicked! The back of her braincase is long and ended in a kind of a point. Powerful muscles reached down from the back of her head. Ear looked normal. The top of her skull sloped down from a high point. The forehead is low and rounded, and the brow ridges are very prominent. The nose is large, broad and well formed. Below her lower lip, the chin does not stick out, but the jawbone is substantial! Muscles flexed around her temple and her brow ridges as she talked.

"Neanderthal." I said.

"Neanderthal." said the bald woman.

"Perhaps you should teach me your language." I suggested.

"Perhaps I should." she responded in perfect English.

"You speak English?"

"This is the first time I have a chance to practice with a native speaker, we have none on this ship. By listening to your radio and television broadcasts, we learned your languages."

"Ship?"

"Yes, we're on a spacecraft. We're heading back to our Planet right now."

The other two women shouted at her.

She turned back to me. "My name may be hard for you to pronounce. Lchnsda Renuxler. You may call me Lucinda. The star you call Alpha Centauri is actually two stars orbiting each other. Our Planet orbits the bigger one at a distance of 118 million miles. You use miles in the United States?"

"Yes, we do. We don't mess with kilometers."

"I was right. As you may know, we are only 4.34 light years or 25.5 trillion miles away. It takes 497 and a half days for Creation to complete an orbit, that is our year. Our name for our Planet, *Chmpashian*, translates into Creation in your language. Do you know about a 'Face Mountain' on the planet you call Mars?"

"Yes. It's in the Cydonia region. Two NASA photos of 1976 caught it. It looked like it was carved. The more recent photo of 1998 shows the Face badly eroded. NASA is now sending probes to Mars, about one every year. Pathfinder and so on. But they don't put a high priority on Face Mountain."

"That's interesting. The Old Records say Face Mountain is a dangerous place. Good thing you send unmanned probes. It was carved by an alien race, not by us or by any other humans. We believe this race still lives, several hundred light years away. Their sun is running out of hydrogen in its core. When the helium ignites, it will balloon up to become a red giant, burning their home planet. They needed a replacement planet, to duplicate the ecosystems of their home planet. They thought of colonizing Earth."

2

"Why didn't they?"

"Several hundred light years. They found some good planets orbiting good stars much closer. Before making the Big Move, they experimented and learned how to do it. They moved Creation into its present orbit and seeded it with Earth life forms."

"And they grabbed a bunch of Neanderthal people from Europe and transplanted them to Creation. These Neanderthals are your ancestors."

"Correct. You're smart. You Cro-Magnons are as intelligent as we."

"Thank you. Can you unstrap me? You can talk to me, and I'm not violent or insane."

Lucinda spoke with the other women in their language. They didn't like her telling me this stuff. She turned back to me. "I can't release you now, but I'd like to. You were indignant when we confronted you on the ground. You thought we were soldiers from Fort Lewis!" She laughed. "You Americans are so insistent on your rights!"

The women left the room, Lucinda telling me that she will be back with the Captain.

They returned a moment later with a gray haired woman. Lucinda asked me, "Is your name Neil Armstrong Peace?"

"Yes it is, you read it off the cards in my wallet?"

"Yes. You have quite a name to live up to."

"My mother's maiden name is Armstrong, My grandfather, my father's father, was Neil Peace, and I was born and named before 1969. I'm not named after the astronaut."

Lucinda smiled. She talked in her language to the other three women. I heard my name; she translated what I said. She returned to my language. "This is Captain Trviea Harsradich."

"I am honored to meet you." I said, trying to be diplomatic.

Lucinda translated my greeting. Captain Harsradich smiled and spoke. Lucinda translated. "Captain Harsradich is honored to meet you." She went on. "The blonde woman you may call 'Wilma' and the brunette you may call 'Betty'".

"Pleased to make your acquaintance." As Lucinda translated I noticed Wilma and Betty each carried weapons with the cool arrogance of police officers.

"Captain Harsradich orders your release." declared Lucinda. "I can have you locked up again. Wilma and Betty are to assist me. Betty is carrying an electric shock device. Wilma is ready with a knockout drug. Take it easy when I release you and you should be all right." Lucinda used a key to unlock the straps. "You may get up slowly."

I stood up slowly, grunting with sore muscles, my butt sore where they stabbed me. "Mind if I stretch?"

Lucinda grinned. "Go right ahead."

I stretched. "It feels good to be loose. Neil Armstrong Peace, citizen of the United States of America on the Planet Earth, I come in peace."

Lucinda translated. Captain Harsradich made a similar declaration, which Lucinda translated. "Captain Trviea Harsradich, citizen of Atlantis on the Planet Creation. I too, come in peace." Captain Harsradich spoke with a stern tone and Lucinda translated. "However, on the basis of a few scattered bones of our ancestors, you think Neanderthals are less intelligent, unable to speak, brutish. We find this insulting. We're just as human as you."

I sat down on the bed and let out a sigh. "I'm deeply sorry about this racist stereotype. You're right to be insulted. I've seen enough of you to know that you're just as human as I am. You're intelligent and most definitely female. Indeed, beautiful."

Lucinda translated and they smiled. I wasn't completely honest. Rounded off chins! Humongus brow ridges. That long bald head. Women with muscles like football players. Beautiful women are found in all human races, but I need to get used to seeing them.

"Uh, there is something else that I have to tell you." stammered Lucinda.

"What?"

"We're under orders not to make love with you during this voyage."

"What a disappointment. Okay, I'll try not to initiate any affection."

"Better not. If you do, you'll spend 25 trillion miles strapped to a narrow bed."

Wait a minute! "There's one little fact we're ignoring. I did not CONSENT to being a passenger on this ship, this is a kidnapping! I was on my way to visit a friend's farm to harvest some broccoli! Now my car is abandoned in the middle of nowhere and no one knows where I am!"

Lucinda sighed. "I understand how you feel. You think this is unethical." She translated my complaint. Captain Harsradich spoke in a quiet, official, this is policy voice.

Lucinda translated her Captain's statement. "We are under orders to bring a human being of Earth back to Creation alive, without revealing our existence. We will not refuse these orders. You were taken by surprise and without your consent. But there was no other way we could do this. We dare not reveal our existence. We know about your wars, your nuclear weapons, your occasional policies of racism, sometimes very hateful, and hey, we are those stoop walking, knuckle dragging, less intelligent, brutish Neanderthals! We will not risk revealing to 6 billion Cro-Magnons the existence of our Race and our civilization, or the location of our Planet."

I said, "You have crossed the gulf between Alpha Centauri and the Earth-Sun system. Yet you profess great fear on your part of the military capabilities of a Race of people who have only been able to build rockets to the Moon and four rocket Shuttles that fly up into low Earth orbit. I don't understand. If you don't want us to approach your Planet, you could easily prevent that from happening." Lucinda translated this and then her Captain's response.

"We can't prevent you from sending a fleet to Creation in a war of conquest. That is something I have to consider. The United States as it now exists would not mount such an effort. Your nation, the leading superpower, would defend our independence and establish friendly relations with us. But will this always be true? In the future, will the United States be the same country? Will it even be the leading country? How much further will your technology develop? How desperate will you become from your population growth? China, India, and the entire African continent have huge populations and great poverty due to the size of these populations."

Lucinda continued to translate. "We know that every nation of North and South America is the result of heavily populated Europe sending huge numbers of settlers to move in with the less numerous Native Americans. We know this happened with Australia and New Zealand. The reason for your World War was the need felt by Germany and Japan for more space. Hitler wanted the vastness of Russia for German settlement."

I responded. "What you're telling me is that you're concerned that Creation would look like a new frontier to my overcrowded Planet. That we might come in with settlers and weapons and overwhelm the Neanderthal population already there."

"That is the fear among our people. There has never been, in your numbers, more than 250 million people living on Creation."

"Yet, you sent a spacecraft across the distance to Earth. You sent a shuttle of some sort to the ground and kidnapped me. If you don't want my people knowing your existence, and you have good reasons for not revealing your existence, you've taken a considerable risk for little ol' me!"

"Yes, an army helicopter could have caught us on the ground and forced our surrender. A squadron of F-15s was a concern until we got up out of your atmosphere. Before we left your Solar System we monitored your people's reaction to your disappearance. Your missing car was found. Your farmer friend was interviewed by TV news. Your ex-wife accused you of running out on your support obligation. Search and Rescue scoured the forest for you. And there were those who claimed that you were kidnapped by a UFO!"

"Wow, a UFO report that's true! Tell me, are these other UFO's Neanderthals from Creation? Have you been making the crop circles? Was that your ship that crashed near Roswell?"

"No, they are not us. Fortunately, the UFO report in your disappearance is taken no more seriously than any other. Anyway, I'm a busy woman and I have a ship to run."

Lucinda accompanied me everywhere on the ship. I picked up some of their language. All woman crew. The ladies flirted with me. Lucinda explained that the trip each way between Earth and Creation took several months to complete. The ship flew far from gravitational fields of stars and planets and then 'warped' across the light years. They kept a safe distance monitoring our broadcasts and mapping out our military defenses. Then they came in to the Far Side of the Moon, which blocked our view of them. From there, the Shuttle was sent to low Earth orbit. They tracked me driving up the lonely gravel road on the Olympic Peninsula. They observed that I am white, they wanted somebody of European descent. They saw me reach the end of the road and turn around. They calculated the distance to nearby military facilities and took their chance. It was an incredible chance; the Bangor Submarine Base was only a few miles away, across the Hood Canal.

The Shuttle dropped through the atmosphere and landed on the road. The descent was vertical and fast, but not free fall, they didn't burn up. Metrola Mornuxler read thermometers connected to the hull and controlled the descent accordingly. They deployed themselves as soldiers in pressure suits and helmets to secure the Landing Zone. There was no response from our military. I drove right into this trap. After they captured me, we went straight up, clearing the atmosphere in 7 minutes. We went to the Far Side of the Moon to join the mother ship. Their physicians, Askelion Lamakian and Meddi Chumkun, examined me. Then the ship started for home.

In spite of Captain Harsradich's no sex order, the women combed their hair and straightened their clothes to look their best for me. They smiled at me and winked their eyes. They bumped me with their hips as they walked by. Lucinda got on their case about it and they ignored her. When it was my turn to shower, all of the crew except the physicians and Lucinda were ordered out of the area. Wilma and Betty stood guard with their weapons.

They would not give me a straight answer as to why there are no men in this crew. Sending an all woman crew to kidnap a man? The Neanderthals of Creation do not suffer from a lack of sex drive!

We were in the Viewing Lounge discussing Greek mythology and the names of our constellations. "In our sky, we call your Sun the Mother Star." Lucinda informed me.

"Because it's the star where your ancestors come from?"

"We didn't know that for most of our history. But it's quite a coincidence! It's the brightest star in what we call the Mother Constellation."

"From your Planet, our northern constellations would look much the same to you, only a bit smaller. Our Sun must be in one of them!"

"Cassiopeia. Your Sun is an extra star in the constellation Cassiopeia from our perspective. The constellation that you name for the mother in your myths, we call the Mother Constellation! And it contains the star that is the mother of every life form on Creation."

"How did your science figure all of that out?"

"That is an interesting story. There is no fossil record older than 50,000 Earth years. The geological record goes back six billion years. We can date with the uranium-lead ratio. But at

5

50,000 years ago, every species of life suddenly appears in the fossils. Everything from earthworms to pine trees to apes, to humans. We have no dinosaur fossils."

"God did create every life form on your Planet in six days and then rested on the seventh!"

"Yes, and every species of life on our Planet is identical to a species on your Planet, as they lived 50,000 years ago. We still have woolly mammoths and mastodons. It's the tropical elephants that went extinct on our Planet."

A tall blonde woman, dripping wet from the shower and completely naked, walked right in front of me. Muscular, larger than average breasts, no fat anywhere else on her body, and a beautifully shaped rear end. I was treated to a glimpse of her private parts, which looked the same as a Cro-Magnon woman's.

Lucinda shrieked at her. She blushed and said something like "Ooops! Sorry!" in their language. She slowly exited the room.

"Lucinda, why don't they take the no sex order seriously?"

Sigh. "You must understand. We've been on this ship for over a year. Some people miss sex with that much forced celibacy. Now they get the musky scent of a man. We have a keen sense of smell, perhaps keener than your Cro-Magnon sense of smell. As long as you have a penis, who cares about the shape of your head?"

"They don't fear your Captain. If they don't want to, why take the ship back? Go to Earth where they would be international celebrities. Just think! Live Neanderthals!"

"A mutiny?"

"Mutiny on the *Bounty*. It actually happened, it's not just a story. The sex drive had a lot to do with it. Fletcher Christian and his men got fed up with Captain Bligh's hard nosed rule. They dumped Bligh into a lifeboat. The *Bounty* went to Tahiti to pick up women to take as wives. They went to Pitcairn Island and lived the rest of their lives there. The people living on Pitcairn today are the descendants of those British mutineers and their Tahitian wives."

The blonde woman who streaked a few minutes before entered the room, this time fully clothed. She spoke to Lucinda. I did not get it all, but she was asking Lucinda to introduce herself to me.

"This is Helga Trvlakian." said Lucinda in English. "She can speak German."

"*Hallo*, Helga." I said. "You are a most lovely woman in the nude."

"*Danke schon.*" she responded with a smile. "*Sprechen sie Deutsche?*"

"*Nein, nein sprechen mich Deutsche.* I know a few German terms: *Furher, panzer, autobahn, Volkswagen.* But I don't speak the language."

"Then you will be happy to know that I speak English too."

"Great! I don't have to rely on Lucinda for communication! You and everyone are flirting with me. Aren't you worried about the Captain's orders?"

Helga broke up into giggles. "Captain's sure full of herself. We don't have to go home. We can go to Earth and tell your people all about Creation and how the Neanderthal Race was transplanted by the same *volk* who carved Face Mountain. Nobody will be punished for making love with an Earthman!"

"So I'm free to screw the whole crew! This trip might turn out to be better than I thought." Lucinda gave me a dirty look.

"We know you don't have AIDS, herpes, syphilis, or any other disease like that. We would have gotten rid of you and gone after another specimen. We know you are healthy. We don't know if you can make us pregnant, your sperm might not be compatible with our eggs. Twelve and nine *kecht* our years or 50,000 Earth years of separate evolution can result in separate species. But maybe we can interbreed."

They think in dozens when it comes to numbers. But I had a more important concern. "This mission is inspired by more than mere scientific curiosity. Tell me, Helga, are there no men on this ship because there are no men on Creation?"

"That's precisely the reason."

Lucinda screamed. "We're NOT authorized to tell him that!"

"Oh, come on!" responded Helga. I liked her. "He'll find out anyway. Here's the problem: About nine dozen of our years, uh, one hundred fifty of your years ago, a terrible Virus infected our people. The epidemic killed every man everywhere it hit. We tried to quarantine the infected areas but we didn't know how the Virus was transmitted. Most of the women survived, from little girls to old women. The men, from newborn infants to the very old and all ages in between, all suffered painful, terrible deaths."

Helga went on. "Our medical research determined that this Virus replicated with the Y chromosome, which exists in men, but not in women. But by that time, it was too late. In three years time, our population of, help me Lchnsda, I'm having a hard time with Earth numbers."

"We use a Base Twelve number system." Lucinda pointed out. "It's a little cumbersome to translate to your Base Ten numbers. Our population of 250 million, men and women, that is for the entire Planet Creation, was reduced to less than 80 million."

Helga started again. "Almost all of us women. We kept the few surviving men in quarantine to protect them from the Virus. We used their sperm to artificially inseminate women in our desperate attempt to preserve our Race. But soon the last of these men died. During this time, every boy fetus died in the womb, often killing the mother. We were left to raise the few girls we had without their fathers."

"Now this mission makes sense. What happens if I come into contact with this Virus upon arrival in Creation?"

"We know it can replicate with Neanderthal Y chromosomes. We don't know if it can replicate with Cro-Magnon chromosomes. One reason we have taken a single specimen of a Cro-Magnon man, you. In case the Virus can replicate with Y chromosomes, we could try the vaccine we've developed. Right now, our physicians are mapping the DNA in your Y chromosome and comparing it with what we know about Neanderthal Y chromosome, where the Virus lined up with it to replicate itself."

"If this happened 150 years ago, why haven't you all grown old and died?"

"We were desperate. We figured out a way to medically stop and reverse the aging process. The Captain lets herself look older to indicate authority. Still, the Fountain of Youth is not Immortality. We have had suicides, murders, and accidents, that sort of thing. There are now only twelve and six *beeyon*,"

"55 million of us." helped Lucinda.

"none of us are children. Lchnsda, he has a right to know."

"You know," I said, "I don't believe that I by myself can be the father of a new generation. You will need genetic diversity. Why don't you go ahead and introduce yourselves to our Planet? I know you fear being overrun, but you need a large number of men to give your Race a next generation. Announce yourselves publicly, describe the problem, and you'll have millions of volunteers."

"You're right. But first we need to find out if we can interbreed. Lchnsda, I think we should throw off the no sex rule and find out if he can make us pregnant. That way, we know by the time we get back home."

Lucinda stated her objection. "We have no facility on this ship for pregnancy or for babies."

"We can figure something out. Maybe early term abortions. Medical can examine the embryos." responded Helga.

"I have an ethical problem with that." I announced. "Deliberately creating human embryos only to deliberately destroy them?"

"Abortion is legal in most of the nations on your Planet." they both said.

"And extremely controversial because of the deliberate destruction of innocent human life. In the case of a pregnancy that results from youthful lust, or from a casual coupling of adult acquaintances, where it just will not work out, abortion solves a lot of problems. We allow abortion because when we didn't, desperate women used coathangers. They went to underground clinics. Many died or were badly injured. Legalization at least allows it to be performed properly and safely. In our society, we have to allow for honest differences of opinion as to morality, and we have to make these decisions for practical reasons. But here, we don't have that desperate situation."

"The situation on our Planet is what I would call desperate. Sure, we can keep you celibate until we get there and then try to make pregnancies where we can care for the children. But if we find out that your sperm doesn't work, this trip will be for nothing. If it will make you feel better, the abortions will take place before the embryos develop consciousness. You will, if you wish, be allowed to participate in the examination of the embryos. If there are any problems, we need to find out now!"

Lucinda had another thought. "Actually, sex is not needed for Medical to determine the compatibility of Cro-Magnon sperm and Neanderthal eggs. He can supply us with a sperm sample, and Medical can extract a few eggs and observe what happens under the microscope."

"Lucinda, you are a killjoy!" declared a disappointed Helga. "Yes, obviously Medical has to perform the analysis that you suggest. But there is only one way to find out if the embryos thus formed will implant themselves in our wombs."

Lucinda was still the Morality Police. "Sure, Medical can place an embryo into a womb to see if it implants. Then an abortion can be performed to avoid a pregnancy during the trip home. The other embryos can be frozen and used on Creation to help create our next generation. No need to violate the No Sex Order."

"This is all fascinating," I interjected, "but there is only one way to get a sperm sample out of me." A man can't live by bread alone.

Medically stopping the aging process in Neanderthal women caused them to cease menstruation, but without the hot flashes of menopause. It is more like what girls experience before puberty. But without menstruation, no pregnancy. Fortunately, they know how to restart menstruation. In the human female, meiosis, the process by which eggs are created, occurs when she is a fetus, before she is born. She is born with all of the eggs she will ever have. They are enough, most of them are unused when menopause happens. Later pregnancies sometimes have problems due to the age of the gametes. These Neanderthal women and their eggs are 150 to 200 years old!

With a man, it is very simple. Meiosis starts in puberty and goes on through adult life. The sperm cells are never more than a few days old.

After Medical restarted ovulation in some of the crew, they came to me for a sperm sample. I refused. I decided not to trade the family cow for a handful of beans.

Chapter Two

I found myself strapped to the bed in the little room. Lucinda furiously tried to extract sperm. The dominatrix theme does not work if the man is not submitting voluntarily. "Lucinda, you're hurting me."

"Good! I hope you're in pain!"

"It's been 150 years since you've had men around. You have no idea how to treat one. Get your hands off my privates!"

She complied and stuffed my manhood back under my clothes. "We can kill you and get another man!"

"That would use up the fuel it takes to get from here back to the Far Side of the Moon. And then send the Shuttle down through the Earth atmosphere to collect another man. And then come back. The more time you spend mucking around this Solar System, the greater the chance you are discovered."

"Which is not your problem if we dispose of you!"

"So be it. But you tell your Captain Trivial Horseradish,"

"Trviea Harsradich!"

"Whatever. You tell her to look at it from the point of view of the President of the United States. You come into our system uninvited. That's fine, we understand exploration. Then you drop a shuttlecraft through our atmosphere to kidnap an American citizen! You don't announce yourselves. You don't request permission to land. You sneak in! In our eyes what you've done constitutes an Act of War!"

"We could always get a man who would be happy to give us his sperm."

"If you can find one who is that easy and who doesn't have AIDS, herpes, or something like that."

Lucinda threw up her hands and stormed out of the room.

"He actually threatened war between Earth and Creation?" asked an amazed Captain Harsradich in their Atlantean language.

"What he said was that landing on Earth and kidnapping him is an Act of War." responded Lucinda.

Sigh. "It is that. Angry at being kidnapped. He believes his sperm is something with which he can bargain. Perhaps we can stop his aging process."

"We could use his sperm, we were successful in our experiments with bonobos and chimpanzees."

"If we can do with humans what we did with apes. We can use that technique to artificially inseminate the twelve and six *beeyon* women." *Beeyon* is Atlantean for twelve to the sixth power, which is 2,985,984 in Base Ten.

"Not all at once. But we can inseminate several *beeyon* women per year and raise a new generation of genetically pure Neanderthals of all ages, thereby saving our Race."

"The alternative is to invite a few dozen *kecht* Cro-Magnon men from Earth and assign each of them a *hekt* women to make pregnant." *Kecht* is Atlantean for twelve cubed, or 1728, *hekt* is Atlantean for 144. "The result will be half-breeds. When Earth develops spacecraft capable of translocating from one solar system to another and puts them into mass production,"

"We will be overwhelmed by settlers, unable to stop them, and the Neanderthal Race will be absorbed.   That's what happened to the Neanderthals of Europe after our ancestors were transplanted to Creation."

"What is all that noise in the corridor?" The door was suddenly kicked open.

Helga and several other women burst into my room. "Neil, are you all right?"

"Yeah, I'm fine. What's going on?"

Helga unlocked the straps and released me. "Come on Neil, get off that bunk!"

I got off the bed and to my astonishment Lucinda was led in with a GUN, of all things, muzzle touching her head! It looked like a policeman's .38 special. Can the hull withstand the impact of a bullet?

They forced Lucinda on to the bed and locked her in the restraints. Only after she was secured did they withdraw the weapon. "Helga," I asked, "I take it this is a mutiny?"

"That's about the size of it." she responded with an idiom she could only learn from our radio and television broadcasts. "We're locking Captain Trviea up in the next room. Wilma and Betty are locked in cages."

"Why are you doing this?"

"They've gone stark raving mad! This whole mission is insane! The ship is secure. Let's go to Conference Room One to discuss this." They showed me the Captain strapped to her bunk in the next room. They showed me Wilma and Betty, standing in cages, ankles and wrists strapped.

In the conference room I found the entire crew minus the four prisoners and the ship's pilot. The others closely watched one of them, Sorby Mishlakian.

Helga spoke to me and translated for the other women. "Neil Armstrong Peace, we owe you an apology. We're sorry we kidnapped you. We're sorry we violated your nation's sovereignty. We're sorry we committed an Act of War."

"The last thing any of us want is a war between Earth and Creation. I accept your apology. It's certainly been more interesting than harvesting broccoli. Len Taylor's a good guy, he really is. He likes the independence of owning his farm and selling his crops."

"Farming is the most honest work there is. If you want, we'll take you back and deliver you to Len Taylor's broccoli farm."

"Len should have his broccoli harvested by now. I want to go back to Earth, but while we're there, we should introduce ourselves to the Planet."

"Let 'em know we exist?"

"Yeah. Earth will find out about Creation, sooner or later. Alpha Centauri is intriguing because it's close, each star a lot like our Sun. You may be practicing some kind of radio silence but signals will get loose that we can capture with our powerful radio telescopes. Even with the latest Global Surveyor photo, Face Mountain on Mars captures the imagination."

"What would be the advantages of introducing ourselves to Earth?"

"It would certainly kick our Planet out of its complacency. Sure, we imagine that there may be life evolving on planets orbiting other stars, but they're so far away and it's all so hypothetical. Never mind Face Mountain. It would sure be a kick in the pants to find out that there is such a life form as close as Alpha Centauri, and that they are HUMANS!" LOVE this idea! "Right now, the political leadership and public opinion in the United States and the other major nations would favor your cause. Racism is now socially unacceptable. How wonderful to find out that the Neanderthal Race lives! Highly advanced human beings who built a spacecraft that made the jump from one star system to another. We haven't done that. We will after we learn that such a thing is possible." About time!

"Like with nuclear weapons. Once the United States built one and used it to end a war, other nations built them. All they needed to know was that it is possible."

"You know a lot about nuclear physics. How stars work. How to date rocks and fossils from the decay of radioisotopes. You Neanderthals don't by any chance have nuclear weapons?"

"I, uh, ooooohh,"

"Yep, I was right. You've built and tested nuclear explosives. Are there any such weapons on board this ship?"

Sigh. "There are no nuclear weapons on board this ship. Trviea wanted to carry a few missiles with warheads. At first, such were authorized so long as they were not made to survive reentry in atmosphere and be a threat to Earth cities. But the electromagnetic pulse of an explosion would damage electrical things on the surface of the Planet. That would be an Act of War. It was decided that we carry no weapons except a few hand held guns and rifles. If attacked we are to run for it. Stealth, speed, and as a last resort, communication, are to be our only defenses. We're not stupid enough to want a war with over an *enbeeyon*, eh, 6 billion Cro-Magnons. Better to be captured or destroyed than to take the chance of committing a hostile act." *Enbeeyon* is Atlantean for twelve to the ninth power, it is 5,159,780,352.

"That's good reasoning."

"Trviea ordered the sneaky invasion and your capture. She didn't think your powerful governments would care about one low ranking person. But then we analyzed the reaction to your disappearance. You refused an order to provide a sperm sample, defiant in the face of death. You called your kidnapping an Act of War, which it is. We needed to end this course of action. I am duly authorized, by orders known to the Captain, to mutiny if there is a possibility, even a remote possibility, of starting a war with Earth."

"How did you determine your origins and our existence?"

"There are no fossils on Creation older than fifty thousand Earth years. We call our Planet Creation because it was created. The geologic record goes back six billion Earth years. But there are no sedimentary rocks older than 50,000 years. The oceans were frozen before that. It was as if our sun suddenly warmed up or our Planet was in an orbit much further out. Many theories were proposed to explain this. About 350 Earth years ago, an expedition led by Lamoan Reducker found the place we call the Old Records in the high central desert of the Opposite Continent. This continent is located on the opposite side of the Planet from our home continent, Atlantis. Numerous legends warned of the dangers of Opposite, some of Lamoan's men were killed. At the site they found ALIENS, not humans, a few of their dead, sterilized of bacteria and viruses. In addition to the bodies, they left an extensive written record of their activities. They used a type of paper designed to last forever. Lamoan and his men learned to read this alien language. Looking for gold and riches, he found something far more valuable."

"Like finding the second copy of the Alexandria Library tucked away in a safe place in the Egyptian desert." I said.

"This was better than that. The alien's home star will blow up into a red giant and burn their planet. They needed a replacement planet to move to, needed to learn how to do it. They invented a spacecraft that can jump from one solar system to another. They explored many star systems. They found Earth, with oceans and clouds, just like their own planet. They set up a base camp on Mars and built laboratories to experiment with Earth life. When they traveled to the Earth surface to catalog its life forms, they found a species as intelligent as them. We humans then lived in huts, used stone and wood tools, and spoke languages. They had an ideal donor planet for transplanting an ecosystem, one that included an intelligent species. Our star is nearby, but Creation was in an orbit too far from our sun. The aliens moved our Planet into its present orbit, almost a perfect circle, 497 and a half days for one year. They tilted Creation's axis

11

to give us seasons and set the rotation at the same 24 hours as Earth. They salted the Creation ocean after it melted. To give us tides, they brought our Moon into orbit around Creation."

"Wow."

"They waited a few years for the creationquakes to settle down. On Mars, samples of Earth life forms were studied in their laboratories. They figured out how to transplant these life forms to Creation and build up Earthlike ecosystems. When they had the ecosystems formed and the climates stabilized, it was time to transplant the humans. And that was the special part. Animal species can be transplanted in the form of eggs and sperm, small, easy to carry. This is how we have large animals like mammoths and whales. Animals can be raised without a mother and released into the wild to survive and reproduce on their own. But human babies and children need the care provided by human adults. A successful transplant required entire communities of humans. They chose the Neanderthal Race then living in Europe."

"Do you know why they chose Neanderthals?"

"We're tough. More muscle and bone. We were living in a cold climate, thriving under adverse conditions. We were as smart as any humans then alive, protective of each other and our children, working together to survive. They believed we were best suited for transplantation to Creation. They kidnapped half of the Neanderthal population of Europe, and released us to survive on Creation. Here we are."

"Congratulations." I quietly said in awe. "The name of your home continent on Creation, Atlantis, is the same as the name Plato gave his Lost City."

"Atlantis was the name we called our home in Europe. When your Ice Age ended, the oceans rose, submerging our old coastal villages. Atlantis may have been the name of a coastal city still existing at that time. It is the name we give to the land to which we were taken."

"We really need to go back to Earth. Us Cro-Magnons have as much right to know all of this as you do."

"We will discuss this among ourselves. Then we will vote on it."

"Fair enough."

I left the conference room to let them talk it over. They put me at a computer station where I could call up files on Creation history, culture, the Planet, everything. It was all in their language. But the maps of the surface of the Planet, the photographs of animals and famous people, and illustrations of events, were nevertheless fascinating. They brought me a dish of fresh vegetables and goat meat. With the meal was a glass of fruit juice.

I pondered the situation. The whole thing could be a ruse. What if Captain Bligh ordered Fletcher Christian to stage a mutiny to trick the Tahitians?

These girls had a problem. I was angry at being kidnapped. Now I am free and they are taking me home. Friendly Neanderthal women would want to spend time with me, to teach me their language. I am now happy, enjoying myself. And in spite of not having any men for 150 years, they know how to flirt; they know how to seduce. That part of a woman's character is instinct. They know how to get a sample of my sperm.

I resolved that they were not going to have it until Earth knew exactly where I was, giving me some LIFE insurance.

I pondered a few other things too. How much of this story of theirs do I believe? The best lies contain grains of truth. They are Neanderthals, that much is true. How did their ancestors wind up 4 light years away? Every woman on this ship is white, their skin the same color as Earthlings of European descent. With all of them, the upper eyelid is folded over the tear duct, like the Asian people. Their hair is all of the different colors seen on white Earthlings.

Other races of Neanderthal are shown in the computer pictures. Some are as black as

Earthlings of African descent. Some have straight black hair, and some have wavy hair. Some have thick lips and light brown skin. Some do not have the upper eyelid folded over their tear ducts.

One thing for sure: Earth people, ALL Earth people living today are Cro-Magnons. NONE are Neanderthal. How can we tell? Feel your chin. Feel your lower teeth. Feel the root of your teeth. Then feel the SHELF of bone jutting out from below your teeth to form the chin. This is called the mental eminence. Neanderthals do not have it. All modern Earth humans have it. The brain is moved forward. The forehead is high. There are brow ridges, but they are not prominent. The back of the head is short and round. This is true for all modern Earth people. Of all races. It is not remarkable that there is some variation in skin color and hair among the Earth humans and that these variations are genetic. What is remarkable is that in basic bone structure there is so little racial difference.

All of the Creation people in the photographs are Neanderthals, with the long braincase and prominent brow ridges. While some are thin and tall, all have the heavier bone structure and carry more muscle. Our football players and bodybuilders have to train long and hard to approach the muscle mass that Neanderthals just grow.

The terraforming of Creation is a fact. The life forms in the photographs are Earth species. They have pet cats and dogs, same species as the Earth cats and dogs. They domesticated bison for meat. Their milk cows are domesticated aurochs, same as ours. Some Creation cultures use water buffalo, also bred from aurochs. They ride horses. Their tropical elephant went extinct about 1728 of their years before. They still have mastodons and woolly mammoths. Marvelous photographs. They have woolly rhinoceroses!

Creation has all of the species of sea life we find on Earth. They used to hunt whales for food and oil. But now they ranch minke whales, confining them in a fjord with a net. Feed them to get them used to human presence. Then selectively harvest them. They catch them live and take them to a slaughterhouse in a truck. The whales in the water have no knowledge of any killing. Plenty of whalemeat and other whale products without depleting the resource.

Atlantean language is represented by an alphabet, each letter representing a sound. I count 30 different letters on the keyboard. Atlantean is one of many languages spoken on Creation.

They have a zero. It is represented by a dot, just like in Arab nations. Numbers zero through eleven are represented by single digits. Twelve is represented by their symbol for one followed by the zero dot. 144 is represented by a one and two zero dots. And so on for the powers of twelve. A Creation Neanderthal counts five fingers, and counts her hand as six. She counts seven through eleven with the fingers of her other hand and counts the hand as twelve. They use feet and inches! Their measuring system is human factors based, just like pre-Metric measures on Earth.

Helga startled me with a tap on my shoulder. "Oh, pardon me!"

"No problem." I replied.

"How are you doing?"

About half of my food had not been eaten. "This database is mesmerizing. How come none of these darker skinned Neanderthals are on this ship?"

"Our Race settled the continents and islands of our Planet just as your Race had done on yours. The people in the tropical climates evolved darker skin and other hot weather features. We have not had movements of large numbers of people in our recent history. No slave trade. As an American you're probably accustomed to seeing Native Americans, blacks, whites, and people of Asian descent, all on the same cross-town bus. We do not experience that on Creation."

She has extensive knowledge of Earth. "The remixing of human genetic material that has always occurred on your Planet, at an accelerated rate since Columbus, guarantees that the Cro-Magnon Race will not diverge into separate species. We can interbreed with the darker skinned Neanderthals, at least when we had men. But we did not interbreed as much as you have. We had a black Neanderthal woman named Harliven from the tropical continent of Graciana scheduled to travel with us. But she was hurt in an accident and could not join our crew."

"I hope she got better."

"We were told that she recovered before we went beyond communication range with Creation."

"I take it all of your crew is from the continent Atlantis?"

"Yes. Almost everyone in Atlantis is white. But we have plenty of people who visit from the other continents. I don't want you to think that there is any racism or discrimination going on."

"I would hope not. It's not a good mental illness to have infecting your society."

"Must not be. We have so far avoided it."

"Trviea is afraid of us Cro-Magnons. That type of fear is what Hitler exploited. It's what made the whites in the southern United States keep down the black folk. It's what made an Army general declare that the only good Indian is a dead Indian."

"That's one of the reasons for our mutiny. Trviea wanted to steal your sperm and prevent Earth from knowing about us. She and many like her fear the Cro-Magnon." She gave me a broad smile to reassure me. "The crew has voted. We need you to advise us on how to do this. I mean, we've never asked to speak to your President before."

Oh yeah! I accompanied Helga back into the conference room. Many smiles and some fear and trepidation. "You all voted to make contact with Earth?" Helga translated and they all nodded yes. All right! "Point the propulsion toward Earth and light up the sky! Perform some maneuvers to prove we are in a ship under power. THAT'll get their attention!"

"What do you mean?" Helga demanded to know.

"This ship is powered by a fusion reactor in a magnetic bottle. Supplies our heat and electricity. I don't know how you're using the fusion energy to propel the ship. But I do know that you have one end of the reactor compartment open to space to exhaust the waste heat as visible light. Heavy shielding on this side to protect us biological humans. There are batteries and fuel cells for when the reactor is down. You're lucky we Earthlings don't yet have an efficient neutrino detector, we would've spotted you coming long ago. You've kept this pointed away from Earth because it would show up as a bright light in the sky."

Helga just looked stunned. "You're an engineer, right?"

"Right. I can figure out some of these things by just looking."

"Okay, how do we warp from here to Creation?"

"Maybe you don't. Our *Star Trek* broadcasts tell you that our science fiction invented the concept of warping to get around Einstein's theory that you can't go faster than the speed of light. You assume I watch these shows. You tell me you use 'warp drive' because that is what I expect. But what's convenient for the TV scriptwriter isn't always possible for the engineer in real life. Since you ladies claim to have medically stopped the aging process, you could come over here on impulse alone. No 'warp drive'. That reactor pushing you all the way. It would take you ten, twenty, maybe thirty years or more, but that is one way of doing it for something as important as obtaining sperm to give your Race a next generation."

"We did make a 'jump' from our Solar System to your Solar System. 'Warp' is not a good word to describe it. You've correctly deduced the fusion reactor and the light energy exhaust."

"That light exhaust could make a nasty weapon against somebody following too close. One other possibility has occurred to me: If you have not been able to medically stop your aging process, just a story you made up for my benefit, then the scenario looks like this: The plague occurred perhaps ten years ago. As soon as your last man died, you started planning this mission. You haven't much time. A woman may live seventy years on average, but she goes through menopause much sooner. You need to start pregnancies right now! Without children, your Race will die off. Your mutiny may be motivated by the belief that Captain Trviea was too slow and cautious. By announcing yourselves publicly, you get as many men coming voluntarily as your ship can carry. All without a war with Earth. Back to Creation you go with a valuable cargo of sperm donors."

"Excellent guess. But we stopped the aging process by medical means. That bought us time. We hit on it while trying to figure out how to clone ourselves, how to reproduce without men, how to generate testicles and sperm cells. We're not able to do these other things. Having thus bought ourselves time we continued all manner of scientific pursuits, engineering endeavors, and of course, space exploration. About three dozen Creation years ago we built the first truly powerful radio telescope. When we pointed it at the nearest star to our system, Planet Earth almost outshone the Sun in the radio spectrum. When we were able to resolve the signals into sound and pictures, we saw everything! We recognized humans, but with flat faces! We recognized familiar species of plants and animals. The story in the Old Records confirmed! Your broadcasts informed us of your wars and conflicts, your protests, peace movements, technological progress, and the general level of science and technology."

"Frightening, wasn't it?"

"Yeah, but we've had our wars and disputes. We can't say we're better than you. But you have both men and women, and you are a closely related human species. Can we interbreed? Can your men give us a next generation? We watched your science shows on human origins. We recognized ourselves in the Neanderthal skulls that were shown. You ascertained that the Cro-Magnon skull is similar to modern Earth humans. But the Neanderthal was either a different race or even a different species. The rotten things said about our ancestors upset us. But we also saw that not everyone had that view."

"All of the old stereotypes will go out the door once people have a chance to meet you. You are very fine specimens of living Neanderthals."

"Thank you. You're right. Earth and Creation need to be introduced to each other. And we need to be honest with each other."

The pilot, Pidonita Hmlakian, came into the room. She said something to Helga in Atlantean. Helga told me in English. "Pidonita has put us on a course for the Earth-Moon system. About halfway there, we will be moving fast, too fast to go into orbit. We will turn tail and point our light exhaust toward Earth. With the light directed in a nice tight cone, your people will see a new blue light in their sky."

"That should get people's attention!" I laughed with anticipation.

"Yeah, it will. We will need your help and advice. This is your idea. You are the Earthman around here. We need you to teach every girl English when she can be spared from duty. We can get started right away in this conference room."

Chapter Three

Angela Peace sat with some of her neighbors outside her apartment in Auburn, Washington. With the kids in bed they relaxed with hot drinks and conversation. It was eleven thirty in the cool evening of November 10, the stars were out and there were no clouds. "I wonder what that blue light is?" asked one of them. Orion was to the southeast, rising with the turn of the Earth. To the right of the bright star Rigel was a clearly visible blue light. It was not visibly moving. "Maybe it's the UFO bringing your ex back."

Angela let out a sudden cynical laugh. "Right. He's either a deadbeat dad who's run out or a pile of bones rotting in the forest. Support Enforcement ain't looking too hard for him. By hooking up with those father's rights Antipeonage Act guys he's got the gov'ment lawyers spooked. Good thing *Phenomena* offered all that money. I know I looked like a fool on the air, but can't say no to the dough!"

University professors and people from NASA, the Naval Observatory, Department of Energy, Jet Propulsion Laboratory, and Lawrence Livermore Laboratory filed into the Oval Office at 10:00 p.m. November 12. General Morton Fairchild represented the Air Force and the Pentagon. The President began the meeting. "Welcome gentlemen. Thank you all for coming tonight. What the Hell is this Blue Light Special, and why does it demand my urgent attention at this time?"

"Mr. President, it's our consensus that we're looking at a spacecraft under power."

"Are you sure?"

"Everyone is sure. It's not visible to the satellites orbiting Jupiter and Mars; the light is pointed at us. It's now shining with a brightness magnitude of 2.0. We parallax a distance of 543 million miles from different spots on Earth and from the Hubble Telescope. Every astronomical observatory on Earth has done this, which is why we have the screaming headlines and television coverage. We're plotting its location every minute and measuring the Doppler shift. Right now, it's traveling at 1100 miles per second."

"Miles per second." The President opposed Metric conversion during his campaign, he signed the Traditional Weights and Measures Restoration Act a week after his inauguration. People who attend meetings with him are advised to convert their numbers into English units.

"Eleven hundred,"

"Miles per second. It IS coming at us?"

"Yes. It's heading for the spot where Earth will be in 11 days, moving in a straight line. It's decelerating at about 6 feet per second squared."

"How do you think it's powered?"

The fusion research scientist answered, "The light is apparently being generated by plasma at 20,000 Fahrenheit, the same as the star Rigel. There are strong spectral lines for hydrogen, helium, oxygen, boron, and cadmium. It's a fusion reactor, a plasma ball, we don't know how big. 10 to 20 feet of hydrogen and oxygen plasma, depending on how dense, can moderate the fast neutrons from fusion. Then a layer of boron and cadmium plasma can absorb 'em. We see faint spectral lines for lithium, what boron 10 becomes when it absorbs a neutron."

"Just like the radiation shields in our nuclear plants."

"Right. The Doppler shift of the spectral lines gives us the speed they're coming toward us. We cross check that by plotting the object's position each minute with the telescope parallax.

Two days ago, when we first noticed this object, already shining at 2.57 magnitude, it was traveling at 1300 miles per second. With this deceleration, they should arrive and be able to go into orbit around Earth in 11 days."

"They."

"They. It could be a robot, or it can have a live crew."

"The light from this fusion reactor is shining in one direction." observed the President. "You NASA guys told me solar sails work because reflecting the light of the Sun generates a small force on every square foot. Is that how this ship is propelled?"

"Solar sails were considered because they use energy that's already there, free for the taking." answered NASA. "But it's a damn inefficient way of using energy from a ship's engine. The formula for thrust from reflected light is $F=2P/c$, half that for emitted light, P divided by c. P is the power of the light, perhaps in foot-pounds per second, c is the speed of light, in feet per second."

"186,000 times 5280,"

"Yes. 983 million, almost a billion feet per second. For each foot-pound per second of light power, you get a billionth of a pound of thrust. One billion divided by 550 is how much horsepower you have to have just to get one pound of thrust."

"Even with a fusion reactor, you'd have to burn a Hell of a lot of hydrogen to generate the thrust necessary for space travel." laughed the fusion scientist. "They may be getting a little extra thrust from emitting the light, but I strongly suspect that it's an exhaust for waste heat."

"Waste heat! At 20,000 degrees Fahrenheit?"

"Undoubtedly they tap some of that for heat and electricity. But you only need so much heat and electricity on a spaceship. In any thermodynamic system, some of the energy is converted to work; the rest is waste heat. However they're using their fusion energy to propel the ship, they certainly have a lot of heat energy left over they can't use. So they exhaust it to space as visible light."

"I take it from this discussion," interrupted the President, "that while we can see the light, we know its magnitude and distance, we cannot estimate the ship's mass or size, or total energy use."

"That's right, Mr. President. We cannot even determine the total power of the light emission. We only know that magnitude 2.0 is a light energy intensity of 4 times 10 to the minus 13 BTU's per second per square foot where we're receiving it. We only know that this energy is concentrated in a cone of less than ten degrees, perhaps less than one degree."

"What does that mean?"

"If it's less than one degree, then they've got damn good technology. They don't need to do that; they may be deliberately getting our attention. The tighter the cone, the less area this energy is spread over, the lower our estimate of total energy. But if it's a wide cone, that's a LOT of energy to be shining at 2.0 magnitude at this distance. It could be a HUGE ship!"

"Marvelous."

"If they can open up one end of that magnetic bottle, the beam could make a nasty weapon. No telling what other weapons they have."

"Who are these guys?"

"Don't know. They could be from Tau Ceti, Epsilon Eridani, Alpha Centauri, or anywhere! We're attempting radio communication with a hailing message."

"We have to make an announcement to the public." decided the President. "If we act like we're in denial, we'll look like idiots. In the meantime get in touch with the Russians, Chinese, and NATO. We need to put our military forces on alert. We go to DEFCON 3."

My students taught me Atlantean as I taught them English. I concentrated on the spoken language because I anticipated voice radio contact before anything else. I learned Base Twelve math as I taught them Base Ten. I learned about *kepfats* and *dollons* while I taught them the English and Metric Systems of measure. It was an incredible experience working with these women: the engineers, mechanics, electricians, and computer software writers needed to run and repair, in flight, an interstellar spacecraft. Brilliant, genius level intelligence. I learned their names: Contrviea Tiknika, Metrola Mornuxler, Nesla Teslakian, and so on.

Helga called me away from language class. Andemona Chmlakian led me to the Switching Room, the radio shack that provides communication services for the ship.

"Oh, glad you have come, Neil! Listen to this!" Helga pressed a button.

"That's the word 'Hello' in about a hundred different languages." There was a lot of fuzz in it, even with the noise reduction circuit engaged.

"That's what I figured. There's another signal that's trying to make out some kind of digital format. It's not analog video or sound."

"Try arranging it in a 23 by 73 rectangle."

"Okay. Twelve and eleven by six dozen and one." She pushed some buttons, it resolved into a picture. "Wow, that's pretty funky."

"Frank Drake's little man figure. The DNA spirals. The Earthlings don't know who we are. So they're sending stuff believed appropriate to start communication with an alien race."

"At least you Earthlings have been thinking about the possibility. These signals are being sent in a beam from one of Earth's communication satellites. For some reason they're using a frequency that has a lot of static from all of the hydrogen in the Universe. We know the beam is aimed at us. We move to the side, we lose the beam. It finds us again when we resume steady course."

"It might be coming from Jet Propulsion Laboratory. They control the probes we send to the outer planets with radio signals. This 'Hello' message in all of the world's languages is the same as recorded on the Pioneer probe we sent out two decades ago."

Helga grinned and opened the door to a cabinet. "You mean THIS Pioneer probe?"

I recognized the gold plated message board with the engraved images of a naked man and a naked woman. "You went and fetched it!"

"We knew it swung by your outer planets and flew out of your Solar System. We knew this probe had information intended for any intelligent species who recovers it. We picked up our mail." She ran her hand over the engravings of nude humans. "Cro-Magnon heads. Cro-Magnon muscularity. What are these dots and dashes supposed to mean? You should use English, we expect that."

"The JPL types who created it were trying to communicate with beings who might not know how to read English, but might understand binary code. Like the on-off switch logic of computers."

"Oh. So what's it supposed to say in this supposedly universal language?"

"I remember one thing that they were suggesting is that you try to communicate with Earth by using the 21 centimeter hydrogen radio wavelength, or 1420 megahertz."

"That's why they're using that frequency!" She giggled. "What's a good frequency, other than this, to talk to Earth?"

"Oh I don't know." I took out a calculator. "You're Base Twelve in your math, we're Base Ten, why don't we take a ratio of the two numbers, say 10/12, and multiply by the 1420 million cycles per second, yeah, 1183 megahertz. A megahertz is a million cycles per second."

"We use *prelates* which are shorter than seconds, and we use Base Twelve numbers. This

1183 megahertz is one ten eleven point one six *beeyon* cycles per *prelate*. We can transmit at that." The Creation women split the day into 24 hours, same as we, the two Planets rotate at the same speed. There are 72 *linits* in an hour, 72 *prelates* in a *linit*. A *prelate* is 25/36 of a second.

"We can tell them 1183 megahertz. But if we send a response at that frequency, will anybody on Earth receive it? We need another way of initiating communication. Our Big Flashlight shows up as a bright light when viewed from Earth."

"Yes. We're deliberately shining it in a tight cone. We can spread it when we get close to Earth. Your radio and television stations are talking about us! Look at this!" She pointed to a video screen. I recognized it as a BBC broadcast. The picture showed the night sky with a blue light next to the star Rigel in Orion. "They're calling us the Blue Light Special!"

"Is there some way of blinking the Big Flashlight?"

"Spread the cone, tighten it back up, it'll look like a blink from Earth." She brought up the key to a code on a computer screen. "Is anyone on Earth still familiar with International Morse Code?"

"There are a few people who can read it still. Our Navy practices sending messages from ship to ship by flashing searchlights. Boy Scouts do the same thing with flashlights. It's one of my ex-wife's hobbies."

November 13. Clear evening sky with the Blue Light Special. The Light started to blink. It blinked for about a minute. Then it stopped. Then it started blinking again. Angela Peace declared, "A natural phenomenon does not blink like that."

"You see it blink, too?" confirmed Yolanda Perez.

"Yeah, if they're using Morse Code they just said 'Hello Earth. We come in peace.'"

"You're right! I-N P-E-A-C-E. Oh my God! H-Ohhh!"

"They're saying something else now. L-A. T-I-E-R-R-A, Hey! That's Spanish!"

"They're now saying 'Hello Earth, We come in peace.' in Spanish! *'Hola Tierra. Nosotros llegamos en la paz.'*"

"That makes sense. This light should be visible to all of North and South America right now. Our radio and television broadcasts bleed into space. We thought we were all alone!"

"Not any more! Get a pad and pencil! We need to write this down! How long have they been listening to us?"

"Long enough to learn that Spanish and English are two of our major languages."

"That ought to make quite an impression!" I jubilantly declared. Helga continued to blink the Morse Code.

A small crowd of people listened intently as Angela and Yolanda translated the flashing message. "Hey! They're flashing again. It's a new message. T-H-E, it's in English, N-A-M-E O-F O-U-R S-H-I-P, The name of our ship, I-S N-E-A-N-D-E-R-T-H-A-L, is Neanderthal? R-E-T-U-R-N, Return."

"They're Neanderthals?"

"I don't know. Maybe Neanderthal means something in their language. But that's what I have here. They're blinking again. E-L N-O-M-B-R-E, *El nombre*,"

"Spanish. It's Spanish for 'The name'. They're repeating the message in Spanish!"

"Yes, you're right. *'El nombre de nos navio es* Neanderthal Volver.'"

"*¡Caramba!* They're humans, of the Neanderthal Race!"

"We don't know that. Let's not get too excited."

Laughter. "An alien spacecraft shows up, blinks in Morse Code, and we're not supposed to get too excited?"

The *Neanderthal Return* repeated its identification message. Then, "New message!" yelled Angela. "W-E A-R-E We are, H-U-M-A-N-S, humans! O-F T-H-E, of the, R-A-C-E, race, Y-O-U C-A-L-L, you call, N-E-A-N-D-E-R-T-H-A-L, Neanderthal!"

"Wow. The Neanderthals live! But how?"

"Hey! They're people! Just like us!"

"Spectacular! They're repeating in Spanish. '*Nosotros somos humanos de la raza llamarseis Neanderthal.*'"

After resting a few hours, we started again in French for Tahiti and New Caledonia, and in English for New Zealand and Australia. The Japanese was transliterated into the Roman alphabet for Morse Code purposes. The Chinese was transliterated into the Roman alphabet by the Pinyin method preferred by the People's Republic. The Russian was performed in the old Soviet Morse Code for Cyrillic alphabet representation. More English for the benefit of India. When Europe and Africa spun into view, the *Neanderthal Return* blinked its messages in Russian, German, French, and English.

Then we rested. Four hours after night fell on the American East Coast we sent another short Morse Code message: "We will transmit voice radio at 1183 megahertz."

The President called the Curator of Anthropology of a major museum. "Yes, Mr. President, the issue of whether Neanderthals can speak has long been a controversy among scientists. It has to do with the shape of the lower part of the skull opposite the jawbone. We modern humans have a curved palate and a deeply set larynx, that allows us to speak rapidly and pronounce the vowel sounds. But with the Neanderthals, the Old Man of La Chapelle and others, the palate is flat, like gorillas, many scientists don't think they could speak the same way we do."

"Well, maybe not. But we have a SPACECRAFT under power coming right at us, and they have communicated, in OUR Morse Code and in OUR languages, that they are Neanderthals. THESE Neanderthals can speak, and they've certainly developed a high level of technology. You say that the Neanderthals of Europe went extinct because we anatomically modern humans wiped them out! Is this spacecraft an avenging angel coming to wipe US out?"

"I don't think so. They've communicated that they come in peace. Let us be glad this is not a shipload of Commanches."

"Being one quarter Cherokee, I might be able to talk 'em out of it. I'm called the first Native American president, even though I'm three quarters white! Is it possible that we carry some of the Neanderthal's genes?"

"If we do, it would be like the descendants of Pocahontas. They have a bit of Native American ancestry. But if out of 256 ancestors, 255 are whites, you're going to be white, you won't look like a Virginia Indian. Likewise, we're not Neanderthals, even if there was interbreeding. It's not believed that the Cro-Magnons and Neanderthals of Europe were capable of interbreeding. Proto-Neanderthals and Neanderthals were separated from the rest of the genus *Homo* for over 200,000 years, perhaps 700,000 years based on the Gran Dolino fossils. We're separate species, not subspecies or races of *Homo sapiens.*"

"This group that we're now dealing with has been separated for an additional 50,000 years or so. How did they get off the Planet?"

"That I cannot answer. They may not be telling the truth. They may not be human at all."

"They'll soon be talking to us. How can they do this if they ARE Neanderthals?"

"As far as speaking, the Moshe skeleton discovered in Israel includes a hyoid bone. The hyoid is a free floating bone behind your jaw that serves as an anchor for your tongue and larynx. Moshe's hyoid is of a shape similar to ours, his larynx might have been low enough to allow the full range of vowel pronunciation."

"Hmmm. They've declared that they will initiate voice communication. Will you please take the redeye to D.C.? I need you in the Oval Office."

"Certainly. I'll bring a briefcase full of stuff on Neanderthals."

"Thank you."

Helga put the headset on. So did I. Mine was reshaped to fit my high domed head. A little microphone dangled in front of my mouth on a metal bar and speakers were held in my ears. "Okay Neil, here goes nothing!" Helga pushed a button, connecting us to the Main Transmitter pointed at Earth, tuned to the 1183 megahertz frequency. Because we were 290 million miles from Earth, normal conversation was still impossible. We talk and wait for a reply.

Helga began. "This is *Neanderthal Return* calling Earth. My name is Helga Trvlakian. I am a human being, much like you are. About 50,000 years ago, my ancestors were kidnapped from their homes on the continent you now call Europe. We were transported to a Planet in orbit around the star you designate Alpha Centauri A. This Planet had been terraformed with life forms native to Earth. We were the last life form so transplanted, an intelligent human Race. In the last 50,000 years our Race evolved on this new Planet. We now have a civilization with a level of technology similar to Earth. Because our Planet was terraformed, we have named it Creation."

"You're doing fine." I said quietly to reassure Helga.

She began again. "We know some things about the race of alien intelligent life who transplanted our ancestors from Earth to Creation. They come from a star located in the constellation Leo. Their sun will soon blow up into a red giant and burn the planet on which they evolved. They needed a replacement planet."

She took a breath. "To transfer their society to a new planet, they needed to reform that planet to sustain their kind of life. They needed to learn how to move a planet to where it will receive the right amount of sunlight. How to form oceans and a suitable atmosphere. How to seed it with life and build up ecosystems. Finally, how to move an intelligent species of life to the new planet. So they experimentally terraformed Creation and transplanted half of the Neanderthal population then living in Europe."

She smiled at me. "I am a descendent of those Neanderthals. Every person living on Creation is a Neanderthal. That is all that I want to say for now. Please transmit a response to us at 1183 megahertz, acknowledge that you have received this transmission, and feel free to ask questions. Your signal will take 26 minutes to reach us at our present distance. We come in peace, peace with all of the people of Earth."

The President, his advisors, General Fairchild, and the Curator of Anthropology sat in the Oval Office listening to the voice transmission from Helga Trvlakian. "They want a reply." the President said to start the discussion.

"It's a protocol thing. Who should be the one to respond? You? The Prime Minister of Canada? Great Britain? The Secretary General of the United Nations?"

"Helga Trvlakian did not identify herself as the captain of her ship. Nor did she claim any rank in the Neanderthal society she claims exists on Planet Creation. So is it proper for a Head of State to be the one to respond to her?"

The Hotline rang. It was the President Korsakov of Russia. "Mr. President, the former Soviet Republics will join you in any military defense. This message would be a good trick by a nonhuman species to get us to lower our guard."

"Come to think of it, Boris, it would be a good trick by a human species, which they claim to be. Our military forces are linked and on alert. We'll stay at DEFCON 3. But who do you think should respond? We need to act fast, they expect a reply."

"They flashed in Russian Morse Code when they were on our side of the Planet. They know Russian. But they initiated voice communication in English on your side of the Planet. Because of our difficulties since the breakup of the Soviet Union, you are the remaining superpower; you have to take the lead. If they initiate voice communication in Russian, then we will take the lead for that. Is this agreeable?"

"It most certainly is. Thank you for keeping in touch."

"You're welcome. When you draft a response, please fax us a written copy and give us a few minutes to comment before you transmit it."

"We will. Thank you." The President hung up.

"Mr. President, we have received messages from 140 other nations and the U.N. that they are leaving the response to us."

"All right then. We respond to the *Neanderthal Return*. Because Helga Trvlakian did not identify herself as a captain or claim any rank with her society, the Secretary of State will voice the reply. We need to draft it fast. It's rude to keep 'em waiting. Voice analysis. Mr. Curator, what do you think?"

"A woman's voice. She pronounces the consonants quite well. Most consonants are made with the front of the tongue working against the palate or teeth, or with the lips, no problem for Neanderthals. But she also pronounces the hard 'g' and 'k' sounds, which are made with the back of the tongue. Her name, Helga Trvlakian, contains those sounds, so they're part of her language. Her English is fluent. She pronounces all of the vowels, confirming a deep larynx as indicated by Moshe's hyoid bone. She may not be Neanderthal at all, she could be an anatomically modern human."

"Thank you. What does CIA voice analysis say?"

"Human, female. Helga is a woman, no sign of an Adam's apple in our voice analysis. No deception indicated."

"Her accent?"

"There seems to be a touch of German or Czech. She may speak these languages as well. Her ship flashed in German when it was over Europe. We cannot determine whether the voice is coming from a Neanderthal or a Cro-Magnon."

"We'll inform the *Neanderthal Return* that we can receive video. We want to see what a live Neanderthal looks like. What should she look like?"

The Curator answered this one. "She'll have very high, wide, arched, and prominent brow ridges. Her forehead will look half as high as ours. The eyes should be big and round, and set very high. The nose will be large and broad with large nostrils, the cheekbones swept back. Her teeth will be larger than ours. She'll have a very strong jawbone with a chin that slopes back from under her mouth. Her nose and mouth will project forward, her braincase lower and extending to the rear. Her face will appear much longer. Her body will be robust, with powerful muscles. Here are some illustrations of what we think Neanderthal men and women looked like."

The President looked at the artwork. "These are all shown as cave dwellers or hunter-gatherers. We're dealing with astronauts in a spaceship."

"Yes, I know. Of course, they could have straight hair, it could be curly, it could be black, blonde, or red. The tear ducts of the eyes could be exposed like modern white people, or covered by the upper fold like modern Asian people. Their skin may be black, white or any shade in between. These characteristics cannot be determined from fossil bones."

"Neil, wake up. It's been an hour. A nap is a good idea. But now we need you awake. A response can come at any time." I stretched myself awake.

23

"Helga, we need another English speaker. Can we release Lucinda and get her services?"

"Might be a good idea. But right now, let's get over to the Switching Room."

Every language specialist was there. Including Lucinda. "Neil, are we still friends?"

"Of course we are!"

She smiled and looked relieved. "I'm told we're signaling our presence to Earth. I told Helga I'm available to help. I asked that Wilma and Betty be released. They would not release them because they fought with some of the other crew members. Captain Harsradich is not strapped down, but she's under guard in her room and is monitoring our radio transmissions. Now that we've announced ourselves, we better play this out." Two women started combing my hair. "You need to be looking your best. They've given all of us the treatment. We're getting prepared for a video transmission. Too late to shave your beautiful manly beard, but we can comb it and trim it." I let these makeup artists do their worst. Then I took my seat at the console.

Waiting. It had been an hour and a half, if Earth had taken thirty minutes to prepare a response it should be arriving. Then it came. "We have both voice and video from Earth!"

I recognized him. "This is Earth calling *Neanderthal Return*. We have received and understood your message. I am the Secretary of State for the United States of America, responding on behalf of the nations of Earth. We appreciate your Morse Code signals in our major languages. We desire peace and friendship with the people of Planet Creation. You are welcome to establish an orbit around Earth low enough to rendezvous with the Space Shuttle *Atlantis*. We have been told by Russia that if you know Russian, you may communicate with their space station *Mir* and approach it for a rendezvous. Please stay clear of our new International Space Station, it is still under construction. We are prepared to receive video images in either analog or digital with your next massage. Everyone wants to see the beautiful Helga Trvlakian. We will await your next message. Over and out."

"Is the video camera ready?" asked an excited Helga in Atlantean.

"Yes it is." came the reply in Atlantean. I understood that much of their language.

"They named a Space Shuttle after our home continent on Creation!"

"No," I responded, "They named it after Plato's Lost City. In his Letters to Timeas and Criteas he described a city on an island 2,000 stadia wide and 3,000 stadia long. A bit larger than Ireland. Perhaps the Grand Bahama Bank during the Ice Age."

"Your oceans rose when the glaciers melted."

"That is the current scientific consensus. The end of the most recent glaciation is believed to be 11,000 years ago. Scientists analyzing ice cores drilled in Greenland theorize that when the Ice Age ended, it ended suddenly, leaving the glaciers in Asia, Europe, and North America to melt away. That could explain Plato's story, Atlantis sinking beneath the water 9000 years before the life of Solon."

"When did Solon live?"

"About 2600 years ago."

"Interesting. Plato himself places the flooding of Atlantis at about the end of the Ice Age when the sea level rose. Flooding our coastal villages."

"Did most of your ancestors live in coastal villages?"

"Yes, the Old Records found by Lamoan Reducker describe the Neanderthal People of Europe as living mostly along the coast. Your archeologists have found only the bones of those Neanderthals who lived inland on higher ground. Most of our people of the Earth's Ice Age lived on the coast where they could dig clams, catch fish, and hunt seals and whales."

"Interesting. Our archeologists should look underwater along the Pleistocene coastline. Ulpp! Looks like you're on!"

"Live coverage of the first voice and video communication with the spaceship that has identified itself as the *Neanderthal Return* now continues!"

"Thank you. It has been about forty minutes since the Secretary of State sent his reply to the *Neanderthal Return's* initial voice communication. It took the Administration a half hour to generate a response so it's not surprising if the *Neanderthal Return* likewise takes a little time to, -- Here it comes!" The television network switched to retransmit the signal from the *Neanderthal Return.*

Angela Peace, our children, and her neighbors were watching television. The video transmission began. Four women sat in a row. "They look like Neanderthals!" someone said. "Brow ridges. Short foreheads. Big noses."

"But they're beautiful! Look at the blonde, her eyes! Those incredible eyes!"

"Yeah, she's cute. But they look like the muscle women of the Ms. Olympia contest."

"Shhh! She's going to speak."

"This is the *Neanderthal Return* calling Earth. Thank you for your response, Mr. Secretary. I am Helga Trvlakian. I can speak German and English."

The camera panned over to Lucinda. "I am Lchnsda Renuxler, I also speak English. Because my name may be hard to pronounce, you may call me Lucinda. As you can see, I am bald. This is a condition that sometimes happens to our people. We are born bald, and never grow hair. To show you that we are indeed Neanderthals, I will turn my head to the side and let Helga show you the features that are the same as the Neanderthal skulls found in Europe."

Helga pointed to the back of Lucinda's skull. "Back here is the occipital bun, a knot of bone at the back of our heads that is not present in Cro-Magnons. Below the occipital bun is the suprainiac depression. You can't see it because of the neck muscles. Lchnsda's jawbone is heavier than the Cro-Magnon jaw, but does not have the mental eminence that makes the Cro-Magnon chin so prominent. Her jaw muscles running in front of her ear are larger and stronger than typical Cro-Magnon jaw muscles. Open your mouth, please. Our teeth are larger than your Cro-Magnon teeth. There is a gap between her third molar, the wisdom tooth, and the back of her jawbone. We have large and broad noses. You see our famous brow ridges. Our eye sockets and eyeballs are larger. The forehead slopes back. Back here, there is more room for the brain. The thinking part of the Neanderthal brain is as prominently developed as the Cro-Magnon, just located a little further back."

Lucinda turned back to the camera with a big smile. "You see? We are who we say we are, human beings of Neanderthal descent. How we moved from Ice Age Europe to Planet Creation is quite a story in itself. But first, let us allow some other members of our crew to introduce themselves."

The camera panned to the brunette sitting next to Lucinda. "*Me nombre es Andemona Chmlakian. Conozco espanol, frances, italiano, y latino.*"

Helga spoke again. "For those of you who do not know Spanish, Andemona Chmlakian knows Spanish, French, Italian, and Latin."

The camera panned to the last woman, a redhead. She introduced herself in Russian; her name is Monoloa Mrvlakian. She also speaks Mandarin and Cantonese Chinese and Japanese and explained so in those languages. Monoloa would be delighted if she were invited on board *Mir* and to visit Kazakhstan and Russia. She would also like to visit China and Japan. Helga repeated her introduction in English.

After all of that, Helga took a somewhat more serious tone. "People of the Planet Earth, we

25

owe you an apology. A few months ago, during your last Northern Hemisphere summer, we visited your Planet in a covert manner. We brought the *Neanderthal Return* to the Far Side of the Moon, using it to shield us from view. We sent a Shuttle to the surface of the Earth. We captured and kidnapped a man from the State of Washington named Neil Armstrong Peace. Here he is right here." The camera showed me sitting next to Helga. I smiled and waved.

"Oh my GOD!" screamed Angela Peace at the television set.

"I am Neil Armstrong Peace. I was on my way to visit a friend named Leonard Taylor where he lived on the Olympic Peninsula. I took a wrong turn on one of those gravel roads and had to double back. I ran into them."

"We were in our spacesuits with the helmets on." Lucinda broke in. "He couldn't see what we looked like. He thought we were soldiers from Fort Lewis. We drugged him, took him on board, and took off to rejoin our ship behind the Moon."

Helga took over. "We decided our Captain, Trviea Harsradich, was on a dangerous course of action. Our orders granted me the authority to relieve our Captain of command if I believe that there is even a remote chance of starting a war with Earth or with any nation of Earth. We apologized to Neil and he has accepted our apology."

Then I spoke. "The last thing any of us want is a war between Earth and Creation, so I accepted their apology."

"Neil suggested we introduce ourselves to you. We are approaching in a straight line in full view of your night sky; we're slowing down to allow orbit around Earth. We thought the Morse Code would be a nice touch."

"We need to know about each other." I concluded. "The Neanderthals of Creation know about us from our radio and television broadcasts."

Helga finished. "We accept your invitation to go into orbit and to rendezvous with the Shuttle *Atlantis*. We will accept a similar invitation with respect to the station *Mir* if it is made. Monoloa would be the one to visit *Mir*. We will stay away from the International Space Station and will maneuver to avoid collision with the other Earth satellites. We have no intention of taking any more Earth people without their consent. This is *Neanderthal Return* signing off."

Angela Peace became an international celebrity. Reporters wanted her to tell about the man on board the *Neanderthal Return*. She said I am a good father to the children and refused to comment on the events that led to the breakup of our marriage. She went to court the next morning and obtained an emergency order sealing the file. She then went to the United States Courthouse. I fought the threat of contempt proceedings in the child support order in our divorce decree as a violation of the federal Antipeonage Act and the Thirteenth Amendment. When she got there, reporters had the case file out.

As Earth rotated to place Russia toward the *Neanderthal Return*, the Russians took over the 1183 megahertz frequency. Monoloa accepted the invitation to board *Mir* and to come to the surface to visit Kazakhstan and Russia.

Over the next few days, the story about how the aliens had terraformed Creation and seeded it with Earth life forms was told to the people of Earth. Helga and Lucinda described the history of Creation, without telling about the Virus Holocaust.

Chapter Four

"Why have they come?" The President started. "Why an all woman crew on their ship? Why steal a man from Earth? People say Neil Peace is the 'luckiest man in the Universe'. He's teaching the crew English. But the comedians joke that he is showing 'em how the English make more English."

"Regardless of how much sex he is having with them," started General Fairchild, "if he is having sex with them, uh, CAN he have sex with them?"

"Of course he can!" the Curator answered. "The Moshe skeleton in Israel had the pubic ramus projecting forward compared with ours. But his is the only complete Neanderthal pelvis that has been found. We haven't found a female Neanderthal pelvis with a complete pubic ramus. That's the bone that goes in front of the vagina, which would tend to be forward of where it is on a Cro-Magnon woman."

"Well, shit!" the President exclaimed. "Maybe we can ask Mr. Peace if he notices any forward placement of the vagina or the pubic ramus when he screws 'em." Laughter.

"Whatever their love life," started the General, "it makes sense that they pick Neil's brain about Earth and to have him teach English to everyone on board. As far as telling us why they come and why an all female crew, it appears they're saving that for later."

"We may know the answers soon enough." concluded the President. "What about diseases, bacteria, viruses? The common cold that is a bother to us for two weeks could kill them if they have no immunity to it. Something they've grown used to could kill us the way European diseases killed Native Americans."

"They've exposed themselves to whatever Neil Peace is carrying. They're still alive and healthy."

"That's apparently true. But they wouldn't transmit a video of sick crew members. What about the people who searched for Neil Peace where his car was found?"

"So far the Center for Disease Control hasn't found anything there that doesn't already occur on Earth. We haven't heard about any unusual illnesses."

"Okay. But we need quarantine procedures for when they arrive in Earth orbit. We've invited them down to the surface. These women are smart enough to consent to quarantine while we check them out, both for bugs harmful to Earthlings and for their susceptibility to Earth diseases. We'll quarantine the Shuttle astronauts too. How's the public reacting to this visit?"

"About what you would expect. Most people are happy that the aliens are human and come in peace."

"Good. Another subject: The publicity surrounding Peace's Peonage Law claim against the child support system has embarrassed the legal community. While he hasn't exploited his current situation to discuss the treatment of noncustodial parents, the press has had a field day with the issues he raised in his federal lawsuit a few years ago. The judges hate it, nobody likes being called a criminal."

"How is it peonage to require parents to support their own children?"

"Take the children away and then enforce the support requirement through contempt proceedings. When a person thus has to have a job to avoid going to jail, we have a condition of involuntary servitude, so says Neil Peace's briefs. California courts have since wrestled with this theory in the *Brent Moss* case."

The Blue Light drifted across Orion. We spread the cone of light exhaust to avoid becoming too bright, then we aimed it past Earth. Two way conversational radio communication with Earth became possible. Pidonita Hmlakian maneuvered the *Neanderthal Return* into an orbit at altitudes between 150 and 250 miles.

With my help, the women negotiated an Agreement with the Earth nations providing for diplomatic status and immunity for the ship and its crew. It provided the ground rules for their visit to the Earth's surface. The host nations agreed to protect them from harm. In return, the women of Creation promised not to remove any Earth persons from the Planet's surface against their will or to otherwise commit any harm or Act of War against any person or nation of Earth. They agreed to not interfere in the operation of satellites and manned orbiters sent up by Earth nations.

The United States Senate ratified the Agreement with a 99-0 vote. Russia and Kazakhstan ratified the Agreement to facilitate the visit by Monoloa Mrvlakian to *Mir* and then to the surface. Then most other nations ratified the Agreement.

At my suggestion, they didn't reveal the purpose of their mission to Earth. Instead, Helga and Lucinda made a videotape for the President to view in private. It seemed only fair to give him a chance to form a position on the questions of our arrival and the women's need, before telling the story to the whole world.

The Shuttle *Atlantis* rose into orbit with an empty cargo bay. Pidonita Hmlakian matched orbits with *Atlantis*. In Atlantean language she warned everyone to prepare for Free Fall, what they call the weightless condition of no propulsion. "*Bly jore!*" is what it sounded like.

We were in Bay Number Four getting ready. Helga, Lucinda, and Andemona were suited up except for the helmets. They wore the same suits they wore when they captured me on Earth. But this time they had gloves on their hands for going out into hard vacuum, and backpacks with thrusters and breathing air. One more time, we went over the planned spacewalk. Andemona now understood some English. *Atlantis* is too big to be brought into Number Four, our largest Bay, and there's no way we can dock.

"Good luck, girls." They had the nervous anticipation of actresses about to go on the stage for the opening night show.

"Thank you." said Helga. "Can we each have a good luck kiss?"

"Sure." I kissed Helga.

"And me?" asked Lucinda. I kissed her.

Andemona wanted more than what I gave the other two. "*Besamos muy bueno, por favor.*" She kissed me full on the lips and cleaned my teeth with her tongue to the amusement of the other two and their assistants. I knew their names from the English classes. Sorby Mishlakian, Nesla Teslakian, and Marla Syferkrip. With the laughter breaking up the tension the helmets were snapped on. They tested their air and other vital functions and gave the thumbs up sign. After this, Sorby cheerfully told me in halting English that it was time to leave the Bay, the air will be sucked out of it. I went into the command center for Bay Number Four. From there, I had a clear view of *Atlantis* through windows. Video screens showed the interior of the Bay. I put on the radio headset.

"This is *Neanderthal Return,* Neil Peace, calling *Atlantis, Atlantis* do you copy?"

"Roger. This is *Atlantis*, Brian Winthrop, commander, we copy *Neanderthal Return*. We see you. You're definitely a large ship! How are you holding up, Neil?"

"Doing fine Brian. Tell Dr. Nguyen I'm as healthy as a horse!"

"This is Dr. Cuc Thi Nguyen. I hear you and I'm ready and standing by."

"If only I can get my stomach out of my throat, what with the fusion reactor shut down." I complained. They laughed.

"Your ex told me to pass on the message that your children love you and to be careful." said Brian.

"Thank you." George Kangley and Joshua Goldstein stood in the open cargo bay. I needed to confirm that their radios worked. "This is *Neanderthal Return* calling George Kangley and Joshua Goldstein, do you copy?"

"This is George Kangley, I hear you loud and clear, Neil."

"This is Joshua Goldstein, I copy. Ready for personnel transfer."

"This is Helga Trvlakian, I copy, I can hear everyone."

"This is Lchnsda Renuxler. I copy all of you."

"This is Andemona Chmlakian. I copy all of you."

"Okay, all of our radios work and we're on the same frequency." I concluded. "Metrola?"

Metrola Mornuxler attended my English classes, but she wasn't yet fluent. She managed to say, "I'm ready." She stood by the controls to the air pumps of Bay Number Four and its huge door, 35 feet 6 inches high and 71 feet wide.

"We're ready for personnel transfer." I declared.

"*Atlantis* is ready for personnel transfer." declared Joshua. "Mission Control, this is *Atlantis* calling Houston. We are go for personnel transfer."

"Roger that, this is Houston, we copy. We are hearing all of you, and your voices are being broadcast on network television. You are go for personnel transfer."

"This is Helga, I am tethered and ready."

"This is Lucinda, I am tethered and ready."

"This is Andemona, I am tethered and ready."

I signaled Metrola to get started; Helga spoke some Atlantean to her. She pushed a button. "This is *Neanderthal Return*. Pressure is going down in Bay Number Four." The dial is marked in Base Twelve Atlantean numbers; the needle approached the zero dot. "Pressure is almost there. Now. Pressure is zero." Metrola confirmed zero pressure in the Bay. The three suited women said in Atlantean that their insuit pressure was fine and their outsuit pressure was zero. There was a video screen with what appeared to be their vital statistics. Metrola flipped a toggle switch. "Door to space is now opening."

"This is Helga." She spoke in English. "The door to space is open. I can see *Atlantis*. It is a beautiful ship. I can see the two astronauts. I'm jumping out, NOW!" Helga ran from fifty feet inside the Bay and leaped from the sill into the vacuum. She hit her backpack thrusters a few times for spurts to correct her course.

"This is Joshua. Helga, you are looking good."

"This is *Atlantis*. You are closing at 15 feet per second. You want to slow down before you hit us. Distance now 100 feet. 80 feet."

"Tension from my cable reel should slow me down."

"You're now closing at 5 feet per second. Distance 20 feet. 15 feet. 10 feet. 5 feet."

"Gotcha," declared Joshua as he caught and steadied Helga in the Shuttle bay. He and George placed her feet in a set of foot restraints. For this mission, a strap was added to each foot restraint for the Creation astronauts. Helga unhooked the tether to *Neanderthal Return* from her waist. She held it with her hand.

"This is Helga. I am secured by my feet to *Atlantis*. I am holding the tether to *Neanderthal Return*." She switched to Atlantean. "I am ready for the bags, Andemona."

In the Bay, Andemona snapped a fifty pound bag on to the cable and spoke in Atlantean. "First bag is secured to line. On its way." She sent the bag sliding over to *Atlantis*. Helga, Joshua, and George caught it. It was placed in the airlock. Andemona sent each of the other bags by the same method.

Helga pressed a button on a little panel attached to her tether line a foot from its end and let go. "Line is now free." The cable reel powered by an electric motor retracted the tether line.

Andemona waited until Helga's cable was fully retracted. Then she jumped off. She used her little thruster rockets in the same manner as Helga. Tension from her cable reel slowed her down. She arrived at *Atlantis* at 5 feet per second. Then Lucinda went. After her tether was fully retracted Metrola closed the door to Bay Number Four.

"All right, ladies, time for us to cycle through the airlock." George announced. "There is enough room for three of us. Two of you go in. I'll follow you."

Helga bent down to look through the airlock hatch. "About a *treefat* in diameter." She then crawled through.

"A *treefat* is a Creation yard?" asked Joshua.

"We have inches, feet, yards, and fathoms, just like you." confirmed Lucinda as she followed Helga into the airlock. "*Treefat* means 'half reach'. In your Base Ten numbers, it's .986 of your yard, or about 35 and a half inches. It's exactly 36 *tig-its*."

George followed the two women into the airlock and closed the hatch, leaving Joshua and Andemona waiting outside. NASA rules prohibit one person outside the Shuttle at a time. "Yeah, the inside diameter of each hatch to this airlock is 36 inches, a yard. How is it you have a system of measures so similar to ours?"

"Human factors, I guess. It's natural to estimate distances and dimensions in terms of the human body."

George turned the handle to pressurize the airlock. Cuc Nguyen helped open the airlock hatch to the cabin. Helga and Lucinda crawled into the cabin and brought their bags in. The airlock hatch was closed behind them. They took their helmets off to breathe Shuttle air. Brian Winthrop came down to have his first close up look at live Neanderthal women.

Helga was the first to speak. "Your *Atlantis*, she's a good ship."

"Thank you." said Cuc. "I'll be ready to perform a medical check on you after I help cycle in George, Andemona and Joshua."

George turned the handle to release air out of the airlock. "Airlock is now depressurized." he declared. He opened the hatch to the cargo bay.

Joshua explained the working of the door to Andemona. "We open the outside door like this. In fact, when the airlock has air in it, we cannot open the door against the pressure. It opens inward. Another safety precaution."

Andemona spoke in Atlantean to her shipmates. "Helga, Lchnsda, please tell Joshua that while Neil has done a good job, my English is not yet fluent. I think he is telling me something about the airlock doors, but I'm not sure what."

The two English speaking girls burst into laughter. "Joshua," addressed Lucinda, "Andemona speaks excellent Spanish. But her English is not yet fluent."

"Oh! Right. We can work on that, I'm sure. Andemona, can you *comprende* this, uh, *esta*? Into the airlock, *por favor*."

Andemona laughed. "I know that much, *gracias*." She crawled into the airlock and Joshua followed her, closing the hatch.

"Allow me to pressurize the airlock." Joshua turned the handle.

"Airlock now fully pressurized, 14 psi." observed Cuc. She pulled open the airlock door and allowed the three spacewalkers into the cabin. The airlock door was closed and secured behind them. They took their helmets off to breathe Shuttle air.

The physician commenced her examination of the Neanderthal women. "Now say 'Ah'." She quickly took some medical measurements as the spacewalkers were helped out of their pressure suits. "Helga, your temperature is 98.8 degrees Fahrenheit. Andemona, 98.7. Lucinda, 98.6 on the dot. Heartbeat, however, is 105 for Helga, 115 for Andemona, and 95 for Lucinda, is this normal?"

"No, we're a little excited right now. When we have a chance to relax, it should be between 60 and 80 beats per minute." said Lucinda.

"I have a question, Lucinda." began Brian Winthrop. "*Atlantis* shifted in her orbit with a delta vee of about three feet per second. But we cannot account for this delta vee from the use of our orbital maneuvering system. We know a fusion reactor powers *Neanderthal Return*. Did your pilot project magnetic fields?"

Helga answered his question. "Earth has a magnetic field. We're in a free fall orbit close to another ship. We can project our magnetic fields to work with Earth's magnetic field to control our location and avoid collision. Pidonita probably did that. Is there any steel on *Atlantis*?"

"Most of *Atlantis* is aluminum. Some titanium in high stress and high temperature parts. The airlock and the cabin are pressure vessels made from welded aluminum. The rest of the structure is made from high strength 7075 aluminum alloy, which cannot be welded. It is tied together with steel fasteners and brackets. There are also some steel fittings."

"That could account for the three foot per second delta vee."

"I suppose it could, thanks."

Dr. Cuc wanted to talk medical shop. "It's nice that your medical records were sent over by radio. But it's all in Atlantean. I need your help in translating it."

"No problem, we'll help you there." said Helga. "Are we on any kind of voice recorder or transmitter?"

"Yes we are. Shut off the Vox. Okay. Vox is now off. We're jealous of our privacy inside this tight little space. We control the cameras and microphones in here. You may speak without it being broadcast all over the Planet Earth."

"You need to know that we've medically stopped our aging process."

"What?!"

"Yes, I am about 175 Earth years old." said Helga. She made the conversion over from Base Twelve and the 497 1/2 day length of the Creation year.

"You look awfully good for 175. I'd like to know your secret!"

"We would tell you, but there are already 6 billion people on your Planet, and you have no problem producing children."

"Yeah. Just knowing that you've done it will have immense consequences on Earth."

"So does revealing our existence."

"True. We had thought the Neanderthals were extinct. Or have evolved into white people." Cuc said that with a wink at her fellow astronauts, who are white.

I decided to remain on board the *Neanderthal Return*. While the English classes have gone well, there is a need for a fluent English speaker on board for the duration of the ship's visit to our Solar System.

A few hours later, I worked with the Russian space station *Mir* to coordinate the transfer of Monoloa Mrvlakian. We did it the same way as with *Atlantis*. Monoloa had taught me some Russian, which was appreciated by the cosmonauts and by the mission controllers at Star City. Monoloa's near perfect Russian impressed them. I complimented the good English spoken by

31

the cosmonauts and by some of the translators for Russian Mission Control, they were accustomed to dealing with Americans. Monoloa unhooked herself from her tether to the *Neanderthal Return* when she was secure on the side of *Mir*. They cycled her through the airlock into the *Kvant* module.

My children were in school, gathered in front of the television set. *Atlantis* was scheduled to land at Edwards Air Force Base in California. My children were very proud of their father. That morning we had a chance to talk by telephone, hooked up to NASA's Mission Control communication system. "Hello."

"Dad? Is it you?"

"Yes Christa, it's me. Is Virgil there?"

"I'm here, Dad. We miss you."

"I miss you too. And I love you both."

"We love you too, Dad. We thought we were never going to see you again. Len and Henry found your car. The door hanging open and everything. They looked for you and called the cops."

"I know, I heard. But I'm back."

"How could they just kidnap you like that?"

"It was wrong. But they realized that and brought me back. I have accepted their apology. What's happening is too important to worry about it. Can you accept their apology?"

"NO!" shouted Virgil.

"Well maybe I can," offered Christa, "if they say they're sorry to me."

"Maybe. But they better mean it!"

"They mean it. They didn't mean to hurt anyone, they didn't know I had children."

"But why did they have to sneak around? Why didn't they just talk to us? Then they could have lotsa people. People who want to go! Enough to fill their ship!"

"That was a selling point I used to get them to announce themselves. But you see, they were afraid of us. Still are. We fight wars with each other. We invade each other's territory and take over. They don't want us to come to their Planet and make war on them. They fear those among us who are racists. I managed to convince them that most of us are good people, and that we don't believe in wars of conquest anymore."

"They're afraid of us. Afraid of racists. I guess all that stuff about Neanderthals as rough cavemen is like calling names."

"That's exactly what it's like. Like referring to stupid or ill mannered men as Neanderthals. That's insulting to these women who are every bit as advanced as we are. We have to admit that, it was one of the things about us that frightened them, that we would show so little respect for the dead. That we would make fun of a Race of people who have no living descendants around. That we would draw such unflattering conclusions from a few scattered bones."

"That's what our teacher tells us about prejudice. That we 'prejudge people' before we get to know them, because we see their skin color or something."

"That's right, sometimes people think they know everything about you because you are white. Which is wrong, because you're not the same as every other white person. It's wrong to judge a person by skin color, or by nationality, or by religion."

"Or by brow ridges!" shouted Virgil.

"Or by brow ridges. You've got it! I'm proud of you two. Always remember this: Never dislike a person because that person is black, Hispanic, Jewish, Muslim, or Neanderthal. Get to know the individual before deciding whether or not you like him. If someone doesn't like you because you're white, well, just stay away from him."

"We know, Dad. With racism and all the wars we've had, we're proud you talked them into letting us see them and coming down to Earth."

"Thank you. I'm in this position by pure luck. I'm only doing what I think is right. Remember, everyone, you, me, your mom, even those kids you don't like at school, are capable of being their very best when the occasion calls for it. And you never know when the occasion comes up."

"We know that. When are you coming down to Earth? We miss you, Daddy."

"I don't know. But I'll remember to talk with you as much as possible."

"Dad, we gotta go. School. They say we're gonna watch *Atlantis* touch down with the three women on TV."

"Well then, I better let you go. Be good in school, study hard, and watch the Space Shuttle land. Love ya!"

"The Shuttle *Atlantis* is coming in for a picture perfect landing."

"Yes, Brian Winthrop makes it look easy. The gear is down. 10 feet. 5 feet. 1 foot. Touchdown! Nice soft landing. *Atlantis* comes to a halt right in the center of the target circle."

"There go the ground vehicles heading out to the Shuttle. They are rolling the stairs to the spacecraft. We now have our zoom lens focused on the crew hatch of the Shuttle. The crew hatch is opening. Somebody is stepping out. It is the doctor, Cuc Thi Nguyen. Dr. Nguyen was born in Saigon. Her family came to the United States in 1974 when she was a small child. She became a U.S. citizen when she was a teenager."

"Now she is a physician with the Center for Disease Control in Atlanta. She has pronounced the three visitors from Planet Creation to be in perfect health. Now she waits at the bottom of the stairs."

"Here comes another person. It is Lucinda Renuxler! Ms. Renuxler has stepped out of the Shuttle. She is taking a deep breath of Earth air. Now she is descending the steps, helped by Dr. Nguyen. Down. Down. She steps foot on the ground, a Creation woman on Earth!"

Monoloa Mrvlakian settled into the *Mir* space station. "Monoloa, there is something we need to tell you before you ride the Soyuz capsule down to Kazakhstan." Pavel suddenly, self consciously, pulled his hand off of Monoloa's shoulder.

"It is all right. I will not bite."

"I am sorry. I do not want to offend you with a touch."

"Of course you do not want to offend me. And I do not want to offend you. But it is all right as long as it is just friendly."

"Just friendly. Uh, I would not want you to misunderstand my intentions."

Monoloa giggled. "You find me attractive?"

"Uh, well, uh, yes! But I just uh,"

"Pavel, it is all right. Just be a gentleman, you know how to do that. Cultural differences I can account for. You may touch me on the shoulder as you would your fellow cosmonauts. We are friends."

"We are friends." Pavel chuckled. "Thank you, Monoloa. I am sure we will get more comfortable as we get to know each other."

"Why don't we have an American on *Mir* right now?"

"Oh. After the Cold War ended, and before we started building the International Space Station, we had a deal with NASA for several years where we would have an American on board *Mir*. The American would stay for about six months or so, then the Shuttle *Atlantis* would dock to take him home and we would get another American. We have hosted people from a lot of different nations over the years. But now, everything is going to the new Station. We are lucky they have decided to keep *Mir* going for the time being. They were thinking of just dropping it into the Pacific Ocean like our garbage capsules."

"What were you wanting to tell me about riding your capsule?"

"Oh. We have not had any problems with reentry in our capsules for a long time now. We now have the defects worked out and it is a safe design. But we had two terrible accidents with them many years ago. The parachute did not open properly on Soyuz 1 and Vladimir Komarov was killed when his ship crashed. The parachute did open on Soyuz 11. We found the cosmonauts dead from exposure to vacuum. A valve popped open when their descent module separated from the orbital module."

"How long ago did these accidents happen?"

"Soyuz 1 in 1967. Soyuz 11 happened in 1971. We have had dozens of reentries since then. No more accidents on reentry. We have fixed the problems. So we are reasonably certain we can reenter safely. But there is always a chance."

"There is always a chance. We too have had accidents that killed people. I knew that when I went into space travel. It is always a possibility. But you can get killed crossing the street. As long as all reasonable safety precautions are taken, the chance of an accident will not stop me from space travel. If I am invited to come down to the surface in your reentry capsule, I will gladly accept the ride."

The President answered the phone in the Oval Office. "Hello. This is the President. Are you Dr. Cuc Nguyen?"

"Yes I am, Mr. President."

"How do our girls look so far?"

"Oh, they are big, strong, healthy! No diseases or pathologies that I can report. They have a LOT more muscle than we Earth Cro-Magnons do! Makes a skinny little Asian girl like me feel puny! They say their muscle tone is a little soft from being cooped up in a spacecraft. But each bench pressed 300 pounds! They're doing calisthenics and stretching exercises. They want to go outside and run!"

"I don't blame 'em. How does their intelligence look?"

"These women are the cream of the Creation crop, scoring over 150 on the IQ test."

"Senses. Eyesight, hearing, smelling?"

"Incredible vision. Standing 20 feet from the chart, each can read the bottom line AND the little paragraph that tells who printed it. No corrective lenses, their natural lenses are perfectly tuned. That could be artificial. But there is more to it than that. We Earth humans can only see so clearly even with perfectly adjusted natural or artificial lenses. The limiting factor is the number of rods and cones in the retina and the amount of brain in the occipital region devoted to interpreting an image from the optic nerves."

"Bigger eyeballs and a bigger occipital region means fundamentally better vision!"

"You've got that right, Mr. President!"

"He-he! I've been getting briefed by the paleoanthropologists. They not only believe that Neanderthals might have had better vision, at least until nearsightedness or cataracts eliminate that advantage, but they may have had telepathy. With telepathy, they didn't need to speak."

"These girls speak, and they don't have any more telepathy than we do. The brain of a Creation Neanderthal works a lot like the brain of an Earth Cro-Magnon. There are no biological radio transmitters and receivers attached to the brain. Therefore, no telepathy."

"While their brains are like ours, there can be differences in function and capability."

"That's possible. I think they were holding back on the IQ tests, because they don't want to frighten us. Their sense of smell is excellent. We tested with a very low concentration hydrogen sulfide, the rotten egg gas. I couldn't smell it. They asked us to quit testing them with low levels of hydrogen sulfide."

"They caught on!"

"Yeah, they expect us to test them. They have a couple of extra cubic inches of brain. Some of that capacity is for the facial senses, vision, smell, taste. Their frontal lobes are at least as well developed as ours. The speech centers, Broca's region and such, are there. But what all is being done with the extra capacity is hard to tell."

"How about mental health?"

"Other than some understandable cabin fever, they're just fine. Oh, here comes Helga and Lucinda, I'll put you on speakerphone."

"When do we get out of this quarantine, Mr. President?"

"Was that Lchnsda Renuxler?" asked the President.

"You said that very good!"

"He-He! When you run for election as many times as I have, you learn how to correctly pronounce people's names. I'm one quarter Cherokee, being an old Oklahoma boy. We had a bad experience with Native Americans suffering from European diseases that their bodies had never been exposed to. We don't want any epidemics ravaging Earth and we don't want to see you hurt. As President, I have to be responsible for that."

"We understand that. But after being cooped up in the *Neanderthal Return*, we're ready to go outside and run! Breathe fresh air! Neil Peace has been with us for some time now, he has not been sick! Our ship's doctor, Askelion Lamakian, tells us your vaccines should protect us. We should be able to mix and mingle with the Earth people with no more risk than they face."

"I think you should, but we'll let Dr. Nguyen make that call. Will you reveal your secret to long life?"

"Not at this point in time. I know it sounds harsh, but there're six billion of you on this Planet! We know that woolly mammoths on Creation, which reproduce very slowly, will nevertheless multiply in the absence of natural predators and human hunting. We humans have overcome all predators and have become the top predator ourselves. So the ability to stop the aging process is an invention fraught with danger. We have prepared a videotape for your viewing that explains our situation to you. Because our measuring system is somewhat different than yours, we have brought a tape player of our own. It feeds the signal out to a coaxial cable. A connector can be fitted on the other end of this that will hook up to your television set. We want you to view this in private and then decide what to do."

"Yes. I've been informed that an Air Force plane is bringing it over. Thank you for talking with me. I will be viewing your tape with interest."

Chapter Five

The tape player arrived at the White House. It was small, the recording tape in a cassette about half the size of a standard VHS type tape. Instructions were written in English. The technicians fitted the cable with an F-type connector. A power converter that I helped design was included to convert 110 volt 60 cycle per second electricity to Creation style electricity.

The President, the First Lady, General Fairchild, the Secretary of State, and the Curator of Anthropology gathered to watch the tape. While the technicians worked, the President asked to be briefed on the latest information about the spacecraft. "200 billion pound mass," began General Fairchild, "enough to have a tiny but measurable gravity. It's about 3,000 feet long, 1500 feet wide, and 800 feet high, 900 feet at the light exhaust. Overall density about 75 pounds per cubic foot, the same as a fighter plane. The fusion reactor burns regular hydrogen. The magnetic fields that contain this fusion reactor are so efficiently used, the presence of the *Neanderthal Return* has NO measurable effect down here unless the pilot deliberately projects the fields."

"Any idea how the ship is propelled?" asked the President.

"The Lawrence Livermore guys have a theory. Nuclear fusion is like a diesel engine, compression ignition. Compress the hydrogen plasma enough, we have fusion. Stars run on steady burning, but we can burn in pulses, like the diesel engine. Most of our experiments involve pulse compression of plasma in a magnetic bottle. So far, while some fusion occurs, we don't get as much energy out as we put in. We just cannot get enough compression in the pulse. The girls from Creation have obviously solved that problem."

"I know that. How are they converting fusion energy into forward momentum?"

"Funny thing happens during a nuclear reaction. The product particles fly with the kinetic energy released in the reaction, accelerated without PUSHING on anything."

"I thought every force had an equal and opposite reaction force."

"There are ways of cheating around laws of physics without violating them. An example: a spaceship and a rocket float in space. The rocket lights up and accelerates away. No effect on the ship's momentum. Let's say the ship has an impact plate. The rocket flies into it. The collision imparts momentum on to the ship accelerating it."

"The rocket's acceleration has no effect on the ship unless it hits the ship."

"Or is connected to the ship. Ordinarily, after a fusion reaction, the product particles fly away in all directions. They hit other particles, and through momentum transfer, like the rocket hitting the ship, they cause the other particles to jiggle around with this extra energy. That's heat. The Creation women don't want heat, they want propulsion. If they can cram protons, hydrogen nuclei, together with magnetic force, they can align 'em so that the product particles fly in one direction with the fusion energy, no canceling effect like we have with unaligned fusion. The protons are temporarily not connected to the ship when they collide and fuse."

"The product particles are accelerated without affecting the ship."

"Just like the unattached rocket. After accelerating, the product particles run into magnetic fields that restrain them. Momentum transfer supplies thrust to drive the ship. But we don't think it's the individual particles that are being restrained. Still not an efficient way of supplying thrust, though much better than relying on emitted light thrust alone. May I have those weights, please."

On a table was a balance scale and a set of known masses. "Sure."

"A one pound mass and an eight ounce mass. The one pound mass travels at one foot per second and hits a spacecraft. It supplies by momentum transfer an impulse to the ship. That is the force of impact times the period of time this force acted. The formula for momentum is mass times velocity. One times one is one foot-pound-mass per second, or one poundal-second of impulse. The half pound mass travels at two feet per second, the same momentum and the same impulse. Upon impact, the ship will be accelerated the same. But the ENERGY to drive these two masses to these speeds is different. One half mass times velocity SQUARED. One HALF foot-poundal for the pound mass. ONE foot-poundal for the half pound mass. Same impulse, TWICE the energy."

"That didn't make sense when I took Physics for Sissies." The watered down physics course for liberal arts majors.

"I know, that's where we lose a lot of students. We think that inside the plasma ball on the spacecraft is a fusion core perhaps six feet in diameter. If it's the density of the Sun's core it contains 1 million pounds of material, an estimate for our simulations. This core pulses perhaps 200,000 times per second."

"Pulses? Like it's compressed to ignite fusion?"

"Exactly. With the protons spin aligned and the core mass tied together with its own magnetic field, the fusion accelerates the entire core in one direction without affecting the ship. Like the unattached rocket. Then it runs into restraining magnetic fields tied to the ship, transferring its momentum, just like the rocket hitting the impact plate. Then it's compressed again. At 200,000 times per second, we have the thrust necessary to push the ship at six feet per second squared. The amount of mass in the core and the pulse frequency could be different, but we'd still get the same result. Now that the ship is in orbit, we can observe 3.6 trillion foot-poundals per second emitted as blue light when it's accelerating at six feet per second squared. Divide that by the 1.2 trillion poundals it takes to accelerate a 200 billion pound ship that much, multiply by two, we get the six feet per second that the fusion accelerates the core with each pulse. The ratio of kinetic energy to momentum is proportional to speed, just like the example with the pound and half pound masses."

"Enough about the ship. What can you tell me about Alpha Centauri?"

"What the astronomers told you, Mr. President. Two Sunlike stars in an 80 year orbit around each other, distance between them ranging from one billion to 11.2 billion miles. Right now, as seen from Earth, the two stars are the farthest apart, orbiting in a plane tilted 11 degrees from edge on. The women say Creation orbits in this same plane. You've been briefed on the Roche lobes?"

"Yes. With only one star, our Solar System is so Sir Isaac Newton. But with two stars, the orbital mechanics of any planets Alpha Centauri may have is Joe Louie Lagrange's worst nightmare."

"Oh, not his worst nightmare. There are lots of multiple star systems around. But even at their closest approach of one billion miles, the Alpha Centauri stars each have enough room within their Roche lobes for rocky planets like Earth and Mars."

"Even the Goldilocks Zones?"

"Oh yeah. Creation's orbit is slightly affected by the Second Sun when it comes in close, but it's still stable enough for Earthlike climates. But any planet orbiting further than 300 million miles from either star will not have a stable orbit because the other one swings in so close. No planets at the L4 and L5 points because the Second Sun has 77% as much mass as the First Sun and the separation distance varies so widely. For a planet orbiting outside the orbits of the two stars, that's a long row to hoe given the 11.2 billion mile maximum separation distance."

"Not likely to have any Jupiter like gas giants. But the third star?"

"Proxima Centauri might have a gas giant or two. It orbits the center of mass of the Alpha System at a distance of one trillion miles. It's a tiny red dwarf that flares to three times normal intensity in only a few minutes, sometimes seconds."

"Catches a spaceship by surprise."

"Yeah! It'll not have rocky planets with a stable climate like Earth or Creation."

"Wasn't Alpha Centauri much further away 50,000 years ago?"

"Yes, 50,000 years ago it was 9 light years or 53 trillion miles away. It moved 23 degrees across the southern sky since then, getting brighter as it gets closer. It'll pass within 3 light years or 18 trillion miles of us in about 28,000 years, heading across our sky along the length of Hydra into Cancer. This can be calculated from the observed proper motion, radial velocity, and parallax. Draw a straight line from here to Alpha Centauri. It's path relative to us crosses that line at a 45 degree angle. We'll see it in the Northern Hemisphere in 60,000 years, heading away from us."

The tape player was turned on. A street scene of a large city with trees consistent with a temperate zone climate. Bright sunshine. The buildings looked well cared for. Automobiles drove the asphalt streets and concrete sidewalks carried people. Flags hung on poles. "We should copy the design of those flags." the President suggested.

A voice came on to narrate. "Hello, Mr. President. I am Helga Trvlakian. By now, I should be at Edwards Air Force Base in California. I thank you for your invitation to visit your country. While you may not be able to visit my Planet, we can let you visit us in this film. This is Cair Atlaston, the largest city on Planet Creation with 1 million people." Helga told about the seaport, the industrial area, environmental concerns. She described some of the technology in daily use. "There is methane and propane that we drill wells for, but we do not have petroleum or coal. We use alcohols and hydrocarbons made from plants and plankton. We get most of our electricity from fusion reactors. Most of our aircraft are powered by external propellers. We have a few jet engine aircraft."

Helga continued, "We won't discuss our space program because of security concerns. If a fleet enters our Solar System with hostile intent, we'll defend ourselves. But we have no intention to bring war to Earth, unless Earth needs our help in defense. We come in peace. The *Neanderthal Return* is unarmed, except for hand weapons for internal security. If we are attacked, our orders are to run. During an emergency rapid acceleration, we might open the magnetic bottle that holds our fusion reactor. But we cannot direct the beam for use as an intentional weapon."

"I will need voice analysis for honesty." ordered the President. "Protocol prohibits a polygraph exam."

"If we cannot get away, then our orders are to surrender, to communicate that an attack is unnecessary, we intend no harm. Of course, we are glad that our ship is safe, in orbit upon your invitation. On more pleasant matters, let's talk about Creation history."

A photograph of Lamoan Reducker and some of his men filled the screen. "This is Lamoan Reducker. He was an adventurer, an explorer. The greatest hero of our history. He and his men set out from Cair Atlaston in a group of sailing ships for a voyage to the Opposite Continent. To help you understand this story, I must beg your forgiveness while I digress and describe Creation mathematics and geometry." She described the Base Twelve number system and their weights and measures. The Appendix titled *Creation Numbers and Units of Measure* describes these in detail.

She explained that *tree* is Atlantean for half or incomplete. *Chm* is Atlantean for full or complete. A *treefat*, which is .986 yard, is a half reach, a *chmfat*, which is .986 fathom, is a full reach. The name of their Planet, *Chmpashian*, is translated to Creation. It means that, and it also means completed structure or project. *Treepashian* means incomplete structure or project. *Pote* is Atlantean for foot, both the thing on the end of the leg, and for the unit that is .986 British-American foot. *Tig-it* is what they call .986 inch. A *kepfat* is 8,640 *potes*, about 8,519 feet or 1.61 miles. Where we divide the circle into 360 degrees, they divide it into 432 *deems*. Each *deem* is 72 *linits*, each *linit* is 72 *prelates*.

After Helga explained the above, she detailed the story of how the Reducker Expedition found the Old Records and learned to read the alien language. She spelled out what they had found there, and this is how Creation people learned of their origins, and of the existence of Earth. The Reducker Expedition occurred 390 Earth years before, about Earth Year 1610, Creation Years Twenty Three Eighty Six through Twenty Three Eighty Nine. After that, Creation technology advanced into an industrial and scientific revolution.

"At about your year eighteen fifty," Helga continued the narrative, "an extremely terrible event happened, a holocaust. A Virus tore through our entire Planet." She then told the story of the Virus Holocaust, the loss of the entire male population of Creation. The desperate medical research that discovered how to stop the aging process. She assured them that there was no possibility of any of them carrying the Virus to Earth and causing a similar holocaust of Earth men. "Now Mr. President, you know why we are here, introducing ourselves to the Planet Earth. The Fountain of Youth is not Immortality. We need to figure out how to give birth to a next generation. We need children."

Everyone was silent. "Pretty soon," began the President, "everyone on Earth will know about their problem."

"No men. No sperm. No children." concluded General Fairchild.

"Feminist paradise." declared the First Lady. "But only for women who want neither men nor children cluttering up their lives. Our ladies from Creation have had enough of that."

"Their men killed off by a Virus Holocaust. They may have a vaccine that will protect men they bring in from Earth. They tell us of a Planet with millions of lonely childless women. They may be Neanderthals with muscles like linebackers, but that's the best offer any Earthman has ever received." General Fairchild smiled.

"Their faces take a little getting used to, but Andemona is pretty and Helga is downright beautiful." The Curator was enthralled by these living Neanderthals. "A Planet full of women who will appreciate the gift that a child is, and will have incentive to treat the father right, will be a siren song for divorced fathers like Neil Peace. That damn Shuttle of theirs can drop down anywhere, anytime, to pick up a load of men who want to leave Earth and try again on Creation. Leaving the single moms to fend for themselves."

"Let's save divorce law for another meeting, please." the President suggested. "Here's what we can do: Several of 'em can stay on Earth to form an embassy. We give 'em frozen sperm samples from as many men as are willing to donate, of all races and ethnic groups, let 'em take Neil Peace and other men who are willing to go, and bid 'em farewell. They go home and make babies."

"Assuming Cro-Magnon sperm is compatible with Neanderthal eggs." said the Curator.

"That's a big assumption." admitted the President. "How closely related are the two Races?"

"It is currently popular in the paleoanthropology community to believe that both Neanderthals and modern humans evolved from *Homo heidelbergensis*. This species is represented by skulls and bones found at Heidelberg, Germany; Petralona, Greece; and Broken Hill, Zambia." The

Curator drew a chart showing these hypothesized relationships. "The 800,000 year old *Homo antecessor* skeletons found at Gran Dolino, Spain might be ancestral to *Homo heidelbergensis*."

"How about Peking Man?" asked General Fairchild.

"Peking Man was a *Homo erectus*, as was Java Man. It is believed that *Homo erectus* did not evolve into *Homo heidelbergensis*, but eventually died out, perhaps much later than we used to believe. But *erectus* and *heidelbergensis* evolved from *Homo ergaster*, best represented by the beautifully preserved skeleton of the Turkana Boy found in Kenya."

"So Peking Man did not evolve into the modern Chinese?"

"No. The modern Chinese are *Homo sapiens* evolved from the same African population of *Homo heidelbergensis* that we have all descended from. This offends some Chinese; they worship Peking Man as their ancestor. The European population of *heidelbergensis* evolved into Neanderthals. The skeletons and crania from the Pit of the Bones near Atapuerca, Spain have proto-Neanderthal characteristics. They are a late version of *Homo heidelbergensis*. It is my professional opinion that *Homo neanderthalensis* evolved in Europe, *Homo sapiens* evolved in Africa, and that we are separate species. Separate species means that while we are closely related, of the same genus, we nevertheless cannot interbreed."

"But there are those who do not agree with you."

"The alternative interpretation looks at the Heidelberg Man as an archaic *Homo sapiens*. He had a large brain, not quite as large as either Neanderthals or modern humans. Because both Neanderthals and modern humans evolved from *Homo sapiens heidelbergensis*, they and we are seen as subspecies of *Homo sapiens*: *Homo sapiens neanderthalensis* and *Homo sapiens sapiens*."

"Our visitors from Creation are obviously as sapient as we." the President said judiciously. "Perhaps we should call ourselves *Homo sapiens cromagnonensis*."

"Perhaps we should. This second theory suggests the possibility that Neanderthals and Cro-Magnons could have interbred. If the population of Neanderthals was reduced, and a much larger population of Cro-Magnons was to move in, then Neanderthal genes would be swamped and Neanderthal bone structure would disappear from the fossil record. Followers of this theory believe that some of the characteristics that define the race Caucasian may have been inherited from the Neanderthal."

"Neanderthal and Cro-Magnon interbreeding is why white people are white?"

"That theory is not popular anymore. At Mount Carmel in Israel, we find a large number of well preserved skeletons of both Cro-Magnons and Neanderthals. This fossil record indicates coexistence between the two groups for as long as 60,000 years. Yet we cannot find a single skeleton that may be a hybrid."

"What about the Tabun jaw?"

"The jawbone from Level C in Tabun, Israel was a Neanderthal with a hint of a chin. But he was not a hybrid. We know that within the Cro-Magnon species, racial diversity of the parents has never prevented healthy offspring. If hybrid skeletons cannot be found in Israel, it may be because Neanderthals and Cro-Magnons cannot interbreed."

"You believe this group in the spacecraft are evolved from Neanderthals?"

"These women are similar to most modern Earth people in the proportions of their arms and legs and body lengths. The European Neanderthals lived in an Ice Age; their foreshortened limbs an adaptation to a cold climate. We see the same thing with Inuit and Lapps. 50,000 years in a temperate or tropical climate, the limbs would become longer. The women believe themselves to be Neanderthals. The examination by Dr. Nguyen confirms Neanderthal morphology. She sent some X-ray photographs." A technician put the X-ray photos up for viewing. "Andemona,

Helga, and Lucinda. Brow ridges, sloped forehead, large eye sockets, occipital bun. Here we see the suprainiac depression. But surprisingly each palate is as flat as the palate of the Old Man of La Chapelle. How is it that they can speak, and speak so well?"

"The same way bumblebees fly, they don't let experts tell 'em they can't. Let's see what we can figure out to help 'em bear children." The President gave his order. "Let's release this tape to the public if the Creation women consent to it. Start the visitors on a vaccine program. If Dr. Nguyen and their ship's doctor, Askelion Lamakian, okays it, release them from quarantine. Schedule a dinner at the White House, whirlwind tours of the Western Hemisphere, the whole bit."

Monoloa and Pavel wore pressure suits in the Soyuz descent module. Originally designed for three cosmonauts, it was redesigned for two cosmonauts in pressure suits after the Soyuz 11 disaster. "Star City, this is *Mir* descent module," Pavel said into his transmitter, "we are go for separation and reentry sequence."

"This is Star City, copy that. We are coming up on separation window in one minute, at mark!"

"We have begun countdown to separation." Pavel looked over to his passenger. "How are you doing, Monoloa?"

"Doing fine, I'm great."

"Good. Let me take care of everything and we'll come to a perfect landing in Kazakhstan." Pavel waited for the countdown to reach zero. "Separating, NOW." He reached up to the control panel and triggered the separation.

They heard a thump. "This is *Mir*, we confirm separation of descent module. Looking good. Pavel and Monoloa, it has been a pleasure flying with you."

"Thank you, *Mir*. Air pressure is fine. Location, altitude, speed, and heading are nominal. Commencing automatic descent sequence, NOW."

Monoloa now regretted not coming down in the Shuttle, which uses magnetic drive and does not rely on a free fall reentry sequence. But the kidnapping of Neil Peace made it politically expedient to allow the Earthlings to bring her down in their spacecraft. That is the funny thing about courage, it sure feels like fear.

"This is Star City. Your retrorockets have fired. We confirm nominal descent profile. You are on course for the Kazakhstan Landing Zone."

"Copy that Star City. Coming up on instrument module jettison." To clear the heat shield for reentry. They heard a boom and felt a jolt. "We have instrument module jettison."

"Copy that Pavel. Coming up on reentry interface and communications blackout. Good luck Pavel and Monoloa."

The descent module is shaped like a large thimble with the heat shield at the base. As the flames of ablation became visible in the window, Pavel held Monoloa's gloved hand to reassure her. "Don't worry, Mono. I've done this four times before. Everything is going like it should."

Monoloa smiled at his concern. "It's not a problem, Pavel. Free fall reentries are part of our training." She didn't want to reveal that the magnetic drive Shuttle is only the fourth one ever built by Planet Creation.

After three and a half minutes as a meteor, the radio crackled to life. "This is Star City calling descent module. Do you read me?"

"This is the descent module, we read you loud and clear." Pavel is always relieved when he can say this, even while desperately trying to keep Monoloa from noticing his apprehension. Another thump sounded above. "Drogue chute is deployed, main chute should be coming out." He turned to Monoloa. "This is where Komarov bought it. If the lines of these chutes get tangled up, we will slam into the ground." The feel of full gravity reassured them.

"This is Recovery Team calling descent module. Your main chute is deploying. It is now fully deployed, a beautiful sight. Welcome home, Pavel. Welcome to Earth, Monoloa Mrvlakian."

Pavel extended the periscope and observed the parachute. He let Monoloa take a look. "It is beautiful. I like the orange and white circles."

Pavel transmitted, "This is descent module. We copy Recovery Team, and confirm chute deployment." Another bang, below them. "Heat shield jettison."

"We confirm heat shield jettison, Pavel."

"Jettisoning periscope."

The landing radar measured the distance between itself and the ground. When the distance became short enough, it triggered the solid fuel landing rockets. They heard the whoosh. "Landing rockets firing, looking good Pavel."

"We confirm that, Recovery Team. We will be waiting for you, feels good to be on the ground." They touched down and the capsule rolled over on its side. Pavel and Monoloa unstrapped themselves from their seats. "I will open this valve, get us some fresh air. They were within sight of us, they will be here soon." They climbed out of their pressure suits. Within minutes, the hatch was opened and the Recovery Team greeted the cosmonauts. "Monoloa, you go first."

Monoloa reached for the open hatch. "Please give me your hands." requested one of the rescuers. She complied and was pulled into the open air by the strong but gentle arms of the Recovery Team. As soon as her feet were clear of the capsule she wanted to walk. "Before you walk, you need to lay on the couches for a few minutes." A pair of couches was laid out on the ground ten feet from the open hatch.

"I can walk, really. I am very strong."

"Yes, I understand. But you have been in space for a long time. Many of our cosmonauts want to walk. But they faint if they don't allow a few minutes for their bodies to adjust to the full 9.8 meters per second squared gravity."

"You are right. Thank you." As an experienced astronaut, she knew they were right. As she was laid down on the couch she noticed that he smiled self consciously, he couldn't help himself. They gave her a large wreath of flowers. "Thank you. I love fresh flowers." The young man tried to hide his smile as they brought Pavel over to lay on his couch. They were surrounded by the foot high grass of the steppe, which stretched off to a horizon as flat as that of the ocean. "What is it?"

He blushed and his friends chuckled. Monoloa has bright red hair and green eyes that look like they could glow in the dark. "You are such a beautiful woman."

She grinned. "Thank you. You are such a beautiful man."

They broke into laughter as a physician quickly took Monoloa's temperature, blood pressure, and pulse. He did the same for Pavel. "In a few more minutes, you may get up and walk around." he informed them.

After a few minutes, Pavel put his flowers down and stood up. While a little unsteady at first, he accepted a large white marker and went over to the descent module and signed his name. Monoloa stood tall and viewed the vast horizon. Someone handed her a big white marker. "Go ahead. Sign your name on the capsule. That is what Pavel is doing. It is a tradition."

"I'll sign it in Atlantean alphabet."

"That is fine." The Recovery Team crowded around as she walked over to the capsule with the marker. Pavel finished signing his name and stepped aside for her.

She wrote the Atlantean letters with broad strokes and when she finished the last letter of Mrvlakian, she was rewarded with a rousing cheer. "Now you are officially on Planet Earth! Welcome to Kazakhstan, Monoloa Mrvlakian!"

Shadowed by a Secret Service detail, the Creation women jogged a trail at Edwards Air Force Base after release from quarantine. They looked forward to the afternoon drive into Los Angeles. They slowed to a walk, panting heavily and coughing. "What is this? We haven't even gone two *kepfats*. Are we out of shape or what?!"

"This always happens after being in space. We will get it back!" They shouted in Atlantean for privacy.

"It is great to be outside! The fresh air!"

"Right! Fresh diesel fumes. Fresh aviation fuel." Sneeze! "Fresh dust and pollen!" Laughter. Their senses of smell, deadened by a year in a spacecraft, were coming back fast.

"Speaking of fresh, the men on this military base sure are interested in us! I hear they have a betting pool going. The winner is the first one to make love with one of us!"

"Figures. What is their favorite phrase in English? '*Fucking A!*'"

"They sure are bright eyed and bushy tailed. But let's hold off the fun and games until after we have been vaccinated. We don't want to get sick."

"It would embarrass them to report to the hospital with dislocated hips. We will have to watch our strength when screwing a Cro-Magnon!" Laughter.

"Speaking of sex, we better consider what Earth religions teach about it."

"You mean '*Thou shalt not commit adultery*'? We prohibit adultery too."

"It is more than that. The non-Hebrew based Earth religions view sex as a sacred thing. They were concerned with fertility. Fertility of the land to produce food and fiber, and animals to hunt. Fertility of the sea to produce fish. And fertility of the women, to produce children to replace the adults as they grow old and die."

"Sex was worshipped not only because it was fun, it produced children."

"Then comes the Judeo-Christian ethic, and Islam, religions that teach against the sinful misuse of sex. The Canaanite religions and their fertility symbols were destroyed because they were considered evil and dangerous."

"Sex is dangerous. Can lead to overpopulation. But homosexuality was taboo in Earth society."

"Still is in American military."

"It is not just the Americans. Their Old Testament declares homosexuality to be as abominable as eating shellfish and pork."

"Understandable with red tide, trichinosis worms, and sexually transmitted diseases. But that is not the reason for their taboos. When we women lay together for comfort and pleasure, we do not generate children. Neither do men when they do likewise. What the Hebrews feared was a widespread failure to produce children because people decided to have fun without the responsibility of children."

"Unlike other tribes, the Hebrews were confident in their ability to produce children within the confines of marriage. Rather than pray to the gods for children, they felt it best to focus the sex drive on producing children and insuring that they are cared for. Hence the bans on premarital sex, on homosexuality, even on masturbation. Those old Hebrew bans continue to affect what Earthlings consider proper. We need to keep this in mind."

After the commercial break, the talk show hostess introduced her next guests. "Speaking of racial harmony, we have two marvelous visitors who are humans descended from Neanderthals transplanted to another Planet. They come in peace in a STARSHIP! From the city of Cair

Atlaston, Atlantis on Planet Creation, I introduce to you Lchnsda Renuxler and Helga Trvlakian!"

Lucinda came out first; they had a makeover at a fine boutique in Hollywood. She wore a blouse with feminine frills that flattered her figure, a short skirt, tan nylon stockings exhibiting her legs and pumps with three inch heels. A sequined band with a corsage wrapped around her head. She took the hostess's right hand with both of hers and shook. She did the same with the basketball player who was the previous guest.

Then came the tall, blonde, and spectacularly beautiful Helga. Her hair was styled marvelously. The strapless dress wrapped around her breasts and midriff like a second skin. The long skirt was cut high on one side to reveal leg to the hip joint as she walked. The sheer nylon wrapped legs terminated a mile below in high heel shoes. She gave the two handshake greeting to the hostess and the basketball player.

After they sat down, the hostess began. "You two are living proof that there is nothing inferior about the Neanderthal Race. While there are many who question the kidnapping of Neil Peace, you have otherwise shown dignity, grace, and considerable intelligence. This is a far cry from the stereotype cavemen that we used to think of with respect to Neanderthals."

"Oh yes," Helga responded, "these anthropologists. They find a few scattered skeletons of our ancestors, and decide that they can tell everything about us from the bones. Can you look at a skull and tell if it contained the brain of a saint or a sinner? You might be able to tell something of the physical health of the person, but you cannot tell anything of his or her intelligence, morality, beliefs, interests, all of the important things about the person."

"Some of the anthropologists thought your Race could not even speak."

Helga, a linguist, smiled. "News flash to the anthropologists: The nerve for our tongue is plenty big enough. We can make the 'k' and hard 'g' sounds because we have flesh where the back of our tongue can touch it. We TALKED about how you thought we could not speak!" The audience laughed.

The hostess went to a more serious matter. "You describe a terrible holocaust on your Planet. You live a life without men, do you miss 'em?"

Lucinda responded, "They were good men whom we cherished. My husband, Chmlee Renuxler, was a wonderful man. I brought some pictures that you may show the audience."

"I have them here." The hostess held each photograph to a camera.

"These are our wedding photos. That big handsome man standing next to me is Chmlee." A young and pretty Lucinda and a sandy haired Neanderthal man, both in elegant clothing. The next photograph showed Lucinda and Chmlee embracing and kissing. "That is where in our ceremony the groom is told that he may kiss the bride. That's us with our parents, my parents both had hair. This is all of us together, with all of our friends and relatives, you see the children down in front. And this shows us dancing. This one was taken a week later, at the balcony of our little bungalow. We were on a hill overlooking the bay. You can see the city, Cair Atlaston, on the other side." Lucinda and Chmlee posed on the rail, the bay and the city behind them.

"Wow. So this is Cair Atlaston?"

"Sure is. We were very happy. We planned to have children. One year later, the Virus came. In the month of Shinoose of the year we designate with the Base Twelve number two, four, eleven, six, the first patient with the Virus was confirmed at Atlaston Hospital. Panic gripped Cair Atlaston. We fled a *hekt* of *kepfats* to the south of the city to ride out the epidemic. Chmlee stayed in a cellar at his uncle's farm wearing a face mask, hiding with the other men. News reports described *kechts* of deaths in the city. The men and boys were dying, the women were living. We didn't know anything about the Virus. All of the men and boys in the cellar fell

45

sick at once. The Virus tore at their brains. They first suffered terrible headaches, then dementia, then coma and" Emotions came flooding back along with the memories. "I'm sorry."

The camera came off of Lucinda. Helga spoke. "Twenty four eleventy six corresponds to your year 1854. We have since studied this Virus in labs. Apparently it is a life form that originally evolved on the home planet of the Face Mountain aliens. It may still exist in the Cydonia area of the Planet Mars. I would advise extreme caution if you ever send a manned mission to Face Mountain. It laid dormant in the Opposite Continent of Planet Creation, somehow left by the aliens. It infected Lamoan Reducker and his men as a benign parasite. It spread throughout Creation."

Helga continued. "Then a virulent form evolved on Graciana, a tropical continent with lush jungles and savannas. The Neanderthal people who live there have dark skin and tall, slender bodies; they were the first to suffer. Eleventy five was the year when Graciana lost all of her men. Then the Virus turned deadly everywhere else on Creation. Eleventy six was when Lchnsda lost her husband. Askelion Lamakian, now our ship's doctor, treated the Renuxler men. There was nothing she could do. The experience left her determined to destroy this bug once and for all. She's an expert on this Virus and can certify that it simply does not exist in either benign or virulent form in the crew of the *Neanderthal Return*."

"How can she do that?" asked the frightened hostess. The basketball player, a man, was also quite concerned.

"The Virus needs to interact with a Y chromosome to reproduce. As women, we don't have Y chromosomes. When our male population died off, the Virus no longer had a host. We have developed an enzyme that is carried by a benign species of bacteria. This enzyme destroys the Virus wherever it finds it. A similar type of enzyme might be what you need to destroy your AIDS virus."

By this time, Lucinda had regained her composure and silently mouthed "Thank you." to the basketball player who had comforted her.

The hostess asked "How are you feeling, Lucinda?"

"I'm fine, I'm fine. There are some things that stay with you for the rest of your life."

"We understand. Maybe we can go to a lighter subject. You come here in sexy clothes that display your arms and shoulders, and your legs. The muscles!"

"Oh yeah." responded Helga. "We Neanderthals grow muscle the way he grows tall. There are some of us who are skinny, there is variation, as there are in Earth people. But we tend to a more robust build."

While Helga rambled on about Neanderthal muscularity, Lucinda suddenly got an idea and whispered it into the basketball player's ear. He smiled and nodded his head.

"How about your running?" asked the hostess.

"Oh we can run for many *kepfats* or miles when we are in shape, LCHNSDA!!"

The tall and grinning athlete was cradled in Lucinda's arms, her right arm under his back bearing most of his weight, her left arm under his knees, not a single part of him was within three feet of the ground as Lucinda stood tall. "I haven't been carried like this since I was a little kid!"

Chapter Six

I remained on the *Neanderthal Return* teaching English and learning Atlantean. I helped link the ship's communications with the Earth telephone systems and with ham radio operators. You should hear the questions I get from Earth.

The Neanderthals from Creation were not the aliens who crashed at Roswell. They have never been to Area 51. They do not make crop circles. They are not telepathic. Except for me, they do not abduct people from back roads.

We don't know whether Sasquatches, Yetis, and Almas are surviving tribes of Neanderthals. These women don't look like Bigfoot.

The Neanderthals from Creation are not aware of any gray bipedal vertebrate aliens with big black eyes. The Face Mountain aliens weren't these; they look like Face Mountain, at least the way Face Mountain looked before being eroded by sandstorms. The braincase surrounds the face and looks like a helmet.

Some people wanted us to go to Mars and look at Face Mountain. But these girls believe the place is booby trapped with a weapon that can reach out into space. It may be what destroyed NASA's Mars Observer. NASA wanted us to look for the Observer, but because they're now sending a probe every year to Mars, we didn't want to get in the way.

We did not maintain a regular orbit. Because people prefer to stick to one surface and not float around, we kept the fusion reactor pulsing to provide acceleration. The light exhaust was pointed past Earth for safety reasons.

I worried about Captain Trviea Harsradich. I was the one who suggested that we use the phrase 'relieved of command' instead of 'mutiny'. She was no longer under guard. She attended daily meetings with the crew. They focused on the mission of establishing relations with Earth and obtaining sperm to solve the problem of reproduction. Wilma and Betty were still locked up; they apparently abused their authority as enforcers of the Captain's will.

After the four women went over to Earth spacecraft and then to the Earth surface, the ship settled into an easygoing orbital routine. One woman at the controls can maintain orbit, a duty they rotated in shifts. The rest performed their duties, but there was plenty of spare time. They brought out musical instruments and sang songs. I joined in and sang Earth songs: Beatles melodies, church hymns, folk songs, and rock and roll.

I was in my quarters getting ready to sleep. They knock when they want to visit you in your private space. "Come in." I said in Atlantean.

Trviea Harsradich entered. "You accept peace offering?" she asked in English. She didn't tell me she was fluent before. She had two cups and a bottle of liquid.

"Sure, Captain, whatcha got?"

"In Atlantean, we call it *manatat*. It's what you Earthlings call rum."

"Where'd you get alcoholic beverages on this ship?"

"I'm Captain. Rank hath its privileges." She poured some into each cup. "Try some, it's good. Do you hate me? Are you angry with me?"

"I fear you. I don't trust you. You didn't want to announce yourself to Earth."

"No, I didn't want Earth to know about us. You didn't like being kidnapped?"

"No. You did it because you need our sperm, but you didn't want to reveal your existence. Tell me, do you hate the Cro-Magnon?"

"I FEAR the Cro-Magnon, but I do not hate the Cro-Magnon."

"That kind of fear is what Hitler exploited. What the Ku Klux Klan exploits. What the anti-gay folks exploit. Fear can become hate, and hate based on race can lead to genocide. Would you kill off the Cro-Magnon Race if given the chance?"

"No. But your Race produced Pol Pot, Hitler, Stalin, and other mass murderers. And what happened to my kind in Europe? Only half of us were hauled off to Creation by the Face Mountain aliens. There were still Neanderthals at Zefarraya, Spain a dozen *kechts* of years later. Plenty of time to double our population back to what it was. At about that time, the Cro-Magnon people, ancestors of you WHITE Earthlings, appear in Europe. Did your Race wipe out mine? We disappear from Earth and you Cro-Magnons have since constantly fought wars! We Neanderthals have also fought wars. But now Earth knows about Creation. Earth knows it's POSSIBLE to build a spacecraft to cover the distance between the stars. One thing our two Races have in common, once we know something is POSSIBLE; we are driven to figure out HOW it is done. I'm afraid Earth spacecraft will eventually visit Creation. I only hope these ships come in peace."

"Are you now reconciled to Earth knowing about Creation?"

"I am. So I now offer you my apology and my friendship."

"Accepted." What else could I do? "But I have to ask, what were you planning to do with me? MAYBE we can interbreed. MAYBE my sperm is compatible with your eggs. MAYBE we can create a healthy child together. But maybe NOT. Maybe we're two separate SPECIES, not two Races of the SAME species. You have no more way of knowing this than we do. Even if we can interbreed, the result would be half-breeds. When Earth builds interstellar spacecraft, Cro-Magnon settlers will provide more genetic material to the Creation population. The Neanderthal bone structure will disappear from Creation just as it did from Europe. I don't think you want this result. So what were you planning?"

She smiled. "Your scientists are learning how to manipulate genetic material, DNA and chromosomes. Our genetic engineering technology is more advanced than yours."

"You shut off the aging gene."

"Yes, it's more complicated than that. Theoretically, we can live *kechts* of years. But we can die, we will die. So we need to figure out how to replace ourselves. Give us a Cro-Magnon sperm cell. One of yours perhaps. We take two Neanderthal eggs from different women for genetic diversity. We remove the chromosomes from the sperm cell. We're not looking to inherit Cro-Magnon characteristics. We remove the chromosomes from one of the Neanderthal eggs and transplant them into the sperm cell. We let the sperm cell heal and let it fertilize the other Neanderthal egg. We place the embryo into a womb. Nine months later, a baby Neanderthal girl."

"So to replace your female population, you need a few good men. A scientist in Britain was able to clone a sheep. Perhaps you could do that to produce baby girls."

"If we get desperate enough. They would be genetically identical to the parent, and we don't want large groups of identical women. If the Cro-Magnon sperm cell has a Y chromosome, we keep that chromosome, take the 22 chromosomes from a Neanderthal egg, except the X chromosome, place them in the sperm cell, let it fertilize another Neanderthal egg. We get a Neanderthal boy, with just a few Cro-Magnon characteristics from the Y chromosome. But these processes are time consuming and expensive. To efficiently make mothers out of the twelve and six *beeyons* of women left on our Planet, we wanted the male stem cells which generate the sperm."

"Stem cells! Oh, no! You're not taking no scalpel to my balls!"

She broke up laughing. She spilled her rum and had to pour more. "Before this mutiny, you would've had no choice in the matter." Strapped to that bunk, I could not stop them from doing it. "We take the stem cells from your testicle. We replace Cro-Magnon chromosomes with Neanderthal chromosomes, except the Y chromosome. We need to make boys. Now we can generate thousands of Neanderthal sperm cells. Make plenty of babies. In fact, from the clone we can grow an entire testicle, two of 'em. We remove your testicles and transplant the Neanderthal testicles. Now you're shooting Neanderthal sperm. You can make our women pregnant the old fashioned way."

"So that was your plan?" Appalling, isn't it?

"More or less. But Trvlakian had other ideas. I hope she hasn't exposed our Race to ultimate extinction. She had the legal right to relieve me of command, IF she can make a credible case that I was risking war with Earth. There will be a hearing on that matter when we get back to Creation."

"What's Helga's plan?"

"I don't know if she has a plan. Her view is that we need to be friends with Earth. If the Face Mountain aliens choose to end their experiment, we would need to cooperate as allies in our defense. She's gambling that your people decide it's in their interest to help us continue our Race. I hope she's right. Racism is socially unacceptable on Earth, but it certainly exists. There are Earthlings who are not happy that we Neanderthals live. But it's the current policy of almost all of the Earth governments, supported by public opinion, that racism is evil and unacceptable. I just hope it stays that way forever."

"I hope so too. I think we'll do all that we can to help you continue your Race. If we can interbreed, then miscegenation can reunite the human species. If not, then we should have two species of humans to face the future together. You have my permission to use my sperm samples for your research."

"Thank you. Ever since you made sure Earth knows about your presence on this ship, you have shown great enthusiasm for making love." A knowing smile.

Oh, that. "Well, what do you expect? I'm stuck on a ship with 43 women who haven't had close contact with a man since twenty four eleventy six!"

"I haven't had close contact with a man since then either."

"Ohhhhh! So you brought me this booze to get me in the mood."

"Whatever works." She drew a line on my leg with her finger. "You gotta understand. Since the death of our men, it's like being sent to prison for a long time! Women who aren't normally homosexual become open to new experiences. But I do miss having close contact with a man."

"Are you telling me the truth?" I asked as she petted my thigh. "Or are you just making up stories to get what you want?"

"Like you've never done that?"

Touché. "You have gray hair. But your body is smooth and strong from the age treatment. The gray hair is just a cosmetic affectation?"

"Yes it is. Lchnsda can have hair but she chooses to remain bald. Why not? She was very popular with the boys and she is beautiful. Chmlee Renuxler was one handsome catch."

"Once I've gotten used to your faces and your muscles, I find you very attractive."

"That's your sex drive talking, kid. You like being with a woman who is strong enough to break your body in two. You're not used to that with Cro-Magnon women."

"It's like being stuck on a desert island with female weight lifters."

The Neanderthal woman is just plain strong, but the shape of her rear end and her build is feminine. After giving in to my sex drive, I could empathize with the wives and girlfriends of football players. But these women are incredibly beautiful.

The eyes are huge, with Asian shaped folds of skin over the tear ducts. Everything else, the powerful chewing apparatus, the large broad nose, and the sawed off chin, becomes exotic, you no longer think of her appearance as weird or strange. When she holds you in her powerful arms, you are not going anywhere. What man does not love being held by a powerful woman's legs? And there is an entire Planet of these females just waiting for us? Wow!

But then I was reminded of my responsibilities on Earth.

"Neil, there's a call for you."

"Thanks, I'll take it in here. Hello, this is Neil Peace."

"Hello. Remember me?"

"Angela! How you doing?"

"I'm fine, thank you. What I'm calling you about is that Helga and Lucinda want to visit with me. They're on the plane to Sea-Tac right now. Should I invite them?"

"Go ahead. They're nice women; you'll like 'em. They should be good with the children. They speak English beautifully."

"I'm sure they're all right. The apartment's a mess; I have to clean up! Get the kids on their best behavior. Virgil and Christa have been the school celebrities lately. They handle it well, but the reporters keep pressing for dirt on our divorce. Christa came home crying! Reporter asked her if you've ever abused her. She said no, of course not! Reporter then accused her of covering up for you, of being in denial. We've never hurt our children like that. Why are the reporters trying to make us out to be unfit parents?"

"Ohhh! I don't know, that's the press for you."

"The court! I got the judges to seal the divorce file. But they want to know how you feel about keeping the file sealed and kept from reporters."

"OH! Yeah! Keep it sealed! I'm all for that under the present circumstances!"

"Good. Thank God! But you have to tell the court yourself!"

"How do I do that? I'm up here in an orbiting spacecraft."

"Your old lawyer said he will represent you *pro bono* for this purpose. You can call him over this telephone and radio system we've got set up with your Neanderthal spacecraft."

"*Pro bono*. In that case I'll talk to him. Maybe he can set something up."

"Thank you. About this visit with the Creation women. You know how I am when it comes to meeting your girlfriends. I filed for divorce so I can't say anything about you having relationships with other women. But I can't help how I feel. Have you been uh, that way, with Helga or Lucinda?"

"Angela, don't worry about that. This is your chance to meet people from another Planet! They have destroyed the racist stereotypes of Neanderthals! They are fully modern humans, just a different Race, perhaps a different species, but they are fantastic! If you pass up this opportunity you will never forgive yourself. Forget the press! Your biggest problem right now is accommodating all those Secret Service agents protecting these Neanderthal women."

"Oh, God! That and cleaning the house! What should I feed them?"

"Feed them what you like. They like fresh fruit and vegetables. There's a Garden Room on the ship. They keep rabbits and a small breed of goat. What they miss is pork, beef, and other big animal meat. No room on the ship for a cow, the goats produce little milk. Give 'em dairy products. Ice cream for desert will be successful. Pizza or spaghetti would be good, they like cheese and tomato sauce. They miss seafood, no fish tank on the ship. Just prepare what you would for any dinner guest."

"Okay Neil, you talked me into it. Now I gotta clean house!"

Andemona Chmlakian traveled throughout Mexico. Her English was halting, but her Spanish flows fluently and flawlessly. With her beautiful black hair, quick smile, and charisma, people fell in love with her. Her command of French and Italian made her a television personality where those languages are spoken.

Monoloa Mrvlakian traveled around Central Asia. Her hosts showed her around Leninsk and the Baikonur Cosmodrome. At Samarkand, Uzbekistan she visited with the bones of the Neanderthal child found at Teshik-Tash. She laid a bouquet of flowers and said the Atlantean Prayer for the Dead. Her Russian language interviews were broadcast throughout the former Soviet Union. She was asked about the Yetis and the Almas that may live in the high mountains of Central Asia. Are the Almas surviving tribes of Neanderthal? If they are, she would certainly like to meet them. She gave interviews to Chinese and Japanese television in their languages. The Chinese call her the Angel of the South Gate because Alpha Centauri is *Nan Mun*, the South Gate.

Helga and Lucinda arrived at Sea-Tac and greeted a crowd at the airport. In Auburn, the Secret Service set up around Angela's apartment and the community hall. "Don't worry, Angela, after this we'll get outta here and let you have your life back."

"Thank you. It's important that nothing happens to these women."

"They were a nation unknown to us until your ex talked them into revealing their existence. For that he should get a Nobel Peace Prize. We know nothing of their military capability. Helga declared that a fleet of spacecraft that enters their system with hostile intent will be fought."

"We would do the same, if we had the capability. Thank God they want to be friends. I wonder why they want to see me?"

"Probably to check out their Cro-Magnon man. They need a father for their next generation. They want to see his children, find out about their health."

"They might want to know why I divorced him."

"Why did you?"

"I don't want to talk about that. Your job is to make sure we can have a little barbecue party without any problems."

"I stand corrected. Well, everyone on the guest list checks out."

"Thank God."

With the Secret Service in place, everything was ready. A Secret Service man announced, "They're arriving! They're coming in right now, the rain's not too bad?"

"Oh no, just a drizzle! I see 'em coming!" A limousine pulled up to the community hall. People crowded around to see. "Okay everybody, make room! We don't want 'em stuck out in the rain too long!" People backed away. The limo driver opened the doors. Helga and Lucinda each stepped out. They wore new windbreaker jackets, jeans and tennis shoes. Lucinda savored the feel of the raindrops on her head.

"Rain! I miss the feel of RAIN!" Lucinda lingered outside.

Helga came around the car, savoring the rain. She said in Atlantean, "We should get inside before we catch cold. Get these children inside!" A nine year old girl caught her attention. Helga crouched down, a CHILD! "Hi! What is your name?"

"I'm Christa McAuliffe Peace, Neil Peace's daughter."

"Pleased to meet you!"

"My father says he's accepted your apology. But me and my brother thought he was dead, we were afraid we would never see him again."

"I am very sorry that we did that. It was wrong."

"I accept your apology. My father likes you ladies a lot. Are you my father's girlfriend?"

"Let's just say that I'm one of 47 girlfriends. Because I can speak English, I got to know him."

"I'm glad you got to know him, you are very beautiful."

"Oh, thank you! Who's that hiding back there?"

"That's my brother, Virgil Grissom Peace. He's still very angry with you."

"Virgil, I'm sorry."

"It's okay, Helga Trvlakian. My dad told us it was a misunderstanding. Now we can be friends."

"We will be friends! I know that. We should get out of the rain before we all catch cold."

Inside, Lucinda shook hands, greeting people. Finally, "Lucinda Renuxler, I'm Angela Peace."

"Hello! I'm so glad to meet you! Where are your children?"

"They're around here somewhere. Oh, your friend is coming in with Christa. I'm her mother, Angela Peace, I hope she's not bothering you!"

"Oh no, it's perfectly all right!" assured Helga. "She's very nice." A gentleman took her coat. She shook Angela's hand. "I'm Helga Trvlakian. I'm honored to meet you. And, uh, hey!"

"That is my son Virgil Peace."

"We've met." admitted Helga.

"Virgil, come over here." directed his mother.

The seven year old came over with a big grin on his face. "Nice to meet you Mrs. Renuxler."

"You look just like your dad!" exclaimed Lucinda.

"Is it true you don't have any kids on your Planet?"

"That is very true. No men either."

"What's that like?"

"Well, we women just do everything! Have to. But we cannot have children without fathers. So we put our time into medical and scientific research, space exploration, athletics, whatever interests us."

"Are you going to take my dad away?"

Silence. Lucinda and Helga thought about that one very carefully. "Nothing has been decided yet. You father, however, has handled the situation extremely well. You can be very proud of him; he is a great man. We admire him."

"You've been taking good care of him?"

"We have been taking very good care of him."

"Well ladies," Angela grinned, "you should meet everyone else. You have the hands of six billion Cro-Magnons to shake." She giggled. "Better get started!"

The women from Creation shook hands and visited with everyone at the party, and met with each and every child. Meeting children was the best part of the party.

The people sat together at the tables for the feast. Helga and Lucinda devoured the beef with gusto. After a year of rabbit and goat meat, fresh beef was a real treat! Dairy products! Pizza and ice cream. But they had to watch their eating; even Neanderthal women can put on weight.

Then the band played. A century and a half of no close physical contact with men left the Creation women eager to slow dance with the Earthmen.

Helga and Lucinda took the microphones and sang some Atlantean songs. Happy, bouncy songs, beautiful love songs, and songs about the laughter of children. When there were children. Then they sang a song of incredible beauty and sadness. The gentle Atlantean words flowed throughout the hall, bringing tears to everyone present. Their stance, their voices, the way they held the microphones communicated grief, pride, and love. When the final Atlantean word drifted off into silence, the singers slowly lowered their microphones to the sides of their hips, arms fully extended. A few nervous hands started to clap. Then more joined in. Then thundering applause.

After the party Angela invited the two Creation women over to her apartment. With the children in bed, the women sat down with coffee to talk.

"Angela, may I ask you a personal question?" asked Lucinda.

"Okay. Sure."

"Why did you divorce Neil?"

Sigh. "I don't want this in newspapers all over the world, two worlds at that."

"We understand. But now we are in private. Even the Secret Service folks are safely outside. We'll keep this conversation confidential."

"We had different ideas about what a marriage should be. What we expected of each other. His ideas weren't inferior to mine, but I was too blinded by my frustration to understand that. He felt the same way. One thing about him is that when he is mad, he refuses sex! I thought that was a woman thing, but. What? You're laughing!"

The Creation women could not help themselves.

"Don't tell me, let me guess." said Angela. "The reason you relieved your Captain of command and flashed Morse Code at us is because Neil absolutely refused sex."

They both nodded their heads. "I HAD to relieve her of command!" pleaded Helga. They told Angela about the mutiny and the decision to introduce themselves to Earth.

Lucinda reminded Helga that "Preventing the Captain from starting a war with Earth is the only lawful reason for relieving her of command."

"That's right. We discussed Neil's suggestion while he was in another room. He wasn't going to make love with any of us until he got some life insurance, namely that Earth knows we exist and that he is on our ship. We discussed it further. It would be immoral to endanger the ultimate survival of the Neanderthal Race on Creation to satisfy our sexual urges. We concluded that Earth will eventually build starships. The Earth starships would blunder into our Solar System. A misunderstanding could start a war. So we all agreed to do what Neil suggested."

"What will you now do with my ex?" asked Angela. "The children miss their father. He had been seeing the kids every week."

"It's his decision." said Lucinda. "He has already given us his permission to use his sperm for the purpose of research and for making babies. If he wishes to go to Creation with us, he will, as our guest. If he wishes to return to Earth, we'll either bring him down or transfer him to one of your Space Shuttles."

"Oh my God. If he goes, that can devastate the children."

"We know. Your children are very precious to you."

"They are the most important things in my life."

"The most precious gift a man can give a woman. The most precious gift a woman can give a man. Neil has offered us the chance for this most precious gift, and we appreciate it. In all of Creation, there is not one single child!"

"You may take his sperm. I filed for divorce, I cannot object to him making love with other women. You didn't RAPE him did you?"

53

"No, of course not! After we showed Earth that we had him on board, he let us make love with him. That bothers you."

"Mmm."

"Just like I'm still in love with Chmlee." confessed Lucinda.

Angela started to laugh. "I just don't believe this! Here I am discussing such intimate things with women who come from another Planet! Let's talk about you. What do you guys like to do back home?"

"I'm a City Girl." informed Helga. "I love Cair Atlaston, plenty of music, plays, good food. But I sometimes visit Lchnsda on her farm."

"I inherited it from Chmlee's family when the Virus killed them all." Lucinda explained. "It's a beautiful piece of land. Almost a square *kepfat*, about 1600 acres. I keep horses, we go riding every chance we get."

"What's happening to your farm right now?"

"Chmlee's sister Jevine Renuxler is living on it. She grows crops and takes care of the horses."

They talked some more, then Angela yawned. "Oh, I'm getting tired. I have got to go to bed. It's been fun having you here. Hopefully we can see each other again."

"We hope so too." They said good-bye. The Secret Service drove the Creation women to their hotel room.

Helga woke up first. She looked out the window, still dark, the winter sun not rising for another hour. She could see the stars; the day will be sunny and cold. Good. They planned to visit the place over on the Olympic Peninsula where they picked me up. The Earthlings want to hear their explanation of the caper.

Lucinda was still asleep. Completely nude, Helga stepped into the shower. Neanderthals have a keener sense of smell than Cro-Magnons. They prefer to be cleaner, to wash up more often. She ran the small bar of soap over every part of her tall and muscular female body. It smelled nice. The hotel supplied small bottles of shampoo and conditioner. A nice fresh scent. The warm water and the steam.

She took her time rinsing the shampoo from her hair and the soap from her body. She shut off the water and let her body drip for a moment on to the shower floor. Then she stepped out of the shower and wrapped a huge towel around herself. She used the towel to dry her legs and backside. She leaned over the sink and wrung water out of her blonde hair. She brushed her hair. The steam quickly disappeared from the mirror.

When she stepped out of the shower room she saw Lucinda laying in the big hot tub with just her face above the water. The Creation women were in the hotel's expensive honeymoon suite, the Secret Service having secured the entire floor. Helga tossed her towel aside and stood at the edge of the tub. "Now why didn't I think of that?" she said in Atlantean.

"The advantage of not having hair on your head. You don't have to shower to clean it."

"You enjoyed the slow dancing last night, didn't you?"

"It would be dishonest for me to say that I did it only to be diplomatic." She grinned. "There is plenty of room for both of us in here. Climb on in. You don't have to wait until I'm done."

Helga laid down in the tub next to her shipmate. "The Cro-Magnons can teach us a thing or two about luxury and comfort. Speaking of which, did you make love with Neil before we left the spaceship?"

"No."

"Why not? After nine dozen years, it felt fantastic. When Neil no longer feared for his life, he no longer said no. Divorced men get to missing it too. And you have a beautiful body."

"Thank you. Quite a compliment coming from Earth's newest sex symbol. But my baldness puts off some of the Earthmen. I don't know why, some of their famous basketball players shave their heads and they are VERY sexy."

"They are not used to seeing bald women."

"They are not used to seeing women like me. Without hair, my Neanderthal features are obvious. Neil pegged me as a Neanderthal as soon as he saw me. At the same time, I am perceived as exotic. For all the Barbie Doll, Playboy Playmate ideal that they have for feminine beauty, there is also a culture here that glamorizes the woman with muscle. The muscle magazines in the convenience store have pictures of beautiful women with powerful arms, large breasts, and long strong legs. I love looking at the men who are photographed with them!"

"Cro-Magnons consider a Neanderthal style build up of muscle to be sexy, on both men and women. So why didn't you take your turn with Neil?"

Sigh. "I don't know. I guess I feel guilty about abusing him when he was strapped down."

"He understands you were following orders. He has forgiven you and told you you're still friends. You enjoyed the time you spent with him before that."

"Yes I did. But I feel a little guilty about that too."

"Oh Lchnsda! Chmlee loved you way too much to want you to be celibate and lonely for the rest of your life. Let the Spirit take care of him. You have to take care of yourself." Helga drew little circles with her finger around Lucinda's nipple.

"I wish you wouldn't do that." She nevertheless shifted and closed her eyes in response to the sensation.

"No you don't."

"Well, maybe not. Chmlee used to do that."

"I would hope so! He was your husband!"

"The Earthlings suspect us of rampant *lesbianism*, and here we are sharing a hot tub."

"He-he. That is because they cannot imagine women being completely celibate in the absence of men. I have no problem with getting you all hot and bothered. That way you will wrap your legs around Neil when the next opportunity presents itself. We want you to do your fair share."

"Ohh. And then Dr. Lamakian's cold stainless steel spoon."

"Small price to pay." They made some gentle lesbian love interrupted by a knock on the door.

The women separated from each other as fast as they could without splashing water. They tried to look nonchalant. "Come in."

A female Secret Service agent came into the room. "We should be getting breakfast soon. The sun is coming up. We have a full day ahead of us! Everyone wants to see the Creation women."

"Why don't you take your clothes off and join us in the tub for a few minutes?" suggested Lucinda.

"I would love to, but I'm on duty. Besides, I don't have any bathing suits. And you don't either!" She just noticed that.

"Don't need bathing suits. Hey, some of your men should be coming off duty."

"One's coming off duty right about now."

"Oh yeah! Ask him in, please!"

"He doesn't have any swimming trunks."

"We don't need no stinking swimming trunks!"

The Secret Service woman laughed. "I'm sorry. He has a wife. He don't need no stinking divorce!"

"Oh pooo! I guess we will have to get ready for breakfast." Sigh.

While the Creation women ate breakfast in the hotel restaurant, the Secret Service prepared their limousine. The girls made conversation with some of the other hotel guests, signed autographs, and posed with them for photographs.

The women and the Secret Service dressed warm, nice winter coats and fuzzy hats for the heads. The limo drove to the ferry terminal in Seattle.

Everything had been prearranged. The limousine was waved past the regular ferry traffic to a special loading area. Parked in the lot used for the Winslow run were the VIP's, news reporters, and other people willing to wait hours and undergo extensive Secret Service searches for the privilege of riding the ferry with the two women from Planet Creation. "Hey! Look at that! That is the flag of Atlantis, our nation on Creation!" shouted Lucinda. "I don't remember showing them our national flag!"

"It was waving from the flagpoles in Cair Atlaston shown in our videos. These Earthlings are very perceptive. They put more emphasis on national flags, at least the Americans do. A nice gesture on their part."

"Some of them have been watching our language videos! That sign is in Atlantean!"

"'Welcome good friends and neighbors'. Another one! 'Peace on Creation and good will toward women.'"

"I keep hearing about Earthlings who don't trust us and are unhappy that we exist. But I've yet to meet any."

"This Secret Service escort is not going to let any of THEM near us."

The limousine drove on to the ferry and parked at the other end of the car deck. Chock blocks were placed under the wheels of the car and a rope like that used at theaters was stretched across the deck behind them. "Okay ladies, you have to get out of the car. We'll escort you up the stairs to the passenger deck before we load the rest of the vehicles."

"Why can't we stay here and watch them load? This is fascinating."

"When we're accustomed to Neanderthal people from Creation being around, I assure you that you'll be treated the same as everyone else. But right now, we don't want either of you hurt in any way. So let's go, please!" The women were escorted up the narrow stairs. They enjoyed their ride across Puget Sound and visited with the passengers and crew of the ship.

The limousine drove off the ferry and across Bainbridge Island. They took the bridge to the Kitsap Peninsula and continued across the Hood Canal Bridge to the Olympic Peninsula. They went to Highway 101 and then up the lonely gravel road I traveled the summer before. The same wrong turn. And then they were there.

At the site, my '66 Pontiac was parked. Reporters were everywhere. News vans with microwave dishes. They were in the middle of a clearcut, surrounded by Christmas tree sized Douglas fir. The Creation women and their Secret Service bodyguard climbed out of the limousine. A man wearing coveralls came up to greet them. "So you are the famous Helga Trvlakian and Lucinda Renuxler."

"Yes we are. With whom do we have the pleasure?"

"I'm Leonard Taylor. Humble farmer of Jefferson County."

"We're extremely delighted to meet you!" exclaimed Lucinda as she and Helga each gave him their warmest handshake. "Neil told us about you, says you are a great guy."

"I've been keeping his car at my farm all this time. His parents drove it over after the police were through messing with it. Support Enforcement don't like coming up here to grab some poor guy's car. We shoot people messing with cars that don't belong to 'em! When we found out about you guys and that you guys had him, the Center for Disease Control was all over the place. Thank God I had already sold my broccoli! They would've impounded it. Didn't know what kind of disease germs you might be carrying! Like the Indians getting hit with smallpox and giving the white man syphilis! That cute Vietnamese doctor, Cuc Thi Nguyen, she was something else again. Oh, I'm babbling, pardon me! How's Neil doing up there?"

"Oh, he's been fantastic!" exclaimed Helga. "He's having the time of his life!"

Len laughed a full throated belly laugh. "I'll bet he is. You just keep feeding him the broccoli! It is nature's perfect vitamin supplement!"

Two Jefferson County Sheriff sport utility vehicles pulled up. The deputies walked right into the crowd. They nodded their heads at the Secret Service agents in friendly greetings. Some of the reporters focused their cameras and microphones on the Creation women and the county mounties. Somebody had tipped them off.

"Are you Lchnsda Renuxler?"

"Yes I am!" she beamed at the correct pronunciation of her name.

"And are you Helga Trvlakian?"

"Yes I am, Sheriff."

"You are both under arrest for the kidnapping and unlawful imprisonment of one Neil Armstrong Peace, a citizen of the State of Washington, such crimes having taken place here in Jefferson County. You have the right to remain silent, . . ."

Immediately the Secret Service surrounded the Creation women. "These two women are under FEDERAL protection. They've been given diplomatic immunity by the Agreement during their current visit! You are to back off and you are NOT to continue your effort to place them under arrest!"

"Hey, I'm just doing my job! A felony information has been filed in Jefferson County Superior Court against these two women. So I'm serving the warrants and informing them of the charges against them."

"Get on the radio to the U.S. Attorney's Office in Seattle right now! We need 'em to take action against this crap PRONTO! As for you, Deputy Sheriff, I strongly suggest you get away from here ASAP!"

"These women have the right to receive copies of the information against them!"

"I'll take them! Now get LOST!"

The agent handed the papers to the women. Helga read them and said, "There is an arraignment scheduled for us next Friday at the county courthouse in Port Townsend."

Chapter Seven

Captain Trviea Harsradich came storming down the corridor about as happy as a caged lioness whose dinner is late. Completely unaware that anything is amiss, I suddenly heard her angry voice, "YOU!!!" She picked me up by the shoulders and slammed me into a wall. Or is it bulkhead? Whether a bulkhead or a wall, it performed its structural function marvelously by not yielding under the load being transmitted through my body from the arms of a royally pissed off Neanderthal woman capable of bench pressing more than 4 *hekt dollons* of weight! A *dollon* is a Creation unit of mass, weight, or force equal to about eight and a half ounces. "*Homo sapiens sapiens*!" she said angrily through clenched teeth. "Double wise is double cross, duplicitous, trickery, Trojan Horse, pulling a fast one, gaining a person's trust and then going back on your word! So says your own anthropologists. The four language girls go down to the surface of Earth. Since then we've been having the biggest love feast since the Treaty of Hiklity Island!"

Oh yes. We had been talking about that. In the year twenty four twelve and eleven, Atlantis and Graciana agreed to study war no more, and negotiated an arrangement on Hiklity Island. That treaty eventually broke down. It turns out that these two societies have quite a long history with each other. A bit like England and France. The Gracians are as black as African Negroes, while the Atlanteans are as white as European Caucasians. So maybe there was, and still is, racism on Creation. Perhaps Harliven's last minute accident was of the political kind. I wondered what Trviea thought of black Neanderthals? Did not seem like a good time to ask. It appeared that her opinion of white Cro-Magnons had suffered a recent deterioration from which it had yet to recover. "Trviea. Would you like to sit down with me and discuss this like adults?"

"Adults? I'm old enough to be your fucking great great grandmother!"

Yup! Her English was coming along nicely! Yessiree! She was definitely getting the hang of it! "Please tell me what happened." This might thrill some men, but sexual excitement was not the accurate description of my emotional state at this point in time. What occurred to me is that she could clamp her huge taurodont teeth in my neck and chomp my windpipe right out with her extremely powerful jaw muscles. If she didn't decide to just beat the shit out of me instead.

She shook a little bit apparently trying to think. Pidonita Hmlakian came running up, ready to intervene. Trviea said to me, "I understand the mutiny was Helga's idea. But introducing ourselves to the entire Planet Earth was YOUR idea!"

"Why don't we get some of that rum of yours, then we can sit down and yu-yu-you can then tell me what happened and maybe I can then be of some help." She opened her mouth wide and exhaled her breath right into my face. "Oh! You've already started with the rum! Excellent!" Not only was she pissed off, she had been drinking too! Always a lovely combination! In a Neanderthal woman who can play linebacker with a reasonable degree of competence!

Pidonita then quietly spoke to her former Captain in Atlantean. By then I knew enough of the language to understand most of what she said. "Trviea, it is not his fault what happened on Earth. One Earthling can give us a promise; a different Earthling can break it. That does not mean we cannot work with the first Earthling who remembers his promise and will work on our behalf. In any event, we need Neil's help, he knows more about Earth politics than any of us." I can kiss Pidonita! In fact I might do that later.

Trviea snapped back in Atlantean: "His fault is for me to decide!"

"No it is not. We relieved you of command. Remember?" I noticed Pidonita casually slipped her arm in front of Trviea's waist, ready to pull her off of me.

Trviea relaxed, and let me go. She turned her head to face down the hall, and let out a long exhalation, blowing the air away from us to avoid entertaining us with her rummy breath. Then she staggered a bit and put her right arm around Pidonita's shoulders and her left arm around my shoulders to steady herself. Without the adrenaline, the proud old Captain suffered from the leg buckling effects of the alcohol. "Last night, our two intrepid ambashadors of good will, Lushindah and Helga, had a nishe barbecue party at your exsh-wife's apartment complexsh." She had switched back to English, but slurred her speech. "A good time wush had by all. After the party they went up to your ex'sh apartment, put your shildren to bed and talked girl talk. Angela wush nishe to them, they had fun. Angie'sh consherned that you might devashtate the shildren if you come to Creation with ush."

"Is that what's bothering you?"

"No. Angela ish right to care about her shildren, uh your shildren, sorry. Then they had a nishe ferry ride thish morning. Everyone wush sho nishe to 'um."

Pidonita took over; at least she was sober and had done a good job learning English. "This morning, Washington state authorities came up with the idea of taking Lchnsda and Helga on a ferry boat across Puget Sound and then over to where we picked you up. Bright sunshine, cold, about 29 on your Fahrenheit scale. They enjoyed the ferry ride. Their Secret Service limousine drove them over to the clearcut where they were greeted by Len Taylor, your farmer friend who brought your car, and a whole bunch of news media types with satellite dishes, cameras, microphones and such. While they were there some Jefferson County Deputy Sheriffs showed up and tried to arrest the women for kidnapping you."

"Have they been charged?"

"There is supposed to be something called an 'information' filed in the Superior Court in Port Townsend accusing Lchnsda and Helga each with felonies related to our little expedition where we picked you up."

"I thought they had diplomatic immunity."

They both exclaimed, "We thought so too!"

"Have they been arrested, are they in jail?"

"No, the Secret Service wouldn't let the local cops arrest them."

"Captain," started Pidonita in Atlantean, "would you like to lay down for a few *linits*? You are looking pretty woozy right now."

"I'll be fine!" Trviea declared in Atlantean. "I'll have some chocolate and coffee, and if it is really necessary Meddi or Ashkeli-li-on can give me one of their magic pills."

"Pidonita, we might need her." I said in English.

"How? What have you in mind?"

"When you came to kidnap me, you were still under her command, right?"

"Yes." She started to smile, beginning to grasp what I was saying.

"You were following her orders. You are of a foreign nation, no diplomatic relationship with the United States on account there has never been contact between our countries before, in a ship under the command of its Captain. As long as you are following orders, our concepts of international law should protect you from criminal charges arising from actions you commit while following orders. If your Captain is operating under a commission and pursuant to orders of some kind from a governmental entity, then she, and only she, can be held responsible for any crimes committed in Jefferson County by persons acting under her orders."

"So they can charge me with the crime of kidnapping you?" asked Trviea.

"Not as long as you are on board this ship, it is Atlantean soil as long as it is an official ship of the governmental entity of Atlantis. If, however, you are just a private citizen who put together a ship and hired a crew and are acting on your own authority and no one else's, then you are a pirate the minute you commit a crime anywhere on the surface or within the atmosphere of the Planet Earth."

"The mutiny! Because Helga told everyone that there has been a mutiny as a result of the aftermath of your kidnapping, the *Neanderthal Return* is arguably a pirate ship!"

"That's why I suggested the phrase 'relieved of command'. 'Mutiny' is a bad word on Earth. It might be what the Jefferson County prosecutor plans to argue. If this is a pirate ship, then the grant of diplomatic recognition and immunity to its crewmembers may not be valid, in theory. But don't worry, pirate or not the President granted diplomatic status and immunity to the crew of the *Neanderthal Return*, and to the ship itself. It was ratified by the Senate in a 99-0 vote for a one year period. Until the year is up, no criminal charge can be sustained in any American court, state or federal."

"That is all well and good, but there's this hearing on Friday in Port Townsend, and Helga shouldn't be charged with a crime at all." the Captain pointed out. "She wasn't on the Shuttle when we came down to pick you up."

"We should so inform the Jefferson County authorities and get the charges against her dropped."

We came to the Viewing Lounge. We had a spectacular view, Vancouver Island, the Olympic Peninsula, and Puget Sound. No clouds over the area except the Cascade Mountains. We sat down in comfortable chairs looking out the window. Sorby Mishlakian sat down with us and said out loud in Atlantean: "Helga, Lchnsda, can you hear me?"

"We hear you loud and clear!"

"All right. You are on speakers. We have Neil here, he has been briefed on your situation."

"Neil, this is Lucinda, can you hear me?" she asked in English.

"Yes, I can. Where are you right now?"

"We're at the place where we picked you up."

"Amazing. So you've been charged with kidnapping me?"

"I'm holding in my hand a document labeled 'IN THE SUPERIOR COURT OF THE STATE OF WASHINGTON IN AND FOR THE COUNTY OF JEFFERSON'. There is a block in which it is written 'STATE OF WASHINGTON, plaintiff,' the letter 'v' and then 'LCHNSDA RENUXLER' in your alphabet, capital letters, underlined, and then 'defendant.' I'm a DEFENDANT! To the right of the block is a number, the first two digits correspond to the last two digits of this year, then there is a dash, and then the number one, I'm told that means criminal, and then a serial number for the case. Below is the word 'INFORMATION' in capital letters. Underneath all of this is some writing, it reads: 'Comes now DONALD MAYTON, Prosecuting Attorney for Jefferson County, Washington, by and through his Deputy, BRUCE ELDERS, and by this Information accuses the defendant LCHNSDA RENUXLER, an alien from another planet, the Planet Creation which orbits the star Alpha Centauri A, who is nevertheless a human being probably descended from the ancient European race designated Neanderthals, of having participated in the kidnapping in the first or second degree and unlawful imprisonment of a person, NEIL ARMSTRONG PEACE, a citizen of the State of Washington, in violation of RCW 9A.40.020 and RCW 9A.40.040, and has assaulted him in the second degree with intent to commit a felony in violation of RCW 9A.36.021(f), and that such acts were committed in Jefferson County, Washington.' It goes on to list these crimes in specific counts and to say that these crimes are Class A, B, and C Felonies and that if convicted I could be imprisoned for quite a few years. The maximum sentence available for a conviction of a Class A Felony in the State of Washington is life imprisonment. My aging gene has been switched off!"

"Well gee Lucinda! Twenty or thirty years of food at the women's prison in Purdy might just switch it back on!" I was kidding with her; no way will a prosecution of a person with diplomatic immunity succeed. "You'll miss the fresh goat meat you get on the *Neanderthal Return*. I like the cabrito myself."

Helga broke in. "I've got the same thing too. There's also an Affidavit of Probable Cause by Bruce Elders for each of us. But I wasn't on the Shuttle. I was in the *Neanderthal Return* parked on the Far Side of the Moon at the time. While I admit that I assisted in the mission from there as a crew member, none of MY actions took place in Jefferson County, Washington! We each have a Summons, another piece of paper, directing us to appear next Friday at 9:00 A.M. in the Superior Courtroom on the second floor of the Jefferson County Courthouse at 1820 Jefferson Street in Port Townsend, Washington to answer these charges. The Secret Service wouldn't let 'em arrest us, now there are a bunch of Marines helicoptered in from the Bangor Base up here and they're deployed all around us securing a perimeter! They're acting like the State of Washington has seceded from the Union and we're at war with your state! It wasn't our intention to start a WAR between Earth humans!"

"The State of Washington is not going to secede from the Union." I assured her. "The Jefferson County Sheriff's Department is not the Viet Cong. They are just a police force, not a military unit. They are not about to take on the Marines and the President knows this. The last time we had a situation like this, President Eisenhower sent the Army to Little Rock, Arkansas to enforce a school board's decision to allow black students to attend a high school with white students. What we have here is a prosecutor making a name for himself. County prosecutors are elected in the State of Washington. He's making a play for votes."

"Should we get out of Jefferson County?"

"You can go anywhere as long as you show up in court Friday. Theoretically, you are subject to arrest anywhere you go in the State of Washington; any local cop can arrest you on a Jefferson County warrant. If you leave the state while charged with a felony with the purpose to avoid prosecution that's a crime too, a federal crime at that. Since you were afforded a fancy hotel room in Seattle, I see no reason why you can't be put up at a bed and breakfast in Port Townsend until Friday. They'll pamper you like crazy because they know the charge is bullshit, and they know that the Port Townsend merchants will make a mint off the media circus that is even now descending upon their town. The federal police will surround the bed and breakfast house to keep you from becoming guests of the Jefferson County taxpayers at their jail. You go into court Friday with your lawyers and your federal bodyguard, plead not guilty to the charges, then your lawyers will move for dismissal on the grounds you have diplomatic immunity and that Helga never committed any such crime in Jefferson County."

I went on, spitting it out between laughs. "If the judge has any sense at all, and I cannot guarantee you that, us noncustodial divorced fathers have been conditioned to think otherwise. But if he has any sense, he will immediately grant the motion, dismiss the case, and demand that you get this CIRCUS out of his courtroom right now! You leave Port Townsend having beaten the rap and a good time will have been had by all!" My sides ached from the laughter.

"He's laughing about it. That's a good sign. You're saying it's not as bad as it looks. But what if the judge doesn't have any sense?"

"If he's a stickler for procedure, he'll declare that they don't hear motions during the arraignment, and note the motions for hearing on a Wednesday or some time like that two or three weeks later on. This will keep you in P.T. or require you to return to P.T. for a hearing where the only rational result is a dismissal because the Agreement very clearly grants you diplomatic immunity, and specifically promises that you will not be subject to arrest or prosecution for any crime committed during the Shuttle mission by which you made me your guest."

"This whole thing is really stupid!"

"Common problem with Earth government. But since the prosecutor wants to make Port Townsend the Center of the Universe, you go right ahead and make Port Townsend the Center of the Universe! Pretty soon some of his voters are going to get really fed up with it!" I still suffered from the giggles. "Meanwhile, I'm going to make some phone calls from up here. Just hang tough! Don't you worry about a thing! Ol' Neil is gonna take care of you!"

"No, no, no! I want to talk to the President himself. I'm not fooling around. I'm the alleged victim of this alleged crime in Port Townsend. I'm the deadbeat dad who has gone the FARTHEST to avoid his support obligation! I can now command press attention beyond my wildest dreams! Maybe a live interview during prime time where I spell out in plain English how using court proceedings to force a divorced father to work to pay money is a FEDERAL CRIME and how the President should be IMPEACHED for failing to faithfully execute the Peonage Law, and for failing his oath of office to protect and defend the part of the Constitution that prohibits INVOLUNTARY SERVITUDE and that an order to pay child support or alimony is NOT a punishment for a crime whereof the party has been duly convicted? I mean, slavery just happens to be illegal! Don't take my word for it, look up *Brent Moss v. Superior Court*, 56 California Reporter, Second Edition 864, the good stuff's on pages 868-870." I didn't mention the California Supreme Court opinion in that case.

"This is the President. Is this Mr. Peace?"

"Hello, Mr. President! How ya' doing?"

"Doing fine! Listen, about the Creation girls, we're taking vigorous legal action to enforce their diplomatic immunity. I made a promise, the Senate ratified it, and I intend to keep it. You can just butt out except when we tell you what to do and then you do it!"

"Mr. President, not even you can order me around! I'm an American citizen and I intend that my rights under the Constitution be respected, period. I've been a good boy not using the bully pulpit these wonderful women have given me to make a public stink about the widespread FEDERAL FELONY being committed in the name of child support! There are far better ways of getting parents to provide for their children than this HATE campaign of practicing slavery by demanding unreasonable levels of child support and VIOLATING state constitutions that prohibit imprisonment for debt. Think about it Mr. President! A state constitution that prohibits imprisonment for debt is a promise that state made to its citizens. Or more accurately, a promise made by that state's citizens to each other. So are the Thirteenth Amendment prohibition of slavery and involuntary servitude and the Fourteenth Amendment requirement for the equal protection of the laws. Promises the citizens of the United States made to each other. That's the promise Ike enforced when he sent the Army to Little Rock. If we're unwilling to honor and enforce promises we make to each other in the form of constitutional rights, why should the Neanderthals of Creation believe any promises we make to them?" Not even Captain Trviea would dare say such a thing to the President of the United States. I know this because her big eyes were wide open and her heavy Neanderthal jaw had just about fallen off of her face! But being an American citizen, I can say anything to the Prez that is not a threat of violence and is protected by the First Amendment.

"So you want me to prosecute those who enforce support orders for peonage? Forget that!"

"Except that I'm up here in their ship and they are far more likely to listen to me than to you. They know I tell the truth and they know politicians don't. I know enforcing the Peonage Law where the debt or obligation is child support would be disruptive to say the least. But then it might not be as bad as fathers fleeing their states, their children never seeing them again, and the huge amount of taxpayer's money spent chasing them down to force them to do something they don't want to do. By simply enforcing the plain language of the Constitution, we can get most of them to do far more than we can imagine. It's amazing how people respond to being treated with dignity and respect. You can spring Helga and Lucinda right now by calling up the Port Townsend prosecutor and telling him that if he doesn't put an end to this nonsense, his deputy prosecutors handling the support cases will be the first people indicted for violating the Peonage Law. Now you can make this threat over a secure phone line, or I can make this suggestion LOUDLY and PUBLICLY."

After a pause to let it sink in, I continued. "You see Mr. President, I like these beetle browed women with sawed off chins." I winked at them. "They have a lot of spirit, and they know and understand what a profound gift a child is. A child is the greatest gift a woman can give a man, the greatest gift a man can give a woman. Under their laws that child shall not be used as a weapon against either parent. The only reason they are here at all is because they need our help. They need to have children so their Race shall not go extinct. Helga and Lucinda are guilty of nothing more than trying to obtain their posterity."

The President slammed the phone down. "How dare that son of a bitch blackmail the President of the United States!" He wiped his brow with a tissue. "We'll get this taken care of lickity split if he would just leave it alone! I mean, as long as he stays up in the alien spacecraft, the Jefferson County prosecution hasn't got their victim available to testify as a witness! And there's no question about the diplomatic immunity!"

"Helga and Lucinda have been getting his advice on how to handle this."

"Oh great! Mr. Antipeonage Act himself! Where did he earn his law degree? Fred's Mail Order Law School?"

A Secret Service agent volunteered some additional information. "We believe Helga and Lucinda are bisexual, there hasn't been a homosexual taboo in their society since the death of their men. The tapes that don't exist show them both in the hot tub in their hotel room in Seattle. They touched each other in a clearly sexual manner. We can now translate some of their language. Lucinda confessed to not having had sex with Neil Peace. Helga bragged that she did. It was wonderful, she said, after nine dozen years when she had no contact with men. In Creation years of 497.5 days, that's about right. Helga then told Lucinda that she wanted her to do her fair share. She had no problem with getting her hot and bothered, so Lucinda would want to mate with Neil Peace. After that, Helga touched her in a very sexual manner. We sent a female agent in and they separated from each other ever so nonchalantly."

"So they're screwing Neil Peace to get sperm from him? Not that I'm surprised."

"Lucinda mentioned her dread of their doctor's cold steel spoon."

"Good work. Burn the tapes. The surveillance equipment never existed. I don't want the problems Nixon and Clinton have had with this sort of thing." Then he turned to the woman from the Justice Department. "What's the legal situation in Port Townsend?"

"The U.S. Attorney's Office over there filed a suit for injunction against Jefferson County in the Tacoma branch of the U.S. District Court. But Judge Meredith will let the state court judge in Port Townsend have first crack at this thing. He considers a Temporary Restraining Order prohibiting the arrest of the women unnecessary because we've got 'em surrounded by a huge number of federal agents and troops! He thinks we should hang tough until Friday and then ask for dismissal based on the diplomatic immunity provided by the Agreement. That should take care of it."

"What the Hell is the deal with this father's rights Antipeonage Act thing that Neil Peace seems to be involved with?"

"In 1988 the Washington Legislature passed a child support schedule law that mandated substantial increases in the support obligation. Since then there has been a low level war, mostly nonviolent fortunately, between fathers who believe the support amounts are way out of line and the state agencies. There are 'mainstream' father's activists who lobby the Legislature, and then there are the radicals."

"Is Neil Peace with the radicals?"

"He doesn't go into the common law court and personal lien crap that some of the others use. He believes in the Antipeonage Act."

"How good is this peonage argument?"

"Pretty damn good I'm afraid. There is absolutely no evidence whatsoever that the 1867 Congress ever intended to exclude child support from the debts and obligations for which a person shall not be enslaved. Involuntary servitude is defined as a legal requirement to be employed; Sandra Day O'Conner said so in a decision. Senator Lane of Massachusetts mentioned the impact that New Mexico Territory's system of peonage had on the debtor with a family to support. Right there in the *Congressional Globe*!"

"This isn't just a bunch of made up stuff like what the Freemen have?"

"No, it's not. The Antipeonage Act is spelled out in 42 U.S.C. §1994 and peonage is defined as a crime in 18 U.S.C. §1581. Anybody can look these statutes up in any law library. In fact, people like Neil Peace encourage folks to do exactly that. 'Don't take my word for it' they say, 'go check it out yourself!' Very effective approach!"

"Aren't there Supreme Court decisions making an exception for child support?"

"No U.S. Supreme Court decisions."

"What's this *Brent Moss* decision Peace is talking about?"

"In 1996 a California appeals court annulled a contempt order against Brent Moss on the grounds that a court cannot punish a noncustodial father for not working. It CITED the 13th Amendment and the Antipeonage Act."

"Oh shit!"

"The state's Supreme Court reversed the decision as to involuntary servitude and peonage issues but refused to apply their judicial reconstruction of the 13th Amendment *ex post facto* to Brent Moss and affirmed the annulment. Still, the father's rights people believe that there hasn't been anything this good since *Brown v. Board of Education*, and that wasn't this good."

Chapter Eight

The county mounties served the paperwork on the women in the presence of news vans with satellite dishes. They remained in the clearcut for an hour deciding what to do. By the time the Secret Service called to secure lodging, it seemed every room in town was booked. The women sat in the limousine watching satellite dishes sprout in the little park across Jefferson Street from the Courthouse while the Secret Service struggled to secure lodging. The women joked about spending the night in the jail so they can have a place to sleep! Finally they found a bed and bath and settled in for the week, the Marines deployed around the house.

Fred Dreyfus grew up in Port Townsend. After he passed the bar exam, he returned to his hometown and practiced law for over thirty years. Most of his practice is criminal defense. He avoids family law because it can get messy. I knew about him from my years as a father's rights activist. I recommended him to the Creation women. He was astonished to find the United States Attorney herself in his office asking him to join the Renuxler-Trvlakian Defense Team. "The deputy prosecutor who signed the Information is named Bruce Elders."

"He's an unethical little pipsqueak!" was his reaction.

The ship had a microwave radio link with U.S. West. The keyboards on the ship have Creation numerals, including single digit symbols for ten and eleven, and Atlantean alphabet letters. The Earth equivalents were written on stickers taped next to the keys. I could type in the area code and phone number. The calls went through, much to the astonishment of the people I called!

During a conference call, the Neanderthals from Creation agreed to pay Fred Dreyfus out of the substantial advances they had already received from publishers for the awesome store of material that they have on the languages, history, and culture of an entire human inhabited Planet. I emphatically seconded the opinion of everyone involved that they needed somebody who spends a lot of time in the local courthouse and who knows the judge, the clerk, and prosecuting attorneys, and is familiar with the local politics.

Fred Dreyfus cleared the afternoon of appointments and told his new clients that he was on his way. Work hard on their memories for details of everything that happened in the Shuttle mission and the negotiations with the President to obtain the grant of immunity. He then dialed up the direct phone number that goes past the annoying voice mail and right into the office of Bruce Elders. Every prosecutor's office has this secret phone number for the benefit of court clerks and judges.

"Fred Dreyfus! I've been meaning. To call you." It was Bruce Elders. Between each comma and each sentence, he pauses for a few seconds. "On the Borden case. I'll accept a plea. To Assault 4. Usual. Slap on the wrist. Recommendation. Deferred jail sentence. Alcohol counseling. Ineligibility. For possession of firearms. As it is domestic violence. Don't operate motor vehicle. Without license and insurance. The usual. Be a good boy order."

"I'll recommend to my client that he accept that." Assault 2 is a felony, if convicted, Mr. Borden will do at least nine months in state prison. Assault 4 is a gross misdemeanor. For a first offense, defendants rarely go to jail unless they violate the be a good boy order or don't meet with the probation officer.

"As for Barlow. We will go down. To Involuntary Manslaughter. Otherwise. We are going. To trial. For Murder 1. With Murder 2. As lesser included."

"Then we're going to trial, you ain't got shit on Barlow unless you've got something that you haven't provided me in the discovery. No deal on Barlow."

"Okay. That takes care. Of those two cases. For now. So why are you. Calling me?"

"The Planet Creation has retained me to represent Miss Trvlakian and Mrs. Renuxler."

"Lucky you!"

"What the Hell are you thinking?! You know damn well these ladies have diplomatic immunity!"

"Well. We have found out. That there was a mutiny. Miss Trvlakian herself. Has so declared. We will enter that. Into evidence."

"It occurred AFTER the alleged kidnapping. It was not a mutiny! Helga is legally authorized to relieve her captain of command if certain conditions exist. We can set up a video screen in the courtroom to receive audio-video testimony from witnesses on board the *Neanderthal Return*. Their deposed Captain herself could testify that yes, under certain circumstances, her shipmates can relieve her of her command. They are out of communication range with their home Planet. Trviea Harsradich could testify that in her opinion this particular event is an unlawful mutiny, but that is a matter to be determined in a hearing back home. The legality of Helga's action relieving her of command is a matter of Atlantean law. The Jefferson County Superior Court is a *forum non conveniens* for any determination of Atlantean law. Because it is a question of their law, the ship is still operating on a commission from their governmental entity. They have transmitted to the U.S. Attorney's Office in Seattle and to me copies of this commission with English translations."

Mr. Dreyfus went on. "But even if it is purely a pirate ship, not operating under the charter of any governmental entity, the President still has the power to grant its crew diplomatic immunity as a condition for any visit to our nation. This was legal as an Executive Agreement, and the Senate ratified it as a Treaty. Foreign policy is a FEDERAL function under the Constitution! State has nothing to say in it but to follow the federal lead."

Mr. Dreyfus continued. "You've got another problem. Your victim has forgiven the perpetrators. He's not available to testify, you've no way of serving the subpoena! He understands that they were following orders from their Captain, who at that time had not been relieved of her command. Only the Captain, under our concepts of international law, can be held liable for any crimes committed in Jefferson County by persons who were following her orders. Since what they did does not rise up to the level of the crimes against humanity as committed by the Nazi War Criminals, Renuxler is immune to prosecution on that basis."

"Renuxler. What about Trvlakian?"

"She was not on the Shuttle when it came down to pick up Mr. Peace. She was on the mother ship on the other side of the Moon at the time."

"Okay. She was an accomplice. To a crime. That took place. In the State of Washington. We can reach her. With the Long Arm Statute."

"Even granting you that, you'll have to amend your complaint! But you have no evidence as to what she was doing! Maybe she was asleep, or confined to her quarters, or assigned to duties unrelated to the Shuttle mission."

"Will she testify? As to what she was doing? At that time?"

"No, of course not! You know the self incrimination privilege as well as I do. She doesn't have to testify at all if you can't define what she was doing! Your best bet is to drop the whole case against her right now! You ain't got shit on Helga even without taking into account the diplomatic immunity per the Agreement!"

"Well," he drew the word out, "I'll tell you what. I'll do. I will talk to my boss. But I think you are right. About Miss Trvlakian. If she was NOT. Actually on the Shuttle. At the time. It picked up. Neil Peace. Does Mrs. Renuxler. Deny being on the Shuttle?"

"No. She was on the Shuttle."

"Does she deny. Stabbing Neil. With the syringe? Did she administer. The drug? Or did somebody else? That is the basis. Of the assault charge."

"I don't know the answers to these questions. We don't know who drugged Peace, and Renuxler does not have to testify as to whether she did or not. So maybe you should drop the assault charge until you have better information and evidence."

"I'll talk to my boss about that too."

"You're doing this because your boss told you to."

"Uhh,"

"I want to talk to him. Now."

"Well let me see if he is in." Fred waited a few minutes.

"This is Don Mayton, is this Fred Dreyfus?"

"Yes it is."

"How ya' doing! Congratulations on getting the Renuxler case."

"Thank you. Now what the Hell are you thinking?"

"Now Fred, you know we can't have UFO's coming into Jefferson County and abducting citizens of the State of Washington. It's a threat to the peace of the State. What if jet fighters scrambled from Whidbey Island? We could've had a nasty shootout endangering our citizens. I didn't know Trvlakian was not on the Shuttle. We'll file a dismissal without prejudice of the charges against her. I've just now gotten the arrest warrant quashed. She doesn't need the Marines and federal police around her anymore. As far as the assault charge, either Mrs. Renuxler stabbed Mr. Peace with the hypodermic or she's an accomplice of the person who did. So we're keeping that on the complaint for the time being."

"Don, the girls were given immunity by the President, period. The Senate ratified it. The State has got to abide by that. It doesn't matter how guilty Lucinda is; she is immune to prosecution as long as she remains in this country under that grant. What you are doing is a complete waste of taxpayer's money. So what is it? A play to get winter business for Port Townsend's tourist industry? Why should the taxpayers fund such an effort? Money for prosecutors and courts is not paid by the taxpayers for such purposes. It is wrong to force Creation to spend what money they have coming from the sharing of their culture on a lawyer like me to defend them from a completely frivolous case like this. I have a good mind to ask for Rule 11 sanctions."

"Now Fred, be nice. Rule 11 sanctions are never awarded against a prosecutor for filing a frivolous criminal charge and none will be awarded now. You know, many folks in this county are skeptical about the benefits of having these people around. It's like the sea lions and Canada geese. Now there are too many sea lions and Canada geese. Maybe it's a good idea the Makahs are hunting whales again. Grizzly bears are now showing up in the North Cascades. They're bringing WOLVES into the Olympic Park to control the mountain goats! And they're DANGEROUS! It's like *Jurassic Park*, it's not necessarily wise to bring back the dinosaurs, even if we could do it. The Neanderthals disappeared from Earth. Like the dinosaurs, they had their time. These women are alive only because an alien race played God. They themselves tell us that a Virus killed off their men. I think God is trying to tell us something. They are a species of almost human, but almost human is all they are. While the spaceship is most impressive, perhaps it's time they stepped aside. They are not meant to be."

"Why you racist, genocidal, bigoted, ignorant, neo-Nazi son of a BITCH!"

"Now Fred, I didn't give any consent to record this phone call. So to record it is a crime in

69

the State of Washington. I didn't say what you think you heard me say, and if you claim that I said it, I'll deny it and say that I don't know why you would falsely accuse me of saying such a thing."

"I'll see you in court." Fred has been at this game long enough to not slam the phone down. Don Mayton liked to try to get his goat and take his mind off the case. He did that to all of the defense lawyers. But in this instance, it is useful to know the animus behind this prosecution.

Fred Dreyfus arrived at the bed and breakfast. A relieved Helga Trvlakian ran up to him. "Nice phone call to the prosecutor! Charges against me have been dropped! Thank you!" She hugged him tightly. This woman is STRONG! Fred has been hugged by grateful and relieved women. Some of whom could unload trucks as fast as most men. But none of them had the Neanderthal physical strength of Helga Trvlakian! "May I kiss you?"

"I have a wife!"

"Your wife won't mind a simple peck from a grateful client!"

"Ha-ha-ha! Oh all right! The Missus won't mind a simple kiss on the CHEEK." Helga kissed him and then let go and stood back. "Now let me give you some advice, it is very important. I don't know what you have for legal process on your Planet but I need to familiarize you with some American process and concepts."

"Okay, we're here to learn everything Earth."

Lucinda broke in. "We have a communications link with our ship. Trviea, how are you doing?"

The Captain's voice came out of a speakerphone. "I'm much better now, thank you. Askelion gave me a magic pill, sobers me right up. She advised me that *manatat* is best drank by the *dollop*, not by the *glup*. Moderation in everything. I have had a rough time of it lately."

"It's not like you're facing a possible life sentence with the aging gene shut off."

"I admit that puts it in perspective. Neil is here too."

"Hi guys!" I said cheerfully. "Way to go Fred, getting Helga off!"

"It was no big deal, really. Any lawyer could've done it. The prosecutor has dropped the charges withOUT prejudice. That means he can file them again if he gets more information and evidence. Uh, how secure is this radio link?"

Lucinda explained. "We anticipated this. This is a direct radio link with the *Neanderthal Return*. We're not going through U.S. West and the regular telephone system for this. We're using a scrambler of Atlantean design. It might be a little while before even the CIA, KGB, or the No Such Agency can crack it."

"Even if they crack your little scrambler, they're not likely to share this information with a state prosecutor who's operating counter to the President's policy." Fred returned to the business at hand. "If you are truly grateful for me getting Helga off, you'll all try your best to make my job easier. The prosecutor is pretending that diplomatic immunity does not apply. He's ignoring the immunity that soldiers and sailors have for actions taken while following orders. Absent the immunity, everyone who assisted the Shuttle mission is an accomplice of a crime that took place within the State of Washington. There's a Long Arm Statute that grants state courts jurisdiction over persons who are accomplices of crimes committed within the state, no matter WHERE those persons were when they assisted in the crime."

"So our entire crew could be charged?"

"Exactly. If such persons can be brought within the physical jurisdiction of the court, that is, within the state. So stay away! Our Constitution grants you the right to not incriminate yourself. So don't! We don't give 'em the list of persons who were on the Shuttle for that mission. We don't say anything about who did what during that time. Without IDENTITY, the prosecutor has

70

nothing. So everybody keep their mouths shut until we get the diplomatic immunity enforced. That goes for everyone on board the *Neanderthal Return* and that goes for Monoloa in Russia and for Andemona in Mexico."

"Andemona is not returning to U.S. territory until this is cleared up. Mexico has strongly reaffirmed their grant of diplomatic immunity."

"Good idea. If the diplomatic immunity fails, and only if the diplomatic immunity fails, which is not likely, not even possible, we can set up an audio-video link so your Captain Trviea Harsradich, are you listening Trviea?"

"I'm reading you loud and clear."

"She can declare that you were following her orders and that she takes full responsibility as the commanding officer. That should get the case dismissed on that basis. But until then, she keeps her mouth shut." He reached out with his right hand and held Lucinda's hand. He simultaneously held Helga's hand with his left hand. "There is something I have to tell you about Don Mayton, the elected prosecutor who's responsible for all this."

"What is it?"

"We cannot talk about this publicly, because he'll deny it. He might even sue for defamation, the tort of making false and malicious statements about him. But I swear it is true. At the end of our phone conversation I asked him what the Hell he had in mind with this. These are his exact words: 'The Neanderthals disappeared from Earth. Like the dinosaurs, they had their time. These women are alive only because an alien race played God. They themselves tell us that a Virus killed off their men. I think God is trying to tell us something. They are a species of almost human, but almost human is all they are. While the spaceship is most impressive, perhaps it's time they stepped aside. They are not meant to be.'"

I turned down the microphone and looked at the stunned Trviea squarely in the eyes. I spoke quietly. "I understand that this is what you most fear, and for good reason. But please know this: Most of us Cro-Magnons, including me, are TOTALLY against this sort of thing. The Germans aren't the only people who have renounced the evil and hatred of the Nazis. Be assured, if your goal is the continuation of your Race, I am firmly on your side."

"I know that. Please turn the mike back up."

In Port Townsend, the women sat there for a minute, stunned. Then Helga declared: "Mr. Dreyfus, you are a good man and we are grateful for what you have done so far." She was shaking, so was Lucinda, each face flushed red. "Next time you have a private conversation with Mr. Mayton, you tell him that he can go to HELL! The human Races that are alive today, yours and ours, are here because our direct ancestors were not in the habit of giving up on life because things looked bad! God, the Great Holy Spirit, He gave us large brains. These brains are there to allow us the opportunity to think our way out of every fix we find ourselves in. MY ancestors, MY Race, survived everything Ice Age Europe threw at us! We survived being transplanted to Creation. And we have every intention to continue cheating death for as long as it takes to bear children, and to raise them, so that the Neanderthal Race of Creation shall not go the way of the dinosaurs!"

"You two hang tough. Enjoy the week if you can. Come Friday morning, we will walk over to that courthouse and KICK HIS ASS!"

Chapter Nine

Helga Trvlakian window shopped Water Street in Port Townsend accompanied by a Secret Service agent. There were plenty of interesting sights to see. A marvelous bronze fountain sits on Taylor Street where it leads back to the cliff. Its centerpiece is a life-size sculpture of a nude woman, perfectly shaped except for a slight bulge in her belly, like she is a few months pregnant. "I wonder if anthropologists of a few thousand years from now will believe this bronze fountain to be a fertility symbol?" she asked her Secret Service escort.

"It is a fertility symbol, in a way. I believe it dates from the days when Port Townsend thought she was going to be the San Francisco of the Northwest, it's a symbol of opulence and wealth. But in the 1890's, everything just plain stopped. Not only was there a recession then, the railroads decided against building a line into Port Townsend. While Port Townsend Bay is a perfect natural harbor, it was easier to build the rails to the harbors on the east side of Puget Sound. That's why we have such a well preserved Victorian seaport here, every major building dates from the 1880's and '90's."

"There is the Bangor Submarine Base."

"That was built a century later, on the east side of the Hood Canal to take advantage of railroads already serving Bremerton and the Naval Shipyard. They just extended the rails a little further to the Sub Base."

Helga grinned, proud and mischievous. "We sure caught 'em napping! Dropped our Shuttle into the Hood Canal forests just a few *kepfat*s from their Bangor and Bremerton Bases. The Marines guarding us aren't upset about that?"

"No, like most people, they want peace, not war, with your Planet. Because you come asking for help in continuing your Race, and because you are beautiful and exotic women, everyone believes it's better to make love than war. But you embarrassed the commanders with responsibility for the security of the State of Washington. Your Shuttle did show up on radar, we have the recordings of it! But no report was made by the radarmen, no alarm sounded, no jet fighters scrambled."

"How come?"

"You dropped straight down from the sky! The radarmen thought you were a glitch in their equipment. Your vertical flight path just didn't look like any aircraft or spacecraft that we knew of! That and all of the UFO hoopla. They didn't want Hood Canal to be another Roswell with the military forces chasing a radar glitch and then saying it was nothing. With the crazy scandals involving our federal government, nobody believes us when we say we were chasing a damn glitch! They would say we're hiding something, that we have gray aliens in custody at a secret base somewhere!"

"Area 51?"

"Yeah, Area 51." He laughed. "You're lucky you're not a prisoner there. Anyway, Hood Canal became another Roswell because the local stump farmers saw your ship come down and then rise up. They found Neil Peace's car with the door hanging open, engine still warm, keys in the ignition. A '66 Pontiac LeMans. Tattered and worn bucket seats, body work done in patches. But the engine and transmission were in virtually perfect condition. Nothing wrong with the brakes, steering, no flat tires. Why would Neil park the vehicle and leave the keys in the ignition? With the door open? Turn the keys, the engine fires right up, plenty of gasoline in the tank. Shift the transmission into gear, it works just fine. The stump farmers, one of whom was

Len Taylor, who was expecting him, immediately thought of the strange object they saw. But nobody wants to be known as crazy. They called in the Jefferson County Sheriff, whose deputies inspected the car and searched the adjacent clearcut and the nearby forest. Nothing. One of the farmers called up the Bangor Base and asked if they had any radar anomalies."

"What did the Navy say?"

"Not a damn thing, as you can expect. But the story of the radar anomaly leaked out. It went right down to the location where Peace's car was found! That's when all Hell broke loose with the UFO story. Then when your bright blue light showed up in the sky and you started blinking it in Morse Code, and then you apologized for seizing Peace and introduced him in your video transmission, I mean WELL! There he is, his beard hiding his pointy chin, with his Cro-Magnon forehead, sitting next to some strikingly beautiful, but obviously Neanderthal women, it was just too much!"

They laughed as they walked back to Water Street to enjoy the quaint shops and cafes. They stepped into a used bookstore. The owner and clerk, an aging hippie, recognized the tall blonde beauty. "You are Helga Trvlakian!"

"Yes, I am! With whom do I have the pleasure?"

"Skeptical Israel, at your service!"

"I study Earth culture, it's part of my job. Are there stories here not yet made into movies broadcast on television? We've only seen the stories transmitted on radio waves."

"We have plenty of such stories, Helga! And of course, what is filmed is sometimes quite a bit different than the story written by the author. Some of Earth's best, and worst, storytelling is available right here in these previously owned paperbacks. There is a lot of obscure stuff in here. But there is one old story I want you to read."

"And what story is this?"

"You are a Neanderthal?"

"Yes. I'm a descendent of the people who have lived in Europe in ages past, that your scientists designate with the term Neanderthal."

"Are you offended by this term?"

"Not at all, we use it in the name of our ship. It's where a skeleton of a man of my Race was found."

"Unfortunately, there was a stereotype, which we now know to be wrong, of the Neanderthals as primitive cavemen who walked around bent over wrestling cave bears, grunting instead of speaking, rough in manners and dim in intelligence."

"Yes, we are painfully aware of this stereotype. It's why we didn't want to reveal our existence for so many years. Like I said on that television show, we let your anthropologists think we're stupid, then we show up in a starship. I'm a modern city girl. I live in Cair Atlaston, which is like Seattle only bigger and a lot older. I don't kill animals with spears and skin them with stone knives. I purchase my meat in butcher shops. I'm on this trip because I'm good at learning foreign languages, religion, culture, and politics. I can work with Base Ten numbers! Not easy if you grew up thinking Base Twelve! I'm not a troglodyte."

"You most certainly are not. And you ain't ugly either, that's the one word that does not describe you. And your muscles are magnificent! Are you typical of Neanderthal women?"

"Yes, I am. There is variation, some women are much stronger than me, and some are thin. I'm taller than average, six feet. But most of us are like Lchnsda and me. It's genetic, like bone structure or skin color. Thank you for telling me I'm not ugly. Why did you mention it?"

"Neanderthals crop up in our fiction. They might be depicted as the ancient European hunter-gatherers. Or a time machine is used to bring them to the present. Or as still primitive hunter-gatherers living in a remote Garden of Eden unexposed to modern society. But I've never seen Neanderthals depicted as modern humans with advanced technology. That's why you've captured our imagination. The story I want you to read was written by Isaac Asimov many years ago. He didn't think of Neanderthals as an inferior race. But he thought that to the Cro-Magnon eye, a Neanderthal would look ugly. He wrote a story titled *The Ugly Little Boy*. It is written from the point of view of a modern nurse hired to take care of him."

"Mr. Asimov is wrong about the ugly part. I have come all this way for the possibility of bearing a child, to become a mother. If the child is a boy, I would never think of him as ugly. I like to carry this photograph. The little blonde girl on the right is me. I was about six Creation years old. The boy is Hmlee Trvlakian, my little brother, four Creation years. As you can see, he is not ugly."

"You were both very pretty as children, your parents were blessed. But I think you'll like Asimov's story. This is a collection of his stories published quite some time ago. *The Ugly Little Boy* is one of the stories. I'll let you have it for free, my gift to you, because it's such an honor to meet a live Neanderthal woman who is so beautiful and so willing to be friends with us Cro-Magnons."

"Thank you. I will accept this gift if you would be so kind as to grant me one small favor."

"And what favor is that?"

"Allow me to pay for it without being offended."

"Certainly, I'm a storekeeper, money must go in the till or I'll have to get a job. Such terrible fate I wish to avoid!" Laughing, he rang up the sale and accepted the money. Another customer came into the store. "Oh no." he muttered under his breath. "He can be a problem, but he's a good customer."

"Well, well, well!" the new customer announced himself. "The charges have been dropped and now you parade around Port Townsend like you're Queen for a Day!"

"Why don't you go somewhere else for a while?" suggested the Secret Service guard as he reached for his small behind the ear radio.

"This store is private property, I'll be the one to decide whether to ask him to leave." reminded Skeptical Israel.

"I don't think Miss Trvlakian would mind hearing from a Cro-Magnon who is NOT in her fan club." said the new visitor. "You've been living a sheltered life behind these Secret Service bodyguards."

"We have already heard from some folks who are not in our fan club." started Helga. "We think they are abusing their office. But I would like to hear from someone who is open with his opinions. So why are you not a member of my fan club?"

"For at least 30,000 years, we have been alone in the Universe. Without your kind around we became civilized human beings. If you are familiar with our history, you know that race has been quite a problem for us! Black and white people still don't quite get along. And then there are the Indians, siwash, if you will. I hear that term is as bad as nigger. We thought of something to call you guys with the same impact. Trogs! Short for troglodytes."

She remembered Fred Dreyfus' advice not to let some guy like this get her goat. But her body nevertheless stiffened in reaction to his hostility.

"At least," he went on, "we all have pointy chins and high foreheads. Even the hippie types you see in Port Townsend. Our brains are all pretty much the same shape and same basic capabilities. Our muscle mass likewise. Men are bigger and stronger than women, and that's the way it should be. But look at you, you're built like a brick shithouse, and you carry a face we haven't seen in 30,000 years. You come back here, ostensibly in peace, asking for our help in making you pregnant because all your men are dead. Hell, you got Neil Peace; he can generate enough sperm cells to impregnate every woman on your Planet. All you gotta do is fuck him! You don't need to announce yourselves and tell us this cock and bullshit story about some Virus that killed your men! What a load of BULL!"

Helga stood there a moment, thinking carefully. A crowd of people showed up. "We're on your side, Helga!" "You tell him what's what!" "You don't have to take that shit off him!" "Give him Hell!" That was reassuring. But then there was: "You sure told her off, Man." "Way to go!" "They're mad because they think we killed them off!" "Maybe we did!" "Perhaps we should do it again!" "They like Earth and they want it back!" "We ain't gonna give it back without a fight!"

"Okay, okay," started Helga. "I'll level with you and tell you the truth. See these guys on these posters back here?" She pointed to some whimsical posters of the gray aliens with the big black eyes. In one poster, a flying saucer is parked next to a beach. Grays are laying on big towels, drinking beer and smoking dope, playing volleyball with Earth humans and swimming in the water. A disgusted shark is spitting a Gray back out, awful taste!

"These gray guys have been our spies." Her voice dripped with total sarcasm. "They have provided us with a lot of valuable information about Earth. I wish they didn't crash one of their ships near Roswell but that sort of thing happens. While we are telling you this sob story to get your sympathy and get you to let your guard down, the Main Fleet, with MEN on their crews, NEANDERTHAL men, and armed to the teeth is even now approaching Earth from all directions. When they get into position they will shower this Planet with nuclear explosives in numbers far beyond the arsenals that you and the Soviet Union have ever possessed! Then come the viruses! And the bacteria. Special little bugs designed to kill any Cro-Magnons who manage to survive the nuclear attack! We've got one nice little animal that will cause your penis to wither up and fall off while at the same time causing your breasts to grow up nice and big! And I mean HUGE, you will look gross! Then we'll kick back for about a hundred years or so while the radiation dies down. With vaccines for everything we use in the attack, Earth will be wide open for Neanderthal recolonization."

Helga just stared at him. Smiled, trying to suppress a giggle. Then everyone present started laughing. And they laughed, and laughed, and laughed! They knew their girl from Creation pulled this bigot's leg right out of its socket! Even the two Port Townsend cops lost it. The racist man angrily stormed out of the store, furious at being made to look like a fool.

One of the cops quietly stopped the man out on the street. He gently told him to cool down; it's no big deal. "Look, after Friday, these women will leave town and everything will be back to what passes for normal in Port Townsend. They have diplomatic immunity! The judge'll have no choice but to dismiss the case and send Mrs. Renuxler on her way. So just play it cool and lay low until then. We really appreciate your help, please don't make my job any harder than it has to be, Okay?"

Helga felt she had to reassure the crowd. "Now people, please understand. None of that story is true. I was just, well, it is just that he, uh,"

"He deserved it! That's all right, Helga. We know you bear us Earthlings no ill will, though we can understand how you might have a problem with guys like him."

"Thank you for understanding." Helga was relieved.

Friday morning, 9:00 a.m., mob scene at Jefferson Street and the courthouse. Those not in Port Townsend to see this show could turn on the television and watch it live. Anywhere in the world. Satellite dishes and microwave antennas stood in the little park as thickly as the small Douglas firs in the clearcut.

In the center of an entourage of lawyers, friends, Secret Service agents, and Marines, Lucinda Renuxler and Helga Trvlakian walked to the red brick and sandstone courthouse for their day in court. Fred Dreyfus quietly gave Lucinda last minute instructions. Technicians carried the audio-video communications equipment for the radio link with the *Neanderthal Return*, which hovered several hundred miles up in the sky, a visible dark spot.

They passed the crush of people and entered the courtroom. Fred Dreyfus set up shop on the right end of the long lawyer's table. Flanked by Marines, Lucinda and Helga sat in the front row of chairs just behind the wooden railing. While most courtrooms have church style pews for spectator seats, Jefferson County sets up several rows of individual wooden chairs. The technicians set up the radio equipment on a display table brought into the courtroom for this purpose. Don Mayton and Bruce Elders set up on the left end of the lawyer's table. The clerk was busy at her station. In addition to Lchnsda Renuxler, several other felony defendants were scheduled for arraignment. Two of them sat in the jury box wearing prison pajamas. Friday morning is also when the motion calendar is heard, so a number of civil and criminal litigants and their lawyers were present or trying to get into the courtroom. A number of reporters, selected by lottery, were allowed into the courtroom to cover the proceedings.

9:00 arrived, the clerk rose from her seat and walked over to the door in the left wall and stuck her head into the judge's chambers. She came back out. "All rise!" she commanded, and everyone in the courtroom rose and stood at attention. "The Superior Court of the State of Washington in and for the County of Jefferson is now in session, the Honorable Judge Rebekah Jacobs presiding." Judge Jacobs, in her black robe and displaying an air of stern judicial dignity walked out of her chambers at normal speed, ascended the steps to her seat.

She sat down. "Be seated." the judge commanded. Everyone in the room sat down. "Call the litigants, please."

The clerk called out the names of the litigants. The first three names were in the courtroom, one in the jury box, all present with counsel. The clerk called the name of Steve Barlow, present in the jury box and represented by Fred Dreyfus. "Richard Borden?" asked the clerk.

"I saw Mr. Borden outside this morning," said Fred Dreyfus about his client, who had agreed to cop a plea to misdemeanor assault. "He may be unable to get in this courtroom what with all the people here."

"That might be a problem today, Mr. Dreyfus." admitted Judge Jacobs. "The clerk will finish calling the names of the defendants who should be here this morning. We will then give a list of those who are not here to Deputy Johnson here, he'll go outside and offer to escort any defendants he can find into this courtroom so they can enter their plea or have their motion heard. They have a right to attend their own court hearings and we wouldn't want them deterred from exercising their constitutional right to due process of law." When the laughter died down, "A bench warrant will issue for any defendant not present and not found by Deputy Johnson. While we're at it, is Lchnsda Renuxler here?" She pronounced the first name correctly.

Lucinda dressed appropriately for the occasion, with a blouse and a midlength pleated skirt, dark nylon hose, and sensible shoes. She sat in the center of the front row of spectator chairs, visible to the judge through the gap in the center of the wooden railing, with Helga Trvlakian next to her. Nevertheless, Fred Dreyfus went along with the ritual. "Mrs. Renuxler is present with counsel your Honor."

"Excellent. Brenda, you may continue." Brenda the clerk read the rest of the roll call of the litigants. Fred Dreyfus sent one of his law clerks on a mission to find Richard Borden and get him into the courtroom NOW!

The aide got Richard Borden into the courtroom, Deputy Johnson rounded up a couple of others and bench warrants were issued for the remainder. The judge announced that she will take up the Renuxler matter last after taking care of the other business for the day. Each defendant entered his plea. For those who pled not guilty, the judge set dates for preliminary hearings and for trial. For those who pled guilty, she set dates for sentencing later because she wanted to deal with the circus in her courtroom. She ran through the motion calendar.

"That leaves us with *State v. Renuxler*." Fred Dreyfus waved his client up to the defense end of the table where she sat in a chair between her lawyers. The lawyers for the federal government also came up to the defense table.

The Assistant United States Attorney spoke first. "Your Honor,"

"In a minute, Mr. McGlothlin." interrupted the judge. "I would like to ask the defendant a few questions if you don't mind. I have never spoken with a person from another Planet. One thing that I have noticed is that everyone addresses you as Mrs. Renuxler. Not Ms. Renuxler, Mrs. Renuxler. Do you prefer to be addressed as Mrs. or as Ms. Renuxler?"

"I was married. To a wonderful man whom I loved very much. He died in the plague that killed all of our men. If it's appropriate in your culture to refer to a widow as Mrs., that's fine with me. If your prefer Ms., I have no problem with that either."

"You have my sincerest condolences, Mrs. Renuxler. I too am married to a wonderful man whom I love very much. He is still with us fortunately; I would miss him very much if he were to pass away. While it is proper to address me as Judge Jacobs, I like being addressed as Mrs. Jacobs when I'm not in the courtroom. Mrs. Renuxler, I must compliment you on your English. You speak our language extremely well."

"Thank you. I have studied your radio and television broadcasts. We find *Sesame Street* and other children's television to be very helpful in learning how to speak and read your language. The actual practice with Neil Peace and then down here on Earth has done wonders for my fluency."

"The situation with Neil Peace and your actions with respect to him are why we are here today. I believe Mr. McGlothlin will argue that you are here under a grant of diplomatic immunity which covers any actions you may have taken previous to this grant of immunity. I may grant a dismissal on that basis. I may grant a dismissal on the basis of the immunity available to soldiers and sailors who are acting under orders. I will not grant a dismissal, nor shall I deny it, on the basis of your Race. The Equal Protection Clause of the Fourteenth Amendment forbids racial distinctions in the law, unless there are extraordinary conditions. I cannot lawfully treat a Native American different than any other American unless there is a treaty right involved. I cannot lawfully treat a white person differently than a black person. And I will not do so. Neither will I treat a Neanderthal differently than a Cro-Magnon. You are obviously an intelligent human being. The technology of your society is well represented by the marvelous spacecraft hovering in our sky. But remember Mrs. Renuxler, with intelligence comes responsibility. We do not consider a shark who kills a human to be a criminal; he is simply being a shark. But a human, a Neanderthal from Planet Creation as well as any person now living on Earth, knows right from wrong. That is why we consider a human who does wrong to be a criminal if that fact can be proven beyond a reasonable doubt."

"I understand that, your Honor."

"And now Mr. McGlothlin, you may say your peace on the behalf of the federal government."

"Your Honor, the defendant in this case has entered this country and remains in this country under a grant of diplomatic immunity. This grant of diplomatic immunity extends back to include any civil or criminal liability for any action the defendant may have committed or participated in prior to this grant of diplomatic immunity. The President made this grant of immunity in the Agreement ratified by the Senate, it extends to Lchnsda Renuxler and to every other member of the crew of the alien spaceship named *Neanderthal Return*, and to the ship itself, for one year subject to renewal, so long as they do not commit any hostile act against any Earth nation. So far they have honored this Agreement. The President has the lawful authority to enter into an agreement with a foreign ship and to grant diplomatic immunity to its crew and he has done so. The Senate has the lawful authority to ratify such an agreement as a treaty, and it has done so."

"I see you have filed a written pleading in this matter. Has this pleading been served upon Mr. Dreyfus and upon Mr. Mayton?"

Fred Dreyfus answered, "We have a copy your Honor."

Don Mayton started, "Your Honor,"

The judge jumped down his throat. "We have a proof of service, Mr. Mayton."

"Yes, we have been served a copy, your Honor." answered the prosecutor.

"Okay. I have read this brief by the U.S. Attorney's Office. There are three Exhibits attached to this Brief of the United States on Behalf of Lchnsda Renuxler. The first Exhibit is an Affidavit signed by the Attorney General of the United States swearing that the second Exhibit is a true and correct copy of an Executive Order signed by the President. On the last page here is the President's signature. Does counsel for both parties see that?"

Fred and Don looked through their copies of the federal brief. They both nodded their heads.

"The third Exhibit is the Agreement Between the United States of America and the *Neanderthal Return*, a Ship Sent by the Nation of Atlantis on the Planet Creation in Orbit Around Alpha Centauri A. Does counsel for both parties see that?"

They both nodded their heads.

"There is no dispute to the fact that Mrs. Renuxler is a citizen of a foreign state?" All three lawyers nodded their heads. "There is no dispute to the fact that the name of this foreign state is Atlantis, and that Atlantis is located on another Planet orbiting another star?"

"Yes, your honor," helped McGlothlin, "the Planet orbits Alpha Centauri A."

"Yes, there is no dispute that Atlantis is located on the surface of Planet Creation, *Chmpashian* in the Atlantean language, which orbits Alpha Centauri A?" Lawyers nodded their heads affirming the answer to Judge Jacob's question. "No dispute to the fact that Mrs. Renuxler came from Atlantis to our Solar System in a ship named *Neanderthal Return*?" No dispute. "And there is no dispute that Mrs. Renuxler transferred by spacewalk from the *Neanderthal Return* to the American Space Shuttle *Atlantis*, which then brought her down into the United States, and that is how she is now within the physical jurisdiction of this court?" No dispute. "And there is NO dispute that Mrs. Renuxler entered this nation at the INVITATION of our President and under the grant of DIPLOMATIC IMMUNITY in this Executive Order? An Executive Order signed by the President BEFORE Mrs. Renuxler entered the United States? That such diplomatic immunity is incorporated by the Agreement ratified by our Senate with a 99-0 vote?"

After the pause, the judge went on. "There is no doubt, under the Constitution and under applicable Acts of Congress, that the President may grant diplomatic immunity to any foreign person so that person may enter our nation without fear of prosecution in our courts. That such can be incorporated in a treaty ratified by the Senate. And there is no doubt, under our Constitution, that matters of foreign policy are matters assigned to the federal government. The States are bound by the grants of diplomatic immunity made by our President and by treaties ratified by the U.S. Senate. Mind you Mrs. Renuxler, it is not a *carte blanche* to go out and commit crimes. If you do while under diplomatic immunity, we can immediately expel you from our country or request that your immunity be waived by your government. But in this case, the crime alleged against you is specifically covered by Section 5 of this Executive Order, and by Section 5 of the ratified Agreement, which specifically declare that no member of the crew of the *Neanderthal Return* shall be liable for criminal prosecution or civil action for tort for the incident involving Neil Armstrong Peace when he was taken from Jefferson County, Washington. This is the Executive Order and the Agreement under which Mrs. Renuxler agreed to come down to Earth."

The judge felt she still needed to remind the defendant of her responsibility to not commit wrongs against other human beings. "Before I make my ruling, Mrs. Renuxler, I must remind you that kidnapping Mr. Peace was fundamentally wrong. He had committed no crime against any person from Planet Creation, yet you take him against his will. This action taken by your ship is wrong, reckless, and is as much an Act of War against the United States as was the attack on Pearl Harbor. How would you feel, Mrs. Renuxler, if a ship from Earth took a person from your Planet against that person's will? What you have done under orders of your Captain could have resulted in a war! If jet fighters scrambled in response to the radar return from your Shuttle, they might have fired upon you. You could have been killed. Neil Peace could have been killed. Some of our fighter pilots could have been killed. People on the ground could have been killed. I can understand part of the prosecutor's motivation. We have an interest in not having this kind of violence take place in Jefferson County."

"I am terribly sorry that we violated Neil's rights and risked lives." confessed Lucinda, a tear flowing from her eye.

"I will note: Helga Trvlakian's actions relieving her Captain of command were motivated by her concern that the kidnapping of Neil Peace was wrong and could lead to hostilities between our two Planets. Miss Trvlakian, I thank you for your efforts at peacemaking and at righting this wrong."

"You're welcome, your Honor." responded Helga.

"Good luck when you get back home. However, the federal government takes the lead in matters of foreign policy. I find that this is a true and correct copy of an Executive Order signed by the President. I find that this is a true and correct copy of the Agreement between our two nations. I find that these grant all crewmembers of the *Neanderthal Return* immunity from any liability for kidnapping Neil Peace. I find that the defendant is a member of that crew and is therefore covered by this Executive Order and Agreement. I find that the President acted lawfully in making this Order, the Senate acted lawfully in ratifying it, authority coming from the Constitution of the United States and applicable Acts of Congress, and that this Agreement binds the State of Washington. Mr. Mayton, I STRONGLY suggest that you will NOT waste this court's time with any more criminal charges this FRIVOLOUS. I hereby DISMISS the information against Mrs. Renuxler. Mrs. Renuxler, you are free to go."

Chapter Ten

"Mr. President, that judge in Port Townsend enforced the Agreement granting the Creation women diplomatic immunity."

"Of course she did. But she lectured Mrs. Renuxler that coming here and kidnapping people is dangerous and wrong. She's right, but what a risk she took! History tells us that people with superior technology CAN just come in and take over, steal people for slave trade and so on. They don't have to justify it as moral. Lecturing is dangerous, you can piss off these people, and it doesn't do any good! They themselves decided that they don't have the right to steal our men. No need to lecture 'em."

"Judges can be reckless in their self righteousness."

"Tell me about it! As Commander in Chief I'm responsible for the security of the United States, that means military security. That's a HUGE ship they have up there! Because the potential threat comes from another Planet, I'm effectively responsible for the military security of the entire Planet. They could push an asteroid into a Dinosaur Killer orbit and destroy us! Or they could run for home and come back armed for war! Each of these ships could carry huge numbers of reentry vehicles containing nuclear weapons."

"I see the problem. But WOMEN in combat?"

"They developed their civilization on another Planet. They don't have to follow our rules. Each Neanderthal woman can bench press 300 pounds. They can hold their own in sword and shield warfare. Also, they have a deadly weapon built into their faces!"

"Their chewing apparatus!"

"Yeah. That Curator has gone over the X-rays and films of these women taken by Cuc Nguyen. He confirms that they can crunch the vertebrae of a horse's neck just like a lioness!"

"And look at their technology! I would love to have our physicists and engineers know how they build that magnetic bottle they are using to contain that fusion reactor! And to contain the magnetic fields themselves!"

"The four girls sent to the Earth surface, language specialists, cultural anthropologists, historians. They are not engineers. They can no more understand how the fusion reactor works than we can. But Captain Trviea, and their pilots, that Pidonita girl, I'll bet they know EXACTLY how to build and operate that fusion reactor! I wouldn't be surprised if Captain Trviea ordered Helga to pretend to relieve her of command to avoid feeling bound by protocol to come to the surface of the Earth."

"Where we might have her reveal the secrets of her Race."

The limousine drove out of Port Townsend on the way to Olympia. The Governor invited them to a dinner and apologized for the inconvenience they experienced in Port Townsend. They were happy, as were their defense lawyers, the Secret Service agents, and the federal attorneys. Lucinda felt remorse, did not feel like celebrating.

They drove Highway 101 through Quilcene and past Seal Rock. From there the road follows the shore of the Hood Canal. Helga read *The Ugly Little Boy* and liked the way it ended, amazed at how a man, Isaac Asimov, can so well understand the maternal instinct. Even with the return of clouds and rain, they found themselves mesmerized by the wild beauty of the Hood Canal.

The Olympic Mountains begin at the water's edge. There is barely space for the two lane highway. Between Quilcene and Hoodsport, only a few tiny villages can be found. Few paved roads lead into the mountains from 101. The pavement usually ends after one or two miles. Then there are gravel roads that come complete with suspension wrecking bumps, ripples, and chuckholes.

In a spot where a clump of trees shield the view of the Canal, the road was blocked by construction barricades. "What is this?" asked the annoyed driver. "Nobody told me about any construction detour!" He rolled down his window and called out to the worker holding the detour sign.

"You have to take the detour, sir. It's only about five miles, it's not bad." For a four-wheel drive truck maybe. But this is a fancy limo!

"We weren't informed of this! Now I demand that you let us through!"

"I can no more let you through than I can bring back the passenger pigeon, sir! Last night, as the frost melted, a bunch of big old trees let go along with the dirt they grew in. Huge mess all over the highway a mile and a half down. Wall of mud and trees ten feet high and a hundred feet long. We're working as fast as we can. Unless you want to pull over and park for about, oh, two or three days, anyway, longer most likely, then going through just isn't an option! If you take the detour, after about five miles it rejoins the highway and you are on your way. Or you can go back and take the Hood Canal Bridge or the ferry to Keystone or go around the Loop and come out at Aberdeen."

"We're calling this in for verification. Nothing personal, but we have a security responsibility here."

"No problem. Hey! Are those the Neanderthal girls?"

"Yes, they are."

"Congratulations on beating the rap! That Mayton's a stupid shit! If that damn woman judge wouldn't let him get away with so much shit, this would've never happened." The construction worker rambled on about how the judges cannot fucking read the Constitution, for crying out loud! Gun laws, for crying out loud! The Second Amendment is clear and plain in its terms. There is nothing vague and subject to interpretation about it! It is not an authorization to either Congress or any state legislature to decide WHICH arms we shall have the right to keep and bear and which we shall NOT! 'Health boards' passing laws to ban Joe Camel, the judges tolerating such laws. What happened to the First Amendment? And then there's child support. What does the state Constitution say? There shall be no imprisonment for debt, except in cases of absconding debtors. He hasn't absconded! He's right here! These judges can't fuckin' READ! They think three years of law school where they teach 'em the fine art of arguing that the word hill means a flat place and then knowing some politician gives them the right to rape the law for which so many fought and died! What a bunch of fuckin' hypocrites!

Helga and Lucinda looked at each other and agreed that they were correct in their assessment that many Americans have serious grievances which their government has yet to redress. I have many of the same complaints, but I was calmer, more civilized, and polite in the way I explained them. This poor fellow was just plain boiling angry! This can be a fatal problem! They were reminded of their own history.

There used to be a long bridge that carried the Shirelind Road across Mother Star Boulevard. The Shirelind Road is a famous highway that heads east across the continent to the great city of Shirelind. It passes through the heartland of old Atlantis with many fine cities and towns. To Atlanteans it has the romance that Route 66 has for Americans. Mother Star Boulevard runs the length of Cair Atlaston and then around the bay to where Chmlee and Lucinda Renuxler had their apartment.

On that hot summer day, the twelve and fourth day of Melandee, twenty two tenty four, twelve and nine judges were hanged from the Shirelind Bridge. Thus began the most violent civil war fought in Creation history. The judges played the same games with hallowed Atlantean concepts of legal rights that American judges play with the American Constitution. What this construction worker was complaining about. Every prohibition against any type of governmental action against citizens, however plainly and clearly written, had its exceptions. Exceptions that weren't written in the law, but INVENTED by judges who felt the policy in question was justified, the constitutional principles impossibly unrealistic. The Atlantean Civil War was eventually settled. A reform provided juries, not judges, with the power to decide whether a civil right was violated.

"Uh, listen, buddy!" the driver called out to him, "I cannot get confirmation of your road blockage. Could we drive up and see?"

"No confirmation! That figures. You gov'ment types don't tell each other what the Hell's going on! Look, we're pretty busy here; this is the only road between the Canal and the Olympic Mountains! There are a lot of people from Port Townsend to Shelton who are depending on us getting the job done. The problem is that it gets pretty narrow and you won't be able to turn that big long car around. Plus I cannot guarantee you that you won't get buried by another landslide! Some of the soil is pretty unstable there! I suggest you take the detour and get your girls to Olympia as fast as possible. I don't wanna see 'em hurt either!"

"What's your name, son?"

"Allen Case."

"Okay, we'll take the detour." They bounced along for a few miles, heading away from Highway 101. They wondered where the unpaved road turned left to go toward the highway. The ridges towered above their heads.

BOOM!!! A loud explosion just ahead! They saw the cloud of smoke! A large fir tree fell across the road a few yards in front of them. They were going slow, the driver slammed the brakes. "What the HELL!!" he screamed. BOOM!!! Another explosion and another large tree crashed down behind the car! Suddenly gunfire erupted from the surrounding forest. "It's an ambush! Get down!"

Helga and Lucinda undid their seatbelts and dived into the footwell in front of their seat. A Secret Service agent jumped on top of their bodies to shield them from the bullets. Thick steel plates of a high strength alloy are built into the doors, roof, and fenders of a Secret Service limo to protect the passenger compartment, fuel tank, and engine from gunfire. But all four tires were shredded. They smelled gasoline. The huge fallen trees blocked them off in both directions; the road is too narrow to allow a long limousine to turn around. In addition, a gunman stood in front of the car and sent a stream of large caliber bullets through the front grill to disable the engine. Shield plates in the hood and fenders protected the engine, but no such plates could be built that blocked the function of the radiator. The pungent smell of hot radiator fluid filled the air after these highly powered bullets crashed into the cylinder block, punching through the cast iron and the water jacket and into the cylinders, hitting the pistons and connecting rods. The engine stopped running with a loud metallic THUMP!

The driver tried to summon help with his radio. "Static! Nothing but static! It's like we're being jammed!"

A voice rang out of a bullhorn. "You are surrounded, your car is disabled. Open your doors, throw out your weapons, and come out with your hands up!"

"Ladies. I'm terribly sorry about this. But the bulletproof glass works fine only with the first bullet. It is simply a very thick laminated glass. All they have to do is pour a stream of machine gun bullets into it and they will punch a hole through it and start killing us. We have to surrender." The car doors opened. "We're coming out! Don't shoot! Please don't shoot! We're throwing our pistols out!" Government issue sidearms were thrown from the vehicle.

"The Secret Service guys come out of the car first." commanded a member of the ambush force. "Are any of you hurt?"

"I don't know. I'm not hurt!" answered several voices. Four Secret Service agents carefully stepped out of the limousine, with their hands up.

"All of you! Put your hands on the back of your heads. Good! You two on the other side of the car, come around to this side. Good. You. Walk up to this tree. Turn around, lean against the tree." The terrorist took out a pair of handcuffs. He cuffed one of the wrists, pulled it around the back of the tree, and cuffed the other wrist. The agent stood with his back to the tree, his arms pulled up over his head and cuffed around the back of the tree. He was frisked for weapons and electrical equipment. This procedure was repeated for the other three agents.

"Okay ladies! You can come out now." Helga and Lucinda cautiously crawled out of the limo with their hands up. Behind them one of the terrorists reached in the car, shifted the transmission to park and pulled the keys from the ignition. The two women stood in front of the car with their hands on the back of their heads. They were frightened, but these are women who have traveled through the vacuum of space. They stood in the cold wet forest tall, calm, and proud.

"Let's take your communicators. We don't wantchew talking to your Trog Ship." The gunman pulled Lucinda's radio from between her breasts. He copped a feel and she winced with pain. "Nice titties." He did the same to Helga and she winced. This guy didn't know how to squeeze a breast. It hurt! She opened her mouth and made ready her teeth! But with several guns pointed at her, she didn't dare chomp his hand. "Smash these radios." He tossed them to one of his comrades who smashed them against a rock.

"Look." started Lucinda. "Neil Peace has accepted our apology. If you're upset about us kidnapping him, we have pledged not to do that anymore,"

"SHUT UP! This has nothing to do with Neil Peace!" Even with the ski mask hiding his face, the women could tell this one was unstable. He walked over to one of the helpless Secret Service agents. He held his .44 magnum up to the forehead and blew his brains out.

"You IDIOT!" screamed one of the other terrorists. "That was not necessary!"

Helga was shocked. "He he he he had sur sur surrendered! He he he was un un unarmed! He he he did did did not do anything to you. He he he was just protecting ting us! He he he had a wife! Why why why?" Suddenly the still hot business end of the pistol used in the murder was pressed into the bridge of Helga's nose, right between the brow ridges. She closed her eyes and said a prayer in Atlantean, speaking very fast. She told the Great Holy Spirit that she is sorry for all of her sins.

"The Great Holy Spirit has answered your prayers, Miss Trvlakian. I killed the Secret Service agent to prove we're not fucking around! It's sad but it's WAR. If you cooperate neither you nor Mrs. Renuxler will be killed. Bring your hands down like this!" He roughly pulled Helga's arm down to her side. "Now put your hands behind your back. You too Renuxler!" Lucinda did likewise, not waiting for someone to force her arms down. Both women held their hands together behind the small of their backs. "Now we're going to put you in the armbinders we bought at this crazy sex shop in Portland. We're using 'em because you Neanderthals, trogs, are extremely strong and we don't wantchew breaking loose. We'll also use special steel gags to bring your mouths under control, your jaws and teeth look like you can gnaw through rawhide like rats!" Two other terrorists came up behind them with the bondage equipment. They still had their rifles, now slung over their shoulders.

Suddenly, the head of the terrorist in front of them exploded in a shower of fragments of ski mask, hair, skull, skin, brains, and blood. A split second later the supersonic bullet was followed by the report of the hunting rifle that sent it. Commonly available hunting rifles are bolt action single shot devices with scopes and bipods. The hunter, aiming carefully, can hit a possum from 150 yards away. Or in this case, a human head. Another terrorist's head exploded and they all started to run. "Let's get outta here!" The two women recovered from their shock and spun around, their fists crashing into the terrorists' faces with roundhouse rights! POW! The terrorists dropped their bondage stuff and fell back from the impact of angry Neanderthal fists.

They were not knocked out. With blood streaming out of their faces into their ski masks, they spun their rifles around and grasped them for use in this immediate situation. The girls were on them and had also grabbed the rifles, trying to pull them away. Lucinda wrestled with the man for control of the weapon. He wasn't giving it up. He may be a Cro-Magnon but his strength was the equal of hers. She bent down and bit into one of his wrists and crumbled the bones under her teeth. She tasted the salty warmth of his blood. Something hard and heavy clobbered the top of her head knocking her furry cap off. Sharp, extreme pain which she ignored.

The terrorist with the badly injured and bleeding hand screamed involuntarily at the pain. He called her something like an apewoman demon bitch who has sex with dogs. She didn't quite hear it all. Having to contend with the strength of only one arm, Lucinda pulled the rifle away from him. He scrambled into the forest and disappeared. Helga's opponent did likewise, she stood there panting and holding his rifle. The women went back to back and scanned their surroundings for hostiles.

"I think we should dive for cover." said one of them in Atlantean.

"Good idea! NOW!" They ran into the shrubbery and dived for the ground. "Now what?"

"I don't know. I never received military training! Captain Trviea and her security goons, we could use them right now! Oh! The Secret Service guys!"

"The one shot by the pistol before the sniper attack is definitely dead. But the other three have all been shot! They might still be alive! Let's check 'em."

"Okay. Let's run zigzag across the road and bob and weave our heads. The sniper might be our friend but then he might not." They ran across the road bobbing their heads, not allowing their brains to become stationary targets for the sniper rifle. All of the Secret Service agents were slumped down. "This one is dead, no pulse, no breathing."

"This one too, and this one."

Helga started crying. Sobbing uncontrollably, she mourned for the men she knew for only a few days. With tears flowing out of her own eyes, Lucinda took over. "Helga, please. Pull yourself together. They were good men; they gave their lives for us. But if we don't keep our heads, we will soon join them."

"Yes. Yes. I understand. We can grieve for them later. It is winter, no flowers. Let us say a Prayer For The Dead." Then Helga noticed the blood. "Oh my Spirit! Your head!"

"Yeah, I got conked during the fight. It does not hurt too bad." Lucinda lied bravely about the pain.

"After I got the rifle away from my guy, he saw you biting down on your guy. He freaked, and tried to throw a big rock at you. I blocked his arm with the rifle, he dropped the rock. It must have hit you, let me look at that." Helga inspected Lucinda's injury. "The skin is broken, there is some swelling here. But you'll live." She wiped off the blood and kissed the injury.

"I hope I don't have an ugly scar!"

"You will wear it with pride. Now let us pay our respect to the dead and get out of here." The Secret Service keeps handcuffs for arrests; the women found the keys. They didn't find any keys to the car nor did they find any radio communicators. They removed the cuffs from the Secret Service men because they believed honorable men should not be in an undignified position in death. They said the same gentle prayer that Monoloa said for the Teshik-Tash Child.

"Our radios are smashed, there are some more in our luggage."

"In the trunk. The keys have been pulled from the ignition. Where'd they go?"

"One of them ran off with them."

"Great. Shoot the trunk open? Smell that gasoline!"

"Make a nice bonfire. With us as the fuel! Let's get out of here!"

"Man, that Renuxler bitch is an inhuman lioness!" He spoke through the salty blood of his smashed mouth. "What kind of woman runs around with a bald head and not only thinks it's normal, but sexy?"

"A dyke." He could barely talk with his broken maxilla. "She's a trog dyke! Her kind is supposed to have been destroyed by the Flood. She's no descendant of Noah and either of his three sons, not even Ham. The Lord's covenant is not with her. What do you expect? Just another minute and I'll get this bandage done. She sure did a job on your wrist! I tried to help you but Trvlakian blocked me like a strong side tackle leading the running back. But Renuxler should have a nasty welt on her head!"

"What a complete fuck up! We should've known that the Secret Service would station sharpshooters on all of the hills around here."

"No they didn't! Some local yokel out varmint shooting decided to play Lee Harvey Oswald! I told 'em Randle Packwood was too unstable for this mission! If he hadn't snuffed the Secret Service guy, that sniper, probably a varmint shooter, wouldn't have dared to interfere. Because the Secret Service guy was snuffed, the sniper thought that we were going to kill our prisoners anyway."

"The trog women, the daughters of the 'men of renown', got away."

Suddenly there was a heavy thump from four feet landing at once! Two angry female voices screamed in unison "FREEZE!"

The two terrorists found themselves staring down the barrels of their own rifles.

"Okay, gentlemen," began Lucinda. She was breathing hard and her face was flushed with anger and grief. Her voice trembled with powerful emotions held under extreme control. "May I inquire as to what this is all about?"

"We are the Avengers of Yahweh. We, of the White Race, are the descendants of Shem, the true inheritors of the legacy of Eber. The Niggers and the Canaanites are descendants of Ham. Because Ham uncovered the nakedness of his father, Noah, his descendants are cursed and must be the slaves of the descendants of Japheth and of Shem. But you women of Planet Creation, you did not descend from Noah! At least the Niggers and the Canaanites are descended from Noah. Your kind is supposed to have been killed by the Flood. But you were on another Planet, unaffected by the Flood."

"What's that got to do with attacking a Secret Service limousine and killing those good men?" Lucinda and Helga were truly puzzled. They thought they had studied Earth religions thoroughly. They had never heard of this interpretation of the Noah Flood story.

"I'll get to that. Okay, here it is: God created the Earth and all that is in it in six days, on the seventh day He rested. He created Adam and Eve to start humanity. You are also descended from Adam and Eve as we are. After getting kicked out of the Garden of Eden, they were fruitful and multiplied. There was a population explosion of humanity. But in those days, men began to get wicked. There were some spirits, godlike supernatural beings, some good, some bad, most neither. Genesis Chapter 6 mentions them. They called them the 'sons of God'. What they did was have sex with women descended from Eve. These women then bore men of great strength. The 'mighty men of renown'. Hercules was probably one of them. The Greeks told of a hero born of a mortal mother who mated with Zeus. Zeus was apparently one of these 'sons of God'. These 'sons of God' were not descended from Adam and Eve. The hybrid children they created are, without a doubt, the Neanderthal men and women whose skeletons we've found. Except your ancestors who were taken to your Planet, these Neanderthals were all killed by the Flood that God unleashed to wipe out the wicked men whom He regretted creating. Noah and his sons survived the Flood because they built the Ark. God repented His act of destruction and made a promise to Noah and to all of his descendants, signified by the rainbow, that He will never again try to destroy the World with a Flood. But His covenant is not with you, you are not supposed to exist. And now you come back to Earth. You are threat to the survival of all of the descendants of Noah because the Lord's covenant is not with you."

Helga answered. "No, we're not! I'm not completely comprehending this whole story of yours. It sounds like Nazi stuff! So what if we didn't descend from Noah! So what if our ancestors included supernatural godlike beings! We have no intention of attacking or invading Earth and of doing any harm to the people who live here. Our only intentions are to establish a peaceful relationship with Earth and to find a way of bearing children so we can continue our Race."

"Yeah. Well Trvlakian, you yourself told of a Plan of Conquest. It's quite possible you can attack our Planet with a shower of nuclear weapons. You tossed in the stuff about Gray Aliens to make it look like a sarcastic put down of a man who thinks like me. You should understand that threats of nuclear war are nothing to joke about!"

Helga thought for a minute, while they stared at each other in silence. "He's right. I owe an apology for that. I let myself get carried away. Did you take my put down of this man so seriously that you decided to go ahead with this attack?"

"If it'll make you feel better, we planned to do it anyway. We cannot afford to let your blood mix with ours, causing the Earth population to include people who are not descendants of Noah and therefore not party to the Lord's covenant. The Lord apparently used a Virus to finish the job begun by the Flood." That last sentence infuriated both women.

Lucinda then spoke. Her face was flushed with shock and anger. "Helga, you do not owe any apology to these hate filled souls who have adopted a twisted, racist interpretation of their Hebrew religion."

"Lchnsda, I have to be true to OUR religion. I am responsible for MY sins regardless of anyone else's." She turned back to the terrorists. "I apologize for frightening you unnecessarily with my fanciful story of conquest and for allowing myself to be provoked into doing such a thing by someone who thinks like you. Now that's accomplished, I see you have some ammunition that fits these guns. May we have it, please?" Helga pointed the rifle at the Avenger's heart. It was not a request!

The Avengers of Yahweh handed over the ammunition. In return the women of Creation allowed them to continue breathing.

"Either of you have the keys to the limousine?"

"No. We don't."

Lucinda took over. "You used these handcuffs to tie the Secret Service agents to the trees so that they were helpless while you MURDERED them! You, the healthy one! Cuff yourself around that tree!" Lucinda tossed a pair of handcuffs to him. He complied. Helga then put one loop of another pair of handcuffs around the healthy wrist of the other one. She then attached the other loop around the chain of the cuffs holding the healthy one to the tree.

"You now gonna kill us?" asked the Avenger with the bitten wrist.

"We will kill in self defense, only if it proves necessary. But NEVER in cold blood! We who have descended from the 'mighty men of renown' are not nearly as wicked as you who have descended from Noah's sons and cannot even look upon the African black people as human beings. We of course, see all of the people of Planet Earth and of Planet Creation as human beings, except those who are consumed with racial hatred. For you, we feel nothing but PITY!"

"Let's get outta here. If we make it out alive, we can tell the American police where they may find these two gentlemen."

The women ran through the forest, not knowing where they were. They desperately tried to figure out which way is Highway 101. The other way goes into the National Park; maybe there are some park rangers there. They came to a clearing where they saw two men. The pair of men and the pair of women pointed their rifles at each other.

"Don't SHOOT!" everyone yelled.

"Len Taylor!" shouted Helga in recognition.

"We're not your enemy! Let us point our weapons to the sky." Everyone did so and then relaxed. "This is my friend, Henry Turnipseed. Henry, this is Helga Trvlakian and Lucinda Renuxler."

The tall handsome Native American man extended his hand in greeting. Each of the women gave him her traditional two handed shake. There was relief and smiles all around. "We saw the whole thing." declared Henry.

"Were you the snipers?"

"That was us."

"I know the taking of a human life is an extremely serious thing, but, under the circumstances, thank you very much!" Helga hugged Len Taylor, and Lucinda hugged Henry Turnipseed in an expression of appreciation for saving their lives. "They said they were the Avengers of Yahweh."

"Oh SHIT!" both men exclaimed.

"Bad news?"

"Bad news. They're a bunch of racist, Christian Identity sort of fanatics."

"The fanatic part we have already observed."

"It's beginning to rain. Let's get outta here before we catch our deaths of pneumonia." With Len leading the way, the foursome ran through the underbrush down the opposite slope and came out on to another gravel road. To their left was the rear end of my '66 Pontiac.

"Is that Neil's car?"

"Yeah. Runs fine." They walked up to it. Len opened the trunk. "Let's put the long rifles in there." They removed the bullets from the chambers, locked the safeties and placed the guns in the trunk. After closing the trunk they got into the car. Len drove them down the dirt road.

"So this is what we took Neil away from?" commented Lucinda as she looked over the worn interior. "No wonder he was so angry with us!"

"Hey, don't knock it! It was a beautiful car thirty years ago! Neil's a much better engineer than certain people gave him credit for. This old buggy sent him on some crazy gremlin hunts, but he was always able to fix it. Could never afford to buy a new one. I wouldn't be surprised if he figured out exactly how your ship runs!"

"He figured out that we have a fusion reactor that we use for propulsion."

"Yeah, and when he comes back down, he probably could work out a design for a fusion reactor, having seen one." They came to a spot where a pair of ruts led off from the gravel road through a locked gate. Len parked the car, and with the engine running got out and unlocked the gate. He drove the car through. Then he went back out, collected his mail, and closed and locked the gate. He drove the party on to his farm.

The rifles were collected from the trunk and they went into the Taylor house. "Let me try the phone." Len picked up his telephone. "Line's dead."

"Can we drive out to Highway 101?"

"We could, but it's pretty risky given the circumstances. We could get ambushed and clobbered. But if I know the Avengers of Yahweh, they're getting away as fast as possible. They have attacked a Secret Service car! They probably thought we were federal agents ourselves. Funny I'm not hearing helicopters. If we're out on the road and there's an Army regiment up from Fort Lewis combing the hills, a mistake could get us killed. It's best to stay right here."

"I wish we had some kind of radio transmitter." said Lucinda as Henry cleaned the injury on her head. "Ours were taken and smashed. Our stuff's in the trunk of the car." She winced as he sprayed on the bacteria killer.

"Your head's not too bad," commented Henry. "But you should get some stitches for the broken skin. Boy, that sure is good fighting when you bit his wrist! You really crunched it! You've got the biting power of lioness when she is bringing down a zebra!"

"You weren't supposed to see that."

"Why not?"

"We came here to ask for your help in continuing our Race. You're not going to give it if you cannot look past our brow ridges, our muscles, and our huge teeth to see us as human beings! We cannot afford to be seen as intelligent lionesses with enough jaw muscle to crunch another person on a whim!"

"Lucinda, you didn't act on a whim! You had just cause! These guys ambushed your limo and murdered your Secret Service escort. Who knows what they were gonna do to you? Nobody in their right mind will blame you for fighting back! We definitely see you as human beings. For a radio, all we have are these little walkie-talkies. We use them to keep track of each other in the forest. They only transmit a few watts. Range is three miles, but that's under ideal conditions out in the open. It's a lot less through these trees and it won't penetrate these high stone ridges."

"Show me how you operate it, please."

"You push this button and speak. Hello, this is Henry Turnipseed calling Leonard Taylor. Do you read me, Len?" His voice boomed out of Len's walkie-talkie.

Len picked up his walkie-talkie and responded. "This is Leonard Taylor. I read you loud and clear, Henry."

"Let me have that, please." requested Lucinda. She pushed the button and spoke. "This is Lchnsda Renuxler calling *Neanderthal Return*." she said in English, and then repeated in Atlantean. She directed Len to "Please turn off the other one."

"Oh, give me a break!" the Earthmen exclaimed. They could not believe that the *Neanderthal Return* had radio equipment THAT good!

"Our ship might be on the other side of the Planet, they have to look after Monoloa in Russia, too."

Lucinda continued to play with the walkie-talkie while Len looked in his refrigerator to decide what to fix for chow.

"This is the *Neanderthal Return*, Captain Harsradich here. We read you Lchnsda, keep transmitting at this frequency. We're getting a fix on your location."

"We're at Len Taylor's farmhouse, Trviea. I'm fine except for a bump on the head and Helga is right here with us and she is all right. But unfortunately there are four dead Secret Service agents down by the limousine. It's a long story but there are two fine men here, Len Taylor and a Henry Turnipseed, they saved our lives!"

"Thank the Spirit you are both all right! Thank you, Mr. Taylor. Thank you Mr. Turnipseed. We cannot see a thing through this cloud cover. There are clouds all over Washington and British Columbia. We know your limo was detoured off Highway 101 by a construction crew. A helicopter sent by the Navy from the Bangor Base has found the limousine; a Jefferson County deputy sheriff is on the scene. The military and police in Western Washington are heading in your direction."

"We were ambushed on the back road. The limo is a mess. The four Secret Service agents with us are dead. We managed to force two of the attackers to handcuff themselves to a tree. They identified themselves as 'The Avengers of Yahweh'. They believe we are descendants of some humans who were wicked and were supposed to have been killed off by their God in the Flood of Noah. God made his covenant with the descendants of Noah. They fear that our existence threatens this covenant. That makes us a threat to Cro-Magnon existence."

"That is positively absurd but then religious absurdity is a problem on both of our Planets. We will communicate with the American authorities and see if we can get some police up there to help you out."

"Thank you, Captain."

Chapter Eleven

"Roger. We do not see a mudslide blocking Highway 101. The road is clear from Quilcene to Lilliwaup."

"We haven't heard from the limousine for an hour now. They have not been seen by anyone in Lilliwaup. There's no way they can go down the west side of the Canal without going through Lilliwaup. They haven't been seen in Eldon. They should be passing Shelton by now. We should hear from them, they have radios. You have not seen a long black limousine?"

"That is negative. They reported a road blockage north of Brinnon. They reported that a highway construction worker manned a barricade and directed them on to a detour route that he said was only five miles. They should have been able to cover that five miles and be on the main road by now. We'll fly west of the highway and search the back roads."

"Roger that. We'll advise the County Sheriffs and the State Patrol of this development. They could send a cruiser up and down 101. There's a Park Ranger in the Dosewallips Recreational Area, he'll come down that road."

The Navy helicopter swung a mile west of 101 and conducted a visual search of the back roads. When the Secret Service limo did not report in, the chopper was scrambled off the Bangor Base to conduct a visual search below the cloud cover.

Jefferson County Deputy Sheriff Mike Carlson was dispatched down Highway 101 in a four wheel drive sport utility vehicle. He had been advised of the missing limousine and the strange circumstances surrounding its disappearance. While there was cause for concern, they could be pulled over changing a flat tire. Nobody was certain of where the limo was stopped by the highway crew that nobody had heard of. What mudslide? There is no mudslide! Hmmmmm.

He drove to a spot where a clump of trees shield the road from view of the Hood Canal. A gravel road led off toward the mountains. The deputy slowed down, and then he stopped! He got out of his truck. Maybe it's nothing. He used a long stick to push aside some brush and looked with his flashlight. Some barricades, just like the ones road crews use. A hand held detour sign! The dirt was freshly disturbed.

A theory occurred to the deputy. One man dressed like a highway worker put up these barricades and used this sign to direct the Secret Service limo up this dirt road off the highway. As soon as the limo had driven out of sight he pulled up the barricades and tossed them into the underbrush. Then he disappeared. No mudslide or construction work on the highway. The deputy did not like this theory. The week before he had to try to arrest these same women on a felony warrant because Mayton had to be stupid. Now he had to help locate the federally owned limousine and its passengers.

"Deputy Sheriff Mike Carlson calling in." He said the milepost number. "Found some highway barricades and a detour sign that appear to have recently been tossed into the underbrush. Proceeding up this side road to see what I can find. There are fresh tire tracks."

"We'll pass that on to the Navy. Be careful, everyone is keen to find that limousine." The Sheriff Department's dispatcher informed the Navy air traffic controllers who then put the deputy sheriff in direct communication with the helicopter.

"Roger, Deputy Mike Carlson, I see you. Can you hear me?"

"I can hear your chopper blades, sir. Imagine, state and federal authorities actually TALKING to each other!"

"What a concept, maaan! Okay, we'll follow this trail and see what we can find." The helicopter flew on ahead. Suddenly, "Oh my GOD! Oh my GOD! Stay back Deputy Carlson! Wait for backup!"

"Wha-wha-what's going on!"

"I see the limousine! It looks like it's been ambushed by the Viet Cong! There's a tree down in front of the car, another tree down behind it! The doors are hanging open. I see human bodies sprawled all over the place, rifles laying at their sides! There are what look like pools of blood! Sheriff, I advise that you approach with EXTREME CAUTION!!"

"Roger," the deputy answered nervously, "Backup's coming?"

"Ohh, you'll get backup, all right. NOBODY ambushes a Secret Service car!"

The alarm sirens screamed at every military base in Western Washington. Army troops and Marines in full combat dress loaded on to helicopters as the engines revved. Heavy lift helicopters were set up to carry jeeps and humvees. Jet fighters scrambled into the sky.

Every available Mason and Jefferson County unit raced into action. Road blocks were set up on Highway 101. Every car was stopped and searched. Officers apologized to the motorists and asked them if they had seen anything. Other officers checked the remote farms located throughout the forest. Their telephones were dead.

Olympic National Park Rangers searched the Park near the limousine for suspects.

Meanwhile, Deputy Sheriff Carlson and the Navy helicopter were on the scene. The Jefferson County truck stopped fifty feet from the fallen tree. "I'm within sight of a fallen maple tree. It's a big one. I'm getting out of the car to get a closer look."

"Roger that, Carlson. I can see through most of these trees and get some view of the forest floor." He was over his initial shock and concentrated on his job. "I don't see any hostiles, or any moving bodies, but be careful."

Deputy Carlson put on a helmet with a radio headset. He slipped a bullet proof vest on over his clothes. He opened his truck door and got out crouching with his gun drawn. Crouched down, he ran around the door and dived behind the fallen tree. Splintered and burnt wood and a pungent fireworks smell informed him that an explosive was used to fell the tree. He peered over the trunk and got his first look at the scene of horror.

"I can see two bodies dressed in camouflage and what's left of ski masks."

"What's LEFT of ski masks?"

"Head shots. I see the limousine. Tires are flat. Oh my GOD! I see men in suits. The Secret Service men! I'm going over to them no matter what happens!"

"Be careful, Carlson!"

Deputy Carlson hopped over the tree and ran to the Secret Service men. Because the Creation women removed the handcuffs, they were laying on the ground at the base of the trees where they were killed. "One of them was shot in the forehead. Powder burns. The other three have multiple gunshot wounds. I'm checking them. This one is dead. And this one. And, oh my God, this one too. All four are dead."

"You see any sign of the women?"

The deputy looked into the limousine. "I smell gasoline. We better be careful around the car, bring foam." He looked around the scene. The four dead Secret Service agents. Government issue sidearms laying in the dirt near the car. They apparently surrendered and got out. Such a well planned attack! Car diverted by a phony highway construction worker. Big fir tree knocked down in front; he could see the splintered and burned wood. The big maple knocked down in back. Large bullet holes in the front grill, smell of hot radiator fluid and motor oil. The engine disabled, the tires shot out. So what happened to cause the two dead terrorists and the four dead Secret Service agents? "I see no sign of the women. They're not here. Possible kidnapping. Something went wrong, probably after the Secret Service surrendered and got out of the car. Two of the perps lie here dead, each of their heads blown open." The deputy was under complete emotional control, proceeding in a businesslike police detective manner.

"You think they were killed by a sniper who happened upon the scene?"

"Can't tell. The one agent with the head wound has powder burns. Execution style. The other men look like they were shot by crossfire. Whoa! Look at this! I see some disturbed dirt and grass, some leather, what the Hell?" Shiny black leather, straps, a zipper that can be pulled up quickly. Two of them! And two of what looked like adult sized leather pacifiers with thick leather straps attached to them. "I believe these are armbinders and gags you can order through catalogues sold in porno shops."

"You're kidding!"

"No. Look, you're planning to kidnap women with the physical strength of football players and the teeth and jaws of lions. What are you gonna tie 'em up with? Regular handcuffs that they can just break? Rope they can gnaw? No, you get equipment strong enough to hold 'em. The women might have gotten away!"

"The first Marine helicopters have just set down on 101 at the base of this dirt road. They've brought some humvees. They should coming up to you soon. You see any footprints leading away into the forest?"

"I'm doing the best I can. There are a lot of footprints and disturbed dirt and plants all around here. No telling where the surviving perps and the Creation women went." The Marines in their humvees arrived and parked behind the Jefferson County utility vehicle. Other Jefferson County deputies arrived. After the Marines secured a perimeter around the site, the police and troops systematically searched the surrounding forest.

Deputy Carlson discovered the two men handcuffed to the tree. They wore camouflage. Their ski masks laid next to an open first aid kit with its contents strewn all over the ground. Blood from the wounded hand soaked the makeshift bandage. "Found two perps, alive. Get paramedics up here, one of them is wounded." He turned to the perps. "Where the Hell are the women!"

"They're not women." responded the man with the broken wrist.

"They're not men in drag." shouted Deputy Carlson angrily.

"They're female all right. But they're not HUMAN. Listen, we've got a pair of dangerous ANIMALS running loose in this forest. They've taken our rifles and they have ammunition."

"Dangerous animals?" asked the deputy. He had already taken out a notepad to record this conversation. He was elated at the news that the two ladies had gotten away alive and are apparently capable of taking care of themselves. "Like the dangerous animals who killed the Secret Service guys. I don't think Helga Trvlakian and Lucinda Renuxler killed the men who were protecting them."

"No. Randle Packwood plugged the one agent. I knew he was too unstable for this mission!"

"Frank! Shut up!" screamed the other terrorist. "No statements without a lawyer, remember?"

"It doesn't matter what happens to me. You can put me in jail for the rest of my life, probably the safest place to be, considering what's COMING."

"So Randle Packwood snuffed the one agent, exactly how did he do it?" Better get any details the perps are willing to give on the killings.

"Yeah, he did, all right. Just put his pistol to his forehead and blew him away."

"And about the other three agents, how did they die?"

"I don't know. They're dead?"

"Yes, they're dead!"

"Bald bitch said they were killed. I didn't see 'em killed, probably happened when we were busy with the demon bitches."

"So the women got away, and they've got your firearms?"

"Yep. They ran off over that way." He indicated the direction with his injured hand. "Here's what happened: Everything was going well. We got the limo diverted on to the dirt road. They went stumbling right into our trap. We blew the trees front and rear of the car, shot out the tires, and shot up the engine. They surrendered. We got the Secret Service disarmed and handcuffed to the trees."

"Wait a minute, the agents were not cuffed to the trees when we found them."

"These here are two pairs of those cuffs. The demon bitches removed the cuffs. We got the demon women out of the car. Randle had them under gunpoint while we were getting out this sex bondage stuff we purchased at this place on Burnside in Portland. The faggots down in that neighborhood! I went into a bar to have a beer and it was full of faggots! We could use some Zyclon B,"

"Let's not reminisce about your days in Portland." The deputy wanted Frank to stick to the day's events. He did not want to be entertained by Frank's hatred of homosexuals, which he nevertheless noted in Pitman shorthand on his notepad.

"Okay, you're right, we're done with Portland. I had to admit the pervert stuff looked like it could hold the demon bitches. But Randle was a nutcase! The bitches came out of the car; they held their hands up and then behind their heads POW style. But they were not cringing. They were very haughty, proud, like goddesses. Randle didn't like women like that. The bald bitch talked to him in a disrespectful manner. That set him off! He then killed the one Secret Service agent to show her he meant business. That seemed to impress them, the blonde bitch started whimpering. Randle put his gun right between her brow ridges, made her think that was it! Then he pulled the gun away and told her that she may live if she cooperates. They were holding their hands behind their backs waiting for me and Jack here to put on the leather armbinders. That's when it all fell apart."

"What happened?"

"Randle's head exploded. A sniper, a varmint shooter who decided to play Lee Harvey Oswald. It was just like the Zapruder film! Glenn Morton's head exploded and everyone panicked. They started to run, somebody yelled 'Let's get outta here!' The bitches spun around and punched us, BOOM! I've been punched before but this is like being punched by Evander Holyfield! That's how strong they are! They really are the daughters of the men of renown. Because we were trying to put them in the armbinders, we had slung our rifles over our shoulders. Now we are on our backs. We managed to swing the guns around to where we can grasp the barrels. But these demon bitches also had them and were wrestling the rifles away from us. The blonde got the rifle away from Jack, but I was keeping the bald demon from taking my gun. That's when she did THIS!" He held up his badly injured hand. "She bit me like a cougar!"

Deputy Carlson couldn't help a laugh.

"You laugh! But no Earth woman of today, no woman who descended from Eve without any interbreeding with the spirits known as the 'sons of God', are capable of biting with this force! They are lionesses, not humans! They did not descend from Noah's sons so the Lord's covenant is not with them. Therefore their existence on this Planet is a threat to us all!"

This is not mystifying to a veteran police officer. Keeping track of Ku Klux Klan type literature is part of a policeman's job. The Noah Flood story has been misused to justify racial discrimination for the last three thousand years. In the slave days in the American South, the African Negroes were said to have descended from Ham, and were therefore cursed because he uncovered the nakedness of his father, Noah. That was supposed to justify holding black people as slaves. After the Civil War, the Ku Klux Klan and other white supremacist groups took up this story. These terrorists are motivated by a racist interpretation of the Noah Flood story! "So you're saying Neanderthals are the descendants of the 'men of renown', born as the result of supernatural spirits, called the 'sons of God', mating with human women?" He remembered his Book of Genesis.

"Yes! That's who they are! They were supposed to have been wiped out by the Flood. But this bunch got taken away to another Planet, keeping the Flood from killing 'em. They are like Hercules, who was the son of Zeus and a mortal woman. Zeus was probably one of the 'sons of God' who married the daughters of Eve, who created the heroic men of renown. Men like Hercules, Achilles, and other legendary heroes. We're certain that Neanderthal skeletons are the remains of these Hybrid People. They're stronger than we are, that is why the heroes were capable of their feats of strength. They can bite like lions! Break your neck vertebrae under their teeth! Look! Everyone KNOWS these demon bitches were holding back when Dr. Cuc Nguyen tested them for intelligence and physical strength! They don't want us to know just how magical their powers really are! Because they're not descendants of Noah, the Lord's Covenant is not with them, they're a threat to us all!"

"Who exactly are you guys? What organization?"

"We are the Avengers of Yahweh."

The deputy switched on his radio. "To everyone. This is important! The perps identify themselves as the 'Avengers of Yahweh'!" That should get every known Avenger taken in for questioning within the next few hours.

He sighed. Find the women, they will be glad to be out of the forest, probably cold and hungry.

The *Neanderthal Return* was parked over Moscow where we engaged in a lively chat with Russian television. Monoloa Mrvlakian translated the dialogue between Atlantean and Russian. The beautiful Neanderthal redhead became very popular throughout the Commonwealth of Independent States. By then, I knew enough Atlantean that my answers to the live call in questions went through one language translation and not two or three.

Suddenly a news bulletin broke in. A map of the Olympic Peninsula with place names rendered in Cyrillic alphabet covered the screen. The announcer described in Russian that the Secret Service limousine carrying Helga and Lucinda was missing. Then a film clip of the limousine leaving the Port Townsend courthouse in triumph as Monoloa translated this news into Atlantean. Pidonita Hmlakian, our best pilot, took off for the Pilothouse, saying to me in English, "We have to get around Planet fast!"

Captain Trviea asked in urgent Atlantean, "Monoloa, how current is this report?"

"Very current," Monoloa answered. "This is coming from Pravda's bureau in Seattle, where they picked it up from local television. This same bulletin is going out on the American television and the international BBC and CNN." We tuned to those stations on separate monitors, and there it was!

Then the Russian announcer started shouting. Monoloa translated it into Atlantean and then we knew we had better move. An American Navy helicopter found the Secret Service limousine.

BODIES laying on the ground. A deputy sheriff found the four Secret Service men dead. He did not find the Creation women. A map of the Olympic Peninsula showed an arrow pointing to the spot near Highway 101 where the limo was found. Then the Russian television showed photographs of Helga Trvlakian and Lucinda Renuxler with their names rendered in Cyrillic alphabet. The announcer suggested that everyone pray for their safety.

Pidonita told us through the ship intercom that "We are going around Planet NOW!" We told Monoloa this; we have to break off from the show. She translated this message into Russian and told her audience. She then told her audience that her two shipmates are very resourceful and had received survival training.

The reports continued to come in. They asked Monoloa about the wrist being chomped by Lucinda in the fight.

"We did not want to let you know about this. We want you to see us as decent human beings. Apparently the 'Avengers of Yahweh' do not see us as human beings, which has led them to violate God's laws. That is why we did not want you to know we can bite with tremendous force. It would distract you from seeing the humanity inside each of us. But we need to be honest with you good people of Earth. You have a right to know everything about us, including things which might frighten you. We know things about you that frighten us. So I need to perform a simple demonstration. May I have a chicken drumstick, please? Thank you. First I eat the meat to expose the bone."

She ate the meat. "Now you can see the bone." She placed half of the bone in her mouth, the bone firmly gripped by her teeth. There was a loud crunching sound as she bit down. She removed the badly mangled bone and displayed it to her audience to loud gasps. "I believe this is what Lchnsda did to the man from whom she took the rifle. We only do this to another person if it is absolutely necessary. For her, it was."

We did not see Monoloa's demonstration of Neanderthal jaw strength. We swung around Earth and parked above the State of Washington. The area was covered with clouds, the cold snap had snapped. We established radio contact with the police and military authorities responding to the situation. An hour after the beginning of the crisis as we had known it, we were contacted by Lucinda with her borrowed walkie-talkie.

We informed the American authorities that the women were alive and well at Len Taylor's farm. I hoped they treat Len well and respect his property!

The Jefferson County Sheriff's utility vehicle raced to a halt next to Len Taylor's locked gate. Several humvees full of Marines parked behind the deputy sheriff's vehicle. A military helicopter flew overhead. The deputy got out of his vehicle and checked the gate, it was locked. "We could break the lock and open the gate!" shouted one of the Marines.

"No you won't!" countered the deputy. "Taylor's a good guy. He don't grow pot like some of the people in these woods. My wife likes to buy vegetables from him when he's harvesting. We WILL respect his property rights! It's bad enough we're fighting the Avengers of Yahweh, we don't need to fight a bunch of angry stump farmers! Oh! Here he comes!"

Len Taylor came running out. "Hey Mike! How ya doing!"

"Doing great, Len!" the deputy smiled, after all of this it's nice to see a friendly face on a civilian. "You got the girls?"

"Yep! They say the construction worker gave his name as Allen Base, or Allen Case, Pace, they aren't sure of the last name, but his first name was Allen."

"Okay, Allen Something. They in the house?"

"With Henry Turnipseed having soup and sandwiches. Henry cleaned and put some Bactine on this really nasty looking cut Lucinda has on her head. When we got past her bravado she admitted it hurts like Hell." He smiled at that. The girl's not a whiner. "She should have some stitches put in. Other than that they are physically none the worse for wear. But they have been through a harrowing experience. They're in good spirits as long as they don't think about the Secret Service agents." He lowered his voice. "But I had to hold Helga for a few minutes while she let it out. Lucinda too. Me and Henry had to do some grief counseling, something for which we are not trained. We should go easy with them, they are strong, very impressive, but right now their emotions are very fragile."

"Everyone's in shock over the killing of the Secret Service agents. Two of the perpetrators have been killed by what looks like sniper weapons, deer rifles or varmint shooters. I'm not going to ask you if you did that, as far as I'm concerned they had it coming. Whoever did the shooting was justified as soon as they started killing the agents, they probably saved the women's lives. We found two of the perps handcuffed to a tree; Lucinda bit down on one of their wrists while wrestling the rifle away from them. The perps tell us that they had cuffed the agents to trees, but when we found them there were no cuffs. The perps tell us that the women used those cuffs to tie them to the tree, they had taken them off of the agents."

"It's an Atlantean belief that when an honorable person is killed, the deceased should not be left in an undignified position. They would have laid the bodies out straight if they had time and laid flowers if there were flowers. As it was they removed the handcuffs and said a Prayer for the Dead. Then they had to move."

Taylor unlocked and opened the gate while he talked with Deputy Sheriff Mike Langston. One of the Marines came up, he had a radio. "Mr. Taylor. The chopper wants to know if he can set down on your plowed fields."

"Those plowed fields put clothes on my back and food on my table. You will NOT set down on my plowed fields. But there is a big lawn behind my house, he can set down there, it should be enough room."

The Marine talked into his radio. "The civilian does not want his plowed fields disturbed. He says you can use the lawn behind his house!"

"I don't like it," shouted the chopper pilot. "But it'll work, I just don't see what harm I can do to a field in the winter."

"Look, this farmer brought the women out of the forest, probably saved their lives." Deputy Langston shouted at the Marine. "If he can set down on the lawn, then tell him to leave the fields alone."

The helicopter set down in the lawn as directed, there was enough room there. The police and Marine vehicles came through the gate and parked in the front yard next to my Pontiac. The Marines secured a perimeter. The helicopter pilot offered to take Lucinda over to the base hospital at Bangor where physicians can look at her head and put in stitches. She agreed to that but insisted on finishing her soup. She finished the sandwich on the helicopter as it flew to Bangor.

The two farmers owned up to having shot the terrorists with their bolt action rifles. They shoot .22 caliber bullets at 4000 feet per second. When they saw the one guy snuff the Secret Service man and put his pistol to Helga's head, they decided they had to do something. So each sighted the head of a terrorist through his gun's scope. The terrorists started to run after their shots. They watched in horror as some of them shot up the other three agents while they reloaded their weapons. They each fired another shot but missed their targets. They watched the two women spin around and punch the two men who were about to wrap their arms in the crazy looking leather binders. They watched the women wrestle the rifles away from these guys and Lucinda's chomping of the wrist. The guy who lost his gun to Helga tried to throw a big rock on

Lucinda but was stopped by Helga. The rock hit Lucinda anyway. Then some of the terrorists, carrying machine guns, came toward them, they had to move!

After running through the forest, they encountered the women, managed to avoid shooting each other and then went to the Pontiac and drove to Len's farm. They surrendered the rifles to the authorities and went into the humvees and rode out to Highway 101.

Lucinda passed Frank Binford in a hospital hallway at the Bangor Base. Binford had just gotten out of surgery for his chewed up wrist. He was surrounded by heavily armed uniformed men. They are tall and powerfully built. Lucinda noticed the Neanderthal style of muscle mass on these determined stone faced Cro-Magnons. Lucinda and her Secret Service guard angled past the Binford party without saying a word. She had fresh stitches on her head.

She and Helga were taken to an FBI office to be grilled by the artist to make the composite of the 'highway construction worker' who flagged them on to the side road. They ran checks on Allens with names that sound like Case or Base. He thanked them for their cooperation. Every American they met was fiercely determined to get these Avengers of Yahweh, for killing their Secret Service agents, and for making a mockery of their Jewish and Christian religion. The Secret Service agents were polite enough, but they were grieving and very angry over the loss of their men.

They were back in the honeymoon suite across the old Pacific Highway from Seattle Tacoma International Airport. In the morning they were scheduled to fly to Washington, D.C. Their nationwide tour had been canceled. Andemona Chmlakian was scheduled to arrive on a plane from Mexico City. They were scheduled to attend the funeral for the four Secret Service agents at Arlington National Cemetery.

Finally alone they embraced, allowed themselves to have a good cry, hugging each other for some comfort after the incredible week they had. Tears, a kiss, and then Helga said in Atlantean: "Let's go to bed. Separate beds, we don't need to push the button these Earthlings have on homosexuality."

"I agree with you there. If we step into the same bed, we will fall asleep in each other's arms and be found that way."

"See you in the morning." One last kiss and they stripped off their clothes and crawled under the covers of their separate beds. Clean sheets are so nice! They were asleep within minutes.

Chapter Twelve

"All this because of a CHILDREN'S story?" asked a perplexed Captain Trviea Harsradich.

"Don't let Earth people hear you refer to the Noah's Flood story as a children's story." I advised her. "There are many who would be offended."

"Well, so they might be offended!" shouted Trviea angrily. "I'm offended by this idea that I'm not supposed to exist! Helga and Lchnsda have had quite a *Twilight Zone* week on the Olympic Peninsula because some Cro-Mags are offended by the fact that we EXIST! We offend by being ALIVE. They were perfectly comfortable with us as a bunch of rotten bones in a few caves! But present them with LIVE Neanderthals, driving a SPACESHIP, they all freak out even though we've clearly signaled that we come in peace! We've done nothing to indicate hostile intention!"

"You did kidnap me."

"Well, yes that is right! I ordered your kidnapping! But the mutiny changed all that. Now we have Earthlings behaving exactly the way I feared."

"Helga Trvlakian and Lucinda Renuxler arrived in Washington D.C. A helicopter is carrying them to the White House. The Secret Service has thrown an extremely tight security blanket around them in response to the terrible attack on the Olympic Peninsula."

"Andemona Chmlakian arrived from Mexico City just a few minutes after the other two. She is popular in Mexico; her trip went smoothly except for the human sacrifice attempt at Teotihuacan. Six teenagers were at the summit of the Pyramid of the Moon. They saw Andemona and her Mexican police bodyguard down in the plaza below, and waved at her. She waved back. In her presence, one of the boys, a seventeen year old, took off his shirt. He laid on his back on the altar. Four other boys held him down, each grabbing an arm or a leg. The remaining boy produced a huge flint knife and held it high for everyone to see. He plunged it into the chest before police stopped him."

"The helicopter has just landed on the South Lawn. The three women from Creation are being escorted into the White House. Ladies! Can you answer some questions?"

"We come in peace. Let us pray there are no more tragedies."

"The women from Creation have restated their desire for peace. They are now entering the White House. Back to you."

The women were escorted to the Lincoln Bedroom and an adjacent bathroom. They were allowed time to clean up and change clothes. Then they were escorted into the Oval Office for a meeting with the President.

The women were introduced to the President, the First Lady, the Curator of Anthropology, and to some of the Cabinet Officers. "You speak extraordinarily well." commented the Curator.

The women knew the Curator wrote a book wherein he described the theory that Neanderthals could not speak the same way we 'anatomically modern humans' speak because of the shape of the roof of the mouth. Helga declared, emphasizing the hard g and the k sounds, "Of COURSE we Can speaK!"

The Curator smiled sheepishly. "Please understand. I'm a scientist. We look at evidence and propose a hypothesis to,"

"Yeah, yeah, yeah."

Sigh. "On behalf of the scientific community of Earth I apologize to any Neanderthal women of Creation who are offended by this,"

"As long as it's the result of scientific curiosity and not from racism, I can accept your apology. Please forgive my short temper. These Avengers of Yahweh make me think I condemned my Race to extinction."

"We don't want that to happen, Helga." assured the President. "I trust you are not too tired from traveling today?"

"We're fine." answered Helga.

"I'm fine." confirmed Lucinda.

"*Muy bien*. My English *es* not as *muy bueno* as Helga's *o* Lchnsda's *Ingles*." answered Andemona.

"*Perro tu espanol es mucho muy bueno*." complimented the President.

"Her Atlantean *es* also *muy bueno*, we can translate." suggested Lucinda.

"For the time being," the President got down to business, "you are invited to stay in the private living quarters of the White House as my guests, and as guests of the American people who own this House. Don't worry about any Monica Lewinsky type thing, I'm not Bill Clinton. Though the damn comedians will tell their jokes. The attack by the Avengers of Yahweh has convinced us of the need to place you under the highest level of security. Most of the people of Earth want to live in peace with you and with every nation on your Planet, and are glad that your Race lives. But there are those who think otherwise, and a few have chosen a violent path."

"If there's anything we can do for the families of the Secret Service men who were killed, they only need to ask." offered Lucinda. "We know what it's like to lose husbands and brothers."

"May I speak, Mr. President?" asked one of the Secret Service men, who normally do not participate in Oval Office discussions when they stand guard.

"Sure." said the President.

"The Secret Service in no way blames you ladies for the tragedy. We appreciate your condolences and offers of help and we join with you in praying for their souls. We appreciate your treating their bodies with dignity and we thank you for your Prayer for the Dead."

"We have medically stopped the aging process." said Lucinda. "But we are still MORTAL. We will die. When that terrorist shot the first Secret Service man to death and put the gun to Helga's head, I was frozen in fear. I couldn't do a thing! Then Helga closed her eyes and said a fast prayer to the Great Holy Spirit apologizing for her sins. In our belief system, we are each responsible for our own sins, and we must make peace. No one but the sinner can apologize for her sins. Even in the presence of a killer motivated by racial hate, we still must take responsibility for our own actions. So I said the same prayers to the Great Holy Spirit, apologizing for my sins. Then I was no longer frozen in fear. We were able to act, to fight back, and to save our lives."

"We're not Christians, Muslims, or Jews." declared Helga. "But we have religious beliefs we draw strength from. We share many values with the major Earth religions. But the one value that we have is that we are tolerant. There's no word for blasphemy in Atlantean. On our Planet, if you don't believe in the Great Holy Spirit, we will not shun you or punish you in any way. We know that faith has to be honest, or it is of no value. That's a basic tenet of our religion."

The President smiled. "I'm happy to hear that you have good strong values. But sometimes religion can lead to people doing terrible things if they misinterpret it or misuse it. Satan is very good at fooling those who want to be fooled. What happened in Mexico, Andemona? Is that kid going to be all right?"

Helga translated the question into Atlantean and translated Andemona's answer. "He is in critical condition. These young men believe in the Aztec religion and the legend of Quetzalcoatl. The Aztecs, actually they were known as the Mexica, and the civilizations before them believed that there had been four suns over several thousands of years. When each of the four suns came to an end the world was torn by great natural disasters. The last time it was flooding, much like the Noah Flood story. The current epoch is the Fifth Sun, and it is prophesied that the Fifth Sun will end with the world engulfed by fire. The Mexica believed that the Fifth Sun was already very old, and that human sacrifices were needed to sustain it and hold off the End of the World. They were killing large numbers of people every year by cutting out their hearts. That was 500 years ago."

She went on. "But there was also the legend of Quetzalcoatl. Quetzalcoatl and a band of teachers came from the Eastern Ocean. They taught mathematics, the calendar, the rule of law, agriculture, writing, the things people need to know to move from a hunter-gatherer existence to a civilization. Quetzalcoatl also taught against human sacrifice and his time was a Golden Age when there were no sacrifices. Then Quetzalcoatl left, on a ship of snakes, with a promise to return. He was often depicted as a pale skinned man with a beard. Some thought Cortes, a pale skinned man with a beard, was Quetzalcoatl come back! He came across the Eastern Ocean in a ship! He taught against human sacrifice. He convinced the Tlaxcalans and other Indians to join him in his conquest of Mexico. But then Cortes and his allies massacred the Indians in Cholula. He conquered the Aztec Empire with terrible loss of life, destroying Tenochtitlan. He was no Quetzalcoatl.

"The people learned the Christian religion from the Spanish priests who came with the conquistadors. The Quetzalcoatl who came back and taught them good values turned out to be Jesus himself. However, there are those who are frightened by we Neanderthals who have returned to Earth for a visit. Some believe Quetzalcoatl came from Plato's Atlantis, and we call our homeland Atlantis. The young men who attempted the sacrifice believe we herald the end of the Fifth Sun. Fortunately, the police stopped it and the young man will recover."

"Maybe we should talk about the Atlantis theory." suggested the President. "Plato described an advanced civilization that existed 9,000 years before the life of Solon. Solon was elected to run Athens after people got fed up with his predecessor, Draco. After he rewrote the laws of Athens, he retired from his position so he could travel. He visited Egypt. According to Plato, Solon heard about Atlantis from the Egyptians. It was a city on a large island beyond the Pillars of Hercules. Atlantean settlers came to Egypt and gave Egypt the start of its civilization. Plato is the only ancient writer that we can find who describes Atlantis and uses that name."

"But most of your archeologists and Egyptologists reject the hypothesis of the existence of Atlantis or an Atlantis like civilization." responded Helga.

"That's true. They don't believe that there was any civilization as advanced as the Egypt of the pharaohs prior to 4000 B.C. Plato describes Atlantis to have existed at least before 9500 B.C. and to have been destroyed by a flood. There were numerous catastrophic floods as a result of the melting of the ice caps that had previously covered Europe, Asia, and North America. If there was a city built on a coastline at that time, the rising ocean would have covered it. A maritime civilization would have lost its home base but might possibly have left bits of its knowledge, language, and mathematics in several different parts of the world, including Egypt."

The President went on. "The Metric System, for instance, is not a mystery. The French invented it during their Revolution in the 1790's. We know how old it is, who thought it up, and how it spread around the world. But who invented the foot as a unit of measure? Who was the first to define a unit of length about this long," he held his hands a foot apart, "and give it the same name we give to the thing on the end of your leg?"

"Maybe it was a Neanderthal who thought it up." suggested Lucinda. "We too have a foot for a unit of measure. *Pote* is Atlantean for the thing on the end of your leg and for the unit of measure. Our measuring system, with feet and inches, has been around as long as our civilization."

"At the time the French invented the Metric System, every nation in Europe used feet and inches. The Romans had feet and inches; they are the first known to divide the foot into twelve parts. The Greeks and Phoenicians had a foot, divided into sixteen fingers. The Hebrew cubit was divided into six palms and 24 fingers. That was the regular cubit in Egypt, they also had royal cubits, divided into seven palms or 28 fingers. The Romans and Greeks considered their foot to be like four palms in the Egyptian and Hebrew measure. On the other side of the Asian continent, the basic Chinese unit, the *chih*, is about twelve and six tenths modern British-American inches. *Chih* is not Chinese for the end of the leg, but the unit has been called a Chinese foot. The Japanese had a unit, the *shaku*, 11.93 American inches. Commodore Matthew Perry called it a Japanese foot, though *shaku* is not Japanese for the foot you stand on. China and Japan now use the Metric System but these are the measures they used since ancient times."

The President went on. "So who first thought up the idea of the foot as a unit of measure? No one knows. There are other mathematical and engineering conventions that we still use today, that were used by the ancient civilizations. The origin of these conventions is unknown. We divide the circle into 360 degrees. So has every ancient culture that we know of where there was geometry, mapping and astronomy."

"We divide the circle into three *hekt* or 432 *deems*. But that is thirty six dozens. Twelve *deems* is ten degrees."

"The number chosen for dividing the circle needs to be a multiple of twenty-four to define the mathematically important angles. Both three sixty and three *hekt* are multiples of twenty-four. On Earth, the number 360 is the number EXCLUSIVELY chosen, perhaps because the year is 365 days in length. That way, the Sun drifts just less than one degree each day along the Zodiac. Who first thought of dividing the circle into 360 degrees? No one knows. Who first thought of dividing the day into 24 hours? Who first thought up Base Ten? The Romans, Greeks, Egyptians, Japanese and Chinese thought in terms of powers of ten. We did not get to the modern method of writing these numbers until the Middle Ages, but Base Ten is an ancient convention, as is the 360 degree circle and the 24 hour day. Who first thought it up? No one knows."

The President went on. "Did the ancients know the size of the Earth? The Greeks actually had a special foot that was just about 1/100 of a second of arc of Earth's surface. The width of the Parthenon in Athens is 100 special feet, about 101 modern American feet, one second of arc of the Earth's surface. 6000 special feet is one minute of arc of the Earth's surface or one nautical mile. How did the Greeks of 2,500 years ago KNOW with such precision the dimensions of the Earth? How did the Egyptians? Their Great Pyramid seems to incorporate in its dimensions, similarly precise information concerning the circumference of the Earth."

"Our *tig-it* is about .986, in decimal numbers, of your American-British inch. Our *pote* is .986 foot. When we walk, we can mark off five *potes* each time our right or left foot hits the ground. As your Curator knows, the European Neanderthals had shorter legs and arms than we do. People who live many generations in a cold climate evolve shorter limbs as an adaptation for survival. After the Transplantation, most of us lived in warmer climates. Our arms and legs got longer, the lengths being similar to most modern Earth Cro-Magnons. Thus our human factors are similar to yours. We can pace off five feet or *potes*. We call that distance a *pfat*, the word means foot reach."

Helga went on. "You had a little problem when it came to defining your nautical mile and your meter. The same problem that the ancient Greeks had if they intended to base a unit, their foot, on some fraction of the Earth's curve. A planet that rotates once every twenty-four hours will bulge at its equator, making it longer than a circle drawn through the poles. A degree of latitude along a meridian thus varies from the equator to the pole. You selected 6076 feet or 1852 meters for your nautical mile because that is right in the middle of the range of distances that you have for one minute of arc. The Greek foot that you describe is right in there. The meter is as good an approximation of a ten millionth of the distance from your North Pole to your Equator as can be had given this equatorial bulge. We have an equatorial bulge on Creation. We therefore made a similar compromise in defining our length units."

"So what is a *pote* in terms of the circumference of Creation?" asked the President.

"Five dozen or sixty *potes* is one *prelate* of arc of the surface of Planet Creation. That is twelve paces or *pfats*. This is in the middle of the range of the distances a *prelate* of arc is due to the equatorial bulge. A *kecht* of *pfats*, or a *kepfat*, works out to two *linits* of arc of our planetary surface. In Atlantis, we mark our road signs in *kepfats*. Graciana marks their road signs in half *kepfats*, which they call *linits*. Local preference. But all of the nations of Creation use the same definition of the *pote*."

"How far back in your history does this system of measures go?"

"As far back as we can trace, as ancient as our Base Twelve convention."

"In our case, we just don't know which ancient civilization first invented our mathematical conventions and the foot as a unit of length. But these conventions crop up all over the ancient world as if Plato's Atlantis did in fact exist!"

"Are you suggesting Plato's Atlantis is the civilization that invented these mathematical conventions?"

"A distinct possibility. Here is my theory: 50,000 years ago, there were Neanderthal and Cro-Magnon people living side by side in Europe. Everyone is living as hunter-gatherers. Because so much of the water from the oceans was tied up in glaciers, the coastline was 300 feet below what it is today. What is now the English Channel and the North Sea was then open tundra. All of the islands are much bigger. If these Neanderthal and Cro-Magnon people learned to catch fish, they would build their villages along this coastline. Once you go out on the water in boats, it becomes easier to visit a place thousands of miles across water than a place hundreds of miles inland, where lived the people whose skeletons we have found. Thus a maritime society can evolve that we know nothing about because its remains are under 300 feet of water."

The President continued. "After the Face Mountain aliens hauled your ancestors off to your Planet this hypothetical maritime society continues to develop. 40,000 years later, there are no more Neanderthals, but the remaining Cro-Magnons inherited this culture and continued to develop it. What happened to the Neanderthals? A Nazi style holocaust? Sadly, that is possible, but maybe the culprit was a disease that the Neanderthal was not immune to. The Cro-Magnons survived the epidemic. You talk about a Virus that killed off your men. But perhaps the Cro-Magnon Y chromosomes are not vulnerable to this Virus."

"Mr. President!" shouted all three women at once. "Have you been talking to our ship's doctors?" asked Helga.

"Well, no."

"Askelion Lamakian has been analyzing Neil's Y chromosomes."

"We all figured she has been doing that."

Helga continued. "But we have not been public with the preliminary findings. Askelion and Meddi have an extensive computer file library on the Virus, and on the mapping the DNA sequencing of all known life forms, including the Virus and our Neanderthal men. She has been comparing Neil's Y chromosome with the Neanderthal Y chromosome and against the Virus. We need to know if Neil or other Earthmen can come to Creation without being killed."

Lucinda finished, "Her preliminary findings are this: There are substantial differences in the portions of the gene that have no apparent effect on the characteristics of the person. But these portions are what the Virus mated up with to replicate. She believes that the Virus CANNOT replicate with a Cro-Magnon Y chromosome. But this is CONFIDENTIAL, because it is PRELIMINARY."

The President whistled. "We need to get Dr. Nguyen into this loop! If this turns out to be true, we have a plausible explanation for the disappearance of the Neanderthal Race from Earth. Nevertheless, an Ice Age maritime culture could, after 40,000 years, become an advanced civilization. Because navigation at sea requires observing the stars, astronomy could be highly developed and maintained over a long period of time. Even the precession of the equinoxes can thus be observed, and the planets, including Earth, could be recognized as orbiting the Sun. Let's say Atlantis developed in the Ice Age and it was a maritime culture. It developed astronomy out of the requirements of navigation. They could thus have created the mathematical conventions we've been talking about."

The President continued his theory. "Then the Ice Age comes to an end. Tremendous floods and catastrophic climate changes result from the melting of the glaciers. The oceans rise flooding the coastal cities and destroying this maritime civilization. But survivors can bring this knowledge, science and mathematical conventions to such places as Egypt, Mexico, China, and Iraq. Wherever new civilizations spring up once the ocean level and climates are stabilized. It is thus possible that Atlantis existed. That Quetzalcoatl, Osiris, Noah, and Gilgamesh were Atlanteans. What do you women think? What do the Old Records left by the Face Mountain aliens tell of the development of Earth culture after the Transplantation?"

"We find it interesting that the President of the United States is spending his valuable time discussing with us some ancient history, not even history, really."

The President smiled. "I see your point. But I'm not the only one to think about these things. We almost had an Aztec style human sacrifice. We had a prosecutor file a frivolous charge against foreign women who are under diplomatic immunity. We had an insane act of terrorism. The only person on Earth who seems to be taking all of this in stride is Angela Peace, Neil's ex-wife!"

The First Lady broke in. "She has children and went through a divorce. Of course she can handle anything!" That brought smiles and a few chuckles.

"Getting back to my responsibilities as President. I'm responsible for the military security of the United States. When it comes to dealing with intelligent life from beyond the Planet Earth, including human beings whose ancestors were transplanted to another Planet in ages past, I am in effect responsible for the military security of the entire Planet. We have two 1976 NASA photos of a mountain carved into a face on the Planet Mars. The new NASA probes photograph this mountain. The Face is not so clear in the pictures since 1998 and our scientists argue that it is just a natural feature. But it could also be argued that a carved face could erode from sandstorms and marsquakes to look the way it does in the new photos! We have a 3,000 foot long SPACECRAFT full of Neanderthal women who tell us that their men were killed off by a terrible Virus, and that their ancestors were transplanted to another Planet. That this Planet was terraformed with Earth life forms by a truly alien race, who carved Face Mountain."

"You want to know what you're dealing with."

"Right."

"So do we. Mr. President, we don't know the answers to your questions. We don't know what killed off the Neanderthals on Earth after the Transplantation, or even when the last Neanderthal on Earth lived and died. Atlantis is the name of our ancient home in Europe. That much we know. How this name got to Plato 48,000 years later, we don't know. Whether there was an Ice Age maritime civilization that could be what Plato referred to, we don't know. We don't know who first thought up feet and inches, or when, but we use them. Either feet and inches were invented prior to the Transplantation 50,000 years ago, or we invented them independently because the human body is an obvious informal measuring stick. What we know about Plato's Atlantis is what you know about Plato's Atlantis."

"Okay, never mind Plato's Atlantis. What about YOUR Atlantis? Did you have a city in Ice Age Europe 50,000 years ago?"

"Plato wrote about a continent of Atlantis as well as a city of Atlantis. We thought of all of our homeland as Atlantis. Today, Atlantis is called Europe."

"We know little about our history on Earth before the Transplantation." admitted Lucinda. "We lived in coastal villages, maybe named one of them Atlantis, they are now under water. We only went inland to hunt. The reason you find some of us in caves, is they served as emergency shelter in storms. One of us dies from the cold or something, we bury him and you find his bones."

"That's a viable explanation of the evidence." admitted the Curator.

"It's the truth as far as we know."

The President changed the subject. "Thank you for your patience and for indulging me. I needed to know what you know about our origins to make policy decisions concerning Earth-Creation relations. We certainly need to establish peaceful relations. I propose we consider all of the planets, moons, asteroids and comets in orbit around Alpha Centauri A and B, and the stars themselves, that is your entire two sun Solar System, to be under the sovereignty of the people and nations of Creation. In return, the people and nations of Creation consider the planets, moons, comets and asteroids in orbit around our Sun, and the Sun itself, to be under the sovereignty of the people and nations of Earth."

"Your proposal is reasonable." said Helga. "I believe we can work out a Treaty of Sovereignty between the nations of Earth and Creation along the lines that you propose. Any such treaty that we negotiate would have to be considered a proposal. We on the *Neanderthal Return* are from only one nation on the Planet Creation, Atlantis. There are 26 major nations and 145 minor sovereignties on our Planet. These nations will want to send diplomats with plenipotentiary power to negotiate formal treaties. We don't have that plenipotentiary power. Still, a pledge by all of the major Earth nations to respect our sovereignty within our entire two sun Solar System would make a very positive impression everywhere on Creation."

"We weren't supposed to deliberately reveal our existence to Earth unless we had good reasons or it happened anyway." said Lucinda. "This is the first close up look we have of Earth. Trviea had orders to study your Planet in a discrete manner, but to somehow obtain a live Earthman to study the possibility of using Cro-Magnon tissue to solve the problem of Neanderthal reproduction. As to HOW to obtain an Earthman, the orders were simply to find a way. We were also told to avoid war with Earth AT ALL COSTS."

"That is the legal basis for my actions relieving Trviea of command." confirmed Helga. "To avoid war AT ALL COSTS means exactly that. After we obtained Neil Peace, I and most of the crew concluded that we risked war with the kidnapping. So we freed Neil and followed his advice, which turned out be incredibly good. We're relieved and happy that most of the people of Earth want peace. Right now, we are treating Captain Trviea Harsradich as another member of the crew. We may need her leadership again. If the situation calls for it, we will restore her to power and follow her orders. We thank you for granting us this time, for your nation's hospitality, and for your forgiveness for how we have taken Neil Peace."

"Thank you. The funeral for the Secret Service agents will be at Arlington National Cemetery after the autopsies. The families want you to attend, they want to meet with you."

Chapter Thirteen

Chuck Carter stepped out into the already warm Algerian sun, it gets hot in the middle of the Sahara desert. This base camp is located 46 miles southwest of the village of Illizi. The American archeologist from the University of Georgia had a hard time reassuring his family about this trip. A few years before, the Algerian government canceled an election. Polls indicated that a fundamentalist Islamic coalition was going to win. While most of this coalition opposes violence, the radical GIS has conducted a terror campaign of incredible violence. But this violence has not taken place deep in the Sahara. Libya is a little over 110 miles away. When in an unstable country, head for a border if trouble erupts. Libya? At least Khaddafy keeps things under control; foreigners are safe there.

The archeology in this area is too exciting for the young black man from Macon, Georgia to worry about the GIS. The rock paintings of Tassili n'Ajjer have excited him since he learned about them in Black Studies class. Painted between 4000 B.C. to 2000 B.C., they show black people, with definite Negro features, living an idyllic lifestyle herding cattle. Strong men with bows and arrows hunt wild game. Men and women sit or stand around the camp in friendly conversation, children play or guide the cattle. There was enough rain in this area at that time to support a cattle grazing culture. He came to search for writing and artifacts left by this culture.

Ali Amoud ran up to Carter. "Chuck! Chuck! A small camel caravan just came into our camp!" he yelled in Arabic. Chuck can speak the local languages, Berber and the Algerian version of Arabic.

"So what is with this caravan, Ali?" asked Chuck.

"They are nomads, on their way to Illizi. But after last night, they decided to come here."

"Why come here, are they low on water?"

"No. No. Nothing like that. It is what they FOUND! They camped for the night at a cave 10 kilometers southwest of here. Six of your miles."

"They find some rock paintings?" This would be a new find.

"Yes. We are letting them water their camels at the pump well. Word gets around that we have a hand pump, this little camp will become a full blown oasis city like Illizi. You come and meet these people."

They went to the camp well to find a man and a woman pumping water into a bucket. There were seven camels, loaded down with burdens. Three children placed the buckets in front of the camels for them to drink. When the two archeologists came over, the children ran to the tall and muscular black man in khaki shirt and pants. "Are you the American archeologist?"

"Yes. My name is Chuck Carter, I am from the University of Georgia. You have already met Ali Amoud?"

"Yes, yes we've met him! Daddy, show him the sketches!" The boy, about ten, grinned a huge, joyous, you are gonna love this grin. "We don't know if the local black cattle people of 4500 years ago made these inscriptions, but SOMEBODY wrote these in the cave we stayed in last night!"

The father took a wire ring notebook from a pack on his camel, and brought it over along with a small 110 type pocket camera and some rolls of film. "My name Mohammed Ahmed Abbas." He shook hands with Chuck Carter. "University of Georgia!" he exclaimed with awe and reverence. "Wouldn't it be something if my children could go there. What we have found should be worth a scholarship or two or three?"

"I cannot make any decisions like that on admissions and enrollment, or for paying for it. But if you have something good, I can see what I can do."

"Have you a darkroom for developing film?"

"Yes, of course we do." answered Ali as he accepted the film.

"These are shots taken of the markings inside the cave. Here are the sketches we made of these inscriptions."

Chuck looked through the notebook. "Egyptian hieroglyphs!?!"

"Yes, ancient Egyptian writing."

"Khufu is the name in some of these cartouches. They report traveling three hundred *aturs* west of Seyne on the Nile. Seyne is called Aswan today. That sounds about right. If I remember correctly, I am not an Egyptologist by specialization, but I seem to remember that an *atur* is seven kilometers, or is it seven modern miles? I cannot remember which right now."

"7.3 kilometers if it is Fourth Dynasty." said Ali. "This is definitely Egyptian writing."

"Yes! But look on the next page!" begged Mohammed. "We copied their images of people at about quarter size to fit them on the paper." He displayed a ruler. White and black paint alternated with each inch on one side and with each centimeter on the other side. "We used this ruler to scale our photographs."

Chuck turned the page. "The figure on the left is what you would expect of an Egyptian. The man has a skirt around his hips, sandals on his feet, and his long hair drawn behind his ears. A cobra symbol is attached to the front of his headband. The figure in the middle is one of these black cattlemen from this time in history, probably during the Egyptian Fourth Dynasty. This is documentation of a meeting between an Egyptian and a Tassili cattleman. But who is this guy on the right, did his face really look like that?"

"That is how he is drawn on the cave wall. He is a Neanderthal."

"Now wait a minute! He cannot be a Neanderthal! Neanderthals disappeared from Earth at least 27,000 years ago! They have never been found this far south in Africa."

"He is a Neanderthal. Look, we know about the spaceship with the women on board. We saw their blue propulsion light when they came in from Orion. We saw them flash in Morse Code." Abbas switched from Arabic to English. "I can speak a little English, and I can speak a lot of French! Just because I live with camels in the desert doesn't make me another dumb Arab. I know what a Neanderthal looks like because I've seen the newspaper pictures of these women who come in the spaceship! Allah Akbar! It's a miracle but it's true!"

Chuck Carter smiled. "No, you're not dumb, I apologize if you took anything that I said wrong. He definitely looks like a Neanderthal. And I see everyone's heard about the *Neanderthal Return* and the women from Planet Creation."

Abbas switched back to Arabic. "I know some of us Muslims, particularly the fundamentalists who would have won that election, are extreme about the role of women in society. The Neanderthal women from Planet Creation, if it is true that all of their men are dead, they HAD to take over the traditional male roles in their society! Our Arab women would do the same, even while keeping their hair covered and praying to Mecca." He noticed the American was not listening. Chuck studied the Egyptian language inscriptions with great intensity. "What do you see?"

"This word. Ancient Egyptian is a mixture of alphabet type symbols, 25 of them with several alternate forms for some of the letters, letters that stand for sounds. Then there are symbols that stand for syllables, sort of like Chinese, and then pictographs that stand for whole words, several hundred such symbols are known to have been used. But this particular group of sound symbols, they spell, well look at this. It is like a single word, this is the one that is standing out for me. It is written from right to left, like Arabic. This is the normal order in which Egyptian is written, but it can also be written from left to right, the way English is written. How you tell is which way the figures face, they face the beginning of the word or sentence. This word starts with this vulture symbol, note how he faces to the right. It is the same as the Arabic letter *alif*."

"Arabic is similar to Hebrew in that respect." contributed Ali.

"Yes, representation of the glottal stop is common in Middle Eastern languages." continued Chuck. "This Egyptian letter, as well as the letters called *aleph* or *alif*, was translated to the letter *alpha* by the Greeks. The first four letters of the Greek alphabet are apparently named after the first four letters of the Hebrew alphabet, *alpha* for *aleph*, *beta* for *beth*, *gamma* for *gimel*, *delta* for *daleth*."

Abbas' wife Labna and their children gathered around for the impromptu lesson in alphabets and languages. "So the glottal stop letter, *alif* in our language, this vulture symbol in Egyptian, is translated into the Greek *alpha* and the Roman A." added Ali.

"Yes. Only in English, Greek and other European languages, the glottal stop becomes a vowel sound. This next symbol, small half-moon, stands for the sound represented by the letter *ta* in Arabic. So these two Egyptian letters spell the syllable 'at'. Then we see a little picture of a lion. He is facing right, just like the glottal stop vulture. This is the symbol that the Egyptians commonly used to represent the *lam* sound where it appeared in foreign words and place names. Egyptian words never included this sound. This is a foreign word or a place name."

"I know the wavy water line stands for the *nun* sound!" exclaimed Mohammed. "Followed by another half moon *ta*!"

"And on the left, a reed leaf followed by this hook like sign. A reed leaf sounds like the letter I in the English word 'it'. The hook stands for the *sin* sound. This is the word 'Atlantis', written in a context consistent with it being a place name."

"Allah Akbar!"

"Where is this cave?"

"Well gentlemen, it is like this: We want our children to have a good education. We want to sell our camels and live in Algiers. There my children can go to school and qualify for University. We have taught them math and Arabic, reading and so on. But all we have are some textbooks and a Koran. I think 100,000 dollars American is appropriate."

"I cannot authorize a payment like that!" protested Chuck. "I can see how you might be entitled to some recognition, but not that kind of money!"

"Oh. Maybe there is some Egyptian gold back there, or even gold from Atlantis. We will just tear the place apart looking for it! What do I care about preserving anything for archeology? You lucky rich American boy! You have no idea what it is like to be poor and living off the land here in the desert! You have a good education! I only want the same for my children! I would like to live in a house. A simple little house or even an apartment. In Algiers. With some electricity, a television set. A nice bed for my wife and I! Schools for my children. You had that! You may be black, but you had that!"

Sigh. "Mohammed Abbas, your concern for your children is commendable. We can hire you to help us excavate this cave. That will earn you some money, good money at that. You can help write books on this find, maybe even give a speaker's tour. You would have to learn good English and French, but that will help you pay for your children's education."

"Right. We can do that. But the location of this cave, and the preservation of the inscriptions, we can go back and destroy them, will cost you 100,000 American dollars deposited in a bank account in my name. Is it not worth it? How much money is your University spending on this camp? For 5000 year old cave paintings of a pastoral lifestyle of some Negroes? What value is a description of a meeting of these Negro cattlemen and some Egyptians of the Fourth Dynasty? Then toss in a NEANDERTHAL man from Plato's ATLANTIS! What is that worth to your University? It is all in Egyptian, which can be read!"

The Algerian nomad had a point. People in the Third World have a valid complaint of Westerners paying them pennies for artifacts that turn out to be of immense value. Off to the British Museum go the local antiquities. Wealth and fame go to the Great White Hunter who stole the artifacts. Nothing goes to the locals who live where these things are found. Chuck Carter and Ali Amoud cannot credibly claim to be different than the old time white grave robbers if they do the same thing! From the Algerian nomad's point of view, these archeologists are going to raid the local antiquities and get rich off of them. He just wanted his cut of the wealth! But $100,000? "Now that we know about this cave," said Ali, "we can find it ourselves."

"We covered our tracks real good. It will take you a long time to find it. By that time we can scour the walls clean of inscriptions and take all of the artifacts. Gold is still valuable after we have melted it down." The archeologists' hearts skipped a beat! "I believe that $100,000 is a reasonable request and well worth it!"

"Mr. Abbas, you seem to be well educated and literate for an Arab nomad. How do I know that this is not just a big scam, that these inscriptions aren't just a big fake job?" asked Chuck.

"Ah, ha-ha! You Americans think you are so smart! Develop the photos." He called to his ten year old son. "Ahmed, bring the bow!" The boy unpacked an ancient bow made of ash wood from one of the camels. "Do a carbon-14 test on this bow. You can't fake 4500 year old wood by selectively removing carbon-14 atoms." The boy handed the bow to the American archeologist. "Note the cartouche just above the handgrip. Probably the name of the owner. Check out this Egyptian language inscription below the handgrip."

"The word 'Atlantis'. This varnish was painted on AFTER this writing was carved. We can do a carbon-14 test of the varnish. Mr. Abbas, you just might be worth $100,000. Why don't you and your family join us for breakfast? We were planning to continue an excavation of a cave two kilometers east of here, but not today; we can go back to it later. We haven't found anything like THIS. It is just more idyllic village life scenes with lots of cattle and happy black people. No Egyptians, Atlanteans, or Neanderthals. Not that there is anything wrong with happy black people. In fact, if this hunk of wood you brought me turns out to be for real, I'LL be a happy black people! I'll be as happy as these happy black cattlemen with their happy wives and their happy children and their happy cows and happy bulls. I was beginning to wonder if this cave artist wasn't getting tired of painting the same thing over and over again! It looks like he decided to paint one of his happy cattlemen meeting a nice happy Egyptian and a nice happy Neanderthal and covering the wall with Egyptian language graffiti. Just for a change of pace! And he included the Egyptian letters that spell the word 'Atlantis'. Oh boy are we gonna analyze this cave for AUTHENTICITY!"

The Algerians shared Chuck's glee and excitement. An archeologist spends his life carefully sifting through ancient dirt and ancient library books and only occasionally finding anything worthwhile. NOBODY has ever found ancient Egyptian writing spelling out the word "Atlantis"! NOBODY has ever found an ancient drawing of a live Neanderthal! A Neanderthal speaking with a black man and a Fourth Dynasty Egyptian. The Neanderthal illustrated in the 4500 year old cave painting is fair skinned like modern white people and has Asian shaped eyes. Just like the women from the spaceship who call their nation Atlantis! They went over to the lab to develop the photographs of the cave and to make arrangements for carbon-14 tests on the bow and its varnish.

The autopsies of the Secret Service men were completed. The bodies were flown to Reagan National Airport for the funeral in Arlington National Cemetery. The families asked that the ceremony be kept simple, no television coverage. The three women from Planet Creation were invited by the families to attend the service. A clergyman selected by the families performed the service. A light rain fell. At the request of the families, the three women said the Prayer for the Dead. They did not understand the Atlantean, but the words were simple, gentle, quiet, and sincere. A military honor guard performed a three gun salute for each of the fallen. A bugler blew *Taps*. Four good men were then laid to rest.

Assistant United States Attorney Shirley Barton in Tacoma was assigned the task of prosecuting Frank Binford and Jack Plotkin for the attempted kidnapping of the two women from Creation and for the federal version of felony murder. When she returned to her office from a morning hearing in the United States Courthouse, an envelope waited in her In Basket. F.B.I. Special Agent Stan Marier also waited for her. "Let me check my mail, please." she asked him. She picked up the letter sized envelope. "The return address is for Babcock, Wilson, and Bates, PS."

"Ooooo! Fancy! Who are you prosecuting that can afford them?" Stan knew they represent wealthy defendants in felony cases. Very expensive.

The prosecutor peeled open the envelope. "A standard Notice of Appearance form filed with the Grand Jury for the Western District of Washington, and another filed with the U. S. District Court in Tacoma. Stanley Babcock is filing notice that he will be the lead counsel for the team being formed to represent Frank Binford and Jack Plotkin."

"Now where did these guys get that kind of money? It takes a pretty penny to retain Stanley Babcock. They only got a few thousand dollars from that bank robbery in Federal Way, if they're the ones that did it, we haven't been able to pin it on 'em. That was a slick job! The Avengers of Yahweh aren't known for drug trafficking, although that's possible. They're not known for being rich either."

"There are some other things that are just not adding up." The prosecutor listed in her mind the anomalies in this case. "It's as if Binford's racism against Neanderthals is feigned."

"Probably is feigned. Possible insanity defense. Avengers are white supremacists, that much is true. They believe whites are superior to people of color. But some of their old literature has it that Caucasians are special because we are the product of interracial breeding between Cro-Magnons and Neanderthals! That made white people superior to all other races of humanity! So what's this story of Creation Neanderthals being a threat to the covenant between the Lord and the descendants of Noah? That doesn't match the previous Avenger mythology."

"Some people liked Neanderthals just fine when they were old dead bones from thousands of years ago. The appearance of these LIVING Neanderthals interferes with their vision of what Neanderthals were. That vision didn't include beautiful women in a spaceship! I can see why the Avengers fear these new Neanderthals as a threat to our existence. Why didn't they just kill the two women when they had the chance?"

"They wanted the drama of a hostage crisis, that's why we have the armbinders and leather covered stainless steel gags. The Secret Service agents were expendable."

"The Avengers knew that trying to imprison and control Neanderthal women is a dicey proposition. The two characteristics that these women show where the paleoanthropologists got it right is muscle strength and chewing apparatus. They are incredibly strong. Their jaws and teeth can and did do a job on the wrist bones of Binford. Binford himself testified to Deputy

111

Sheriff Mike Carlson that being punched by Lucinda is like being punched by Evander Holyfield."

"Even if they got away with these two women, bound in the armbinders and gagged, how were they gonna keep 'em? They have to ungag 'em to feed 'em. They shit and piss just like we do." The FBI agent liked to exhibit a little masculine crudeness in front of the woman prosecutor. "And they're smart! They would think or talk their way out of bondage somehow. They would even use their female charms. 'Could you please loosen up my arms? This is very uncomfortable.' while looking at 'em with those big pitiful eyes."

"And as soon as the arms are free, POW! So you have a gun in your hands, so what? You can't pull the trigger if your neck's broken. I'll make a call to Stan Babcock, put him on speakerphone." She dialed the number.

"Law office, Stanley Babcock." answered the receptionist's voice in the speakerphone.

"This is Assistant United States Attorney Shirley Barton calling for Mr. Babcock concerning the Binford and Plotkin matter. Is Mr. Babcock available?"

"He is in a meeting right now, I can have him call you back. What is your number?"

"He has my number. I'll be in my office for the next hour or two." About thirty seconds later the telephone rang. "Yep, a meeting in the real sexist room that allows men only."

Stan Marier chuckled. "Defense lawyers also shit and piss just like we do."

"U.S Attorney's Office. Shirley Barton speaking."

"Hello Shirley! How ya' doing?" It was Stan Babcock.

"Doing fine, Stan. Our information on Binford, Plotkin and the other Avengers of Yahweh is that they're not exactly millionaires. In fact, they could qualify to proceed *in forma pauperis*. Are you doing *pro bono* work Stan? Or is somebody rich paying their legal fees?"

"Now Shirley girl, you know I don't discuss matters such as fee payments without a court order. Anyway, we'll be seeing you in court in a few days for a bail hearing."

"And you're not likely to get it. Four Secret Service Agents killed and for a few minutes there was the unlawful imprisonment of two foreign women who were under federal protection. This can have international, even interplanetary, consequences."

"Shirley, they were duped by Randle Packwood into going along with this whole charade! They didn't pull any triggers during the incident. They certainly didn't know Packwood was going to suddenly snuff a Secret Service agent like he did. As far as the other three agents are concerned, my clients were pretty busy when that happened. Are you sure the snipers, the two stump farmers everyone's calling heroes, didn't put a bullet or two into the agents? From the distance they were shooting at, they could miss their intended targets and hit the agents."

"Len Taylor didn't miss Packwood, he got him good. Typical defense lawyer trick, put all of the blame on the dead guy. And Henry Turnipseed nailed Glenn Morton, the other terrorist found dead at the scene. None of the bullets recovered from the Secret Service bodies are .22 caliber, what the two farmers were shooting. No friendly fire there, every bullet recovered from their bodies is heavy caliber, designed to pierce Kevlar, the vests were penetrated. We'll send you the discovery as soon as we have indictments. Even if your clients are just a couple of naive country boys from small wheat towns in Eastern Washington who got caught up in something they didn't understand," she rolled her eyes, "we'll oppose bail. They pose a danger to the community, flight risk, and considering the theory that dead men tell no tales, it might be in your clients' best interests to remain in custody where they're nice and safe. As far as charges are concerned, you know about Section 2." She referred to 18 U.S.C. §2. "They aided and abetted an attempted kidnapping of persons under federal protection and the murder of four Secret Service agents who were in the line of duty."

"Not to mention destruction of government property." contributed Agent Marier to the speakerphone.

"Not every case is an easy one for the defense lawyer." admitted Babcock. "You would, however, be hard put to establish the intent element of the crime of aiding and abetting the murders of the federal agents."

"But there are many Avengers involved in this incident still at large. We could use some cooperation from your clients right now. Like names. The phony construction worker. Allen Case, Cayce, Pace, Base, or Gayce? He might as well be named D. B. Cooper. Who planned and financed the effort? Information like that. If they wish to ever be on the outside of federal custody someday, that cooperation might be the key to their eventual freedom."

"I'll inform my clients of your position on that. But while Binford babbled like a brook for a few minutes during his arrest, neither of my clients are going to give you anything more for free. Is there anything else?"

"Not right now, thanks."

Chapter Fourteen

I was very comfortable. My head laid on the lap of Pidonita Hmlakian, she fed me grapes. Trviea Harsradich had my legs on her lap. Contrviea Tiknika sat on top of me between the other two women. Wlsmda Hotlund, originally introduced to me as Wilma, sat across the room, not allowed to speak, not allowed to touch me. She wore a chrome plated collar that monitored her blood pressure, heartbeat, breathing, muscle exertion, and the signal flow in her spinal cord. If she moved too fast or got too excited, a warning buzzer sounded. If she didn't heed the warning, it induced temporary paralysis. She calmly obeyed every order given her. She and Bchsda Bentlakian, Betty, used their position and power as security officers to abuse other members of the crew. Captain Trviea herself suggested the disciplinary collars.

"Anyway," started Contrviea, "again how much did you say I should get from General Electric or Westinghouse for showing them how to build a fusion reactor?" Contrviea runs the Machine Shop, she knows how everything on the ship is built.

"Oh, a billion dollars anyway, plus a nice percentage of the price of every unit sold." I would estimate Contrviea as having the equivalent of Phd's in mechanical, electrical, and nuclear engineering, physics, and chemistry. She has had 150 years to learn this stuff. We Earthlings have barely enough time to earn one degree in one discipline and then we must go to work where the skills atrophy as companies hire us to do some damned office job. Engineers are not allowed to work in the shop and shop workers are not given any incentive to study engineering. It's amazing that we build any working machines at all! Contrviea not only knows her science and engineering, she gets to tear into things with a screwdriver!

"Billion dollars? What's that in Creation numbers? How many *beeyons*?"

"It's *beeyon* me! About one fifth or one sixth of an *enbeeyon*. You might get up to an *enbeeyon* of dollars in total wealth, even after taxes. Why go back to Creation? You might be able to get a green card or even American citizenship because you have a valuable and unique skill!"

"I'm afraid not. There's no way we'll give up our technological advantage over Earth until we've solved our problem of reproduction and rebuilt our Planet's population. While a few cities are still metropolises, most are ghost towns, and vast formerly inhabited areas have been taken over by the forest. We need to resettle this territory."

"You don't want it settled by Cro-Magnons."

"It's not that we don't want Cro-Magnons immigrating, it's that we don't want Cro-Magnons taking over. We need to restore our population before overcrowded Earth figures out fusion reactors and interstellar space travel. Otherwise, we Neanderthals will be crowded off of our own Planet. It's as if Native Americans went exploring and discovered the overcrowded Europe of the Year 1500. When King Montezuma reads the report brought back by his explorers, he wouldn't want the Europeans to know how to get to America."

"Even if Native Americans had a technological advantage over Europe," broke in Trviea, "Europe's history of war and conquest, with its vast numbers of poor dominated by the wealthy few, combined with the low population of America, would have made inevitable the European settlement of America. That's what we have here. The Cro-Magnons of Earth are more of a threat to us Neanderthals of Creation than the other way around, even while we fly a big interstellar ship."

"I understand your point of view, Captain." I said. "I know it's sometimes hard to believe,

115

but we've come a long way since 1500. Our American system of civil rights is the result of revulsion and rebellion against the abuses that have occurred."

"Well, yes, but those abuses continue. There's a hate campaign against good men like yourself, who are guilty of nothing more than being unable to sustain marital relationships with the mothers or their children. We understand the need to have a father involved in the raising of children. But throwing the father out of the child's life, taking all of his money, and coercing his employment so he can continue to pay money, doesn't makes sense. As you yourself have said, peonage is an evil that still exists in your nation. You let judges, not juries, decide what your Constitution means. They twist its words and destroy its meaning. How can WE trust your leaders if YOU have reason not to?"

"Trviea, you're absolutely right. But I assure you that there are noncustodial parents who have not abandoned their children, but do not kowtow to the tyrants who hate us. We drive 'em nuts by simply telling the truth of the Antipeonage Act. Because it's a felony to enslave a person for a debt or obligation, the Peonage Law frightens 'em, especially with the *Brent Moss* case."

"We were talking about fusion reactors." interrupted Contrviea.

"Yeah," I responded, "think of the wealth and comfort you can live in by selling to us Earthlings the secret to your fusion reactor! You can buy anything you want. I'm not asking you to sell the secret to how you hop from one star to the other."

"I'm not tempted by the possibility of living the rest of my life on Earth with vast wealth because I can live just as well on my own Planet. Lchnsda has title to a farm that in the United States would be worth millions of dollars. But she cannot sell it because anybody can claim an abandoned farm and scavenge what they need from other abandoned properties. But here's something I don't understand: You Earth Cro-Magnons have hydrogen bombs, uranium fission reactors, particle accelerators, and you know how stars work. You understand nuclear physics and the fusion process. So why don't you have fusion reactors?"

"We can't figure out how to build the magnetic bottle to contain the plasma."

"Figures. Your ancient Greeks built little steam powered toys but couldn't build steam engines to drive ships. You know how to use magnetic fields and you have electricity. How do you start your car?"

"I turn the key."

"What happens when you turn the key?"

"My starter motor engages the flywheel of the engine and spins it until the engine starts."

"How does the starter motor engage the flywheel of the engine?"

"When I turn the key, a switch closes to allow a current through the solenoid and the starter motor."

"Describe the solenoid, please."

"A simple coil of copper wire wrapped many times. The current spins around in a spiral helix pattern creating a magnetic field." I smiled. "An iron bar within this field moves in an axial direction with sufficient force to slide the little pinion gear to where it meshes with the flywheel."

"Excellent! You know that by moving charged particles, in this case electrons within a copper wire, you create a magnetic field strong enough for a simple function of mechanical machinery. So if you know this, why can't you build a fusion reactor?"

Trviea broke in. "Contrviea, what you're doing is extremely dangerous. He may have a cubic *tig-it* less brain, but he makes the most of what he's got!"

"Contrviea," I started, "either you've given me a billion dollar clue or you've deliberately led me astray."

"Now why would I lead you astray?"

"You have good reasons to." Pidonita playfully dropped another grape into my mouth. I quickly chewed and swallowed it. Trviea took off one of my shoes and started tickling my foot. "Trviea, please! This is important!"

"That's what I'm afraid of."

"Look. If the three of you want to party while Wilma the Chastised Slave in a Control Collar watches and listens, hey, I'm open to new experiences." They laughed. "But first, let's talk about magnetic fields and the Secret To Your Success." They sobered up. "A week ago, before Helga and Lucinda had their trip into the Jefferson County Twilight Zone, I walked past your Shuttle Bay. Contrviea here and Metrola Mornuxler had some inspection plates off the Shuttle."

"Routine maintenance, I assure you." said Contrviea. "There's nothing wrong with the Shuttle, and we keep it that way."

"Of course. After Helga relieved Trviea of her command, the things that were in my pockets, including a magnetic compass, were returned to me. The south pole of my compass needle pointed to the Shuttle. I walked around the Shuttle. Ah-ha! The south pole pointed to the Shuttle! From all directions. Later on, you were finished. Now my compass didn't point, it spun around aimlessly. The inspection plates apparently shield off a magnetic field. I made a phone call to a retired Boeing executive I know who lives on the Kitsap County side of the Hood Canal. I'm surprised you didn't monitor it."

"Maybe we should monitor your calls." interrupted Trviea. "Though we too have a tradition of respecting people's privacy. Go on."

"He was in his yacht when your Shuttle came down to pick me up. He saw the south pole of his boat's compass point WEST to the Olympic Mountains. After you were gone, it went back to pointing south. He made a few phone calls. A Skokomish Indian was in his boat near the Bend in the Hood Canal, the south pole of his compass pointed north! He also found out that our Navy boys at Bangor and Bremerton saw the same thing at the same time they saw the glitch on their radar screens."

"So you figured out how our Shuttle is powered?" asked Contrviea.

"Yep. If you can create an intense magnetic field for a fusion reactor, you can use such a field to repel against the Earth's magnetic field and overcome its gravity. Anyone who plays with small iron magnets knows the principle. They stick together, but turn one around, they repel each other. You drop straight down and you rise straight back up. No jet engine, no rocket. All you need is a nice intense little source of energy to power the magnetic field drive. Perhaps a fancy set of gigafarad capacitors."

"So why don't we power the *Neanderthal Return* that way?"

"You need a fusion reactor anyway, for your energy source. If you can align the protons so the product particles go in one direction, only to be restrained by the magnetic bottle, that would be your propulsion. No need to be near a planet with a magnetic field."

"So why can't you Earthlings build a fusion reactor?"

"Maybe because we're short a cubic inch of brain. We can manipulate the flow of charged particles as long as we have a medium to channel these particles in a path. Electrons flowing in a copper wire. But copper cannot carry enough electric current to generate the kind of magnetic field we need for a fusion reactor without turning into plasma! You obviously thought up something else."

"You figure out what it is, we'll lock you up in a steel collar like we have on Wilma here and tell Earth that we've had a terrible accident with our fusion reactor. Your body was just vaporized!" They were laughing.

"Is it because it not only allows you to have fusion reactors and magnetic drive flying saucers, but it allows you to wink out of existence here and then wink back into existence near another star in less time than it takes a flash of light to get there?"

No answer.

The three women from the Planet Creation were at a reception. Senator Carla O'Donnell, liberal Democrat and very feminist, declared "If anyone doubts the capabilities of women, look at these women from the Planet Creation. Without men, they designed and built a starship and crossed the 25 trillion miles between their star and ours. Without men, they stopped the aging process so that their lives are actually long enough for them to accomplish any great thing they set out to do!"

"Without men we are not complete." Lucinda responded. "Without men, we cannot bear children. Without children, our Race will die out; we will be no more. There is nothing that we can achieve without men that we cannot achieve even better with men. We our proud of our achievements. But if the Great Holy Spirit, how we refer to God, made the offer, I will gladly trade it all away to have Chmlee Renuxler alive again." Applause. "We would all make that trade, to have our men back. But the Spirit, He does not offer that deal, such is the finality of death."

"But is it not true that you women were afforded opportunities not there before? During our Second World War, millions of women worked in factories for the first time. They did well when given the chance."

"Perhaps we had a different relationship between the genders. Neil Peace told us that the general difference between men and women of your Race in size and muscle strength affects their relationship. The men think they are better suited to doing the heavy work necessary to provide for the family. The women think they have the right to be protected and provided for while they take care of the home and raise the children. So women are discriminated against in the workplace while men are discriminated against in the home and required to go fight the wars."

"You realize that is an oversimplification."

"Yes, Senator, I realize that. But now consider the situation on our Planet. As you know, muscle development is affected by the genes. With us, the lack of testosterone does not prevent us from growing powerful muscles because our DNA commands it. This varies from woman to woman, just as other features vary. With our Neanderthal Race, oh, how is the best way that I can say this? I understand how this can be misunderstood with disastrous political consequences."

"Don't worry Lucinda," assured Senator O'Donnell, "we know you're not racist or sexist."

Helga broke in. "Allow me to make the point that Lchnsda is trying to make. Neil told us about human factors that he used in his work. Units of measure are derived from human factors: feet, yards, fathoms and such. There are also measurements of force exerted by each muscle group. Percentile levels are based on such measurements of a large number of men and women. Neil noticed that at every percentile level, a woman's physical strength is about half of a man's physical strength. Where a 5th percentile women can exert ten pounds of muscle force, a 5th percentile man can exert twenty pounds. A 95th percentile woman is stronger than a 5th percentile man, and sometimes they get married." Laughter. "But for the most part, Cro-Magnon women are about half as strong as Cro-Magnon men."

"But Neanderthal women, at a given percentile level, are stronger than half of the strength of Neanderthal men?"

The women from Creation laughed. Helga began again. "At each such level, for our Race, the physical strength of a woman is between ten and eleven twelfths of a man's strength. The effect is like your track meets. The world records are held by men, the women's world records are somewhat slower. But all of the women who compete in the Olympics are considerably faster than the AVERAGE man. That's the way it was for us in muscle strength."

"That would lead to a different relationship between the genders." concluded Senator Carrell, a conservative Republican.

"Well, yes! With all due respect to Jean Auel, we have read her novel *Clan of the Cave Bear*, and seen the movie with Darryl Hannah; we have NEVER allowed ourselves to be dominated by our men like that. Sure it's fun watching Darryl Hannah portray the plucky Cro-Magnon girl Ayla who stands up to the men who are just a" Helga changed her voice to a mocking tone, "bunch of Neanderthals." She rolled her eyes. "But I assure you that it would never take an independent thinking Cro-Magnon girl to set things right in the tribe. We Neanderthal women, gifted with our muscle power, would have slammed Broud into the cave wall. The other men would have said, 'Broud, get real. We have to live with these ladies!'" Laughter.

"Just how strong are you girls?"

"How strong?"

"Yeah, we've been hearing that you've been bench pressing 300 pounds or more in the White House weight room."

"Oh! I see what you mean. Lucinda, you care to take this one?"

"Look at Helga here. Six feet tall! Beautiful. I can see the effect she has on men." Laughter.

"Some of that is in reaction to you and to Andemona." declared Helga as she stood.

"I like to think so. But in this lovely evening dress, you can see that Helga has a beautiful body." Helga blushed. "So beautiful that the men here do not notice her funny looking face. But note how this dress, with its bare shoulders and no sleeves, emphasize the muscular build of her arms and back." Helga turned around like a fashion model. "She bench pressed 350 pounds."

"Only once." Helga showed false modesty. "You bench pressed 350 too."

"Yes, I did. Almost everyone on our crew is capable of lifting, in the exercise equivalent to your bench press, four *hekt dollons* of force, about 300 pounds. A few are not that strong, and we have a few who can press over five *hekt dollons*. We do six reps of 300 pounds each time we take our turn with the barbell. A good workout for the arms."

Whistles. "How much can you leg press?"

"About four or five hundred pounds. On our ship, we usually set the leg press at six *hekt dollons*, which is about 450 pounds." They let that sink in.

Helga then spoke. "Our men were strong like that too. You asked about the relationship between the genders. As you can imagine, there was a lot more equality, we women had it better in a lot of ways. But our men also had it better. Muscle strength has a psychological effect. Nobody is submissive if everyone is capable of killing with bare hands and bare teeth. If a married couple isn't getting along, one of three things happens: they work it out, they separate, or one of 'em dies."

"So domestic violence tends to be a two way street?"

"Yeah! Rape was not as big a problem. Murder, yes. We've had murderers, we can kill by clamping our jaws on a victim's neck and ripping out the windpipe or crushing the vertebrae. But raping a Neanderthal woman is like raping a she bear." Laughter. "We've had sex offenders, we just didn't have REPEAT sex offenders." Laughter and cheering. "Victims so often kill their attackers, that self defense is almost always an issue in our murder trials."

"What effect did this have on the crime rate, the level of violence?"

"The rate of crime and violence was rather low, criminals preferred burglary to robbery. The invention of gunpowder, particularly hand held firearms, made robbery more attractive to criminals. But violent crime was rare, except during wars and revolutions, in which case the level of violence can be extreme. Free and democratic governments are the norm on Creation because practicing tyranny and slavery against Neanderthal people is a dangerous proposition. We try to accommodate grievances as much as possible. But there have been times when tyrants take over, resulting in civil war as we regain our freedom."

"What happens to those who are convicted of murder?"

"Mitigating circumstances, if any, are taken into account. But if the murder was planned and deliberate, or the result of a planned and deliberate crime, if the defendant was the attacker and not acting in self defense, then the penalty was almost always death. I believe that's equivalent to what you call first degree murder."

"You carried out the penalty?"

"There is one automatic appeal, where every bit of evidence is reviewed and investigated, the appeals court has awesome powers of investigation in reviewing a capital case. If you are a police officer, you have an incentive to play by the rules; there is no police code of silence. You never know when you find yourself in a murder investigation, where first, both prosecution and defense can look into your job performance, then in the event of a conviction, the appeals court. Sometimes, such a conviction is reversed. We take perjury very seriously, either life imprisonment or, in the case of perjury by a witness in a capital case, death. But when the appeals court affirmed the conviction, the hanging took place twelve days later, after the condemned person was allowed this time to prepare. The twelve day preparation period is provided to all persons sentenced to death. Hangings were public, and did not happen very often because murders did not happen very often."

"Was the low level of murder and other violent crime due to the deterrence of the death penalty or because of better moral fiber of the people?"

"Our societies are sometimes healthy, sometimes not. The deterrent is the fact that the victim has the right, and the teeth, to fight back. To kill if necessary. But only if necessary. People have the right to defend themselves, and to defend children, the sick, and the elderly, anyone who is frail. If you try to hurt a child, nearby adults will kill you. Attackers who kill were sentenced to death. Defenders were usually not charged. It was pounded into us when we were children that it is wrong to start a fight, because with our muscle and teeth, we can kill or be killed."

"That made it safe to walk the streets at night."

"Usually. We humans, of both Races, are the most awesome killing machines ever evolved. We need some way of keeping the evil that is within our souls under control. On Creation, we have tried to build an ethic, in religion, in law, in our relationships, where we respect each other. If you mistreat a person, you can turn on that person's dark side, and that is very dangerous. We have a criminal justice system, but we understand the practical limits of government. So our government, like yours, figures out some rules designed to limit the tendency to dominate and abuse the people it governs, to operate with the consent of the governed."

"Have you got it all figured out?"

"We're still working on it."

"This is very interesting, we should do this some more. Why don't we talk about lighter subjects? Like recreation and entertainment. We know you like to sing songs, but what else do you do for fun?"

"Lots of things." Helga answered. "I love to go horseback riding, we can't do that on a spaceship."

"Yes! Me too." seconded Andemona, "Helga's a good horse rider. Lucy, too."

Lucinda smiled. "Yes, I miss riding horses. I had a few on my farm. Our Secret Service bodyguard won't let us use the horseriding place at Rock Creek Park without closing it to the public. We won't consider inconveniencing the public for our pleasure."

"We have a few acres in Maryland, just a few miles beyond the district line." offered a gentleman. "We have some horses and riding trails, I think you would enjoy them. If you would be so kind as to take my card, you can give me a call and make arrangements."

"Thank you, uh, Mister,"

"Allen Fairfax Washington. This lovely lady is my wife, Dorothy."

"Pleased to meet you."

"It is an honor. Well, maybe we can find time to come over to ride horses. We thank you very much for the offer."

Hrtinsla Pliklakian asked me to help her in the ship's Garden Room. Like Lucinda, she owns a farm. It is not as big, three dozen *plowdats* located four dozen and three *kepfats* north of Cair Atlaston. She showed me the lights that are designed to mimic sunlight. How water and plant nutrients are delivered in precise quantities to each plant, according to its species and state of growth. We went past small fruit trees, melons, berries, and vegetables. Grains growing on short plants, bred for use on a spacecraft. We went into the fiber growing area, cotton, sisal, and flax. I recognized a familiar species from my college days. "I didn't know you guys are dopeheads! This is marijuana!"

She smiled. "What do you think we make our paper out of? Hemp linen is as comfortable to wear as flax linen. The oil from hemp seed is what we use to make lubricant for our metal machinery. There's no petroleum on Creation; we have to use vegetable oils. We don't smoke the flowers and the leaves of this plant like you do."

I smiled. "Yeah. Before the 1930's there was no law against growing hemp. The instinct for Prohibition turned itself to recreational drugs other than alcohol and tobacco. Now we have these crazy drug laws and this terrible problem of people ruining themselves with cocaine, heroin, and other dangerous drugs. We make paper out of trees, those who own the trees and paper mills don't want competition from hemp paper. Oil for lubrication is made from petroleum. We're not going to see any common sense with hemp until there is a vital need for its products."

"Before we sent the four women down to the Earth surface, we made certain there were no hemp products in their possessions. No hemp linen in their clothing. We wanted to respect your laws."

"Do you make any use of the THC, the cannabin?"

"You mean the drug compound in the leaves and flowers?"

"Yes."

"We use a medicine made from cannabin to fine tune the lenses in our eyes. This medicine doesn't alter the mind like the raw cannabin. That's why we see perfectly without glasses."

"THAT might convince our people to legalize this plant. Everyone wants to be able to see without glasses! I thought your perfect vision was the result of some medical procedure. Nearsightedness, astigmatism, and cataracts are natural. Perfect focus of the natural lens is not the usual condition."

"That's true. The hemp extract is preferable to glasses and contact lenses."

"Why haven't your physicians provided me with this treatment?"

"You haven't asked for it, though you didn't know about it. But also, we don't want to put you in a position of violating your laws."

"I'm already not paying my child support."

"True."

"I'm a bit of a rebel. Sometimes we break our laws in protest. Rosa Parks refused to give up her seat on the bus. Susan B. Anthony voted. Richard and Mildred Loving got married in violation of a Virginia law prohibiting mixed race marriages. People helped runaway slaves. Our Declaration of Independence was treason if we were unable to win our Revolutionary War. Many positive changes are the result of this kind of protest. So please allow me to be an American and grant me this cannabin treatment for my eyes. I want clear vision!"

Hrtinsla smiled. "The United States has passed many foolish laws. The rule of the majority is no guarantee that the majority will always be wise and fair. What sets your country apart is the willingness of Americans to fight for what is right." We were in a soft grassy spot surrounded by seven foot hemp plants. The tang of their odor filled the air. "I like this spot." She laid down in the grass and took off her shoes. "Does the State of Washington have any laws about sodomy, sex outside of marriage, or interracial marriage or sex?"

"Actually, no." I laid down beside her. "Adultery often leads to divorce, but it seems to have no bearing on the decree. The Legislature in Olympia repealed sodomy laws twenty or thirty years ago. So we could do anything we want, sexually. There have never been any Washington laws that I know of banning interracial marriage. So we could get married, a Neanderthal and a Cro-Magnon, and the marriage would be legal."

"A crowd of 10,000 people has gathered here in Port Townsend, Washington to protest racism. I'm here with Angela Peace, the former wife of Neil Peace, who has come here to show solidarity with the Neanderthal women from Planet Creation and with all Earthlings who are opposed to racism. Angela, why do you think it's important to come here to Port Townsend for this demonstration? You could have this rally in Seattle."

"John, you're right that we could do this in Seattle, and maybe we should. But it is here in Port Townsend that we had public officials, using our tax money, prosecuting these women in violation of a grant of immunity. Neil has forgiven them and he has talked them into introducing themselves to us. If that isn't worth a Nobel Peace Prize, then I don't know what is. We need to establish a peaceful relationship with this other human Race. But given the racism and hatred we Earth Cro-Magnons have exhibited, who can blame Captain Harsradich for not wanting to let us know that there are Neanderthal people still alive somewhere in the Universe?"

"Angela, how about the campaign to 'go after' deadbeat dads? If your ex heads off to another Planet, he'll be too far away for anyone to 'go after'."

"I miss the support payments. But if we were still married, we would be missing the paycheck as a result of his layoff. We'd be working through it without this business of anybody going after anybody. Many fathers disappear because we threaten to JAIL them for not having a job! I thought that's what happened! He left his car in the middle of nowhere! Door hanging open, key in the ignition! I was hoping he wasn't dead. Child support is only money. I wanted Neil ALIVE and I'm glad he is. I don't care about the money. More of us ex-wives are that way than you think."

"So you think enforcing a parent's obligation to support his children is not that important?"

"It's the way we're going about it. It's not productive to define somebody the 'obligor', to strip him of his property and freedom, to impose an unreasonable monthly payment, to toss the state and federal Constitutions aside, and then 'go after' him when he doesn't do what you want him to do. Divorce is enough of a tragedy as it is, but we have an unconstitutional system that makes it considerably worse. It exists because it's a money tree for lawyers, bureaucrats, and social workers. I wouldn't blame Neil if he stays on the *Neanderthal Return* and rides it back to Creation where he's free of all this."

"But what about the single moms who NEED the child support and are not getting it? What about the deadbeat dads?"

"Calling people names and 'going after' them doesn't help whatever problem you're trying to solve. You might as well ask 'What about the honkies?' Or 'What about the gooks?' Or niggers? Or faggots? Or siwash? Or trogs? I hear the nasty term for these Neanderthals is trogs, as if they still live in caves! That's no cave up there in space! These women are good people, even if they did kidnap my ex! The situation they describe is extremely desperate! No men, therefore no children. Stop the aging process? Fine, but your Race goes extinct if you don't solve the problem of reproduction. So we call 'em trogs. Or demon women because of their physical strength and courage. Too many of us Americans have hated, but there is nothing American about hate! That is what we have gathered here in Port Townsend to declare, to protest, to celebrate our opposition to hate."

"It's for you, Neil."

"Thank you. Hello."

"Hi Neil, it's me, Angela."

"I saw you at the demonstration in Port Townsend. Way to go! All of the women up here appreciate it. I appreciate it."

"Yeah, I'm glad. The people of Port Townsend were wonderful. The prosecutor, Don Mayton, I don't think he'll be reelected. People will stand against racism once they understand what's going on. White, black, Asian, and Native American men and women, boys and girls, we marched down Water Street side by side. They came from all over the state, other states, and from Canada. A *kepfat* was marked off from the Jefferson County Memorial Field down Water and Sims Streets. That took us to the supermarket which let us use their parking lot as a staging base. Everyone had flags and banners and signs. Some of the signs were written in Atlantean. Along with American and Canadian flags were flags from around the world. We had an Israeli and a Palestinian carry their flags side by side. A group of South Africans, some white and some black, carried along with their new national flag a banner that read 'No more apartheid between Creation and Earth.'"

"I'm glad you had fun."

"Yeah. It was fun! The kids enjoyed it too. You don't mind?"

"Not at all."

"We finally got the march organized at one o'clock in the afternoon. We headed out of the parking lot on to the street. The police closed it off during the march. The ferry from Keystone didn't dock until our parade passed. The captain blew the ship's horn, the passengers watched and cheered. Along the way we sang songs, *We Shall Overcome, God Bless America*, John Lennon's *Give Peace a Chance*, the South Africans entertained us with *God Bless Africa*. Crowds cheered us as we walked between the Victorian buildings of the old downtown. Then we turned left to go into the athletic field. Food, games, a stage was set up, bands played and we all gave speeches. I gave a speech. I hope it was nice, I was pretty nervous."

"You did fine, we watched it up here."

"It was televised?"

"Yeah, live."

"Oh wow. We had a moment of silence for the Secret Service men. But we also had joyous celebration for the victories against racism and hate and we celebrated the miracle of the survival of the Neanderthal Race and the fact that they come in peace."

"You also got a phone call from the White House!"

"Yes! The President called us and spoke to us! Then he put Helga, Lucinda, and Andemona on! Lucy and Helga thanked me, by name! For the hospitality that we showed them at our party in Auburn. They spoke with our children for a few minutes, that was special! The three of them serenaded us with a song in Atlantean language celebrating peace between Earth and Creation. We clearly heard the English word 'Earth' in their song. Then they explained that *Chmpashian* means 'Creation' and is the name of their Planet in Atlantean. *Chm* means full as in *chmfat* for full reach or fathom. The word can also mean 'finished' or 'completed'. *Treepashian* means 'not completed', just as *treefat* means half reach or yard. They told us that the process of establishing peaceful relations between Earth and *Chmpashian* is in a state of *treepashion* and that we all need to continue working hard to bring it to a state of *chmpashian*. They thanked us for our march and celebration. No way are they going to let a few criminals get in the way of the most important introduction between nations in history."

"Are you back home now, where are you calling me from?"

"Oh! At nine in the evening, we had a candlelight parade back down Water Street from the athletic field to the supermarket parking lot. From there, many of us headed for home. I just now got the kids into bed and I dialed this phone number Helga and Lucinda gave me. It got through! To an orbiting spacecraft!"

"Ain't technology wonderful! Makes me proud to be an engineer!"

"Yeah. And I'm proud of you too. There's something else I want to discuss with you. You've been making love with these women?"

"Why do you ask?"

"I know you are making love with every woman on that ship who wants you."

"You divorced me, what are you complaining about?"

"Not complaining. But I'm concerned about you."

"About me? I'm doing just fine!"

"Typical man. Give him lots of sex, he thinks he's doing just fine. I'm a little worried about your safety."

"Since when have you ever worried about my safety? You weren't when you filed for divorce and kicked me out of the house and sicked the state support bureaucracy on me leaving me without enough in my paycheck to pay RENT!"

After a pause while she composed herself, "I didn't call you to rehash ancient history."

"Sorry about that."

"Yeah. We women can be irrational when it comes to men. There really is no such thing as 'casual sex'. There's the old communication problem: we wonder why you can't take a hint and you wonder why we can't understand plain English. We get frustrated. Some men beat the shit out of their women, that's true. We women verbally abuse our men because we know we'll lose a physical fight. We use the divorce system because it's such a marvelous system for abusing a husband. And some of us murder our husbands. That's with us physically weak Cro-Magnon women. But here you are, making love while cooped up in a tin can with over 40 Neanderthal women, not a one of them incapable of bench pressing 300 pounds. What if you piss 'em off? You men have a talent for that. Any one of 'em decides to eat your windpipe, you're dead in two seconds!"

"Actually they're handling things pretty well, they're not gonna eat my windpipe." I decided not to tell her about my confrontation with a drunken and frustrated Trviea Harsradich. "They all worry that they may have made a big mistake. Commodore Matthew Perry opened Japan to the outside world. The Japanese learned the technology of the rest of the world and industrialized. Overcrowded islands with shortages of raw materials and disputes with many other nations. Commodore Perry didn't intend to cause Pearl Harbor, but that was one of the results of his mission. The Creation women hope they never reap a whirlwind like the Pacific War."

"Whew! They have good reason to be afraid of us. They need your sperm to continue their Race. The sex probably calms 'em down. I hope you're not 'playing games'. That could get you killed. They appreciate your efforts to advise them about Earth politics. But if things go sour, they can learn to hate you with a depth you cannot imagine. That is, unless there's something about female Neanderthal psychology that's different than female Cro-Magnon psychology. I don't think so, they're just putting up a *Right Stuff* front. Be careful. Please be very careful."

"These three ladies are good with horses."

"Yeah, they know how to ride 'em. It took the animals a bit of time to get used to Atlantean commands. But the way they petted them and allowed each horse to eat out of their hands, they got their confidence." Lucinda rode her horse over to Allen and Dorothy Washington. "How ya' doin' Lucy?"

Lucinda was happy, she had just galloped over a furlong of trail, she and her animal were sweating and panting. "This is excellent therapy! This sunshine, spring is coming. I have not seen Andemona and Helga so happy in a long time! Russians have horses, I'll suggest to Monoloa that she go riding. Thank you very much!"

"We're just happy to do whatever we can to help. Frankly, we didn't expect you to come, this is a big thrill for us, we are honored."

After the women from Creation rode their horses, they took them to the stable, brushed them, fed them, and even performed some shovel work. All three obviously had experience with horses on Creation. They had to decline, with apologies, the Washingtons' invitation to dinner, and returned to the District of Columbia with their Secret Service escort.

Chapter Fifteen

Mustafa Khedr studied the Tassili n'Ajjer mountain range from the window of the small propeller plane. After taking a 737 to the international airport at Tamanrasset, Algeria, where he cleared customs, the Egyptian Antiquities Organization official transferred to this small bird for the trip out to Illizi. Security was extremely tight because of the GIS. The GIS existed in part because the Algerian government is oppressive. Fortunately for Khedr, his clout protected him from having to fill out currency forms; Algerian Antiquities needed an Egyptologist.

He tried to imagine a time when this place was wet enough to support a cattle herding culture. Perhaps clouds would float across the desert and bunch up against these mountains to drop rain. Nowadays, that rarely happens. A high pressure system permanently keeps rain clouds away from the Sahara.

But during an era when the high pressure system was not so strong, we could have plenty of water and grass for raising cattle. Who were these Negro cowboys? Perhaps they were Kushites, who were depicted in ancient Egyptian art and described in ancient Egyptian writing.

He gave up trying to see a pattern of ancient habitation in the yellow brown landscape, and went back to the photographs taken by the nomad, Mohammed Abbas, blown up to 8 by 10 inch size. Three men standing together, apparently in a conversation. The Egyptian, the Negro cattleman, and the Neanderthal. 4500 year old rock painting depicting a Neanderthal. Old enough for Egyptians and Tassili cattlemen. But nowhere near old enough for a Neanderthal. At least a Neanderthal from Earth. This guy from Planet Creation? Not likely, but who knows? Okay, Neanderthals were still alive on Earth during the Egyptian Fourth Dynasty, unless this artist is drawing from an ancient legend. He's got the Chinese shaped eyes, just like the women from Creation, and he has blonde or gray hair.

The Neanderthal is dressed appropriately for a white skinned person in the desert. He is wearing a stylish white robe tied at the waist with a broad cloth belt. The Negroes evolved black skin for protection from the tropical sun. The Arabs developed loose clothing for the same purpose. The women in the spaceship and this man in the painting are as pink skinned as Germans. Without plenty of clothing, such a person would suffer skin cancer in the Sahara.

The pilot asked everyone to fasten their seatbelts, final approach to Illizi. Mustafa Khedr put the materials away and prepared to disembark. After the plane landed, the pilot handed the passengers their bags. They descended to the pavement. There are no buildings at Illizi Airport, it is just an airstrip three miles from Illizi town along the Route du Tassili N'Ajjer. Mustafa was relieved to see Ali Amoud's car parked by the side of the road. Ali Amoud greeted him. "Mustafa! How are you doing? We are pleased that you have come! Let us get into my car, I will drive you out to the camp."

"Yes, that would be a good idea. You find a wife yet?"

"No, not yet, I am still a happy bachelor!" They got into the Land Rover and drove through Illizi and then on to the makeshift road for the one and a half hour trip to the archeological Base Camp. "Algerian Antiquities has taken possession of the site. They are allowing us to conduct the excavations by standard archeological procedures. It is nice to have the soldiers protecting us and the site from the GIS. Chuck Carter and Mohammed Abbas, that's the Bedouin nomad who found the place, have the cave floor marked out in a square meter grid."

"Bedouin? This is Tuareg country."

"His wife, Labna, is Tuareg, the locals have accepted him as a nomad. We have also been poking around the surrounding area, and found evidence of an ancient campsite, possibly a village. Good place for this meeting with the Egyptians and the Neanderthal from Atlantis."

"Hold it right there! Atlantis?!"

"I know. The writing definitely contains the word 'Atlantis'. Atlantis is written on the bow, below the handgrip. The name 'Avenor' is written in a cartouche above the handgrip. We are wondering why Avenor left such a nice gift in the cave. What is your take on the writing?"

"Before I go into that, have you done any carbon-14 tests?"

"It has not yet been confirmed, but the preliminary result for both wood and varnish, is between 2500 and 2600 years Before the Common Era." Before the Common Era is another way of designating Before Christ years. Anno Domini becomes the Common Era.

"Fourth Dynasty. Right time for an expedition sent out by Pharaoh Khufu. All right, here is what the writing says: Pharaoh Khufu sent an expedition into the Western Desert. The expedition went by boat up the Nile to Seyne, the ancient name for Aswan, accompanied by the Pharaoh. At Aswan, supplies and camels were put together for the march due west. Water was loaded in large skin bags. Astronomical instruments were brought so they can keep on a westerly course. A wheeled device to serve as an odometer was dragged behind a camel."

"This is the first time we have any evidence that I know of that the ancient Egyptians used such a device. This writing is very specific about the units of measure."

"It is that. The wheel was 3 cubits, 1 palm and 1 finger in diameter and clicked off ten cubits with every revolution. Royal cubits of 28 fingers, not regular cubits of 24 fingers."

"You sure about the cubits being royal, not regular?"

"No doubt about it. Here is where the cubit is defined. You see the two ten symbols." Mustafa pointed to two symbols that look like the letter U from the Roman alphabet turned upside down. "These tally marks they used to represent one are clearly broken in the middle. So there are eight tally marks, not four. We have the number 28, not 24. Seven palms, not six."

"You are right, now that I see. I owe 200 dinars to Chuck, he said it was royal cubits, I said it was regular."

Mustafa laughed at Ali's financial misfortune. The sum is less than ten American dollars. "Americans have an easier time with ancient units of measure than we do!"

"What they use is a modified version of the ancient systems of measure. Why don't Americans want to adopt the Metric System?"

"They have a foot fetish."

"You've heard it! Old joke. Anyway, they went marching off into the desert with a wheeled odometer clicking off 10 cubits with each turn."

"That is what it is saying here. 1400 turns is an *atur*. *Atur* of Edfu, 14,000 cubits. In the evening, when the sun went down, the group set out from Aswan. They refilled their water bags after 20 *aturs*. That would be Dunqul Oasis, perhaps. But then they went through a stretch of desert with no water for 130 *aturs*. Probably missed the Cufra Oasis in what is now Libya. They camped during the day and marched at night using the stars to keep on course. Then they found a dry river bed, and they followed it upstream, toward the north, bringing the North Star a degree higher in the sky."

"Thubin? It was not Polaris then."

"Probably Thubin, Alpha Draconis, precession of the equinoxes and all. In the river bed, pools of water slacked their thirst and they refilled their bags. They set out west again. Another 100 *aturs*, the sand dunes gave way to grasslands. They finally found black cattle herders. After a tense moment when the Egyptians convinced them that they come in peace, the cattle people proved hospitable. The Egyptians were then directed to the area around this cave. They estimated that they were 300 *aturs* west of the Nile River. About the actual distance we can measure today."

Mustafa went on. "The Egyptians spent a season living with the black cattle people. They learned their language and taught them Egyptian. They gave an astrolabe to the local chieftain, his name spelled in Egyptian phonetic symbols inside a cartouche, these symbols are equivalent to the letters *mim*, *ba*, the reed leaf which could be like the *ya*, another *ba*, *ta*, and a *ha*." As they were speaking in Arabic, Mustafa referred to letters in the Arabic alphabet. "Mebibetah is the name of the black man depicted in the middle of the three figures, his name is set in a cartouche because he was the 'pharaoh' of these cattle people.

"After the Egyptians and Mebibetah learned enough of each others' languages, Mebibetah called for the white skinned man that had been living with one of the family groups. The Egyptians knew of white skinned people. But this guy was different, he was the reason for this entire expedition across the desert.

"The rock painting is representing the meeting, Mebibetah was translating between the Egyptian and the Neanderthal, because he knew Egyptian, his own language, and the Neanderthal's language. The Neanderthal's name was Afenor, set in a cartouche."

"Afenor, I prefer Avenor."

"Why Avenor? After the *alif* vulture, the name is spelled with the viper symbol, which always stood for the *fa* sound. Now you are showing a preference for the English V sound."

"Well, maybe the name is Euenor. The same name as the 'Adam' of Atlantis as described by Plato in his Letters to Timeus and Critias."

"Sure, why not? Afenor came from a land far, far away. Across the desert, across the oceans. The name of this land, as you have already found, is Atlantis. I confirm your reading of the Egyptian symbols. The lion symbol can also stand for the sound combination *ru*. Atruntis does not seem as likely as Atlantis. Afenor explained that in the *Zep Tepi*, the First Time of Egyptian mythology, Osiris and Isis traveled from his homeland to Egypt, and carved the Sphinx, then as a statue of a lion with a lion's head. The lion faced due east, because at that time in history, the lion constellation rose due east. When the sun rose in the spring due east, the vernal equinox, it was in the lion constellation."

"This is an Egyptologist's worst nightmare!"

"Tell me about it! I am a patriotic Egyptian. I like to believe that we built the Pyramids and the Sphinx. We developed this language, the hieroglyphics, hieratic, and demotic writing styles. We developed the religion based on the sun god Ra. Don't get me wrong, I am happy to be a Muslim. But I also have pride in the pharaohs and their civilization. So we at the Egyptian Antiquities Organization, along with the international Egyptology community, have been hostile to the theory that the Sphinx was originally carved thousands of years before Pharaoh Menes Narmer established the First Dynasty, even before the Ice Age finally came to the end. We have been hostile to the theory that the three Giza Pyramids were not built by the three pharaohs for whom they were named. We are hostile to the idea that there is an Atlantean Hall of Records below the paws of the Sphinx. We are hostile to the idea of the existence of Atlantis because that demotes us from our status as the inventor of civilization."

"Not to mention the inventor of the 360 degree circle, the 24 hour day, Base Ten numbers, or even the concept of standard weights and measures!"

"People credit the Sumerians or other ancient Iraqis with inventing the 360 degree circle and the splitting of the hour into minutes and seconds. But we Egyptians usually get the blame, or credit if you will, for numbers based on powers of ten. We invented both feet and cubits, though some dispute that we used a foot of four palms or 16 fingers. Or so we thought until the

Neanderthal Return showed up. I do not know if the Creation Neanderthals have anything like a cubit, but they sure do have feet and inches."

"I thought it was the Romans who came up with the idea of splitting the foot into twelve parts. How is it that these people of Planet Creation think it up?"

"There are only so many different ways to break up a foot. Since the Creationists use a Base Twelve number system, they are not likely to split their foot into ten parts."

"Why not? The Romans, with Base Ten numbers, chose to split the foot into twelve parts, because their fractions were Base Twelve! Just like the Creation Neanderthals! It was the Chinese and the Japanese who split their *chih* and *shaku* units into ten parts."

"Like Americans when they measure lake levels. They split their foot into ten parts for this use, while splitting it into twelve inches in all other cases."

Ali took a deep breath. "Now that we are alone in this Land Rover, kilometers from anybody else, hopefully from the GIS, we have to talk about Atlantis. This makes me nervous, because I am not independently wealthy like Heinrich Schliemann." Schliemann was the wealthy German businessman who in the late 1800's found Troy. "If I am fired from the archeology profession, I might have to settle for another boring office job in the Algerian bureaucracy. If the government will have me. Or I could always be a terrorist with the GIS."

"We like to think of ourselves as scientists. But we can behave as emotionally dogmatic as the Catholic clergymen who placed Galileo under house arrest. Ali, we are friends. I will not run you out of the profession for talking about Atlantis stories. These women in the spaceship have certainly upset a few paradigms already."

"They upset the guys who tried to kidnap them. It rains too much in Washington State, makes them insane. To hear these women tell it, Atlantis is the name they gave their home in Europe. The end of the Ice Age with the melting of the glaciers and rise of the ocean, can explain the Plato story and the flood myths we find all over the world. Plato wrote that Atlantis existed and fought a war with Athens 9000 years before his time. This war involved all of the nations inside of the Pillars of Hercules on one side, led by Athens, against the Atlanteans who led a confederacy of nations based outside the Pillars."

"So we and the Greeks fought a war with the Celts, American Indians, and Atlanteans around the end of the Ice Age."

"Yes. The women profess no knowledge of Plato's Atlantis. They argue that in their conception, the continent of Atlantis is Europe itself. The sea around Europe gets deep within a few kilometers of the modern coastline until we get around Spain from here. Then we have the Celtic shelf, the English Channel and the North Sea, all less than 100 meters deep, and were dry land 9000 years before the time of Solon. So all of the coastal communities, be they Neanderthal or Cro-Magnon, are now under water."

Ali continued. "Me and Chuck reread Plato's Atlantis story. The city of Atlantis is described as an island surrounded by three lakes crossed by bridges. Similar to Tenochtitlan." The Aztec city was on an island in a lake and connected to the land by bridges. "Plato mentions the Region of Gades. Gades was a real city in Spain; we now call it Cadiz. Some think that Tartessos, or Tarshish, which was located near Cadiz, is a good candidate for Atlantis. But while Tarshish is just beyond the Pillars of Hercules, it is not nearly old enough to be Atlantis. Plato describes the island of Atlantis as 2000 stadia wide by 3000 stadia in length. That is like 360 by 550 kilometers." 230 by 340 miles. "Plato also mentioned that beyond this island of Atlantis, is 'the opposite continent that surrounds what can truly be called the ocean.'"

"I remember that! Columbus did not discover America, he merely confirmed a rumor!"

"So by this description, Atlantis was not Florida! Now redraw the Atlantic Ocean with the sea level 90 meters down from what it is today, and start looking for a 300 to 400 by 500 to 600 kilometer landmass between the Strait of Gibraltar and North America. What do we find? The Grand Bahama Bank comes to mind, the Bimini Road being an alleged Atlantean artifact."

"Okay, I'll bite. If an advanced civilization existed during the Ice Age on Grand Bahama Bank, then an island, only to be covered by the ocean when the glaciers melt, why do we not find any trace of it in the nearby land masses, Cuba, Florida, and such?"

"Some people think the Olmec Heads are such evidence. Images of African Negroes carved in Tabasco State in Mexico thousands of years before any such African would have ever been on that side of the Atlantic. Not to mention the downright European looking images that we also find in their ancient carvings. The bearded walker carrying a flag. He looks like a Celt, definitely European. And the descriptions of Kukulkan or Quetzalcoatl as a bearded white man whose symbol is a feathered snake."

"Feathered snake as a symbol has a vaguely Pagan Celtic feel to it for me."

"Yeah! Like the snakes that St. Patrick chased out of Ireland! Maybe that was a metaphor for a Pagan religion that Patrick's Christianity overturned. There are theories that it was the Phoenicians, not Atlanteans, who visited the Olmecs in Mexico. Rome fought wars with Carthage because the Phoenicians controlled trade in the Western Mediterranean and beyond the Pillars of Hercules. They kept their trade routes secret, so when they brought tin from Britain or silver from wherever, including possibly Mexico, people buying the goods from them may not have known where they came from."

"I do not doubt that Phoenicians, from their bases in Spain at Cartegena and Tartessos, could have crossed the Atlantic to Mexico. But if they did, why did they not bring back food plants like squash, peppers, potatoes, and maize? These plants were unknown in Europe and Africa until Columbus brought them back."

"It is a matter of what is considered important to a society. All cities back then grew their food locally. Food carried on ships was for the sailors, not for trade. Trade goods were durable goods and wine. It may be that the Native Americans with whom they came into contact were strictly hunter-gatherers and had not yet developed agriculture. Therefore, no potatoes or corn available to bring back. Consider the difficulties experienced by Captain Bligh when he attempted to transport breadfruit plants from Tahiti to Jamaica. So for long distances across the ocean, it might not have been profitable to carry mere food or even seeds. But if you have some gold, silver, tin or some other valuable and nonperishable goods, then you might be able to justify the expense of crossing the Atlantic Ocean. But the Phoenicians are not old enough to be the Atlanteans that we have represented here as a Neanderthal man named Afenor."

"Then there is Plato's description of Atlantean society and impending destruction in Critias. It sounds very familiar."

"Well yes! Poseidon handed down his laws which were inscribed upon a column of *orichalcum*. Just like the Code of Hammurabi! Engraved on a pillar of black stone, handed down by the sun god Shamesh. I wonder if *orichalcum* is a black stone?"

"Some people say it was copper or some kind of corrosion resistant naval brass. But the idea of a law code handed down by a divine being and engraved on stone occurs in a number of ancient cultures. Egyptian laws handed down from Osiris, Nut, Thoth and a few other gods and goddesses."

"The Ten Commandments. Chuck tells me that Moses came down from Mount Sinai leading a pair of oxen. The oxen dragged a huge ox-cart, piled high with stone tablets. Hundreds of stone tablets, with very small writing on each of them. The Hebrews looked at him with a mystified expression. Moses says 'Tax Code'."

131

Laughter. "Chuck does have a sense of humor."

"Anyway, as the centuries go by, the people of Atlantis become debased, are no longer obeying the laws of Poseidon. Zeus becomes angry, decides to punish them. Then Plato's story comes to a sudden end, and so does Atlantis. This, of course, sounds like the Noah Flood story, people becoming evil, and Allah punishing them by destroying them in a flood."

"Interesting parallel. Now we have the word 'Atlantis' showing up in this site in the Tassili Mountains. We have a painting of a Neanderthal identified as an Atlantean. The Atlantean, named Afenor, claims that his nation sent a colony to Egypt and carved the original Sphinx at a time when the lion constellation rose due east. Leo looks more like a lion than any other constellation. Due to the precession of the equinoxes, what we call the astrological Age of Leo was a thousand years each side of 10,000 B.C.E. This was when the Sun was in Leo during the vernal equinox. Leo rose due east every day during that entire epoch. The vernal point was in Taurus and Aries during the classical times, been in Pisces since about the time of Christ, and will soon be in Aquarius. Pisces and Aquarius now rise due east today."

Ali switched into English and sang the Hair song, *Age of Aquarius*.

"Please! Your singing is quite unnecessary!" Mustafa protested in Arabic. "The Age of Leo is about when the Ice Age came to an end. We Egyptologists have been confronted with alternative theory amateur archeologists wanting to mess around with the Sphinx so they can 'prove' that it was built in 10,000 B.C.E. by people from Atlantis!"

"So Atlantis was a coastal community before the end of the Ice Age. Not exactly as Plato described it, but after 9000 years, he got a few details wrong. It might have been populated by Neanderthals and our Cro-Magnon ancestors. How would we find any evidence of a coastal community or a maritime society that existed on a coastline 100 meters below the present ocean surface? But being a maritime society, they would need to develop astronomy and mapping for navigation. That means writing and mathematics. Numbers and geometry. A standard set of weights and measures."

"The circle divided into 360 degrees. The day divided into 24 hours. Base Ten numbers. A foot or a cubit or both. Now we have these women from another Planet, obviously descended from a population of transplanted Neanderthals, who define their nation as Atlantis, say that Atlantis is their name for their old home in Europe, and use a foot divided into twelve parts."

"It is enough to make a good Muslim take up drinking!"

"At least the girls use Base Twelve numbers and don't split the circle up into 360 degrees."

"No, what they do is split it up into 36 dozen *deems*, while we split it up into 36 TENS of degrees. They have a human factors based set of length units that looks a lot like the British-American system, with the rest of their weights and measures looking like what the Metric System would be if invented by people using Base Twelve numbers."

"So what is with this Neanderthal man illustrated on a rock in the middle of the Sahara? There is some evidence of Neanderthal type stone tools on the Algerian coastline. But we have never found Neanderthal bones to positively prove that Neanderthals were present in Algeria at any time in history or prehistory. Now we have this painting, he is identified as being from Atlantis. Atlantis theorists have never suggested the possibility that some or all of the Atlanteans were Neanderthals."

"Plato did not suggest that they were Neanderthals."

"Plato would not necessarily consider their facial features or the shape of their heads any more significant than their skin color. He would have recognized Neanderthals, if he ever met any, as a foreign but nevertheless human race. There is this most interesting practice of skull deformation in many Stone Age cultures around the world: Chehalis Indians of Washington and Oregon, Mayans, ancient Egyptians, and others."

"The practice of head binding!"

"Not done anymore, child abuse. An infant's skull is very flexible. The brain grows rapidly during the first few months. The skull plates are separated and also grow fast, eventually catch up with the brain to fuse together to form the braincase. With wooden boards tied to press the skull, it grows into a radically different shape, like with King Tutankhamon. The usual practice caused the forehead to slope back,"

"Resulting in a shape that is superficially like the Neanderthal! Ancient people for some reason imitating the look of Neanderthals! Thousands of years after Neanderthals have disappeared."

March 17. The St. Patrick's Day parade on Constitution Avenue. The three women from Creation waved at the crowd from a float shaped like a 1930's *Buck Rogers* spaceship. The Secret Service scanned the crowds watching the parade. The float carrying the women reached the Ellipse. The South Portico of the White House can be seen in the distance. The Creation women smiled and waved to the crowd. A Secret Service agent suddenly shouted, "Gun!" A tall dark haired woman pointed her .38 Special at Lucinda and fired. Before she could get off a second shot, the Secret Service was on top of her and pulling the gun out of her hand.

"For what it is worth," she said to the agents pinning her to the ground in the center of the commotion, "I'm not with the Avengers of Yahweh."

Secret Service agents leaped to cover the bodies of Helga and Andemona. But blood spurted from a wound an inch below Lucinda's left breast.

Chapter Sixteen

"Where are they taking her?"

"That's what I'm trying to find out! The Navy hospital's half mile down Constitution Avenue from the Ellipse."

"Your Navy's still angry with us for dropping the Shuttle past Bangor."

"If they take Lucinda to the Navy hospital and we lose her, that's what people will be saying. They could be going to George Washington University Hospital. If I remember correctly, that's where they took Reagan when he was shot."

"Are they good?"

"Reagan lived. If George Washington's where they take the President for bullet wounds, you bet they're the best! The news reports that the ambulance is going up Virginia Avenue, they're going to George Washington."

The spaceship raced across the Atlantic Ocean. "We've got to get over Washington, D.C. Where on the coast is it?" Pidonita was anxious, using maps and my help to find Earth cities.

"You know what Chesapeake Bay looks like!"

"Okay, Okay, I see. Which one's the Potomac?"

"Fourth big estuary up from the bottom. That big fat one, there." I pointed to the Potomac on the map.

Pidonita looked at the map and out the window. "The one that's six *kepfats* wide?"

"Yeah. That's the Potomac. Follow it upstream, where it narrows down to a river is where you find Washington, D.C. You see the road net converging on it, and it's surrounded by a big circular freeway."

"The Beltway. Okay, got it. We'll park a *hekt* of *kepfats* above the District of Columbia. Hope that doesn't make your military nervous."

"144 times 1.6. Two hundred, oh, 230 miles. I don't think so, but there's just been an assassination attempt. I just thought of something. Is Neanderthal blood compatible with Cro-Magnon blood?"

"I don't know. Sometimes a donor's blood isn't compatible with a receiver's blood. Blood is typed by the presence or absence of chemical compounds. These compounds cause it to gum up if they're mixed wrong. I think, uh, Lchnsda's blood type is A negative, unless it is B negative."

"You don't know if it's A or B?"

"We call 'em different things in Atlantean. But Askelion and Meddi have been studying your televised medical shows."

I called up Medical on the intercom. "Doctor Lamakian? Doctor Chumkun?"

"This is Doctor Meddi Chumkun. We should get down to the ground to help Lchnsda."

"This is Washington, D.C. we're talking about. We need clearance to get the Shuttle down without being blown up by an F-15. They're watching us now, the Navy's still smarting over you slipping that baby past 'em to the Hood Canal. But what we're concerned about is blood compatibility."

"Lchnsda is A negative. Andemona should be donating a, what you call a pint, right now, she is A negative."

"I believe a pint is equivalent to 3 *glups*."

"Yes, Andemona can give 6 *glups* in an emergency, that would be two pints. She'll be woozy for a while but she'll survive it. There are five crew members on this ship who are A negative, another twelve and four who are O negative. That should get us twelve and nine units of four *glups* each. Normally we only take three *glups*, but this time we can take four."

"Yeah, you do that. Do you have any blood in storage?"

"No. We're on a spaceship. Things can happen in storage. We believe the safest storage for blood is in the body. So in an emergency we are set up to take blood for immediate use. We have four *glup* bags for storing the blood. We can take these on the Shuttle. We don't know if the racial difference is a problem with blood compatibility."

"Fortunately, it's not been a problem on Earth. A negative blood from a black person is compatible with A negative blood of a white person. And type O's are universal donors, of course. But with pointy chins and high foreheads, we're all Cro-Magnons. A and O blood that is Rh negative from Cro-Magnon donors should be compatible with Lucinda. But we don't know that and if we're wrong,"

"I understand. We'll get all of the girls with compatible blood in here."

The ship's astronomer, Sabar Duradich, was also in the Pilothouse. She, Nesla Teslakian, and others pilot the ship when Pidonita does not. "I'm the same blood type as Lchnsda, I'm going to Medical now."

The ambulance pulled into the George Washington University Hospital Emergency Entrance. The rear doors flew open. Emergency paramedics carried the gurney out the doors. They extended the wheel carriage below the gurney and raced into the hospital entrance. Lucinda was pale, unconscious, and in shock. She was covered by a heavy blanket and strapped down. Helga, Andemona, and Secret Service bodyguards ran in with them.

Dr. William Gladstone had already suited up and washed his hands to perform surgery. He pulled on the rubber gloves and greeted the paramedics and gurney in the hallway outside the emergency operating room. The paramedics immediately shouted the patient's current status. "Patient five foot ten 185 pound Neanderthal female, little body fat, well muscled. B.P. 70 over 40, heartbeat 103, core temp 100.6 and rising. Patient in shock. Entrance wound one and half inches below left breast. No exit wound. She has lost blood."

"Get her into O.R. and prep her for surgery. Take a blood sample and type it." Dr. Gladstone turned to the two Neanderthal women who accompanied Lucinda into the hospital. "I cannot allow you into the O.R., of course. Can either of you give blood for her?"

"I'm the same blood type as Lchnsda." said Andemona. "I believe you call it A negative in your language. I can give blood."

"Good. Nurse Ramirez, take a pint from her stat. And you,"

"I'm B positive." said Helga. "I don't think my blood's compatible."

"Take a sample anyway, we can test it for compatibility. Can we use Cro-Magnon blood for her?"

"I don't know. There are five other women on the *Neanderthal Return* with A negative blood. A bunch more with type O negative. Each can give three or four *glups* depending on body weight. Since this is an emergency, all will give four *glups*. That is about twenty of your fluid ounces, a pint and a quarter. Five such units is six and a quarter pints of A negative. And we'll have many pints of O negative."

"Okay. We have A negative blood in storage, but it's Cro-Magnon. We need that Neanderthal blood. We don't want to risk racial incompatibility. Can your Shuttle land on our helicopter pad?"

"It might be too heavy for that. Can they block off the street out front?"

"The street out front. If we can get the police to cooperate."

"One of our ship's doctors will be on that Shuttle."

"They're not licensed to practice medicine in the District of Columbia. Are they qualified?"

"They're both educated at Atlaston Hospital, none better on the entire Planet Creation. They have, uh, what you'd call a medical license for Atlantis, and by agreement, that license is valid in all of the nations of Creation. They're responsible for the medical care of all crew members of the *Neanderthal Return*. Furthermore, they're the foremost experts on Neanderthal physiology in this Solar System."

"How's their English?"

Sigh. "Neil's been teaching English language classes for the crew. Askelion and Meddi have been attending. But I don't know if they're fluent, particularly in medical terminology. You may need me to translate."

"Okay. Stand by, Helga. How's Andemona doing? We need that pint stat!"

Andemona flexed her fingers open and closed to pump blood into the bag. Nurse Ramirez coached, "Almost done here. Just a few more ounces, another minute. You're doing great, Andemona."

"Thank you." responded Andemona. A sample of her blood had already been taken to the lab to test for compatibility.

"Bring that blood into O.R. as soon as possible!" shouted Dr. Gladstone. "Get Air Traffic Control to clear their Shuttle! We need Neanderthal blood stat! How's the patient?"

"B.P. stable! 85 over 65! Heartbeat 65! Got it calmed down. Bringing her out of shock. Core temp down to 100.2, getting blood circulation to the extremities."

"Anesthesia?"

"She's knocked out. Local applied to wound. Can't leave that bullet in there. But we need blood if we're going to operate."

"Lab report!"

"Donor is compatible with patient, both A negative!"

"A negative in storage?"

"Ten units available, all Cro-Magnon."

"Keep it on standby. Run test for agglutination. We'll use it if no choice."

"Donor pint is now available!"

"Good! Set it up. Let's get to work."

Andemona sat up sipping from a small cup of apple juice. "Nurse Ramirez. You speak Spanish?"

"*Si.*"

Andemona switched to Spanish. "This is an emergency. I can give a second pint right now."

"We are supposed to wait at least a week before taking another unit from the same person."

"But Lucy needs my blood NOW."

"I know. Without it, we will find out whether there is incompatibility between Cro-Magnon and Neanderthal blood." Sigh. "Finish that apple juice. Drink another cup and I will set you up for another pint. But we will not chance a third one."

Helga came over. "How are you doing Andy girl?" she asked in Atlantean.

"I am fine. How's Lchnsda?" They spoke in Atlantean for privacy.

"Don't know. She is on the operating table and they are digging the bullet out now."

Sigh. "That Mexican kid was willing to have his heart cut out to prevent the end of the Fifth Sun. Here I sit on this table ready to allow myself to be drained of blood to save Lchnsda. And that woman who shot Lchnsda, she probably thinks we are somehow a threat to human existence. Did we do the right thing? Most of these Earth people are good people. They love us. They are glad to know our Race lives. The way they cheered at us when we were on the float in the parade. Lchnsda blowing kisses at them, they loved that. Just a few *linits* ago. But some of these Earth humans are not so happy that we live. We could have just floated back to Creation with Neil and his sperm and started having babies, baby boys. Did we do the right thing?"

"It has to be the right thing. We knew about Earth. They thought they were all alone, broadcasting their radio and television. With our spaceship, we could explore all of the stars near here, without the Cro-Magnons knowing. Neil was right. Earth has the right to know about our existence. As far as solving our problem of reproduction, we would have had to compel Neil's cooperation. That is rape, any way you look at it. We did the right thing. Which is not always easy."

"I know. Can we say a prayer for Lchnsda?"

"Sure." They clasped their hands together. "Great Holy Spirit, we beseech thee in our hour of need. Our dear friend Lchnsda Renuxler is on the edge of crossing over to you. We love her dearly and will miss her if she goes. We humbly thank you very much for the time that we have already had with her. She is a beautiful, wonderful person. We respectfully request that she be returned to us and that her injuries heal. Grant these physicians your strength, your wisdom, and your compassion. Grant Lchnsda your full support to her will to live. We thank you for our lives and for Lchnsda's life, and we thank you for these compassionate people of Earth who care for us in our hour of need. Thank you for the power and the glory of your love."

They kissed each other on the lips and then gently let go of each other's hands. "Nurse Ramirez," began Andemona in Spanish, "I am now ready to give the second pint."

"Okay, so we're clear for the Shuttle to come down into Washington, D.C.?"

"To where George Washington University Hospital is. It's straight up from the Lincoln Memorial. That's 23rd Street. If you can put it down on the north side of the Memorial, we can have a van waiting to race you up to the hospital. Police will block off the side streets and clear the parade crowd away from there. Can you do that?"

"I'll check. Pido, can your Shuttle pilot find her way once she gets down close to D.C.?"

"I don't know. She's giving blood now. Doctor will give her a booster shot to keep her alert after giving blood." She called over to Medical. "We need to talk to Metrola Mornuxler."

"She is still on the table, but she can talk."

"This is Metrola."

"How do you feel for piloting the Shuttle?"

"Have the Americans given us clearance?"

"You are cleared to land on the north side of the Lincoln Memorial."

"Then I'm good to go! But to find my way, Neil'll have to ride down with me."

"I'm native to Washington STATE. I've never been to Washington, D.C."

"But you're an American. Lincoln Memorial, Washington Monument, the Reflecting Pool, these are places you've been hearing about all your life! If you don't help me I might land in Virginia!"

"Okay! Okay! I'll ride down with you. Lucinda's life's on the line. Okay, Air Traffic Control. We'll be coming down as soon as we're ready!"

"We'll stand by and help guide you. Good luck Neil Peace and Metrola Mornuxler!"

I ran the halls to Medical. I was greeted by Metrola, tape and gauze still on her arm. "Neil, come help us load the blood on to the Shuttle."

"Sure." I followed her into Medical. It was crowded, the donors were recovering. The Rh positives and the Type B's were over in the Shuttle Bay preparing the Shuttle for flight. Six were going to ride it down. The two physicians were loading the units of blood into a plastic box.

"I'm coming with you." declared Askelion Lamakian. "Meddi is staying. One of us needs to be here for the crew. This box has two compartments. In this compartment are the type A's. I labeled them with your Roman letter A, as you can see. In this other compartment are the type O's, which I have also labeled. The staff at George Washington can heal Lchnsda without me. But they'll be asking me a lot of questions. I'll be more valuable for the post-op recovery of the patient. I can reassure her with my presence. But this blood is what's vital. Lchnsda needs it. Andemona can give only two pints, and we don't want to take a chance with Cro-Magnon blood."

The blood was in plastic bags similar to the pint bags I've seen before. These were covered with Atlantean writing and were bigger, carrying four *glups*, not the 3.2 *glups* that is the U.S. pint. "Did Dr. Nguyen draw any blood from them when they were first in her care?"

"On my orders, they did not consent to any blood being drawn."

"So Dr. Nguyen was unable to determine whether your blood is compatible with our blood. Afraid she might determine how you've stopped the aging process?"

"That's not fair Neil! There's over an *enbeeyon* of you already! Without some kind of control over your reproduction, the Fountain of Youth would bring a disaster to your Planet that would exceed both your World Wars and Hitler's Holocaust! Starvation and slaughter would be the means of death if you no longer have old age! I'd love to talk about this some more but we haven't time!"

"All right! All right! I'm sorry! Let's get this over to the Shuttle before they use up Andemona's second pint!"

We hurried over to the Shuttle Bay and carried the blood into the Shuttle. Metrola was there in the pilot's seat. There were six other women there, wearing pressure suits with the helmets open. "We would get you, me, and Askelion into pressure suits but there's no time!"

"Great!" Sure, I'll ride without a pressure suit! No problem!

"Neil, sit right here next to me, strap down. Here's a map of Washington, D.C."

"Yeah. This is the Mall, the Capitol over here. This is the White House, the Ellipse, this is Constitution Avenue, they're still clearing it from the parade. Lots of crowds and chaos, with the shooting. This here is the Washington Monument. It's a giant obelisk, 550 feet tall; we don't want to come down on top of it. This is the Tidal Basin. Straight west of the Monument is the Reflecting Pool, points you right to the Lincoln Memorial. You see the Potomac River right behind it. The road going straight north of the Lincoln Memorial is 23rd Street, leads straight to the hospital Lucinda's at. This road going at a slant is Bacon Drive, runs past the Vietnam Memorial here. Where they want us to set down is in this little triangle bound by Bacon, Constitution, and 23rd."

"Okay. Don't want to land near the Vietnam Memorial. We might land halfway over the Wall, and topple over smashing all of that shiny granite!"

"Smash a few names. That would require some apologizing!" We both smiled at that.

"Give me a kiss for good luck, please." We made a quick kiss on the lips.

"Shuttle door is closed and secured, Metrola." came a voice in Atlantean.

Metrola called on her microphone to Pidonita. "Shuttle is secured. Let's run through the checklist." Following that, Metrola listed each item on the Shuttle in Atlantean, followed by someone saying the word "*chm*" for complete. After the checklist, "Everyone strapped down?"

After affirmative responses, Askelion declared, "Blood is secured."

"Shuttle is ready for launch." Metrola called into her headset. I had one on too, adjusting it for my funny shaped head.

"Good." declared Pidonita. "Shuttle Bay is clear of personnel." Video cameras scanned the

Shuttle Bay to make sure. "Pumping air out of the Shuttle Bay." We watched the gauges. Twelve and six *dollons* per square *tig-it*. Now just twelve. Eleven, ten, nine, soon pressure was Zero. "Shuttle Bay is now in vacuum. Shuttle Bay doors opening now." Looking through the Shuttle's window, we watched the doors open into space. Below the black sky we saw the blue white curve of Earth. "Shuttle launch is good."

They do not say "go". Metrola flipped open a cover exposing the button underneath. She pressed it and a mechanism attached to the mother ship gently pushed us down some guide rails out the opening. We exited the *Neanderthal Return* at a relative speed of about 3 *potes* per *prelate*, or 4 feet per second. I felt like I was tossed out of an airplane without a parachute. I was strapped in good but my stomach was not. My heart was pounding! Metrola operated some controls and the *Neanderthal Return* was a small toy in the distance.

We tilted over and I was looking straight down at Earth. We started falling straight down! "Ohhhh! This is worth at least an E ticket!"

"What?" asked Metrola.

"Never mind."

"Fun, isn't it?"

"Most fun you can have with your pants on! Okay, there are some clouds over Maryland and Delaware, but northern Virginia and the District are clear. Beautiful weather for St. Paddy's Day."

Suddenly, the Air Traffic Control for the District of Columbia called in. "This is District of Columbia Air Traffic Control calling the *Neanderthal Return* Shuttle."

"Okay, Neil. This is where you start earning your pay."

"Pay! I've been meaning to talk to you about that!"

"Really. Prostitution services should be worth one hundred dollars per trick!"

"Which is exactly the price of the sperm sample you obtain thereby. Funny how it cancels out!" We both laughed at that. These Creation girls can be earthy! Not like Earth girls who get all offended by a dirty joke.

"We heard that!" exclaimed ATC. "Metrola Mornuxler, we compliment you on your English."

"Uh, thanks." she responded sheepishly. "I thought this microphone was turned off. Sorry."

"You are dropping down fast, you're gonna burn up like a meteor and dig a crater if you don't slow down. We don't need a second Tidal Basin."

"We'll slow down when we start feeling atmospheric friction." assured Metrola.

I tried to give them some status of the ship. "Our current altitude is tenty five *kepfats*."

"What?"

"That is the Creation numeral ten followed by five. A hundred and twenty five *kepfats*. Now a hundred and twenty four."

"We are more accustomed to Base Ten numbers and units like feet and miles."

"You're lucky I'm not using Greek stadia considering these girls call their nation Atlantis."

"I'm sorry." apologized Metrola. "I'll just push this button there. Now Neil, your console should be giving you digital readouts in Earth numbers and miles."

"Okay, altitude is now one eight seven miles." I said.

"I get one six zero nautical miles." claimed ATC.

"What's a nautical mile?" asked Metrola. "I thought your miles are five two eight zero feet."

"They are." I said. "A nautical mile is longer, no time to explain. Look, DCATC, I can use STATUTE miles and feet, that okay?"

"That's fine."

"Uh, Metrola, you did factor in the .986 ratio between feet and *potes*?"

"Of course I did. I could do it in meters."

"Not necessary. Aviation uses altitudes in feet the world over."

"I thought the Metric System is the international system."

"It is, but some things are in feet and inches the world over. How do I switch from miles to feet?"

"Push this button."

"Okay. I now report altitude at eight eight zero thousand feet. Still falling fast!" The Beltway was noticeably getting larger. I could see the Potomac getting wider.

"We suggest that you slow down when you get to 400,000 feet, or you're going to be a very bright fireball coming right at us!"

"Don't worry." assured Metrola. "We've done this before. Last summer come to think of it. We have a heat shield, like your Space Shuttle tiles, and parachutes in case of malfunction. But our ship's in excellent condition."

We fell and fell. I watched the numbers scroll on the console. "Six four zero thousand feet." I called out the altitude with each ten thousand feet. Soon, "Four hundred thousand feet."

"Okay, now I'll start slowing us down." assured Metrola. Thermocouple gauges recorded the skin temperature of the Shuttle hull. In Creation numerals and their temperature scale. 12 *deems* is the triple point of water, a little above 32 degrees Fahrenheit or Zero Celsius. 144 *deems* is the normal body temperature of a human being. 370 *deems* is about the boiling point of water at our standard atmosphere.

Metrola did not let the hull temperature get above 6 *hekt deems*, about 458 Fahrenheit. Our supersonic fighters get hotter than that but Metrola has no need to get that hot. She slowed down as necessary to keep the hull temperature below 458 F.

After about two minutes, "Altitude is now 30,000 feet." I called out. Metrola had slowed us down to about 600 miles per hour. We felt heavy against our straps, more than one gravity as we slow down. Free fall is weightlessness, an acceleration of 32 feet per second squared in Earth's gravity. We feel one gee when dropping at a steady speed, no acceleration. Metrola decelerated so we can make a nice soft landing, adding to the one gee. "Okay Metrola, we can now see the Mall right below us, the Tidal Basin, and the Potomac River. The Lincoln Memorial is right by the River."

"Yes I see. I'm driving toward the spot north of the Lincoln Memorial."

"N.R. Shuttle," called ATC. "You are right on course. Our compasses are reacting to your magnetic field. Keep slowing down."

We got closer. The Washington Monument drifted off to the side. We could see the parade crowd being held back by the police. They heard that the alien Shuttle was going to land. Everyone would want to see that. The roof of the Lincoln Memorial grew larger. "We're now at 1000 feet. We're easing down slowly. Metrola, you see where the grass is cleared for us, is that big enough?"

"It should be. Washington Air Traffic Control, we are preparing to land."

"You are looking good. The truck is standing by."

"Yes, we see it now. We also see the police have blocked off 23rd all the way to George Washington."

"23rd is one way the wrong way for part of the distance. You'll be routed around that to the Emergency Entrance, you can take the blood in that way."

Metrola brought us into the triangle between Constitution, Bacon, and 23rd. 40 feet above the ground she righted the ship and guided us using a video screen wired to a camera mounted on the bottom. She extended the landing gear, three wheeled assemblies that look like they were each taken off of a Cessna.

"Looking good N.R. Shuttle. 20 feet, 10 feet, 5 feet, touchdown!" We set down very gently.

We immediately unstrapped ourselves from the seats. Two ladies opened the Shuttle door and extended the ramp to the ground. Askelion unstrapped the plastic box containing the blood. "Neil, grab this other end, please!" she yelled to me.

"Got it!" We carried it out into the late St. Patrick's afternoon.

A paramedic ran to us. "Truck's over this way!" We followed him to the open rear doors of the van, its engine running. Motorcycle police deployed fore and aft of the van. A dozen Army troops in full battle dress and carrying loaded M-16 rifles deployed around the Shuttle while letting us through.

We hopped on board the van, the paramedic followed us and closed the rear doors. "You secure back there?" asked the driver.

"Yes we're in." I answered. The driver immediately shifted into gear and accelerated. The police motorcycles flew ahead while the van's driver floorboarded it. "How's the blood?"

Askelion opened the box and inspected the plastic bags carrying the precious fluid. "Blood is intact."

The driver turned to his radio. "Van en route to G.W. Emergency. Inform E.R. Neanderthal blood is intact and on the way!"

"Okay, I see the bullet. Thank God it's not a hollow point. I hate hollow points, they break up and scatter all over the insides. Make me earn my pay while the patient passes away. One piece, just the way I like it. Got it! Tray." Dr. Gladstone deposited the missile in the tray alongside the bone chip from where it grazed the rib. "She still needs more blood, still showing signs of blood shortage."

A nurse ran into the viewing area above O.R. She called in over the intercom. "The Shuttle from the spacecraft has landed by the Lincoln Memorial. Many units of Neanderthal blood are in the van on the way. Should be here in a minute. One of their doctors is coming, Askelion Lamakian."

"Good. That second pint's about gone. No more coming from Andemona. Okay ladies and gentlemen, let's get her closed up."

Chmlee stood in the distance. He saw her, and smiled. "Lchnsda!" he yelled. They ran to each other, husband and wife, embraced and kissed, a deep passionate kiss.

"I love you! I missed you. Chmlee, you look beautiful! You smell good!"

"You're not so bad yourself, lover girl!"

"Let's make love."

"Sure."

They did. In the warm afterglow Lchnsda noticed that there was no pain, only pleasure. Every *tig-it* of her body felt so wonderfully healthy and strong. As did every *tig-it* of her dear Chmlee Renuxler. "I do not want to ever leave you again. I want this to last forever."

"And perhaps someday, it will."

"What do you mean?"

"You are not dead."

The shock of reality hit. Cold. "I am not dead. But you?"

"The Virus killed me. You cremated me. The other women had to hold you with all of their might to keep you from throwing yourself on the funeral pyre. But this bullet wound, you will survive it, it will heal up. You are going back. You have to go back."

"Life. I was in this parade. On Earth. The Planet Lamoan Reducker found out about.

142

Where our ancestors were taken from. The people there today, their heads are shaped differently, they have less muscle. But they own Earth, while those of our Race died out sometime after we were Transplanted. No one knows why. Now it is coming back." She told him about the trip to the Earth Solar System and what had happened so far. She told him about meeting children.

"Children?"

"Yes, children! Forgot what is was like to have children around! For all the problems Earth has, we envy them for their children and their men. What we have done on Creation we are very proud of. The spaceship and the endless youth by our medical technology. But existence on Creation is joyless compared to life on Earth."

"Creation needs children. Creation needs men. No doubt about it."

"Today is St. Patrick's Day, a national holiday in Ireland that is celebrated wherever there are people of Irish descent. I blew kisses to the people along the parade route, Constitution Avenue. Many children with their parents. All happy. We started at the Capitol Building and headed west toward the Potomac River. Fancy old buildings on both sides of us. We were passing right between the White House and a huge obelisk they call the Washington Monument. I heard a loud noise. I felt a thump in my chest, just below my breast. There was commotion, I fell down, then I started to hurt. My chest was on fire. Then everything went black and here I am."

"You have to go back. You will go back. There is much you need to do. Our Race needs you to do it. And also, they may not know it, the Other Race that now lives on Earth needs you too. Everyone from your spaceship are praying for you. So are *beeyons* of people of Earth. You need to live and you need to have children."

"Children. You don't mind if I make love with a Cro-Magnon man? Even marry him?"

"Of course I'll mind. You are my wife and I love you very much. But you have a LIFE! You have a destiny. You need to have children. You need to carry them in your womb. Listen! If none of the Neanderthal women still alive have children, then we cannot be reincarnated. You cheat death with a youth serum, but accident, violence, and disease can still happen to you. You could have died today. The bullet missed your heart, the Earth physicians will save you. Eventually, every Neanderthal woman alive today will die. Then we who are now in the care of the Great Holy Spirit will fade away. Nothing even He can do to prevent this. So my love, go back. Work with the Earth people to solve our problem of reproduction, and raise and love the children that you are destined to have."

Lucinda did not remember her dream.

Chapter Seventeen

As we raced off to the hospital, the dozen Army troops deployed around the alien Shuttle as a precaution. The commanding officer addressed the two women standing in the door of the Shuttle. "I'm Second Lieutenant Pete MacGregor, United States Army. May I speak with your commanding officer?"

The two women looked at him quizzically. "We don't have a 'commanding officer'. Captain Trviea Harsradich was such a leader, but she's up in the *Neanderthal Return*. She's not with us in this Shuttle."

"I compliment you on your English. Mr. Peace has taught you well. Then if nobody is in command of this mission, could I speak to you and your pilot?"

"Thank you for your kind words about us speaking your language. But understand, sometimes we designate someone in charge for missions away from our ship. It's just that this is an emergency and we didn't have time to get so organized. We are, as you say, making this up as we go along. But this whole thing is like that. I mean, there's just no procedure written down to follow when it comes to meeting an entire human species on an entire Planet for the first time. So we are, what is the word for it, uh, improvising, yes that's it, we are improvising it."

The young officer laughed. "You're doing fine. I want to assure you that we're deploying around your ship in full battle gear as a precaution. We mean you no harm."

"We know that. If we thought you meant us harm," she pointed to one of the other heads looking out at the Army officer, "Metrola would have lifted off immediately. As it is, if you are not shooting us, then we're Okay."

"We just have to be careful. For some reason it's open season on Neanderthal women among our nut cases."

"She has been arrested?" Metrola asked. "The one who shot Lchnsda?"

"Immediately."

"Well then, I guess we're as safe as we ever are. Since Lchnsda wasn't killed outright, she should be all right. Your physicians are good at digging out bullets. Our physician, Askelion, is good with the recovery."

"Our prayers are with her. We Americans admire astronauts. You are astronauts. I love the way you set this Shuttle down so softly. Can you take off right away?"

"Yes, we can take off right away. But that's not necessary. Can we step out of our ship? We've been cooped up in a spacecraft for over a year and a half!"

"Well, uh, I don't know. I understand the Agreement provides diplomatic immunity to the entire crew of the *Neanderthal Return*. You and your Shuttle were cleared for landing. Uh, our orders are to protect you, not keep you prisoner, but if you step out on to the grass,"

"This hull is not bullet proof. Only a twelfth of a *tig-it*, our inch, thick sheet of a high strength aluminum alloy. If someone shoots at us, well, so be it. But please, understand, we NEED to breathe fresh air and to walk on a planet surface, to put our feet on solid ground." They walked out of the Shuttle, stepping tentatively on to the grass. Seven women, six of them in pressure suits without the helmets. "What a beautiful white temple. May we go over to look at it? We will be respectful. We will not dishonor President Lincoln."

The Second Lieutenant ordered his men to keep up with the women. He called into his radio. "The landing party is headed over to the Lincoln Memorial! What are my orders?"

"You're like the Secret Service!" ordered the voice on the radio. "You stay with them! Let 'em explore the Mall and the monuments. Christ, Pete! This is the first shore leave they've had since they've left Creation. They're not prisoners, they are guests. Any of them armed?"

"I don't think so, they haven't shown any weapons."

Some of the women yelled at each other in Atlantean. Two of them made sounds that expressed disappointment in any language. They jogged back to the Shuttle to avoid leaving it unwomanned. At MacGregor's orders, several soldiers protected them and their Shuttle. The rest followed the other five women to the Lincoln Memorial. Metrola stood before the huge statue of Abraham Lincoln. "So this is President Lincoln." she said. "Nice carving work."

"He was a great man. It is what he believed in and what he accomplished that we honor. He fought and died for the ideal that no man, and no woman, shall bow before another, shall be slave to another, that we are all equal in the eyes of God and in the eyes of the law."

"This is like the Parthenon in Athens. Inside was a giant statue of Athena. Maybe she wasn't a goddess. Not originally. Maybe it was her wisdom, they called her the goddess of wisdom, that was honored. The Greeks came to think of her as a goddess, they forgot about Athena the woman."

"How do you know about Athena?"

"I'm just speculating. But here is Abraham Lincoln, honored the way gods used to be honored."

"We remember that he was the man who ended slavery and brought the nation back together."

"Yes, that is worth remembering and honoring. There are legends on Creation of a woman who was very wise. She developed mathematics, laws, the idea of human rights, the sort of thing President Lincoln believed in. That sounds a lot like the Greek goddess Athena."

"So there was a Neanderthal Athena?"

"Yes. Her name was Arleesia. She is a legend, we do not know if she ever lived or if she's just a story. Our ancestors came from Europe. But it was a completely different Europe then. The Face Mountain aliens took us before we started to develop past the hunter-gatherer way of life. You Cro-Magnons thought you were superior to us, because you are still here, and we were not. But at the time of the Face Mountain aliens, your Race was no more advanced than ours. They selected us for seeding Planet Creation because we had more muscle and were thriving in adverse conditions. So we populated Creation and developed our civilizations and technologies there."

"But there were still Neanderthals living on Earth after the Face Mountain aliens. What happened to them?"

"We don't know. Your scientists say that the Ice Age got real bad after that. It is like your Inuit, or Eskimos. They live and thrive in a tundra landscape. But there are not very many of them. When our European homeland became more like Greenland, our population probably dropped to match the landscape. But we had the example of technology. Both Cro-Magnons and Neanderthals had seen spaceships and gizmos, electrical stuff, surveying instruments. That sort of thing. This must've had an impact upon culture, language, religion. Gods and goddesses who come from the sky! Who hand down laws. Notice how so many of your cultures around Earth look to the sky for religion, for information, for the stars! You take a tribe of hunter-gatherers. Some go down to the sea to dig clams, to catch fish, even to hunt whales and seals for meat, which is hunter-gathering. This is done long before people figured out how to plant and harvest crops. Both farmers and fishermen require a little science, a little technology. The farmers need to know the seasons, the solstices and equinoxes. The fishermen need to navigate. Thus the beginnings of astronomy, the First Science. Just to study the stars requires the measurement of

146

angles and the keeping of time. Which requires math. Which requires numbers. If records of astronomical movements are needed, then writing is needed. Units of measure are needed. All this just to map the sky for the purpose of navigation, of keeping track of where you are, and of the seasons."

"And our ancestors, your ancestors, needed all of this long before civilizations such as the Egyptians and the Sumerians."

"Which might explain why your 360 degree circle and your numbers based on powers of ten do not have a point of origin. Ships used them, ships took them everywhere. Plato described Atlantis as being a maritime civilization 9,000 years before Solon's lifetime. He also mentioned the great continent beyond Atlantis that surrounds what can truly be called the ocean. How did he know about America if it wasn't discovered until 1492?"

"People crossed the ocean long before Columbus, long before Leif Erikson. The Indians were here, they got here somehow. And they, at least the Mayans and the Aztecs, had astronomy, math, and engineering. Well, I'm just a soldier, I don't know about all of this cosmic ancient stuff. All's I know is that I'm guarding some beautiful exotic women from a faraway place. Is there anything I can do for you ladies?"

The five woman visiting the Lincoln Memorial came around. "Could you get us food?"

"Food?"

"We're not hungry or starving or anything like that. We have plenty to eat on our ship. Fresh vegetables, fruits, and grains, we have a Garden Room for that. We have rabbits and a small type of goat for meat. We sometimes have trouble maintaining calcium in our bones. Periods of low gravity in spaceflight. Helga and Lchnsda described some of the wonderful foods here on Earth, beef, pork! Dairy products!"

"Pizza!" yelled one of the others. "Could you order us a pizza! I understand that we have a bank account in our name to receive money we get from publishers selling Helga's and Lchnsda's lessons in Creation history and politics and Atlantean language. So we can pay for it!"

"Yeah PIZZA! With all the fixings! Lots of cheese!"

"All right!" MacGregor laughed. "Don't worry about paying for it." He turned on his radio. "This is MacGregor. Can we get a couple of pizzas here? Extra cheese with all the toppings? These Creation girls are hungry for pizza. They're tired of ship food!"

"Okay, this is a type A negative. Fine, set it up. Good. Lucy's now getting a third unit of Neanderthal blood. Look at this strange alphabet! It's not too much bigger than a pint."

"So Askelion, is there anything about Neanderthal physiology that I need to know right now?"

Helga watched through the glass. She translated Dr. Gladstone's question into Atlantean for Askelion. Askelion was in the O.R. wearing a surgical gown with rubber gloves and shoe covers. "Your emergency trauma procedures and surgery are fine. The bleeding has been stopped and the bullet removed, that is good. With the wound clean and closed up her tissues shall now heal. That process will take a while. Several more units of blood should be enough, keep adding blood until she shows signs of a full tank. Thank you, Doctor. If you don't mind, I need to go check on Andemona. If we don't need all of these units, we can put one into Andemona. She's two pints down."

I was in the blood donor room sitting with Andemona. "Keep drinking that juice, *muchacha muy hermosa*."

"*Si*. I would, but I have to lift my head to do it. Oh man, do I feel groggy! Next time, I'll give ONE pint. That's it, one pint. Three *glups*, four *glups*, but not six *glups*! Man I'm feeling ambitious. NOT!"

I laughed. "You talk too much. Now shut up and drink your apple juice." I smiled when I said that.

"Yes daddy. If I don't will you spank me?"

"Only if you buy me dinner and take me to a movie, and then we'll see."

She looked at me askance and smiled sardonically. She downed the rest of the apple juice. I took the empty cup from her. I looked for something other than apple juice to avoid monotony. Andemona laid back, her eyes closed. "You awake? Here take this. Some pineapple, some kiwi, some other such juices, you'll like it. Here, have a cookie."

"Thank you."

Askelion arrived with her bag. A doctor's little bag. Brown, not black, she pulled out a stethoscope. After checking heartbeat, blood pressure, body temperature, all in Atlantean language, numbers, and units of measure, she pronounced Andemona healthy. "Would you like a four *glup* unit of blood put back into you?" she asked her in Atlantean.

"Yes!" was her emphatic answer.

"When we know for sure that there is a surplus unit of blood, we'll get you some. Meanwhile, you are doing fine. That is a brave thing, giving a second pint for Lchnsda."

"How is Lchnsda?" We both wanted to know.

"The hospital is still listing her under their designation 'critical'. But the bullet is removed, bleeding is mostly stopped, the wound is sewn shut. Her left lung will not be able to pull in as much air for at least a few months, she'll be sore. But the prognosis is very good!"

We all shouted in relief. The physician and I gave each other a hug and a kiss. We did the same with Andemona. Helga came in. We haven't seen each other since she went over to the Shuttle *Atlantis*. She rushed over with glee and gave me a bone crushing bear hug. After a kiss she said "They're going to wheel her out of O.R. and put her in a regular patient room. Here, I brought a unit of Neanderthal Type A negative, excellent year, exquisite bouquet, fruity, can go with red meat or with fowl, just because I want Andemona to have it! Gotta liven her up a little!"

They set up the unit and drained four *glups* of the juice into her. She felt a lot better.

"You are not going to believe this." announced Special Agent Bernie Walker of the FBI. They were at the FBI office at Buzzard's Point in Washington, D.C. They have already made phone calls to the seventh floor of the Federal Building in Seattle, Washington. Avengers of Yahweh. Damn! Who could blame the Creation girls if they went back to their spaceship and abandoned us Cro-Magnons to our fate? Mistakes are what humans make. That proves Neanderthals are human. They could admit they made a mistake and leave.

"What am I not going to believe?" asked Special Agent Raymond McCleary. The grizzled veteran has seen it all.

"This gal who shot Lucinda Renuxler during the parade,"

"Michelle Smith?"

"She's not Michelle Smith. Try Michael Schmidt of Port Orchard, Washington. She's a guy in drag."

"Great! The press will have a field day with this one!"

"You see, Michael's real serious about becoming Michelle. Hormone shots, the whole bit. Got his breasts up to a nice respectable size B."

"A she-male."

"A she-male. But her fingerprints match up with Michael Schmidt of Port Orchard. The State of Washington wants him for a whole bunch of felonies. Bank robbery. Pipe bombs. Malicious mischief. Armed robbery. Hate crimes against gays. And he's reputed to be a member of the Avengers of Yahweh."

148

"I thought the Avengers hated homosexuals, transvestites and transsexuals. Mockery of God's Creation and all that."

Bernie laughed. "That's what the Avengers say. They also have a problem with these Neanderthals who show up in a spacecraft. They don't like blacks. They don't like Jews. They don't like Arabs. They don't like Mexicans. They don't like us white guys who are traitors to our race."

"Equal opportunity hate-mongers. So what's the story with Michael, now Michelle?"

"How much time you got? Graduated from a high school north of Seattle. Grew up there most of his childhood. Parents divorced when he was ten, saw his father on weekends. Lived with father during high school. Played football in high school, cornerback. Got three interceptions, ran one back for a touchdown. Went out for track, 800 meters. Best time two minutes three seconds. Took his 3.6 grade point average to Simon Fraser University in British Columbia. Got a degree in anthropology. Lived in Chilliwack, B.C. for a few years after graduating from Simon Fraser. Drove trucks because he figured he could study lots of anthropology visiting small towns and big cities everywhere in Canada and the U.S. But nobody would publish his thesis. We're trying to get a copy. Then he moved from Canada to Port Orchard, Washington, where he got hooked up with the Avengers of Yahweh. That's when his life of crime is known to have started. Then he disappeared, nobody could find him."

"Seems he decided he'd rather be a girl than do time in a jail."

"Laughing at his male image shown on *America's Most Wanted*. Nobody would connect this cute brunette woman living in the District of Columbia with that bank robber on the lam from Port Orchard."

"But if he passed himself off as a woman to avoid prosecution, then why did he shoot Renuxler with a pistol from a crowd where he was sure to be arrested? I mean, going to jail as a she-male? They LOVE she-males in prison! Long soft hair, lipstick, perfume, the prettier the better!" He broke out into a belly laugh. "He'll get what he deserves! Oh boy, will he ever!" His laughing ended and he became serious. "But he would know that. So why did he not shoot from a distance with a sniper rifle? A varmint or deer shooter with scope and bipod?"

"Like the bolt action Lee Harvey Oswald used? He got caught."

"But not the guys who shot from behind the Grassy Knoll."

"Oh, don't give me that Grassy Knoll business! You and Mark Lane! Well, I think it may be the chance to become famous. Shoot the President? It's been done. But no Cro-Magnon has killed a Neanderthal for 30,000 years! I dunno. We'll just have to try to find out why Michelle blew her cover by shooting Lucinda."

The drugs wore off slowly, bit by bit. Lucinda drifted at the edge of awareness. She opened her eyes briefly. A vague and numb soreness defined her whole body. She couldn't move anything but her head. The fuzzy whiteness that she could see out of her clouded eyes resolved itself into a black Cro-Magnon woman in a bright white nurse's uniform checking some equipment. Lucinda went back to sleep. The nurse turned to her and asked, "Did you just open your eyes? Take it easy, hon, don't rush. Wake up when you're ready, but get your rest. Hmmm. Your EEG is showing some brain activity. You look like you want to wake up. I'll be back in a minute."

Nurse Taney went into the hallway and found four people with that look of exhaustion seen with those who keep hospital vigil. "Askelion Lamakian, you're a physician, right?"

"Yes."

"Please go in there and look after her, she's beginning to wake up."

"Sure." The physician went into Lucinda's room.

"How's she looking? Can we go in?"

"Well I don't know. I'll have to speak with Dr. Gladstone to okay that." She went over to the nurse's station. "Get Gladstone, please. Tell him Mrs. Renuxler's waking up."

In the room, Askelion went over to Lucinda. Looked closely into her face. Put a hand on her patient's chest and listened to the heartbeat. Perfectly normal for a sleeping woman recovering from a gunshot wound. Breathing a bit labored, half of her left lung out of action. "Looking good Lchnsda." she said in Atlantean. "Hang in there. You are going to be all right." She took Lucinda's right hand, not disturbing the wounded left side, held it. Kissed it. "Well girl, let's take a look at these cathode ray tubes hooked up to you. Hmmm. Metric units. Base Ten Earth numbers. Roman alphabet. English language, an esoteric dialect at that. I'm the best there is in the healing arts, but this is a culture shock! At least I know what brain activity looks like on an oscilloscope. You are waking up, my dear." She looked closely at Lucinda's head. "The scar you got on the Olympic Peninsula is healing up nicely, the stitches have been removed, I see." Then the physician turned to study the EEG some more.

Lucinda's eyes opened suddenly. "Askelion! Where are we?"

Askelion turned with a surprised start. "We are in the George Washington University Hospital in Washington, D.C., United States of America, Planet Earth."

"Oh. Was I shot?"

"You took a bullet from a type of handgun they call a thirty eight special. The bullet did not fragment, it stayed in one piece, grazed a rib and tore through your left lung."

"My breast?" Every woman wants her womanhood intact.

"It missed your breast. You are still a beautiful woman."

"How big was the bullet?"

"Thirty eight caliber. I think that means a diameter of thirty eight *hundredths* of their *tig-it*, inch." She used the English word "hundredth". The Atlantean equivalent is like 'eighty-fourth'. "Let's see, that translates to about forty seven *hekers* of their inch, oh forty eight *hekers* of our *tig-it*." *Heker* is Atlantean for the fraction one forty fourth. In her translation, forty means four dozen. She was saying 55/144 inch or 56/144 *tig-it*. .38 inch actually works out to 55.5/144 *tig-it* or 666/1728 *tig-it*.

"How you come down here?"

"They gave us clearance for the Shuttle. They did not want to take a chance with Cro-Magnon blood. They had plenty of A negative, but if there was a racial incompatibility, who knows what would happen? You received two pints or six *glups* from Andemona. We brought five four *glup* units of type A negative and a bunch of O negative in case you needed more. You received four of the units we brought down. One went into Andemona to bring her back from Woozy City. I put about three dozen *keecoilons* of Healing Factor into each unit of blood before coming down."

"That'll make me grow a third breast!"

"It won't do that." Askelion gently laughed. "But it'll sure speed the healing of your lung and rib. It will have its other effects. Be careful, people here might misunderstand a sexual response. Neil Peace came down with us. Metrola did not trust herself to land in the right place in D.C. Neil guided her and spoke with Air Traffic Control as we descended. He's out in the hallway, along with Helga and Andemona."

"Bring 'em in!"

A man in a white coat came into the room. "Ah! You're wide awake I see. I'm Dr. Gladstone. I'm the surgeon who pulled the bullet from your chest. It went in clean, not a lot of damage. We probably did more damage removing it, but you can't leave a bullet in if it's feasible to remove it. Prognosis is excellent! You're a lucky girl Lucinda! You're in the best trauma unit on Earth!"

"Thank you, Doctor Gladstone. For everything. Are my friends in the hallway?"

"Sure. Let them in." We went into the room. When we saw Lucinda's eyes open and the smile on her face, there was rejoicing all around. We all kissed her and thanked Dr. Gladstone for his successful surgery. Lucinda sat up, wincing with pain, but there was no stopping her.

Nurse Taney popped into the room. "Lucinda Renuxler, are you awake?"

"Yes I am!"

"You have enough visitors right now, you should be getting your rest. But there is a gentleman out here who wants to see you. His name is Henry Turnipseed."

"Henry's here? Show him in! Show him in!"

"I don't know about this,"

"Is he tall, dark, and handsome?"

"Well, yes he is."

"That's all we need to know! Along with Len Taylor, this man saved my life and Helga's life, over in the State of Washington. He's our friend for whom we thank the Great Holy Spirit. Let him in! I want to see him."

Dr. Gladstone spoke. "Well, Dr. Lamakian, you are the expert on Neanderthal physiology, health and psychology. Do you believe it would be helpful for Mrs. Renuxler's recovery that the esteemed Mr. Turnipseed be allowed in here?"

"The more friends that Mrs. Renuxler sees she has in this world, the less desire she will have to go on to the Next World. Since the will to live is a powerful component of the healing force, we need to do everything we can to nurture it. I vote that we allow Mr. Turnipseed in for a visit with our patient. Do you concur Dr. Gladstone?"

"I'm a trauma man. I'm on call 24 hours at a time for one purpose: to dig lead and steel out of human flesh. I'm very good at it, I hate to lose a patient. Sometimes the damage is too much and that is that. But in most of the other cases, it's the will to live that makes the difference. Some patients survived that I didn't believe would make it. And some give up and pass away with less damage than I've seen with Lucinda. Lucinda is awake, alert, in a little pain, right?"

"It's not that bad." Lucinda lied bravely.

"I believe the stress on her system imposed by the gentleman caller would be more than offset by the boost that it gives to her will to live. Let the gentleman in!"

"You may come in Mr. Turnipseed."

Henry Turnipseed came in bearing a dozen roses.

"You didn't tell us about the roses!"

"Get a vase! Put some water in it! Henry! You didn't have to! But I'm glad you did."

"I'm so relieved that you are going to be all right."

"I'm so glad that you are here." Lucinda reached her right hand up behind Henry's neck, pulled him down and gave him a kiss as we laughed.

"You sure are STRONG for a woman who's just been shot."

"If it don't kill me right away, it don't kill me! So you catch a plane here when you heard I was shot?"

"No, no, no. I was in town for an art show. Native American art. My sister's big in the art world. We were at the St. Patrick's parade, we saw you shot. After we watched your ship's Shuttle come down, we decided to buy you these roses."

"Well that was sure sweet of you! Nicest thing anyone's done for me since you cleaned the dirt out of the cut on my head. A lot less painful, too!"

"We'll all leave you two alone. Yeah we'll just go out into the hall here."

"Yeah, duty calls, I've got to make my rounds, busy doctor and all."

"Guys!" Lucinda protested. "There's no need."

"It's all right Lucy my friend. We know when there is something going on between a man and a woman."

"Oh come on! There's nothing going on. We're just friends."

"Just friends. Right. The way you two look at each other. Hey, I was with you when we were in Taylor's house, remember?" Helga teased her friend.

Lucinda switched to Atlantean. "This is nothing more than a little sexual desire on my part. Henry's cute, but I'm not ready for a relationship, meaningful or otherwise."

"Sexual desire is good." responded Helga in Atlantean, nodding her head. "Isn't that right, Andy?"

"Right. Nothing wrong with a little sexual desire. Does wonders for the will to live and the quality of life."

"I must agree," I said in Atlantean, "Lucinda ought to live a little, Henry's a good guy. You might even fall in love."

"Your Atlantean is getting good, Neil!" exclaimed Lucinda.

"What are you all saying?" asked an anxious Henry. He did not know Atlantean.

"We should switch back to English." I suggested in English. "It's not fair to poor Henry here. What we're talking about is that Lucinda just admitted to being sexually attracted to you."

"Whoa! Maybe I should beat a hasty retreat!"

"Ah come on, Henry!" I urged. "I'm your friend. You can trust me."

"Us Indians ought to learn to quit trusting you white men!"

"You're the one that came here with the dozen roses! You KNEW that such a gesture can have that affect on a woman. Don't trust me, trust yourself. The divorce was a terrible experience for me. I'll admit that. It wasn't a lot of fun for Angela either. But I'm the father of two wonderful children and I've drank from the silver cup. And for that I'm glad. I understand your fear, but cowardice is the one thing Indians are not known for."

Henry smiled. "But we are of such different races."

"What if Pocahontas said that?"

"We would still own the continent."

"Bad choice. Sorry. What if Fletcher Christian said that? They would have just taken the breadfruit plants to Jamaica and helped maintain the institution of slavery. Or Richard and Mildred Loving? Mixed race marriages might still be illegal. Besides, I don't believe the Neanderthals of Creation have come to take over Earth. She is a pretty lady and she's looking at you in the way I have never seen her look at me."

"So, Lucinda, why are you looking at me like that?"

"Some guys have it, some guys don't. Besides, Helga is Neil's girlfriend. I cannot compete with her, she is just too beautiful."

We all laughed at that. We left the room leaving Henry alone with Lucinda.

Ali Amoud drove with his Egyptian passenger into the archeological camp. They were greeted by Chuck Carter and camera crews from the American cable channel, Science and Humanities. "What's with the film crews?" asked Mustafa Khedr. Egyptologists don't like new finds being announced to the world before they have a chance to analyze them.

"Mustafa Khedr!" greeted Chuck Carter. "Welcome. Glad you can come! The S&H people? They're bringing us lots of money. Now we can get the best equipment! Besides, we had to get Mohammed Abbas his hundred grand somehow."

"You confirm the dating of the bow?"

"We sent samples of both wood and varnish to the lab in Switzerland. They can carbon date with milligram quantities nowadays. If the varnish checks out, than we'll know that the words 'Afenor' and 'Atlantis' in Egyptian hieroglyphics were carved into the bow during the Fourth Dynasty. What's your reading of the writing on the wall?"

"The Neanderthal is named Afenor. The story tells that he came from a place far away and that the name of that place is Atlantis."

"How's the Egyptology community taking it?"

"About what you would expect. They think this whole place is a hoax. You know how we are. Plato's Atlantis did not exist. Civilization started in Egypt when King Menes or Narmer united Upper and Lower Egypt. Nothing but New Stone Age villages before then. That is the doctrine. The Sphinx was carved during the Dynasty Period, not thousands of years before. Khufu built the Great Pyramid and so on."

"So what do they think of the spacecraft?"

"Neanderthals somehow got transplanted to another Planet. We'll concede that. They developed their civilizations and technology there. Just like we did. But no way was there any contact between Neanderthal civilization and ours over 41 trillion kilometers of space! 44 trillion kilometers back then."

"Everywhere in the ancient world, the circle is split up into 360 degrees, each degree split up into 60 minutes and 3600 seconds. But this system of angular measure does not seem to have a point of origin."

"The ancient Iraqis get the blame or credit for that, but the evidence that the Sumerians invented the system of angular measure that we still use today is thin. That's mainly based on their reckoning of numbers in 60's."

"The Sumerians reckoned 60 as 6 tens, not as 5 twelves, as our Creation Neanderthal friends would reckon it."

"The evidence that the Egyptians used the 360 degree angular measure is mostly from the fact that the astronomical observatory of Elephantine Island is exactly seven degrees of latitude south of the two outer ends of the estuaries of the Nile. Other than that there is no direct evidence of the use of degrees for angles in ancient Egypt."

"Well, we know your ancestors used some kind of angular measure, how else could the Pyramids and the monuments be built?"

"Of course, if the Elephantine observatory was deliberately set seven degrees south of the seacoast, that would require that they knew, with that degree of precision, the size of the Earth or at least the rate of curvature."

"Ahh. The nautical mile, or the meter, based on an estimate of the Earth's curve. Did they define the foot as one hundredth of a second of arc of the Earth's surface?"

"Oh give me a break! You Americans are always trying to justify your crazy ancient system of measures as being based on something superior to the Metric System."

Chuck laughed. "In the absence of the Metric System, it's perfectly natural for people to measure distances in human factors. One second of arc is 101.26 modern British-American feet. The Egyptian royal cubit is about 20.6 modern inches. Do the math, one second of arc comes to about 59 royal cubits. Shrink the cubit a little, and you have 1/60 of the second of arc. As good a basis for a system of measure as one ten millionth of the distance between the North Pole and the Equator. The royal cubit was divided into seven palms and 28 fingers. Why seven palms? That would make sense if your ancestors were estimating π as 22/7, which works out to 3.14.

But they weren't, they estimated it as 3.16."

"I know. But you know the traditional tricks. If you make a cylinder 11 centimeters in height and 11 centimeters in diameter, you have a volume of about"

"One liter! π as 22/7 and the tricks are why we have a seven foot unit of length throughout the Middle Ages in continental Europe. The Russians used the same feet and inches we use, by order of Peter the Great, but defined the sazhen as 7 feet. We English speaking types prefer the six foot fathom to the seven foot sazhen because a fathom is an even two yards."

"And the yard is what makes English measures English. π as 22/7 explains your furlong being 220 yards."

"Yeah, a circle 70 yards in diameter has a circumference of about one furlong. But let's get back to the ancient units of length. The royal cubit was seven palms but the regular cubit, particularly as used by the Hebrews, was six palms. Three palms was the Hebrew span. Goliath stood six cubits and a span. We know the Greeks used a foot of sixteen fingers, equivalent to four palms. We've recovered cubit rulers from Egyptian tombs and such. There is definitely a mark of some sort at the four palm division."

"There was no Egyptian foot. Just as there was no Pyramid inch."

"I agree with you on the Pyramid inch. But there are marks in the ancient limestone and granite quarries that are four palms apart. There was an Egyptian foot, even if it was only on this informal basis. Without sea charts, the existence of the fathom in American civilization would also be an unproved rumor. This Egyptian foot, lets see, 20.6 divided by seven multiplied by four, it was 11.77 modern inches. That would be 103 or 104 Egyptian feet to the second of arc."

"You're reaching Chuck, the ancients didn't base their units of measure on the curve of the Earth. Even if you believe in a special long Greek foot of one point oh one modern feet. What brings up all of this discussion of metrology anyway?"

"Ahhh! Well first, there are the pretty ladies from another star. They use feet and inches, yards and fathoms, and they define their units in terms of their Planet's curve and their 432 degree circle. They use Base Twelve numbers. We use Base Ten numbers, and that was widespread throughout the ancient world."

"There is no doubt that the Egyptians used Base Ten."

"As did the Iraqis when they stopped this sixty business. As did the Vedic Hindus of ancient India, as did the Chinese and the Japanese. You have to go over to Mexico to find different. The Mayans thought of twenty as four fives. Fingers and toes. The Far Eastern units of length prior to the Metric System were 12.6 inches for the Chinese *chih* and 11.93 inches for the Japanese *shaku*. *Shaku* is not Japanese for the thing at the end of your leg I'll admit, and neither is *chih* Chinese for foot. Still, we can think of these units as feet."

"So Chuck, what did you find?"

"Something truly amazing back in that cave."

Chapter Eighteen

We walked down the hospital corridor wondering what to do next. I made a suggestion. "Why don't we go for a bite to eat?"

"The hospital cafeteria?"

"No, no and Hell no! That wallet you gave back to me? It still has some money in it. We could go for pizza or burgers, or a steak and seafood place, gotta have some beer. I don't know about you, Askelion, but I'm tired of spaceship food. I want to enjoy a good lunch."

"There are these Secret Service guys following us!"

"So what? Hey gentlemen, we're not under arrest or anything like that?"

"No, of course not. But we're under orders to keep you from being killed."

"But we're free to go. I AM an American citizen. If I'm not under arrest, I KNOW I'm free to go. I still have my driver's license in my wallet, it's not expired, maybe we can rent a car and drive around. Go see some Virginia and Maryland. Better yet, use that Shuttle and get my car from Len Taylor. Then we can drive all the way across the country back to here. With a load of foxy chicks from another world!"

"That would be like driving the Shirelind Road!"

"Exactly! We bring enough money for gasoline and emergency repairs, motel rooms, we could have a lot of fun! I could show you how to operate the vehicle, but then we would have to make sure that the taillights are working and you would have to stay at the speed limit. Can't have cops pulling us over with an unlicensed Neanderthal girl driving. Spring is coming. Maybe, just maybe."

"That much freedom to move around? What about the Avengers of Yahweh?"

"What about 'em? I face death every day of my life. We all do. We Earthlings, not just us Americans, we like to get into automobiles and drive around. Every time we do that, we run the risk of death. One time, I was in Oregon. I was driving up I-5 from Salem to get to Beaverton. Suddenly the traffic in front of me stopped. I slammed the brakes, noticed that the lane next to me was open and went over there. I passed the car I would have clobbered if I didn't move. And it was over. Just like that."

"What did you do the rest of the day?"

"I went on with my business. Not that I'm callous toward death, even my own. But if no harm done, no harm done. I didn't stop driving my car. There's no point in reliving every such experience, in letting it stop me from living my life. We didn't stop launching Space Shuttles after *Challenger* exploded. We fixed the thing that caused *Challenger* to explode, but it's possible that some other malfunction can happen. Don't stop men and women, who have families, who have children, from riding the Shuttles. The point I'm making is that you ladies from another Planet need to be able to visit Earth without worrying about somebody trying to kill you."

"We would love to be tourists like that."

"Exactly! One of the things we do that helps keep nations on friendly terms, prevents war and all that is the exchange of regular people from one country to another. Canadians and Americans cross the border back and forth all the time. Our two nations are in such peace that the border is not fortified in any way. This peace is maintained by the close contact and the travel. People traveling to other nations for pleasure, for business, on student visas to study at Universities, these things help knit the world together. The best way to learn American culture is to live in America for a while, and not as part of a tour group. That is the best way to visit Mexico, or China, or Russia, or any country. I would love to take a few of you girls on a car trip across the United States. There are 47 women in your crew. While a few would need to stay on the ship, you can rotate that duty, we could distribute you all over the Earth and local folks can then show you their countries, their culture, teach you their languages."

"That's an awesome proposal! And in return, we can then tell them a little bit about ourselves. Our language, customs, and beliefs."

"I'll settle for some lunch right now." said Andemona.

"As a physician," started Askelion, "I'll say that Lchnsda has the best post-op therapy any woman can have: a new boyfriend. No need to hang around here. I'm tired of ship food. I need some therapy, lead away my friend!"

We left the hospital with the Secret Service in tow, they were chattering away into their ear things. We found a Chinese place. It advertised Hunan, Szechwan, and Cantonese. "Want some Chinese food?"

"Chinese food? But we're in America!"

"That's Okay! We have styles of food that originate from all over the Planet. Because we consider variety to be the spice of life, we allow all types of food to be available in restaurants and supermarkets."

"Sold in pounds and ounces. You're the least metricated of all the Earth nations and yet the most international. I mean, three types of Chinese food?"

"Not metricating is our way of saying we are a sovereign, independent nation. We decide our national language, not anyone else. But at the same time, feel free to offer to your American customers all that they'll voluntarily pay for. If you can sell, you thrive, if not, your business closes. Three types of Chinese food. Monoloa should be able to fill you in on it. But this is what I can tell you: Hunan and Szechwan are two provinces in China. These provinces have very spicy styles of food. A good Hunan hot and spicy soup should clean your sinuses. But it's GOOD! Cantonese cuisine comes from the Chinese city that was once called Canton and is now called Guangzou. It includes most of the classic Chinese dishes, such as chow mein, sweet and sour pork, fried rice and so on."

"Any meat dishes? We have plenty of vegetables on ship. It's meat we want."

"Meat and fish. Prawns. Not convenient carrying salt water in a spaceship, if it spills, you have the corrosion to worry about. I would suggest Mongolian beef, or beef and broccoli, or sweet and sour pork, almond chicken, lets go look at the menu!"

That sold them. We went into the place. The waiter found us a table, and an adjacent table for our Secret Service bodyguards. We ordered meat dishes and shared a chow mein. Hot and sour soup came first. It did clear sinuses. It was also a hit after the bland ship food. I suggested we get some spice seeds for the Garden Room. We had a great time.

"I hope we are not setting up Henry Turnipseed to be hurt." said Askelion. "He seems to be such a nice man."

"How would he be hurt?" I asked.

"Something happened between the two over in Len Taylor's house." contributed Helga, who was there. "It's the sort of thing that both will deny. We had been through a harrowing experience. When we got to Len's house we were finally able to relax. Len has a perimeter alarm system to protect his farm. Well, Henry was so caring and so gentle when he cleaned the injury to Lucy's head. She was touched by that. They also liked to talk, to the exclusion of me and Len. When we let go crying for the Secret Service men, Len held me in his arms, and Henry held Lucy in his arms. I was happy to be comforted, but it seemed to be something more than that for Lchnsda."

"How would you know that?" I asked.

"Lucy loved being married. She was really in love with Chmlee. I've never felt that. That is what the Virus stole from me. The opportunity to feel that level of love with a man. The Virus stole the man from Lucinda, but at least she experienced that love."

"The thing that was holding Lchnsda back with Henry," broke in Askelion, "is her memory and undying love for Chmlee. She has to first let him go before she can give herself to another man."

"I can tell you my dear Neil," Helga again, "if I felt the same way with Len that Lchnsda was feeling for Henry, we would be engaged to be married right now."

"Oh gee, Helga! What about me?" I pleaded, only half joking.

"We tolerate you. We REALLY tolerate you." Andemona repeated a popular Earth joke.

"Don't get us wrong, Neil." assured Askelion. "We do love you. But it's kind of a group love, what the people of a community have for a hero. You suggested that we announce ourselves to Earth, and convinced us to do it. We didn't have the courage otherwise. The semen that you have supplied us will be taken back to Creation. There, we will take each sperm cell, remove all of the chromosomes except the Y chromosome, and replace with the 22 non sex chromosomes from an egg. Revive the sperm, and that sperm will fertilize another egg which we then implant into a womb. For some reason, we need the sperm cell to make the delivery. The resulting boy will be a Neanderthal except for your Y chromosome. We believe that will make him immune to the Virus."

"Do you know that?"

"Our Race died on Earth. Your Race lived. The Virus may be the reason why. The intelligent life forms who carved Face Mountain and transplanted us may have invented the Virus as a safety valve. We don't know this for a fact, but we have a theory. They left the Information Repository where it would be difficult for us to find. That was deliberate. We think it was booby trapped. The Face Mountain aliens were conducting an experiment. They wanted to practice a full blown terraformation of a planet including the transplantation of an intelligent life form. This experiment was successful. But our physical strength, our powerful bite with our large teeth, combined with our intelligence frightened them. They apparently decided that they did not want to share the Galaxy with us, should we develop technology."

"So," I concluded, "your theory is that if you develop a dangerous level of technology, you will find the Information Repository and release the Virus. But as long as you did not find the Information Repository, they let you live."

"That is one theory we have."

"So why did they not prepare a Virus for us? We are immune as your studies of my Y chromosome seem to indicate."

"They may have believed that you Cro-Magnons were not capable of crossing over to civilization and technological development. The Virus may have gotten loose on Earth, killing the Neanderthal, leaving the Cro-Magnon. Maybe it didn't occur to them that you are immune to the Virus and we are not. Some of your paleoanthropologists have an interesting theory about Cro-Magnon muscle and teeth and the final crossing over to civilization and technology."

"Aren't those the guys who thought we couldn't speak?"

"Well, yeah, the roofs of our mouths are flat. But the theory is this: The Neanderthal can survive on muscle alone. We didn't need to cook our food because of our powerful chewing apparatus. The Cro-Magnon, without the special adaptations the Neanderthal evolved in the Ice Age European climate, had to live by his wits alone. Thus the final crossover to civilization and technology by the Cro-Magnon. The flaw in this theory is that living in a cold climate like Ice Age Europe, we needed fire and clothing. Preparing animal skins can require a lot of chewing. Thus evolved our special faces. You need a large brain to have fire, to make clothing, to find or build shelter, to live in a cold climate when your body is evolved for a warm climate. Once you have a large brain, you can make the crossover to civilization regardless of your muscle build and your facial features. We made this crossover on our Planet. We beat the Face Mountain aliens by stopping the aging process and by building a spacecraft to find Earth. Now we can take your sperm and maybe, just maybe, we can have our next generation."

"That is what we appreciate about you Neil." assured Helga. "We also like the sex." she assured me with a wink and a smile. "What you call 'lesbian', well, we do that, but it's not the same."

"Okay," I said. "Maybe it's just as well we did not have that mad passionate love, it allowed you to share me with the crew. Most men I know would call that seventh heaven. I tried the true love route. Like Lucinda, been there, done that. But the end result was painful for both me and Angela."

"But you have children. That too, the Virus has taken from us. And you have to finally let Angela go before you can give another woman the love necessary to justify a marriage. We are not sure you have done that."

"You said that you were worried about Henry getting hurt?"

"Well, has Henry ever been married?"

"No."

"Has he ever been engaged? Had a girlfriend whom he really loved?"

"He has not been engaged. As far as I know, his girlfriends are dates. He never has gone steady with any one for any length of time as far as I know."

"Yeah, that's me." said Helga. "Been there, done that. He might be a little naive about this. You see, Lchnsda has to let Chmlee go before she can marry again. And if she can't, Henry can be hurt. Lchnsda herself will tell him about her love for Chmlee and how ready she is to finally let him go."

"But there is one other concern that I have for Lchnsda," said Askelion, "right now her mind is a bit intoxicated."

I sat next to Andemona and she held my hand. "What the good doctor means is that she is still affected by the mind altering nature of certain drugs."

"That's right. First there are the effects of the pain killing and knockout drugs used by the emergency surgery team. After that they drained into her 4 units, twelve and four, uh, sixteen *glups*, 5 pints of the blood we brought down from the *Neanderthal Return*. I added some Healing Factor to each unit of blood to speed the healing of Lchnsda's wound."

"Healing Factor has a side effect." declared Helga as Andemona started kissing my hand. "It's like nothing you have in Earth medicine."

"At least I don't believe you have anything like it in Earth medicine." hypothesized Askelion. "We had a 4 *glup* unit of A negative left over, which we put back into Andemona, because she was so weak from having given two pints. It too had some Healing Factor. It won't hurt Andy, even though she has no injury to heal. But it increases her sexual awareness."

Andemona stopped kissing my hand long enough to look at me with a silly grin. The other two broke up laughing. After all of the tension, it was good to hear them laugh, especially when I said, "So Andemona, you doin' anything tonight? Maybe we could go dancing or something.

Then we could go up to my room and look at my stamp collection."

While we laughed, a woman wearing a Georgetown University sweater came looking for us. The Secret Service immediately stopped her and patted her down. When they were satisfied she meant us no harm, she was allowed to talk to us. "I tried the women around the flying saucer parked by the Lincoln Memorial. They didn't understand me but told me that I could find you here in this restaurant. It seems you communicate with some kind of walkie-talkie?"

"Yes, we do." answered Askelion.

"Well, here's the thing. I'm a graduate student with Georgetown University's Anthropology department. We were on the phone with a University of Georgia anthropologist named Chuck Carter. What he told us is stupendous! He's really keen to talk to a Creation woman. We're sorry to hear that Lucinda Renuxler has been shot."

"Lchnsda doing fine. She is awake, alert, and has a new boyfriend."

"Great! I'm glad to hear that. It's really important that a Creation woman come and talk with him."

"What's this find that's got you so excited?" asked Helga.

"I'm not at liberty to say. But Carter is in Algeria, 700 miles south of the Mediterranean Coast, smack in the middle of the Sahara Desert."

"With Lucinda in the hospital, that leaves me as the fluent English speaker. Where can we go so I can talk to him?"

"We have him on the line in a lab at Georgetown University. I have a van outside, your Secret Service escort can ride along."

The Secret Service grumbled about security, we could use the White House phone system. But we were adamant about getting out and about. So we all piled into the Georgetown University van and drove over to the Anthropology Department.

"You are Chuck Carter?"

"Speaking."

"I am Helga Trvlakian."

"Wow. I'm really talking to a woman from another world. You are not offended if I refer to your Race as Neanderthal?"

"No! Of course not! There's nothing offensive about the Dussel Valley."

"Okay. Here in and around the Tassili n'Ajjer, there are paintings made on cave walls and other rock walls under protected overhangs. We've known about these for some time. Today, this area is extremely dry desert. But several thousand years ago, there was more rain. The mountains here rise as high as 6,000 feet above sea level. This is high enough to catch clouds coming across the desert and squeeze some rain out of them. So there was grass on which cattle can feed. The rock paintings depict black people with Negro features and herds of cattle. Women taking care of children, men hunting game, children milking the cows, that sort of thing. These paintings date to between 2,000 and 4,000 B.C. About contemporary with the Early and Middle Kingdoms of ancient Egypt."

"Did you find a painting that depicted more than cattle herding and tribal village activities?"

"Yes. An Arab nomad named Mohammed Abbas and his family found a remarkable set of paintings and WRITING on a cave wall six miles southwest of here."

"Where is 'here'?"

"Oh. We're at an archeological base camp 75 kilometers, oh, 46 or 47 miles from a town named Illizi. Anyway, these paintings are radically different from all of the other rock paintings in this part of Algeria. It shows three men in a meeting. A Tassili cattleman, an Egyptian of the time, and a Neanderthal man in a white robe."

"A Neanderthal man. Is that interesting?"

"I would say so! Neanderthals are supposed to have disappeared around 25,000 B.C. at the latest. Neanderthals have not been found this far south in the Sahara Desert. Stone tools that may have been made by Neanderthals were found on the Mediterranean Coast north of here, but no Neanderthal bones. No ancient paintings of Neanderthals have EVER been found. This is a first. There is Egyptian hieroglyphic writing that describes the trip made by the Egyptians, they were sent by Pharaoh Khufu. He was of the Fourth Dynasty. They recorded a travel distance of 300 *aturs*. That's accurate."

"What's an *atur*?"

"Egypt had defined weights and measures. An *atur* was 14,000 royal cubits. A royal cubit is about 20.6 modern inches. We know this because cubit rulers have been recovered from Egyptian tombs. 300 *aturs* is 1365 miles. We're that far from the Nile River. What drew them over was this Neanderthal man who was living with the Tassili cattlemen. His name is Afenor. According to the story on the wall, Afenor came from a land far away."

"That is believable."

"So far, so good. But the name of the place Afenor is from, spelled out in Egyptian phonetic symbols, is Atlantis."

"Now that is interesting."

"This is the first time this word, used as a place name, has been found anywhere in ancient writing outside of Plato's Letters to Timeas and Critias. We brought in Mustafa Khedr from the Egyptian Antiquities Organization. He confirms that this is the story told on the wall. We found a bow in the cave. It is inscribed with the name 'Afenor' in a cartouche, and the word 'Atlantis'. There is varnish painted on after these names were inscribed. The carbon-14 tests have come back. This bow was made during the reign of Pharaoh Khufu. There is no faking that!"

"A little hard to remove carbon-14 atoms to make it look ancient."

"That would be a good trick." The archeologist laughed. "An extremely good trick. We found some other neat stuff! Before we go into that, I need you to do me a small favor. Would you be so kind as to write on a piece of paper the Atlantean alphabet with Roman alphabet equivalents? Then please write the Atlantean numbers with Earth equivalents. By Earth equivalent, I mean the Western Arabic numbers that are commonly used. Count these Atlantean numbers from zero to thirty six. Show me some representative numbers from beyond thirty-six. And how you represent fractions, numbers between zero and one."

"We use a place value type of system, like your numbers. That way, we can do simple arithmetic calculations without using a counting board or abacus. We use a dot to represent zero, just like your Eastern Arabic still in use in the Middle East. So we use a wavy line for the same purpose that you use a decimal point or comma."

"So left of the wavy line, you have units, twelves, grosses, and so on? Right of the wavy line, your digits represent twelfths, one forty fourths, and so on?"

"Yes, that is correct. The wavy line in a horizontal direction is how we denote fractions in general, other than twelfths and *hekers*. Numerator above the horizontal wavy line and the denominator below."

"That sounds like a perfectly serviceable system of numbers. Just how ancient is this place value system of numbers? How ancient is your zero?"

"Very ancient. *Kechts* of years."

"Hmmm. Our modern place value decimal system of numbers didn't get into general use in Europe until about the time of Columbus. The Arabs used this system, written two or three different ways, from the first century of Islam. They seem to have gotten it from the Vedic

Hindus of India. The earliest we can trace it is about a few centuries after Christ. Most of the world's civilizations used tally marks to represent numbers. These marks had different shapes for units, tens, hundreds, and so on. Fractions tended to be twelfths, sixteenths, twentieths, and so on. That's why pre-Metric weights and measures are divided by those types of ratios. So evidence of a place value number system in ancient times would be just awesome. How are you coming on that paper?"

"Just about done. I also have written some typical Atlantean words and their English equivalents."

"Excellent!"

"I'm done. Some simple Atlantean stuff written on an 8 and a half by 11 inch piece of paper. Before I send this on the facsimile machine, may I inquire as to why you want this?"

"This is very preliminary. We have found the mummy of Afenor, in a sarcophagus, in a burial chamber with some of his possessions. These possessions include some items with writing and numbers in his language and in ancient Egyptian. There is an Egyptian cubit ruler and a yardstick with Afenor's numbers marking off the units. It looks just like a modern American yardstick, divided into 36 units with 3 major divisions. But the numerals appear to be Base Twelve place value type numbers. I compared this yardstick; it is wood, good for a carbon 14 test, with a tape measure of modern American make. 35 and a half inches! A *treefat* stick!"

Helga sent the fax.

FBI Special Agents Peter Kent and Clark Parker met in a backroom office of the Portland sex shop with a former employee of the shop. "You are positive that the Michelle Smith who shot Lchnsda Renuxler is the one who made the purchase?"

"Yes, she even used the name Michelle Smith. She purchased two Number AB40 Armbinders illustrated on page 46 of the Millennium Catalogue. Shiny black leather, zipper to close, extra roller buckling straps for greater security. Can hold an NFL linebacker, perfect for a Neanderthal woman. She also purchased the two of the Number T7B Plug Gags of page 52 of the Millennium Catalogue. This model is usually made with a leather gag. Miss Smith special ordered it with a stainless steel core inside the leather so that it cannot be bitten through. The steel reinforced rawhide strap wraps around the head below the curve of the skull, adjusted tight, and is locked back there. A neck collar comes attached to further control the jawbone. A Neanderthal woman may be capable of crushing bones between her teeth like a great white shark but she ain't getting out of this baby without a key. This item comes in several different colors, Miss Smith selected black."

The FBI had already identified the items recovered from the Hood Canal crime scene as the above numbered items sold by the Millennium Fetish Company. "You have any record of the purchase?"

"What we have showed you. As you can see, we sold these items last January 15. They were paid for with cash. Most customers pay with cash, for obvious reasons. Michelle did not fill out any questionnaire about her fetishes or sexual preferences, nor did she ask for help in selecting the items. She knew what she wanted and gave us the order and this phone number to call when the order was ready. She came in, paid with cash, and left with the items."

"Michelle did not confide that she used to be a he?"

"We don't pry. Some customers are quite open and will let us help by giving us such detailed information about themselves. We keep their trust by being discrete. We sell to women of both sexes. We notice Adam's apples but don't say anything, unless the customer is open about that."

"What can you remember about Michelle's demeanor when she made this purchase?"

"Businesslike. Not nervous, cool. Like she was picking up a dry cleaning order."

"She let you fill out the purchase order in your handwriting?"

"Yes, she did. But we made her sign for it."

"We have samples of her signature, we can compare this signature. It'll be very useful. Thank you. Please inform us of any address or phone number change, we'll keep in touch. Call us if you have any concerns."

The two agents left the building by a different exit so no one would connect them to the sex shop. In the Bureau car they considered what they had. "Have either of our two perps in custody in Seattle said anything more?"

"Nope, that fancy lawyer has 'em under control. Our U.S. Attorney friends in Seattle are trying to negotiate a deal to get 'em talking."

"Anything more on the highway worker, Allen Case or Pace?"

"Nope, nothing on him. But now that we've identified Michelle Smith as the purchaser of the items recovered at the crime scene, maybe we don't NEED those two perps! They can ROT!"

Chapter Nineteen

After wolfing down the pizza, the Creation women climbed out of their bulky pressure suits, revealing shapely bodies well endowed with muscle. They wore simple pants and shirts made out of linen and cotton. The women went everywhere around the Mall, in groups of two or three. Some explored the Capitol and the Supreme Court, others toured the Museums. Second Lieutenant Pete MacGregor's soldiers had difficulty keeping track of them.

As the evening fell, the women put on coats and jackets. Three of the women were unaccounted for. Great! MacGregor's men desperately tried to find the missing women.

"This part of town is not beautiful like the government area. Broken windows. Drunks and dope addicts strung out on the pavement. The smells!" Metrola Mornuxler made these comments in Atlantean as they walked around a sleeping homeless person. "What was the name of that large building complex we passed a few blocks back?"

"My reading of the English, I believe the sign said *Dunbar High School*." responded Nesla Teslakian. "What's a *high school*?"

"I don't know. I wonder if every Earth city has a rundown section like this?"

"Probably, this is the capital of the richest nation on this Planet." commented Sorby Mishlakian. "Many a palace looks down on a shanty town. No matter the resources that they develop, there is always poverty. They debate this a lot."

"Well, what do they expect? They drink alcohol until they are bombed out of existence! We make paper, cloth, and rope out of hemp. We don't smoke it! And some of these poor souls, look at them! Shooting opium products or Spirit knows what into their veins! How can a person VOLUNTARILY put himself through this kind of Hell?"

"Don't be so judgmental. We have these problems on our Planet. The Cro-Mags are as human as us. Trviea likes her rum a little too much! But we know how capable she is when she can focus on a job. We would not have made it into the Earth system without her leadership. With these people, it may be a vicious cycle. They cannot get a job to focus their energies so they turn to drugs, reckless sex, or violence. But nobody wants to hire someone prone to these activities. The Earthlings don't know the answer, I am certainly not going to pretend to have one."

They walked a few more paces in silence. It is sobering to see for themselves the down side of Cro-Magnon society. A down side that also exists in their society on Creation. With or without brow ridges, humans are humans.

Suddenly a man jumped in front of them waving a large knife. "Gimmee all yo money or I'll cut yo up!" The knife was six inches in front of Metrola's face.

"I'm sorry." Metrola switched to English. "But we don't have any money. I suppose we could get some, Helga and Lchnsda have that deal with the publishing house that should be pouring money into a bank account in our name. But we just came down from our spaceship. We didn't have any American currency to bring down."

"Spaceship? Yo jiving me, honky bitch?!"

"What is 'honky bitch'?"

Nesla explained in Atlantean. "Neil explained to us that the word *bitch*, which means female dog, is often used as an insult to women. Or it is used to describe a woman with a disagreeable temperament or who does not cooperate."

"That's us," affirmed Sorby, "we don't have any money so we cannot cooperate with this gentleman who wants some so bad that he threatens us with a knife."

"It seems to be important to him." Metrola switched back from Atlantean to English. "We're terribly sorry sir, we just don't happen to have any money with us."

"Listen, honky bitch! Yo not gettin' out of givin' me yo money by talkin' in yo fo'in language! Oh by talkin' nonsense! Now hand it over!"

"I don't believe this poor fellow comprehends who we are. Note how he refers to us as 'honky bitches'. If I remember correctly, the word 'honky' is an insulting term for a white person. Just the way 'nigger' is an insulting term for a black person."

The man's eyes flashed angrily at the word 'nigger'.

"I see. This gentleman has an emotional response to the word 'nigger'. Interesting. So I am correct that 'honky' is that kind of insult to white people?"

"It is." confirmed the robber. He began to think and decided to move from his slang to a more standard form of English. "You have white skin. Ain't you honkies?" But it wasn't perfect English.

"Technically, no. We are of an entirely different Race than the flat faced Europeans whom, you have to admit, seem to have taken over the entire Planet Earth. If you would please pull your knife down and look at our faces closely, you will see that we are Neanderthals, not Cro-Magnons."

The black man produced a small flashlight and pointed it into Metrola's face. "Man! Youz an UGLY bitch!"

The women giggled. "My, what big eyes you have, grandma!" exclaimed Sorby gleefully. "And what big teeth!"

"Haven't you been paying attention to what's going on? We come in this spaceship, we tell you that we are humans of the Race you call Neanderthal."

"Yeah. I seen you guys on TV. The bald one, Lucinda, who misses her husband. The blonde, Helga, who is as pretty as a Neanderthal can be. But how you come down from your ship?"

"Oh, we have our own Shuttle for going down to a planet's surface. Didn't you see us come down today? Lchnsda, that's the bald one, was shot during the St. Patrick's Day Parade. We came down to bring her blood, because we don't know if there is a compatibility problem with blood from our two Races."

"Wait a minute! Ah was in the hospital a year ago wif knife wound. They gave me a bunch of O negative. They didn't worry if it came from white donors oh black donors. Ah'm still here. So racial compatibility must not be a big issue in blood."

"Your physicians know that there is no such incompatibility. It's sad to see you and white people calling each other names like 'honky' and 'nigger'. You really are very closely related, the same species, the same Race. We however, though we are human, are of a different Race, perhaps species. Our bone structure is different, radically different. We don't know if there is a racial incompatibility problem with our blood and your blood. We just didn't want to find out with Lchnsda."

"I understand that. Saving her life was the Number One priority. The cops went crazy today, screaming through here with their sirens. You in this flying saucer thing that came down?"

"That was us."

"Wow. And I thought that was the crack I smoked. Well, Okay. I believe you don't have any money. But I gotta get somethin' outta dis ya see. So I think I'm gonna rape you. That's right, rape you. Lay down bitch! I'm gonna have me some cavewoman poontang!" The women broke up laughing. The knifeman looked around, wondering what was going on. Rape victims usually do not break up laughing! This is a big eight inch knife, a dagger. "What're yo laughing at? I'm gonna cut yo up bitch!"

The 'bitch' grabbed his wrist faster than he could blink. He could no more move his knife hand than if it was cast in a block of concrete. Man! This bitch is STRONG! Suddenly everything went dark. Next thing he knew, the back of his head hurt and his eyes saw a blur that slowly cleared. He looked up from the ground to see Metrola holding his knife, inspecting it with his flashlight. Nesla bent over and looked at his face. "How many fingers am I holding?"

"Three. What da fuck happened? Man, my head hurts!"

"You Cro-Magnons don't have a big knot of bone in the back of your skulls like we do. I hit you with a measured force. I didn't want to kill you. But I don't think anyone would blame me if I did. How dare you threaten us with a knife?" Nesla grabbed his shirt in front of his chest. She lifted him up over her head, his feet dangling in the air. "We Neanderthal women fortunately have the muscle to defend ourselves. But this is no way to treat a person. We're not calling the cops because we've seen enough American government to not want to waste our time!" She threw him to the ground. "Now get lost!"

As he picked himself up to leave, Metrola said, "Thank you for the knife and the flashlight. We always appreciate gifts." After the unsuccessful mugger scrambled off, Metrola switched back to Atlantean and discussed the knife with her shipmates. "*Vanadium Stainless*, it says here. Is *Vanadium* a company that makes knives?"

"I don't think so. Maybe *vanadium* is a metallic element used in the alloy. We better get back to the Shuttle. Poor Lieutenant MacGregor will freak if he finds out about this."

"We should be more careful. He could have used a gun. Firearms are rampant around here."

"Dr. Cuc Nguyen, glad you could come!" The President greeted the Center for Disease Control physician as she entered the Oval Office.

"I'm honored to be here. But your men made me feel like I was under arrest."

"My apologies. But as you know, Lucinda Renuxler was shot at the St. Patrick's Day Parade. She's gonna make it, she'll be all right. One of Neil Peace's friends from the State of Washington, Henry Turnipseed, is pushing her around the hospital in her wheelchair. That's not a big problem. We can always give her a green card or something if she wants to marry an American citizen. No, what I'm concerned about is something their physician, Askelion Lamakian, talked about when a bunch of them were at a Chinese restaurant."

"Askelion come down on their Shuttle?"

"Yes, she did. Helped 'em patch Lucinda back together and brought Neanderthal blood from the donors on her ship. Now we've got an additional eight Neanderthal women down on Planet. That's a total of twelve, eleven here in Washington, D.C. Leaves 35 up on the ship. If you look out over the South Lawn, you might see some of them on a morning jog around the Mall. They're all running to regain muscle tone now they're in gravity."

"It's true that their muscle tone is a little loose after a year on the spacecraft. But these women are incredibly strong. I've heard about the fellow who checked into a free clinic with a mild concussion."

"What about this fellow?" asked the President. "I haven't heard about this."

"Well, Mr. President," began General Fairchild, "last night, three of the Shuttle girls, including the Shuttle pilot, Metrola Mornuxler, got completely away from Lieutenant

MacGregor's unit. We didn't know where they were! About ten thirty, they suddenly arrive at the Shuttle to go inside for the night. They were laughing. Poor MacGregor. He was screaming at 'em. Telling 'em he cannot be responsible for their safety if they're gonna run off without at least giving him a chance to send a soldier to accompany them. They responded with an apology. Then Metrola asked him if there were many foreigners in Washington at any given time. He answered yes, of course, a national capital, embassies, tourists, and everything. Then Metrola asked him if they always had a United States Army soldier following each of them around to insure their safety. Well, uh, no. So all of these foreign persons are free to travel around on their own, responsible for their own safety, and willing to take their own chances. Well, uh yes. But we don't have terrorists specifically targeting these foreigners. Are you sure of this? What about Israelis?"

"Whoa, there!" interrupted the President. "Okay, I get that three of them wandered off and when they returned they had an argument with the poor soldier responsible for keeping them alive. What about the man who checked into the clinic with the concussion?"

"Yes. Robert Freeman. Last night at eleven o'clock, his mother dragged him into the clinic to have his dizzy head checked. Seems he got hit with a rabbit punch. No big surprise, he's a small time hood, been in prison, a registered sex offender. Has a conviction of third degree rape, plea bargained down from second degree. He's now in his thirties, has a string of misdemeanor convictions and a couple of felonies stretching back to when he was a juvenile. Has a reputation for stealing stuff, mugging people, and shooting drugs."

"Your basic run of the mill hood. No stranger to Judicial Square."

"Exactly. But then he tells the clinic staff that he ran into three Neanderthal women from the spacecraft and they thumped him and stole his knife and flashlight!"

Laughter broke out in the Oval Office. "He probably threatened them with the knife and they whacked him and took it!" exulted the President. Cracking down on crime is a standard stump speech of his. "We should give 'em a heads up about the Great American Crime Problem. There are some neighborhoods not safe to walk the streets at night. Some of these thugs use guns. Being able to bench press 300 pounds does not protect one against a gun."

They sat around giggling for moment, savoring the blow struck by the alien women for law and order. "But now, getting to the reason I called you here today, on admittedly short notice, we now have two individuals on the surface who have expertise that I'm really interested in. Not like the four girls who have been down. They know languages, history, literature, OUR culture. Whoopee! We already know about OUR stuff! What we need to know about is THEIR stuff."

"Their languages, culture, history, and so on?" Dr. Cuc asked. "Helga and Lucinda are selling that for money."

"No." answered the President emphatically. "I mean their medicine and technology."

"Oh. Metrola piloted that Shuttle."

"Which we know works on some principle of magnetism. When that ship flies, it knocks magnets and compasses out of kilter. Now the Shuttle is at rest and the compasses are back to pointing north as usual. It repels the Earth's magnetic field to an extent sufficient overcome its weight in our gravity. Metrola knows how its engine works, she would have to in order to fly it."

"Not necessarily. I can drive a car, and I haven't a clue how it works." protested Cuc Nguyen.

"But you do know it has something to do with pistons and cylinders."

"Does it really? I used to know how the '60's and '70's vintage cars worked. My boyfriend in high school liked to work on them. He would rail about the Metric conversion, the stupid new designs, parts made inaccessible, the idiot government regulations, all the pollution crap. I look under the hood of my car, and I ask 'Where's the distributor? A COMPUTER distributing spark?' What I know about computers is they suddenly malfunction for reasons nobody can understand. 'Carburetor?' The salesman said 'fuel injection', but I cannot tell you what that is. All I know about how a car works is that gasoline goes in and miles come out. When this doesn't happen I take it to a mechanic, an 'automobile physician' if you will, and he tries to cure it. I get a bill that's like a hospital bill. It's listed with a bunch of items that are impossible to understand and looks like something compiled by a hospital nurse."

The President laughed. He won the election by speaking out against this kind of nonsense. "Well, it may be that Metrola doesn't have a clue as to how the Shuttle works. But we should bring her in here and let her explain that. Now about Askelion. Our Secret Service people guarding her, Helga, Andemona, and Neil Peace, clearly overheard her suggest a theory about the Virus that killed off their men." He turned very serious. "The theory is that the Face Mountain Race MANUFACTURED the Virus and used it to booby trap the Information Repository that Lamoan Reducker found."

"An engineered Virus?"

"Yeah. The Information Repository is located in the center of a remote desert. Deliberately difficult to find. But if the Neanderthals build an airplane or an orbiting satellite, it would be easy to find. As it is, they found it after sailing their ocean in ships. Something to attract their attention if they develop a dangerous level of technology. Until then, the Face Mountaineers were content to allow this species of humans to live on their manufactured Planet. But they apparently didn't want them exploring the Galaxy in spacecraft."

"To work the way they describe it, the Virus would have to be benign at first so that the explorers would bring it back and infect the rest of the population. The Creation Neanderthals would live for a few more generations. Then some kind of mutation or recessive gene would be triggered and their men are killed off by an epidemic. Women cannot reproduce without men. So their Race dies off when they grow old. They beat that part of the strategy by shutting off the aging gene."

"Could such a Virus be engineered?"

"Theoretically possible. But then the Virus would have to be made dormant and be able to survive a long time. However, we have been able to revive bacteria that were holed up in 'spores', what we call the bacterial type of cocoon, for as long as 25 million years in insects caught in amber."

"And where would the Cro-Magnon version of this Virus be hiding?"

"We've been allowed to develop a higher level of technology than the Neanderthals had before they stumbled into the Information Repository. But I would suggest that we approach Face Mountain on Mars with extreme caution, given the little that we know about Creation and what her women have told us."

"We need to get Askelion Lamakian in here ASAP! Arrest her if you have to! This is a national security matter of the highest order!"

"Arrest her?" protested General Morton Fairchild. "We've given her diplomatic immunity! We could risk war with Planet Creation! All they have to do with their great big spaceship is push an Earth crossing asteroid into a different orbit and we have a Dinosaur Killer on our hands! Besides, it sounds like the Face Mountain aliens are the real threat. We've been bleeding radio and television signals into space with reckless abandon since Marconi. His signals are now about one hundred light years out. 250 light years to the Face Mountaineers' new home planet according to Helga and Lucinda. They find out we've not succumbed to the Virus trap, having been warned by the Creation Neanderthals, they might come here with a fleet to exterminate us!"

"I can see why there are laser cannons installed all over the Creation Solar System." conceded the President. "Okay, when you bring Askelion, be tactful and polite. But get her in here!"

Helga withdrew some money from the Creation bank account. We rented a large American built van with plenty of seats. I drove the Jefferson Davis Highway. In the van with me were Helga, Dr. Askelion, Metrola, Sorby Mishlakian, who looked like Captain Trviea Harsradich, and one Secret Service agent. There had been a rainstorm, but now it was partly sunny. March in Virginia. We drove into Fredericksburg, looking for a place to eat.

Askelion was on the car phone with the nationally syndicated radio talk show host, Rusty Limburger, who is very popular with the conservative audience. Rusty and his callers wanted to hear from the rest of us, so the car phone was passed around.

"Now that we have practiced some capitalism, we have Neil Peace holding the car phone. How ya doing, Neil?"

"I'm doing fine. It's great to be back on the ground, right here in the good ol' USA!"

"How is it that you can forgive these women for kidnapping you?"

"Well, Rusty, it's like this:" I struggled through Rusty's hearty laughter. "When you're with a bunch of beautiful women who offer you a heartfelt apology and treat you real nice, well, shucks! Life's too short to be angry all the time! It's like John Smith being a prisoner of Powhatan. He used the opportunity to start a dialog with the Virginia Indians." My voice took a more serious tone. "We need to understand that they snuck up on Earth and kidnapped me because they were afraid of us. Still are. But they know they need us. What we need to realize is that we may need them. We need to help them find a way to have children so they can continue their Race. That's the only human thing we can do. Given that an entirely alien species of intelligent life carved Face Mountain and played God with the Neanderthals, and probably played God with us, we humans need to stick together. Right now the Creation Neanderthals are our best and only friends in the Universe."

"I heartily agree with that. It must also be said that they didn't expect any handouts from us or from our government. They entered into contracts with publishing companies and television media to raise the money to purchase provisions and pay for their activities on Earth. That's the way it's supposed to be done! And Askelion, we certainly appreciate the warning about the possible origin of the Virus. It's extremely imperative that we do everything we can to avoid any possible Cro-Magnon version of this Virus. We have Ronald in Denver, Colorado, with a question for Helga Trvlakian."

I handed the phone over to Helga. "This is Helga Trvlakian."

"Welcome to the show, Helga Trvlakian. Ronald, of Denver, you're on!"

"I'm honored to be on this show and to be speaking with the beautiful Helga Trvlakian of Planet Creation."

"Thank you, Ronald!" Helga answered pleasantly.

"I'm a single guy, not attached, I was wondering if you were busy and,"

"Ronald, I'm flattered!"

"No, no! Just kidding. Flattery will get you nowhere."

"Try me."

"But seriously. I am a Christian, I have a friend in Jesus, my faith is very important to me. I am also sure that your faith with the Great Holy Spirit is important to you."

"It is. I am glad to hear that your faith is important to you."

"You are not here to be like a missionary, to try to convince us that your faith in the Great Holy Spirit is the way?"

"Absolutely not. It is NOT our intention to injure any person's Christian faith. Everything we've heard about Jesus Christ indicates that he was a wonderful man. He may even be the Son of God. We are not Christians, we have our own religion. But just like Jesus teaches, our religion is that we are to be tolerant of how other people believe. No one in our society is denied any liberty or property because of their belief or lack of belief in the Great Holy Spirit. Belief in the Spirit is either completely voluntary, or it is of no value. We do not go out and try to sell faith to each other, that faith must originate in the heart. There are several women on our ship who are what you would call atheists. But we love them and respect them just the same, and they likewise love us and respect us. If your Christian faith is heartfelt and honest, wonderful! But if it is not, to pretend belief does a disservice to yourself, to Jesus, and to God."

"You're right. But there are times I have doubt. And I see all the evil and sin in the world."

"Ronald, that is because we're HUMAN. Humans make mistakes. Humans sin. That's what we do. Jesus had his moment of doubt. On the Cross. Because of hate and intolerance and fear among other people in his society. I have felt that doubt. The thing to remember, whatever your faith, is that we all have evil in our souls. You have it. I have it. But we also have good in our souls. And it all boils down to which one you choose. It is a choice only you can make, no one can make it for you. And you have to make that choice again, every day of your life, for every situation that comes up."

"Thank you, Helga. You'll make some lucky man a wonderful wife."

She laughed softly. "Thank you."

Rusty Limburger took over his mike. "This reminds me of George Washington's speech about how important it is for our democracy that we have faith. But now we have a call from Chuck Carter, the famous American archeologist from the University of Georgia. He has been studying rock paintings from several thousand years ago in the middle of the Sahara Desert. From Afenor Cave in Algeria, six miles from the Tassili Archeological Base Camp, 53 miles from the city of Illizi, how are you doing Chuck?"

"I'm doing great, Rusty! It is true, all that you've heard about this. We've found the preserved mummy of a Neanderthal man with the name of Afenor, written in Egyptian in a cartouche. We have not yet removed the mummy from his sarcophagus. But we were able to positively identify Afenor as a Neanderthal by using a portable X-ray machine to get a picture of his skull. He is a classic West European Neanderthal."

"That's what I am!" exclaimed Helga.

"Yes, I've seen the published X-ray photographs of you ladies. There is no doubt that you and Afenor are Neanderthals. Afenor is preserved just like the Egyptian pharaohs. In the coffin with him are some of his personal possessions. These possessions include an Egyptian cubit ruler and a yardstick with apparently the units of measure of Afenor's society. The cubit ruler is consistent with other cubit rulers found at ancient Egyptian sites. It is a royal cubit, divided up into seven palms and 28 fingers, equivalent to 20.6 modern inches. It is marked in ancient Egyptian writing, with Egyptian numerals. Tally marks for units, the letter U marks for tens."

"But what about the yardstick? I thought the yard was a British invention."

"Yeah, you, me, and everyone! Though many of the continental European pre-Metric systems had three foot units. The Romans had a foot divided into twelve inches, the first known to divide the foot into twelve parts. They had measuring sticks of one, two, three, or more feet in length. They've never described a three foot unit, a Roman yard. The Greeks and Phoenicians used a foot divided into 16 fingers. The Hebrew cubit, as Bible readers know, was 24 fingers, and the Egyptian royal cubit was 28 fingers as we've just said."

"The Greeks defined their foot in a way that related to the existing cubits then used in Israel and Egypt."

"Apparently. The western Phoenicians, based at Carthage in Tunisia and in Spain traded with the Etruscans and the Romans. This is probably how the Romans got to using the foot as a unit of measure."

"How did the Romans go from dividing the foot into 16 fingers to dividing it into 12 inches?"

"It's how the Romans reckoned numbers. As we know from Roman numerals, they grouped their numbers in 5's, 10's, 50's, 100's, and so on for numbers greater than one. But their fractions, numbers less than one, were twelfths and one forty fourths. Just like the Creation Neanderthals."

"Ahh. So what is the significance of Afenor's yardstick?"

"1500 years before the Romans were known to be using a foot divided into twelve inches, we find a measuring stick that looks a lot like a Roman three foot stick. The total length of this measuring stick is divided into 36 parts. Like the cubit ruler, some of these parts are divided into smaller fractions. We see this in modern rulers. Centimeters divided into millimeters. Inches divided into sixteenths or tenths or whatever. But what proves the 1/36th divisions as units are the numbers written at each of these divisions."

"Numbers." commented Helga. "You asked me to fax you a piece of paper with some Atlantean numbers and alphabet."

"Yes, I wanted to compare with Afenor's yardstick. They look like a predecessor to the Arabic numbers we use today. One is represented by a line, that seems to be universal. But two, three, and so on are represented by individual symbols. Not common until the Hindu and Arabic numerals were developed. Some of these numbers look a lot different from the corresponding Creation numbers. But three, four, and six bear a resemblance. The striking thing about Afenor's ruler is that ten and eleven are represented by single symbols."

"And twelve?" asked the talk show host.

"By a one and a zero dot. The inches in the second foot are numbered with one and one, then one and two, and so on, until 24, which is represented by a two followed by a zero dot. The inches in the third foot are numbered with two and one, two and two, until at the end of the yardstick, where there is the number three followed by a zero dot."

"Rusty, Chuck," interrupted Helga, "that is exactly how our *treefat* sticks are marked, with Base Twelve numerals."

"But there's also the length of Afenor's yardstick, about 35 and a half modern British-American inches! Isn't that the length of your *treefat*?"

"Yes."

"Helga," asked Rusty, "How ancient are the Creation weights and measures and the Creation Base Twelve numbers?"

"Very ancient. We can trace the use of *kepfats, chmfats, pfats, treefats, potes* and *tig-its* back three *kechts* of Creation years. That is a couple thousand years before the First Egyptian Dynasty. The definition of these units has been remarkably stable. Our system of numbers as we know it today came into use about two *kechts* of Creation years ago, but it could be older than that. Somebody back then was able to determine the size of Planet Creation. Our *pote* is about one sixtieth of a *prelate* of arc."

"Amazing. So Chuck, what else did you find?"

"Afenor was mummified and buried the Egyptian way. In the burial chamber are a bunch of items, all piled up like in King Tut's tomb. There is a desk with drawers. In one of these drawers, there are what appear to be clear plastic bags."

The Creation women in the van lit up. Askelion said urgently, "Give me the phone! Please!"

"This is Askelion Lamakian, the physician."

170

"Yes, Askelion." said Rusty. "You have a comment on what Chuck Carter is finding?"

"Chuck! Can you hear me?"

"Yes, Dr. Lamakian. I hear you loud and clear."

"Please describe the plastic bags."

"They are small, about two by three inches, flat, less than a quarter inch deep."

"What's in them?"

"A light tan powder. We have not opened these bags,"

"Good! Don't open them! Quarantine the archeological site! Has anyone left the site since you have found these bags?"

"No. Labna Abbas, Mohammed's wife, was going to Illizi to purchase supplies for us. She hasn't left yet."

"Don't let her go. I don't want to create a panic. We're on the radio. But let's be cautious. Nobody leaves the site, nobody should go into the site until I can get there to check these bags and everyone there for the Virus."

"The Virus?"

"The one that killed our men. It might be just like I explained. Maybe this is a booby trap left by the Face Mountain aliens. If so, it's possible this is the Cro-Magnon version of this Virus. But before we have a worldwide panic, it's most likely not such a Face Mountain artifact. The site is too new for that. But we need to make sure."

"What do we do now?" I asked.

"Get me and Metrola back to the Shuttle. We gotta fly! Now!" With that I took a turn at the next intersection where there is a sign pointing the way to Interstate 95. I drove about 5 to 10 miles above the speed limit on the freeway. We discussed the matter. The girls didn't think the Face Mountain aliens left a Virus booby trap on the surface of the Earth. We would have found it by now. Face Mountain on Mars is the most likely place for that.

Chapter Twenty

I parked the van next to the Shuttle and handed the keys to the Secret Service agent. "Helga, make sure this van gets back to the rental company. He'll drive it over and his agency can bring you back."

Askelion and Metrola signaled me to follow them to the Shuttle. Askelion told us what she was thinking. "This should not be too much of a problem if everyone in Algeria keeps their heads screwed on straight."

"Algerians haven't been keeping their heads the last few years. Gov'ment canceled an election a few years ago because the wrong people were gonna win. Since then, the radical fringe of the wrong people have been killing people. You just told everyone around the archeological site that they may be standing near a plague germ. It's human nature to get away fast. Half of them would be in Algiers by now if that city wasn't so unsafe!"

"That's why we need to get there quick. I only need Metrola to fly the Shuttle, and you to talk with the Air Traffic Control, both American and Algerian. No one else needs to go to Algeria. I need to stop at the *Neanderthal Return* to pick up my Virus test equipment." She switched to Atlantean. "Anyone need to get back to the ship?"

Two women needed to get back to the spacecraft. The rest chose to stay, they were enjoying their shore leave. As we were climbing into the pressure suits for the ride in the Shuttle, the black limousine with the Presidential flags arrived with its Secret Service escort. The President and Dr. Cuc Nguyen jumped out and ran to us. "Doctor Lamakian, we need a quick briefing on this! What is it you are worried about in this archeological find in Algeria?"

"Mr. President, Dr. Cuc Nguyen, it's a pleasure to meet you. Please bear with me while I put on this pressure suit. It's a precaution, in case air leaks out of the Shuttle while we're in space. Chuck Carter described plastic bags. There were some plastic bags in the Information Repository. We don't know if the Virus was left inadvertently by the Face Mountain aliens or if it was a deliberate booby trap." Askelion was making sure the CDC physician was taking this in. "It might be a naturally evolved Virus, but evidence supports the theory it was engineered. Chmlee Mornuxler, a scientist with the Reducker Expedition, opened the plastic bags to determine what was in them. He rubbed the contents between his fingers and tasted them with the tip of his tongue. He became infected with the Virus. At first, it was benign. It replicates with the Y chromosomes in men. The Virus can spread by casual contact from man to man. Every man in Reducker's Expedition became infected, but none became sick. They stopped at many ports on their way back to Cair Atlaston. For 245 Earth years, the Virus spread until it infected the entire male population of Planet Creation. Then, in our Year Twenty Four Eleven Five, the Virus turned virulent in Graciana. The tropical climate probably allowed more replications. The epidemic hit Atlantis the next year, Twenty Four Eleven Six. All efforts at quarantine failed because every man was already infected. What happens is that the Virus had a gene that did not switch on for a certain number of generations. Then it turns on and within days destroys the nervous system of the victim."

"So the Virus lives as a benign parasite within its host," Cuc started to ask her question.

"For quite a few years. This gives it time to spread. We had no warning we were carrying a deadly contagion. A man can live with it in his body until he dies of old age. Neither he nor his physicians would know anything is amiss. But he's spread it to his sons and grandsons and to every other man he's met. So it is important that we get over to Algeria and eliminate the possibility that the Face Mountain aliens planted the Virus there."

They stood there for a moment while the President and the CDC physician took it in and thought about it. Then the President spoke. "Please take Dr. Nguyen with you."

"We need to limit exposure to as few people as possible." protested Askelion.

"Dr. Lamakian, I am a fully qualified physician. University of Washington medical school. As a student I participated in AIDS research. I interned at Fred Hutchinson, also in Seattle. The latest in cancer treatments. I specialize in infectious viruses and took a job in Atlanta with the Center for Disease Control. I have been on the last two ebola outbreaks in Zaire now Congo, anthrax in Iran, and bubonic plague in India."

"Iran, I thought you Americans weren't getting along with Iran."

"The Iran trip is kinda secret."

"Kinda secret?"

"The press reports it but we and the Iranians officially deny it. When there's a dangerous bug on the loose killing people, politics are tossed aside and CDC is welcome. In addition, I know a little bit about Neanderthal physiology and a lot about Cro-Magnon."

"One other thing about Dr. Nguyen," added the President, "she has been fully briefed on the current situation inside Algeria. She is authorized to brief you while you're on your way there."

"Yes, we've heard about it. Okay, Cuc, get into a pressure suit. It wouldn't hurt to talk shop with an Earth physician."

Cuc Nguyen went back into the limousine and brought out several bags of her equipment. Metrola and I loaded them into the Shuttle. We were already in pressure suits. Mine fit, sort of. It was made for a Neanderthal woman, a Cro-Magnon man required some adjustments. The chest felt roomy, my breasts are of the masculine variety. The shoulders fit fine, Neanderthal women are built strong. After loading Cuc's equipment, she brought suits of a different variety from the back seat of the Presidential limousine. "We call these 'moon suits'. We need to put them on when we go into the field. They'll protect us from any bug that might be in the environment."

"Are these like pressure suits?"

"No. They're designed to work in an atmosphere. But this backpack provides you with sterile air. Instead of the bulkiness of a pressure suit, you'll have full freedom of movement for your fingers. Everything seals up, Virus may touch the outside, but it does not get inside. After a possible exposure, we have equipment to spray you down with disinfectant. Then you can get out of the moon suit, which can then be incinerated."

Askelion looked at the Earth technology with skepticism. But she knew she had to get along with the Earth medical community if indeed there was a Virus present in the Algerian cave. "Let's get this stuff on board. No offense, Cuc, but how are we going to get you into a pressure suit, you are so small!"

Cuc smiled. "Yeah, I'm five foot one. When I pig out, I get up to 105 pounds. I am gifted with the curse of not being able to gain weight."

"Oh I feel SO SORRY for you!" we all called out! My pot belly disappeared while on the *Neanderthal Return*, but I gain weight too easily with Earth food. This can be a problem for Neanderthal girls as well.

Cuc laughed. "Yeah, I get that a lot! Being thin and pretty has its advantages." We managed, with a lot of adjusting and shortening, to get the pressure suit on Dr. Cuc. We all strapped in, me next to Metrola as before. With the ramp withdrawn and the door closed,

Metrola fired up the Shuttle. People on the ground backed away and held out compasses to watch the needles point at the Shuttle.

The Shuttle silently lifted off and rose up out of Washington. People on the ground did not hear any sound other than the landing gear retracting. We had clearance from ATC, the President had already talked to them. Sabar Duradich brought the *Neanderthal Return* around. Metrola brought us up out of the atmosphere to rendezvous with the mother ship. After we cycled into the Shuttle Bay, Meddi Chumkun was there waiting for us. The two passengers disappeared into the ship. We then loaded about a *kecht* of *dollons* of equipment on to the Shuttle, including two *hekt dollons* of a special disinfectant designed to destroy the Virus. We left the *Neanderthal Return*, Meddi came with us. Sabar brought the ship over the Sahara Desert while we were on board.

I was strapped in next to Metrola, looking down into the center of the Sahara. We had maps of Algeria brought in from the ship. They were faxed up from Earth and printed out. Dr. Cuc briefed us on the latest State Department and CIA information on Algeria. The Tassili area should be safe, just stay away from the Tell in the north. "Okay, Metrola, this is where we need to go. This is the little city of Illizi. From there, about 40 miles in a straight line this way, about two dozen *kepfats*, is the archeological Base Camp. When we get down close, we should see it because the Algerian Army has the place surrounded."

"All those mountains around there."

"Mountains shouldn't be a problem. The Base Camp has lots of flat places to land. They land helicopters there. Can you actually hover this thing?"

"Sure, we ride the Earth's Magnetic Field."

"N.R. Shuttle, this is Tamanrasset Air Traffic Control, do you copy?" The Algerians, like air traffic controllers everywhere, communicate in English and use feet for altitude.

"This is N.R. Shuttle, we copy. We are maintaining 550,000 feet altitude. Shall we drop in for a visit?"

"The sooner the better, everyone is waiting at the Base Camp. Labna Abbas is very upset. She wants to get her children out of there! But the scientists understand the need for quarantine. The Americans have already told us about Dr. Nguyen from CDC. Who all is with you?"

"Metrola Mornuxler is piloting the Shuttle. I am Neil Peace, U.S. citizen, helping her. Our passengers are three physicians, Dr. Nguyen, and Doctors Lamakian and Chumkun from Planet Creation. I hope you don't mind woman physicians?"

The ATC controller laughed. "Some people are very traditional about the role of women in society. But we don't object to women in medicine. This is an emergency. Bring them on down, they just have to be modest, that's all."

Metrola gave me an angry look. She turned off the microphone. "What's he mean by 'modest'?"

"Uhh, Algeria has been Muslim since the Seventh Century. The period of French Rule helped Algeria become more modern about women. Berber women often don't cover their hair. But Islamic fundamentalism is a force and has led to violence. A lot of violence. They'll allow you to be a pilot, because you've earned that. They'll allow our three passengers to be physicians and test for the presence of the Virus. But I strongly suggest you don't take ANY clothes off in public or flirt with any of the men. That's what he means by being modest. It's a culture shock for liberated women from places like the United States and Planet Creation."

"It's not too big a problem." commented Dr. Cuc, who has been in Muslim countries on bug hunts. "Just be tactful and respectful. It sometimes helps that I'm not white, but I often wore a head to toe chador. In the Algerian desert, we can show our faces, our hair should not be a problem. But if someone offers you a hejab, a head covering, put it on. We're not coming to offend local sensibilities. Our job is to make sure we don't have a dangerous bug on our hands."

Meddi and Askelion nodded their heads and told our pilot in Atlantean, that it is Okay. "Please Metrola." I begged. "You don't have to leave the Shuttle if you don't want to. That would be modest. Wearing the moon suits should maintain modesty."

Metrola took a deep breath and turned on the microphone. "This is N.R. Shuttle, Metrola Mornuxler, PILOT." She emphasized the word loudly. "Do we have clearance for descent into Algerian airspace?"

"You have clearance, N.R. Shuttle. Can you see Illizi? It's on a road called the Route du Tassili N'Ajjer."

"We can see Illizi, and the road." I confirmed. "We will aim for a point seventy kilometers southwest of Illizi. Do we have clearance for this flight plan?"

"We've canceled all flights between Tamanrasset and Illizi. The airspace is clear. When you get low, you should be able to see the Base Camp. Then I can turn you over to Lieutenant Hussein Ibrahim who is in charge of the Base Camp Force."

"This is Lieutenant Ibrahim, do you copy N.R. Shuttle?"

"We copy Ibrahim. We will begin descent when we have clearance." I turned to Metrola. "Seventy klicks is about two dozen *kepfats*. You see Illizi?"

"Yes, I see Illizi." Metrola confirmed.

"N.R. Shuttle, you are clear to descend into Algerian airspace." affirmed Tamanrasset ATC. "You are clear to approach the Base Camp."

"You are clear to land at the Base Camp." Lieutenant Ibrahim declared.

Metrola operated the controls and we rode down through the atmosphere. After we landed, we got out of our pressure suits. Metrola talked to Ibrahim through the radio. "We need a few minutes to get out of our pressure suits and to put on the CDC moon suits. I'll pull down the screen over our window"

"But you have a MAN in there!" responded Ibrahim. I could tell that he had a humorous accent to his voice. He represents the government, which has been fighting the extreme fundamentalists.

"I'm a decadent American. I'm already beyond salvation." I could hear Ibrahim and other men laughing. "Don't worry, these women are fully clothed under the pressure suits. They're not giving me a strip show while changing into the moon suits."

Askelion and Meddi gave a quick lesson in how to use the test equipment. "This device tests your breath. You attach a sterile tube like this. Ask the person to blow through it like so." Askelion blew through it. After a moment, an Atlantean word appeared. "This is the Atlantean word for 'negative'. Memorize it. Can you remember what this combination of letters looks like? Cuc?"

"Yes."

"Neil?"

"Of course. It's the word *jerofan*. I know that much Atlantean."

"Okay, as long as this is the result, we are Okay. If the Virus is present, a different word will read out and you will hear this warning tone." She pushed a test button and we heard the tone. It sounded like a test by the Emergency Broadcasting System.

Meddi took over. "This machine works by reading the DNA sequence of every virus detected in the breath. If any virus shows a significant portion of the sequence of the Holocaust Virus DNA, then the alarm sounds. This alarm should sound with any of the known benign forms of the Virus. It should also sound with any possible Cro-Magnon version of the Virus that we could mathematically model.   Analysis of Neil's Y chromosomes presents a different sequence than the Neanderthal Y chromosome.   Cro-Magnon men should be immune to the Virus that killed our men."

"But if this Virus was engineered," started Dr. Cuc, who knows about engineered viruses, "It could be engineered to replicate with Cro-Magnon Y chromosomes.   Why would the Face Mountain aliens do this to us?"

I fielded that one. "We're competitive, we're aggressive, we fight wars.   Viet Cong and the ARVN, they did an excellent job of killing each other, did they not?   It is true that we were primitive hunter-gatherers when the Face Mountaineers transplanted the Neanderthals to Creation.   But both Neanderthals and us Cro-Magnons must've shown our Killer Instinct even then.   Even then we must've shown them our ability to master technology, which makes war even deadlier.   But no matter how murderous we are to each other, we're not a danger to THEM as long as we cannot get off Planet."

"Neil Armstrong walked the Moon!"

"Now we are a danger to them.   Rockets are rather inefficient even if spectacular.   But the magnetic field technology that powers this Shuttle and contains the fusion reactor in the *Neanderthal Return* is not far beyond Earth capability.   We are now a significant threat to the Face Mountain aliens.   That's why the Virus booby trap at the Information Repository.   They knew about our curiosity.   Fast forward 45,000 years.   We have Afenor here.   A Neanderthal man, preserved with Egyptian mummification technology.   He is interned with an Egyptian cubit ruler and a YARDstick for crying out loud!   At the time he lived, what did we have in Egypt and Iraq?"

"Writing, numbers, mathematics, defined units of weight and measure."

"So if the Face Mountaineers were still around, they'd be saying 'Damn!   The Cro-Magnons are just as capable as the Neanderthals!'   You are absolutely right, Askelion, we better check this place out!"

"Anyway," Meddi began again, "These other machines are set to analyze blood and urine samples for the presence of the Virus.   These swabs work by wetting with this special fluid.   You rub a surface if you suspect a Virus in a cyst.   This liquid dissolves the cyst and awakes the Virus, just like when you inhale it or pick it up with your skin.   Then you put the swab into the machine, and it compares the DNA for a match.   As long as you see the Atlantean word '*jerofan*' everything's fine.   If you get a positive, then you use one of these spray cans with our special disinfectant.   It does three things: It dissolves the cysts in which these Viruses lay dormant.   Then an enzyme tears apart its DNA chain without affecting other types of virus.   It is an engineered enzyme.   There is also an engineered bacterium that seeks out and consumes these Viruses.   It does not eat anything else, it will die if there is no Virus present.   But we do not want to release it into the Earth environment unless we get a positive reading on our machines."

"Everybody know what to do?"   asked Askelion.   We all nodded yes.   "Okay, lets zip up these moon suits and get to work."

We opened the door and lowered the ramp.   Out we came in our moon suits carrying the test equipment.   It must have been ninety degrees!   Getting hotter inside the moon suit!   Lieutenant Ibrahim greeted us.   "Welcome to Algeria, my friends.   Can you hear me?"

We all answered yes.   We asked him if he could hear us, he answered yes.   Cuc Nguyen came up and addressed him.   "I'm Dr. Cuc Nguyen, of the Center for Disease Control in Atlanta.   I am honored to be in Algeria, we come in peace and friendship.   We will need to test everyone's breath, blood, and urine for the presence of the Virus.   Then we need to test surfaces that might have the Virus in cysts.   Last, we need to test Afenor Cave."

"Sounds like this is going to take the rest of the afternoon and most of the evening. We will take breaks for prayer and for meals. Today we pray to Allah that there is no Virus, and if there is, that we can eradicate it. We also thank Him for the survival of the Neanderthal Race and the warning that you have brought us. My men are under orders to cooperate in every way. All of the civilians will submit as well."

It was tedious work. The breath samples went quick. Urine samples are disagreeable to work with, but at least we could not smell them while in the moon suits. The blood tests took the longest, because only the three physicians could draw blood. Neither I nor Metrola had any experience finding veins. The Science and Humanities Channel camera crews followed us around, documenting the tests. Ian Miller narrated for the world audience. Meddi demonstrated the use of the test equipment for the video cameras. We found out that two Canadians with the S&H crew had been paramedics. We put Donald Colburn and Ben Roy Sumner to work. An Algerian soldier serving as a muezzin called the prayer. We stopped work and retired to the Shuttle for a break. Inside the Shuttle we tested the outside of our moon suits for the Virus. When the machine tested negative, we took off the head coverings to cool off and eat a snack. Metrola turned on what we call an air conditioner and the Shuttle air cooled slowly.

"So far, so good." started Askelion. "We'll soon be done with the Base Camp and the soldiers. Then we will have to go to Afenor Cave, ten kilometers or four *kepfats* from here. The soldiers guarding the Cave itself have cycled between there and the Base Camp, so we got all of them. We go into the Cave, we will have to test the little bags with the brown material. We believe the bags in the Information Repository is where the Face Mountain aliens stored the Virus. At the time Chmlee Mornuxler opened these bags, our medical science did not know about viruses, prions, and such. Once in his body, the cysts dissolved and the Virus replicated with his Y chromosomes. Because there were no symptoms, the entire Reducker Expedition was infected by casual contact with Metrola's ancestor. That's why we reacted when Chuck Carter told me about the bags."

Meddi then spoke. "You can't come into the Cave with us, Neil. Neither can Donald or Ben. We're going to test the contents of these bags. If the Virus is there, we are prepared to disinfect them and everything in the site, regardless of the loss to archeology. If the Virus gets into a man with Y chromosomes with which it can replicate, that one man can spread it to the entire male human population of Earth. We cannot take that risk. If it gets into a woman, it can survive for a while, but it cannot replicate. Our bodies will overwhelm it with antibodies. Also, we can isolate ourselves and take the bacteria that eats this Virus. We believe that because none of these bags have been opened, the Virus, if it is there, is still safely contained. That is why we are having the negative readings. This is good news. But you understand. It has to be just us girls in the Cave."

"Yes, I understand. I can relax and shoot the breeze with Chuck Carter, it's nice to meet a fellow American in this foreign land. What about Afenor? He was a Neanderthal. What if he died of the Virus?"

"Well, if he had any form of the Virus in him when he died, it would form cysts and become dormant. For a long time. We'll test tissue samples. Good thinking, Neil."

After we finished the meal, the prayer was over, we put the moon suit helmets back on and resumed the testing. When the three physicians certified the Base Camp to be free of disease, we all breathed a sigh of relief. We climbed out of the moon suits. "Do you want us to cover our hair?" asked Dr. Cuc.

"You don't have to if you don't want to." assured Labna Abbas. "But I have some extra hejabs, if you want to cover your hair."

"No, but thank you anyway."

Lieutenant Ibrahim declared the Base Camp lifted from quarantine, but that the quarantine still held for Afenor Cave. This was announced to the rest of the world.

We put the equipment away and visited with our hosts before going to sleep.

The next morning the girls went over to Afenor Cave to analyze Afenor and the plastic bags for the Virus. I took it easy. For the first time in my life, being male got me out of having to do work! The archeologists invited me over to view the photographs and drawings of the site. As I studied the X-ray photo of Afenor's clearly Neanderthal skull, Mohammed Abbas, Ali Amoud, Mustafa Khedr, and Chuck Carter relaxed. The Muslims had their soft drinks. Chuck and I each had a nice cold beer.

"Not only do I get to drink beer, but I have also been known to eat BACON!" bragged Chuck.

The other men laughed. "I wouldn't brag about your decadent Christian abominations if I was you, Chuck."

"Speaking of abominations against God, Chuck, you happen to have some clam chowder?" I asked, but not seriously.

"No, no. But since you are from the State of Washington, maybe you can arrange to have Dungeness crab flown in. Now that is my favorite fish without scales."

"You laugh, but we don't get red tide poisoning."

"But seriously, folks," started Mustafa, the serious Egyptologist, "this Cave may the archeological find of the new Millennium, it is such an anomaly."

"The Neanderthal girls from Creation are anomalous." I commented.

"And not too bad in the sack?"

"I don't kiss and tell! It's RUDE. No way to treat a lady."

"They find out you been talkin' 'bout dem, dey'll kick yo' ass!" warned Chuck, now on his second beer.

"That too. We already had quite a few historical and archeological anomalies. The Giza Pyramids. Almost every other stone structure from ancient Egypt is covered with writing. But except for the graffiti found by Vyse, almost no inscriptions whatsoever were carved by the ancient Egyptians on the Giza Pyramids. And the geometry of them! 440 royal cubits to a side, within inches of a perfect square. Such are the dimensions of the Great Pyramid. Divide the 880 royal cubits of two sides by the height of 280 royal cubits to which it was originally built, and you get π!"

"Speaking of interesting coincidences," started Mustafa, "The perimeter of the base of the Great Pyramid is 1760 royal cubits, which is the number of yards in your mile."

"Yeah, how about that? Here is what we do: We define 220 royal cubits as the Egyptian furlong. Got that? A square Egyptian furlong should be 10 Egyptian acres. Since the Great Pyramid is 2 Egyptian furlongs long and 2 Egyptian furlongs wide, the Great Pyramid covers 40 Egyptian acres. The perimeter is eight Egyptian furlongs, an Egyptian mile. That would be just like the 'Back Forty' in the U.S. It is a square, two furlongs by two furlongs, and you need a mile of fence for the perimeter. Who needs the Metric System? We've got something better!"

Laughter. When the Egyptologist recovered, he admitted, "Yeah, I have to admit it is a problem for Egyptology. Somebody told Herodotus that the Great Pyramid was built for King Khufu and that has been the official line since. Never mind the incredible mathematical precision to which the thing is built. Never mind the complete lack of inscriptions and the absence of the Pharaoh's body. We've always had grave robbers, but they usually don't take the time to sand off inscriptions while stealing the gold and artifacts. When inscriptions are vandalized, it was usually for political reasons and we can find evidence of that. But we still refuse to believe that the Pyramids were built before the Fourth Dynasty, even though the glorified tomb theory wears thin."

"Speaking of pre-dynastic theories, there is the heavily eroded lion body of the Sphinx! There hasn't been rain like that in Egypt since King Narmer put it all together! Anomalies? How did Plato know about the 'opposite continent that surrounds what can truly be called the ocean'? He describes a 2000 by 3000 stadia island beyond the Pillars of Hercules, that's Atlantis, beyond which he describes America 1300 years before Leif Erikson! 1800 years before Columbus."

"Yeah, and I hear Quetzalcoatl was a white man from Plato's Atlantis."

"One possibility. Hey, the Mormons have Jesus Christ going to America and ministering to the Indians. Who are we to say they are wrong? And then there is the Kennewick Man. What's a white guy, not an Indian, doing on the bank of the Columbia River 7,300 years before Jesus?"

"Getting shot by a spear, that's what he was doing. It healed some, but the infection probably killed him, like Richard the Lionhearted."

"Cayuse never did like white men invading their territory. First the women in the spacecraft. Now a 4500 year old Neanderthal mummy buried among Egyptian hieroglyphics describing an expedition sent out by King Khufu. For whom the Great Pyramid is named. I think it's high time for the archeology community to quit being so obstinate about considering alternative theories to explain the evidence. Indeed, the science community at large. They were so annoyed by those NASA photos of Face Mountain!"

"That's the last bag. No Virus in any of them!" Askelion declared to her relief and jubilation. "No Virus in any of the tissue samples from Afenor. He didn't have it when he died."

They ripped off their moon suits. "The bags are made of some kind of cellophane. Afenor's people figured out how to make it from wood. The material inside appears to be finely ground hemp leaves."

"Marijuana." confirmed Dr. Cuc. "I bet the THC content was pretty high. No seeds. Maui Wowee quality. Pretty stale now, too bad."

"4500 year old controlled substance. Let's go give 'em the good news. I'm sure the archeologists will be happy to carbon-14 date the cellophane and the marijuana. Cuc, do you mind if we say a prayer for Afenor?"

"Not at all. Go ahead."

The three Creation women spoke quietly in Atlantean, the Prayer for the Dead.

Chapter Twenty One

"Mr. President, here are the latest Keyhole Satellite photos of Algeria and Libya."

"The *Neanderthal Return* has not interfered with the operation of our spy satellites?"

"No, they've been scrupulous about honoring the Agreement. But they should be scanning the Tassili n'Ajjer region as much as we are. Terrorist Training Camp M165 in Libya is deserted. This is from HUMINT confirmed by satellite photography." HUMINT is a CIA acronym for human intelligence. A spy. "It might be an idea if the Algerians allow us to send a Blackbird in return for a share of the intelligence." A Lockheed SR-71. If the Algerian government granted the clearance, the spy plane can fly along the Libyan border and take oblique photographs of TTC M165. The terrorists duck inside whenever a satellite flies over. The Blackbird can catch them by surprise.

"TTC M165 is deserted, what does that mean?" asked the President.

"That's the terrorist camp closest to Illizi and Fort Tarat in Algeria. Three Creation women and two American citizens dropped in yesterday on the Creation flying saucer. The Creation physicians were worried about a possible Virus booby trap, and said so on the radio. With another 20 non-Algerians there with the Science and Humanities Channel, about half of them Americans, the rest Canadians, British, and one German, this place is now a juicy terrorist target. The S&H people broadcast live through the satellites."

"Is there any evidence of an impending attack against the Base Camp?"

"GIS is raising Hell in Algiers and other cities on the Mediterranean coast, as usual. But up 'til now, the desert's been peaceful. The people in Illizi were just as pissed off about the election cancellation as Algerians elsewhere. It's hard to determine the level of GIS support in Illizi. The ordinary bandits in the Sahara are not likely to attack a well defended target like the archeological Base Camp. But the GIS could take on Ibrahim's troops and reap the publicity."

"Okay. Inform the Algerians that TTC M165 is deserted. I'll inform the Creation girls and suggest they get their Shuttle outta there as soon as they're done sweeping for the Virus."

After the President hung up the phone, he and his Secret Service bodyguard went over to the Lincoln Bedroom. Henry Turnipseed answered. "Mr. Turnipseed, may we come in?"

"Sure, Helga and Lucinda are in here."

"How's Lucinda doing?"

"She's glad to be out of the hospital. Glad to be alive. Yeah, come in."

"Hello, Mr. President!" greeted the women cheerfully.

"Thank you for letting Henry visit with us here." said Lucinda.

"Henry, how long will you be in town?" asked the President.

"Got a plane this afternoon out of Reagan National for Seattle. I need to get to my farm and plant my crop."

"I understand. There is something that I have to tell you that we cannot have in the media. Can I get your cooperation on that?"

The women nodded, but Henry was skeptical. "Watergate, Iran-Contra, Whitewater, Monica Lewinsky, please Mr. President, I don't want any part of anything like that."

"He has been a perfect gentleman with us," reassured Lucinda, "he hasn't made any passes or improper suggestions to us."

The President chuckled. "Aren't you glad I'm not Bill Clinton. Don't worry, Henry, it's not another scandal." He took a deep breath. "Algeria has been in a state of civil war since an election was canceled several years ago. The opposition wanted to change the laws to a fundamentalist Islamic model of society. They were going to win the election according to all of the polls. When democracy was canceled, the people were understandably angry. The mainline part of the opposition eschews violence. But the radical wing, called the GIS, has engaged in a campaign of incredible terror. It is not unusual for 2,000 people to be killed in a month. However, in the desert where your Shuttle went, it has been peaceful. But the terrorist camp in Libya closest to Illizi is now empty. This is the camp that was training Algerian GIS terrorists. With all of the live reports from the Science and Humanities Crew about the Neanderthal mummy and the Egyptian hieroglyphs, and with your physicians checking for a potentially catastrophic Virus, we think this place might be a target."

"Thank you for telling us this, Mr. President." said Helga. "What should we do?"

"You have a communicator with your ship?"

Helga held out a small object in her hand. "I can talk to the *Return*. What do you think I should tell them?"

"I suggest that the Shuttle with the Creation women, Dr. Nguyen, and Neil Peace get out of there as soon as your physicians certify that Afenor Cave is clear of the Virus."

"I see. I shall also suggest that we take the position that Algeria's internal affairs are not our concern. We just wanted to make sure that there was not a dangerous contagion hidden in an ancient tomb." Helga then contacted her ship and spoke with them in urgent Atlantean.

Everyone at the Base Camp was happy. No Virus. The archeologists were ready to resume the dig, the happy news broadcast to the world by the S&H crew. The physicians, Metrola, and I were invited to a celebration lunch in a large tent. As we enjoyed the Algerian food, we engaged in conversation with the archeologists, proposing theories, each wilder than the last, to explain how Afenor was alive 4500 years ago, and why the ancient Egyptian writing described him as a man from Atlantis. It has never been unusual for the dead to be buried with personal possessions or offerings. But such items usually do not include measuring sticks.

"The Arabic name for Egypt is Al Misra." Mustafa Khedr restated a fact that everyone knew. "That means 'The Measured Land'. The reason for this is that Egypt has the reputation of having been surveyed to the last cubit, palm, and finger since very ancient times."

"Not to the last millimeter?"

"That's been since Napoleon. Today, we're surveyed to the last millimeter. If you look at the precision of the Pyramids, the need to survey the farm plots on the banks of the Nile, the need to control the quantity of water distributed to each farm; you know they felt the vital need for science, mathematics, engineering. Until Aswan Dam was built, the Nilometer was closely watched by everyone during the annual flood. If the River did not reach 16 cubits, then famine will be in the land. So writing, numbers, weights and measures, the fertility of the land, vital to the survival of the nation, were originally considered the gifts of Amon-Ra. Now that we have been corrected by Mohammed, Peace Be Upon Him, we consider these things the gifts of Allah."

"I thought the Metric System was the gift of the French. I stand corrected, it is a gift from God." Laughter. "But in the time of the pharaohs, was there a religious significance to cubits?"

"Under the pharaohs, there was a religious significance to everything. The pharaoh was an image of God on Earth. Tutankhamon, 'Living Image of Amon'. So his laws are the laws handed down from a god. This is a common thing in the ancient world. The Code of Hammurabi was handed down from Shamesh. In Plato's Atlantis, the laws were handed down from Poseidon. The Ten Commandments handed down from Allah."

"Basic problem of government." stated Chuck Carter. "How do you get the people to obey the laws? Whatever laws you write, they don't work if the people don't comply. So you tell them these laws are handed down from gods, and they'll have Hell to pay if they don't obey. The American idea of separation of church and state didn't occur to them because they couldn't imagine one without the other!"

"Some folks are still a little weak on that!" responded Mustafa. "The problem with weights and measures is definition. Without definition, you cannot have precision. Without precision, you cannot have the Giza Pyramids. Or navigation. Or desert-gation across the Sahara. Can't have those cubits varying in length all the time. Merchants cheated by using different sized shekels. Without a standard shekel, you cannot have honest trade. The pharaohs' solution was to declare that the Royal Cubit was defined by the gods. Cubit rulers have been recovered from tomb treasuries along with the other odds and ends that a mummy would be supplied for the trip into the next world."

"So what's with Afenor? A cubit ruler and a measuring stick that is definitely NOT Egyptian was placed in the coffin with him."

"Weighing on a scale is part of the imagery of the Egyptian Book of the Dead. The deceased is brought before the Goddess Maat. His heart is placed on a balance scale. If his heart is heavy due to the weight of his sins, it was fed to a lion and he was sent into oblivion for real. If his heart was light in weight, because he lived a good life without too much sin, he was allowed to continue on his journey. This is a final judgment, a reckoning. The weight of your heart is the weight of your sins."

"Were Egyptians buried with standard weights?"

"Standard weights have been found in tombs. Hmm. Maybe Afenor had a belief system where his sins were measured in length. So he was supplied with rulers to help him pass the Judgment of Maat."

"With some people I know, they would need a hundred meter tape measure." Laughter.

Metrola heard a soft beep. She took out her communicator and spoke softly into it. She listened. "Lieutenant Ibrahim,"

"Yes, milady?"

"The American CIA reports that Terrorist Training Camp M165 in Libya has been deserted the last few hours. Our infrared scanners on our ship confirm the lack of living human bodies."

"M165. That's 105 kilometers inside Libya across from Illizi and Fort Tarat. It often gets above human body temperature in the desert afternoon. But right now it's still well below that. So 165 is deserted. I'll alert my men, thank you and thanks to the American CIA."

"What does this mean, Lieutenant?"

"Nothing, probably. We get these alerts all the time. The GIS has been a bother, but they usually don't cause trouble this deep in the desert."

"We usually don't have living Neanderthals who are worldwide celebrities in this Base Camp." I pointed out. "I haven't noticed a great deal of press worldwide about the troubles you have in Algeria. The GIS might want attention, which is the terrorist's greatest craving."

"You are welcome to stay, but you are free to leave."

The ten jeeps were parked just behind the dune under covers made to look like desert sand. The engines hadn't run for a while, to keep them from showing up on the satellite infrared or whatever sensor technology the *Neanderthal Return* has. An American built Jeep, some Land Rovers, and some Toyota Land Cruisers. Five to ten years old, the vehicles were selected for their ability to blend in with the local trucks. The GIS got them into position while the Army scrambled to surround the Base Camp and Afenor Cave for quarantine. Now the commander viewed the Base Camp through his binoculars. "You read the report from the Avengers of Yahweh?"

"Yeah. Neanderthal women are tough, deadly. Demon Women, they call them."

"Just kill them. They say their ship is unarmed. They may be strong, the daughters of demons, but they're women. They are not hard as steel like us desert rats."

"Trogs." He spoke in Arabic, but used the racial epithet for Neanderthals. "I agree with the Avengers. They were supposed to have been wiped out by Allah in the Flood. They are not supposed to be alive. Besides, they have allied with the Great Satan." His reference to the United States.

"Their physicians now certify that Afenor's Cave is clean of their so-called Virus. Ibrahim has reduced his force. Wait a minute." The soldiers looked like they were under an alert. In that case, now or never. The commander grabbed his radio and gave the click-click signal for the attack. The Land Cruisers, Land Rovers, and his Command Jeep roared to life and charged over the hill.

"We're under attack!" a soldier screamed in Arabic. Explosions and gunfire erupted all over the Base Camp. Ibrahim's troops formed a skirmish line. Some sortied out in their own Land Rovers, the battle was on.

Metrola screamed at me in Atlantean, "Neil, to the Shuttle!"

"On my way!" I answered in English. I followed Metrola up the ramp into the Shuttle. The three physicians were already there. As we strapped ourselves into the seats, other civilians clambered on board. Chuck Carter. Mustafa Khedr.

Mohammed Abbas. "Don't worry about Labna and my kids. They're in Illizi." Praise Allah for that.

Science and Humanities Channel people ran into the Shuttle. Several were staying to report on the attack, but the others wanted out. "Close the door!" Metrola screamed in Atlantean. "We cannot take any more passengers!" It was crowded and we were probably overweight. With the door still open, we lifted off. Somebody got the ramp retracted and the door closed. As we passed 100 feet in altitude, we could see the battle over the camp buildings. The GIS attempted to flank the skirmish line by driving around it. Several vehicles were on fire, bodies littered the ground. "Okay Neil," said Metrola after a quick survey of the scene, "we're going up, figure two, three gees, considering all this weight."

A rocket flew past us. Bullets crashed into the ship. Holes in the window in front of me. "Anybody hurt?!" I screamed in English.

"Fred Graf. Two bullets in his leg! Get him to a hospital, he should make it!"

"We have three physicians on board! Tend to him ladies!"

Metrola studied the bullet holes in the window. The Creation Neanderthal version of Plexiglas. "We ain't leaving the atmosphere 'til that's fixed. Passenger needs hospital. Where to, Neil?"

She really did not have any idea. "We don't want to go to Libya. Chad, Niger, Mali, forget it. Tunisia? Too close to Libya. Head for Morocco. They may be tolerable, if not, head across the Med for Spain or France." I looked back at Mohammed, Mustafa, and Chuck. "No offense, guys, but right now I have a preference for someplace modern, Christian, and European."

"Understand." "No problem." They had that same preference.

Metrola screamed "Missile coming after us! What is it?"

One of the S&H men looked out the rear window. "Stinger!"

"Oh shit!" I exclaimed.

"I don't like the sound of that 'Oh shit!', Neil." complained Metrola. She jerked the ship all over the place to evade the missile. The wounded Fred Graf screamed involuntarily. Cuc, Meddi, Askelion, and the two former paramedics, Don Colburn and Ben Sumner, tried desperately to treat his wounds, his blood smearing the floorboards. Air whistled in through the bullet holes near him. Jagged aluminum bent inward, threatening to shred any skin that got near.

"Let the missile come close, and then jerk away." I suggested.

Metrola was frightened and not entirely cool under fire. "Let it CLOSE! Are you NUTS!"

"I read it somewhere."

"Oh thank you, Mr. Expert in Air-to-Air Combat." What is it about women? You get to know one of them, and she gets nasty and sarcastic with you about things like this.

"'E's right! I was a chopper pilot in the Royal Marines."

"The missile follows me as I juke back and forth." observed Metrola.

"'Eat seeker." observed the former Royal Marine. "You 'ave a 'eat source on this flying saucer?"

The missile ran out of fuel and fell to the desert floor. Everyone cheered in relief. "Nice flying, Metrola!"

"Thank you." Metrola turned to the British man who knows about Stinger missiles. "What do you mean by 'heat source'?"

"The Stinger 'as an infrared detector that it 'omes in with. If you're in a jet fighter, it's difficult to evade a 'eat seeker, though with training, you usually can. They're rather effective against 'elicopters. Is your engine 'ot?"

"No, not much hotter than anything else. The energy is not heat. It's nothing like your combustion engines."

"Another missile! Off to the right!"

"Another Stinger, all right!"

"What is it with these Algerians?" screamed Metrola. "We come in peace! We're not concerned with your local disputes!"

"The GIS likes to kill foreigners."

"Why?"

"To make it impossible for the government to govern the country."

"That's very productive. This missile is also following my evasive movements. I'm going to duck behind that dune!" Metrola brought us down to the deck. The missile followed. She cleared the top of the dune by inches. She followed the contour of the backside of the dune. The Stinger flew into the sand and exploded.

Applause and cheering. "WOW!" Sheer terror followed by relief. "Cracking! Metrola, did you receive any kind of military training?" asked the former British Marine.

"Not THIS kind of military training."

"Oh, pardon, where are me manners? My name is Ian Miller." The S&H narrator drops the h's when he's not on microphone. Metrola reached back to shake his hand as she drove the ship higher and faster. "Ma'am, this ship operates by creating a magnetic field that counters the Earth's magnetic field, does it not?"

"Yes. I wonder if the GIS knows this too?"

"Blimey! They could've modified their missiles to seek your magnetic field!"

Metrola sighed as she stared out the window at the desert passing below. "A magnetic field that causes compasses to point at me is not exactly Stealth."

As she thought hard on the concept, "Another Stinger!" someone yelled.

"No dunes this time!" screamed Metrola. The Sahara was flat and sandless.

"Do a juke move that sends us upward as the missile gets within two *hekt potes*," I suggested, "then suddenly cut power."

"Free fall. But going upward we can do it for a few *prelates*." She juked the missile, it followed us. She let it get within one *hekt potes*. I didn't suggest THAT! Then she shot us upward at 45 degrees, while changing our ground course 120 degrees around the compass. Everyone not strapped down was thrown. We became weightless when Metrola suddenly cut power. We were just under Mach One, the air screaming past the bullet holes.

"Look at the Stinger!" shouted someone excitedly. The rocket flew below us, in a wide curve toward the south.

"I'll be buggered!" exclaimed Miller. "She's seeking the South Magnetic Pole!" We watched as the missile found the desert floor and exploded. We were weightless. It is no fun being in an artillery shell. Ears were popping. We were nearing the top of the parabola, about 20 seconds passed. Metrola turned on the motor and restored gravity by flying level. I checked the altimeter, 9,600 feet.

"That missile suddenly lost track of us when I cut the magnetic field generator." declared Metrola quietly, her anger building. "Those three rockets were DELIBERATELY modified to attack US!" She blew a large amount of air in a long slow breath. "We come in peace. We agreed to not take any hostile action against any Earth nation. But people keep trying to kidnap us or kill us! What did we do wrong?"

"Nothing." I assured her. "Pull yourself together. Now we're between 9,000 and 10,000 feet. This is a good altitude, considering we don't have pressure suits on and there are holes in our cabin."

"Thanks, Neil. Morocco, right?"

"Yeah." She checked the Global Positioning System computer she rigged off of our satellites. Compared the latitude and longitude reading to the map of North Africa. One second of latitude is about 100 feet. The GPS is accurate to less than that. We were 100 miles northwest of the Base Camp. She pointed us toward Morocco and accelerated.

"We can get supersonic and still not burn up. But given the bullet holes, I'll keep our airspeed below two *hekt kepfats* per hour. And I'll keep us below 10,000 feet."

"The bullet holes will scream." I observed, as their whine got louder. "How's Fred Graf?"

"Banged up like the rest of us." answered Dr. Cuc.

"I'll be all right." confirmed Fred.

"Well, I don't know about that. He hasn't gone into shock, we managed to keep that from happening. Patient is in good spirits as you can see."

"Of course I'm in good spirits! Three Sting-kers? Ve all come vithin zentimeters of getting killed three times. But the marvelous Metrola Mornuxler saves our lives every time. However, remind me to send note to German motor vehicle authority not to grant her driver's license. Ve don't vant her driving on our autobahns!" In spite of all of the groans from the bruises and bumps, there was laughter.

Metrola reacted well to the banter. "Question Fred."

"Shoot."

"Your autobahns have no speed limit?"

"That is correct. It really is no speed limit."

"Uh-huh. And they call us Neanderthals crazy."

"Neandertal is a place in Germany."

"I know. Do people shoot at you while you drive the autobahn?"

"Not since the surrender in 1945. No, it isn't like America."

"Fred, you've been reading too many newspapers." I assured him. "They do exaggerate."

Metrola explained the situation. "We're heading for Morocco. It'll take about two hours. We can't go faster because of the damage to the ship. We can't go into space with these holes. Are there decent hospitals in Morocco for Fred?"

"Yes, there are qualified trauma surgeons in Casablanca." answered Dr. Cuc.

"I wonder where the Air Traffic Controllers are?" I asked. I put on the headset. "This is N.R. Shuttle, calling Algerian Air Traffic Control. Come in please, do you copy?" I repeated this several times. No answer. Has the GIS downed the ATC system?

Suddenly, there was an answer. "This is Morocco Air Force Command calling N.R. Shuttle, do you copy?" It was faint, full of static.

Then on the same frequency, much stronger. "This is the *Neanderthal Return*, calling N.R. Shuttle, do you copy, Neil?" Pidonita's familiar voice sure sounded good!

"This is N.R. Shuttle calling both Morocco Air Force Command AND the *Neanderthal Return*. Yes! We copy!"

"This is Morocco, please let us explain the situation to the best of our knowledge. After years of street violence, the GIS is making its bid for power. We don't think they'll win, this time. But they have shut down all ATC and radio communications within Algeria. The archeological Base Camp appears to have been successfully defended. But it's a mess, we haven't any broadcasts from the S&H Channel guys. There is house to house fighting in progress in Illizi, Djanet, Tamanrasset, Algiers, Oran, and most other cities. French Navy is approaching the coast. Why haven't you cleared the atmosphere and gotten outta there?"

"This is Metrola Mornuxler, pilot of the N.R. Shuttle. We got out of the Base Camp a minute after the attack started. We have bullet holes in our front window and in the aluminum of our hull. We have, how many passengers? 21 passengers, all civilians. One passenger has bullet wounds in the leg. We cannot go into space until the holes are repaired. After we cleared out of the Base Camp, we were attacked by three Stinger missiles that apparently were modified to seek the magnetic field of our Shuttle. We evaded all three missiles. But many of our passengers were not strapped down. We have a lot of bumps and bruises. Our three physicians and two paramedics are doing the best they can, but we need a hospital."

"N.R. Shuttle, you are cleared to enter Moroccan airspace. We have a fine hospital for your wounded passenger in Casablanca."

"Thank you!" we both exclaimed in relief.

BOOM! "What was that?" someone screamed. We became weightless.

Metrola furiously worked her controls and read her gauges. "We've lost the magnetic field generators. We're in free fall! I can't turn 'em back on!" She punched an emergency button. Another Foom! sounded above. The ship stopped falling and swung back and forth. We could see the parachutes deployed above. "Emergency 'chutes." stated Metrola as a matter of fact. She went back to trying to figure out what went wrong. We were smack dab in the middle of a nation engaged in full scale civil war, dangling from three parachutes like an Apollo capsule.

I worked the radio. "This is N.R. Shuttle, calling Morocco and the *Neanderthal Return*, do you copy?"

"Yes, we copy." they both answered. Good, the radio still works! "We've had a malfunction. The magnetic field generators are gone, Metrola has deployed the parachutes."

"This is Morocco Air Command. We copy, you are disabled and landing with parachutes. We cannot enter Algerian territory at this time. We are neutral with respect to the civil war, for us to come would be an act of war. Good luck, N.R. Shuttle." They signed off.

Metrola had more bad news. "The hydraulics are not functioning, I cannot lower the landing gear. The 'chutes are designed to drop us with a three *pote* per *prelate* terminal velocity with the nominal weight. We are heavy, so we are falling at maybe four or five *potes* per *prelate*. We'll hit hard. Brace yourselves everyone!" We hit, a hard landing. "Everyone all right?!" Everyone answered yes.

"We're in the middle of a desert. How's our water supply?"

Metrola suddenly looked very tired. She's done well, but this is not pleasant for any of us. "After the doctors declared the Base Camp clear of the Virus, we refilled our water tanks from the Camp well. We have two dozen *shlopons* of fresh water. If the tanks aren't damaged."

I punched a calculator. "We should have water adequate to last a while, 135 gallons." Ian Miller's British. "American sized gallons." I multiplied by 3.78. "512 liters for those who Think Metric. If, as Met says, the tanks aren't damaged."

The physicians broke out their medical equipment. Meddi checked a water faucet. A *dollop*, half a fluid ounce, poured into a small cup. "Tank Number One works. That's 12 *shlopons*." Half of our supply is intact!

Askelion checked another faucet, another half ounce! "Tank Number Two works. Our supply is intact, unless the tank is leaking through a bullet hole."

"I'll go outside to look," volunteered Ian Miller.

"I'm the pilot, I'll come with you." answered Metrola. She switched to Atlantean to talk to me, I had become almost fluent. "Neil, get on the radio, inform the *Neanderthal Return* of our current status and try to get help."

I got on the radio. The mother ship was in contact with the world governments. Pidonita managed to get in touch with General Hakim of the Algerian Army. She relayed him to me. "I'm extremely glad to hear you're still alive, no one dead yet?"

"Fred Graf, German national, was one of the S&H guys who came with us. He has suffered bullet wounds to the right leg. The bullets came through the hull as we were pulling out of the Base Camp. He is still alive. We have 500 liters of water for 21 people."

"Good. Ibrahim's men did well, but Lieutenant Ibrahim is dead. The assault on the Base Camp was repulsed, but with many casualties. The GIS retreated leaving 18 dead. We suffered 22 dead at the Base Camp and many more elsewhere. War's nasty business in the desert. There is fighting in the cities at this hour except Illizi, Djanet and few other desert towns where we've managed to gain control. But our Air Traffic Control is wrecked, all of our aircraft and radar were destroyed in the initial attack. We cannot get anybody out to help you. Maybe we can invite American help from the carrier *Abraham Lincoln* which I believe is now in the Med. But we cannot grant clearance to enter airspace we don't control."

"Okay," started Pidonita in the *Return*. "I'll see if we can get the President to authorize some kind of mission from the *Lincoln* to your location."

In the burning Sahara sun, Metrola and Ian carefully inspected the outside of the wrecked Shuttle. "I don't see any water leaking out 'ere." noted Ian cheerfully.

"The water tanks are intact." confirmed Metrola. "But what was that explosion? I cannot think of anything that would explode in our Shuttle machinery. We don't work with any combustible fuel. You smell anything like burned electrical wiring? I don't, and I have a good sense of smell."

"There was definitely an explosion, look at the damage. You mind if I peek in 'ere?"

"Go ahead, soon all of Earth will know how to build a magnetic drive flying saucer. All your engineers need to know is that it is possible. Then they are funded and they get to work."

"Do Boeing and Airbus a lotta good. Overnight, their beautiful planes are obsolete! And the American Space Shuttles! Spectacular and beautiful, but oh so expensive and inefficient. Well,

I'll just look in 'ere, 'ello! I'm getting a fireworks smell. Like cordite! You smell that?"

"I smell it now. It smells like the explosive you call dynamite. We use it for mining in the Creation Solar System. I've transported *gunds* of it through space. We tow it on *kepfat* long cables. I hate being close to it."

"I don't blame you there. Let's look down here. Can we take this inspection plate off?"

"Yes, we have tools. But lets look under here. Well, at least we landed in nice soft sand. Please help me dig this sand out." They both dug underneath the hull to expose part of the bottom.

"I see something." declared the British television narrator. "I need a torch."

"I don't think we need any fire under there."

"You've learned your English from an American. They don't know 'ow to spell colour or favour, and they think a pint is sixteen ounces. Americans think a torch is that flaming thing they carry at the Olympics. But we British know better. It's what they call a flashlight."

"Oh! Here. It's the one I took off that mugger in D.C."

"I 'eard about that on the BBC. What's the story there?"

"Three of us got away from the soldiers their President sent to protect us. We wanted to see the town for ourselves. When we got out of the government area, we noticed things weren't so affluent. We saw people who were strung out on alcohol or drugs."

"Every city has that, a worldwide plague. I've seen it in London and Liverpool, from Soho down to Brighton."

"Sad. This guy jumps out of nowhere and waves this eight *tig-it* knife in my face. That's eight inches, you British still use inches?"

"The government's in love with the Metric, but the people prefer the customary."

"Anyway, it's a big weapon and he wants money. We didn't have any, not American currency. We try to tell him who we are, and finally he points this flashlight in my face and calls me an 'ugly bitch'!" That really hurt, now that she's had time to think about it.

"Sweetheart, you are most certainly not ugly. You are different, the way a black woman is different. But you are beautiful in your difference, just as the black woman is beautiful in 'er difference. And you are not a bitch. You are a damn fine woman you are. If you weren't, we'd be dead by now."

"You are a charmer. Thank you. Then he demands sex from us! Now I like sex as much as the next woman, and being without it for so many years leaves me open to suggestion. But at knifepoint? Sorry, I'm not that open to suggestion."

"'E was definitely going about it the wrong way. I understand 'e's been convicted of other sex offenses. You Neanderthals are quite capable of defending yourselves. But most Cro-Magnons don't have your physical strength. The rapist usually does not pick on Ms. Olympia. Each one of these guys will terrorize 'undreds of women before 'e's finally put away to jail. I bet there are many women in America who wish you killed 'im."

"Well, it was Nesla Teslakian who punched him. She didn't want the responsibility for taking a human life. She could've, you know. All she had to do was aim a couple of inches lower and hit the vertebrae with full force."

"'E'd been dead before 'e 'it the ground. I'm not about to criticize Nesla for using the minimum force necessary for defence. Well, let's see if Mr. Freeman's torch still works for us." He peered under the Shuttle with the flashlight. "Oh shit!" he exclaimed.

"Every time you Earthlings yell 'Oh shit!', something bad happens. What is it?"

"I'll be buggered. Somebody planted a BOMB on this ship! We are very lucky indeed! I count five sticks of dynamite that did not explode. What did explode must've wrecked your magnetic field generator and your 'ydraulics."

"Unexploded dynamite. Best news I've heard all day!" Her voice was sarcastic. She ran around the Shuttle to the door. The physicians and the uninjured men were setting up the tent and operating table to work on Fred Graf. The Shuttle included a portable MASH unit. "Everyone!" she shouted quietly, afraid that a loud noise might set off the dynamite. "Get everyone out of the Shuttle! We were disabled by a bomb that was planted. There is unexploded dynamite under there, we have to get away from the ship!"

"What about the water? We'll each sweat a gallon an hour in this desert heat."

"One problem at a time, please! Yes, we'll have to remove the dynamite and get it away from here, but first evacuate the ship!"

Everyone got out of the ship, and we started to carefully dig underneath the hull. Hydraulic fluid dripped everywhere. I hoped it wasn't anything like Skydrol. The stories you hear at Boeing about that stuff! I got one stick unstuck. The timer apparently detonated only one or two sticks. The three inch thick ablation shield muffled the explosion and limited the damage. But the magnetic field generator was right above where the dynamite was planted. As I brought it out, I said "I got one stick off."

"Don't wave it in my face, Neil!" Metrola, a fearless and brave lass, seemed to have a phobia about dynamite. Did she once have a bad experience with explosives?

"I'll take it a couple of hundred yards that way."

"The farther the better." She turned to Ian. "What do you mean by 'buggered'?" she asked quietly.

"Oh!" He whispered the answer in her ear.

"Sorry I asked."

Chapter Twenty Two

"Did you see those parachutes over there? That is the trog Shuttle! It is disabled!"

"Yeah, looked to be about 50 kilometers that way."

"Check our GPS position, please." Bandits in the middle of the Sahara now have hand held GPS computers.

"Got the GPS reading. Problem is they did not declare their GPS location in the clear. I think they have a coded communication between them and their mother ship. Okay, why should we go after them?"

"They are unarmed."

"Great! They are unarmed. But the Army is armed and is probably on its way!"

"Are you kidding! The GIS has gone all out today! The Army will probably win but it will take them awhile. Both Army and GIS are busy. Leaves the trog Shuttle available to us!"

"Okay. We are not interested in politics or religion, just profit. What about the Americans? They usually have a carrier task force in the Med. They still have bases in Europe."

"Americans might be a problem. Does their President have the balls to send an Airborne force to rescue the trogs and their passengers? If so, how fast can they get here?"

"It might take them a while. If we're going to hit them, we have to hit them now. Figure the trog mother ship and the American satellites will be watching us. It is broad daylight."

"Can the trog mother ship do anything?"

"Warn the trog Shuttle of our approach. Tell the Americans and the Algerian Army. Nothing else unless they have a second shuttle."

"Okay. Here are the risk factors: The trogs up in the spaceship might have a second shuttle. But they have never told anyone that. The Americans or French or NATO might arrive in force. Our Army might spare a unit from their current preoccupation with the GIS. The GIS might come. What can the passengers of the trog Shuttle do about us if they are warned of our approach?"

"Nothing! Run into the desert?" They laughed. "They will surrender as soon as we show them our guns. Okay, what have they got that is worth stealing? That is worth the risk factors?"

"The magnetic drive unit."

"Yeah. It obviously malfunctioned. But engineers can take it apart and figure out how it works. Then they can repair it or build another one. A plane works on the lift generated by the wings passing through air, it can only operate within the atmosphere. This thing only needs the Earth's magnetic field. Instant space program! A fraction of the cost of big rockets. We charge millions of dollars to be deposited in a Swiss Bank Account. We could spend the rest of our lives drinking pina coladas in Acapulco."

"Yeah. The Iranians, the Chinese, any former Soviet Republic,"

"Or Argentina, Brazil. Don't forget South Africa, they have repealed apartheid."

"Maybe that is why the GIS targeted it. Okay, if we're going to hit them, let's hit them NOW."

Sabar and Pidonita watched the desert around the Shuttle. "Look!" cried Sabar. "Those three trucks are approaching the Shuttle! Focus the telescope on them, how good is the resolution?"

"Theoretically a *tig-it*. But realistically three or six *tig-its*." Pidonita called General Hakim

191

on a coded signal. "Do you have any Army units off the roads and highways around 28 degrees north and 5 degrees east of Greenwich?"

"Your Shuttle is halfway between the Route du Haggar and the Route du Tassili N'Ajjer, close to the edge of the Erg. We do not have at present any units anywhere near there. We have only a few companies of men on the entire road net outside the cities and villages. Where are these jeeps?"

"Less than a dozen *kepfats* west of the Shuttle. 30 kilometers."

"Not ours. Could be GIS, could be bandits, could be just people. I'll see if I can spare a helicopter for your Shuttle."

"I am looking at the picture from our telescope. Visible light, high resolution. One truck is a covered flatbed. They have rifles. They are not just people."

"Any uniforms?"

"Just white shirts and blue jeans, and some kind of blue and white head covering."

"The head covering is a tagelmoust, a Tuareg symbol. Blue jeans. They're ready for a fight. Okay, I'll see what I can do."

"Thank you, General."

"That is the last stick of dynamite I can see." Ian Miller carefully detached the stick of explosive from the belly of the ship. "Are you sure these jacks are safe?"

"No." admitted Metrola. She helped me open the wheel well doors for one of the landing gears. If we can get the wheels lowered and locked, than we will have the Shuttle up high enough to repair the magnetic field generator. Ian passed the dynamite to Mohammed Abbas who carried it 200 yards to our dumping place. The portable operating room was relocated further away from the Shuttle in the opposite direction. The physicians had Fred Graf under anesthesia and were performing surgery on his leg. Donald Colburn and Ben Sumner were in the tent helping out.

"Okay, Met, is there something locking the wheel in the up position?"

"This little latch here." She reached up and unhooked it. I could see how the hydraulic actuator rotates it to lock and unlock the gear. Unfortunately, the fluid was squirting out of the hydraulic pump where it was damaged by the bomb. "Help me pull this wheel down, careful."

The wheel came down slowly. We pulled with what felt like 60 pounds of force. We got it almost all the way down. "Let me dig some of this sand out of the way." I swept the sand out from under the wheel. We pulled the wheel some more. Click! It locked into position.

We looked at each other and smiled. We were covered with dust and hydraulic fluid. "I'm sorry I yelled at you before." she apologized.

"Don't worry about it."

"Just two more to go." Her communicator buzzed. "I have to get out from under this ship. Interferes with the radio signal." After she crawled out, I went to work on another landing gear with Ian.

"I think she likes you." announced the ever cheerful Englishman.

"She does. But she snaps at me sometimes. Although getting shot at tends to shorten anyone's temper. Ian, may I ask you a favor?"

"What?"

"Why don't you take her off my hands? That way I can go back to Helga."

"The tall blonde."

"Sure. Well, maybe not. Metrola can get passionate. All of them are just sexy like that. Who would have thought of Neanderthal women as sexy? But when it comes to strong and lean female bodies, Cro-Magnon women are just not the same."

"Most Cro-Magnon women cannot lift 20 stone off the ground."

"No, they cannot. Is that it? Physical strength in the female. But with muscle that is genetic, not built with testosterone or steroids like some of our woman bodybuilders."

"So the shape of their bodies is natural and female. It's also the effect of their eternal youth. They are incredibly 'ealthy, 'ave the energy of people in their twenties, but at the same time, they 'ave the wisdom that can only come with age. They've beaten the cruel paradox of our life span. By the time we 'ave a chance to learn from our mistakes, we're too old to take advantage of the lessons. There, the wheel well doors are open."

"Let me get that." I detached the latch. We pulled the wheel down.

Metrola ducked her head under the Shuttle to give us an urgent message. "We have visitors on the way. Three trucks charging through the sand ten *kepfats* west of here. They have rifles."

"Sixteen miles. Even through this sand, not very long before they get here."

Everyone gathered around for an emergency conference. "Here is the present situation:" Metrola announced, "Just a few miles away are two Toyota Land Cruisers and a flatbed truck with a cover. They are coming this way. There are about ten to fifteen men, carrying rifles. They might have other weapons. The Algerian Army says these guys aren't them. They could be GIS, or they could be bandits. They'll be here before any Algerian, American or French force can get here. The French Foreign Legion has landed on the coast, but that is 600 miles from here. And we have not a single gun among us. So what do we do? Do we go out to them with a white flag and tell them we are unarmed and come in peace?"

"Absolutely not!" screamed Mohammed Abbas, who knows the mentality of these bandits. He switched back to Arabic and explained to Chuck Carter.

Chuck translated Mohammed's Arabic to English. "We do that, they'll just slit our throats and then rummage through our stuff for anything worth stealing. Got some money in your pockets? Algerian dinars? American dollars? British pounds? Even euros will do. If they are smart enough, no guarantee of that, they might realize the black market value of the magnetic drive unit in the ship."

"I have an idea." I said. "It's psychological. Look, we haven't any weapons. Hopefully, they haven't any brains. But look at us. We have a television crew. Ian used to be a Marine. I'm an engineer. We have three physicians. Metrola's sand dune trick was the result of her quick thinking. We all figured out that those Stingers were specially modified for our ship, just in time to fool the third one. So we're pretty smart. *Psyche*, that's Greek for using the old noggin. Psycho Logical Warfare."

The two Toyotas and the truck pulled to a stop 150 yards from the Shuttle. The bandits could see the parachutes folded up in a pile. The Shuttle had been jacked up and stood on its landing gear. The tent where surgery was being performed on Fred Graf could be seen in the distance. Sand dunes and rocks were all around. The place looked deserted. The men disembarked from the trucks.

Suddenly small metal cylinders rained down all around, spewing fog. The bandits were surrounded by clouds of fog. They panicked, firing their rifles, covering their faces. "Cease fire! Cease fire!" screamed their leader in Arabic. "Get away from this stuff! Over here!" he commanded. The men got away from the trucks and the fog. Some were on their bellies, like soldiers, facing the hills. The leader remained standing. "These trogs have no guns! What are you worried about?" He went over to one of the hissing cylinders. He sniffed the fog. He let it blow in his face while his men watched. "It is just cold mist! Compressed air squirting water droplets."

The men started to laugh. Then they were laughing big time. Firing their guns into the air.

"Nice try TROGS!" one of them yelled at the top of his lungs.

"They know who we are." observed Chuck Carter. "That last sentence was 'Nice try trogs.' The trog part doesn't need translating." We were all whispering. And wishing these dunes had more than sand for stopping bullets.

"What does that mean?" asked Metrola.

"Trog is supposed to be the insulting term for you Creation Neanderthals. Like calling me a nigger. Trog is short for troglodyte, which means cave dweller or cave man. You are a Neanderthal, and Neanderthals used to live in caves."

The physicians were still in the tent, working on Fred. What else could they do? They absolutely had to close him up or the leg's gone and with it, perhaps the man.

"Are you ready, Mohammed?" I whispered.

He nodded "yes". He was nervous, frightened, but he was going to do it.

Mohammed Abbas walked out from behind the dunes carrying a white flag. "What is this?" cried out the bandit leader with derision in his voice. Mohammed was selected because he speaks Algerian Arabic and the Tamahag dialect of Berber.

"I come under a flag of truce to deliver to you a message."

"Ha! Ha! Ha! A message! We should shoot you where you stand!" Mohammed stood his ground and did not flinch. He did not show any reaction to the threat. But his stomach did not want to stick around.

"Maybe we should listen to the message." suggested one of the others. "Then we can shoot him. Okay flag boy, what message do the trogs have for us?"

"Those cylinders sprayed the bacteria that on Planet Creation causes Ballzat Disease. You've all been exposed to it."

"Ballzat Disease? I feel fine!"

"It takes a few hours for it to take effect. What it does is that it destroys your testicles, painfully, and makes your breasts grow up to a nice female size." Some of the bandits felt their chests. "But you will not care about that because of the roaring headaches, the convulsions, the vomiting, the itching skin, the diarrhea, and other wonderful symptoms. You will be dead in about four days, and glad of it, but sometimes it takes a couple of weeks."

Mohammed paused to let it sink in. Some of the bandits started to look nervous. "Fortunately, there is a vaccine. It kills the bacteria and lets you live. This used to be a scourge disease on Planet Creation, like smallpox. But they solved it with this vaccine. Just like smallpox is no longer a problem for us."

"You are full of shit!"

"I most certainly am. When that diarrhea kicks in, you will be amazed at the amount of shit you are full of." Mohammed turned and started to walk away.

"We'll kill you all and then find the vaccine and administer it to ourselves!"

They are buying it! Mohammed turned around slowly. He always wanted to be an actor. "Can you read Atlantean? It is all in Atlantean. You inject yourself with the wrong stuff it will do you no good. Besides, the stuff has to be mixed up. Instructions are written in Atlantean. The Neanderthal physicians are not going to do that dead."

"Okay, we will kill all of you except the trog physicians. They will do it under gunpoint! If they refuse, we can torture them!"

"All they have to do is hold out until the symptoms kick in. Then you will be too weak to lift even a finger off the ground. Then again, they might not let themselves be tortured. Neanderthal women are not like any women I've ever met. How many women do you know can pick 150 kilos off the ground?" Exaggeration. "And carry it around like it was nothing? And they are quick! Like a kung fu master. All I can say, gentlemen, is good luck!" He turned around and started walking away with the white flag.

As Mohammed walked away, panic started to set in. "What in the name of Allah do they want us to do?" screamed the leader of the bandits.

Mohammed turned around again. "Well, it is like this: You come here to kill us and steal our stuff. We know that. Now, you are most certainly capable of doing that, nothing we can do to stop you. But if you do, you will be dead or wishing death within a week, guaranteed. You want the physicians to mix up the vaccine and inject it into you? Then you are going to have to stack your guns in front of your trucks. We don't trust you, can't blame us for that, can you? Because we don't trust you, you will have to take off all of your clothes and leave them in a pile next to the guns in front of the trucks. And then you must walk 100 meters over this way and stand in a group while we seize your guns and search your clothes for weapons. You can have the clothes back when we have made sure that there are no weapons in them." Mohammed turned around and walked away.

"Kill him! Kill him!" demanded the leader. But his men were stacking their arms as instructed. One of them had his gun to his leader's head.

"I'm sorry. We cannot take the chance that they are telling the truth."

We watched in amazement as the bandits stripped and piled their clothes in front of their trucks as instructed. They then walked in a group the 110 yards as instructed. Metrola walked out from behind the dune, tall and proud. She imperiously pointed to the spot where they were to stand. A trog woman looking upon their nakedness and giving them orders! We did not wait for their reaction to this latest humiliation. We all sprinted as fast as we can down to the guns and grabbed them! As soon as we had secured the guns we whooped and yelled and screamed for joy! That Mohammed Abbas! Gotta love him! Not only were we going to live, we were armed and ready for the next gang of bad guys that comes this way!

Chuck, Ian, and I walked up to the group of naked men and pointed our rifles at them to make sure they continue to behave themselves. Mohammed and Metrola stood in front of them. Cuc Nguyen and Meddi Chumkun came running up. "What about Fred?" Metrola asked in Atlantean.

"Surgery is now completed." Meddi answered. "We removed two bullets and a shred of aluminum from the Shuttle hull. Askelion and the Canadians are watching him. We saw the last part of it."

"I know a little Arabic." declared Cuc in English. "What's Ballzat Disease?"

"I don't know." answered Metrola in English. "Never heard of it."

"Me neither." admitted DOCTOR Chumkun, also in English.

"WHAT!?!" screamed the bandit leader.

"You know English?" Metrola asked.

"Yeah, I know English. I also know French, this used to be a French colony."

"So what's a well educated fellow like you doing running around with bandits?"

"Had a nice government job. Then the elections were canceled and the GIS declared a *fatwa* on us government employees. Fortunately I'm a Berber, and the GIS don't fuck with us Berbers. Quit the government and here I am. Don't like either the government or the GIS. We just take what we want when we want it. Until we ran into you. You could at least cover your hair WOMAN!"

Cuc held her hair across her face. "This better? Sorry, forgot to bring my hejab." She shrugged her shoulders.

"There is no such thing as Ballzat Disease." the bandit leader realized. "You will burn in Hell, devious Trog woman!"

Metrola quickly grabbed the naked bandit's neck. He felt her Neanderthal strength and was forced to stare into her angry face. "Please do not call me 'trog'." she ordered through clinched teeth. "And no, I'm not going to cover my hair. I'm not going to wear a veil. Don't you talk to me about modesty while you stand here naked. You had all of the guns. Yet you surrendered and took your clothes off, because you are a COWARD. One who believes in nothing, who only lives for profit and murder."

"Wrong. I do believe in the Prophet and in Allah."

"Sure you do. But I didn't know Islam considered banditry to be acceptable. I thought 'Thou shalt not steal' is as much a Commandment for Muslims as it is for Christians and Jews. I was under the impression that the Five Pillars of Islam did not include Murder and Theft." With that Metrola threw the bandit leader to the ground with great force. He and his fellows thus learned that Neanderthal women do not suffer from a lack of physical strength.

Metrola stalked off, she had a ship to repair. All these damn interruptions! Mohammed spoke to his prisoners in their language. "Magnificent woman. Now we know why the Pagans and Infidels believed in goddesses. She may be a Demon Woman, but I both envy and pity the man who marries her."

After we had searched the clothing and removed all knives, bullets, pistols, and anything else we did not want the prisoners to possess, we let the prisoners put their clothes back on. We then bound them hand and foot and placed them under a makeshift tent made from one of the parachutes.

"Hi, Mr. President." greeted Metrola. We were on a radio link through the *Neanderthal Return*, a satellite, around the curve to the White House. "Sorry if I'm not following protocol. Right now I'm extremely tired. The magnetic drive unit can be repaired. It was just knocked off its mountings and bearings. But that takes some very careful alignment. If not, I cannot control it and we can slam into a mountain or float off into space without pressurization. Two days before we can fly it. We are down to 18 *shlopons* of water and we've got 13 bandits we are keeping prisoner. They only brought a few liters of water, and it tastes TERRIBLE."

"I just cannot get over how you disarmed these bandits!" The President was just amazed. "18 *shlopons* is about"

"100 gallons. For 34 people. In the middle of the Sahara. We've been doing a lot of heavy work, which uses up body fluids. We ration the water, but everyone wants more. We dare not short ration Fred Graf. He NEEDS plenty of fluids. We have food, but everyone is going hungry. Again, the bandits did not bring very much. We could use the bandit trucks to drive some people out to the Route du Haggar, if we can be sure we don't run into any more bandits or the GIS."

"Sounds like you could use some help. Here is my problem: If you can just fly into Morocco, you'll be safe. Morocco is a stable modern Arab nation. But you need two days at least before you can fly your machine. It's too heavy to lift out by any other means. Morocco is not going to cross into Algerian territory, they have to get along with whoever wins this civil war. The French are giving us guff, as usual. This is one of their former colonies, never mind that they had no right to conquer it in the first place. They will neither confirm nor deny the reports that their Foreign Legion has landed on the Algerian coast. They are there, we see them with our satellites. But they do not appear to be interested in coming down into the Sahara at this time. They don't want us coming in either. The Algerian government officially opposes any foreign intervention, as does the GIS. We are officially neutral with respect to the civil war."

"So we're on our own."

"I didn't say that. I keep trying to get the Algerian Army to come to your aid. I keep getting excuses."

"Well, they are busy with the GIS."

"They are, in the populated north. But the desert is pretty much secure. Tuaregs and Berbers of the desert have never been as enthusiastic about the GIS as the northern Algerians. The government has roadblocks set up every 100 kilometers along the Route du Haggar and every desert town is garrisoned. They could send somebody over."

"Why don't they? They were pretty hospitable at the archeological Base Camp."

"That was before the GIS attacked. That Brer Rabbit trick you pulled on the bandits has everyone in Algeria spooked. Maybe you did let a dangerous bacteria loose in the Algerian environment. Or they think you bewitched the bandits, you are truly a Demon Woman. A sorceress or a witch. Some even think that you are one of the Three Goddesses mentioned in the Satanic Verses."

"The what?"

"The verses that were deleted from the Koran by Mohammed because they were the work of the Devil. Muslims are very touchy about that, and we are at wits end trying to figure out how to deal with it. Nobody in North Africa wants to get near you. At least you don't have to worry about bandits, they're afraid of you."

"Mr. President. Please reassure everyone that I am not a goddess or a witch. I am a flesh and blood human being. Put a bullet through my brain, I die. Cut my skin, I bleed red blood. Just like every other flesh and blood human being. As far as the 'Brer Rabbit' trick, we had NO CHOICE!"

"I understand. I'll keep trying to get the Algerian Army to at least bring you water and take your bandit prisoners off your hands."

"Metrola! Give me that thing!" As an American citizen, I just about had enough of this President! So did Chuck, he was sitting right next to me. "Mr. President, this is Neil Peace!"

"And this is Chuck Carter."

"Hello gentlemen,"

"Listen to us for a minute, please! With all due respect, sir, there are a bunch of American citizens in a tough spot here! We didn't violate any Algerian laws. We're neutral with respect to the civil war. We don't give a damn who runs Algeria and whether she is a strict Islamic Republic or an insane socialist government that harasses with ridiculous currency regulations and excessive taxation. The mass of the Algerian people are in the shit hole either way! There was no reason for the GIS to attack US when they attacked the Base Camp! We would have just gone up out of the atmosphere if they didn't shoot holes in our passenger cabin! Three Stingers, how the HELL did they get STINGERS?!!! That's an American made thing! These Stingers were specially modified to home in on the Shuttle's magnetic field."

"You sure about that?"

"We'll brief you when you get us outta here!" assured Chuck.

I continued my tirade. "And somebody planted a BOMB on our ship when we were peacefully parked at the Base Camp. Were it not for that, we would have been outta their hair, and they could have their stupid civil war!"

"What do you want me to do about it?"

"Send in the 101st Airborne for crying out loud! Tell 'em to bring some water, food and a medivac chopper for Fred Graf. They could evacuate the civilians except those of us needed to repair the Shuttle magnetic drive. All three physicians and half of the S&H Crew. And deliver these damn bandits to the Algerian authorities!"

"Christ, Peace! We haven't had a chance to consult with our allies! Many of them won't sign on to this military action you propose."

"Well, let's see. We have some Canadians, some British, and a German. I'm sure those governments wouldn't have too big a problem with a rescue. There are some citizens of the Nation of Atlantis on the Planet Creation here as well, they won't have a problem with it either. If you sit there and do nothing but plead with the damn Algerians, you're going to have to explain it to the American people! I'll guarantee you that the Science and Humanities Channel won't let 'em forget it!"

"There is one other thing, Mr. President." pointed out Chuck.

"Yeah, I'm getting a lecture from some uppity civilians."

"As American citizens, we are your boss." reminded Chuck. "The one other thing is the magnetic field generator. Now it seems that every Muslim on this continent is spooked. They think Metrola is some kind of Satanic Demon Sorceress and are afraid to approach this spot. But I can think of ONE Muslim who suffers from no such superstitious belief. Khaddafy would love to have the magnetic field generator. Instant space program. He could claim the Moon and Mars for Libya. He could go over to Tranquillity Base and tear the American Flag down! And we couldn't stop him unless we ask the Creationists to intervene in Earth politics. They'll not interfere with our sovereignty over our own Solar System. That's to preserve the precedent for their Solar System. How the sovereignty of the Moon and the planets is distributed among the Earth nations is up to us to sort out. Khaddafy would love to sort it out in his favor. The other thing he could do is float up out of the atmosphere, around the Earth and then drop nuclear warheads in reentry vehicles all over the North American continent."

I added my two cents worth. "Either you order our troops in here or Khaddafy might order his."

"Shit!" exclaimed the President. "Hang tough."

Chapter Twenty Three

The prisoners rested under the parachute tent after their sunset prayer. Mustafa Khedr and Mohammed Abbas did their best under the circumstances to perform the prayer with the prisoners. They helped each prisoner perform the ritual purification with sand and pointed him in the direction of Mecca. They prayed. They did not have food and water as often as they had prayer. Mustafa explained that sinners need to get right with Allah more than they need food or water. There is no limit to Allah, but there were only 14 *shlopons* of water left.

Metrola brought a two *jug* container of water and a measuring cup. When the prisoners saw her they shrank back. But their leader, who identified himself as Maurice Jafar, held his ground. "Why do they shrink back from me?" she asked him.

"They fear you. They believe you are a Demon Woman."

Sigh. "Is it because of my Race? They did not shrink back when Askelion and Meddi examined them."

"It is not your Race. We know Askelion and Meddi are physicians. We know Cuc Nguyen is a physician, and we care not that she is a Vietnamese turned American. They did a good job on Fred Graf. For this we praise Allah. But while I know you are a mortal woman of the Neanderthal Race, they believe you are one of the Three Goddesses mentioned in the Satanic Verses."

"I see. Well, I'm not a goddess of any type, Satanic or otherwise." She poured exactly one *glup* of water into the measuring cup. "Please drink your water ration."

Maurice could not hold the cup because his hands were tied behind his back. Metrola held the clear plastic cup to her prisoner's lips and allowed him to drink. He noticed the Creation numbers along the graduated marks. Two, four, six, eight, the single symbol for ten and at the top, the Creation twelve. Halfway between each pair of numbers, is the line for the odd number of *dollops*. "Metrola, please explain your liquid measures." he requested.

"We have feet and inches, like the Americans."

"Like the Romans had."

"Yes. A *dollop*, you see that is what this cup is marked in, two, four,"

"I see."

"A *dollop* is the volume of a cylinder one inch, our inch, not the American's, one inch high and one inch in diameter. Our numbers are Base Twelve, the way your numbers are Base Ten. Twelve *dollops* is a *glup*, that is the amount of your ration. Twelve *glups* is a *jug*, which is pronounced just like the English word jug."

"What's a *shlopon*?"

"Twelve *jugs*. It is the volume of a cylinder one foot high and one foot in diameter."

"Thank you for telling me this."

Metrola tried to get another prisoner to drink from the cup. "Maurice, please tell him I'm not a Satanic witch. He can drink from this cup without selling his soul to the Devil. I will not put a spell on anybody."

Maurice laughed. He switched to Arabic and told his men to drink the water. Metrola is a Neanderthal woman, not a supernatural being. With that, their thirst overcame their fear. Each prisoner drank the water as fast as he could to limit his contact with the Demon Woman. He had to look into her face as he drank. She was not so fearsome. But faces can be seductive, that is why Arab women wear veils. A Demon Woman might well try to seduce him. After everyone had a drink, Maurice felt bold enough to ask Metrola a personal question. "What do you believe? Your faith? Do you believe in the Great Holy Spirit?"

"Before I answer your question, what is your opinion of non-Muslims?"

Maurice thought it over, bound hand and foot, the prisoner of a woman. She exhibits feminine emotions and Herculean strength. Dangerous combination. Yet she took time away from repairing her ship to give them water. Probably needed a break. Might as well the truth, one less lie to explain to Allah. "Christians and Jews we refer to as 'People of the Book.' They have a Bible. The Old Testament is the Hebrew Bible. The New Testament is the life of Christ. We believe that Islam is what their prophets tried to teach them. We believe that Noah, Abraham, Moses, and Jesus were prophets. But it is the revelations of Mohammed, Peace Be Upon Him, that we know of as Islam. He is the last and the greatest of the prophets, to us, he is the Prophet. The Koran, which is the book where these revelations are recorded, restates many things that these previous prophets had revealed and are recorded in the Bible. But it is the Koran that defines the one true religion of Abraham."

"So I take it that you believe that Christians and Jews are people who are part way down the right road, but have yet to go the rest of the way?"

"Yes, you could say that."

"What about people who are not Christian, Jewish, or Muslim?"

"Infidels, Pagans. We think they should convert or die. But most of us do not believe in violence against Infidels. I do not agree with the GIS that faith can be properly coerced."

"What do you think of us Neanderthals from Creation? Are we Infidels or Pagans?"

"If you were to convert to Islam, Allah considers woman of all races to be equal."

"I'm not going to convert to Islam."

"But do you believe in the Great Holy Spirit?"

"If I do, does that make me a Pagan or an Infidel?"

"Not necessarily. Your people have been on a different Planet. We understand that you have not received the revelations given to Mohammed, or even to Moses or Jesus. It depends on whether Great Holy Spirit is your way of saying the name of Allah."

"Most of the crew are pretty religious. They believe in the Spirit. The Spirit could be thought of as God. We would never think of Him as Satan. Actually we don't have a concept like Satan. But I'm what you call an unbeliever, an atheist. I don't believe in any god or spirit."

"You said we were cowards because you thought we believed in nothing. Wrong. We were cowards because we were after booty alone. We weren't willing to risk death from disease for mere money. But here you are. You profess to believe in nothing. And yet you show no lack of courage. You are credited with wondrous feats, of evading three Stingers modified to seek your ship's magnetic field. That is one reason so many believe you are more than human. A demon or a goddess. Now you might actually repair your ship, out here in the middle of the desert hundreds of kilometers from anywhere. You are a remarkable woman, indeed!"

"My religion, or lack of religion, is not your concern."

"Dear Metrola. Allah, the Great Holy Spirit, He gave you your abilities. He gave you what you needed to evade the missiles. He gave you your brain, your sight, your marvelous physical strength. He gave you your brow ridges. He gave you Earth and all of the Cro-Magnon people who live on Earth. He gave you Creation, even the Face Mountain aliens who remade Creation and transplanted your ancestors there. He gave you all of your friends, and He gave you us. Are you not the least bit grateful?"

Metrola stared past him with cold emotion.

"You once believed in the Great Holy Spirit, didn't you?" he asked with a gentle voice.

"What kind of God, gracious and good, would allow something like a Virus that murders all of our men!" She turned away, not allowing the prisoners to see her face. She walked out of their sight. They heard the muffled sobs of a woman.

Metrola came back from her break. Her eyes looked like she had been crying. "Are you all right, Metrola?"

"I'm fine. I took water to the prisoners, and I managed to get 'em to drink it. Their leader, Maurice, convinced 'em to take water from me. I don't believe he convinced 'em that I'm not a Demon Woman."

"Did they say or do something to make you cry?"

"I didn't cry!"

End of subject. Chuck, Ian, Mohammed, and Mustafa came back under the Shuttle. "We've got all of the new brackets set, now we can try the final adjustments."

"There is a screwdriver stuck to the side of the cyclotron." she observed. The steel shaft of the tool was held tight by magnetic force to the casing. She read the Roman alphabet letters on the handle. "STANLEY. Where did you get this Earth tool?"

"We borrowed it from one of the bandit trucks." answered Ian. "Since we're sharing our precious water with 'em, we could at least make use of their resources."

"I see. I have no problem with the morality of using the bandit tools. However, this is a MAGNETIC device. Our Creation tools in the Shuttle kit are excellent general purpose tools, but they are made from the metals you call titanium, aluminum, and chromium. This is the reason we use NON-magnetic tools." She gripped the handle of the Stanley screwdriver and pulled with all of her great strength.

"We've already tried that ourselves." we said.

She laced her fingers around the handle and lifted her feet off the ground. The magnetic force was greater than her weight. "Have you tried this?"

"Yeah, it's stuck good. Our fingers give up when we add a second body to the weight."

"My fingers are pretty strong. Let me try something first." She placed her right hand against the cyclotron casing and pushed while simultaneously pulling on the screwdriver with her left. She could barely move it laterally along the casing.

"It moved!" Mustafa yelled excitedly. "Maybe we can brace it with some kind of tool."

Metrola let go. "One of the titanium crowbars might work."

Chuck picked up the longest titanium bar. "This eight foot bar?"

"Yes." She inspected the wide, flat end of the bar. It was designed to wedge under the cyclotron and control mechanisms and move the stubborn parts while we readjust the mountings. "Place this wedge under the screwdriver. Careful." She gripped the handle of the screwdriver. Not as much finger room with the bar in there. "I need two or three of you to hold this bar in tight while I pull on this handle." Mohammed and Mustafa joined Chuck in holding the bar. "Ian, Neil, I need you to grab me around the waist and chest and help me pull this screwdriver."

"Okay," I said, "I'll wrap my right arm across your ribs, and I'll grab your forearm with my left hand."

She redirected my right arm up between her breasts. "Hold it right here, and pull as hard as you can on the count of three. Brace your feet right behind mine so we both use our full strength. Ian, come around in front of me, please. Push on me like you are tackling me in rugby."

Ian put himself in position. "My face is pressed against your breast. You don't mind?"

"Just don't kiss my nipple." That brought a chuckle from everybody. "Okay, on three. One, two, THREE!" The screwdriver slowly slipped on to the flat blade of the bar. "Okay, stop!" Metrola commanded. "Let go of me, please." We let go of her and stood back. "Chuck, Mohammed, can you push the bar forward?"

"Yes, it is moving." Mustafa answered.

"Careful, gentlemen, my fingers are in there." Metrola held the screwdriver in position on the bar as it slipped forward. She watched as the distance between the screwdriver blade and the magnetic casing slowly increased. The end of the bar slowly extended into midair. Finally she could wrap her hands around the screwdriver and the bar. She pulled hard. "Everyone! Grab the bar and pull!" We wrapped our hands around the bar, standing in a row. "One, two, THREE!"

The bar and the screwdriver suddenly let go of the cyclotron and we fell into the sand. Metrola tossed the screwdriver away from the Shuttle. "No more STEEL tools in here!"

After we got up, we inspected our work with flashlights. "See where we placed the new brackets and repaired the wiring?"

"Yes, looks good." answered Metrola approvingly. "You guys really come through! Let me get my fine measuring tools to adjust the alignment."

She brought back a tool case. She laid a blanket on the sand. There was little wind, which was good. She did not care to have sand get into her expensive stuff. We had already used calipers and scales to set dimensions to the nearest 1/24 of a *tig-it*. But for flight readiness, we needed accuracy to the nearest 1/144 of a *tig-it*. Metrola carefully opened the case to reveal high accuracy micrometers and calipers. "These tools are made from a nonmagnetic alloy for use around fusion reactors and magnetic drive units such as this. This alloy has almost no coefficient of thermal expansion. We check these tools on a regular basis. In this protective case, they should be in fine shape after our rough flight." She lifted a caliper out of the case.

"What's your President been doing?" asked Ian.

"It seems that us getting this Shuttle out of here is the easiest thing for him." answered Chuck.

"But we're using up our water, having to take care of some unexpected guests." commented Metrola.

"We have been giving the President accurate updates on our water situation." responded Chuck. "He knows exactly what a *shlopon* is, figuring that as long as we have that much water left, he doesn't have to send in troops."

"So maybe we should punch a hole in the tank and then tell him that we lost all of the water in a leak." suggested Metrola as she readied to measure Dimension One.

"Have him send the 101st Airborne on false pretenses? Not a good idea." I knew better. "Trust me on this, Metrola. Lying to a bunch of bandits in self defense is acceptable. Lying to the President of the United States is not. We need PEACE between Earth and Creation. That means peace between the big countries of both Planets."

"All right." she protested. "Not a serious suggestion. At least Fred Graf is doing well. Dr. Cuc, our infectious disease girl, prevented infection while the leg was open. It would have been nice to airlift him out."

"I think the President is taking into account our own resourcefulness."

"So what did he do to keep the Libyans from showing up?"

"Two F-117 Stealth fighter-bombers buzzed Tripoli and Benghazi." answered Chuck. "Each dropped a leaflet bomb."

"What's a leaflet bomb?"

"A nonexplosive device, not intended to hurt anyone, spews hundreds of leaflets. A leaflet is a piece of paper with a message on it. The Stealth planes freak out hostile people like Khaddafy and Saddam because their radar just does not pick them up. They fly in at night so people cannot SEE them with their eyes. The engines are QUIET, and have infrared shielding. The bomb explosion is the first they know of a Stealth plane and then they can't find it to shoot it! Yesterday, it was leaflets they delivered to Libya. On each sheet of paper is a message in English and Arabic. It said: 'Greetings. This message is brought to you by the United States Air Force. Please make sure Mr. Khaddafy receives a copy. He'll know what we are talking about.' What has already been communicated to Khaddafy is our desire that Libya not intervene in the civil war in Algeria and that they especially stay away from us."

"Dimension Three needs an adjustment of two *hekers*. Hand me a half *tig-it* wrench and a 5/14ths." In Base Twelve, sixteen looks like fourteen. The bolts have hex heads. These titanium wrenches might have enough allowance to be used on the corresponding Earth inch hexes. Metrola loosened a locking bolt with a half *tig-it* hex. She used the 5/16 *tig-it* wrench to slowly and carefully turn an adjustment screw. She measured with her micrometer as she turned the adjustment screw. A little too much, she turned it backward a bit. She reset the locking bolt. She measured it again. "Dimension Three is now perfect. Okay, so your President has kept Libya out of our hair. What's going on with the Algerians? They could at least take the prisoners off our hands."

"The Algerian situation is this:" started Chuck, who had been in country for seven months. "The government has control of the desert. Ali Amoud, our fellow archeologist, is alive and busy repairing the Base Camp. Mohammed's family is alive and safe in Illizi. But the GIS controls much of the Tell, and nobody controls the capital city, Algiers. There is fierce fighting going on there. Where the French have landed there is no fighting. The French are staying in their beachhead and have an informal truce with both the GIS and the government."

"So if the government has control of the desert, why don't they come here and take the prisoners off our hands?" asked Metrola as she rechecked Dimension One. "That would stretch our water supply."

"I have an answer to that." volunteered Mohammed Abbas, the desert nomad. He then explained in Arabic, with Chuck translating. "Most of us in the desert are Tuaregs and Berbers, though I am an Arab. The bandits reflect this ethnic mix. A couple of Arabs with the majority of them Berbers and Tuaregs. The government cannot politically afford to be seen as oppressing Berbers and Tuaregs, at least not until they regain the Tell, the rich part of the country. So they leave them with us. One less problem for them to worry about."

"I see. So it is still up to us to get ourselves out of here." With that, Metrola went through the long tedious process of checking and aligning and rechecking the entire magnetic field generator and all of the control mechanisms.

We worked through the night. Mohammed and Mustafa took a break for their nighttime prayer with the prisoners. It was some time after they came back that we were finally satisfied with the alignment. We agreed to get some sleep.

After another difficult day representing his client, Michelle Smith, the former Michael Schmidt, Larry Bookbinder walked into his home and the embrace of his wife. After dinner, the attorney kicked back to do some light reading. He did not want to watch television. His client is too famous, and he tired of watching himself say "no comment" to the cameras. By shooting a Neanderthal woman who is visiting from another Planet, his client brought she-males off of the daytime talk shows and into the Media Big Time.

"Honey, here are the books you wanted from the library."

"Thank you, sweetheart." A large glossy science oriented book with photos and illustrations, *The Last Neanderthal*, by Ian Tattersall. Larry always liked science. But he was lousy at it in school so he went the liberal arts, law school route. Another library book, *The Neandertal Enigma*, by James Shreeve. He started reading.

In all fairness to Tattersall and Shreeve, their books were written before the spaceship arrived full of women descended from a population of transplanted Neanderthals. What were they saying on the news? Helga dies. Bury her in a cave in Israel. Wait a few thousand years. Except for the limb and body lengths, we have a skeleton similar to the six foot Neanderthal found at Amud, Israel. The limb proportions of the Creation women are similar to modern European people, not the ancient European Neanderthals. But the European Neanderthals lived in the Ice Age, their limbs adapted to the climate. The women report that people who live in the cold climate parts of Creation also have foreshortened limbs. Helga, Lucinda, and Andemona are descendants of a population of West European Neanderthals, that much is clear from Cuc Nguyen's X-ray photographs.

Lucinda Renuxler is a Neanderthal. And his client is accused of shooting her. What would be an appropriate charge? After reading the first chapter of Tattersall's pretty coffee table book, he had an idea.

The reporters surrounded an angry Helga Trvlakian. "Let me get this straight. A man who took hormone shots and dressed up like a woman, to escape justice for the crimes he committed when he was a man, is not guilty of attempted murder because Lchnsda is not a PERSON!! If the Secret Service hadn't jumped this PERSON, this PERSON would've aimed the second bullet at ME. But that is okay. I'm not a person either. I'm just an ANIMAL! Never mind that I can speak English, German, and ATLANTEAN! Never mind that we have developed our own languages, Base Twelve numbers and mathematics, religions, laws, medicine, and technology! Never mind that we came in a spacecraft of our design and construction. We are ANIMALS, not persons. We're just a bunch of Neanderthals!"

A nice beautiful morning in the Sahara. It was actually beautiful! After Mohammed and Mustafa performed the morning prayer with the prisoners we were ready to test the ship to see if we can get out of there! "Does everyone have their compasses?" asked Metrola.

We all nodded "Yes".

"Everyone to your positions." she said cheerfully.

A dozen of us had compasses and spread around the Shuttle, the way the numbers of a clock surround its center. Metrola climbed aboard and took her position in the pilot's seat. We each had a radio headset, adjusted to fit our Cro-Magnon heads. "Is every compass pointing north?"

"Yes." we answered in turn.

"I'm turning the magnetic drive on NOW"

"My compass south pole is now pointing at the Shuttle!" each of us yelled in turn. "It is working!" The Shuttle lifted off! We all cheered!

"Looking good!" Metrola shouted in Atlantean. "Sorry, I'll try to keep my speech in English. Let me try some control maneuvers." Metrola went up, down, and all ways sideways. She landed and turned off the magnetic drive, our compasses went back to normal. She came out of the Shuttle in triumph and we rushed her. Hugs, kisses, and cheering.

We packed for the trip out. "What about the prisoners?" Good question.

The prisoners sweltered for an hour without the parachute cover. We repacked the parachutes into the top of the Shuttle. We did not want to lift off without them, having just repaired the magnetic drive unit! Mohammed and Mustafa conducted one last prayer with the prisoners. Several of us came around. The prisoners looked up at Metrola, Chuck, and me.

"I have a question to ask of you," started Metrola. "Do you still think that I am a Demon Woman?"

Maurice Jafar translated the question into Arabic. The prisoners talked it over, and came to an agreement. Maurice gave the answer in English. "After you brought us water, we realized that you are indeed a flesh and blood human being. After having a close look at your face, we have decided that you should wear a veil, because you are so beautiful. You are of a Race of people we haven't seen for many thousands of years, but that does not make you a demon or a goddess."

"Thank you for your kind words, Maurice. Here is the situation: The Shuttle is repaired, we can fly out of here. We are packed up and ready to go. Nobody from any Algerian government we can contact wants to come and get you. The civil war is still going on in the north. We've checked your trucks, they run. We filled your water canteens, you have 20 liters. You will have to find your own food. We removed the firing pins from your rifles, and dumped the ammunition in the desert, you can go look for it if you want. The rifles are stacked under the canopy of your flatbed truck. We will release you if you promise not to harm us in any way."

As Chuck repeated the offer in Arabic, we took out knives and made ready to cut the rope binding their wrists and ankles. "We promise on our word of honor." declared Maurice.

We cut the ropes and freed the bandits. "There are your trucks, go to them." Chuck told them in Arabic.

As the bandits limped with their sore muscles to their vehicles, we sprinted back into the Shuttle. I strapped down next to Metrola at the pilot's console. With everyone on board and the door closed, we took off. We saw the bandits as they reached their vehicles. Then Metrola headed for the sky. "Hey! the bullet holes in the window have been repaired." I noticed.

"Yes. We can now leave the atmosphere! Would any of you like to see an interstellar spaceship?"

"Are you inviting us on board the *Neanderthal Return*?" someone asked.

"Maybe we better check this out with the girls up above." I suggested as I put on the headset and operated the radio. "This is N.R. Shuttle calling the *Neanderthal Return*. Come in *Return*. Do you copy?"

"This is the *Neanderthal Return*." announced Trviea Harsradich's voice. "We copy N.R. Shuttle. You are flying high, your bullet holes repaired?"

"This is Metrola. Yes Trviea, the bullet holes have been patched. I'm eager to get the Shuttle up for proper repairs by Contrviea's crew. But we have a full load of Cro-Magnons. Three women, including Dr. Cuc. Fifteen men, including Neil. Our Medical ought to be better for Fred Graf than any Earth hospital."

"Okay, I guess we can invite your passengers on board for a visit, uh that is what everyone is telling me, excuse me." We heard a bevy of excited voices speaking unintelligible Atlantean. "Yeah, bring 'em up if they all consent. Because we agreed not to kidnap any more Earthlings, you will have to take them back down if any do not agree to come. Those are the rules."

"Okay, Trviea. We'll let you know what we decide."

We turned and looked at our now excited passengers "Is there anyone who does not want to visit a starship?" asked Metrola. "What William Shatner and Patrick Stewart pretend to do, we do for real. We can let you visit our ship if you agree to come."

"That sounds very exciting." said Ben Sumner. "What happens if one of those bullet hole patches fail when we are in space?"

"We're exposed to hard vacuum and we die." was Metrola's matter of fact answer.

"After everything else that has happened, I can accept the risk."

"Fred," started Meddi Chumkun, "how ya feeling?"

"Great! My leg's feeling good. How did you do that?"

"Healing Factor. Our secret recipe. We mixed it in with the blood our Canadian friends donated. Good thing you are of the same blood type. Now if you want, we can take you to a hospital on Earth. Above the atmosphere we can go *kechts* of *kepfats* per hour. We can drop you into Germany within a few minutes."

"*Ja*. But German hospital no fun. I don't think I need to go to a hospital."

"We can monitor your recovery just fine in our Medical."

"*Ja. Ich* can visit the *Neanderthal Return*."

"Dr. Cuc, would you like to see our Medical and learn Creation Medical Science?"

"You have to ask? Of course I would. No Earth physician has EVER had the chance to see another Planet's advanced medical science. It's like a shaman being offered the chance to go to Johns Hopkins."

"You flatter us, Cuc." reminded Askelion. "Atlaston Hospital is our equivalent to Johns Hopkins, and we were both educated there. One little problem we have. We keep the means of eternal youth well hidden, but of course we carry this knowledge with us. If you learn our secrets, we may not let you go back to Earth. You will become a permanent citizen of Planet Creation. We have promised not to kidnap any Earth person. But if you voluntarily come, then we can ask that you consent to this condition. Do you consent?"

"We have always dreamed of stopping the aging process. But with billions of us already, I can see why you want to keep it a secret. When we Earthlings figure it out, it'll be the biggest moral dilemma we have ever faced. I'll try not to find out this secret, and if I do, I'll go with you to Creation."

"Then it's settled." announced Metrola. "Is there anyone who does not want to go up to our ship?"

Everyone wanted to see the inside of the *Return*.

"This is the Shuttle calling *Neanderthal Return*," Metrola announced in Atlantean. "We will approach for docking."

"Shuttle, this is the *Return*. Shuttle Bay is ready."

"We did not repair the hydraulics. The landing gear is extended."

"Then please take care as you enter the Shuttle Bay."

Chapter Twenty Four

Chuck Carter flopped down next to me in the Viewing Lounge. "It was sure nice to take a shower and get cleaned up. This is one Hell of a ship! But how did they make clothes that fit me, and are of masculine style?"

I laughed. "They are very resourceful, these ladies. You've seen the Garden Room yet?"

"Nah. We're just cycling through the showers. Neanderthals claim to have a better sense of smell than we, so they are eager to get us all cleaned up."

"They grow flax, cotton, and hemp."

"Hemp. Like marijuana?"

"Yeah, but they don't smoke the leaves and flowers. These clothes are made from hemp linen, flax linen, and cotton."

"Ahh. The traditional uses of hemp. Do they do anything with the THC?"

"Askelion and Meddi make some of their drugs from the THC. The main thing they do is make a substance that tunes the lenses of their eyes to perfect vision. That's why they see so good. They claim that this substance has no effect on the brain. Which as we all know is the main problem with THC. Or benefit, depending on your point of view."

Chuck laughed. "Speaking of Askelion, how come she wants a blood sample from each of us?"

"They want to test for every virus and bacteria that might be a contagion. The machines that they used to test for the Holocaust Virus can be adjusted to find AIDS, ebola, polio, herpes, anything you can think of that they just don't want to deal with. Especially AIDS."

"AIDS. Well, HIV positive is not the same as AIDS."

"Not from their point of view. Having the virus is having AIDS. That is one bug they don't want at all. Period. They have no problem with political correctness. You have the human immunodeficiency virus, they'll take you back to Earth. Or drop you into the Sun. Even if you're only HIV positive, and not yet suffering from full blown AIDS. They don't see the difference, they want you CLEAN."

"Why do they want us CLEAN?" He was smiling, he knew the answer.

"They need our sperm. No men. No children. That's why they're here. That's why they built a 3,000 foot ship. They bought themselves time by stopping the aging process. But with no children, their Race goes extinct. They may not grow old, but they are not immortal. They have plenty of my sperm. And they have my permission to use it in any way that'll help them procreate. They will ask your permission, should you prove to be HIV negative. And then they'll want samples of your semen."

"Why? As you say, they have plenty of your sperm."

"Genetic diversity."

"Oh. I'm black."

"Bingo. They might go to Japan for one of their men. Lucinda appears to have herself a full blooded Native American man."

"And how do they propose to take such samples?"

"By the method women have always used." Chuck looked at me like he just could not believe it. "After visiting you in the privacy of your room, she quietly goes to Medical and one of the physicians removes the semen and puts it into storage."

"So this is like a whorehouse in the sky!"

"Don't say that. To them it's not a matter of morality, it's survival. Besides, can you blame 'em for wanting a little sex after all these years?"

"No, I guess I cannot."

"The Virus replicated with Neanderthal Y chromosomes. That's what killed their men. They are hoping, indeed Askelion believes it to be the case, that this Virus won't replicate with Cro-Magnon Y chromosomes. So we're immune. The procedure that they propose is this: Take two eggs from different Neanderthal women. Genetic diversity. Take one of our sperm cells. The eggs and the sperm each have 23 chromosomes. They remove 22 chromosomes from the sperm, leaving the Y chromosome."

"How they do that?"

"I think that's what they're working on. They remove 22 chromosomes from one of the Neanderthal eggs, leaving the X chromosome. These 22 Neanderthal chromosomes are inserted into the sperm cell. The sperm cell is revived and sent after the other egg. There is something chemical that goes on when the sperm penetrates the egg that allows fertilization. The egg becomes an embryo with the cells splitting again and again. Implant into a womb, nine months later we have a Neanderthal boy. One Cro-Magnon Y chromosome, 45 Neanderthal chromosomes. This should guarantee Neanderthal bone structure combined with immunity to the Virus."

"I see. Not a half-breed. But could we have true half-breeds? A jawbone found at Tabun, Israel has a space behind the wisdom tooth and is heavily built like the Neanderthals, but it has a chin like us Cro-Magnons. Makes me wonder if Junior Tabun was the product of a mixed marriage? Daddy Tabun a proud Neanderthal hunter and Mommy Tabun a tall slender Cro-Magnon?"

"That's possible, another experiment we can try. But don't worry. Right now, these women have their menstrual cycles shut down. They won't get pregnant. They're saving that for when they get back home."

Deputy Prosecutor Bruce Elders opened the weekly meeting in Port Townsend. In the room were Don Mayton, the Chief of the Port Townsend Police, several other police officers, and Jefferson County Deputy Sheriff Mike Langston. While waiting for his secretary to arrive with the viewfoils, he made small talk with the meeting participants. "My eight year old. Had his friends over. Last night. They watched the *Lion King* movie. Twice. That *Hakuna Matata* sung by. Elton John. Ohhh maaan! Kids would not stop. Singing it. Finally. Got 'em to bed."

"*Hakuna Matata*. I wonder if it really means 'no worries'."

"Maybe we should call the U. of W.'s Language Department and find out." Don Mayton referred to the University of Washington. "Wouldn't it be funny if it turned out to mean 'Two zebras doing it in the savanna'?"

Laughter. "The zebras don't have no worries!"

Mike Langston spoke up. "I remember talking to Henry Turnipseed about this sort of thing."

"Yeah. Uh, full blooded. Puyallup-Nisqually. I believe. What's he doing. Out in our woods? Doesn't he have, uh, fishing rights or, uh, something?"

"Henry earned his money selling a book of poetry. Good poetry too. Bought a copy, he autographed it for me. He's a good guy. He paid for that 10 acre plot fair and square. Just wanted to get away from Fife and Tacoma."

"Can't say as I, uh, blame him. But why. Way out here. In our County? It's NOT. Like we haven't. Our own Indians: Jamestown S'Klallam, Clallam, Makahs. Uh, Hoh in the piece of our County. On the other side. Of the Olympic National Park."

"Because Federal Way isn't far enough. If he has money of his own, earned fair and square, it's none of our business where he buys property and chooses to live. He's an American citizen." Langston is a good friend of both Len Taylor and Henry. "With all due respect, Elders, I'm getting a little tired of your racism against Indians."

"Uhh, well uh, look! I'm NOT. Racist against Indians." No, of course not! "As long as. Uh, Henry does NOT. Break any laws. He's entitled to our protection. Same as anyone else. But with all of the Indian place names. We HAVE around here. I wonder if the Indians didn't have. A bit of a sense of humor. 'Touch my *Humptulips* and I'll kick you in the *Hoquiam*!'" He laughed softly at his joke.

"Yeah. I was shooting the breeze with Henry one day. I asked him if *Tacoma* was really the Twillshootseed name for the mountain we now call Rainier. He said 'That's what my ancestors told this guy Tolmie. Sometime later, a feller named McCarver wanted to build a new town on the side of Commencement Bay opposite of where the Puyallups were given a reservation. We told him that *Tacoma* is the name we gave the mountain. Well, here's the scoop: We named the mountain *Tacoma* because that is the part of the female body it looks like.'" Laughter. "I still don't know if he was just pulling my leg!"

"I understand. He visited with Mrs. Renuxler. When he was in D.C." pointed out Elders. "Gossip columnists are making an item. Uh, out of them two. I wonder if, uh, the trog woman wants to be. His wife or girlfriend. Out here in Jefferson County?"

"You really shouldn't use the term 'trog'." reminded Deputy Langston.

"Well, uh, well, uh, what should I call her? Neanderthal? Creationist? Atlantean? How about, uh, Demon Woman? She sure did a number on Frank Binford's hand."

"Not Demon Woman. Neanderthal or Atlantean is fine. Creationist makes her sound like she doesn't believe in evolution. She and her shipmates are living proof that evolution happened. After listening to you for the last ten years, I believe they've evolved further than we." Laughter.

"Well, yeah, yeah, funny." Elders stood there with the silly grin he uses when someone zings him with a funny insult. "Well, if Mrs. Renuxler, uh, wants to be Mrs. Turnipseed. The diplomatic immunity. Will eventually lift. And. We can charge her again."

"Judge'll toss it on soldier and sailor immunity, and be pissed off at us for wasting her time." reminded Don Mayton. "Nothing they did to Neil Peace rises to the level of Nazi War Crime. Neil's enjoying their company too much for anything like that to stick. Besides, I've caught too much political heat for that as it is. Now that our old friend Michael Schmidt shot her in D.C., Lucy's got the sympathy of the public. And everyone loves a love story. Henry's publisher has released a new printing of his poetry and it's selling like mad."

A knock on the door. "Hi. I hoping I'm not disturbing your weekly meeting. I'm Assistant U.S. Attorney Shirley Barton."

"You're the one prosecuting Binford and Plotkin?"

"Yes, that's me."

"Well, come in, then. Come in."

"And I'm Special Agent Stan Marier, FBI." The G-man held out his badge. "And these are some U.S. Marshals." Five Marshals fully armed with guns and handcuffs filed into the meeting room.

Ms. Barton held out a yellowed copy of the Port Townsend newspaper several years old. "Bruce Elders. You are quoted here describing Michael Schmidt as having communication problems. That's why he was a failure as an anthropologist and as a truck driver. Although he seemed to be pretty good at compiling a nice long list of felonies, well planned bank robberies, that you and other counties in this state want him for. The she-male bit was actually rather brilliant. It was like Michael Schmidt disappeared from the face of the Planet Earth. We were wondering if the Creation girls kidnapped him. Nobody, and I mean nobody, connected Michelle Smith with Michael Schmidt. That stupid lawyer of his raised a hornet's nest trying to characterize Lchnsda Renuxler as an animal, not a person. This morning the judge denied the motion. Whether Neanderthals from Planet Creation are a race of *Homo sapiens sapiens*, a separate subspecies *Homo sapiens neanderthalensis*, or an entirely different species than us, *Homo neanderthalensis*, they exhibit sufficient intelligence, emotion, and ability to make mistakes to be considered fully human, not animal, and are therefore persons for all purposes under the Constitution and laws of the United States. So sayeth the United States District Court for the District of Columbia."

She let this news sink in, and then went on. "Now we were wondering why Michelle Smith, having so successfully evaded justice with her disguise, would draw attention to herself by shooting a woman on a parade float. Well it turns out that she didn't have any racial hate toward Neanderthals. In fact, she was sympathetic to them. They didn't ask to be born Neanderthal. But God in His wrath intended to wipe them out in the Flood. The Virus was another attempt by the Lord to eliminate them. Smith really believes this. She actually believed that if we who are descended from Noah help them in their effort to frustrate the wrath of God, then the covenant granted to Noah and his descendants will no longer be in effect."

"That has been the Avenger of Yahweh line since the spacecraft showed up."

"Right. Michelle began to worry about life as a she-male in prison. Daunting prospect I must admit. And that her lawyer would do something so stupid! Anyway, those communication problems that you mentioned, Mr. Elders? Perhaps a side effect of the hormone shots is a vast improvement in communication skills. Or do you suppose the incentive to make a deal would also improve communication skills?"

Special Agent Stan Marier, FBI, whipped out the *Miranda* card. "Mr. Elders, you are under arrest. You have the right to remain silent, . . ."

Mrs. Elders and her eight year old son watched in horror as the FBI conducted a search of their home. She just could not believe the words she read in the search warrant the federal police handed her. Her husband is an honest prosecutor. There are a lot of scumbags in the world; one cannot always get 'em playing by Marquis de Queensbury rules. It is amazing how much dope is grown, sold, and smuggled by the hippie and biker communities around the Olympic Peninsula. And then there are the interracial marriages and the homosexuals, bisexuals, and Lord knows what else, even in our nice quiet small town. Canada is right across the Strait, so we have all kinds of smuggling. People just get into a boat and don't bother with going through either nation's border posts. And they don't just carry themselves, but anything they do not wish to declare at the border crossings. Didn't Bruce help put away those coin dealers who were smuggling Roman gold staters into Canada? Some of Richmond, B.C.'s Hong Kong Chinese didn't want to mess with things like GATT, NAFTA, antiquities regulations, taxes, duties and so on. They were also bringing Hong Kongers across the Strait who wanted to see miles on road signs without bothering with American immigration and visa regulations.

Her Bruce has done an excellent job! The trog women from Creation needed to learn that they must obey our laws while they are here. But here is the FBI, search warranting their house on the word of that scumbag Mike Schmidt! What is the world coming to! Her Bruce would have nothing to do with the Avengers of Yahweh except to be their prosecutor!

Peter Kent and Clark Parker went through Bruce's tool shed in the basement. "Hey, this cardboard box is heavy, full of magazines."

"What are they?"

"*National Geographics*."

"Dump 'em out and look through 'em."

"Okay." Peter dumped the magazines out on to the table. "Welllllllll! Lookee! What have we here? A genuine, honest to gosh, Millennium Catalogue! I wonder if the missus knows anything about this?"

"I doubt it, she don't seem the type to do anything weird. Just missionary position as few times as possible to produce a kid."

"Well let's take a lookee through this kinky catalogue. What are those page numbers again?"

"46 and 52."

"Okay. First we look at page 46. Oh wow, a transvestite harness on page 40. Our girl Michelle'll like that, maybe we'll order one for her. Yep, on page 46 is the AB40. Hey! This page is dog-eared! Circles are drawn in ink around 'AB40 DELUXE ARM BINDER', the list price, $249.95. And in the paragraph, the word 'zippered' is underlined in the same black ink. It 'Comes zippered or laced.' Look at the photograph. Replace the lacing with a zipper for fast work in a kidnapping, and these are the items found at the crime scene."

"Michelle's telling the truth. Let's look at page 52."

"The T7B locking gag trainers. Those are the animals all right! The whole display is circled in ink! Look down here below the description paragraph and the list price of $249.95. I wonder if this is Bruce's handwriting? 'Special order, stainless steel core in gag, $50 extra.' A phone number. 503 is Portland's area code."

"That's the sex shop's phone number all right, I wonder if Bruce is stupid enough to make any calls there from his own number or from a phone owned by the Jefferson County taxpayers?"

"With some of these public service geniuses, anything like that is possible! I'm sure we'll find out soon enough! Put it in the evidence bag. Neat thing about these rubber gloves, gives the fingerprint boys in the lab a chance!"

"Who me? Stupid?" Larry Bookbinder asked his smiling law partners. "The Avengers of Yahweh will now face justice for their crimes. The Olympic Peninsula is rid of a corrupt prosecutor. Name me a defense lawyer that doesn't want to nail a corrupt prosecutor. A guy like that can cost the local taxpayers a shitload of money and get innocent people thrown in jail. Meanwhile, real criminals run free and kill Secret Service agents. The Creation girls now have a useful precedent they can point to when it comes to their legal rights within the United States. The rest of the Planet Earth will follow with legislation or court rulings establishing that Neanderthals are persons for all purposes under the law. Our client? Federal Witness Protection Program! Not bad considering what he or she has done with his or her life!"

There were seven Neanderthal women in Washington, D.C after the Shuttle took off for Algeria, including Helga, Lucinda, Andemona, and Sorby Mishlakian.

Nesla Teslakian is rumored to have helped design and build the Laser Cannon defenses of Creation. She discreetly read *Aviation Week & Space Technology* and other technical manuals and engineering magazines. The Metric System drives her nuts. It will do that to a Base Twelve thinking Creation Neanderthal. She wishes we Americans would use our American measures more often in our science. At least the metallurgy and the thermodynamics are in inches and foot-pounds and such.

The other two women are software writers. Marla Syferkrip and Wlmsda Gtslakian were cooped up in a spaceship with the finest computer equipment ever built on either Earth or

Creation. Seventh heaven for computer nerds! When I first came aboard, they obviously hadn't been too prissy about their appearance. Hair tended to be unkempt. When a Neanderthal woman puts on weight and doesn't exercise, she looks like she's been drawn by R. Crumb. But with a man on board they took more showers, combed their hair, and worked out in the ship's gym. They lost a few *dollons* and improved their muscle tone.

The White House hosted a reception for the Ambassador from Saudi Arabia. The Ambassador's wife visited with the Creation women. "Our biggest problem now is that we're all cooped up in here." Helga complained. "With all of the attacks on us, and then with Metrola, Sorby, and Nesla getting loose and thumping that mugger, they put us under even tighter security."

"Can you get back to your ship?"

"No, our Shuttle got banged up in Algeria. It ain't coming down until Contrviea says it's coming down. That might be a while."

"You really would like to get out now and then?"

"We do get out. But we have this tight Secret Service escort. Spirit bless 'em, their Number One and Only Priority is to keep us alive and unhurt. We go for enchiladas and the Secret Service tastes the food first. We all know there is danger out there. But it's the same danger you yourself face, that every American faces. We've spent most of our lives the last few years with nothing but three *tig-its* of aluminum between us and the hard vacuum of space. This Security Cocoon is a bit frustrating to us who are used to a higher level of freedom."

"Us Saudi girls understand how that can be like. I have an idea."

A group of women in chadors walked down the sidewalk past a kosher restaurant. Not an unusual sight in Washington, D.C., given the foreign embassies. Their heads were completely covered; the Neanderthal women worried about getting high on carbon dioxide like the Apollo 13 astronauts. They were used to breathing free, not through a piece of cloth! They could see through the thin silk across their eyes, it hid their brow ridges. They looked around. Not a Secret Service agent in sight! Gave them the slip!

The restaurant is decorated with Hebrew letters, menorahs, and Israeli and American flags. "We Arabs aren't supposed to eat pork either." announced the ambassador's wife. "If the Palestinians and the Israelis can kiss and make up, or at least try to, I don't see why we should continue to pretend hate for Jews." She lowered her voice to a conspiratorial whisper. "You Creation girls have no beef with the Israelis, or with Jews? Do you?"

"Absolutely not! Given the kosher rules, at least not the rump roast!"

The giggly group went in and were seated around a large table in the back by a waiter gifted with a New York Yiddish accent. They looked at their menus for a few minutes and then made their orders.

The food was brought to them. Beef briskets, lamb shoulder, lentil loaf, and falafel. The Saudi woman removed her face covering so she could eat. The waiter was not surprised, a nice tan Arabian face. But he did a double take when he saw the other faces. He looked around. "Where are the Secret Service guys? I've heard they can be discreet, but this is really discreet!"

Helga grabbed his hand; he felt her great strength, even though she was being gentle. "Please. Be a *mensch*." Helga knew that Yiddish is derived from German and that *mensch* is a Yiddish way of asking him to be a good guy. "Please don't call anyone. We needed to get away. Don't we all desire a little freedom?"

"I understand. And I'm honored that you have chosen our restaurant. Let me know if there is any problem with the food."

"I'm sure the food will be fine. Smells great. Thank you."

Sabar Duradich showed Chuck Carter her astronomy equipment. As an archeologist, he knew about the astronomy that apparently went into the Mayan pyramids, Teotihuacan, Stonehenge, the Giza Pyramids and the Egyptian tombs. He knew about proper motions of stars and the Precession of the Equinoxes and how they affect astronomical observations over the ages. "So that's what those who believe the Sphinx was originally built around 10,000 B.C. argue. In that time, Leo rose due east, where the Sphinx faces. The Sun was in Leo when it rose on the Vernal Equinox."

"That's very interesting." responded the five foot three inch astronomer. "You are not married, are you Chuck?"

"Uh, no. No girlfriends either."

"I see. Not much chance of a social life in the middle of the Sahara, is there? Unless you're gay?"

Chuck laughed softly. "I'm not gay. No, not much of a social life in the desert. Islam is a wonderful religion, but it doesn't make for wine, women, and song. Not for us Christian American type guys."

"Your medical tests came back. No AIDS, no herpes, no nothing that is really bad. You had a common cold virus about a year ago. There were some antibodies, but not the rhinovirus itself." She dropped her eyes for a moment and took a deep breath. "So we can use your sperm."

"Is that why you spent this time talking shop with me? You aren't really interested in archeology and ancient Earth history, are you?"

"I'm sorry. I really am interested in those subjects, I am a scientist." She turned around and bent over to apparently look at a setting on her equipment. Chuck had the perfect view of her rear end inside her form fitting pants. "It's all right if you don't want us to have your sperm, if you don't want to make love with me or any of us. I won't bring it up again."

"It's Okay, Sabar. Not a problem. I wouldn't mind making love with you." She smiled. She also thought she saw something. In Leo, right on what the Earth astronomers call the 'ecliptic', below the Lion Paws. The planetary plane. "Look, with all of the sex harassment and other garbage that goes on with our damn lawyers and feminazis, men and women on Earth are afraid to talk to each other."

Sabar kicked off her shoes. There is something more important going on here than some faint fuzz spot in the Lion Constellation. It still looks like a lion when viewed from Creation, four light years above Australia. She turned around and leaned over Chuck. He put his right hand around behind her back. With his left hand he cupped her right breast. She gently grabbed hold of each wrist and then firmly forced Chuck's hands off of her body and down by his side. "Wouldn't mind making love with me, you say? Question is, would I mind making love with you?"

"I thought you weren't as strong as the others." complained Chuck, marveling at how strong such a small woman can be.

"I'm not as strong as the others. I'm the only one on this crew who cannot bench press four *hekt dollons*. Only three *hekt* and ten dozen *dollons*." She wore a teasing grin.

"Four *hekt dollons* is 302 pounds. You're admitting that you can bench press 'only' 290 pounds." He whistled. "Mo' than I can bench press."

She laughed. "You're being modest. You can bench press 300 pounds if you really wanted to. I keep hearing stories about little old ladies lifting cars off of people trapped under them. Adrenaline and incentive can make all the difference. I'm flattered that you tell me you don't mind making love with me."

"Well, right now I cannot move my arms."

"Don't worry, I won't rape you. You may consent to sex, but what we NEED is consent to use your sperm in any way we need to allow us to bear children. I'll go to Medical after we are through here, and Askelion or Meddi will remove your semen from me and put it into cold storage. If our research and experiments bear out, you may become the proud father of twelve *kecht* baby boys and make an entire Planet deliriously happy. By our method, each boy will have 45 Neanderthal chromosomes so that we continue to be Neanderthals, with these brow ridges and heavy muscles, and your Y chromosome. That is what you have to consent to. If you do not, no sex. Not with me, not with any of us." Her grin was wicked. Her thigh could feel the arousal of her male prey.

"Maybe I could jack off into a Petrie dish."

"Why would you want to do that?"

"I don't. Sabar, it is not fair to ask me to make a decision like that after getting me all hot and bothered. It makes it very difficult for me to think."

"I plead guilty as charged. It's no worse than when an Earth girl gets you in bed, then refuses to get an abortion and refuses to marry you. And then sicks the state support agency on you for the money to pay for HER decision. At least I offer you the opportunity to make your decision BEFORE I extract your sperm. I won't take your sperm and then make the decision without regard to your feelings. I won't violate your Constitutional rights as an American citizen. Not like your American girls."

"I appreciate that but,"

She let go of him. She moved away and sat in a chair. "I'll leave you alone for a while. That way you can make your decision without any pressure. I apologize for trying to seduce you into it. We are an endangered species, but we will not cut ethical corners to secure your help in continuing our Race. That is why we knocked Trviea down a notch."

"You can use my sperm in any way that'll help you continue your Race. Uh, is this room secure?"

"I took the liberty of locking the door."

"Did you do this with Neil?"

"I don't kiss and tell. It's rude."

Chapter Twenty Five

I was sound asleep. Off in the distance I heard some kind of buzz. As I slowly started to come to, I felt the warmth and comfort of a woman's body next to mine. Angela? No, we divorced. Or did we? Wait a minute, this woman is taller and has more muscle than Angela. The woman turned around, got up and turned on a soft florescent light. Trviea Harsradich. Oh. Now I know where I am.

I used to be a lot more careful with whom I went to bed. Even before I met Angela, I never went to bed with Neanderthals. But then where do you go to meet one? I can just see the personal ad:

SWNF, HWP, age 188, NS, professional astronaut, enjoys music, dancing, moonlit nights and rum. ISO SM, any race, HWP not mandatory, no STD, NS, for procreation and possible LTR.

SWNF is single white Neanderthal female, of course. SM means single male, not that other stuff.

I watched Trviea's nude body as she talked quietly on the phone in Atlantean. Then suddenly, "Neil, it's Sabar."

"This is Neil."

"I need you to come to Astronomy right away. Bring Trviea."

"What did you see?"

"Just come, please."

After getting dressed and running a comb through our hair, we went up to Sabar's station. "Check this out." Sabar showed us a photograph of the sky taken by the ship's telescope.

"Fuzz spot. Looks like a comet."

"That's exactly what it is. Infrared shows it's as cold as a comet. That's hydrogen, methane, cyanogen, and such boiling off of it. I asked Pidonita to stay within the planetary plane but get away from Earth, about a *hekt kecht kepfats*. With this initial parallax, I can roughly triangulate the distance to the comet. Now Pidonita is running us in a parallax estimating pattern. We move laterally exactly twelve *kecht kepfats*, takes two hours with acceleration of about 5/12 gee, and measure the displacement of the comet against the star background, we know exactly how far it is. Two more hours to go back and again measure the displacement. A few such cycles and we know it's speed, heading, and orbit. It's in free fall like every natural object."

"What do you know so far?"

"Coming in from Leo. One *hekt* and two dozen and one *beeyon kepfats* from your Sun. That's 860 million miles, 20 to 30 million miles inside the orbit of Saturn. It's really close to the planetary plane. Closer than Jupiter's North Pole. Probably closer than Earth's North Pole. And it is BIG! The core is about thirty, err, three dozen *kepfats* across."

"Thirty six times one point six,"

"58 miles in your numbers and units."

I whistled. "Hale-Bopp was only 25 miles across."

"It's a big one. Should be a spectacular show from Earth two years from now. It might get within several *beeyon kepfats* of Earth. In your numbers, I'd say ten or twenty million miles."

"If I remember, Hyakutake flew over our North Hemisphere at a distance of nine or ten million miles. It was pretty then. Hale-Bopp never got closer than 120 million miles or so, but because it is so huge, it was much better than Hyakutake. Now it looks like Comet Duradich is going to pass at a Hyakutake distance while being over twice the diameter, 10 times the overall size of Hale-Bopp. Let's call the International Astronomical Union."

"I think I have their number here. Can we hook up with Earth's telephone system from this distance?"

"Yeah, we can," answered Captain Trviea, "there are a couple light-*prelates* of distance, but we can get a transmission through." She put on a headset and used the ship's radio. She dialed in the frequency for contacting the telephone satellites. "We're in, I'm getting dial tone. Here Neil, take it, you know these Earth systems."

I put on the headset. The keyboard was marked in Creation numerals. Earth numerals written next to the buttons. I punched in the number for their voice phone in Massachusetts.

"Astronomical Telegrams. Hello."

"Sabar, you're on!"

"Hello. My name is Sabar Duradich, I have discovered a new comet." she then read off the right ascension and declination in Earth terms. "Constellation Leo, right on the ecliptic."

"When did you record this location?"

"Over the last two hours. In fact, it's there now."

"Okay, I note the time. Where are you located? We need to note your longitude and latitude. You seem to take a long time to answer."

"I'm in the *Neanderthal Return*. The spaceship. We are about, uh, 400,000 miles away from Earth, on the centerline of Earth's orbit on the lag side. The Earth was where we are six hours ago."

"Oh! OH! I'm sorry. That explains the time it takes for you to answer. 400,000 divided by 186,000, 2 seconds each way. Are you a Neanderthal woman from Creation?"

"Yes, I am."

"Oh wow! We'll name this comet after you if we confirm it! Please send us your data on it, here is the number for the computer transmission."

Sabar took down the number. She punched it in, her computer confirmed hook up. "Okay, got it! Sending." The data included her estimate of the comet's size and the transliteration of her name into Roman alphabet. Sabar used her computer to quickly translate the data into Base Ten numbers, British-American units, and Metric units.

Chuck came into the Astronomy room. "Oh, are you busy? I can come back later."

"Oh, come in, come in." invited Sabar.

"I brought some flowers from the Garden Room."

"Oh, that's sweet!" Sabar accepted the flowers and put them in a tall thin cup of water. She kissed him.

"I saw Earth out one of the windows. How come we're so far away?"

"We discovered a comet. We just called it into your International Astronomical Union. They are going to name it after me. Do I really want that?" She wasn't sure.

"Way to go. I'm happy for you. But why is Earth so small?"

"We moved away to get a better look at the comet. Pidonita Hmlakian is our current pilot; she is performing parallax maneuvers at two hour intervals. From these we can accurately determine its distance, location, speed, and orbit. It's coming in from Leo." She pointed to a video screen with a diagram of our Solar System, Zodiac constellations around the outside, showing current locations of the planets and the comet. At the scale used, the ellipses looked like circles, but the orbits of Mercury and Mars were visibly off center. Mars is furthest from the

Sun when it is in the direction of Cancer and Leo. "If you'd been looking up at midnight, you'd have noticed that Leo and Virgo are right above you. In late March, almost April, Earth is currently on the side of the Sun toward Leo and Virgo. The comet is out here, inside the orbit of Saturn. Saturn, Jupiter, and Mars are too far away in their orbits to have much effect on the comet's orbit." She pressed a button and a parabolic curve appeared wrapping around the Sun with one leg going through the comet. "This is a preliminary calculation of the comet's orbit. The Earth will complete two full orbits between now and when this comet crosses the Earth's orbit. It should pass within 10 million miles."

"Wow. It's not going to hit us, is it?"

"No! Its orbit would have to be precisely in the planetary plane and it would have to cross the Earth orbit at precisely the right time. *Beeyon* to one odds against that. It's in the planetary plane now, but it's probably crossing, going north or south. We don't know which way, yet."

"One other thing," started Trviea, "the core of this comet is around 60 miles across. I'm told that Hale-Bopp was only 25 miles. It should pass close to Earth, and be very large in the sky."

"I see. Uh, Hrtinsla helped me pick these flowers for you."

"Thank her for me, please."

"You might not be so thankful. She tried to seduce me."

We all laughed. "Word has gotten around. Your African heritage makes for genetic diversity."

"You're not jealous?"

"Why should I be? If you are going to give us sperm, then we need as much as you can supply. It's a long way back to Creation and this ship is big enough to carry plenty of those little vials."

"You should go find her before she gets a hold of one of the Canadian boys." Trviea suggested, as we giggled.

"Oh wow! What about the three Earth girls? They might feel left out."

"I see no reason why our physicians cannot remove semen from them as easily as from us. But I warn you, Earth girls might not be as easy as us. It's not like they've been without men since Twenty Four Eleven Six. They might slap your face!"

Chuck was no longer able to contain his laughter. "I'm sorry. Ah gotta get outta here! You guys are just too much! Ahh don't fuckin' BUHLIEVE this!"

"*Achtung*! How you feeling Fred?" Dr. Lamakian was bright and cheerful when visiting her patient.

"*Ja. Ich* feel great! I can walk on this leg. You, Meddi, and Cuc did a good job. How come it's healing so fast?"

"Healing Factor. Wonderful stuff. Maybe we can share this medical technology with Earth. Healing Factor is perfect for gunshot wounds. I managed to slip some into Lchnsda with the blood we brought down to Washington, D.C."

"*Ja*! There is still a lot of warfare and gunfire on Earth. Even in Germany. As a defeated nation, we followed a policy of peace while hoping the Warsaw Pact and NATO don't start a war on our soil. Then the Soviet Union fell apart and the East European countries rejected Communism without a war! There was some violence there, in Romania, but that was a nasty dictatorship. Still, reunified Germany has its violent crime, there are neo-Nazis. Our standard of living has fallen as our factories moved to other countries for cheap labor. Real violence is as close as Bosnia, as far as East Timor. America is a fantastic nation, but it's known for its crime and gun culture. In both peace and war, guns and knives take their toll. Your Healing Factor is a *wunderbar* gift and only fair in return for the sperm we provide."

"Healing Factor is a boon to innocent victims of crime and war. But part of the deterrent to war and violence is the horror. Healing Factor might reduce this deterrent and that in turn might cause more innocent lives to be taken."

"The horror of war did not deter Hitler. The horror of the Holocaust did not deter the ordinary Germans who participated in it. Horror did not deter Stalin from starving millions of Ukrainians and Russians to death while exporting grain to pay for industrialization. Horror did not deter the Viet Cong, the Khmer Rouge, the Bosnians, the Serbs in Kosovo, the Rwandans, or any other fanatic or tyrant. Deterrence is in the possibility of LOSING the war or being PUNISHED for the crime. And that does not always work. Please Askelion, we NEED that Healing Factor."

Sigh. "You're right. It is a dilemma. Can we morally withhold technology that can benefit people in a society? Or is it moral to share that same technology and risk the possible consequences? It is one thing if a society develops its own technology and applies it. It is another thing to introduce it."

"Actually, the technology has already been introduced. Before you came and introduced yourselves, science fiction described everything you have that we did not. We imagined that these things are possible. Now we KNOW that these things are possible. We will work hard to develop the technology. It's like the atomic bomb. H.G. Wells wrote about it before it was invented. It was in the popular science fiction. Then the Americans dropped two on Japan to end the war. Now, almost every nation has at least a workable design on the shelf, if not an actual bomb in its inventory. Now that we know Healing Factor exists, we will develop it. You can save lives and ease suffering by sharing with us this technology now. Share it on the Internet at a Web Site, so that everyone has access to it. Think of it as *quid pro quo*. You want our sperm to solve your problem. Share with us your medical technology and allow us to deal with the resulting dilemmas. Fair trade."

"You are not married, are you?"

"*Nein*. Divorced, no children."

"Why no children?"

"*Mien frau* was barren, I'm fine, I have a good sperm count."

"I see. If you consent to the use of your sperm for research and for giving us a next generation of children, I'll share the formula for Healing Factor with instructions as to its proper use. Deal?"

"Sure. I agree to this. But my leg is still healing, so please be gentle."

"Oh-kay." Askelion removed her shirt with a smile.

"You weren't kidding!"

"*Nein*."

Mohammed Abbas was in Medical receiving a check-up from Dr. Cuc Nguyen. They were speaking mostly in Arabic. "Your blood pressure is 123 over 85." reported Cuc, using her own equipment which is in Earth units of measure. "Not bad, temperature is a perfect 98.6."

"Algeria was a French possession, we are fully Metric. What's that in Celsius?"

"Oh. 37.0."

Donald Colburn was helping the physicians. He spoke in English. "Back in Vancouver we have this Metric stuff, one of Trudeau's ideas. But old habits die hard. We still think in feet and inches, and weigh ourselves in pounds. I went into a bookstore to buy some reading material for the trip to Algeria. And there it was, the Ray Bradbury classic. *Celsius 233!*"

Dr. Cuc giggled. "Sounds like Trudeau went a little too far."

"Can you both agree to doctor-patient privilege?" Mohammed asked in broken English.

"Sure." they both answered.

He switched back to Arabic. "I know these girls have been taking sperm from the men. From Donald, here."

Donald blushed when Cuc translated. "Well, yes. But I don't kiss and tell."

"Please don't." in English. He continued in Arabic. "I know what they want to use the sperm for. I have no problem with that. It will be a wonderful thing when they have children, *Inshallah*. I'd be happy to contribute! Why haven't any of them asked me? Is there something wrong with me? Am I unattractive?"

Dr. Cuc laughed. "No, no, no! You're not unattractive. Not at all! But you have a wife. And children. You are not divorced."

"Oh. I see."

"They did not come here to ruin marriages. They understand the value of the relationship between a man and a woman. None of them want to inflict on you, your wife, or your children any of the pain that they themselves have suffered."

"You're right. 'You must not commit adultery'. That is Allah's Commandment. Not bad advice either."

Dr. Cuc slipped on a rubber glove. Pointed her index finger. She could not resist a wicked grin. "There is one thing we have to do that your wife will HAVE to forgive."

"Do we hafta?"

The Vice President lives at the Naval Observatory. He walked over to the Navy astronomers and asked for a briefing on Comet Duradich.

"90 to 100 kilometers in diameter."

"Excuse me, gentlemen, please explain in miles."

"55 to 60 miles. But Sir, much of our equipment works in Metric."

"I know. We recently passed the Traditional Weights and Measures Act because the American people don't want the Metric System. I don't either." He winked and smiled, us politicians have to do this, you understand.

"All right, here it is. Comet Duradich is coming in from the Constellation Leo. About 860 million miles from the Sun, 767 million miles from Earth. Right on the planetary plane. More specifically, the plane of the Earth's orbit, which is called the ecliptic. This comet has not deviated from the ecliptic. We believe that it'll pass within 10 million miles of Earth about two years from now."

"Is it possible that this 60 mile cometary core will HIT the Earth?"

"Well, I guess it's possible. If the comet was passing through the ecliptic plane, then it'll pass high in the northern sky like Hyakutake did. Hyakutake was never a threat because the plane of its orbit is tilted compared to the plane of Earth's orbit." He held two business cards at right angles to each other to illustrate the point. "Most comets are that way, so they don't hit us. But this comet is steady in the ecliptic plane." He held the two cards flat against each other.

"What are the odds that it'll hit Earth?"

"Long odds. Very long odds. It's timing. It has to pass a point in the Earth's orbit at the same time Earth passes that point. It could just as easily hit the Moon. For it to hit the Earth is like winning the lottery."

"As the second string Commander in Chief, I'm responsible for national security. The dinosaurs won the lottery. I don't wish to have a repeat of their luck. What are the Creation girls doing in their spaceship?"

"They moved a half million to a million miles away from Earth and are performing a parallax maneuver, repeating every four hours. They're staying in the same position relative to the Sun

219

and the Zodiac while we orbit away from them at 66,600 miles per hour. Makes for a very accurate parallax."

"Parallax maneuver?"

"They move exactly perpendicular to the line between them and the comet, a distance of twelve *kecht kepfats*. That's 33,460 miles. They're using their units and numbers. They can triangulate the distance to the comet with increasing accuracy. They must have a much better estimate of its orbit than we do."

"I see. The President spoke with the *Neanderthal Return* a few minutes ago. They were full of non-answers then. The President's gut feeling is that they are having an increasing level of concern. When you have an accurate calculation of its orbit that positively answers the question of whether it's a Dinosaur Killer or not, please give me a call."

We watched Sabar perform the calculations from the latest data on the comet that now bears her name. She suddenly let out a quick breath and angrily spat out an Atlantean word that I did not know. "What does that word mean?" I quietly whispered this question in Trviea's ear.

"It's obscene." she whispered back. "You don't want to know."

Sabar double checked every calculation by hand. She didn't want to believe her computer. She covered page after page of hemp paper with Creation Base Twelve numerals. I recognized her shorthand symbols for the Atlantean units of measure. I also recognized the Creation versions of Newton's and Kepler's equations with Einsteinian corrections. "My equations account for the gravitational pull of Jupiter. The gas giant is now between the Sun and Gemini. When this comet, falling in from Leo, crosses the orbit of Jupiter next summer, the Planet will still be four dozen and four *beeyon kepfats*, or 250 million miles away, between the Sun and Cancer. Not close enough to significantly affect this comet." In her stress she made arithmetic errors that she hastily corrected. She hit her calculator again and again, the same equations. Finally she was satisfied that she was not going to get a different answer. "Please inform the Earthlings that I do not want my name on this comet."

"Dinosaur Killer?"

She nodded her head. "April 12 two years from now. Between the Equator and 60 degrees north."

Chapter Twenty Six

"That is the best guess I can make right now," Sabar was depressed. It is an honor for an astronomer to have her name on a comet. But no one wants her name associated with a holocaust. Enola Gay was by all reports a wonderful mother to the bomber pilot she raised. But no one thinks about that when they hear her name. "It'll hit the Earth at between 20 and 30 degrees north latitude. That is the easy thing about converting from *deems* to degrees, a dozen *deems* is ten degrees. It'll be about eleven p.m. local time, between 80 and 120 degrees west longitude."

"Texas, northern Mexico."

"Into the Gulf of Mexico, and we have tidal waves, uh, tsunamis, *kepfats* high circling the Earth several times. On to land, a dust cloud will black out the Earth for years. Not a single life form larger than an amoeba will survive in the impact area. This is a Dinosaur Killer."

"Does Earth know about this yet?"

"They'll know soon enough. What'll happen when they know?"

"The murder rate might go sky high." I said glumly. "Why worry about prison or death penalty if the world is going to end April 12 two years from now? People will quit worrying about AIDS and other such diseases, so we'll have a repeat of the free love of the sixties. Why care so much for children or the consequences of divorce? What's a little adultery between friends? For those who are already divorced, why not kill the ex-spouse, or the lawyer, or the judge, or all three?"

"Okay, fine. Social consequences of the End of the World. But the question is, what are we going to do about it?"

"Destroy or deflect the comet."

"How?"

"We could point our light exhaust right into it and boil it off on one side. That might cause it to rocket off its present course."

"And destroy our ship." Captain Trviea was originally given the responsibility of keeping the ship intact. "I don't like getting close to comets. The fumes boiling off eject solid chunks. We have to find the core. There are *kechts* of *kepfats* of fumes surrounding the core of any comet bigger than a single *kepfat* any time it gets close enough to the Sun to boil the frozen gasses. Where this thing is right now, low boiling point gasses like hydrogen and cyanogen blow out. Water ice stays nice and solid. We get close to that thing we could be hit by an iceberg as big as this ship."

"Smashing, just smashing!"

"How about laser cannons?"

"We're unarmed, except for hand weapons. We have no laser cannons."

"We can build one."

"With the help of Earth engineers and machinists, we could have a laser cannon up and running in about, oh, two years. Just in time for the comet to blow a *kecht kepfat* crater in Chihuahua State. If we hurry, we may get it built quicker. But every month we wait, that comet gets closer. The best time to deflect it is now. But how?"

"Nuclear weapons. Earth still has plenty."

"Nukes. We didn't bring any. So we take an Earth nuke out to the comet and bomb the comet. What happens if a nuclear bomb detonates inside the ship?"

"We become a nebula."

"That doesn't stop the comet from hitting Earth."

"Nuclear bombs might work, but that is a big comet, it takes a big bomb sent in close to the core."

"10 megatons enough? Let me do some calculations. What's a megaton?"

"Yield energy of the explosion. It's suppose to be equivalent to the yield of a million tons of TNT. That stands for trinitrotoluene."

"I see, Metric or short tons?"

"I dunno. Does it matter? Figure 2000 pounds of TNT for each ton, estimate on the high side in case it's Metric tons. It's an awful lot of BTU's or foot-pounds of energy."

Sabar worked with her computer. "Two point three, our numbers, *gunds* of TNT for each ton. Look it up, now I got the energy value of TNT in our numbers. Okay, now I got the explosive value of two and a quarter *gunds* of TNT in *pote-dollons*. Multiply by ten million converted to Base Twelve. Now I've got the energy yield of a ten megaton bomb. Three dozen *kepfat* comet core, hmmm. A ten megaton bomb would warm it up some. Boil off some of the lighter gasses." She did further calculations. "Three things we could do. 1) Evaporate it. 2) Break it up, or 3) Deflect it. Let me look up the enthalpy of sublimation of cometary ice."

"I seem to remember 1200 BTU's per pound."

"Got it. Let me do the conversion from British-American units to Creation units. Your 1200 BTU's per pound matches up with our data for water ice. Now we know the size and volume of this cometary core, three dozen *kepfats* in diameter. But what is the mass? We have to make an assumption of density. It's like the density of water ice at very cold temperatures. Look that up. Eight dozen and nine *dollons* per cubic *pote*. That is as good a number as any for the density of a comet core. Now I can calculate the total mass of the comet, multiply by the *pote-dollyals* of heat to evaporate each *dollon* of ice, convert back to megatons, the unit of yield for atomic bombs. Oh my!"

"What?" I had to giggle, I knew the answer would be truly astronomical.

"In Base Ten, it takes 264 MILLION megatons to evaporate this comet! So evaporation is out!"

"That leaves Complete Break-up or Deflection."

"For Complete Break-up, we need to calculate the energy it takes to accelerate all of the chunks to the escape velocity from each other. Otherwise, we can separate the pieces, but they'll fall back into each other, and we'll still have a comet falling into Earth in more or less one piece. Still a Dinosaur Killer. I have worked out the equation for that, it is basically Newtonian. I assume, I hate assuming, but we're estimating here. I assume that density does not vary within the core, and that the core is a perfect sphere, which simplifies the calculation. It is:" She wrote it down.

$$(16/15)^2 (\text{density})^2 (\text{Gravitational constant})(\text{radius})^5 = \text{Minimum Breakup Energy}$$

"I see. If the length units are feet, the mass in pounds, and the time in seconds, the break-up energy would be calculated in foot-poundals."

"Yeah. But understand I prefer Base Twelve and our PDP system to your FPS system, let alone your MKS or CGS."

I laughed. "*Pote-Dollon-Prelate*. Foot-Pound-Second. Meter-Kilogram-Second. Centimeter-Gram-Second. It was a standing joke in my college physics classes that Archimedes used the Cubit-Shekel-Second system of units."

"He probably did. Let me enter in the figures for this comet, in Creation numbers and units, I'll get the break-up energy in *pote-dollyals*. Convert back to megatons and Base Ten numbers." She worked the equations. "31,000 megatons, plus the energy it takes to overcome the tensile strength of the ice. To fracture it into pieces. You Earthlings don't happen to have a nuclear bomb that big?"

"Afraid not. I think 60 megatons is the biggest that the Soviets ever built. Hopefully they might still have a few like that in storage. They might have theoretically designed 100 megatons but they never tested anything that big. We Americans topped out at about fifteen megatons, then concentrated on accuracy of the missile guidance so as to hit the target and destroy it with smaller bombs."

"So Complete Break-up is out. That leaves Deflection."

"A much simpler delta vee calculation. Figure we can get to this comet about 400 days before it is scheduled to hit Earth. We need to deflect its core at least 20,000 miles in those 400 days. Pull the breakoff pieces away from Earth. We can still have quite a meteor shower, including chunks big enough to hit the ground. The farther we can deflect it, the better."

"Okay, for this I'll use your numbers and your American units. 20,000 miles divided by 400 days. Convert to feet and seconds by multiplying in numbers like 5280, 3600, and 24. Three feet per second. Okay, we just need the energy to deflect a 36 *kepfat* or 58 mile diameter comet core with the density of ice at very cold temperatures. In your units that density works out to about 57.57 pounds per cubic foot. Total mass of this sphere, uh, 8.7 times ten to the 17 pounds. With $(1/2)mv^2$, that is, uh, 3.9 times ten to the 18 foot-poundals. Hey, a megaton is about ten to the 17 foot-poundals. 39 megatons."

"That's assuming 100% efficiency with an explosion. But now it starts to look possible with a single bomb of 58 megatons like the Soviets used to have, or with a series of ten megaton bombs."

"I would like as few bombs as possible, very large yields. Each bomb attack will endanger the *Neanderthal Return*. We have to place the bomb as accurately as possible. That requires remote control from here. That requires a detonation code transmitted from HERE, from on board the ship. That requires mapping of the comet core with radar, from HERE. We'll have to get CLOSE to the comet. A few *kecht kepfats* perhaps. Really too close to the coma."

"The bomb burns the side of the core. The material flashes to steam and jets out, providing the delta vee. That is what we need to do in order to deflect this whole mass away from Earth. But it will be like letting go of a balloon. Air jets out of the balloon, but the balloon goes all over the place, not in a straight line."

"This comet core is already rotating, all natural objects in space rotate. No matter how well we place the bomb, it'll be impossible to accurately calculate the directional effects of the shock wave or the jetting material. That jet will be flashing around everywhere, including right at US. With chunks as big as a mile coming at US. Small pieces can come off at very high velocity. We'll have to track them and get out of their way! This is not a process I want to repeat too many times. So I want big bombs, as few as possible. When you take a chance each time, sooner or later your number comes up. So I don't want to use little ten megaton bombs again and again."

"I sure hope the Russians still have a Blockbuster in their inventory."

The President met with as many people as can fit into the Oval Office. Several generals of the Joint Chiefs of Staff, including Air Force General Morton Fairchild, were there representing the military. NASA was represented. The Ambassador from Mexico was there; it is his country that is Ground Zero. So was Russian Ambassador Peter Kerensky. Helga and Andemona were there. Key Senators and Representatives were there, including several from Texas. So were scientists and engineers. "Please explain this crazy Cookie Cutter idea, Jim Hunter."

"Mr. President, it is a kinetic energy device." the NASA engineer began. "We lace thousands of small steel missiles together in a wire rope net. Send it into the comet at thousands of miles per hour. The comet is sliced and diced into nice small pieces."

Nobody was convinced. General Fairchild had a response. "That might work with an asteroid, a nice solid hunk of rock. But this is a dirty snowball. The steel net will go right through that thing without having any effect! The comet will fall back into itself under its own gravity, with perhaps the mass of the Cookie Cutter added to it. I'm still saying the only thing we can hit it with that'll have any effect is a nuke!"

"Nuclear bombs in space! You are absolutely NUTS!"

"Now, Jim." interrupted the President. "Nuclear bombs have the virtue of already existing. We know a lot about 'em, and about the physics of explosions. But do we happen to have one of these Cookie Cutters on the shelf?"

"Well, no. But if we got more funding,"

"Everybody needs more funding. Forget the funding. What you're telling me is that we don't have a Cookie Cutter right now, and we certainly don't have one designed for a 60 mile comet core, RIGHT NOW!"

"No, Mr. President, we don't. But we can build one."

"Not in the two years we have. And we don't have that long. We need that comet taken care of as soon as possible, not when it's gotten close. So the Cookie Cutter is out. What about a laser?"

"The best lasers we have are very powerful, we can deliver a short burst in the terawatt range. But there is the problem of attenuation. We can shine a billion BTU's per second of power through a circle the diameter of a quarter inch. But a thousand miles away that billion BTU's is now going through a circle a foot in diameter. Two thousand miles and the circle has expanded to two feet, the area is four times greater. The intensity decreases with the square of the distance. By the time we are a million miles away, the laser is nothing more than a bright light, if that. We have the same problem with particle beams. So either we get the laser out to where the comet is, or we wait until the comet is within a few hundred thousand miles of Earth."

"That is a problem. Helga, Andemona, what is the thinking on board your ship about carrying weapons out to the comet?"

"We don't want to get close to it." Helga responded. "We don't like the idea of lasers because of the attenuation problem. For the laser to be effective, we have to get CLOSE. We could point our light exhaust at the comet, even open one end of the magnetic bottle, creating a particle beam. Again, we have to get CLOSE. We would risk getting clobbered by a cometary fragment as big as a mile. Then we are in free fall until our fusion reactor is recharged. In the neighborhood of a comet. We don't like this idea."

"Aiming the particle beam from your fusion engine is an interesting idea." observed Jim Hunter.

"We could hit the side of a 60 mile comet core. But it wasn't designed to be a weapon. Another problem we have with any laser or particle beam, is the coma around the core of the comet. Fumes boiling off the core form a layer thousands of miles thick before being turned into the tail by the solar wind."

"Hundreds of thousands of miles thick, for a comet this big." corrected Jim.

"Yeah, that's right. This bright layer will reflect and absorb any laser or particle beam before it reaches the core. It's the core that needs to be taken care of, blowing the fumes around doesn't solve the problem."

The President thought for a bit. "So that leaves a missile. With a nuclear warhead."

"Nuclear warhead! You can't be serious. The treaties prohibit nuclear weapons in space! We just cannot take the chance of introducing nuclear bombs into space!"

"Jim Hunter, you just don't like nukes. Or anything nuclear. I know your type. Your kind has an almost religious opposition to anyone splitting an atom anywhere for any reason. Your kind will file lawsuit after lawsuit against any power company that dares to build a nuclear power plant. And then after forcing delay after delay with your incessant lawsuits and protests, you have the audacity to complain of the COST to the ratepayers of nuclear generated electricity! Well, Jim, here is the Real World: The Sun and every star is a fusion reactor. The *Neanderthal Return* is powered by a fusion reactor. We have volcanoes and continental drift because of the heat generated within the Earth from the radioactive decay of uranium. That's the way the Universe is. After spending billions of tax dollars on nuclear bombs, not using them will make no sense at all to the people."

The President let that sink in. "Mr. Ambassador Kerensky, does the Russian government have any objections to the use of nuclear explosives against this comet?"

"Absolutely not!" affirmed Kerensky, "Mr. President, we will be happy to contribute the nuclear explosives."

"You still have a Blockbuster?"

"*Da*! We have several. We keep them in a special Vault behind a coded lock. With all of the unrest since the Soviet Union came to an end, we wanted to prevent an unauthorized use of them."

"What exactly is a Blockbuster?" asked Helga.

"A 58 megaton bomb. Andrei Sakharov figured out that if you alternate layers of lithium deuteride with depleted uranium, you can build as big a bomb as you want."

"That was the Joe 4 design, half a megaton. Sakharov and his gang went with the Teller-Ulam concept to get the megatons." The President is fully briefed on all things nuclear. "The 58 megaton device, is that the design you tested at Novaya Zemlya the day before Halloween, 1961?"

Kerensky smiled. "We did have quite a series of tests back then. 30 atmospheric explosions in two months. The Halloween Blast was 58 megatons. It was never deployed as a strategic weapon because of its size and weight. Not even our RS-20 missile, what you call the SS-18, was capable of delivering it. A 25 megaton warhead designed for the RS-20 is the largest bomb we have ever deployed. The Blockbusters are kept at a special Vault in a secret location."

"Can a whole Blockbuster be delivered into orbit? It might be too much for an SS-18. But the 14,000 pound weight of a 60 megaton device should be a piece of cake for an Energiya rocket that can lift 330,000 pounds into orbit."

"*Da*! *Da*! An Energiya rocket can bring several Blockbusters up to orbit."

"Okay," said the President. "So the Russians can bring Blockbusters into orbit. Is it necessary to use a bomb so large?"

"I have an answer for that." said Helga. "Sabar Duradich has been working without sleep on this. She is our astronomer, she knows more about comets than anyone else on our crew. First, I must tell you, she does not want her name on this comet."

"We'll respect her wishes." A general murmur of agreement. "I propose that we call it Comet Wormwood. That's from the Book of Revelations."

"Neil told us that a 'megaton' is your unit of measurement of the yield of nuclear bombs. At least of the very large bombs. He explained that it is supposed to be the energy yield of the explosion of one million tons of TNT. We have information like that on file in our computers, we use explosives in mining. It is all in Creation weights and measures and in our Base Twelve numbers. But with this information, we can convert. The only thing Neil didn't know is whether we are talking short or Metric tons of TNT."

"Neither." answered General Fairchild. "The detonation of a specific weight of TNT can vary from experiment to experiment. What we can figure is that one ton can release around a billion gram-calories of energy. That is the heat that will raise one billion grams of water one degree Celsius. We just arbitrarily define the ton of TNT as one billion gram-calories. That is about 100 billion foot-poundals if you want an easy conversion to mechanical energy units. 100 trillion foot-poundals is about a kiloton, 100 quadrillion foot-poundals is about a megaton."

"I'll so inform Sabar. With this information, she was able to model the effects of nuclear explosions on the comet. Here is what she found:" Helga was a little nervous, she is not an engineer. "We need to do one of three things: Vaporize the comet completely. Break the core apart with enough energy that the pieces do not fall back together from their gravity. Or simply deflect it."

She took a breath. "First option. We're not going to vaporize the comet. The core is about 58 miles in diameter. It probably has the density of frozen water ice at very cold temperatures."

"Excuse me, Helga," Jim Hunter interrupted, "The core of Halley's Comet turned out to have a density of a loaf of bread. It's honeycombed with gas voids."

"Yes, comets in short period orbits get that way after 40 or 50 visits close to the Sun. But this one might be coming for the first or second time, having thousands of years to get cold and fall in on itself. So ice density it is. 57 or 58 pounds per cubic foot, give or take 20 pounds. The heat needed to vaporize ice at very cold temperatures is around 1220 BTU's per pound, assuming no increase in temperature. A BTU is 252 gram-calories. 4 trillion BTU's is about a megaton. Work the numbers, and it takes at least 264 million megatons to evaporate the comet core. So first option is out."

Another breath. "Option Two. Break-up the comet. We have to overcome its gravity. The equation for this is a little complicated, but it's derived from Newtonian type mechanics. We still use the density of 57.5 pounds per cubic foot, the radius of 29 miles times 5280 to get feet and the gravitational constant in FPS units. If a megaton is about ten to the 17 foot-poundals, we get a more reasonable energy requirement of 31,400 megatons to break up the comet core, still a bit much. So the second option is out."

"So that leaves Deflection." concluded the President.

"Yes. A simple delta vee calculation. The mass of this thing is maybe 8.6 times ten to the 17 pounds. If we can budge it before it is 400 days away from hitting Earth, then we could deflect it 20,000 miles relative to the Earth by accelerating the total mass about three feet per second. Using the $(1/2)mv^2$ equation, we get 3.9 times ten to the 18 foot-poundals, or about 39 megatons. That is within the realm of possibility. But we risk the ship EACH time we approach for such a nuclear attack. We need the biggest bombs you've got, ideally move that thing with a single bomb. A Soviet Blockbuster."

The Oval Office was silent for a minute while everyone thought through the implications of using an old Soviet Blockbuster bomb. Jim Hunter felt he had to make one last attempt. "Helga, I remember you talking about your laser cannons. You specifically said 'long range laser cannons'. If you can build one of these, can't you strike this comet from a long ways off, and therefore not endanger your ship?"

"What you suggest is the ideal solution. The problem with all Earth designed lasers and other beam weapons is attenuation, the rays spread apart. You triple the distance, you have one ninth the intensity. We have a mechanism, it is classified, it sends the beam in a truly parallel path. It does not spread, but a little. With this in the laser cannon, we can strike from three dozen *beeyon kepfats* away. That is why we believe we can defend our Solar System from a hostile invasion. Farther away, even that will start to attenuate. We have used comets and asteroids for target practice. It warms up the comets, the jetting of steam changes their orbits. With a continuous beam from a laser cannon, yes, we can burn through the coma and move the comet. Unfortunately we don't have time to build one. We have to use the biggest nuclear weapons available right now."

"Can't you go back to Creation and get a laser cannon?"

"By the time we get back, this comet will have hit Earth. It'll take that long."

"You can't just warp over and back in hyperspace?"

"You've been watching too many *Star Trek* shows. No, we can't do that."

"All right." the President concluded. "The Russians can lift their Blockbusters into orbit. Now the trick is to deliver 'em to the comet while it's still far away from Earth. After the initial explosion, we can then look at the results and see what we still have to do. Ms. Trvlakian, how are you ladies for carrying such a huge bomb out to the comet?"

"If you can vouch for the safety of the bomb. I understand that you have secret codes and mechanisms to arm the bomb and to detonate it. We can approach the comet, get within, oh a *hekt kecht kepfats*, or four hundred thousand miles. We can then let go of the bomb on a course that takes it toward the comet while we turn away."

"Can you actually DROP the bomb into the comet?"

"The *Neanderthal Return* is not a B-29." she laughed softly. "A rocket would have to be attached to the bomb to guide it into the comet. Our guidance is probably not as good as yours. When you have continuous propulsion, you can just steer your way to your destination. Your entire space program is designed to deliver payloads on such precise free fall trajectories that you can send a probe past Neptune. We cannot do that dropping a bomb with our starship."

"A rocket attached to the bomb to guide it." commented Ambassador Kerensky. "It would have to be an American rocket, your guidance technology is the best. An American rocket delivering a Russian bomb. The whole assembly taken there by the spaceship from Planet Creation. Need one Israeli and one Palestinian to complete the crew." Laughter. Everyone's mood is better! Discussing actually doing something about the comet.

General Fairchild pointed out that, "Since it's impossible to know the best trajectory, the missile would have to be directed by remote control. An American crew can steer the missile, a Russian crew can then signal the detonation code. That would require interactive communication between the missile and the mother ship. For it to be interactive, the ship will have to be within a light second. 186,000 miles."

Helga whistled. "Captain Trviea's not gonna like it."

"But then the people of Mexico don't like us doing *nada* about this comet." commented the Mexican Ambassador. Andemona had been at his side quietly translating the discussion into Spanish.

"*Nosotros comprendomos.*" reassured Andemona. "All 47 of us have to meet and discuss the use of our ship this way. All have a say, all 47 have to agree to this mission."

"How likely is that?"

"We should be able to come up with a consensus." answered Helga. "None of us want to be known for standing by in our splendid spaceship doing nothing while a billion people die. But at the same time we don't want to risk our ship in a futile effort. We need to be sure that we have a plan that will likely deflect or destroy the comet, a benefit that will be worth the risk to our ship. I believe that this use of a 58 megaton bomb, perhaps several in series, delivered by a remote controlled rocket has the best chance of success."

"You agree, Mr. Ambassador?" asked the President.

"I agree. It will have to be approved by our people in Moscow and by the former Soviet Republics, particularly Kazakhstan. I don't see any problem with that. Then we'll put together a team of our people to work with your people on the details, the engineering necessary to adapt American rockets to an old Soviet bomb. Energomash has a joint operating agreement with Lockheed-Martin. I believe there are Centaur upper stages in Kazakhstan right now. We'll also need to put together additional multimegaton bombs for the follow up, if the first bomb isn't enough. Helga, is there a bay on your ship that can contain a Blockbuster bomb? It's 3 meters long and 65 centimeters in diameter."

"Bay Number 4 can be used as a weapons bay." Helga answered. "It has a 36 by 72 *pote* door that opens to space. Is this big enough?"

"The *pote* is like a British-American foot?"

"It is .986 British-American foot."

"Okay, it'll fit. The Centaurs will fit."

"Good. After all of the bombs and American rockets are inside, the door can be closed and air pumped in to a pressure of 24 *dollons* per square *tig-it*. 12 psi, your technicians can work without pressure suits. When it comes time to launch the missile, we can rig up a mechanism to gently push it out the door at a speed of several feet per second. When it is clear of the ship, a radio signal can be used to fire the rocket engines. Bay Number 4 is big, there is plenty of room for missiles and warheads."

People around the room smiled and nodded their heads. The President closed out the meeting. "Ladies and gentlemen, it looks like we have a feasible plan. We'll call this Operation Rainbow. God promised that He will never again try to destroy humanity with a flood. The rainbow was the symbol of His covenant. This covenant applies to the Neanderthals as well; I don't care what those criminals say. We have a dirty snowball in a bad orbit. Our job is to help the Lord keep His promise. So Operation Rainbow it is."

Sabar Duradich searched the corridors to find him. "Moooostafa! Mustafa Khedr!" She sang the name as she ran after the Egyptian archeologist. "I want to talk to YOU!"

Mustafa smiled at the attention from the astronomer who first saw Comet Wormwood. "You want a sperm sample?"

"Not tonight, I have a headache. If you consent to the use of your sperm for our procreation, we'll find a girl to come and take it from you. Unless you're married?"

"My darling passed away two years ago from cancer. But we have three beautiful children, who are now grown into fine adults."

"My condolences for your wife and congratulations for the children. But that's not what I want to talk to you about."

"What do you want to talk about, Sabar?"

"What's all this I keep hearing about the 'Atlantean Hall of Records' under the Sphinx?"

Mustafa burst into laughter. "An American fellow named Edgar Cayce dreamed that there is a secret chamber underneath the Sphinx wherein the records of the refugees from Plato's Atlantis were stored. Because of this, we have had a lot of people mucking around the Giza area looking for such underground chambers. We at the Egyptian Antiquities Organization have been going crazy protecting the Sphinx and the Pyramids from their attempts at amateur archeology."

"I see. I've looked down at the Giza Plateau with our telescopes. The three Pyramids look like the Belt Stars of Orion."

"The Fourth Dynasty did not deliberately mimic the Belt Stars when they laid out the Pyramids. That son of a bitch Bauval,"

"Mr. Khedr! I don't like hearing someone's mother insulted. It's clear that everything built on the Giza Plateau was done to a deliberate plan, if only because of the precision to which the structures were built."

"Yes, the Great Pyramid, 230.4 meters by 230.4 meters at the base."

"It's my understanding the Metric System was invented in the 1790's."

"Yes. The Pyramids were built before then."

"So what unit of measure were the Pyramids designed in?"

"It is the current consensus of the Egyptology community that the Pyramids were built to a Royal Cubit of 52.3 centimeters or 20.6 modern British-American inches. In terms of this Royal Cubit the base of the Great Pyramid is 440 cubits by 440 cubits, a perfect square. It is perfectly aligned with the cardinal directions. The height of the Pyramid is about 280 cubits, which is why many people think it is a representation of π, a ratio of the circumference to the diameter of the circle. The other two Pyramids are built to this same degree of accuracy. Same ratio between height and base dimensions. They are just smaller. Why are you concerned about whether they were intended to look like the Belt Stars of Orion?"

"One of my jobs on this ship is to figure out where we are. There is a 11/12 chance that we will go right where we intend to go when we make the 'jump'. But there is a possibility that we might end up somewhere else. In determining where, I would look at the star field and try to locate familiar stars. Triangulate with several stars, and we know where we are. Mustafa, which stars would you seek out if this was your job?"

He thought for a moment. "I suppose I would use the brightest stars. Easy to find."

"The three Belt stars are perfect. Three incredibly bright stars, all in a nice recognizable row, all over a thousand light years away. You call these stars Alnitak, Alnilam, and Mintaka. Arabic names adopted by the Earth astronomy community. Were the ancient Egyptian names of these three stars Khufu, Khafre, and Menkaure? Whatever. Once you find these three stars, you can easily find the star you call Rigel. Another incredibly bright star that is very far away. Then there is Canopus, Deneb, and other superbrights. After we find these superbright and far away stars, we sight the nearer stars to accurately locate ourselves. It is just amazing that your Pyramids are laid out to look like the three stars that any starship astrogator in this part of the Galaxy would use. We know that the Face Mountain aliens came by for a visit or two."

She let that sink in while the professional Egyptologist considered the implications of what she said. Sabar, an actual starship astrogator, confirmed the usefulness of the Orion stars for astrogation. It is well known that the ancient Egyptians identified Osiris with Orion. No one denies that. But Egyptology has always vehemently denied space alien or Atlantis origin theories of Egyptian civilization. It has always denied the existence of any advanced civilization earlier than 3100 B.C.

"To use an Earth saying, cat got your tongue?" teased Sabar. "Never mind the Pyramids. Let's get back to the Sphinx. Faces due east, does it not?"

"Yes, it faces due east. I know what you are thinking. You have bought into the idea that it was originally carved thousands of years before the pharaohs. When Leo rose due east. When the Sun was in Leo during the Spring Equinox."

"I have not bought into anything. The lion body sure looks like it has been rained on."

"It has, we do get some rain in Egypt."

"True. And you had PLENTY of rain when the Ice Age ended with the glaciers melting like crazy! The oceans rising, conveniently covering any coastal city of Atlantis that might have then existed! The deep erosion of the limestone of your Sphinx that I can see through my telescopes required years of heavy rain. You have not had enough rain since the start of the First Dynasty to cause it. I can believe the pharaoh's head was carved from a much older and badly eroded lion head."

"Sabar, you can believe what you want, but"

"Please, Mustafa, I'm not done yet. The Egyptian Antiquities Organization is a governmental entity, right?"

"Yes it is. We answer directly to our head of state. Mubarak, before him Sadat, Nasser, and so on. We are responsible for the entire Giza site."

"You decide whether to allow any excavation, and you have the power to prevent any and all excavations."

"We most certainly do have that power. It is the responsibility that the Egyptian people have given us for preserving our legacy. A legacy that belongs to the world."

"I understand. Of course, you also have the power to perform your own excavations, and keep them secret."

"What are you saying, Sabar?"

"You control the Sphinx, access to the Sphinx, and therefore any and all chambers underneath the Sphinx. Or chambers within the limestone cliffs on either side of the Sphinx, it is located in a trench that was dug in ancient times."

"What in the name of Allah has gotten you on this whole subject?"

"Comet Wormwood is in an orbit of 12,498 years in length. It was seen by everyone on Earth last time, including people living in Egypt. It came in from Leo, just like it does now. Leo then rose due east, the vernal point being in Leo. The Precession of the Equinoxes is a steady process, easy enough to program into a computer. The comet missed Earth, obviously. It passed through the Earth's orbit, about 9 million miles or 14.5 million kilometers ahead of Earth, on October 13, 10,495 B.C. That's a five and a half day miss. Five and a half days later, Earth passed through the comet's tail. It dominated the sky the months before and after this close encounter."

"You sure you have Wormwood's orbit calculated that accurately?"

"Yes, we do. What has the Egyptian Antiquities Organization found that has not been revealed to the rest of the world?"

"We recovered some artifacts from chambers near the Sphinx." Mustafa admitted quietly. "We have not been able to figure out the writing. But there are some astronomical illustrations: A comet. The Constellation Leo. The Constellation Centaurus with a circle drawn around Alpha Centauri, your star. It was drawn in the position it was in 10,495 B.C., 10 degrees farther from Hadar than it is now, in the middle of the Constellation Norma. All of the star positions illustrated are consistent with that era. Proper motions, radial velocity, and distance from parallax."

"Yes, I know what you mean."

"There are also illustrations of people of several known races: Ancient Egyptians, possible ancient Hebrews, African Negroes, white Europeans, Chinese, and one who seems to be a Native American. And there is no mistaking the Neanderthals."

Chapter Twenty Seven

Anatoly Donovon is a spry, healthy man in his eighties. 120 rems of lifetime radiation exposure and he has yet to develop a cancer. He eats right, drinks vodka in moderation, and gets plenty of exercise. When people ask him his secret, he tells them that his grandmother is Georgian; they are famous for living past 100. That and the radiation exposure, including a dash of strontium 90 in his bones, kills the bacteria and viruses that plague those not exposed to nuclear energy. Or so he claims.

Good thing Anatoly is resistant to cancers, the Soviet nuclear program has always been sloppy when compared to the American, French, and British programs. He worked under Sakharov when he was a young nuclear engineer. He remained with the nuclear weapons program after Sakharov left. He worked on the large yield single warheads for the RS-20, what we Americans call the SS-18, before he retired.

With a letter of appreciation signed by Gorbachev himself, the state gave him the dacha near Moscow as a reward for his long years of loyal service. He resumed his friendship with Andrei Sakharov when he was elected to the Congress of People's Deputies. He had a prominent place at the funeral of the man everyone finally recognized as a true Hero of the Soviet Union.

He learned from the telephone that he will soon receive important visitors. He picked up the house, put his great grandchildren's toys away, and put on his best clothing. The doorbell rang. Anatoly answered the door to greet the polite KGB men. "Comrade Donovon, greetings. May we come in and secure your home for President Boris Korsakov and the envoy from Planet Creation, Monoloa Mrvlakian?"

"Certainly, you will find everything in order. Come in, come in. Have some tea if you like."

"I will not. But thank you anyway. After we check through your house, we will take up positions and the President's personal bodyguard will accompany him and Miss Mrvlakian in."

"That will be fine. Thank you."

"Thank you. For your service to the Rodina." Rodina is a Russian way of saying Mother Russia.

"You look about fifty?"

"I am 59. I remember the humiliation of when we had to pull out of Cuba in '62. At least the 58 megaton blast on October 30 the year before gave Kennedy something to think about. Thank you, Comrade Donovon." The KGB officers made their usual inspection of his home. "Your house is in good order Comrade Donovon. My compliments."

"Thank you."

The KGB man spoke quietly into his ear thing, then announced "They are coming now."

Accompanied by several personal bodyguards, President Boris Korsakov and Monoloa Mrvlakian ascended the steps to the front door. Anatoly greeted them. "Welcome Boris Mikhailevich. It is an honor and a pleasure to welcome you to my humble home. Please come in."

The President kissed the retired bomb engineer on the cheeks. "I am honored to be invited into your home. This beautiful lady is Monoloa Mrvlakian, from Planet Creation."

"Yes, yes, I know. I recognize her from television. It is an honor."

"The honor is mine Anatoly Donovon." Monoloa held his hand with both of hers and shook it gently. Anatoly added a little firmness to his grip to show her that while he is old, he is not frail.

"Miss Mrvlakian, I must compliment you on your Russian. It is impeccable."

"Thank you."

"Let's go in, I have some tea."

They went into Anatoly's living room and sat down. A tea service imported from Britain was placed on a low table, steam and a wonderful tea aroma rose from the pot. Anatoly poured tea for his guests. Boris went right down to business. "Anatoly, we have not much time. We must ask for one more service from you for the Rodina. This time it is all of humanity that needs your service."

"The comet. You want the large bombs to blast the comet?"

"Yes. You are the only one left alive who has the code for opening the Vault with the Blockbuster bombs. Sergei Potemkin destroyed his copy of the code because he wanted these bombs to stay buried forever. Who would have guessed that a 90 kilometer comet core would be on a collision course with Earth in our lifetimes? But there it is, and we need the biggest bombs we have ever built to divert it. It is possible to force this huge snowball, as big as it is, into a course that will miss Earth, if we use a big enough bomb. To accomplish this, we need a Halloween Bomb."

"I see. With all due respect Boris, what we are talking about are State Secrets. There is a foreign woman in our midst."

"Miss Mrvlakian does not represent a hostile power. Their ship is unarmed. They come in peace, and they have abided by their agreement not to commit an act of war against any Earth nation. If they wanted to conquer us, they would have done it by now. Or they could just float away in their spaceship and let the comet come in. As it is, the women from Creation are willing to use their ship to transport our nuclear weapons out to the comet. Because of this, I have briefed Monoloa. Monoloa, please tell Anatoly some of what you know."

"All right." Monoloa began. "After the coup attempt against Gorbachev failed, the government decided to give you and Sergei Potemkin the secret codes to the vaults where the old Blockbuster bombs are stored. Indeed, you and Sergei were allowed to write the codes without sharing them with anyone else. It was believed that you two had no ambitions for power. It was hoped that you would be beyond coercion. This arrangement is top secret. It is not secret that the superbombs are locked in vaults at secret locations. Unless the code is entered in exactly, any attempt to access the bombs will result in the detonation of one of the bombs. With Sergei Potemkin's death, you are the only person who has the access code for the Bomb Vault. It would take more time than we have for either the Russians or the Americans to put together a whole new bomb of the 50 megaton range. Our astronomer, Sabar Duradich, believes that 40 megatons is the minimum yield needed to divert this comet from hitting Earth. We need more than that, we need the bombs in the Vault."

"Okay, Boris, Monoloa, I will key in the code to open the Bomb Vault."

"Certainly!" a relieved Boris Korsakov shouted. "If you write down the code sequence on a top secret notepad in my office at the Kremlin, we can send people out to the Vault and recover the bombs."

"No, President Boris, I will not do that. I will go out to the Vault and key in the codes myself. We cannot take the chance that a miscommunication on my part will detonate the 58 megaton bomb that is booby trapped into the locking mechanism."

"Are you sure you are up to it?"

"My grandmother was a Georgian. She lived to 113. I am only 84. Plenty of time left! I am still in the prime of my life!"

Everyone smiled. "Very well." decided Boris. "You will go to the Vault. Then you can have your old job back for the purpose of preparing the bombs and for planning the attack on the comet. You may pick some of the youngsters, only in their 50's or so, in the atomic weapons bureau, to accompany you into the Vault."

Anatoly, his younger associates, and their GRU escort walked down through the dark personnel access tunnel. Anatoly used a simple five number combination to open the main door to this tunnel. It is a standard bank vault door, hidden behind a false wall in what looks like a cabin typical of this region 220 miles southeast of Archangel. The cabin itself was never lived in and was allowed to look abandoned. A chain link fence and a padlocked gate kept the idle curious from wandering on to the remote plot of land on which it was built.

"Quite like an Egyptian tunnel, isn't it?"

"I have never been to Egypt, sir."

"Now you be nice and friendly with us or we will commit suicide and take you with us." admonished Anatoly with a twinkle in his eye.

The GRU man did not flinch. "You have children, grandchildren, and great grandchildren."

"Ohh, a nice Stalinist threat, huh? No way you could get away with it nowadays."

"No threat. Without the big bombs, all the trog girls can do is chip away at it with old RS-20 and American Titan warheads. Knowing the Americans, they probably did destroy their multimegaton warheads just like they say. They can pound on it with smaller nukes, but that 90 kilometer mass is going into Earth unless they can really push it. That would not be good for your grandchildren."

Anatoly smiled. "Lighten up. I have no intention of entering the code improperly. It is amazing that weapons so destructive that we have never deployed them, weapons we thought could bring the end of mankind, are now the only things we have that can save us from the fate of the dinosaurs. Andrei Dimitrievich would love the irony. So would Sergei Nikolievich, may they both rest in peace. Ahh, finally, here we are." The narrow personnel tunnel ended in a door. Anatoly dialed in another combination, he opened the door to reveal a room of about 60 by 100 feet. Seven very large locked doors were there, all of heavy steel construction. "The Seven Seals. For a government that was officially atheist, we sure had a thing for Revelations. At least in the nuclear weapons business."

"We will see you, and we wish you good luck." The GRU men went back into the personnel access tunnel and closed the door behind them. It locked.

"Don't worry, we are not entombed. We can open this door from the inside." Anatoly demonstrated, and then closed the door again. Svetlana Lebed and Mikhail Dostoevski worked with Anatoly the last few years he was with the bureau. "Check the walls for bugs."

They inspected the room, augmenting the room light with flashlights. "I do not see any sign of bugs, Anatoly. The walls are smooth."

"I don't think there are any. Remember, this place is booby trapped. Planting a bug or a hidden camera is a good way to commit suicide in spectacular fashion. I am an old man; I will not be around for many more years. I want you to learn the access code, so pay attention." Anatoly opened up his note pad. Nothing was written on it. He took his pen. "Repeat after me: Square mile minus square verst plus a sazhen."

"Huh?"

"It is the code. This is what you do to remember it." The other two repeated the strange formula. "Very good." With a pen, performed arithmetic on his notepad. "There are 5280 feet

233

in a mile. Because Lenin and Stalin converted Russia over to the Metric System, we no longer think in terms of feet and inches, sazhens and versts. So Sergei and I thought that it would be a little harder to crack if we used pre-Metric measurement concepts. I multiply the number 5280 by itself to get the number of square feet in a square mile, 27,878,400."

"I see."

"3500 feet in a verst. Before Lenin, we Russians used the same feet and inches that the British and Americans use. But instead of yards and miles, we Russians used arshens, sazhens, and versts. An arshen was 28 inches. 3 arshens were a sazhen, which was also 7 feet. 500 sazhens, or 3500 feet, was a verst." They tolerated Anatoly's repetition of an old school lesson. "Square the number 3500. The number of square feet in a square verst, 12,250,000. Subtract the square verst from the square mile, then add 7 for the sazhen. The resulting number: 15,628,407. I can't remember a number like this worth a damn. But I can remember 'Square mile minus square verst plus a sazhen.'" He took out a deck of cards. "Please use these cards to number the doors from left to right skipping the number three. Ace, deuce, four, five, six, seven, eight. The doors must all be opened, in the order of the number we calculate from 'square mile minus square verst plus a sazhen'. First, Door Number One, then Door Number Five, Number Six, and so on. If we do not follow this precise order, we find out if the bomb still works. A simple code. One that even an old man can remember to reconstruct. But one that no one in Metric Thinking Russia would guess at. And if anyone even tried, they would get one chance. Try to open any door out of order, you become a shadow on the wall."

He took out a New Testament and opened it to the Book of Revelations. "We use this dual language Bible, the left page in the original Greek, the right page in Russian. We go to Door Number One." He turned a simple latch with a sudden jerk. "BOOM!" he shouted. "Are we still here? We are, that is a good sign! Turn the latch on any door out of the order given by the special number, the bomb goes off. This latch opens the cover to a panel of buttons labeled in the Greek alphabet. The Book of Revelations was originally written in Greek by Saint John of Patmos. We decided that these doors shall be analogous to the Seven Seals."

He handed the Bible to Svetlana. "Please turn to Revelations Chapter Six."

Svetlana turned to the page where Rev. 6 began. "Got it, Revelations Six. The first six Seals are opened here and horses and riders come out to do terrible things."

"Exactly! Notice how on the Greek language side I underlined certain words."

"I see."

"Good. The first door is the First Seal. We type the words 'white horse', 'bow' and 'crown' in Greek, using these exact spellings." He carefully typed the words. A sudden loud CLANG! made all three jump. Svetlana screamed. The door slowly swung open. "Loud clang GOOD! Blinding flash of light, BAD!" He had a wicked grin on his face. "This is the equipment access tunnel. We roll the bombs out this way. It leads to an underground rail station. Plenty of Interior Ministry troops there. Tough veterans of Afghanistan and Chechnya. They will help us load the bombs on to the train."

He went to Door Number Five. Opened the cover to the Greek alphabet panel. "Red horse" in Greek. Then "power" and "sword". CLANG! The door opened. An empty room behind it. Door Number Six. "Black horse". "Pair of balances". CLANG! Another empty room. Door Number Two. "Pale horse" and "Death" in Greek. CLANG! Empty room.

Door Number Eight. Seven doors, but there is no Door Number Three. So at Door Number Eight, he opened the panel of buttons in Greek alphabet. In Greek language he typed "Souls of those who had been slain for the word of God".

"Get that wrong and we join them." he warned. But he got it right and was rewarded for another sudden, loud CLANG! The door opened to another empty room.

Door Number Four. In Greek he typed the words "earthquake", "black sun", "blood moon", and "falling stars". CLANG! The door opened to reveal another empty room.

"Pick up the cards, we don't need them any more. We will shuffle them back into the deck, and put it away. We have only one door left, sixth door from the left, but it is indeed, the Seventh Seal." He opened the cover to the button panel. The same Greek alphabet. "Now we do something a little different. We type 144,000 in Greek alphabet numerals. Alpha, Delta, Delta, then Omicron three times." CLANG! The door opened.

This room is huge. The walls are built out of reinforced concrete and lined with thick steel plate. In it were dozens of large megatonnage bombs. "See the bomb with wires leading up to it. That is the booby trap bomb, we will have to disarm it. It is a 58 megaton Halloween Bomb."

They went to the bomb attached to the wires. "Take these screwdrivers and help me remove this panel. Look at the keyboard! Nice Cyrillic letters and Arabic numerals. I type in '7 trumpets', the word 'trumpets' in Russian." He heard an audible click. "Whew! The bomb is no longer armed. We get to live a while longer, at least until April 12 two years from now. Let us remove the booby trap wires, just unhook these connectors."

"Looks just like the wiring harness connectors in a car or an airplane."

"Yes, they are. Put these cover plates back on and wheel these six bombs," Anatoly pointed out the six he wanted, "to the equipment access tunnel. That's the brake, you unhook it by kicking this." The bombs were on wheeled carriages. "The GRU man was ordered to walk back out of the personnel access tunnel and lock the bank vault door after he hears the seventh CLANG! He should be using the secure telephone in the cabin to inform his superiors that they can now come in from their bunker 100 kilometers away."

They wheeled the six Halloween Bombs into the equipment access tunnel. "Close the other six doors." instructed Anatoly. "Each door should automatically lock. You want to reset the booby trap on one of the other bombs?"

"No way. We don't want to be killed next time we come to retrieve a bomb."

"Me neither. You are entrusting us with the access code?"

"Yes, I am," affirmed Anatoly. "but we can let everyone believe that we reset the booby trap to another bomb."

"I think that is a good idea."

"Me too. Don't want our politicians and generals being too eager to retrieve these doomsday machines."

"Will one of you please go up the personnel access tunnel and see if the bank vault door is closed and locked?" Anatoly asked.

"I will go." Mikhail volunteered. A minute later he returned and closed the door to the personnel access tunnel, it locked. "Bank vault door is closed. GRU man followed orders."

"Good. Check the six Doors we have already closed. Make sure that the covers of the Greek Alphabet panels are closed and latched."

They checked. "All panels closed and latched." reported Svetlana.

"And so is this one to the equipment access tunnel Door." reported Anatoly. "All right. Let's get into the tunnel with the bombs and close this door behind us. It will lock. Next guy that comes down the personnel access tunnel from the house will see a room with seven identical doors. Nothing to tell him which one is which. Let's get these bombs to the rail station. Once loaded on board, we can have a drink of Stolichnaya vodka."

They pushed the bombs the length of the equipment tunnel, one at a time. It led through several bank vault doors that opened from the inside, but required combinations to open from the outside. They arrived at the rail station. The five foot gauge tracks lead out through a tunnel to a spur line. A short train with a special car designed to carry nuclear bombs was parked on the tracks. The Interior Ministry troops loaded the bombs on to the train. The three nuclear bomb engineers went into the dining car and relaxed with their drinks.

Suddenly, it seemed as if the *Neanderthal Return* was in drydock. Everywhere on the ship inspection plates and covers were pulled off and women worked with their tool chests. Several women put on pressure suits to go outside and inspect everything around the hull of the ship.

Chuck Carter, Mohammed Abbas, Mustafa Khedr, Ian Miller, Metrola Mornuxler, and myself were all drafted by Contrviea Tiknika to go over to the Shuttle Bay. She wanted us to tell her everything we did to repair the magnetic drive unit. It took some time, she was very thorough and precise in her questioning. She wasn't in any way rude or demanding, but she made it clear that she wanted precise answers. Then she complimented us on the fabulous achievement, in the middle of the desert, of getting this thing working and off the ground. We complimented her on the repairs so far. The bullet holes completely disappeared from the aluminum hull and the window. Fred Graf's blood no longer stained the floor inside the cabin.

Then tools were put into our hands and under Contrviea's direction, we replaced every structural member that was damaged by the bomb. Then we remounted and readjusted the magnetic drive unit. Contrviea didn't seem worried that we might now know enough about the thing to help an Earth company figure out how to build one. But then again, how the cyclotron was built inside was the secret. We didn't take that apart, not necessary. Everything else was a matter of precise mounting and adjustment to the nearest *keetig-it*, though we know it works when adjusted within 12 *keetig-its* or 1/144 *tig-it*. This allows for slight misalignments that may occur in normal service. Then we installed a whole new lower hull and ablation shield. Contrviea's shop started building these parts as soon as they received a detailed report of the damage while we still were in the Algerian desert.

We were pretty tired when we were let go. That Shuttle looked as good as new! Gotta love the can do spirit of these girls! Comet coming to hit Earth? Well by golly we're gonna hafta do som'thin' about dat! Yesiree! Gotta get dis ship in tip top condition for dis mission!

I was almost into my quarters looking forward to a few hours of sleep when some fingers massaged my spine in between my shoulder blades. "Hi Trviea."

"Neil, may I speak with you in private?"

"You may join me in my room. But I'm really tired. One in and out then I roll over and make like a beached whale." Trviea started giggling. "Angela never did this but I had one girlfriend who really got pissed off and pounded my face in with her fists for wanting to sleep because I was dead tired. She wanted more sex and I was saying wait until morning, I'm better when I've had some rest. At least she didn't have the physical strength of a football player. You can kill me if you lose your temper. Just please don't have higher expectations than what I can deliver."

"Maybe that's what happened to us on Earth." she giggled. "Neanderthal women are strong enough to KILL our men when we lose our tempers. Fewer pregnancies are bound to result under such circumstances. But there is something else I want to talk about."

We went into my room and closed the door. It locked, and it was understood that when a woman went into a room with one of the Earthmen, the DO NOT DISTURB sign was on. She handed me a stapled printout on hemp paper. I quickly figured out what it was. "Book of Revelations. In English. Looks like King James Version."

"You're the only Earthman I can trust, Neil. The rest of you scare the Hell out of me."

"I can't blame you there. But is the reason that you trust me because we make love and it doesn't hurt?"

She blushed and smiled. "That helps. I suppose I could trust Chuck Carter. The girls like him. He's black AND beautiful. But he's serious about being a Christian. He's having fun and consents to the use of his sperm. Yet I get the impression that he thinks of us as a bunch of whores. We're not doing this for money, or even just for fun. We're doing it for children. For the survival of our entire RACE. How can we get him to understand that? It's not a sin given the circumstances."

She took a deep breath. "That's why everyone wants to help blast the comet. We want to help your Race survive in return for helping us. The thought of nuclear weapons in Bay Number Four gives me the creeps. The thought of OLD Russian bombs of 58 megatons each REALLY gives me the CREEPS." She smiled and kissed me. "Don't worry about that. I'm willing to take the risk. Just a big old adventure. We get to be the Archangel Michael sallying forth to slay the Dragon. The Posse Comet-tatus. The Golum. I've heard all of that. How often does anyone get the chance to save an *enbeeyon* of lives?"

That is the thing about having a relationship with a woman. Sometimes she wants to talk and will be happy if you just nod your head while generally keeping your mouth shut. I was almost asleep.

She noticed that I was not paying attention. She grabbed me in a tender spot. "Attention K-Mart Shoppers! There is an important conversation going on here and it is appreciated that you pay close attention!"

It cracked me up. I couldn't help myself. I was just laughing! "OW!"

"Neil, can I speak with you about Earth religions without worrying about you getting offended?"

"Sure."

"Yeah. Chuck's pretty serious about his Christianity. And I don't dare bring this up with any of the Muslims. They want me to cover my face and hair. Forget that! The Canadians are too busy cracking jokes about the Metric System, Quebec, French and English, and differences between Canadians and Americans, for me to have any confidence that they'll take anything seriously. Ian Miller, the British guy, he's too busy trying to get in the sack with Metrola."

I laughed. "He is smitten with her. Go easy on the Canadians. I like their sense of humor. We all need to laugh. But I understand your reluctance to discuss religion with anyone but me. I'm too much of a skeptic to try to save your soul or be offended by anything you say on the subject."

"Thanks, Neil. Is there anyone else on Earth who recognizes that Revelations is simply a work of fiction by John of Patmos?"

"It does look that way. The Lamb opens the Seventh Seal. And everything is still. Quiet. For half an hour." I said this very dramatically. "After all of the *Sturm und Drang* of the first seven chapters of Revelations, we have a dramatic pause. Builds suspense. Every writer knows that trick."

"Yeah. But I don't like being called the Whore of Babylon. It's not like Cro-Magnon girls never make love outside of marriage!"

I could not resist more laughter. "But they don't arrive in a spaceship that could be said to be the Multiheaded Beast."

She spat out an Atlantean oath. I think it meant "Shit!" But sometimes they refer to any old garbage with that word. Just like we do.

"I'm sorry you women get insulted like that. Even after you generously offer your ship to

237

carry us out to bomb Comet Wormwood."

"At least your people aren't calling it Comet Duradich. She has never done anything to deserve that. Well. We are NOT the Whores of Babylon. Whores of Atlantis, yes. But not Babylon. We've tried to talk to Saddam Hussein, the guy in charge of Babylon. He's nuts! I think some of that nerve gas of his got to him!"

"So Damn Insane! It's too bad that the Mesopotamia Basin, one of the Earth's special places, is under control of a bunch of crazy thugs who cannot even be counted on to act in their own best interests."

"Well. I guess we cannot let ourselves worry about those who just cannot accept the existence of us Neanderthals as flesh and blood human beings. We're neither Angels From Heaven nor Demon Women From Hell. We're not goddesses or witches. We're just people who happened to build a spaceship."

"You're people all right. Gifted with these wonderful muscles!" She's talking about Life, the Universe, and Everything, and I had pussy on my mind.

"I'm just a little concerned about the Mission. We cannot just drop that big Russian bomb out of the ship and send it into the core. We have to put a rocket on it. We have to get close to map the nucleus with radar. Then we can program the rocket's guidance. The nucleus is a constantly changing thing, rotating, so we have to keep updating the radar map. The Americans, whose rocket we'll be using because the Russians have more confidence in American guidance than their own, want to remote control the rocket from the ship. Then the Russians want to send the detonation code from the ship to set off the explosion. All of these considerations means we have to get within a *kecht* of *kepfats*. Maybe closer."

"That's a problem?"

"Yeah, that's a problem. We can get hit by a mile wide iceberg BEFORE setting off the bomb. Then we set off a 58 megatonner. That comet will spiral around like a toy balloon let go. Solid chunks up to a mile in size will come out of the jetting hole, the small ones will move fast! We're going to have to haul ass outta there!" I'm amazed at how they pick up American idioms.

"Ohhhh! Look at this!"

"Not as pretty as it once was, huh, Anatoly?"

"It isn't. We will have to replace all of these detonators, indeed, all of the electrical parts on each of these bombs. The wires are hard and brittle. We don't want to send a dud into the comet. The uranium 238 looks fine. The plutonium pits are fine. Might want to replace the initiators. We'll pull them out and test them. The lithium deuteride is all right. But we will want to mix in lithium tritide to increase the yield. I can think of a few other modifications to boost the yield and the reliability. 65 megatons perhaps."

"We will order the parts. We should also test the plastic explosives around the plutonium pits. That we can replace. The old Klaus Fuchs design."

"The design Fuchs STOLE. It's the basic American design. Dates from Nagasaki, even Trinity. Heavily modified and improved, of course. Now this stuff can be read in college textbooks and on the Internet. Anybody with some plutonium can build a bomb."

"I think we will have to test one of these."

"You are right." Anatoly agreed. "Atmospheric, it is too big for an underground test. Korsakov will have to get the Americans to agree to an exception to the Test Ban Treaties. A little more environmental damage at the old Novaya Zemlya Test Range weighs favorably against letting that comet come in. It is not like we have not shot off a hundred large megatonnage bombs there. I will tell Boris myself."

Chapter Twenty Eight

"Another judge has been found killed in his home today. That brings to 34 the number of judges and court commissioners murdered in the last few days. We have seen some of the same thing with tax collection agents, both state and IRS. Support enforcement officials, lawyers, police officers, and others are also in considerable danger."

"What do authorities believe is the motivation for this wave of murders?"

"The comet on a collision course. Why not get your revenge if you're going to be dead in two years anyway? Divorce and child support orders ruin people financially. This is not opinion, it is fact. The court system abuses fathers with impossible orders to pay as much as 60% of their income, while federal tax laws don't allow deduction of these enormous payments. This is ignored by politicians and newspapers who demand that we 'crackdown' on 'deadbeat dads'. The fathers complain about the violation of their constitutional rights. They claim the Thirteenth Amendment ban on slavery and involuntary servitude and the federal Antipeonage Act is violated by contempt proceedings used to force them to get employment, a contention argued before the California courts in the *Brent Moss* case."

"Most judges don't agree with it?"

"No, they get angry with any father or lawyer who cites it. Divorced fathers aren't the only people who have a--"

Metrola shut the set off and turned to me. "Huge increase in violent crime, just like you predicted. There have been some mass suicides. In Colorado, Nova Scotia, France, and Russia. Civil wars are breaking out anew in many of what you call the Third World countries. We have to get the people of Earth to believe we CAN deflect this comet. That there WILL be life after April 12, two years from now."

"It's Korsakov, Mr. President."

"Thank you. Hello Boris! This is the U.S. President. You get those bombs out of storage?"

"Yes, we have. But Anatoly Donovon, our senior atomic scientist, tells me that they are in that 'sat around for years' condition. Brittle wires. Electrical components that need to be replaced. Some corrosion. That sort of thing. But the nuclear materials, the depleted uranium, the plutonium pits, the lithium deuteride, are in good shape. Here is the situation: We have six Halloween Bombs. Design yield is about 58 megatons for each. We can handle the parts replacement. That's no problem. We'll have to restore the tritium mix in the lithium hydride to get the yield back up to that level. Anatoly wants to put in some modifications to increase the yield beyond 58 megatons, by a more complete burn of the uranium. Every scientist and engineer is saying that we do not know what bomb yield will be necessary to push the comet away from its collision course with Earth. We know the minimum, 40, 50 megatons or so, but that doesn't account for thermodynamic efficiencies of using a nuclear explosion. You never get 100% efficiency converting heat to work. There are so many variables that can affect that. The more megatons, the better."

"Good, you're working the problem. Our Lawrence Livermore Lab engineers appreciate the information you have sent on the Halloween Bomb. We like Anatoly Donovon's idea of the Penetration Vehicle. Now we can adapt a Centaur rocket to guide this bomb into the nucleus of the comet. Your people at Energomash have already been working with the Lockheed Martin people on the Atlas 4AR project. If we can mate Energomash RD-180 engines to a Centaur upper stage, I see no reason we can't mate the Centaur with a Halloween Bomb inside the Penetration Vehicle. Thank you for keeping me up to date."

"Uh, there is one more thing. Anatoly has advised me that we need to make sure the bomb will work. He wants to test one of the bombs. With the megatonnage, we'll have to take it out to the old Novaya Zemlya Test Range and fire it in the atmosphere."

"I see." It took him only a moment to make the decision. "We agree to make an exception to the Test Ban Treaties. I'll consult with Congress and call up the world leaders. I'm sure that under the circumstances, a test explosion will be allowed. One more thing, we'll need to call a press conference to explain Operation Rainbow to the public. We'll need one of the Creation women; Helga's pretty good with public speaking. And we'll need a Russian general to explain the Russian part of this thing."

"We have a man in our embassy who was a Strategic Rocket Forces general. General Fyodor Pushkin, he is knowledgeable of our bombs."

"Excellent, get him in the loop. Thank you for calling."

Charts, graphs, and models were set up on easels and tables around the stage for the press conference. It was carried live around the world. The Press Secretary walked out to the microphone. "Ladies and gentlemen, the President of the United States."

As the band played *Hail to the Chief*, the President walked down an aisle through the seated audience with an entourage of advisors, General Fairchild, a NASA official, Helga Trvlakian, Russian Ambassador Peter Kerensky, and General Pushkin. The President took the microphone away from his Press Secretary and waited for the applause to die down. "It has come to my attention, that we have had a skyrocketing rate of murder in the United States, and all around the world. It seems that everyone who feels that he has had the short end of the stick is now taking the opportunity to even the score with violence. People believe our civilization will come to an end April 12 two years from now. Well, we have to take care of some of the grievances, some are legitimate. We have to think of something else than constantly cracking down on divorced fathers, calling them 'deadbeat dads'. After all, one of them did talk the women from Planet Creation into introducing themselves to us. Now they are here, not only to establish a peaceful relationship with all of the nations of the Planet Earth, but to help us in our hour of need. So fathers, I'm putting an end to contempt proceedings. I'll enforce the Peonage Law against all state officials who are still prosecuting parents for contempt or nonsupport after June 1 of this year. In 1996, a California court did admit that the Antipeonage Act applies to child support orders in the *Brent Moss* case. The 1998 California Supreme Court decision is a state court order declared null and void by the 1867 Act of Congress. So you fathers no longer need to engage in violence. If you do, you will pay the full penalty provided by law."

After a pause to let that sink in, the President continued. "As far as all others who feel the need to settle scores, just remember this." The President inhaled and shouted the next sentence. "The world will NOT, I repeat, NOT come to an end in two years. Your prison sentence will NOT end on that April 12! If you are sentenced to death, the world will continue after your execution! I say this because of the need to stop the violence! I say this because we have a PLAN! This plan is code named Operation Rainbow."

The President paused while the audience applauded. He pointed to the Russian Ambassador. "Mr. Ambassador, you may take over."

Ambassador Peter Kerensky unveiled the first easel. "Russia will supply for this mission up to five bombs, each with a yield of 58 megatons, of the type that we tested on October 30, 1961. Because a bomb of this design was detonated the day before Halloween, we informally call it a

Halloween Bomb. We have recovered six from an underground storage unit. Because these bombs are old, we plan to test one in our old Test Range on Novaya Zemlya Island." He pointed to the Arctic island on a map of Russia. "It will be the first atmospheric explosion of a nuclear device since the Chinese stopped testing their bombs. We need to do this so we can have confidence in our bombs for use at Comet Wormwood. Back to you, Mr. President."

"Thank you, Ambassador. Astronomers estimate the nucleus of Comet Wormwood to be 58 miles in diameter. This is a huge mass, but we CAN deflect it. It would take as little as 40 megatons to accelerate this entire mass at least three feet per second. If we can move it that much or more before 400 days before it hits Earth, it won't hit Earth."

The President waved his hands to quiet the applause. "But to do this we need cooperation between diverse nations. We need the 58 megaton bombs that the Russians once built and tested. We need American missile guidance technology. The preliminary plan is to use a Centaur rocket. And we need a spacecraft to carry these missiles out there. Fortunately, we are being visited at this time in our history by the descendants of a group of human beings who were transplanted to another Planet. They have come to visit us in a spaceship of their design and construction. The *Neanderthal Return* is therefore available if its crew so consents. From the nation of Atlantis, here is Helga Trvlakian."

"Thank you, Mr. President." Helga unveiled a model on a table. "This is a model of the *Neanderthal Return*. We have designated Bay Number Four, here," she indicated it with a pointer, "as the Weapons Bay. The door to this Bay is 35 by 71 feet; large enough to admit the American Centaur rockets. This bay is 200 feet deep, plenty of room for rockets and warheads. When the door is closed, the Bay can be pressurized to allow people to work in it without pressure suits. We have excellent radio equipment all around the ship, that will allow American missile controllers to control the flight of the rocket. And it'll allow the Russian bomb controllers to send a detonation signal for the bomb. We will have to map the core of the comet with radar, to determine its axis and rate of rotation. We can do this. We are capable of bringing the missiles, bombs and people for Operation Rainbow out to the comet."

"Thank you Miss Trvlakian. And now the Air Force. General Fairchild,"

"Thank you Mr. President. We bring the *Neanderthal Return* into position near Comet Wormwood. We map the core with the Atlantean radar and determine its axis of rotation." The general pointed to a white globe, spinning it. "We place the bomb at one of the poles of rotation. The idea is to heat up a portion of the comet to very high temperatures, which is what a nuclear bomb can do. Then the steam that is generated from the cometary material will jet out providing a very large force to shift the comet to a different orbit. We don't want to place the bomb away from the poles of rotation. The jet of steam would spin around, canceling itself out. So we have it jetting from a pole of rotation, pushing the comet in more or less the same direction. Before we use the big Soviet Blockbuster, we propose to punch a relatively small hole in the core into which the Blockbuster can be inserted. That way we don't lose half of the energy of the Blockbuster by radiation into space."

After a pause, Fairchild continued. "We propose to use the upper stage of a NASA Aries rocket, which was also the upper stage of Minuteman I missiles. This rocket can be guided into the rotation pole of the comet, delivering a 100 kiloton warhead housed in a B61-11 Bomb Vehicle made by Sandia National Laboratory. The missile will go in at a velocity of ten to twenty thousand miles per hour relative to the comet. This bomb package was designed to allow us to destroy underground targets. It is designed to penetrate 10 to 20 feet into earth, where the explosion generates the largest possible ground shock for each kiloton of yield. In this case, it'll penetrate about 20 to 100 feet into the comet nucleus and then detonate. The nuclear fireball should drill deep within the comet, perhaps a mile, and eject steam out to make the hole. We can monitor the steam jet from the ship. There are several guidance mechanisms available with the B61-11 and Aries, our first choice is a manual control by a remote operator stationed on board the *Neanderthal Return*. If we can punch a hole a few hundred feet wide and over a half mile deep, then we can deliver the big Russian warhead to effect deflection. To deliver the Russian warhead, we propose to use the Centaur, the well used upper stage made by Lockheed Martin for satellite launchers. It is liquid fuel, we can shut off and restart the burn at will. We are currently rigging up some for remote control, and to follow infrared to seek the heat left by the B61 warhead. Now I'll turn this over to my Russian colleague, General Pushkin,"

General Pushkin took over. "Our senior nuclear weapons engineer, Anatoly Donovon, whom we have recently taken out of retirement, has come up with some ideas. He worked with Sakharov and was instrumental in building the huge 40 to 60 megaton bombs that we tested in 1961 and '62. His idea is to insert the bomb into the hole made by the American Aries missile with a Penetration Vehicle, similar in concept to the American B61-11 just described. The Penetration Vehicle consists of a 5 centimeter thick steel casing the shape of a bullet. It'll look just like a great big artillery shell. Inside the steel casing is a layer of shock absorbing material, into which the bomb is packed. Simplicity itself, the drawings are completed, the machine shop should have six Penetration Vehicles finished and ready by the end of the week. The bomb itself is a cylinder 65 centimeters in diameter and 3 meters long as you already know." Laughter. "The Penetration Vehicle will be 4.5 meters long and one meter in diameter. The mass of the entire package will be about 20,000 kilograms or 44,000 pounds. Yield should be over 60 megatons, Anatoly can get a few extra megatons with his tricks up the sleeve. The American Centaur will guide this package into the hole left by the American Aries missile. A Russian Bomb Crew on board the *Neanderthal Return* will send a coded signal starting a 10 second countdown for detonation. This will give the Penetration Vehicle time to carry the bomb into the hole. There, the detonation will inject the maximum amount of energy from the bomb into the cometary material. That material will blast off the side of the comet with tremendous force, shifting it off its collision course with Earth. Helga, to you."

"After we confirm detonation, we will turn tail and run for our lives! The *Neanderthal Return* will be at maximum normal acceleration, about one and a half gees. We will be tracking the comet including any piece that is big enough to be a threat to our ship. If necessary, our pilot could order everyone to strap down and initiate an emergency rapid acceleration of 5 gees. After that is over we determine the results on the comet's orbit and whether another nuclear attack is necessary. Back to you, Mr. President."

"Thank you, Helga. Everything is now on an accelerated schedule. Every previously scheduled payload on the Space Shuttles has been postponed, putting the construction of the International Space Station on hold. We will use the new Space Station as it now exists, and we will use the old *Mir* station, for receiving supplies from Earth and transferring then to the *Neanderthal Return*. All four Shuttles are now dedicated to delivering payloads for Operation Rainbow. The Russians plan to use the two Energiya rockets and most of the Proton rockets in their current inventory in the next week. Available Atlas and Titan launchers are now reassigned to Operation Rainbow. The European Ariane 5, the Japanese M-5 and the Chinese Long March rockets are similarly being rededicated to Operation Rainbow. As soon as the Shuttle for the *Neanderthal Return* is repaired from its recent trip into Algeria, it too will be pressed into service. The *Neanderthal Return* is capable of picking up every object that makes it above the atmosphere. Our civilization will not come to an end April 12 two years from now. It cannot. Income tax forms are due three days later." Laughter.

The President ended on a lighter note. "When I throw out the first baseball to start the major league season tomorrow, Helga Trvlakian has promised to hit it out of the park! I have promised to strike her out!" Cheering. Helga grinned and pantomimed swinging a bat. "And these wonderful women will not be the last of their Race. We'll solve that problem too."

"Here we are at Camden Yards for Opening Day for the Baltimore Orioles. If you just joined us, the National Anthem has already been played. Here comes the President to take the mound. The band is playing *Hail to the Chief*. This time, the President will do more than just toss out the first ball of the season. He was once a pitcher for his college baseball team, the Oklahoma Sooners. He will go up against the beautiful Helga Trvlakian, the 6 foot blonde bomber from Cair Atlaston, Atlantis, on the Planet Creation. He is going to try to strike her out, she is going to try to hit it out of the park. She is wearing short pants showing off her long muscular legs. She is also wearing an Orioles jersey, an Orioles batter's helmet, and cleated shoes. Whoa! The helmet fell off!"

"My helmet fell off again!" Helga giggled.

"Dang! I thought I got it adjusted for your head!" protested the Orioles equipment manager.

"Yeah, for my funny shaped head." She reached down and picked it up. "You see, the front with the bill rests fine on my brow ridges. But it just sticks too far up in front here. That is not too much of a problem, the problem is caused by the fact that the back of the hat doesn't go far enough back here."

"I see. I have an idea. The purpose of this cap is to protect your ear from a wild pitch. That is why it has only one ear cover." He felt the back of her head. "Is this the occipital bun?"

"Yes. I'm a Neanderthal. I have a thick knot of bone on the back of my skull."

"Okay, Helga. My idea is to cut out the back of this cap here. That way it'll no longer interfere with the back of your skull. We should then be able to get this cap to settle down, protect your ear, and stay on. It'll take a few minutes while I saw this."

"There is a short delay in the start of the game while the Orioles equipment manager adjusts the helmet to fit Helga. Look at this! He's SAWING on the back of the cap! Neanderthal heads are LONGER than our Cro-Magnon heads. While we wait, the President warms up with a few throws to the catcher. Helga swings her bat. She has selected a 28 ounce Louisville Slugger."

Helga took a few practice swings. Inhaled deeply through her broad nose. Fresh cut grass, dirt, oiled leather, the breeze off Chesapeake Bay. The ball has an odor all its own. Every baseball ever made seems to have this same scent. A pleasant scent. The wood of the bat likewise has a pleasant scent. These smells are subtle, you don't usually think of them. But they put you in the mood for an afternoon of a game that cannot be allowed to die.

"The hat is ready, Helga." The equipment manager brought it over. The strong tangy odor of fresh sawed plastic. "Try it on."

"Thank you. Hey, it fits much better!" Her ponytail flowed out of the space cut in the helmet. She smiled and walked out to Home Plate. The crowd cheered. Above the home team dugout, the women of Creation sat in VIP seats. They cheered Helga. Yelling at her to go get 'em in Atlantean.

The batting coach gave her last minute encouragement. "You know the Strike Zone, don't you?"

"Of course. Width of the Plate, from knees to shoulders."

"Good, just be aware that sometimes the umpire expands the Strike Zone just a little bit. Watch the ball. If it's outside the Strike Zone, you don't have to swing at it. Inside the Strike Zone, it's just a matter of eye-hand coordination. The pitcher tries to throw it past you; you try to hit the ball. It's that simple and it's that complicated. You know the stance, good luck Helga Trvlakian."

"Helga Trvlakian is now stepping up to the Plate. The catcher and the umpire are now in position. The President catches the ball with his mitt. His uniform has the Presidential Seal. Pitcher and batter now stare each other down. Here's the windup, the throw,"

The image from the eyes are interpreted in the back of the brain. In the Neanderthal, this part of the brain is larger. The eyeballs are larger in diameter, that many more rods and cones in each retina. And their medical technology has allowed them to keep their lenses in perfect tune. Helga saw clearly the ball and the path that it took. She held the bat and did not swing.

"Ball one!" calls the umpire.

"High and outside! Ball One. The catcher tosses the ball back out to the President. Count is one and oh! The catcher makes a signal to the President. Now he is ready to receive the pitch. The windup, the throw,"

The President threw a knuckleball. Helga watched the ball move back and forth in its path. Interesting study in aerodynamics and the lift generated by the ball's spin through the air. It was in the Strike Zone. She swung.

"Grounder down the First Base Line, it is foul! Strike One. Count is now one and one. President receives the ball. The catcher signals again. President takes his time. The windup, the throw,"

The President threw a change-up. The ball dropped like a wounded duck. Helga did not swing. "Ball Two!" calls the umpire.

The crowd cheered. They enjoyed watching this plucky woman carefully handle each pitch so far. "Way to watch it, Helga!" screamed a man in the crowd.

"The count is two and one, the President receives the signal from the catcher. The windup, the throw,"

The President spun his hand around the ball for a perfectly thrown curve ball. Helga watched the ball as it flew in its path. It is curving outward, it should be beyond the Plate. She did not swing. "SteeeRIKE!" yelled the umpire, drawing out the word and pointing his thumb and two fingers. Helga dropped her mouth wide open in apparent shock and stared at the umpire. But it is not wise to argue with the umpire. She was thrown a curve, that's baseball. She made a show of recovering her composure as the crowd applauded the President for his pitch.

"The count is now two and two. The President catches a new ball thrown out to him by the umpire. Another signal by the catcher. The President takes his time. The windup, the throw,"

Another knuckleball. This time it was inside the Strike Zone. Helga swung and hit the ball.

"Foul ball into the bleachers behind Third Base. Look at the grin on the face of the kid who caught it. What a souvenir. A ball pitched by the President and hit into the stands by a beautiful woman from Planet Creation. Count is still two and two. The President receives a new ball. He takes his time, thinking about his next throw. Pitcher and batter stare each other down, locked in psychological combat. The windup, the throw,"

The President shouldn't throw change-ups; the ball actually hit the dirt in front of Helga.

"Full count, three and two. This is it. The President makes ready for another throw. The windup, the throw"

The President is in pretty good shape. He accelerated the five and an eighth ounces of horsehide to a full 89 miles per hour in an effort to burn Strike Three past her. But she has excellent eyes. She grinned as she watched the fastball travel the 60 feet 6 inches in a virtually straight line. CRACK!!! She put the bat down and took off at full sprint for First Base.

"It is going, going, GONE!!! Outta here! Right over the centerfield fence. Looks to be about 450 or more feet! The crowd is going wild. Home run off the President of the United States!"

Helga danced around the bases in triumph blowing kisses to the cheering crowd. She shook hands with the Orioles players as she approached Home Plate. Even the President was grinning. He tipped his hat to the crowd, he is a good sport. Not a poor loser. He walked over to Helga as she was being mob hugged by Andemona, Lucinda, Sorby Mishlakian, and the other Creation women who are currently down on Planet. Monoloa Mrvlakian couldn't make it, she was on her way to attending a nuclear explosion being given by the Russians. Helga broke away from her shipmates as the President approached. "Congratulations, Helga."

"You are not mad?"

"Heck, no! You hit my pitch fair and square!"

"That Strike Two. The ball was OUTside! Nice pitching, though." Helga not only shook hands with the President, but hugged and kissed him on the lips to the delight of the baseball crowd.

"HEY!!!" screamed the First Lady in mock jealousy to the laughter of the spectators.

Helga broke away and hugged the First Lady. Then she took a more serious tone. "Mr. President, I have a concern here. We have a tremendous amount of work to do. All of us. In fact, in two days, we're all going to pile into Air Force One to attend a nuclear explosion on Novaya Zemlya Island. 58 megaton explosion, and it's the Social Event of the Year!" The President couldn't resist a laugh as Helga continued. "And here we are, playing baseball."

"What we're doing here is just as important as what everyone else is doing." informed the First Lady.

"That's right." agreed her husband. "Right now, as we speak, the Shuttle *Columbia* is in the Vehicle Assembly Building getting ready to take the first load for Operation Rainbow into orbit. I've done pretty much all I can do signing the necessary Orders. Congress is going as fast as it can with the necessary appropriation bills, but they are not ready to be signed. I know you girls have been teleconferencing with engineering offices, machine shops, factories, and launch sites to consult with people who need to know how the *Neanderthal Return* works and how to match Creation technology with Earth technology. But there's not much we can do until after this nuclear test in Russia."

Helga whispered. "Me and Lucinda are going to Egypt!"

"Shhh! That's Top Secret. Don't even let anybody see you studying Arabic language or Ancient Egyptian. I know about what Mustafa Khedr told Sabar. But the Egyptians aren't going to cooperate if we don't keep this secret. It's like Kissinger going to Paris to talk to the North Vietnamese, using Jill St. John as a cover. You will wear chadors to hide yourselves, like you did when you snuck off to the kosher restaurant with the Saudi ambassador's wife. Anyway, this baseball is important! Many of the players on these two teams and around the league are making a point of extending their contracts for next season and the seasons beyond. They plan on playing! That's a vote of confidence that deserves recognition on our part."

"There is this thing about baseball." contributed the First Lady. "When the Sun is out and the teams take the field, the hot dogs are sold and the umpire yells 'Play Ball!' after the National Anthem has been played, people have a feeling that God is in his Heaven and that all is well with the World. This is an important feeling, it keeps people from killing each other. If we are to have a chance to get your ship, our rockets, and the Russian bombs together for this mission, then we have to foster the belief in the public that we can succeed in this and that it is RIGHT that we do this."

"What we have done is shown that we can work together and put on a show to entertain a crowd." concluded the President. "This improves the people's confidence that we can succeed with Operation Rainbow. And you hitting the ball out of the park has made everyone believe that maybe, just maybe, you Neanderthal women CAN do anything that you put your minds to."

Chapter Twenty Nine

The United Parcel Service 757 landed at Cairo International Airport. After it taxied to the cargo apron and parked, two women covered from head to toe in chadors, hejabs, and very dark veils descended the stairs and disappeared into a nondescript looking government car. As the driver headed out to the perimeter road, the gentleman in the passenger seat looked over into the back seat to greet the two women. "You ladies have a nice flight?"

"As nice a flight as can be had on a cargo jet." answered Lucinda Renuxler.

"The UPS crew made us as comfortable as possible." commented Helga Trvlakian. "We rode with them in the cockpit. We were allowed to sleep in the bunk beds."

"Good. I'm Charles Sheehy, Egyptian Antiquities Organization."

"We're honored. I'm Helga Trvlakian."

"And I'm Lchnsda Renuxler." They shook hands. "How does an Egyptian have a first name like Charles?"

"My mother's Coptic Christian, she wanted Charles. Nothing my father could do about it!" He laughed. "Okay. Now we get down to business. After we drive through town and past the Giza Plateau we'll head out into the Western Desert. We won't visit the Pyramids or the Sphinx. Too many people, one of them is bound to recognize you as Creation Neanderthals. The local Islamic fundamentalists have been targeting tourists, killing the tourist trade. They are angry at how your friend Metrola treated the bandits in the Algerian desert. We don't want to take any unnecessary chances. Besides, we've already cleaned out what the Edgar Cayce people would call the 'Atlantean Hall of Records.' Nothing there for you to see. The artifacts are stored in a secret location 200 kilometers southwest of here. Hope you don't mind a two hour drive. Did you, uh, relieve yourselves before leaving the plane?"

"Yes we did." they both answered.

"Good. See the Army truck full of soldiers about 200 meters ahead?"

"Yes."

"There is another one the same distance behind us. Security that does not call attention by being too close. But they'll be here in a jiffy should trouble arise. We have some aircraft flying ahead, they'll warn us if somebody's trying to set up a desert ambush. Our driver is a fully trained bodyguard, and he has a little Uzi nice and handy. A benefit from Camp David."

After driving around Cairo, they saw the Pyramids from inside the car. Then they were on the highway to Bawiti. After a few miles, the two Army trucks were the only vehicles in sight, cruising at 140 kph. The traffic cop waved as they passed by, he knew it was a government car. The air conditioning in the car kept them comfortable. "We shouldn't have any problems today. The road has been scouted all the way to Bawiti. The terrorists don't come this way. No tourists to kill."

"As long as the terrorists don't know we're here. But wouldn't even the terrorists consider themselves as having an interest in us shifting the comet?"

Charles laughed. "They all think they're going to Paradise if they die in the name of Islam. It's like explaining Einstein's Relativity Theory to the average person. You get a polite nodding of the head, but you might as well be speaking Ancient Egyptian. The guy who'll machine gun a bunch of Greek tourists or the guy who sends him probably doesn't comprehend orbital mechanics. If you actually get him to comprehend that the comet will HIT Earth, he probably thinks it's all an American trick or a trick played by the Demon Women From Outer Space."

"That's us."

"That's you. Another reason to keep those chadors on nice and tight."

"Metrola told us how the Algerian bandits were so afraid of her. She had to get the one who could speak English to tell the rest to take their ration of water from her." She paused for a moment. "Would you be offended if we asked you a question about Islam?"

"No! No! Of course not!"

"I mean, you will not be offended no matter what we ask. You are not just saying that."

"I will not be offended. You won't be offended either, will you Anwar?"

"No, I will not be offended."

"Good, keep your eyes on the road, this 140 kilometers is faster than the speed limit. This road isn't like a German Autobahn or a Montana Interstate. This Anwar, he's a young guy, his mother named him for Sadat. Doesn't want to take two hours. So what's your question about Islam?"

"Well, me and Lchnsda here, we are what you call cultural anthropologists. It's been our job for many years to study Earth radio and television broadcasts and learn as much as we can about the other human Race. We were both offended and amused at how Neanderthal was the term applied to 'primitive' humans."

Charles laughed some more. "Yet your civilization and technology is as advanced as ours. We understand. The Europeans and the Americans think they are culturally superior to us, while at the same time they admire the monuments and the technology of our ancestors of 4500 years ago. We Arabs think we're superior to them. We're nice proper Muslims while they are decadent pork eaters."

"We learned the European languages first. English, Spanish, French, German, and Russian. These languages are broadcast a lot. Arabic is also broadcast, but it was very hard for us to learn, as was Chinese and Japanese. Once we learned these languages, we started to learn about the culture, including religion. We thought we were experts on Christianity and Judaism, and yet we were caught by surprise on the Olympic Peninsula."

"Noah's Flood story being used to justify racism."

"Yes. These guys in Washington State think we are the Daughters of the Men of Renown. That is what they think Neanderthals were, and we were supposed to be wiped out by the Flood of Noah. Those of us who descended from Neanderthals who were transplanted to another Planet are defeating God's intention and our presence endangers the covenant between God and the descendants of Noah."

"I wonder how those Avengers of Yahweh view Comet Wormwood?"

"Unfortunately, like too many other people. Comet Wormwood is the Lord's Judgment against the sins of modern man. Many of these people believe it to be sinful and arrogant to even try to deflect the comet with nuclear explosives. At best, they pray, confess their sins, and clean up their lives. They believe that with the power of prayer they can turn the comet. We could use all the help we can get. But there are those who condemn us as the Whores of Babylon who come to trick modern people into following us with a false promise."

"And you want to know how Islam views all of this?"

"I want to know what's all this about the Three Goddesses mentioned in the Satanic Verses. What is all that about?"

"I see. Too many believe that the Three Goddesses are among your crew, Metrola Mornuxler one of them. Then again, who says that there should be only three, why not 47 Goddesses?

What this is all about, uh, it's like this: Islam is the religion taught by the Prophet Mohammed, Peace Be Upon Him. We think of Mohammed as an ordinary and decent man who received the final instructions from God through the Angel Gabriel. He is not the first to receive prophecy from God; Adam, Abraham, Noah, Moses, and Jesus all received prophecy, all were messengers of God. But we believe that Mohammed is the last and greatest messenger of God. 'There is no god but God, and Mohammed is his Prophet'. That is what we say."

He held up a copy of the Koran. "This book, the Koran, is the Prophecy as revealed to Mohammed by the Angel Gabriel. The Koran is the uncreated Word of God, dictated word for word by the Angel Gabriel to Mohammed in the Arabic language. This book in the Arabic language is an exact copy of the Divine Book kept in the Seventh Heaven. Mohammed performed only one miracle during his life, the miracle of the Koran. I'm not laying it on too much, am I?"

"No, no. Part of our job is to study Earth religions. This is a major religion of Earth. It has a lot in common with Judaism, which is based upon the Torah, the Five Books of Moses, which are the first five books of what the Christians call the Old Testament. And it has a lot in common with Christianity, which is based upon the teachings of Jesus. So the Koran is the Word of God revealed to Mohammed by Gabriel. Do the 'Satanic Verses' have anything to do with this?"

Anwar's back stiffened visibly, but he kept his mind on his driving. Charles also had a visible reaction. But he remembered that these are non-Muslims who ask their questions in good faith and with honest curiosity. "This is a touchy subject for Muslims. Salmon Rushdie is a Muslim. He wrote a book titled *Satanic Verses*. In it he wrote commentary that many Muslims find offensive. So offensive, the Iranian Ayatollah Khomeini declared a *fatwa*, a sentence of death, on Rushdie for blasphemy. The Americans, Canadians, and Europeans reacted by reaffirming their belief in freedom of speech. Copies of *Satanic Verses* were in the windows of every bookstore in those nations. Salmon Rushdie himself went into hiding behind considerable protection by the authorities in Britain where he lives. But that is not the question you asked."

He took a deep breath. "Mecca was the site of a Pagan shrine prior to the time of Mohammed. He told his wife, relatives, and friends about the prophecy that was coming from the Angel Gabriel. He was an uneducated orphan saying things that no uneducated orphan could say; his prophecy must be genuine. Other people in Mecca were not happy about this. They were Pagans. They put Mohammed and his followers under siege with the intent of starving them to death. Mohammed then told them that he received a prophecy that said that the Three Goddesses of Mecca were genuine, along with Allah, there were thus four Gods, not just one. The siege was lifted. Mohammed later revealed that this revelation about the Goddesses came from Satan, it was a trick. These verses were removed from the Koran, and are known as the Satanic Verses. The fundamental principles of Islam are that there is one God and only one God, and that Mohammed is his Prophet. The Satanic Verses are evil and are properly banished from existence."

"So if the verses about the Three Goddesses are a lie, that no such Goddesses exist, then how can we women who arrive in a spaceship be said to be these Goddesses, or that we have the Three Goddesses in our crew? That Metrola Mornuxler is one of them? She is most certainly not, she is, we all are, flesh and blood human beings who'll eventually die. We are just people, our spaceship is an artificial device, no more magical or supernatural than this automobile."

"I know. It's not logical. The Three Goddesses never existed, and you ain't them. But people are often not logical. They just don't know what to make of you. In our religion and culture, women should be modest. The woman's job is to take care of the home and family. The reason for the chador and veil is that a woman should display her charms only to her husband. If she is not married, she should not display her charms to the public. Here you come along, in a spaceship, exploring the Universe. That's guy stuff! Being Neanderthals, you have a level of physical strength that most women, even most men, simply do not possess. If people believe you to be goddesses, it is because you behave like goddesses. You kidnap an Earthman, and you seduce him by apologizing for kidnapping him! We've always thought that Neanderthals either never existed, or were primitive almost-humans wiped out by the Flood of Noah. Such almost-humans were hideous with brow ridges and large noses, exaggerated muscles. Then we see you in the flesh, and you're BEAUTIFUL! Incredibly sexy! You can seduce any man! You arrive in a spaceship, you can travel from star to star. Modest you are not! And to obtain sperm to continue your Race, which I do not condemn, you are doing what you sincerely believe you have to do, you turn your spaceship into a Whorehouse in the Sky! It is well that you wear these chadors when you come to Egypt."

"We have the audacity to believe that we can deflect a comet with a nuclear bomb. That we can use Cro-Magnon sperm and with genetic manipulation, create Neanderthal boys. Thereby continue our Race. AND continue your Race by deflecting the comet."

"Yes! We used to expect that with the Russians, they built the huge bombs. And the Americans! They think they can do anything! There is one other fundamental tenet of Islam of which you should be aware. We believe in a Judgment Day, just like the Christians. We don't believe in the Christian Book of Revelations, where Jesus comes back with a sword in his mouth. But we do believe that that there will be a final day when the Angel Gabriel sits in judgment. When the wicked are punished and the virtuous are rewarded. To those who believe Judgment Day will be the day that comet slams into Mexico or Texas, your proposed plan to carry American missiles and Russian bombs to the comet is the work of people who are deceived by the Devil."

The women sat quietly, thinking, the miles passing beneath their feet. "It'll be a Judgment Day all right." announced Lucinda. "The day that Comet Wormwood crashes into Earth, is the Day of Judgment of all those who stand by and do nothing. Of all those who were capable of taking action, but who did not. If this comet is truly the Will of God, then we WILL fail, but God will not punish us for TRYING. But we do not believe this comet is anything more than an accident of orbital mechanics. It presents a simple mechanical problem. Deflect it. That is all we have to do. A hundred years ago, none of us could've done anything about it. But today, we have the spacecraft. The Americans have the rockets and guidance. The Russians have the huge bombs. We have radio, and we know each others' languages. We CAN move this comet. If the Great Holy Spirit has any intention with this comet, then it is to TEST us."

"We CAN deflect the comet." announced Helga. "The question is, WILL we? We CAN work together, Russians, Americans, Egyptians, and Atlanteans. The question is, WILL we? We could be KILLED. Do we have the courage to risk it? This is the test God gives us, time and time again. Throughout our history, both on Creation and on Earth. We will blame ourselves for the horrible loss of life if we do not even attempt to deflect it."

"I agree." admitted Charles. "Most people agree with you. It is consistent with Islam and all of the major religions that we go out to this comet and deflect it with a bomb. But there are those who don't see it this way, that's why we have troops in trucks ahead and behind."

They drove on toward their destination. Finally, Anwar announced, "The turnoff is up ahead, we are almost there."

The truck up ahead turned off to the side road. They followed it, they were 120 miles from Cairo. The side road wound a half mile between hills that prevented the warehouse from being seen from the Bawiti highway. A fence surrounded the warehouse, the road went to a guard gate.

The truck that preceded them pulled off to the side, its soldiers deployed in a defensive arc around the gate. The other truck did the same behind them. Anwar and Charles Sheehy presented their identification to the guard who had stepped out of the guardhouse. The guard looked into the backseat. Two women in full chadors, just like he had been told. He didn't like it. Prostitutes have been brought in this way, but he didn't dare say anything. The other problem with women in chadors and veils is that terrorists can easily dress up and pretend to be women. "Show your hands, please." he ordered in Arabic.

"He wants you ladies to show your hands," Anwar advised in English, "to make sure you're not holding weapons on us." The women complied.

The guard nodded his head. He signaled to his colleague in the guardhouse who pushed a button. The barrier lifted, and Anwar drove into the parking lot. They got out into the hot sunshine. Anwar stayed with the car. Charles led the women into the building and the relief of air conditioning. They went down a hallway to a second locked door. Charles held his finger up to a fingerprint reading device. Charles had the right fingerprint, the door unlocked. In they went.

After closing the door behind them, Charles opened the door to the inner sanctum and guided the women in. "You can remove your veils now, you will want to see with the clearest vision."

Lucinda made the first observation of the artifacts. "Everything here is made from stone and gold."

"Yes." responded Charles. "Stone and gold have the virtues of not tarnishing or decaying with time. If you want permanent writings, carve it in stone, or etch it in gold. The next room is a replica of the chamber we found in the limestone cliff north of the Sphinx. They were not under the Sphinx, Edgar Cayce got that part wrong. That the chamber is not below, makes sense. The Nile River is near by, it gets wet down below. The chamber inside the cliff is up high, about as high as the back of the lion body of the Sphinx. Nice and dry. We got in secretly, and we hid the entrance after we removed these artifacts. Some wood we found in there carbon-14 dated to about 10,500 years Before the Common Era. About the time of the end of the Ice Age and the previous visit by Comet Wormwood. Because of the great age of these artifacts, we call this the *Zep Tepi* culture, after the Ancient Egyptian phrase meaning 'First Time'. We cannot read the writing, it seems to be like an alphabet, but that is not certain. We do not know if the symbols are letters that stand for sounds or are symbols that stand for ideas. But we can recognize the astronomical data, they seemed to use a 360 degree circle, but also a 432 degree circle, like you do."

"432, that is three *hekt* in Base Twelve."

"Yes, the numbers seem to be Base Twelve, but also seem to be Base Ten. We cannot get a handle on the units of measure. They look like feet, inches, yards and fathoms in some instances, and look like nice proper Egyptian cubits of seven palms and 28 fingers in other instances."

Lucinda studied the writing on a gold sheet. Each gold sheet was mounted on an iron frame when it was originally made. The iron rusted just enough to show that it was not a stainless alloy of steel. A modern frame of glass and a wood now protected it. Helga looked through the glass at an astronomical plate showing the southern constellations, all the way to the South Celestial Pole as it existed 12,500 years ago. There is the Southern Cross, Hadar and Alpha Centauri. Alpha Centauri is shown much further from Hadar than it is today, surrounded by a quarter inch diameter circle. "That's our home star, drawn in a circle."

"Yes."

"Why is all of this secret?" asked Helga. "This is one stupendous archeological find! Doesn't science like this belong to the public? What's so wrong with archeological evidence of an advanced civilization in Egypt 12,500 years ago? Any good sound religion, which Islam is, which Judaism and Christianity are, can survive scientific revelations whatever they be. I mean, religion tells us that our Universe, our lives, and everything is the creation of God, it is God's gift to us. All science ever tries to do is quantify and explain God's gift, to explain how He created the Universe, and how we developed throughout our history."

Charles laughed. "You're right, faith can survive any scientific revelation. But clergy, of any religion, can be downright political! That is why Galileo was put under house arrest! Some of the extreme Muslim clergy would BURN these artifacts, just as the Spanish Catholic priests burned the Mayan codices. Our duty is to PROTECT these artifacts from those who would destroy them as the work of the Devil! One big reason we keep this find secret is right over here."

Lucinda pulled the plate indicated by the Egyptologist, out from behind some other such plates. She lifted it out and laid it on the table.

"Weren't you shot just a couple of weeks ago?" asked the amazed Egyptian.

"Yes, I was. It's healing up, but it still hurts."

"That sheet of gold and its iron backing weighs 60 kilograms! You lifted and carried it like it was nothing."

"We're goddesses, remember?" They looked at the images worked into the gold. "Just like these three."

On the three by four foot sheet are the images of three beautiful Neanderthal women. The women are wearing skirts that went halfway to their knees. Leather shoes cover their feet and ankles, each has a buckle on the top of the foot. The heels are flat, the shoes look both comfortable and practical. The waist of each blouse was drawn in to flatter the figure, a halter covered the breasts and wrapped around the back of each neck. "They look like they could be students at UCLA." commented Charles, who has been to UCLA. "Except for the muscle build and the faces, not even the woman athletes look like this. This artwork is extremely well done and detailed. Look at the eyes, they are Chinese shaped, just like you."

"Why don't you let the world see this?"

"The Three Goddesses. The Satanic Verses. We have enough trouble with Islamic extremists. They could say these women are the Three Goddesses. They are very strong. Goddesses are strong. Look at their bearing. They are very proud, haughty. Goddesses are like that. That was the impression you left on the Avengers of Yahweh. They said you were haughty, proud."

Helga smiled. "Yeah. But if they thought we were proud and fearsome when they had us under gunpoint, what did they think of us when we punched their faces and took their rifles?"

"Like I said, goddesses are very strong. You can't treat them like you can mortal girls. Of course, I believe you treat the smallest woman with the same respect you treat a goddess with the strength of Hercules. I also believe that women should treat men with that same level of respect. These three women are incredibly beautiful. Goddesses are beautiful. This is true for almost every Pagan goddess, except when being ugly serves her purpose."

"I don't believe that a passing resemblance to the Three Goddesses of the Satanic Verses is the only reason that you keep these artifacts secret. The fundamentalists don't seem too offended by the ancient monuments and pre-Islamic religion and culture that they represent."

"No they aren't. And we can explain this truly extraordinary find as being thousands of years before Mohammed, before the pharaohs even, and therefore has nothing to do with Mohammed, Mecca, or the Pagan religion that was practiced in Mecca before Mohammed. There is another reason, and it is totally political. We Egyptians are proud of the ancient monuments, the

Pyramids, and the pharaohs who built them. We honor the pharaohs by preserving their bodies TODAY. We even leave Tutankhamon to rest in peace in his own tomb. The influence of our ancient forebears is still felt with the Algerian Berbers, who speak a language that is similar to Ancient Egyptian. Probably derived from the Egyptian spoken by the expedition to Afenor Cave. We've always rejected theories that the pharaoh civilization that began with King Narmer about 3100 B.C.E. was started by people from somewhere else, be it Plato's Atlantis, Iraq, or Outer Space. We wanted to believe that EGYPTIANS created this wonderful civilization. That we Egyptians invented writing, Base Ten numbers, astronomy, astrology, religion, law, agriculture, irrigation, engineering, weights and measures. We invented everything that modern man still uses, even as he walks upon the Moon and contemplates bombing a comet."

"And here is solid evidence that somebody had already invented the basics of technology and civilization 7,000 years before King Narmer."

"Yes. It's pretty humbling."

"This writing, it looks vaguely familiar, but that is all I can say about it right now. Do you have anything that might pertain to the time when Comet Wormwood last passed by Earth?"

"Yes. We think we do, now that Sabar Duradich told Mustafa Khedr when it did. Many astronomers are verifying her finding that Comet Wormwood passed by in October of 10,495 B.C.E. Here, let's put the Three Neanderthal Beauties away. We'll get out this other plate." They did so and carefully laid the next sheet of gold on the table. Behind the glass is a panorama of the sky and a horizon. "This horizon looks like the terrain east of the Nile. You see the Nile in the foreground, this looks like the view from Giza. The background stars are Sagittarius, consistent with proper motions back to 10,495 B.C.E. This looks like a view of the sky just after midnight."

"The comet dominates the sky, starting just above the horizon, the tail pointing up, tilted from the vertical about two dozen *deems*, uh, 20 degrees." observed Helga.

"The head of the comet is right on the ecliptic plane, its tail follows that plane," declared Charles, "which is consistent with Comet Wormwood and Sabar's calculations. Additional evidence of the *Zep Tepi* date of these artifacts."

"This is a view of the comet as it passed through the Earth's orbit five and half days ahead of Earth. Just like Sabar calculated. Uh, can we have some photographs and drawings of these artifacts to take with us? We promise not to reveal your secret until you do."

"We plan to call a press conference to announce this to the world. After you are up in the *Neanderthal Return*, with the missiles and bombs, on your way to the comet. Then nobody can stop you with their protests. This comet has come back, I suspect this writing predicts that it'll come back and smash Earth. This could explain all of the doomsday predictions we find in religions around the world, including Revelations and the Islamic belief in Gabriel's judgment. Because of security considerations, we need to keep your visit here secret, until you are safely out of Egypt. We don't want to see you hurt, we want to see you blast this comet. We have a suitcase full of photographs of these plates, with inch and centimeter scales, and a CD-ROM that can make exact size printouts with the right equipment. The Americans will help you with that. This is waiting for you at the airport. We just wanted you to come out here to see this stuff for yourselves, so you know we aren't trying to hoax you."

"We don't believe you are trying to hoax us. Thank you, Charles, for bringing us out here and letting us see these artifacts ourselves. May we take our time here and look at as many of these gold sheets as we can?"

"Certainly, we can stay until three this afternoon. Then you'll have to put the veils back on and start back for Cairo."

"Thank you. Is there anything here that tells of the Face Mountain aliens?"

"No, not that we can tell. There might be something about 'em in the writing, we cannot read it, but there are no illustrations of true aliens. The Neanderthals that are illustrated, and the circle drawn around Alpha Centauri, are the only hints that we can see of your existence. Because of the Precession of the Equinoxes and its proper motion, your star was less than 20 degrees south of the celestial equator in 10,495 B.C.E. It hung high in the Egyptian sky. It was still prominent in our southern sky during the time of the pharaohs, worshipped as the herald of autumn. Today your star sits at 61 degrees south declination, we never see it from Cairo and Giza and it gets barely above the horizon during the late summer in places like Luxor and Aswan. Whether the Neanderthals illustrated here had any knowledge of some of their ancestors being taken to another planet, we cannot tell from these illustrations. Many of the known Cro-Magnon races are represented here: Native American, Chinese, European white, African black, Egyptian, Hebrew, and so on. But all of the Neanderthals look pretty much like you. Maybe all of the Neanderthals of that time were of the same ethnic group, white skinned with Asian shaped eyes. Other ethnic groups of Neanderthal, if they ever existed, may have already become extinct at this time."

"I am naturally bald." Lucinda pulled down her hejab to reveal her smooth dome. "I was born this way, it sometimes happens to us. Are there any bald Neanderthals illustrated?"

"There is a Neanderthal man illustrated with a bald head. Let's get it out. I don't know whether this man was naturally bald like you say, or if he shaved his head. Sometimes the ancient Egyptians shaved their heads. Rameses II is often illustrated as a boy with a shaved head."

They got the sheet with the bald Neanderthal man out on the table. "He's cute." both women commented. The man had no hair on his obviously Neanderthal head. He was also very muscular, flat belly, and had a handsome face. He wore pants, shoes, and a tunic, looked great. The women liked this picture.

"I miss having men like him around." pined Helga. She spat out an Atlantean obscenity. "Sorry." she apologized in English.

They spent the day until 3 p.m. looking at the artifacts. Charles insisted on a lunch break. They ate sandwiches, beans, cheese, and falafel. Charles explained the meat was lamb, proper for Muslims. Yes, it is very much like the Jewish kosher food. At 3 o'clock, the women put on their veils, they climbed into the car, and started for the Cairo Airport with their Army escort.

"There is a government car on the Bawiti Highway heading for Cairo, they should be passing by soon." The two Islamic fundamentalists spoke in a little cafe in a tiny roadside village.

"Okay, so what?"

"They have two women in chadors in the back seat with them."

"Great. Prostitutes are not a high priority. As far as ruining the tourist trade is concerned, whacking hookers on a back road far from the Nile will not buy us much. It's not like Egypt is known for hookers. Sex tourists go to places like Belgium and Germany."

"Something tells me they are not prostitutes."

"Oh?"

"They have Army trucks escorting them in their 'nonchalant' mode. 200 meters before and aft. Some Egyptian Air Force planes above, scouting the highway. They spent the day at the secret facility near Kilometer 206."

"I see. The women could be the wives of important officials. Or prominent women hiding their identities in chadors. What is in that place anyway?"

"The Antiquities people spend a lot of time there. Ancient artifacts shouldn't be secret, but when they are not on display, it makes sense to store them in a secure place. But the women are not Egyptians, they are not even Arabs."

"How do you know?"

"This morning, the guard at the gate of the place, checked the car before letting them in. Charles Sheehy himself was in the front passenger seat."

"I see!" That impressed him. "The man in charge of the Sphinx. Maybe whacking HIM might be worthwhile."

"Antiquities people have friends all over the world, including our fundamentalists. We want our Islamic art treasures protected. The Saudis consult with them on the preservation of the Kaaba and the shrines at Mecca and Medina. I don't think it would be a good idea to whack a high ranking Antiquities man. At least not if he is the only one in that car. But when the guard asked the women to show their hands, they did not understand him. The driver, that Anwar guy, had to translate his request into English."

"They don't speak Arabic! Foreign women in chadors. Okay, so they're EXPENSIVE prostitutes. Everyone wants white girls. British, Canadians, or Americans if they speak English."

"Army trucks and air reconnaissance for foreign prostitutes? I don't think so. No, I think they are Creation women."

"Trogs? HERE?! Why would two Demon Women take time off from preparing to bomb the comet to come HERE?!"

"Because the artifacts stored at Kilometer 206 are from Atlantis. Not THEIR Atlantis, PLATO'S Atlantis! They were found near the Sphinx. It is all hush, hush. But a piece of wood from the site carbon-14 dated to 7,000 years before King Narmer!"

"9,000 years before the time of Solon, just like Plato said."

"The plates have illustrations of people, stars, and writing of a language unknown to us, and probably unknown to the pharaohs. The people illustrated look like Egyptians, Hebrews, white Europeans, black Africans, Chinese, and one Native American."

"Pretty international for that time."

"There are also Neanderthals illustrated."

"I see. Are you SURE the two women in chadors are from Creation?"

"It was the way they moved when they got out of the car and walked. They are tall, 180 centimeters or so. Even in chadors, we could tell that they are different than Cro-Magnon women."

"The Moshe Neanderthal found in Palestine had a pelvis that would indicate a different walk."

"Well, I don't know how Moshe walked, but I have seen the Creation girls walk on television. These two in the chadors moved like that, with the confidence of great physical strength. Today, in America, Sorby Mishlakian, Nesla Teslakian and the others are making public appearances. But NOBODY has seen Helga Trvlakian and Lucinda Renuxler since the baseball game yesterday. Those two are tall, 6 feet for Helga, which translates to 183 centimeters. Those two are reputed to be the social science types, the other girls being engineers."

Charles Sheehy answered his cellular phone. He spoke softly in Arabic. "Change in plans. Anwar, take the detour, we don't want to go through this next town." He winked at his guests. "Digital and scrambled. Can be intercepted, but you just get fuzz."

Anwar sped to catch up with the lead Army truck, which slowed to take the side road. The rear Army truck sped to close the distance with the car. Separated by about 30 yards between each pair, the three vehicles bounced down the detour road. There was asphalt, complete with potholes and jarring ripples. "There's no truth to the rumor that the last time this road was repaired, the crew was sent by Cleopatra." Charles joked. "It was repaired at least once, during Nasser's time. Just a precaution. Somebody noticed that you didn't understand the guard when he asked you to show your hands in Arabic."

The young man sat on the stool in front of a gap between buildings. He had a good view of the highway. A second young man stood further back, ready to come forward with the rocket launcher. They waited for the Antiquities car. Their leader told them that Paradise waited for them if they successfully destroyed the car with the Demon Women. The weapon was hidden in a pile of laundry. Several policemen came up. "Hello gentlemen." they greeted. "Your papers please?"

The two young men calmly handed the police their identification. Sometimes the cops visit these little jerkwater towns and check everybody. One of the officers inspected the laundry bin. "Did either of you know that there is a rocket launcher, of all things, in this pile of laundry?"

"No sir. I don't know how that got there. I know nothing about it." A rifle butt crashed into his head. Same thing happened to his buddy. An object rolled out on to the ground.

"Grenade!" shouted the policemen. They dived to the ground away from the grenade. The young men got up and sprinted. The grenade did not explode. Two of the policemen got up and raised their guns to shoot the fleeing suspects. The grenade exploded.

"Good thing we took this detour." announced Charles. "We have a report that three policemen were just hurt by a grenade while in the town we bypassed. Two of them very badly, they may die. Hopefully nothing more will happen."

Fortunately, nothing did. Helga and Lucinda were safely on the UPS 757 with their suitcase full of photographs of the artifacts.

Chapter Thirty

"Then it's all set. Air Force One is to land at Matochkin Shar Airport, on Novaya Zemlya."

"*Da*. Then we use the train to get you and the Creation girls out to the bunker for the bomb test. It is code named Thor's Hammer. The facilities are primitive and in disrepair. You'll have to rough it. But it's the only place where we can test any nuclear device larger than 10 megatons. You can refuel at Archangel, Aeroflot has modern facilities there with good jet fuel. Then you don't have to refuel at Matochkin Shar."

"We'll refuel at our base at Keflavik. The Icelanders will want me to step off the plane for a public appearance. We'll let 'em meet with the Creation women."

"Who'll steal the show, as usual!" Boris Korsakov laughed. "From the operational standpoint of Operation Rainbow, we need to have some Creation women and the Americans who are going on the *Neanderthal Return* to witness a 60 megaton explosion. We want them to know exactly what they are working with."

"I agree. Our Missile Crew for Operation Rainbow, led by General Morton Fairchild, will be on Air Force One, along with all of the Creation women currently in Washington, D.C. I trust your Bomb Crew will likewise be there."

"They are there right now. Anatoly Donovon is at the test site. They've got the bomb inside a Penetration Vehicle. Because the 60 megaton yield will dig enough of a crater as it is, they want to hang it as high as practical above the ground. They're hanging it from a blimp tethered to the ground by thousand meter ropes. They have the remote control radio device installed, so this is a test of our remote control detonator as well as the bomb itself. Our Bomb Crew will send the detonation code from the bunker while you, your people, and the Creation women watch. Everyone on this project is acting like a kid given a new train set for his birthday. I have never seen this much enthusiasm in a nuclear weapons project before."

The President laughed. "This time, they get to save the world, not plan its destruction, and not worry about what they could be responsible for. It's like that with our people. They have a test missile rigged up. The B61-11 Bomb Vehicle is rigged with a non-nuclear test bomb. It's just like a real bomb with two differences. U-238 instead of plutonium in the pit."

"Test the high explosive trigger without the nuclear explosion."

"Yep, we inspect the uranium pit and determine if the test was successful. The lithium hydride has no heavy hydrogen. The B61-11 works just fine when sent into dirt. But our people want to test it on a glacier, because ice is more like the material of the comet. Sandia engineers may make a few modifications, and call it a B61-12. We are planning on sending it on a cruise missile into the glacier near Yakutat, Alaska."

"That should work. You can test a dummy bomb in Alaska if you want, but why not test the B61-11 or 12 with a live nuclear bomb? We need to know if the nuke will actually work and how it will work with an actual glacier. We have plenty of glaciers on the North Island of Novaya Zemlya. Why don't you test your bomb on one of them?"

"Boris, this is the first time Russia has INVITED us to test one of OUR nukes on Russian soil. Nuking an actual glacier in the Arctic? The environmentalists will have a shit fit and a half!"

"Screw the environmentalists! We've had quite a testing program in the early sixties at

Novaya Zemlya. The polar bears and the whales didn't go extinct, they survived all those nuclear explosions just fine. At least the ones who weren't too close. A couple more won't kill 'em off. But we let that comet come in,"

"I understand. Just like the Dinosaur Killer. We can send a B-52 with an Air Launched Cruise Missile, packing the B61 with a 100 kiloton warhead, live, not dummy. It can carry General Fairchild and his Missile Crew. Perhaps reduce the yield of the warhead to about ten kilotons. We only need to test the plutonium pit, to see if it works after impact with the ice. Pick a nice thick glacier, we'll see if the fireball will continue moving through the ice after detonation to drill a hole. That should work! You sure about this Boris?"

"I'm sure! Priority Number One is deflecting that comet. If it comes into the Gulf of Mexico, the resulting tidal waves will be many kilometers, or miles, high. Our whole Arctic and Pacific coastline will be washed. These waves will wash over Denmark to hit everything along the Baltic. The whole Plain north of the Carpathians is flat as a billiard table. Belorus, Ukraine, and Russia all the way to the Urals will be washed. The tidal wave will pile up at the Strait of Gibraltar and then wash into the Mediterranean. It'll come up into the Aegean and past Istanbul. The Turkish and Georgian coastline of the Black Sea is mountainous, but the Ukrainian and Russian coasts are flat and low. If the comet comes in on land, in Mexico or Texas, the dust cloud will cut off the Sun for years. Our land will get extremely cold and no crops will grow ANYWHERE on Earth. We have no problem with letting you test a nuclear device at Novaya Zemlya. We cooperated to defeat Hitler, we can cooperate now to deflect this comet."

"Thank you, Boris. We can have the B-52 take off at Keflavik. From there they can get into the Berents or Kara Sea and launch the cruiser into the North Island glaciers."

"That would work. But they can take off from Archangel or Murmansk. It is that important, we will allow that if you believe you need to."

"Thank you, Boris, we will keep that in mind."

Sabar was holed up in her astronomy lab with Mustafa Khedr and Chuck Carter. They were poring over the photographs of the gold sheets sent up by Helga and Lucinda. "You still think it's a bad idea to have a seance and call up Jean-Francois Champollion?" asked Mustafa, only half jokingly. Champollion figured out how to read Ancient Egyptian, using the Rosetta Stone.

"If we can raise him on the psychic network, why not just get the *Zep Tepi* people who made these gold sheets?"

"Because we wouldn't understand a word they say. This is as indecipherable as Indus Valley script. So how would we understand their speech? How could we get them to understand ours?"

"I see. We were able to figure out English and other European languages. We can thank Helga and Lucinda for that. Monoloa figured out Russian, Mandarin Chinese, and Japanese. I still don't know how she figured out Japanese."

"What gets me," observed Chuck, "is the coincidence of you using inches, feet, yards, and fathoms, just like we English speaking Earthlings do."

"Not really Chuck, it's perfectly natural to base units of measure on human factors. If human factors are not Base Ten, it's because the natural world, including the human body, is not Base Ten. Which leads me to another question, maybe Mustafa can answer it better than any American. Why did most of the Earth give up human factors units of measure? I can understand the rationale behind a measuring system that matches up with your Base Ten numbers, but the meter is just not a half-reach, a *treefat*! It is not a yard! And it sure is not a cubit or a foot. So what gives?"

Mustafa smiled and took his time before answering. "It was political. Which is the answer to just about any question of why folks do something that is not logical. It was

GOVERNMENTS that led the movement to convert to the Metric System. The people were reluctant in almost every case. The Americans still haven't changed their road signs to kilometers."

"That's because while the American government wanted to kilometerize the road signs, it also wanted to get reelected." declared Chuck. "Therefore, the signs stay in miles and the Traditional Weights and Measures Act gets passed. End of Metric conversion in the United States. Our current President got a lot of votes by pledging to stop Metric conversion, and he did. Road signs are touchy because you FORCE people to Think Metric when they drive their cars. You might get away with that in Canada or Australia, but not in the United States."

"Britain has a very active anti-Metric movement." added Mustafa. "Which stands to reason. They're called English measures because the British definition is the basis of feet and inches used the world over. Peter the Great redefined Russian feet and inches to match the British definition. The Soviet Union continued Czar Peter's policy by agreeing with the English speaking nations to define the inch as 25.4 millimeters. Feet and inches were used throughout Europe before the French Revolution. But they varied in definition from nation to nation. Every sovereignty used a different pound, a different foot, a different mile."

"I supposed people considered that to be a problem." deducted Sabar.

"Yes. A common definition of the foot and other units would've improved things. But whose foot do you accept? With the new Metric System, everybody gives up their native units, including the French, who were introducing Metrics wherever Napoleon went."

"Which ironically saved feet and inches as a viable system of measure." added Chuck. "Every machine shop on Earth can use the same inch, defined as 25.4 millimeters. While Metrics are international in usage, we can use feet for airplane altitudes, feet and inches for railroad gauges, and other uses where feet and inches are international. The meter is kinda impractical from a human factors standpoint, which makes it unpopular with people accustomed to estimating distances and dimensions with their own bodies. Because EVERY nation is to give up its native measures, Metric conversion seemed acceptable to many governments. It's just that the American and British people don't see the need and they live in democracies."

"The reason I asked you my question about units of measure," informed Sabar, "is because I think I can figure out the numbers and units on these plates. In modern times most of the Planet Earth has accepted a common Metric System, and the rest of it accepted a common foot. This process happened on Creation in ancient times. Everyone uses the same *potes* and *tig-its*, based on the circumference of Creation as well as human factors. We knew that circumference in ancient times. You have your nautical mile and your meter, based on the Earth's circumference. Question is, did Earthlings know the size of their Planet in ancient times? Did THESE Earthlings know that size?"

"We've had this conversation, Mustafa." remembered Chuck. "I suggested that the ancient foot might have been one hundredth of a second of arc of the Earth's surface, and that the Egyptian royal cubit might have been one sixtieth of a second of arc."

"Which is possible if we have a slight redefinition of either." declared Sabar. "And I think that is what we have here on this sheet. Sheet 4AB-16. See these two lines up the side, next to the writing?"

"One of them is a foot, the other a cubit?"

"Possible. An inch and centimeter scale is conveniently located next to the sheet in this photograph." Sabar used a pair of dividers. "Four inches. I take it that they are the British-American definition?"

"Yes, 25.4 millimeters." answered Mustafa.

Sabar set the dividers on the shorter line and counted off three divider lengths, corresponding to 12 inches per the scale of the photograph. "We have a little bit left over. It's just a little bit longer than a modern Earth foot. About an eighth of an inch longer. One hundredth of a second of arc of Earth's surface. Interesting. Now let's measure the longer line." Sabar counted five divider lengths, 20 inches per the scale of the photograph. "There is a little bit left over here. About a quarter inch. A foot of twelve and an eighth inches, a cubit of twenty and a quarter inches. This foot is a hundredth of a second of arc, this cubit is a sixtieth. I believe the writing on this plate is an explanation of these two lines, there appears to be some numerical calculations described here."

"If they could so accurately measure the size of the Earth, could they have calculated the orbit of the big comet they illustrated on Sheet 3BR-13?"

"Anything is possible. The comet illustrated is right where I calculated Wormwood to have been on October 13, 10,495 B.C. Sagittarius as the background constellation, looking east at midnight. They might have determined that it would hit the Earth 12,498 years later. What I really want to know, is if they believed this comet to have been DELIBERATELY set on this course."

"Why would they believe that?"

"The same reason there was an engineered Virus set on our Planet. Killed our men. You get clobbered by a Dinosaur Killer. Face Mountain aliens don't have to share the Galaxy with us humans. I'll bet they meant this comet to hit the last time around or the time before. But even with this miscalculation, it's possible to have a direct hit the next time around. Anyway, Base Ten numbers, 360 degree circle, 24 hour day, feet and cubits seem to be rather common in your ancient world. Almost like they were spread the way the modern Metric and English systems of measure have been spread. Like it wasn't an accident."

"Why do you think Neanderthals disappeared from Earth?" asked Mustafa. "We had your brothers and sisters as recently as Afenor."

"Well, if you Cro-Magnons are immune to the Virus as Askelion believes, that explains it. If not, I don't know."

"We are reporting live from the airport in Archangel, Russia. General Morton Fairchild's B-52 is parked on the apron. It has under wing a Boeing Cruise Missile carrying a special type of nuclear bomb that is designed to drill into ice or dirt and then explode. The Russians have invited the U.S. Air Force to test this nuclear bomb on a glacier in the remote Novaya Zemlya Island, high in the Arctic Ocean. Novaya Zemlya means 'new land'. The test of the American bomb is code named 'Spear of Longinus'."

At Matochkin Shar, Monoloa Mrvlakian found herself in a joyous group hug with her shipmates who came on Air Force One. The Russians directed them and the American contingent on to a train parked by the airport. They took the train to the bunker, which barely had room for them. The Russian Bomb Crew, led by Anatoly Donovon, were there at the ready. On television screens, they saw the blimp with the bomb suspended from it, ready for Thor's Hammer. These screens showed the images from a dozen cameras located around the test site and in Russian Air Force planes. Another television screen was dedicated to the transmission from the B-52, getting ready to take off at Archangel to conduct Spear of Longinus. Another set of television screens showed several different views of the target glacier on the North Island of Novaya Zemlya. These images were available to the world's networks for the benefit of live broadcasts. A weather monitor kept an eye on several storms in the Arctic Ocean. But around Novaya Zemlya, the weather was generally sunny, with only a few thin clouds.

And finally, several screens showed the view from the telescope cameras of the *Neanderthal*

Return. The Science and Humanities Channel received these, it was covering the nuclear tests. "This is *Neanderthal Return*, we copy." I said into the microphone. I was surrounded by screens showing transmission from the Russian Arctic. In front of me was a huge bay window with a spectacular view of the Arctic Ocean. The Viewing Lounge was crowded. 200 miles below us was the Berents Sea. We saw the Kola Peninsula through bands of clouds. Looking the other way are the islands of Novaya Zemlya. We were moving into position above the test sites. The ice had broken up, surrounding the islands with floes. Beyond Novaya Zemlya, we saw the bright white of the permanently frozen ice of the polar region. Less than a month past the Spring Equinox, the North Pole was just this side of the line between night and day. "We are moving into position."

"We copy that, *Neanderthal Return*." replied the Russian air traffic controller at Matochkin Shar. His English had an accent but he spoke it well.

"Can we be heard at the bunker at the Test Range?" I asked.

"Yes *Neanderthal Return*, this is the Test Range, we copy."

"Excellent, we have Captain Trviea Harsradich here, she wants to speak."

"Put her on."

"This is Captain Trviea Harsradich."

"Hi, Trviea!" we heard the Creation women greet her in Atlantean.

"First, we have rigged up a neutrino detector for these bomb tests. We use them to monitor our fusion reactor and for other purposes. Today, we plan to count the number of neutrinos that hit our detector during the flash of each explosion. With the number of *kepfats* between us and the explosion, and your measurements as to megaton yield, we can calibrate our instrument. This way, when we detonate a bomb at the comet, we can, within *prelates*, er, seconds, we'll know the energy yield of the explosion. On another subject, I need to speak with Helga Trvlakian in Atlantean."

"Right here, Captain." Helga went up to a microphone in the bunker. She switched to Atlantean.

"You may or may not have had legal authority to remove me from command. I'll admit that kidnapping Neil Peace was a risky policy. But now we have an entirely different mission. For us to successfully perform it, somebody needs to be in command. If the crew of this ship votes to perform this mission, will you follow my orders as Captain?"

"If the women vote to perform this mission, and we agree to restore you to command, I'll follow your orders. That promise I solemnly make. But I need a promise from you. Will you promise not to abuse your authority in any way with respect to me and to make full use of my abilities and training?"

The Captain's face flushed, her eyes flashed. "I have to be honest with you Miss Trvlakian, I am still angry with you. But I don't need to be told that I must behave as you demand, or my authority as Captain will not be respected by anyone on this aluminum tugboat. Pardon me for a *linit*." Trviea turned to me and whispered in English, "Neil, what do you think?"

"I love you both. I think all of you are the most fantastic women I have ever met. Now will you and Helga please kiss and make up! We've got a comet to divert!"

"How do you and Angela get along?"

"Admittedly, not that well during or since the divorce. But we do have to cooperate and communicate at least a little bit when it comes to our children. Which is another reason you and Helga need to kiss and make up! I have CHILDREN! MY children! Let's give 'em a chance to become adults."

"You're right." She smiled sardonically and turned her microphone back on. She spoke in

Atlantean. "Helga Trvlakian, if I am reinstated as Captain, I will not treat you any differently because of what has happened. This is my promise. Neil is a father, and his children alone are more important than our differences."

"Thank you, Trviea."

Trviea switched to English. "All right, that takes care of the business between me and Helga Trvlakian. This is the *Neanderthal Return*, standing by for Spear of Longinus."

After some activity back and forth, one of the screens in front of me showed the B-52 in flight. Then we could hear the voices of its crew. "This is General Morton Fairchild, in command of the B-52 code named *Spear Thrower*."

"Matochkin copies, *Spear Thrower*." acknowledged Matochkin air traffic control.

"*Neanderthal Return* copies, *Spear Thrower*." I said.

"Commander in Chief copies, *Spear Thrower*." acknowledged the President.

"We are approaching the Initial Point in the Kara Sea, one two zero statute miles east of target on North Island of Novaya Zemlya. Our altitude is four zero three zero feet. Is Russian authorization for Spear of Longinus confirmed?"

"*Da*. This is President Korsakov, you are authorized for Spear of Longinus."

"My Commander in Chief, do you give the final order to arm and launch the nuclear missile?"

"This is the President of the United States. *Spear Thrower*, you are authorized for Spear of Longinus."

"Thank you, Mr. President. Do you confirm our orders to land at Matochkin Shar Airport?"

"That is affirmative *Spear Thrower*. You have the Missile Crew for Operation Rainbow. Our Russian hosts are keen for them to witness Thor's Hammer."

"Very well. We are now moving into position to launch Spear of Longinus. Arming warhead. Warhead is armed. Missile is ready for launch. Launching missile. Missile away." On our television screens we could see the ALCM drop from the B-52, its wings deploy. Its jet engine fired. The B-52 turned south to put distance between it and the missile. "We confirm that missile engine is on. Spear is now flying due west at 3,000 feet altitude and ground speed of 560 miles per hour. We will now test the remote control mechanism. Major Easton, turn Spear 10 degrees to the right, please."

The missile turned as indicated. "Excellent, now turn Spear 20 degrees to the left." The missile turned. "Increase Spear altitude 100 feet." The missile gained 100 feet in altitude. "Bring Spear back down to 3,000 feet and set course for the target area. Spear is now at 3,000 feet and 570 miles per hour. We will now send it to the target. Spear is now ninety eight statute miles from target. Estimated time of arrival at target is ten minutes and 45 seconds."

We watched the cruise missile fly. "It's not a solid fuel rocket in the vacuum of space." commented Trviea.

"I understand. A cruise missile of this type is propelled by a jet engine, and rides on the lift of its wings. A jet airplane can be easily remote controlled with its ailerons. But rockets in space have gimbaled nozzles and can be remote controlled. It is the remote control equipment that needs to be tested, and right now, it's passing the test."

"The missile is now within a *kepfat* of the target. Look at the target area! The Russians painted the ice!"

"The origin of the cross-hairs is the target. The dark blue circles are intervals of 70 feet, the dark red circles are intervals of 25 meters."

"Why 70 feet?"

"10 sazhens. They're Russians. The missile is now gaining altitude."

Another voice was heard, "This is Major Roslyn Easton, Missile Controller on the *Spear Thrower*. The Spear is now rising to 10,000 feet over the target area." She used the image from a video camera mounted on the ALCM to help her remote control it. "Now the Spear is diving for the target."

The missile flew in an arc topping out at 10,000 feet. Then it curved down into a vertical dive. It went supersonic. Roslyn Easton slammed it into the ice five feet from the center of the target at 2,000 miles per hour. We saw the nuclear flash. Even at this distance, it was blinding to those of us watching out the window. The window automatically darkened in response to the flash, so our eyes weren't hurt. "We'll have to put on the dark goggles for Thor's Hammer." commented Trviea.

We watched the explosion as a number of voices declared the obvious in a variety of languages. "We confirm detonation."

The shock wave expanded through the glacier. It behaved like a piece of loose plywood slammed by a heavy sledgehammer. It rattled in the dirt basin that contained it. Before we could blink, the fireball blew out the ice and then formed the traditional 10 kiloton sized mushroom cloud. "Look at the dark brown color of the mushroom cloud." observed Trviea. "The fireball penetrated through the ice and dug up some of the dirt and rock below."

"Trviea, how come you know so much about nuclear explosions?"

"I am fully trained and experienced in the design and operation of nuclear explosives. We build 'em and shoot 'em off too. I have personally conducted seven such tests. If you Earthlings had a decent neutrino detector, you would already know that." She grinned.

"Initial estimate of yield of Spear of Longinus, 10.3 kilotons." we heard through the radio.

"Look at the clouds straight above." Trviea observed. "The bomb was about two dozen *potes* inside the ice when it detonated. The steam coming out of the hole was superheated to say the least. So you couldn't see it. But it punched holes in the clouds above. Look! Three dozen *kepfats* above the ground, you see the ice crystals forming, that is how far the steam flew before cooling enough to freeze. The fireball shot down through the ice, when it hit dirt, it blew out. How thick did the Russians say the glacier was?"

"About 70 meters."

Her lips moved silently as she did the math in her head. "I hate meters. I like your feet and yards much better."

"A meter is like one and one twelfth of a *treefat*. More accurately 40 *tig-its* or three *potes* and four *tig-its*."

"I know, but I still hate 'em. 230 of your feet. One *hekt* and seven dozen *potes*. It is well that you limited the yield of the test bomb to ten kilotons. That way we can observe the ice digging and steam jetting phenomena. Which is what we need to place the Russian Blockbuster in the Comet." She touched the button on the intercom. "Pido girl!" She meant Pidonita Hmlakian. "How many neutrinos did you count?"

"Is Neil there?"

"Yes."

"Okay, I'll try to answer in English and Base Ten. We received 16, that is twelve and four, neutrinos during the nuclear flash. All of the neutrinos are from plutonium 239 fission, none from fusion or from the fission of any other isotope. Our distance, in Base Twelve, is One two zero *kepfats*. With the Earth declared yield of 10.3 kilotons, we have a data point for calibrating our neutrino detector."

"Thank you, Pido. Move us into position for the next test. This one's going to be a LOT bigger!"

"144 plus 24, 168 times one point six, 270 or so miles. We are at a slant from the Spear test site."

"Of course we are. You don't think we're foolish enough to place ourselves DIRECTLY above a bomb that is being drilled into ice before explosion? I would rather not be hit by the jet of steam superheated by a nuke!"

We waited for the next test. An hour passed by as the triumphant B-52 landed at Matochkin and its crew minus a security detail rode the train out to the bunker.

"Everyone here?" asked Boris Korsakov in English.

"All my people are here, Boris." answered our President. Then Boris asked the same question in Russian, and received affirmative responses. "Okay, Bomb Crew. You are hereby authorized to conduct the test code named Thor's Hammer. Anatoly, please take over."

Anatoly Donovon addressed his audience in English. "American Missile Crew, Women of Creation listen up and observe. We have the bomb suspended from the blimp about 800 meters or 2600 feet above the ground. The original design and tested yield of this device is 58 megatons. I am one of the engineers who designed this bomb. In the few days since we retrieved this bomb from the Vault, I have added a few small design changes that should push the yield to as high as 62 megatons. Even though we are 37 kilometers from Ground Zero, I urge everyone to put on the dark goggles for the flash, because boy, we are going to have a FLASH! After the flash, you may remove the dark goggles, but do not look directly at the fireball until I give the go ahead. There will be TWO shock waves from the explosion. These shock waves travel a little faster than the speed of sound; they'll take a little less than two minutes to arrive. Everyone put in the ear plugs and put on the ear muffs, because it's going to be a BOOM! TWO booms! That is why we are in this bunker, to keep the bomb from knocking us flat! The equipment we'll be using is identical to the equipment we want to install on your spaceship. It'll arm the bomb by coded signal, and it'll start a 10 second countdown to detonation with a coded signal. The bomb is installed in a Penetration Vehicle that we designed and built in record time, so this will test the receiver antenna for the bomb within this Vehicle." Then he gave the same instructions in Russian.

"*Neanderthal Return*, are you standing by for Thor's Hammer?" This question was asked in English.

"We are on station and standing by." I confirmed. Everyone watched the South Island of Novaya Zemlya through the window, this time with dark goggles at the ready. "*Neanderthal Return* has now shut off and secured all electronics not nuclear hardened. We have our neutrino detector at the ready."

"We copy *Neanderthal Return*. We are now shutting off radio transmissions to protect our equipment. This is the Novaya Zemlya Test Range Bunker, signing off."

"Dark goggles ON! Everyone, dark goggles ON!" This call went out in English and in Atlantean. People rushed to place the dark goggles and made sure that they had a view out one of the many windows of the ship turned toward the Test Site. We weren't going to hear the countdown, but we knew it was going to happen. We waited.

Down in the bunker, the call for "Dark Goggles!" went out in both English and Russian. Everyone had the goggles ready.

Then Anatoly gave his orders in Russian. "Arm the bomb, please."

"Arming bomb, NOW. Confirm! Bomb is armed." Maria Romanov, no relation to the Royal Family, operated the bomb. All of her speech was in Russian. "Ready to send the Detonation Code."

"Please send the Detonation Code, Maria." commanded Anatoly.

"Sending Detonation Code. Mark. *Dyesat, dyevyat, vosyem, syem, shyest,*" Right about five in her countdown, everyone fixed their dark goggles in place. "*Pyat, chetirye, tri, dva, odin, nol.*"

FLASH!!!!!!

Pidonita had backed the ship off to where we were over 500 miles away from the blast. The blimp shielded us from the nuclear flash for about half of a microsecond, then it evaporated and we received the full treatment. The flash seemed to overwhelm the Atlantean dark goggles we were wearing. I closed my eyes and I could see the red imprint on the inside of my eyelids. If I looked upon the bomb explosion without the goggles, I would see the vein structure of my eyelids. But within a few seconds I saw the Atlantean words for "Safe to Remove", flash on inside the goggles. I lifted the goggles carefully, just a crack. It was bright, but not blinding. I slowly removed the goggles. The window was incredibly dark; it had the material that darkened automatically in response to intense light. Given that Creation knew we Earthlings had nukes, had lasers, and with all of the beam weapons depicted in our science fiction broadcasts, it was a reasonable precaution to design into the ship's windows. Still the fireball glowed bright white, like looking at the Sun. Everyone was silent as we watched the spectacle below. We could see the surrounding landscape. The fireball expanded, but not as rapidly as one is conditioned by films of nuclear explosions to expect. It was the SCALE of the blast. We could see the shock waves slowly expand like ripples across land and sea.

From the standpoint of the people in the bunker, the shock waves were not slow at all! The people had removed their goggles. The wall of the bunker was between everyone and the explosion. Looking backwards, the land was lit to a brighter white than snow in the sun, it was painful to look at. "Everyone! Fix the ear plugs and muffs!" This order rang out in both Russian and English. "Fireball past 10 kilometers diameter, still growing. Confirm at least 40 megatons of yield. 12 kilometers. Confirm at least 50 megatons." A moment later, "Thirty seconds to shock wave." Everyone put in ear plugs and fixed their ear muffs in place. These ear muffs were specially designed. Once on, with the plugs, you were deaf, you could hear only your heartbeat. Everyone grabbed a hold of something and braced themselves.

"Pidonita," whispered Trviea softly into her headset. "How big is that fireball?"

"Four *kepfats*, now almost five. Great Holy Spirit! Over five *kecht* neutrinos from fusion, same number from Uranium 17(10) fast fission." Pido was in awe. Her designation of Uranium 238 was in Base Twelve numbers. "From the number of plutonium fission neutrinos, I'd say that there were nine pits inside that uranium pressure vessel."

"If you can set the detonators of one pit to all go off in the same nanosecond, why not the detonators of nine pits?" I said. "We know the bomb is hot dog shaped, 3 meters by 65 centimeters, plenty of room for nine pits. Make the pressure spike that much higher for the fusion."

"We have nukes." Trviea confided to me quietly. "But we've never built them that big."

A digital clock counted the seconds to shock wave. As the count reached zero, everyone gripped harder. Everyone was now genuinely frightened. What if this bomb somehow ran away to over 100 megatons? The steel Penetration Vehicle somehow reflected fast neutrons back into the U-238? Burning a larger proportion of the nuclear fuel? If so, they could be badly injured or killed. It didn't help that Anatoly himself looked to be in fear for his life. He's the one who designed this thing! What kind of 'enhancements' did he build into it?

BOOM! The shock wave was deafening, even through the ear protection. Everyone was lifted off the ground and slammed back into it hard! Legs did not break, but there will be a few sore ankles. The shock wave didn't care if you were an elderly Soviet nuclear engineer or a strong and muscular Creation Neanderthal. It treated you the same. Like a grain of sand on a drum! Anatoly signaled everyone to keep the ear protection on. BOOM! The second shock wave characteristic of nuclear explosions hit. Outside the bunker, dust filled the air from the disturbed earth.

Anatoly gently removed his ear muffs and pulled out his ear plugs. Everyone followed suit. Now everyone heard nothing but a seashell sound coming from their ears, very loud. "We now estimate the energy yield to be 62.3 megatons." someone said in Russian. It was repeated in English. It seemed very far away. Like someone shouting at you from a hundred yards away on a beach with the waves crashing.

"Anatoly!" shouted Helga. She was shocked by how far away and quiet her own voice sounded, even though she KNEW she yelled at the top of her lungs. "What has happened to my ears?"

"If you did not wear the ear protection, you would be deaf right now. Permanently. As it is, it is just like going to a rock concert and standing too near the stage. In a few hours, your hearing will start to come back. It'll heal up and return to normal in a few days."

"Anatoly!" shouted Monoloa. She spoke to him in Russian. "Look at my face. My eyes are bigger. My nose is bigger. The back part of my brain is larger. The ear holes in my skull are SLANTED, while yours are straight. Our senses are just more sensitive! Seeing, smelling, HEARING!"

"Not right now." Anatoly laughed. He walked out from behind the bunker and looked straight into the fireball. He signaled for everyone to come and look. Everyone's throat was dry from breathing the dust. The dust floated all smoky on the ground covering the whole of the world as far as they could see. It seemed about a fathom thick, the height of a man. The fireball cooled enough for people to be able to look at it. It had risen enough now to form the mushroom. A huge 8 mile diameter mushroom. The top was flattening as it reached the top of the atmosphere. Anatoly grinned with the satisfaction of an engineer whose design worked perfectly! "Monoloa my beautiful friend, THAT is what we are going to take on YOUR spaceship and put into the comet."

Chapter Thirty One

"Which way is the wind blowing the mushroom cloud?"

"Local winds are from the west, the nuclear clouds should drift out over the Kara Sea. That is where the radioactive fallout will be. The ocean is vast, it'll dilute it. But you don't want to be caught in the fallout, too much radiation exposure at once is bad for your health."

Trviea lost some of her enthusiasm for Operation Rainbow. "I'll feel better when we hear from the Test Range Bunker. Eight Creation women are now at the Bunker: Helga, Lchnsda, Monoloa, Andemona, the four who went down originally. Then the four left over from the emergency Shuttle trip bringing Neanderthal blood to Lchnsda. Sorby Mishlakian," she had an affection for Sorby, they looked alike, "she is experienced at going outside in a pressure suit for inspection and repairs. We need her up here, right now. Nesla Teslakian is an engineer. She knows magnetic fields, very good at designing and repairing electrical and magnetic equipment. Knows high energy physics, I would like to hear her evaluation of Thor's Hammer. She's also good at mechanical design, tubes, wires, plumbing, structure. Our computer software is in good shape right now, but I would feel better having Marla Syferkrip and Wlmsda Gtslakian. They can troubleshoot any computer problem."

"You seem to think of Sorby Mishlakian as special."

"We all consider her special. Her father, Demoan Mishlakian, was the very last man to die from the Virus. We had him in a quarantine. He was providing sperm. We could not risk exposing him to the Virus, so we had to use medical equipment to make women pregnant. What we didn't know was that he had the Virus, it just hadn't mutated. He fathered over a *kecht* of beautiful little girls, all of them named Mishlakian. But all of his sons died in the womb. Many of their mothers died too, but we saved some of them. The daughters survived and were born. Sorby was five months along when the Virus in her father mutated and killed him. One of the reasons we think of her and her sisters as special, is that as she was born four months after her father went to the Great Holy Spirit, she is Innocent of the Grief. That is special."

"Innocent of the Grief is special?"

"It IS special. Those of us who went through the Virus Holocaust, you have NO IDEA what it was like! But that's GOOD. I'm GLAD you have no idea what it was like! Makes you Innocent of the Grief. Makes you special."

She kissed me to emphasize the point. "All of the Mishlakian girls, we look after them. Even though they've now been adults longer than any of our ancestors lived. Because we know that they are our daughters and nieces. They sometimes resent it. Sometimes it is a problem for a woman like me who went through the Virus Holocaust if her name happens to be Mishlakian. But we love Sorby. We think of her as our daughter because she is younger than any of us, and we are proud of her."

"Is she YOUR daughter? Are you her mother?"

"Family resemblance. Neither me nor her acknowledge it much. Because I was Captain, and may be Captain again, we don't want any of the crew to think I treat her as a favorite because she's my daughter. And I didn't. Even Helga will say that. If anything, I was harder on Sorby than I was on anybody else. And she was harder on herself. Necessary if she puts on a pressure suit to go out into the vacuum to inspect the hull and poke around the fusion reactor. Anyway, everyone allows me to love her as a mother should. I'm sure that everyone at the Bunker is all right. But I'll feel better when I hear that from the ground."

"We'll need 'em all. There is your problem with Helga. I hope that hasn't been solved permanently." I like Helga, I would miss her.

"I certainly don't want Helga dead. I'm not that angry with her. We had a relationship, her and me."

"I'm sure you will be friends again."

"Uh, you don't understand. It was sexual at times."

"I see. I've been kidnapped by bisexual Neanderthal women from Outer Space. Sounds like a comic book sold only to those over 18."

That cracked her up. When she recovered from her laughter, "Our men are all dead. So what's a little homosexuality between friends? But I agree, we shouldn't advertise this embarrassing fact to Earth. Monoloa tells me that the taboo against homosexuality is as strong in Russia as it is in America."

"Or on Creation. Your religion had strong teachings against homosexuality, your old laws punished those who were caught, women as well as men."

"How did you learn that? It's true, but how did you learn that?"

"I can read Atlantean now. I've been reading your history." I said it in Atlantean.

"Well, sometimes laws are repealed before they're repealed. The Revolution of Twenty Two Tenty Four. Like the United States, we had a set of basic laws designed to protect our people from abuses of government power. And like the United States, our judges came up with excuses and exceptions galore to prevent these basic laws from getting in the way of the government abusing its power. One of those abuses involved long prison terms imposed for homosexuality. It didn't always matter that the accused homosexual was actually innocent of the crime. So homosexuals joined the Revolution. The Revolution succeeded, and now we have juries, not judges, decide whether a basic right is violated. Juries are less apt to invent excuses that weaken civil rights."

"Was that when your sodomy laws were repealed?"

"Uh, no. There were still many who considered homosexuality a sin. The Revolution could no more repeal the sodomy laws then a handful of Hawaiian judges can legalize same gender marriages. But the result was that these old laws were no longer enforced. After the Virus killed our men, these laws were 'suspended'. Which is as good as repealed. After all, what are we going to do?"

"I think we'll wait until AFTER we deflect the comet before we tell Earth about this part of your history."

"Good idea. Why don't you try the radio? The static from the bomb should be dying down, see if you can contact Matochkin or the Test Range."

"This is *Neanderthal Return*, calling Matochkin Shar, and calling the Test Range Bunker. Do you copy?"

There was a lot of static on the receiver. I pushed the button to suppress the static. It did, but the result was distorted. *"Neanderthal Return*, this is Matochkin Shar, we copy. We have an underground line to the Bunker, everyone is alive, no major injuries."

Trviea smiled and cheered in relief. She wasn't the only one. "We copy. That is good to hear, Matochkin Shar."

"Their ears were affected by the shock waves, but other than that they should be all right. All eight Creation women are there. You want to come and get them with your Shuttle?"

I handed the microphone off to Trviea. "This is Trviea Harsradich. Metrola Mornuxler is reluctant to use the Shuttle this close to the Magnetic Pole."

"Yes, it is just across the water in the Canadian Islands. I guess the bomb explosions affected the magnetic field too."

"Fortunately, nuclear explosions, even as big as Thor's Hammer, have a transient effect on the Earth's magnetic field. Metrola can get the Shuttle down to Novaya Zemlya; she just has to have more confidence in the repair job. Frankly, I think the problem is the remoteness of your location. She would rather come down to someplace like St. Petersburg or Moscow, where rescue and repair is more feasible."

"I see. Better than the Algerian Desert." He laughed. "Give us a few hours. We're still recovering from the nuclear explosion."

The people at the Test Range Bunker watched the mushroom cloud slowly drift to the east. The two Presidents stood together on a little hill and spoke as quietly as they could with their ears still hissing. "I wonder if it was a mistake to have the women watch this explosion from here?" asked the American. "I've never seen them so frightened."

"It's a matter of history. This is the first contact since the beginning of civilization between our two Planets. Everything we do now will profoundly affect our relationship with them for the next thousand years. If Stalin and Truman handled it better, we might not have had an Arms Race. We might not have these huge bombs."

"Even the Cold War had a positive side to it. The bombs we feared as Doomsday weapons are now the only things we have that can PREVENT Doomsday. These girls are scared. We need them and their spaceship for this mission."

"These girls NEED to be afraid of this bomb. Maybe they have nuclear explosives themselves, maybe this crew has participated in such tests, so there is no reason to impress upon them the seriousness of these bombs. But you know how gung ho and can do cosmonauts are. These women are cosmonauts. We cannot be overconfident, that is the one thing that can lead to disaster more than anything else. For the future of our relationship, their participation needs to be voluntary, and we need to make sure that nobody can say their agreement was uninformed. That we tricked them. That we didn't make sure they knew exactly the magnitude of the weapon that we send with them to use."

"They already know the magnitude, we gave them the definition of the megaton, which they could convert to their units."

"Abstract numbers on a piece of paper. Why don't you Americans want to use the Metric System? Because you visualize distances and dimensions in feet. It's not so clear to you if stated in meters. But how do you visualize anything that is measured, however familiar the units, if what you are talking about is immense in scale? We needed to have these women EXPERIENCE a sixty megaton explosion. Otherwise 'sixty megatons' is an abstract expression. It means nothing."

"I just wish I could get this wind to stop blowing through my ears. I can barely hear myself speak, let alone hear you."

They laughed.

Monoloa came up the hill and joined them. "Hello, Mr. President. I've been told a lot about you, it is all good. But please forgive me, I speak Russian much better than I speak English."

"That is quite all right. No apology necessary. I've heard nothing but good things about you too, Monoloa." Our President offered his handshake.

"Thank you." She used both of her hands to give him a proper Atlantean handshake. Then she turned to President Korsakov and spoke to him in Russian. "Did your military actually consider using one of these," she pointed at the drifting mushroom cloud, "on China?"

Boris smiled. "Brezhnev's cooler head prevailed. The suggestion was never serious. The one thing nuclear weapons have done to us. We don't let a few companies of soldiers shooting it out in a border skirmish escalate into a general war. At that time China could have hit every major Siberian and Central Asian city with their nuclear explosives. We did not want to risk that nor did they want to risk the millions of civilian casualties that we could inflict. There have been civil wars, proxy wars, and interventions in the smaller and poorer nations. But no one has had the stomach for a general conflict between major powers."

"Losing our men had a similar effect on us. Women soldiers took over the combat duties in our armies and navies. After we buried a few *kechts* of them, it dawned on us that we CANNOT have children. We CANNOT replace our losses. Diplomacy became a very attractive option. Without children, once we're dead, we're dead. And when we figured out how to stop the aging process with a medical treatment, then throwing a life away in something as foolish as a war is throwing away centuries of existence, not just decades. But we still have the courage to risk our lives if it is truly necessary. Comet Wormwood makes it truly necessary. Thank you for letting us see and FEEL this bomb explosion. We will still do it, but we will now take our duties seriously." She shook his hand and went down to join her group.

"What did she say?" asked our President.

"She confirmed what I just told you. Look at Anatoly and his Bomb Crew. Chatting with the American Missile people. Recording all of their measurements, like typical scientists. They sure look happy. But we already know everything we really need to know from Thor's Hammer."

"The bomb works. It yields 62.3 megatons in Anatoly's current design. For the Creation women and the crews slated for Operation Rainbow, they felt the explosion. What more do we need to know?"

"There is one thing. The Thor's Hammer bomb was in a steel Penetration Vehicle. Basic bridge construction steel. Anatoly wants to substitute U-238 for the steel."

"How much would that increase the yield?"

"With lithium deuteride-tritide packed in between the outer casing and the old Halloween bomb, he thinks between 120 and 150 megatons."

"But would the Penetration Vehicle still perform its function of getting into the hole we punch with our B61-11 nuke?"

"*Da*! Of course. Uranium is just as strong as steel. Put a heat shield on the leading cone, like you have on any reentry vehicle. It'll race down that hole at thousands of miles per hour against all of the hot gasses and solid chunks, then detonate. The idea is to push that comet as much as possible with each explosion. The Creation girls want to do this with only one bomb run, if possible."

"So why did you not detonate the enhanced bomb with the U-238 Penetration Vehicle?"

"We might not have survived the test standing in this Bunker. People are panicking enough as it is with Comet Wormwood. 62.3 megatons they'll accept because that's not much more than we've done before. But to reveal to the public that you can enhance the yield of nuclear bombs to truly incredible levels by just packing in more U-238 and lithium deuteride? Depleted uranium is cheap and plentiful, you Americans left a few tons of it in the Iraqi desert in the form of expended ammunition. Natural uranium will also do nicely, banana republics and terrorist states have pitchblende deposits. Once you make a plutonium pit, just pack in the LiD and surround it with a uranium casing designed like a pressure vessel. For pressures as high as in the core of the Sun, only has to hold for a few hundred nanoseconds. There is fusion, and fast neutrons from the fusion split the U-238 nuclei. Put that into another even bigger uranium pressure vessel with more LiD. Combine Teller-Ulam with Sakharov layer cake. The limiting factor is how much lithium 6, heavy hydrogen, and uranium you can get your hands on. India and Pakistan each have nukes. Everyone is frightened that they might lob a few missiles at each other over only a few hundred miles. But by packing these same nukes into a uranium pressure vessel with LiD, Pakistan can deliver megatons to New Delhi with a truck, Timothy McVeigh style."

"Boris, you're just a pleasant and optimistic kind of guy! In going along with your policy of making sure that nobody can say we tricked the Creation girls, don't you think somebody should tell them about making the Penetration Vehicle out of depleted uranium to enhance the yield beyond the 62 megatons of this test?"

"Look at Anatoly now, he's speaking with Monoloa."

"Monoloa," Anatoly addressed her, "I have something I need to tell you."

"What is it?" They spoke in Russian.

"The test bomb we just shot off was in a Penetration Vehicle made of steel."

"You want to substitute uranium 17(10), excuse me, 238?"

"Yeah. With lithium deuteride-tritide as the packing material."

"120 megatons or more. In a package one meter in diameter and 4.5 meters long, weighing about 20,000 kilos."

"How did you know?"

"Give us some credit. We have a fusion reactor on our ship. I was talking to Nesla, she's an engineer. She suggested your idea just now. Each time we get near the comet, we will put our ship at risk. A Blockbuster bomb in the comet could break off a chunk as big as a half *kepfat*. But the big chunks aren't the threat, they'll move comparatively slow, we can see them, we can evade them. It's the forty or fifty *pote* chunks, they'll be moving FAST. We have a 3,000 *pote* ship, but a fifty *pote* chunk moving at *kechts* of *kepfats* per hour can do real damage. This is true whether we use a ten megaton bomb or a 100 megaton bomb. The ten megatons won't move the comet away from Earth. The big bomb can. The bigger the better. We'll discuss this in the meeting scheduled when we all get on the ship."

"Ian Miller, want to help me test fly the Shuttle?" asked Metrola.

"Test fly the Shuttle?"

"Sure. You used to be a Royal Marine, didn't you? Chopper pilot?"

"Well, yes, uh, in the Falklands War."

"Good! Neil has done well helping me with the air traffic controllers. I'm sure you can do just as well! Your English is the original English! And for test flying, you helped rebuild the thing, once in the desert, and once up here in our Shuttle Bay and Repair Shop. Contrviea's Garage and Lube. We'll fix your engine, guaranteed, or you're going nowhere! If you are not happy with our work, feel free to sue us! Your process server will only charge you for 25 trillion miles! Each way!"

"That's a lot of mileage." Ian laughed at her joke about Earth legal process. "Maybe I'll just come in for an oil change and a tune up. What kind of test flying are you talking about?"

"Going down to the Russian Arctic to pick up the 8 Creation women."

"Some test flight. You sure you want to just go get 'em?"

"Well, I was thinking about a test flight within a *kepfat* of this ship first. We don't go any further until we know she's as good as new."

"Good idea."

"So, you're coming?"

"Well, sure. I've nothing else to do except,"

"Plenty of time for that. Maybe this time not only will I let you put your face in my chest, I'll let you kiss my nipples."

"You are a tease."

"One of the things we have in common with Cro-Magnon women. Let's get into pressure suits. Askelion took your measurements. In *tig-its*, of course. Contrviea adjusted a suit to fit you."

"She did that?"

"We don't know what all Earthlings we're taking on this mission. Neil Peace for sure, he has been with us the longest, he knows us best and we trust him the most. He has given us excellent advice for dealing with Earthlings. He is an engineer, too, and that's not bad to have on a spaceship. He'll be an asset for both Creationists and Earthlings."

"You're Creationists? You don't believe in evolution?"

Metrola pointed her finger at his face with a stern look on her face. "Don't. You know what I mean. We're proof of evolution. We're much further advanced than you." She grinned. "Meddi and Askelion want to take Cuc Nguyen along. They feel that they'll need a third physician for their regular duties, not to mention emergencies. Cuc is licensed to practice medicine on Earth and she knows Earth medicine. The Earthlings for this mission will feel reassured having her on board. Mohammed Abbas needs to go back down, his wife is already suspicious, we don't want to ruin his marriage."

"'E has not been,"

"No, 'e hasn't." she unintentionally picked up his accent. "And we've not been approaching 'im. We don't want to ruin a marriage and break up a family. Adultery is a sure fire way of destroying a happy marriage. Trick is to convince Labna that 'er husband has honored his vows to her."

"While being on a spaceship with 39 beautiful, muscular Neanderthal women who came 'ere for the specific purpose of obtaining sperm and maybe even a live man or two to bring back to Creation. Tough sell. But maybe we ought to reconsider having Mohammed along. The way 'e talked to those bandits, the courage and steadiness with which 'e pulled it off. It was valour."

"Yes, that speaks well of 'im. It was beautiful. 'E was the demon who put a spell on them, not I! We do 'ave plenty of extra room on the ship, we could double up the bunks for sleeping arrangements. Our life support is running at about one third capacity, we could easily take on four dozen Earthlings for Operation Rainbow."

"Even to take back to Creation?"

"'Ow'd you guess?" She grinned. "Ah, 'ere we are at the Shuttle Bay. Contrviea, Ian has volunteered to 'elp us test fly the Shuttle."

"Somehow, I knew he would if you are the one to ask him." smiled Contrviea.

"If SHE asked me!?" protested Ian.

"A woman can tell these things, Ian. The way you look at her. Either you've fallen in love or it's the darndest infatuation I have ever seen."

Ian was shocked. She had him read. But he managed to recover. "I'm infatuated with all of you. You're all very special."

"Thank you! We have more important things to do right now than flattering each other. Let's get you into this pressure suit, you do work so well with Metrola."

"Let me get this straight. The purpose of these pressure suits is to protect us in case the Shuttle loses air?"

"That's right. You already know the first thing about basic astronautics. We've tested the Shuttle cabin integrity. We read the pressure gauges inside the Shuttle. We reduce the air in the

Shuttle Bay to vacuum. We open it to space. Just like when we launch. So far the pressure hasn't dropped and we haven't detected any leaks. It maintains a full two dozen *dollons* per square *tig-it*. That's about twelve or thirteen pounds per square inch. You should be able to breathe easy, but the suits are a precaution."

The test flight lasted several hours, where Metrola practiced flying in Earth's magnetic field and moving in and out of the Shuttle Bay. Ian practiced radio communication with cooperating Russian air traffic controllers, who gave him pointers. They congratulated him for his fast learning. Finally, Metrola landed in the Shuttle Bay and closed the door to space. The air filled the Bay and Metrola pronounced the Shuttle shipshape.

After the successful test crew got out of the pressure suits, Metrola spoke quietly with her man. "Ian, in one hour we're going down to Matochkin Shar to pick up our women. We can take down any Earthlings who wish to leave the ship and not go on this mission. Nobody is being drafted. You can leave too, if you so desire. The Russians have promised to fly them out of Matochkin and eventually get them home. Although they certainly can stay on board if they wish to be taken to a better location at a later time. Mohammed Abbas might need to leave immediately to take care of his home life. I understand that 737's are now able to get into Tamanrasset. The old Algerian government holds the desert. The GIS holds the Tell, except the Berber areas. The Berbers are governing themselves and have entered into negotiations with the old government. Labna and the children are safe in Illizi, not hurt in the fighting. If we can get Mohammed into Tamanrasset, he can find his way to Illizi and his family."

"I agree. We need to get Mohammed home. I understand Air Force One is 'eading to Moscow, the two Presidents need to work together on this some more. Maybe Mohammed can 'op a ride, that gets 'im to Moscow. From there 'e can get to Cairo, and an Egyptian 737 can take 'im to Tamanrasset. Those of us with the Science and Humanities Channel, we want to stay on board to film and document this 'istorical mission. We can all be of assistance, we're accustomed to adjusting and repairing technical equipment in remote locations."

"I see. A film crew recording this mission is a good idea. But we may have to limit the size of your crew, there is only so much ship. You might have to meet and choose who can stay and who can go. Rank yourselves in priority. Now, one other thing. We have an hour. Do you consent to the use of your sperm for our reproduction?"

"Of course I do! I've already contributed some."

Metrola dropped her mouth open in mock shock. "And I thought you loved me!" She had a smile and winked when she said that.

"Of course I love you. I love all of you, and I'll be happy to love you right now."

"Glad to hear that! Let's go to my room. I have a *glup* and a half of *manatat*, you call it rum. With this Shuttle working, we're going to have to go shopping on Earth. Some good French champagne, California wine, sides of beef from both America and Argentina, sausage from Germany, and so on. The Garden room grows fresh vegetables for which we are grateful, the rabbits and little goats provide us with meat, but we need to restock our meat locker with the big animals, beef, horse, bison, deer, pork, I can get used to Earth food!"

"We can get Stolichnaya vodka when we go down to Novaya Zemlya!"

"Good idea! The sale of books and tapes about Creation prepared by Helga and Lchnsda, the Spanish language versions of which prepared by Andemona have given us plenty of hard currency to spend. Perhaps the Russians will sell us some of their finest vodka."

"Did you say you eat horsemeat?"

"Back on Creation we did. We also ate minke whale, perhaps we can get some from Norway or the Faeroes. I understand we can get horsemeat in France. Andemona wants to try out her

French. Helga wants to go to Germany and talk Deutsche, in addition to her speaking that language with Fred. Get some pork from the people who know pork. I miss having big animal meat almost as much as I missed making love with men!"

"Speaking of which,"

"Ah! Here's my room, come on in!"

The *Neanderthal Return's* Shuttle landed at Matochkin Shar. Ian Miller assisted Metrola with the air traffic control. American F-18's and Russian MIG 29's flew CAP for the Presidential planes. The B-52 that was *Spear Thrower*, Air Force One, and Korsakov's Illyushin were readied for flight. The train arrived at the airport. Metrola hugged each of her shipmates, glad to see them again.

"Are you healing up, Lchnsda?" she asked in Atlantean.

"I am. Thank you for bringing me the Neanderthal blood, the Healing Factor, and Askelion Lamakian. I am almost all better now. My left lung still hurts a little if I take a deep breath. It sure keeps me from wanting to run a few miles like everyone has been doing."

"Miles? When in America, do as the Americans do. Well, maybe Monoloa has been running kilometers, or *versty*." Plural in Russian language ends with the vowel sound similar to 'runny'.

"Whenever I can, Metrola!" exclaimed Monoloa. They hugged and kissed.

"Ian suggested something. Since we are in Russia, we should get some of their best vodka, to add to our *manatat*. We can pay for it of course."

"I'll ask."

Monoloa approached President Korsakov as he waited to greet the three people who came down on the Shuttle. Mohammed Abbas, the famed Algerian who pulled the Brer Rabbit trick in the desert, decided to come down. Monoloa spoke with Boris. "Mr. President, Metrola was wondering if we can get some of your finest vodka. We'll pay for it. But if there is none to be had in this remote location, we understand."

Boris Korsakov laughed. "I'm the President! There is some on my Illyushin, it is Stolichnaya, the best. Want one case or two cases?"

"Cases?"

"Yes! A case is a box of 24 bottles, that is two dozen in your numbers. Each bottle is a liter. So you want 24 or 48 liters?"

"Well, we don't want too much on board, we can take one case."

"Take two cases, and don't worry about paying for it, our compliments!"

"Not pay for it? All right. Thank you!" Monoloa did not want to offend by turning down a gift.

"Listen. You ladies don't have to go out to this comet and help us bomb it. We could work out something. With two Energiya rockets and American Space Shuttles, we could assemble a Blockbuster bomb with some Centaur upper stages and send it on a trajectory to hit Comet Wormwood while it is still millions of kilometers away. That may or may not work. But with the *Neanderthal Return*, we can do so much better than that. So enjoy the vodka! We appreciate everything you have done so far. Tell Sabar Duradich we appreciate her finding the comet as soon as she did."

"Thank you." She knew what he was doing. By letting her accept a gift of vodka, he was making her feel obligated to carry out the mission. But she can also give Russia a gift from Atlantis in return. The gift should also go to the Americans to avoid the appearance of favoring one superpower over the other. She went to Metrola and spoke quietly in Atlantean. "Met, I need to use the printer. Let's give them the formula for Healing Factor. We know it works on Cro-Magnons because it works on Fred Graf. They have seen it work on Lchnsda and are impressed. It won't tell them how to stop the aging process, but it will help immensely with all of the trauma, violence and physical injuries they suffer."

"I agree, let us talk it over with everyone. Then we can print it out, no time to translate it into English or Russian."

"That is all right, they have a complete description of Atlantean language and Creation numbers, weights and measures that will allow them to translate to their languages."

"Come to think of it, maybe the vodka is a gift in return for that."

"Perhaps. But we need a spectacular show of good will. It will overcome any bad feeling people might still have over the kidnapping of Neil Peace. I don't know about this Whores of Babylon and Three Goddesses stuff. Such a gift might be considered the work of the Devil by those who refuse to believe we are anything other than witches in a pact with Satan."

"We cannot worry about that, they are a minority. Most Earthlings are modern technological human beings who consider engineering and medicine part of the gift of God, the gift of their fellow human's genius, talent, and invention."

Mohammed basked in the glory for having saved the Shuttle from the bandits with his acting skills. His English was halting in spite of having been in close contact with Americans, Canadians, and British. Arabic speaking Russian and American officials competed for his attention. "This is wonderful!" he exclaimed. "I am offered a ride to Moscow on Air Force One and on the Russian Presidential jet. I am sure the accommodations on both are the best one can ever have on an airplane. But how do I choose? I do not wish to offend either Russia or America, for I consider you both my friends and friends of Algeria. How do I find my way out of this dilemma?"

"I have an idea," suggested the American, "why don't you ride with the Russians to Moscow." The Russian nodded his head. "Then you can ride Air Force One to Paris. From there, we can find a flight to get you to Illizi, somehow. The airport at Algiers is closed right now, but anything can happen in the next few days. You could fly to Tunis or to Casablanca, from there, we can get you to Tamanrasset or someplace like that and you can find your way to Illizi."

"That is a good idea. I will fly with the Russians to Moscow, and with the Americans to Paris. Ohhh! France! We used to be French, but I am proud we kicked them out of our country! Well, I guess I can suffer being in France for a little while. Paris in the spring, we all have to make sacrifices."

They laughed at that. "Then it's settled."

Monoloa and Metrola came back out of the Shuttle, each bearing several sheets of paper stapled together. "We have an announcement to make." Monoloa shouted this in Russian, Metrola in English. Monoloa first spoke in Russian each sentence, followed by Metrola in English.

"We have contacted our ship by radio, and they have agreed to a gift we shall now make to the entire Planet Earth. We thank you for your hospitality and your friendship. We thank the Russian people for the gift of vodka that is now being loaded on our Shuttle. Our gift to you that we make in return is the information contained in these sheets of paper."

They held up the paper, the cover sheets had large size print. On one was Cyrillic alphabet and Russian language, the other Roman alphabet and English. It read: "A gift from the People of Planet Creation to the People of Planet Earth."

"We have not had time to translate this information into English, Russian, or any Earth language. But we know that you now have enough information on Atlantean language and Creation weights and measures, and numbers, to perform your own translation, into any Earth language, and into the Metric and English systems of measure. It is the formula for Healing Factor. You have seen it work on Lchnsda, healing her bullet wounds. We know it works on Cro-Magnons, with Fred Graf's bullet wounds. In addition to the formula, it contains instructions for its use and when NOT to use it. The formula is simple, place it on the Internet, no one shall have a patent on it, even the poorest nations can set up labs to make it. We only ask that you make Healing Factor available to all who need it and to get it into production as fast as possible. Do not withhold it from anyone for any reason, except when its use is dangerous or unnecessary, that is all that we ask. It has one side effect, it increases the patient's sexual awareness and appetite."

Laughter. "No! That is not a joke, it is serious. It is medicine, treat it as such, respect it for what it is. Use it wisely, use it for healing, NEVER use it for an evil or inappropriate purpose. One of these we will hand to the Russian President, and one we will hand to the American President. Please promise that neither of you will abuse your power by withholding this information."

"We promise." they both said as they solemnly accepted this profound gift.

Chapter Thirty Two

The women put on their pressure suits to ride the Shuttle back up to the *Neanderthal Return*. The suits used for the spacewalks over to the Shuttle *Atlantis* and to *Mir* were brought to Matochkin Shar. Other suits were stowed on the Shuttle. The women bade farewell and boarded their ship.

Ian Miller returned on the Shuttle and performed his communication role with air traffic controllers. His employer wanted him on the *Neanderthal Return* to film and document Operation Rainbow.

During the Illyushin flight, President Korsakov came over to Mohammed Abbas. A translator accompanied him. "I trust you are comfortable, Mr. Abbas?"

"Everything is fine, thank you."

"Excellent, anything I can do for you?"

"No. The stewardess brought me this fruit juice and fresh fruit. Delicious. She knew enough not to offer a Muslim anything with alcohol or pork."

"Good. I would like to get down to business. The Americans will ask you these questions when you ride their 747 out to Paris. Then the French will get you. Then the Algerians whenever you get that far. Please tell me your impressions of these women from Planet Creation."

"What do you want to know?"

"Technical competence. Intelligence. Emotional stability. Sanity. How do you think they can handle themselves in a crisis?"

"The two physicians operated on Fred Graf in the desert, with help from the American physician and the Canadian cameramen who used to be paramedics. He is doing great! Even accounting for the Healing Factor, I would say that the five of them are the best emergency surgeons you could have. They know their stuff. The thousands who built and provisioned the *Neanderthal Return* back home have done an impressive job! Who would think of stowing a portable hospital on their Shuttle?"

"The Shuttle. What can you tell me about how the Shuttle operates?"

"I am not an engineer. My education consists of learning to read with a Koran, and knowing what one needs to know to survive in the Sahara. The Shuttle operates by repelling against the Earth's magnetic field, and it seems to derive its energy from that field."

"Are you sure?"

"Well, no. I am not sure. Like I said, I am not an engineer. It is just that I could not see anything that looked like a fuel tank when we were working on the guts of that ship."

"You participated in the repair of the Shuttle?"

"Yes. I took my orders from Metrola Mornuxler. Translated by the American archeologist, Chuck Carter, his Arabic is perfect. Metrola knew exactly what she was doing. Allah prevented the bomb from destroying the Shuttle, we removed seven sticks of unexploded dynamite from the bottom of the hull."

"What is your impression of Metrola Mornuxler?"

"I can see why many people think she is a Goddess or a Demon Woman. But she is a flesh and blood human being, with her imperfections and emotions. She just happens to be of a Race of people we may not have seen since Afenor was alive. We will see more of her, *Inshallah*. As a pilot, she was wonderful. Working as a team, we handled the bandits and got up out of the desert."

"What about the rest of the crew?"

"Too bad I'm married, Muslim, and in love with my wife and children. Beautiful, strong women. Once you get used to the shape of their faces and the muscular build of their bodies; you understand why the Pagans believed in Goddesses. To be on this ship, each must have had connections, or have beaten out thousands of highly qualified women. There is a big split between Helga Trvlakian and Trviea Harsradich. They're working hard to resolve it."

"Did they ever approach you for sex?"

"No, they will not suggest adultery. They did not come here to ruin marriages and break up families. Now I have to get back to Illizi and convince Labna that I remained loyal to her this whole time."

"I hope you succeed in that. How about the two called Wilma and Betty?"

"They are under discipline for some infractions that none of them will discuss. They are soldiers. Extremely tough. When I saw them, I was glad to know that they were under the tight control of their metal collars. But if they were to turn Wilma and Betty loose, with orders to kill, they could break your neck in two seconds. Take the two toughest paratroopers in your Army, make them Neanderthal women strong enough to throw 100 kilograms across a soccer field, with large teeth with the jaw strength of lions, that is what Wilma and Betty are."

"Are they trained in hand to hand combat?"

"That is the story. If Wilma and Betty were in the limousine when the Avengers of Yahweh attacked, the Avengers would all be dead, and the Secret Service men would have lived. Because of their status of punishment, they are off limits for sex. Which was all right with the Earthmen who were enjoying the rest of the crew. As for me, all of them are off limits, because if I did, Labna would know."

"How about mental stability?"

"It seems pretty good. They have a keen sense of smell. So when there were men present for the first time in such a long time as they describe, there was some, uh, tension. But they handled that. If they can handle that, hey, bombing a comet with 60 megaton nuclear weapons ought to be a piece of cake!"

"What do you think of the *Neanderthal Return*?"

"The spaceship? It got them here. But there is nothing on that ship that is beyond our grasp if we make space exploration our Number One Priority. You know about Nikola Tesla? Neil Peace believes the Creation women went in directions Tesla started to go."

"I've heard that from my own people. No chance that they might try to take control of the nuclear weapons and use them against us or threaten us with them?"

"What for? All they have to do is float away in their spaceship and let the comet do the damage, if that is what they wish. They want to move the comet and be our friends. If we Earthlings are just as competent, disciplined, and emotionally stable as they are, then we can move the comet."

"Thank you, Mohammed Abbas. Good luck with your wife."

The women met in Conference Room One. Metrola had pilot duty. She participated in the proceedings through her headset. We Earthlings weren't allowed to attend. We sat around the Viewing Lounge making small talk and cracking jokes to hide our nervousness. While we could not imagine the women deciding not to participate in Operation Rainbow, we knew there were skeptics. We worried about the antagonism between Helga and Captain Trviea.

"This is the President of the United States calling the *Neanderthal Return*. Do you copy?"

"Yes, we copy, this is Neil Peace. You're on speakerphone in the Viewing Lounge. We're looking down upon South America. I think we're looking at Buenos Aires."

"Yes, I see. You're on speakerphone here, we're in Moscow, at the building where Boris Yeltsin held out against the attempted coup."

"This is Boris Korsakov, hello Neil Peace."

"Hello President Korsakov. My compliments on the nuclear tests. At least we have the bombs for this mission."

"This is Mohammed Abbas. Nice to talk to you again, Neil!"

"Thanks, Mohammed, nice to hear from you. Everyone up here feels that way, isn't that right people?"

"That's right!" "We're doing great, Mohammed!" "Allah *akbar*!"

"I am the German ambassador to Russia. May I speak to Fred Graf?"

"Fred, you wanna speak to your ambassador?"

"*Ja*, sure." Fred came up to the microphone. Even though we were in low gravity, it was still remarkable how the Healing Factor has enabled him to resume his duties with the Science and Humanities Channel. They were filming us in the lounge. Fred and his ambassador spoke in German. "*Guten tag, mien* Ambassador."

"*Guten tag*, Fred Graf. How is your leg?"

"I am healing up great. The pain is now gone, I can use the leg, but it will be a while before I have full strength in the muscle. Is it true that Metrola and Monoloa gave you the formula for Healing Factor?"

"*Ja*, it is true. The Russians are working on the translation right now. The American President faxed his copy around the world and posted it on the Internet. Will you be on the ship for Operation Rainbow?"

"I don't know. First, the women have to decide to participate in Operation Rainbow. Then they have to decide how many of us from the cable channel are needed to film and document this mission. I may be sent down because I was shot."

"You may be sent down because every trauma physician on Earth wants to look at you. The Americans at George Washington Hospital are thoroughly impressed at the progress Lucinda made, Askelion admitted that she added Healing Factor to the Neanderthal blood she brought down. I'm glad to hear that you are healing up well. All of Germany is proud of you."

"*Danke*, Ambassador."

"This is the American President." He said it in English. "May I speak with Cuc Nguyen?"

"Right here, Mr. President."

"You are still a federal employee on the CDC payroll. Have you seen any possible sign of the Virus on the *Neanderthal Return*? The one that killed their men?"

"There's no sign the Virus is on board, not even as a specimen in a jar. It's true the Virus can survive a long time in a cyst, but there are enzymes they use to kill any such Viruses. Everything on the ship has been so treated. The Virus needs Y chromosomes to replicate. If a woman is pregnant with a male child, the Virus could kill her as well as the child. But absent such a source of Y chromosomes, the Virus cannot replicate and is soon outnumbered and destroyed by the woman's antibodies. In a man the Virus can keep ahead of and overwhelm the antibodies."

"Does Askelion Lamakian believe we Cro-Magnon men are immune to this Virus?"

"In the Medical computer files they keep the DNA sequence of the Virus and the Neanderthal Y chromosome it needs to replicate. After determining the DNA sequence of Y chromosomes from Neil and the other men on this ship, Askelion and Meddi are now positive that the Virus cannot replicate with Cro-Magnon Y chromosomes. I've looked at the evidence myself, and I'm inclined to agree with them."

"Why do they think the Virus is engineered?"

"The epidemic occurred in Twenty Four Eleven Five and Six. Lamoan Reducker's expedition took place from Twenty Three Eighty Six through Twenty Three Eighty Nine. About 180 Creation years or 245 Earth years between the Reducker Expedition and the Virus Holocaust. The Virus was dormant in cysts when Neanderthal men were exposed to it. It survived within them as a benign parasite. Over that many years it spread to the entire male population of Creation. A certain number of replications turns on a recessive gene and the Virus eats the brain of its host, killing him within days. Why would a natural virus evolve a gene that 'counts' with each replication? That's a characteristic of an engineered Virus."

"Like a DO loop in computer software. A Cro-Magnon version of this Virus could exist."

"Yeah. One of our concerns was with our archeology. With all of the tombs we have dug into, did we ever expose ourselves to a Cro-Magnon version of this Virus? That's the reason we tested people in Algeria. We all turned up negative. The Virus is thought to have been planted in a plastic bag of brown powder at the Information Repository that someone would be tempted to open. So we checked the similar bags found in Afenor Cave. Then we checked Afenor's body for Viruses in cysts and for evidence that he died of the Virus. We found none."

"Exactly how could you tell?"

"When a Neanderthal man dies with the Virus, it cocoons itself into a cyst. That's why they cremated the bodies, contrary to tradition. There were no Viruses in cysts in Afenor's body. When we were done, Askelion and Meddi said a prayer for him."

"No Virus on Earth that we know of. Are the women meeting now?"

"Yes they are." I confirmed. "They went in a few minutes ago."

"Is there anything we can do now?"

"Not until they come out to announce their decision. It's like when a jury deliberates."

Helga started the meeting. "First the invocation. Trviea, would you like to say the invocation?"

"Why should I? You took me down, I am no longer Captain. You say the invocation, you wanted command, you've got it."

"Captain, we have to work together, whatever we decide to do. Very well, I will lead the invocation. Unless any of the Atheists object?"

"No, I don't object." "Me neither."

"Metrola, do you object to an invocation?"

"No, go ahead, Helga." responded the electronic voice.

Helga lead the prayer. "Great Holy Spirit, we thank you for our lives, for our food, water, and oxygen, and for our good fortune so far. We thank you for the *beeyons* of women who helped build this, our first interstellar spaceship. Now there is a comet on a collision course with Earth. If it hits, terrible damage and loss of life will result. We meet here to decide what to do. Please grant us the wisdom to make a good decision, for good and decent reasons, and the courage and cooperation to carry it out."

Nesla Teslakian stood up to take the floor. "Before I begin my statement of reasons against our participation in Operation Rainbow, I believe we need to resolve the differences between Trviea Harsradich and Helga Trvlakian."

"Yes, I agree." added Metrola's electronic voice. "A feud between two of our best people can be fatal for all of us."

"Trviea," Helga addressed the Captain she deposed, "if we vote to participate in Operation

Rainbow, we will need a Captain who can make decisions and give orders, orders that we can have faith in. You know a lot of different things to qualify as Captain: you can pilot the ship, the Shuttle, your knowledge of physics and engineering, fusion reactor and its control, you have all that. But on each of these things, you are not as talented as at least one other crew member. Your talent is that you know ALL of these things. Since we propose to accept nuclear explosives ON our ship, it is comforting to know that you have led nuclear tests. Most important, you have the ability to make good decisions in a short time and under pressure. THAT is what we need, and if you accept command, I will follow your orders."

Trviea turned and faced the crowd, tried to read the faces. "Will all of you follow my orders?"

There was some murmuring and nodding of heads. "We have to vote you back in as Captain." declared Lucinda. "I did not participate in relieving you of command. So I hope you can trust me when I say this. Our orders on this mission were few and very simple: Travel to the Earth Solar System. Observe the Planet from a safe distance until we have a better view of current politics. Then decide on a plan to obtain an adult man from the Planet. Carry out the plan. BUT, and this was the big one: AVOID war with Earth at all costs. They left the specifics up to us. Technically, Trviea was obeying the orders. We had obtained a man and determined that he is healthy and not carrying any contagious diseases. But he was very angry with being kidnapped. Earth television and radio broadcasts indicated that we weren't invisible in our Shuttle. We could not be sure that the American government would not determine exactly what happened to Neil Peace."

Lucinda let it sink in for a moment. "Trviea knows Earth politics, culture, law, technology, and war capability. But Helga knew these things better than any of us. That is why the Atlantis Council gave her the extraordinary power of relieving the Captain of command if she determined that we were risking war with Earth or any Earth nation. I now believe that Helga was right in her analysis that if the Americans, their military and science establishment, determined that we actually INVADED their territory and KIDNAPPED an American citizen, we could have war. By taking over the ship and freeing Neil Peace and finding out what he believed was needed to resolve the situation, Helga acted properly and within her responsibility. Now the situation is completely different, Trviea can become Captain again without risking war. Earth will be grateful if we succeed with Operation Rainbow."

Trviea stood there, stone faced. Thinking. Helga came close and whispered "Come on, Trviea, please." Trviea became alarmed at the close distance between their two faces, their two sets of teeth. She angrily opened her mouth and made ready for a bite fight. Helga responded and the two lionesses faced each other.

"Mother!" screamed Sorby. "Helga, please!" She feared her mother's death more than her mother, who could ill afford to look like a coward. "This is not necessary!"

"I think we should chain them together by the neck with a two *pote* chain." suggested Wlmsda Gtslakian. "The one left alive can be patched up by Medical and be our Captain."

"Why only two *potes* in length, Wlmsda?" asked Trviea. "The tradition calls for six *potes*, a *chmfat*, and by the waist, not the neck."

"To keep you two from licking each other."

Everyone except Sorby broke up in raucous laughter at Wlmsda's filthy remark. Helga and Trviea each smiled, they could not help themselves. Helga stepped away from Trviea and stood straight, her feet 18 inches apart. She put her hands behind her back and lifted her chin up, appearing to look at the ceiling. "I won't fight you, Captain. You may kill me if you like."

"Trvlakian, this is completely unnecessary." protested an exasperated Trviea.

"Captain, if we don't trust each other, the Earthlings cannot trust us, we cannot trust them. We have to trust them. If they were to deliberately detonate a bomb in Bay Number Four, well, it is no different than what we need to demonstrate now."

"Go ahead, Trviea." urged Monoloa.

"Mother! Helga! Please!"

Trviea sighed. Took a deep breath. Somebody handed her a pair of wrist cuffs, heavily built to withstand Neanderthal strength. She bound Helga's wrists behind her back and stood at her side. She firmly gripped the back of Helga's neck with her left hand. She placed her teeth on Helga's throat, around the windpipe, firmly against the skin. She could rip Helga's windpipe out of her neck, no one could stop her. She placed her free hand between Helga's breasts. The heart was pounding. Good! She wasn't quite sure. Girl's got courage, but she's not crazy. It still matters to her whether she lives or dies.

After a minute of breathing through her nose, Trviea released Helga's throat and kissed the teeth marks left in the skin. The skin was not broken, the marks soon disappeared. She unlocked Helga's wrists and handed the cuffs to her. "Okay, Helga, your turn. You may kill me if you like." With that Trviea stood straight with her feet 18 inches apart, her hands behind her back, and her chin lifted up.

As Helga bound Trviea's wrists, Sorby declared through her clinched teeth: "Yes, Helga, you may kill her if you want, but then I'll kill you!"

"Sorby, this is a free choice thing." reminded Contrviea as she held Sorby back. "If Helga chooses to kill your mother, we will have to strap you down. We may have to leave you on Earth."

Helga performed the ceremony and then released Trviea's throat and kissed the teeth marks. After removing the wrist cuffs, the two women sat down. They both looked extremely tired. Their feud was ended.

"Are you all right, Sorby?"

"Yes, I'll be fine." The relieved Sorby composed herself. She patted her mother on the shoulder. "I think my mother and Helga will be fine. We're still friends, aren't we, Helga?"

"Of course we are, Sorby. Nesla, you may begin."

"Thank you. Our orders for this mission do not include intervention to prevent a natural disaster. To help the Earth Cro-Magnons deflect the comet is a major departure from our mission. Our orders grant us the freedom to make such a departure, but it is to be done with an informed and free vote by the entire crew. We must keep in mind that we are responsible for this ship and to our people back home."

Nesla paused. "It is my solemn duty to present the reasons against participating in this venture. This does not mean that I have any malice or racial hate toward the Cro-Magnons, I don't. But the Cro-Magnons have demonstrated considerable racial hatred toward each other. The Nazi Holocaust and the Rwandan mass murders are two examples of this. We must consider this, for we are not only of a different Race, but perhaps of a different SPECIES. There are also examples of mass murder not motivated by racial hatred: the deliberate famine in the Soviet Union during Stalin's dictatorship and the terror perpetrated by the Khmer Rouge in Cambodia."

She let it sink in. "Aside from mass murder, there are many examples of one Cro-Magnon race or ethnic group moving into the territory of another race or ethnic group. The native group is overwhelmed by larger numbers, superior technology, or both. This happened in North and South America, Australia, New Zealand, and Hawaii. English and Spanish supersede the native languages. The Arab conquests imposed Arabic language and Islam upon Northern Africa, and even into Spain. The Chinese have more recently conquered Tibet. The Japanese and the

Germans tried wars of conquest in which they were defeated, in part because they did not have the numbers."

She continued. "Now consider the situation with numbers. Today, there are more than an *enbeeyon* of Cro-Magnon people alive on Earth. While there were once Neanderthal people living there, people like us, there are none today. They are now beginning to recognize themselves as one Race, the variations of skin color and eye shape to be superficial. Differences in language, culture, and religion are the product of the imagination and persuasion of *beeyons* of people. There is a sameness in some things around the entire Earth. The Metric System, counterbalanced by a commonly defined inch. English seems to be spoken almost everywhere. Movies, books, and manufactured products are now sold to worldwide markets. While this seems good, there is also widespread poverty and starvation from the incredible population growth that continues unabated. Overpopulation in Europe drove the settlement of white people in the American continents and Australia. Many of these same places now see large numbers of people immigrating from the nations of Asia and Africa, driven by population pressure. Overpopulation can and will make the Cro-Magnon desperate."

She paused to let that sink in. "They now know that there is another Planet very much like Earth, stocked with Earth life forms including us. They now know it is possible to build a spaceship that can travel between our two Planets. And they know that while there are an *enbeeyon* of them, there are only a dozen and six *beeyons* of us left alive, all of us women, we cannot have children. Even if we can use the sperm we have obtained to start having children, we will be no match for an intensive Cro-Magnon colonization program. We will eventually be a minority on our own Planet. Overwhelmed like the Hawaiians, the Native Americans, and the Australian aborigines."

"We have the laser cannons." commented Trviea.

"Yes, that is true, but any weapons system can be overcome. Our lack of numbers can leave the laser cannons unwomanned, and therefore inoperable. We must consider the risk to our ship and to ourselves. We have the courage to risk our lives, but because we have not been able to have children, there are three dozen and eleven fewer of us permanently if we die. More important, we now have a precious load of sperm to take back to Creation. All we have to do to complete our mission is go home, and maybe, just maybe, we start having children again. This won't happen if we lose the ship."

"Thank you, Nesla." praised Trviea. "We all know the particulars and risks of the proposed Operation Rainbow. If we allow nuclear bombs to be placed on board our ship, then we are in the same position of trust that Helga put herself in with respect to me. Let a detonation code be transmitted, or an accidental explosion, and we are suddenly dead. I believe the probability of an accidental explosion of a nuclear bomb is very low. It is the liquid fuel rockets bouncing in and out of the Four Bay that is more of a risk. An explosion and fire there would end the mission and possibly destroy the ship. Then if we get past that possibility, we need to get very close, as close as a few *hekt* of *kepfats*, to this very large comet."

"We could be destroyed BEFORE sending the missiles to bomb the comet." added Nesla. "I understand that Anatoly Donovon has placed each of his old Halloween bombs into what he calls a Penetration Vehicle. This is to allow it to get into the hole left by the small yield American bomb. It turns out that he wanted to make the heavy metal shell out of uranium with lithium deuteride-tritide packed inside with the bomb. We may get 120 megatons of yield that way. Possibly move the comet in one shot, the ideal result. But it also has risks for this ship. A *chmfat* sized piece of comet would come out of there extremely fast, could we dodge it? Yes, we can turn tail so the heavy structure and light exhaust can help protect us from impacts. But that is where our drive is. Not good to be drifting in free fall *beeyons* of *kepfats* from Earth and more than one and 9/12 *tibeeyons* of *kepfats* from Creation."

"So there is a substantial risk to this mission." concluded Trviea. "It is also possible that without us, the Earthlings can still place their nuclear weapons on this comet as it comes in and either reduce the damage it does to their Planet, or even deflect it to a complete miss on their own. Helga, it is your turn. Are you all right?"

"I am fine, Trviea. We did not kill each other, we can work together again." Helga hugged Sorby and went to the front of the room. "I will not minimize the risks to our ship, our mission, and our lives, of this proposed Operation Rainbow. But if we do not do this, the descendants of the few Earth people who survive will remember that we stood by in our splendid spaceship and did nothing. So will OUR descendants should we succeed in having children, with the sperm we have already been GIVEN by the Cro-Magnon men we have invited on board our ship."

She let that sink in. "I will not minimize the numerous cruel and terrible things that Cro-Magnons have done to each other. But there is one very simple reason for us doing this. After I hit the home run off of the President, we sat down to watch the game. Children, *hekts* of CHILDREN came up to us asking for autographs. We saw them sitting in the laps of their parents. For all of the evil in this world, even with a Comet Wormwood on the way to destroy everything, everyone was there to have a good time, to enjoy their families and their friends. Everyone was very nice to us. And it was fun! The Seventh Inning Stretch was fun. Everyone knew the words to the song and sang it. They were glad to be in the ballpark with their friends and their children, and they were glad to have US there as well. We stand by and let these people die, we would be as evil as the worst of both Races. We have to give it a try."

"Is that all, Helga?" asked Trviea.

"That is all, Trviea."

"All right," announced Lucinda, "let us pass out the ballots and vote. It is a secret ballot, mark them and seal them. I will carry this box to Metrola to receive her ballot, then I'll come back here to receive your ballots, and I will vote and place my ballot as well. We will mix the ballots so we cannot identify who cast which vote. Then we will count them." They did as directed.

After Lucinda collected the ballots, she mixed and counted them. "Three dozen and eleven. Now we open them and count the votes. This first one is, Yes." Each ballot was marked Yes. "And this is the last one, it is, Yes. That is it, three dozen and eleven Yes, zero No. Operation Rainbow is a go."

Monoloa brought out a bottle of Stolichnaya vodka. "Let us pass out the cups and have a drink. We are going to need it."

"We need a Captain." announced Helga. "Trviea, are you willing?"

"No more mutinies?"

"No more relieving you of command, working together to bomb the comet is not likely to risk a war with Earth."

"In that case, I will accept command if you all consent."

"Everyone agrees to Trviea being Captain?"

Everyone declared their desire for Trviea Harsradich to be Captain.

"Very well. I accept command of the *Neanderthal Return*." announced Captain Harsradich. "Monoloa, please pour everyone each a *dollop* of vodka. Except Metrola, she's driving the ship." Laughter. Soon, every woman had a small glass of vodka. "To the success of Operation Rainbow!"

Chapter Thirty Three

The women came into the lounge led by Trviea Harsradich. Monoloa brought a half full bottle of Stolichnaya vodka. They gave little glasses to all of us and Monoloa filled them. "So, what did you girls decide?" I asked.

"First, let me give you a big hug, Neil!" I let Lucinda squeeze me almost half to death and gave her an affectionate kiss. "Thank you. We all decided that, considering what's at stake, we just could not afford to take the risk."

"You could not take the risk to your ship?" asked Mary Ellen Martin, a camera grip with the Science and Humanities Channel. A fundamentalist Christian from the Bible Belt, she is offended by homosexuality. She could tell that much of the touchy-feelyness of the Neanderthal women is not platonic. But she remembered the teachings of Christ. Love thy neighbor and judge not lest ye be judged. And to not be rude to a host in her house. She was polite but standoffish, and did not know these women well enough to read their moods the way I could.

"Oh no. Sorry Mary Ellen." apologized Lucinda. "I meant we could not take the chance of NOT going after this comet. When we were down on Earth, we met thousands of children. The women up here spoke with children, often in school classrooms, talking to them the way the Space Shuttle astronauts talk to them. There are no children on our Planet and there haven't been since Sorby grew up. No way could we allow that comet to crash into Earth and kill all of those children without at least trying this insane plan to move it into a different orbit. The vote was unanimous."

We whooped, shouted, clapped our hands! Since the radio was on connecting us with the Russian White House in Moscow, there was cheering there. The news spread around the Earth at 186,000 miles per second. "Uh, Monoloa, how much of that vodka did you guys drink?"

"Oh. I believe this is our third bottle."

"Third liter. 46 women, not too bad. We Earthlings had better help you drink it. Thank you, President Korsakov!"

"You're welcome." came his voice through the radio. Then he spoke in Russian. "Monoloa, can you hear me?"

"I hear you loud and clear, Mr. President."

"Good. Do you have a Captain?"

"*Da*! Trviea Harsradich is now our Captain!"

Helga then repeated that declaration in English while wrapping her arm around Trviea's shoulders. She drank a shot of vodka from a glass held by Trviea while Trviea drank from Helga's glass. Then Trviea gave a command in Atlantean. "Helga, I order that we kiss and make up!"

"Thought you would never ask." Their kiss was too affectionate for Mary Ellen's comfort, but she held her tongue, respecting their foreign customs.

I came up to Mary Ellen. "How you feeling, Mary?"

"I'm glad we're going out to bomb the comet." she said judiciously. "But perhaps the Cro-Magnon women to ride this ship ought to be people like Martina Navratolova, k. d. lang, and Ellen Degeneres."

"Now be nice, Mary. Most of them are naturally straight. Just like most of us. But the Virus

285

Holocaust was an extraordinary event which put them in an extraordinary situation. Imagine if you were stuck on their Planet with no men. Forever! If Jesus can defend the adulteress, surely you can defend the lesbian."

"I can forgive them. I can love them. Christians love the sinner and hate the sin. Jesus told the adulteress to go and sin no more. But these women do not consider gay sex to be a sin and will not give it up even now that men are available. Men who act like bull moose during the rut."

I laughed. "They are beautiful. It was impossible for me to stay angry with them."

"I'll bet. But I have been a bit lonely. How can a pudgy Cro-Magnon Christian girl like me compete with tall, muscular, Neanderthal, Pagan, bisexual, AMAZONS? Even if I were gay too? Look at Helga. She is the most beautiful woman I have ever seen in my life."

"She is a babe."

"But look at me, Neil. I carry twenty pounds too many and it ain't muscle. Even if I lose the weight, which would require a permanent change in my eating habits, which probably wouldn't work anyway because it's a set point thing. Even with that, my face is not Julia Roberts'. And these women never worry about this kind of thing."

"Well, I guess we should be glad they're willing to participate in Operation Rainbow. You have to admire their courage. They came here, flying through trillions of miles of vacuum, survival dependent upon a machine. They do not risk their lives needlessly, because they are painfully aware they cannot replace themselves. Which is why they want the sperm. But they will put themselves at risk when it is necessary. They've had their Apollo 1 fires, their Soyuz 1 and 11 disasters, and their *Challenger* explosions. Look at this plaque on the wall. I know you cannot read the writing, it's in Atlantean, but you can tell it's a list of names. They died in rockets and spacecraft. All this they were willing to do because they knew that there was another human Race, with men, and the possibility that we could help them have children. And now they're willing to risk their ship and their lives to plant a huge nuclear bomb on a comet to deflect it. To save US. They couldn't make any other decision. I think we can forgive them their sexuality, and toast their courage and compassion. You don't have a problem with drinking vodka, do you?"

"No, of course not." She smiled and accepted a small glass of Stolichnaya.

"To the success of Operation Rainbow!"

"Neil!"

"Hi, Helga! This is Mary Ellen Martin. Mary Ellen, this is Helga Trvlakian."

"Pleased to meet you." Mary Ellen politely greeted. She accepted Helga's two handed Atlantean handshake.

"Neil, it has been too long." Helga opened her arms and I gave her a hug. I'm still getting used to the incredible strength of these women!

"Will you give me the same kiss you gave your Captain? I thought you two hated each other."

"New mission, Neil. That old stuff is behind us. I'll give you the kiss and much more!"

"Sounds wonderful, but for now, the kiss."

After we kissed, Mary Ellen blushed with a sheepish smile. "Damn you, Helga! Plain Jane girls like me just cannot compete with glamour blondes like you!"

"Actually, Mary, you can. You are a very nice girl with strong religious beliefs and sound values. With the better class of men, that is more attractive in a woman than physical beauty. But you are physically beautiful in your own way."

"Are you just flattering me for the same reason some men flatter me?"

"Mary, I will not ask you to violate your principles. I will insist that you stop selling yourself short! You have what we desperately want and do not have. The opportunity to find a man with whom you can make a lifetime commitment, and with whom you can raise children. Thank the Lord for that every day. Then promise the Lord that you will do everything in your power to help us keep it that way and then live life to the fullest until you find a man. When you do, then give him your commitment and be the best wife and mother that you know you can be."

"Your religion. Is the Great Holy Spirit, is He God?"

"He may be. I don't know. We believe He works in mysterious ways too. Anyway, we believe that He gave us the Twelve Gifts. The Gift of Life. The Gift of Reason. The Gift of Mystery. The Gift of Hope. The Gift of Beauty. The Gift of Tenacity. I think that is the English word that best defines it, Tenacity. We never give up, we die hard. The Gift of Strength. The Gift of Genius. The Gift of Language and Numbers. The Gift of Hard Work. Anything worthwhile requires it. The Gift of Time. We do not believe that time will ever come to an end, there will always be a future. What it will be is up to us. And then there is the Gift that makes it all worthwhile. The Gift of Love."

"And you believe that these Twelve Gifts must be used wisely?"

"Yes. We believe that each of these Gifts can be used for good or for evil. It is our choice. But it is a choice we must make with care and consideration, each and every day we live."

"And now you plan to use these Twelve Gifts to move the comet?"

"We have to. All of us. The Great Holy Spirit, or God, He gave us the comet. He also gave us each other. He gave us two different types of human being. A multitude of languages. He gave us radio, spacecraft, electricity, rockets, fusion reactors, magnetic drive engines, and very large yield nuclear bombs. Actually He gave us the talented people who invented and built these things and the materials from which they are made. He gave us a challenge and a job to do. So lets do it."

"Neil, Mary Ellen, your President wants to talk to the American citizens on this ship."

"Okay, we will be right over. One more drink, to Operation Rainbow!"

"Here, Here!"

We went over to the microphone and joined Chuck Carter, Cuc Nguyen and the three other American employees of the Science and Humanities Channel who came up from Algeria. "We're all here, Mr. President."

"Excellent, how are you all doing?"

"We're all doing great!" exclaimed Juanita Asturias. "We're ready for Operation Rainbow!"

"Glad to hear that. We'll soon have more rocket launches per day than ever before. From Cape Canaveral, Kourou in French Guiana, Baikonur and the new Cosmodrome at Svobodny in the Amur Oblast. The Shuttle *Columbia* is now rolling out to the launch pad carrying two Aries missiles. Each missile consists of a Minuteman I upper stage and a B61-12 warhead with a yield of 100 kilotons."

"B61-12? I thought we're using a B61-11."

"Sandia rolled the part number. They made a few design changes for this mission. The missile is 44 inches in diameter and about 25 feet long. Each is in a packing crate designed for use with the Canadian Arm to transfer it over to the *Neanderthal Return*. There will also be a six foot wide box containing the equipment to remote control the missiles. We will be sending four United States Air Force officers to come over to the *Neanderthal Return*. They will be the Missile Crew. I'm sure you'll like General Morton Fairchild, the commander of the Missile Crew for Operation Rainbow. I want you all to give 'em your full cooperation and to help 'em learn to get along with the Creation women."

"I'm sure we can do that." I responded cheerfully.

Captain Harsradich broke in. "This sounds like a feasible plan to me. I was thinking of having Neil put on a pressure suit and have him help transfer the missiles and equipment. His Atlantean is really coming along, he can quickly translate to facilitate communication during the Payload Transfer. We also trust him, he tells us the truth. Uh, Mary Ellen, would you like to put on a pressure suit so you can go out into Bay Number Four to film the Payload Transfer for your employer?"

"Well, uh, I uh, YES! I would like to do that!"

"Excellent! I'm going to ask Sorby and Wlmsda Hotlund to put on pressure suits and train you in the Bay before *Columbia* is ready to launch. Metrola will run the controls for the Bay, I think, uh, Marla Syferkrip, she can help you into the suits. We have a lot of work to do, so we better get started soon."

"All right, we'll work this out." I declared. "Mr. President, we need the dimensions, mass and center of mass of the missiles in their present configuration in their packing crates. You told me that they are 44 inches in diameter and about 25 feet long, but we need the crate dimensions. Then we can go to Contrviea's Machine Shop and make brackets and straps to secure the missiles as packaged into place. When we are out near the comet, our Missile Crew can work out the details of physically removing them from the Weapons Bay and sending them into the comet."

"Yes, that's important information. I can tell you that the packing crates are 25 feet and a couple of inches long, and four feet by four feet. There is a payload grapple on the end of each for grasping with the Canadian Arm and there are two eyebolts on the side two feet from each end for hooking with your tether cables. The total mass of each missile in its packing crate is about 24,000 pounds. The box of equipment is six feet in all three dimensions, the NASA folks are calling it the cubic fathom box. It has a mass of about 3,000 pounds. It too has a payload grapple and an eyebolt. The Space Shuttle has a lift capacity of 60,000 pounds so 51,000 pounds plus four Air Force personnel in spacesuits is just about a full load for *Columbia*."

"Thank you, Mr. President, this information is useful." I remembered as an engineer that we need something more than just verbal descriptions. "Could you radio up drawings of these packing crates with the information we need?"

"Consider it done, Mr. Peace."

After the President signed off, Captain Trviea called over the language specialists in her language. "Helga, Lchnsda, Andemona, Monoloa! You have an assignment starting right now!" The four came over to receive their orders. "I want you to prepare and place English and Russian placards for every safety and emergency sign and label on this ship. I want to see 'Oxygen' in all three languages everywhere we see that word written now. The fire equipment, the medical first aid equipment, strap down, Free Fall procedures, depressurization, excess carbon dioxide, everything like that. When you are done with that prepare pamphlets in those languages to hand out to our visiting Earthlings. Then you are to prepare lesson plans and get ready to teach classes and have them practice emergency procedures. If we are going to get close to that comet, then EVERYONE on board had better be ready to strap down, fight fires, give first aid, and everything else like that. The leader of the American group, General Fairchild, may be a big shot in Washington, D.C. but on THIS ship, he learns the Atlantean words for 'Strap Down' (*Tix jord*) and 'Free Fall' (*Bly jore*), and he learns to follow those orders. I also want them to be able to read Creation Base Twelve numerals and to know our weights and measures. And we need to make sure they at least know basic astronautics."

Each of the four women acknowledged and understood Trviea's orders.

"Good, get to it. Report back to me when you are done with the placards and have your lesson plans drawn up."

Sorby Mishlakian and Wlmsda Hotlund, the 'Wilma' I met when I was first kidnapped, gave me and Mary Ellen Martin a crash course in spacewalking. Contrviea had already adapted pressure suits to fit us, we put them on. Marla Syferkrip helped us. We were in Bay Number Four.

"Getting enough air, Neil?" asked Marla after I was in my suit.

I took a deep breath. The air had a slight odor of metal and hard plastic, which was to be expected. But there was plenty of it. "Yes I am."

"Mary?"

She took a deep breath. "Yes, me too."

"Either of you woozy?" Sorby needed to make sure.

"No." We both answered.

"Can you think clearly?"

I performed a simple calculation in my head. Half mile is 880 yards. High school track before they metrifornicated it. The new law should change it back. Full mile is 880 fathoms. Sixteen miles, the estimated depth of the ice covered ocean on Europa, that would be, uh, 8,800 fathoms plus, uh, 5,280 fathoms, oh, 13, no, 14,080 fathoms. "Yes, I can think clearly."

"Mary?"

"Yes, I can think clearly."

"Good. Do you taste a faint sour odor and a sour taste?"

"No." They had us each breathe a sample of air loaded with carbon dioxide so we could learn what it smells, tastes, and feels like. It's the fumes from dry ice, only warmer. It was just a one breath exposure.

Then Marla instructed us. "If you have too much carbon dioxide, it will replace the oxygen in your blood, and your thinking will not work right. That is the first symptom, but there is no symptom that is an obvious warning of too much carbon dioxide. Remember, you're not thinking very good. It's a little like carbon monoxide poisoning. If you do not have enough oxygen, you will feel tired. If your pressure is low, especially if it is sudden, your ears will pop and everything will start to hurt. If you pass out, which can happen with carbon dioxide, that is a BIG problem. Because we don't want that to be your first warning, there is a warning sound in your helmet if any of these things start to happen. It sounds like this," she pressed a button on my helmet.

A loud warble screamed in my ears for two *prelates*. Marla brought my left hand, encased in the pressure glove, surprisingly thin and flexible, up to a button. "You can test the alarm system by pushing this button. Go ahead."

I pushed the button. I was rewarded with two *prelates* of warbling. "Yes, it works."

"Good." She repeated this with Mary Ellen. "When you hear that sound without pushing this button, the first thing you do is check the digital readouts on the lower inside lip of your helmet. Can you read them?"

"Yes, I can." I answered.

"Yes, I see 'em" Mary Ellen answered. She and the other Earthlings have received instruction in Creation Base Twelve numbers.

"Good. On your left are two pressure readings. The upper display is outsuit pressure, the pressure outside your suit. The lower display is insuit pressure, the pressure inside your suit. This number is VERY important. What are your readings?"

"Both two zero." we each answered.

"Good. I'm glad you both can read Creation numerals. Two dozen *dollons* per square *tig-it*. About twelve pounds per square inch. It is designed to maintain two dozen *dollons*. But you will normally see the insuit pressure drop to one eleven and one ten. It is not a problem even if it drops to one zero. You feel like you are in the high mountains. A sudden drop, even within this range, will pop your ears and set off the alarm. You could even get a mild case of the bends. Below one zero, or further, below zero eight *dollons*, we can start to have real problems. To the immediate right of your pressure readings, is another digital display. What does it read?"

"About one." All we saw was the number one.

"That is your carbon dioxide reading. It is one *kechter* of carbon dioxide. It'll read one even if it's actually half of that. The air on Creation has about that much carbon dioxide as does the air on Earth. What you would call one hundred percent would be equivalent to a *kecht* of *kechters*."

"So a *kechter* is one seventeen twenty-eighth?" Mary Ellen asked.

"Exactly. You are fine as long as it does not read over four zero *kechters*. But if it exceeds that level, your ability to think will be compromised. At one zero zero *kechters*, you're in big trouble. It's just like the Apollo 13 astronauts when they were adapting the lithium hydroxide canisters. Speaking of such canisters, there are some built into the breathing apparatus of your suit. They are changed with every use. The way you tell if yours were not changed or if they are overloaded, your carbon dioxide reading will start to climb, 2 *kechters*, 3 *kechters*, 4 and so on. Your warning signal is programmed to sound if this number climbs too fast or if it reaches four zero. Can you read the third digital readout?"

"Yes. Two six."

"That is your oxygen reading. It is in *hekers*, or one forty fourths of the air. It is equivalent to about twenty or twenty one percent, the amount of oxygen in Creation and in Earth air. As long as you are getting air from the mother ship through this line, that will be your reading. But if you are cut off from the mother ship, or go on a spacewalk on your own air, this oxygen reading should climb to one zero zero or to the high eleventys. No nitrogen taking up space in your own air supply. Your insuit pressure will reduce to zero ten *dollons* to keep you from getting too much oxygen. You will have about four hours of oxygen on your own at normal breathing rate. All right, let's test your radios."

"Yes. This is Neil Peace, can anyone hear me?"

"This is *Neanderthal Return*, I can hear you, can you hear me?" asked Metrola.

"I read you loud and clear, Metrola."

"This is Mary Ellen Martin, I read you loud and clear, can you read me?"

"Yes, we can hear you."

"This is Sorby Mishlakian, I read you loud and clear, Neil, Mary Ellen, and Metrola, can you hear me?"

"Yes, I read you loud and clear." We all answered. "Wlmsda?" asked Metrola.

"Yes, I can hear you just fine." Wilma answered in Atlantean. "I can hear Sorby, Mary Ellen, Metrola, and Neil." And then we confirmed that we could hear her. Whenever Wilma or Betty put on a pressure suit, Captain Harsradich disabled the paralysis mechanism. But as they were still under discipline, she did not unlock and remove the collar. Instead, she connected it to the biosensors that are in every pressure suit.

"Excellent." commented Marla. "We will get out of this Bay and close the airlock. After we get out of here, Metrola will start the air pumps and your outsuit pressure will drop. The warning should sound if your insuit pressure also drops. But keep an eye on it anyway and let us know FAST if you see your insuit pressure drop. Good luck!"

Marla and the other two helpers exited the Bay and closed the air lock. Then we heard Metrola. "Nonsuited personnel are out of Bay Number Four. The airlock is closed and secured. Ready for vacuum?"

We all answered yes. "I am now removing air from the Bay." We heard air pump sounds and watched that the outsuit pressure reading drop. One eleven. One ten. It seemed to drop a *dollon* every few seconds. "How's your insuit pressure?"

"Fine." we all answered. The outsuit pressure fell past one zero. Twelve *dollons* per square *tig-it*. The last few *dollons* took longer, as would be expected. Then the outsuit reading was zero. My insuit pressure read two zero. I felt fine. Oh man! Being an astronaut takes courage! "Pressure in Bay Number Four is now zero. How are the four of you doing?" asked Metrola. I gave her the thumbs up and said I was fine. So did Mary Ellen. Sorby and Wilma each also said that they were fine. "All right. Pidonita, are you ready for a Free Fall Drill?"

"Yes I am." answered Pidonita from the Pilothouse. Then she called out on the ship's public address system in Atlantean. "Prepare for Free Fall Drill. Prepare for Free Fall Drill. Free Fall in two *linits*. Free Fall in two *linits*." We heard "*Bly jore!*" Atlantean for free fall. We have to match orbits to transfer equipment and personnel with Earth spaceships. That means shutting down the fusion reactor and becoming weightless. We waited. "Free Fall in one *linit*. Free Fall in one *linit*." The crew tied down everything that was loose to keep it from floating around during weightlessness. They took the opportunity to instruct the Earthlings on this procedure. We've done this twice before. When we sent the three over to the Shuttle *Atlantis* and again when we sent Monoloa over to *Mir*.

"*Bly jore.*" announced Pidonita. It was like being in an elevator that suddenly dropped. The floor of the Bay fell away from me and my stomach rose to my throat. There were magnets in my shoes and a thin steel plate in the floor.

"The magnets in your shoes exert only a few *dollons* of force." instructed Sorby, who demonstrated by walking around. Wilma, Mary Ellen, and I also walked around. Sorby then jumped off of the floor. She grabbed the ceiling with her hands and then let it go in such a manner that she floated in the middle of the Bay. "There are several things you can do if you are stuck in a position like this." Wilma walked over to where she floated and reached up and touched her. "Your buddy can come over and pull you down. You can float for a while and admire the scenery. Or you can do this." She operated a little joystick located just above her waistband. Little jets spurted out of her backpack thrusters and gently pushed her. "In your backpack is a canister of helium gas that is held at a very high pressure, several *gunds* per square *tig-it*. Helium is a lightweight atom that spits out very fast through the nozzles. It is inert, so it is safe to repressurize the Bay with air. This gives you a few *dollons* of thrust for the expenditure of only a few *keecoilons* of mass."

She maneuvered herself back into her floating position. "The other thing you can do is this," she pushed a button on a little panel attached to her line. The cable reel was located near the outer door of the Bay. It turned on and drew in Sorby's line. "The air line is made stiff enough that the cable reel does not pinch it. You can control the speed of the reel, and you can turn it off."

The line drew taut and drew Sorby toward the reel. She grabbed the line with her hand and thrust it upward, her body moved downward in reaction. The magnets in her shoes grabbed the floor and she shut off the cable reel. "The cable reels can also be operated by controllers at Metrola's station in case you are unconscious. There is another control panel on the reel itself. All right, Neil and Mary Ellen, let's practice all of these maneuvers in here, then we'll open the door and do some outside maneuvering."

We floated around inside the Bay, and we performed all of the maneuvers. There was appropriate emphasis on the emergency procedures but much of the time was spent on work procedures. Plenty of cables in the Bay that had latch hooks on the end. They could be hooked to D-rings on the waist band of the pressure suit to bring a person in. Or they could be hooked to cargo being transferred in. There was also a selection of nets and slings made of wire rope and fabric straps, all in bright colors so we can see them. A small plastic control panel, about three quarter inch by two and a half inches, tapered at the ends, was built into the cable a foot from the end. Another control panel was at the cable reel and another inside the ship. We performed several training drills.

After performing training drills inside the Bay, Metrola opened the door to space. We were on the night side of Earth. Wilma pretended to be a piece of cargo. She floated about two hundred feet outside the ship. We saw her in the candlepower cast by the ship's lights. I ran and leaped off the sill of the Bay to bring a cable and a sling assembly out to her. I wrapped the sling around her body, tightened the straps and then hooked the cable. I turned on the cable reel and drew Wilma into the cargo Bay.

Mary Ellen performed the same drill a little better than me. She laughed and shouted and exclaimed how much fun this is. We all agreed, but Sorby emphasized that this is serious work and that less than one *tig-it* from our skin is hard vacuum.

In another drill, Wilma pretended to be a distressed astronaut who has passed out.

"Wilma! Can you hear me! This is Neil calling Wilma Hotlund! Do you copy?"

"Neil! Mary Ellen! Sorby! I'm reading carbon dioxide at five eleven from her pressure suit! Her insuit pressure has dropped to eight *dollons*! I don't know, she should still have some response! She has heartbeat, but it's weak! Breathing is irregular! Get her in here! NOW!"

We could hear Wilma giggling as she floated 150 feet out in space at the end of a slack line. She had two dozen *dollons* of pressure, plenty of oxygen, and a normal CO_2 level. And here was Metrola describing her as half dead! But it is an important drill. Sorby ran over to Wilma's cable reel. "Cable reel is not working. Repeat! Cable reel is not working!" Sorby pretended to pull on Wilma's line. "Line is disconnected from Wlmsda! Neil, Mary Ellen, you have to get another line out to her and hook her!"

The line did not disconnect from Wilma. That would be too dangerous for a training drill. We just pretended it did. A spacewalker can be recovered if she gets away from the ship. If the ship can maneuver close enough, she could be brought in with a tether, either hooked to her waist rings or wrapped in a sling, and reeled in. "I've got a wire rope. I'm unlatching the cable reel. The line comes easily. Mary, get ready with the sling! I'm ready to jump!" I took a running start and leaped out of the Bay into space. I could see that I was going to miss Wilma by about ten feet. "I'm adjusting course of flight." A quick blast of helium out of my jet pack sent me toward Wilma.

I collided with her body with the impact of a football tackle. I wrapped my arm around her torso and grabbed a hold. Tension from my cable reel brought us to a halt. I saw that I could simply hook one of her waist rings. Sorby had quietly whispered to me before the lesson that we needed to include Mary Ellen as much as possible. She suggested this: "I can't get a hook on her waist ring! Mary, bring the sling, NOW!"

Mary Ellen hesitated just a second and then ran for the sill. She leaped. She tried to adjust her course with her helium jets but missed us by twenty feet. Her rope drew taut when she was fifty feet past us. "Don't worry about it, Mary!" reassured Sorby. "This is your first time. This happens in real emergencies with experienced spacewalkers. Just squirt a little helium, pull your joystick in the direction you want to go, like we showed you!"

"All right! Got it!" Mary Ellen brought her line in contact with us.

"Now use the cable reel to bring you in toward Wlmsda!" instructed Sorby. "That's good! Keep going!"

Mary Ellen drew herself in until she was with us. "I'm shutting off my cable reel."

"Good." I praised. "Now lets get this sling wrapped around Wilma, fast. How you doing, Wilma?"

"I'm fine. Just don't tickle me." Wilma was giggling while otherwise trying to play the part of a limp, unconscious body. Ironically, her punishment collar probably would offer a little extra protection in case of low pressure.

We got the sling wrapped around Wilma and hooked the cable to it. "I'm reeling her in!" called Mary Ellen as she pushed the button on the line. Immediately the cable reel whirred to life to pull Wilma in.

We each operated our cable reels by pushing the buttons on our lines. "I'm coming in!" we each declared.

Sorby was at Wilma's reel and turned off the motor when Wilma was within 30 feet. She caught her and then pulled in her other line. The one we pretended was broken. I shut off my cable reel when I was within 30 feet. I remembered high school football. 10 yards is 30 feet. I could still estimate distances that way. I landed and brought myself to a halt 20 feet inside the Bay. Mary Ellen did the same.

Wilma was still pretending to be limp. Sorby got her line pulled in. "Bay Door is clear for Emergency Closing and Pressurization."

"Emergency Closing and Pressurization commencing." called Metrola. A lot of this is being said in Atlantean. In an emergency you go with what you know. I glimpsed the view out the door before it slammed shut.

Wow! I have never seen Libra so clearly. Virgo with the bright star Spica. Door. It shut fast! 36 by 72 *potes*! Big door!

We ran over to where Wilma was floating limp while being held in place by Sorby. The outsuit pressure, heretofore zero, started to scroll. I could hear the 'Whoosh!' of blowing air through my feet. Sound travels through metal and other materials. It does not travel through vacuum. When the outsuit pressure passed five *dollons* I started to hear the sound of the air vents through the air itself.

"There is a one way valve built into these suits that will allow air in when the outsuit pressure exceeds the insuit pressure." commented Sorby. "A distressed spacewalker needs air and pressure as fast as possible."

When the outsuit pressure reached two dozen *dollons*, Sorby popped Wilma's helmet off. Then we popped our helmets off.

Wilma grinned and said in Atlantean, "I have bad news for you. I am not dead yet!"

"All right guys." declared Metrola. "Drill's over! Neil, Mary Ellen, you both performed well. But Neil, if you're actually bringing in a hurt astronaut, you don't waste time staring at the distant stars while the Bay Door closes."

"I'm sorry, Metrola. But Wilma's constant giggling took me out of the mood of thinking of this as a real emergency. The stars are beautiful up here on the night side of Earth."

"I understand. You'll get better with practice. And practice you shall have. *Columbia's* coming up soon. Then we have payloads coming up from French Guiana, Kazakhstan, and the new Cosmodrome in Amur Oblast. I understand the Russians have contracted the use of a Long March with the Chinese. And we have stops to make at *Mir* and the new Space Station. I also need you to ride with me on our Shuttle a few times. Ian works for the Science and Humanities Channel part of the time."

Pidonita's voice rang out in Atlantean on the public address. *"Jore put!"* It means "Commence acceleration!"

Chapter Thirty Four

RUSSIA-KAZAKHSTAN BORDER (Bishop News Service). Today at 9:35 a.m. local time, a heavily armed train escorted by Interior Ministry troops and MIG 29 jet fighters crossed the border into Kazakhstan after passing through Orsk. We have been following this train since it went through Vyatka, the former Kirov, several days ago. Officials are closed mouth on the question of whether this is the train carrying the Khrushchev era nuclear bombs of the type recently tested at the old Novaya Zemlya Test Range. Nor are they saying whether this train's destination is the Baikonur Cosmodrome.

Baikonur Cosmodrome is located 3 miles north of the Orenburg-Tashkent Railroad that runs along the Syr Darya River Valley. It was known in the West as Tyuratam for a nearby railroad town. The city where the space workers live was named Leninsk. Leninsk has been officially renamed Baikonur but the signs still say Leninsk. Leninsk is still generally closed to the public. The nearest public airport is at Kzyl-Orda. This train can reach the Cosmodrome by turning on to the Orenburg-Tashkent at the Kandagac Junction. After several hundred miles a short spur takes it into the spaceport.

We watched the progress of the train from our perch 200 miles up. "They sure are putting on a show about this train." Monoloa commented.

"Potemkin is a Russian name. All this show of military force and security. This big show of officials refusing to deny or confirm the presence of nuclear weapons on board the train. Ballyhoo press coverage, most likely orchestrated."

"You don't believe the big nukes are on that train?"

"Monoloa, you of all people should know about the Russians. You know exactly what the phrase 'Potemkin Village' means. I suspect the bombs were delivered by a shabby looking Antonov transport to the secret airport at Leninsk. They may even have been delivered by a different train, with a few cars hauling cotton or wheat as part of the camouflage. Or even by a truck down the highway."

I paused, and then went on. "I remember when the Bangor Submarine Base in my state was first opened and had some actual Trident submarines. Some general in the Pentagon watched the movie *Dr. Strangelove* one time too many. So there was this big fancy White Train that would roll across the United States and eventually arrive at the Bangor Base. The cars were painted shiny white, as if to withstand the flash of a nuclear explosion. It would be accompanied by visible military security and local cops called out to keep the protesters in line, or at least drag 'em off the tracks so the train can go by. It would follow an irregular schedule and take a different route every time with no announcement. And of course, the officials would not say what was in the train. It attracted protesters the way a turd attracts flies."

"But of course it didn't contain any actual nuclear warheads." Monoloa concluded.

"It might of. But I think the real bombs were delivered by more discreet means. With the Russians, I suspect they split the five bombs up to deliver them to Baikonur with five different conveyances. One of them might even be on this train."

"In the event of a crash, there would still be four bombs. I know they plan to deliver them to our ship on two different Energiya rockets, so we don't lose all five if one rocket explodes."

"*Columbia* is go for launch. T minus ten. Nine. Eight. Seven. We're go for main engine start. Five. Four. Three. We have main engine start. One. Lift-off! We have lift-off! *Columbia* is clear of the tower and on her way with the Missile Crew led by Air Force General Morton Fairchild and the first payload for Operation Rainbow. Two Aries missiles that each consist of a modified Minuteman I upper stage and a B61-12 warhead with a yield of 100 kilotons. A cubic fathom box of equipment is also strapped in *Columbia's* cargo bay. General Fairchild will direct his people and equipment over to Bay Number Four on the *Neanderthal Return*."

Contrviea, Wlmsda Hotlund, Wlmsda Gtslakian, Sorby, Nesla, and Marla were in Bay Number Four with me. Mary Ellen was also in the Bay in a pressure suit, she had a video camera to record the Payload Transfer. We were in our pressure suits and ready with the tether cables for bringing over the two Aries missiles and the cubic fathom box. We used four cable reels located just inside the bay at the corners. I was on the right side holding the hook ends of the two lines on my side.

Sorby stood ready on the other side of the Bay with her two tether cables. The other women were ready to deploy the catch net across the mouth of the Bay after we hook each box to the cables. Metrola was ready to operate the cable reels to draw it in.

NASA has used the Aries as a 'sounding rocket' in recent years. It delivers a payload of up to several thousand pounds into a suborbital trajectory. What that means is that the payload is delivered to an altitude of several hundred miles. The payload takes a reading of an astronomical object such as Comet Hale-Bopp or performs an experiment and then falls back to Earth where it is recovered. Such sounding rockets usually consisted of a Minuteman I upper stage on top of a first stage to give it extra boost. Such a package, including payload, would weigh as much as 35,000 pounds before lift-off.

In the weeks since the discovery of Comet Wormwood a lighter weight package was put together consisting of the Minuteman I upper stage, the B61-12 warhead and a remote control inertial guidance system. No first stage as in the NASA sounding rocket.

Metrola was at her station controlling the Bay air and its door. Pidonita was in the Pilothouse. "This is *Neanderthal Return*, Pidonita Hmlakian, pilot, calling *Columbia*. We can see you now, your cargo bay doors are open, you are looking good. Do you copy?" Pidonita's English was much better than before.

"This is *Columbia*, Brian Winthrop, commander, we copy. Pidonita, we read you loud and clear, your English is excellent. We can see your ship now. We have established orbit. We have opened the doors to the cargo bay. All systems are nominal. Laura Duncan is our mission specialist, she will be operating the remote manipulator arm." The official term for the Canadian Arm. "General Morton Fairchild, United States Air Force, is in command of the Missile Crew. Major Roy McKenna, Major Roslyn Easton, and Major Wilbur Davenport, all of the Air Force, will comprise the Missile Crew."

"We copy, *Columbia*. We now introduce the other personnel involved in this Payload Transfer."

"This is Trviea Harsradich, Captain of the *Neanderthal Return*, standing by in the Pilothouse."

"This is Metrola Mornuxler, at the controls for Bay Number Four. All systems are ready. Nonsuited personnel are now out of Bay Number Four, the airlock door is secure. Is everyone in Bay Four ready for vacuum?"

We all answered affirmatively and introduced ourselves for the benefit of *Columbia*.

Metrola got down to business. "I am now removing air from the Bay." We could hear the air pumps and we watched the outsuit pressure gauge drop.

Pidonita took the com. "We are closing on *Columbia*, to a distance of one *kepfat*, NOW. We are matching orbits with *Columbia*. *Columbia*, be advised, when we cut the fusion reactor and go to Free Fall, we will project our magnetic fields. We will use the interaction of our magnetic fields and the Earth's magnetic field to control and adjust our orbit during the Payload Transfer."

"We copy *Neanderthal Return*." responded Brian's voice. "Be advised that there is steel on board *Columbia*. *Columbia* is built with an aerospace type of structure, 7075 aluminum alloy ribs and spars tied together with steel fasteners. Our ship is just like *Atlantis* in basic design."

"Yes, I see, we did this once before, it did not seem to bother *Atlantis* too much that we projected magnetic fields. How many pounds of steel are we talking about?"

"Several hundred pounds total."

"I will take that into account. If we get too close, I can use the magnetic properties of your steel fasteners to push *Columbia* away to avoid a collision." Then Pidonita switched to Atlantean and used the ship's public address system. "Free Fall in two *linits*."

We tuned our ears to hear the words "*Bly jore!*"

As we prepared for Free Fall we watched the outsuit pressure fall to zero. "Bay Number Four is now in vacuum." announced Metrola. "Is everyone fine?"

"We're fine." we all answered. The status of our insuit pressures and levels of oxygen and carbon dioxide were also being transmitted to her station by little radios in our pressure suits. Meddi was with her monitoring our heartbeats, breathing rates and other vital statistics.

Sorby wanted last minute verification of her information from me. "The outer dimensions of each missile crate?"

"25 feet long, by four feet by four feet. That's in Base Ten and American feet. Two dozen and one *potes* should easily fit sideways through the six dozen *pote* wide opening of this Bay."

"It should. How much mass are we talking about?"

"Each Aries missile package has a mass of 24,000 pounds. The cubic fathom box contains 3,000 pounds of equipment to remote control the missiles. That's 51,000 pounds total for Payload Transfer."

"Six feet in all three dimensions." Sorby translated the specifications into Atlantean for her shipmates. "Each missile in its packing crate has a mass of about two dozen and two and a half *gunds*."

"Got that, Sorby." acknowledged Metrola. "We'll try to keep it to less then one *pote* per *prelate* when it hits the catch net. Got that ladies?"

They answered affirmatively. They had already been briefed on the dimensions and mass of each of the packages. In Free Fall, the women can wrestle the missile to its storage location and lash it down. 12 tons of mass is no weight in Free Fall. Momentum is the problem with large heavy objects in Free Fall. A person can be crushed if caught between a large flying mass and a wall.

Pidonita continued calling the Free Fall warning over the public address. Finally we heard her declare in Atlantean: "*Bly jore.*" She quickly repeated it in English. "Commencing Free Fall." The elevator fell away from my feet but the little magnets in my shoes kept me attached to the floor.

"All right everyone," addressed Metrola, "we are now opening the door to space." The door opened, and we saw *Columbia*, 200 feet away. It filled our view of space. I stood at the ready.

Sorby went to a position about fifty feet from the sill. I did likewise, we each held our cables. We crouched, ready to run, like competitors in a track meet. "We're ready for Payload Transfer." we both testified.

Pidonita called out in English. "*Neanderthal Return* is in position and ready for Payload Transfer. Does *Columbia* copy?"

"*Columbia* copies, *Neanderthal Return*." confirmed Shuttle commander Winthrop. "Laura?"

"I am ready for Payload Transfer, Brian, *Neanderthal Return*." confirmed Laura Duncan.

"Houston, *Columbia*. We are go for Payload Transfer." confirmed Brian.

"*Columbia, Neanderthal Return*, this is Houston, we copy. You are go for Payload Transfer."

"This is Harsradich, *Neanderthal Return* Captain. Metrola, Sorby, Neil, everyone, you may commence Payload Transfer."

Then we heard Metrola's voice. "On your mark, set, GO!"

We both sprinted for the sill and leaped into space carrying our cables. Metrola controlled the tension in our cable reels. We aimed for a point about twenty feet above the open cargo bay of the Shuttle. Metrola gently slowed us to a stop. We were next to each other at an arm's length distance. "We are in position twenty feet above the cargo bay." I declared. "Everything in the cargo bay looks good. Two missile crates, clamps holding them in place. The cubic fathom crate, also locked into place. Looks small in this 60 foot bay. I like the Leonardo da Vinci drawing on the fathom box." The famous drawing of the naked man with his outstretched arms inside the square and circle. The square formed the edge of the side of the box, so only the part of the circle inside the square fathom could be seen. "The Canadian Arm looks ready. Standing by for Payload Deployment. Laura, it's up to you."

"This is *Columbia*, Laura Duncan. Commencing payload deployment procedure now." The Canadian Arm grasped a payload grapple built into the cubic fathom box. "Cubic fathom box grapple is captured, releasing clamps." We saw the clamps suddenly release. "Lifting box." The box was lifted thirty feet from the bottom of the cargo bay.

"I'm maneuvering to place my hooks into the eyebolt." I brought myself to the box with my helium jets. I slipped both hooks on to the eyebolt. Sorby did the same. We checked to make sure our lines weren't tangled up with the payload lines.

"Eyebolt secure to all four lines from *Neanderthal Return*." announced Sorby.

"All right Laura, please lift and release the cubic fathom box." I requested.

"Lifting box to full extension above *Columbia* bay." Laura lifted the box until the Arm was fully extended. She released it. "Cubic fathom box is now free of *Columbia*."

Sorby and I maneuvered ourselves down and away from the payload box. Our lines went to the floor of Bay Number Four just inside the sill. The four payload lines went to the corners of the Bay. We saw the catch net deployed across the opening of the Bay. Metrola asked, "Please confirm mass of the box?"

"3,000 pounds." I answered in English. "Is that correct *Columbia*?"

"That is correct, 3,014 pounds." answered Laura.

"Thank you, *Columbia*." In Atlantean Metrola added, "Between three and four *gunds*. Be advised payload transfer crew, I'll bring it in slow." Metrola started the cable reels. The lines drew taut and slowly accelerated the cubic fathom box. As soon as Metrola judged that the cargo had enough momentum, the lines became slack. Then she drew the lines in at the same speed as the drifting box to keep them from tangling. The box entered the Bay and settled into the center of the catch net. It never exceeded two feet per second as far as I could tell, it took about two minutes for the box to travel the distance between *Columbia* and *Neanderthal Return*.

After the box landed in the net, the women in the Bay removed it from the net and moved it to the rear of the Bay and lashed it down. Mary Ellen recorded it all on film. Her camera also sent a live image to Mission Control in Houston and to the Science and Humanities Channel's main studio in Portland, Oregon. The net was reset for the missiles. "*Neanderthal Return* is now ready for the missiles." announced Metrola. "Sorby, Neil, please come back in to pick up the cables." She switched to Atlantean. "These boxes are two dozen and one *potes* in length and have a mass of over two dozen and two *gunds*. I will keep its relative speed to less than one *pote* per *prelate*."

We operated our cable reels to draw ourselves back into the Bay. We took up the four cables and resumed our positions. On Metrola's signal we again ran and leaped out into space. Again we were slowed to a halt twenty feet above *Columbia's* cargo bay. I was toward the front of *Columbia*. Sorby was twenty feet from me toward the rear. I saw the vertical fin rise behind her. "All right. Standing by for one of the missiles. Go ahead Laura."

"Commencing missile transfer." The Canadian Arm grasped the payload grapple built into the end of one of the missile crates. "Port side missile package grapple is captured, releasing clamps. Lifting package."

The crate was lifted thirty feet from the bottom of the cargo bay. "I am maneuvering to the forward eye bolt to attach the cables from the *Neanderthal Return*." I used the helium jets from my backpack to slide over to the eyebolt two feet from the forward end. I latched the two hooks of my cables on to the eyebolt. "Forward eyebolt is secured to both lines from the *Neanderthal Return*."

Sorby likewise maneuvered to the eyebolt two feet from the aft end. "I am hooking my lines from the *Neanderthal Return* to the rear eyebolt." She deftly hooked both of her lines on to the eyebolt on the first try. "Aft eyebolt is secured to lines from the *Return*."

The eyebolts were on the side of the box facing the Atlantean ship. We did not have to rotate the 24,000 pound mass. "All right Laura, please lift and release the missile package." I requested.

"Lifting missile package to full extension above *Columbia* bay." Laura gently lifted the missile until the Arm was fully extended. She released the long wooden crate. "Missile package is free from *Columbia*."

We looked back at Bay Number Four to make sure the net was deployed across the opening. "Net is deployed and ready." declared Nesla Teslakian. "We are now moving into position to receive the payload." The women inside the Bay moved to the rear and tucked themselves into the little rooms cut into the side walls. The women were out of the way in case two dozen and two *gunds* of mass broke through the net.

Sorby and I dropped ourselves down out of the way. We made sure our umbilical lines were clear of the cargo cables. "Everything and everyone is ready for bringing in the payload." Sorby told Metrola over the radio.

"This is Metrola. Bringing in the missile, keeping the speed below one *pote* per *prelate*. It is two dozen and two and a half *gunds*."

"Of which twelve and six or seven *gunds* is solid rocket fuel and one *gund* is a nuclear bomb." I reminded her.

"Uh, Neil. General Fairchild." Captain Harsradich interrupted. "Hold on for a *linit*, Metrola. Just exactly what is this solid rocket fuel made of?"

"It's a concoction of aluminum powder and ammonium perchlorate crystals suspended in some kind of organic polymer." I answered.

"That is correct." admitted General Fairchild.

"Organic polymer?" asked Trviea.

"Plastic. It's actually a pretty stable mix. The purpose of a Minuteman missile was to sit in a silo year after year ready to launch. When the missiles were taken out of deployment, NASA and other agencies snapped them up for use as sounding rockets. There are thousands of them in existence. So we can put a few of them to good use as comet bombers."

"Neil Peace," interrupted General Fairchild, "how do you know this stuff?"

"I used to be a Boeing guy. Some of my friends worked on the Minuteman program. It's also public information, I made some phone calls to the ground to learn as much as I can about these things. My ex-wife was able to find this stuff in the regional library in Federal Way. So I know it's in the public domain."

"Yeah, information about the NASA sounding rockets is public information, and so are many things about the design of rocket engines. But Neil, it's not necessary to inform everyone of the number of rockets we have in our possession."

"Ahh, come on, General. Everyone knows about our mass production capabilities. Any item that we can make one of, we can make a thousand of. Curing plastic with stuff mixed in is a process quite adaptable to mass production. Besides, we need to cooperate with the Creation women and the Russians to pull this off. There is nothing like being secretive and refusing to give straight answers to cause people to mistrust you. Trviea asked a reasonable safety related question for which she is entitled to an answer. It's general knowledge that we had one thousand missile silos. For every Minuteman deployed in the silo with a live warhead, there was at least one spare in storage. Maybe two. Standard military procedure about spares. When the Minuteman I was replaced by the II, and then by the III, all rockets of each model became surplus. All three stages of each rocket. That doesn't mean we destroyed them, except for the few NASA has been launching, they still exist. As for the operation of the rocket, it doesn't matter what the payload is, whether it's a nuclear warhead or a scientific payload, it works the same. You light the solid fuel, it spurts the rocket forward. NASA has no shortage of sounding rockets. We could literally pound the comet out of existence if we just had enough Space Shuttles and Energiya rockets to bring them up here."

"You made your point, Neil, enough already!" pleaded the General. I could hear the other Air Force people giggling.

"Captain Trviea, does all that answer your question about the fuel in these Aries missiles?"

"I'm satisfied. Aluminum powder and ammonium perchlorate in a plastic binder should be safe unless somebody deliberately lights it off. Which we plan to do when we get out to the comet. Proceed with Payload Transfer, Metrola."

"I am now proceeding to bring the missile package into the Bay." The lines to the missile slowly became taut and accelerated the missile toward the net. Metrola did her job extremely well. The missile remained lateral relative to the net inside the bay. It slowly closed the distance. The lines became slack when Metrola judged that the momentum of the missile was sufficient. She drew in the lines as slowly as the missile crate moved, keeping them from tangling. The long box went through the very center of the opening and gently landed on its side in the net. The ropes of the net pulled on braked reels as the net gave. The missile came to a halt fifty feet inside the Bay.

"Missile is now stationary inside the Bay!" Nesla triumphantly announced in Atlantean. The women unhooked the tether lines and removed the missile from the net. They gently brought it to the rear and lashed it down on the floor. "Missile is secure."

With the net out of the way, Sorby and I pushed the buttons on our cable reel controls to draw ourselves back into the Bay. We took a hold of the lines and ran out of the Bay leaping toward the Space Shuttle to bring the lines out to hook the other missile. By the same procedure as before, we brought it into the Bay. Then we brought our selves back into the Bay.

"Payload Transfer is complete." announced Metrola. "Now we are ready for Personnel Transfer."

"This is General Fairchild, all four of us have gone through the EVA preparation procedure. We are ready to transfer over to *Neanderthal Return*. Permission requested to come aboard, Captain Harsradich?"

That caught Captain Harsradich by surprise. "Uh, hold on for a moment, General Fairchild." She shut off her headset and turned to Chuck Carter. "Chuck, why did he request permission to come aboard? I thought we worked that out, of course he has permission to come aboard. We've got two of your American NUCLEAR BOMBS inside OUR Bay! Not to mention three dozen *gunds* of flammable plastic."

Chuck chuckled. "It's a courtesy thing. When we come on board a ship, it's a tradition to ask the Captain for permission to come aboard. General Fairchild is a military guy, this sort of tradition is pounded into him from the Air Force Academy on. Just say 'Permission granted.' You're the Captain, it's up to you to grant permission to come aboard."

"All right. I thought I already had." Sigh. She turned on her headset. "Permission granted, General Fairchild."

"Thank you Captain. Major McKenna and myself will cycle first into the airlock. We'll bring our bags of personal belongings. After we get out of the airlock, Majors Easton and Davenport will cycle through with their bags."

As they went into the airlock, General Fairchild quietly ordered his Majors to each request permission to come aboard. "Captain Harsradich, this is Major Roy McKenna, in the *Columbia* airlock. Permission requested to come aboard?" The other two Majors each introduced themselves and requested permission to come aboard.

Captain Harsradich rolled her eyes. "Permission granted. For all of you." She turned off her headset and smiled at Chuck. "Cro-Magnons." She turned her headset back on. "Now please get on over here. We need to free up Metrola Mornuxler. She's got to take our Shuttle down to Kazakhstan to pick up the Russian Bomb Crew. They've been observing the loading of the Energiya rockets at Baikonur. But before they launch the rockets, the Russians want their Bomb Crew up here on the *Return*."

"We copy that, Captain." the General acknowledged. "We are now ready to exit our airlock."

While this has been going on, the women in the Bay rigged up two personnel retraction cables. Sorby came over to me and handed me the two hook ends. "Would you like to go get them, Neil?"

"Well, Sorby, you have more experience doing this than I."

"True. But you've done well so far. I can go get 'em, but you are the American, and we want you to be the one to bring the Americans over. Here, take these tethers and show 'em how its done!"

"Aye, aye, Sorby." I took the cables. "Ready for Personnel Transfer."

"We're now both outside the airlock in *Columbia* cargo bay. Ready for the bags?"

"Just toss 'em over slowly, we'll catch 'em." Fairchild and McKenna tossed their bags. The women in the Bay caught them.

"Please commence Personnel Transfer, Neil." requested Captain Harsradich.

With cables in hand, I ran and leaped off the sill of the Bay. I drifted over to *Columbia*, watching the two astronauts standing there. Metrola brought me to a halt right in front of them. "One for you, General, and one for you, Major." I handed the hooks to them. I noticed that their feet were anchored in the footholds in the cargo bay.

"You're quite an astronaut, Neil Peace." complimented the general. "You should apply for NASA."

"Thank you. But what chance does a washed out, laid off, divorced Boeing engineer have with NASA? I mean, to even have a chance, I have to have a clean life and a glowing work history. By that, I mean supervisors had to put me at the top of the totem. I got laid off, guess where I was on the totem? Like most REAL people, I have my flaws. I've made my mistakes. Shit has happened to me. Doesn't matter if it was my fault or not! Why should NASA take a chance with a guy like me when they can choose from a legion of perfect people with perfect life stories?"

"I see your point. But you just have to believe you can do it." Generals are accustomed to giving pep talks.

"Oh, I believe I can do anything I set my mind to, if only given the chance. It's being given the chance, that's the trick." Every unemployed person has that complaint.

"Well, at least you are making the most of the chance you've been given." The spacesuits each had a parachute type harness wrapped around the torso. Each Air Force officer took a hook and latched it on to his parachute harnesses.

"Good, you're latched to *Neanderthal Return*. Now please unhook your feet from *Columbia*." They jumped clear of the cargo bay. "Since you gung ho Air Force officers can do anything you set your minds to, set your minds to pushing these buttons on these control panels." I pointed to the button that would activate the cable reel. "This button activates the cable reel, this button turns it off. Just get enough pull to move a few feet per second no need to exceed the 70 mile an hour speed limit, this ain't Montana. We want you ALIVE after you land in Bay Number Four. The cable will tend to pull you right into the center of the Bay. Let's go!" We each operated the cable reels and pulled ourselves toward the Bay. "When you get within 10 yards, if you've played football you know what 10 yards looks like, shut off your cable reels and coast in, you'll be going plenty fast enough. The girls in the Bay will try to catch you or at least render emergency medical aid after an emergency pressurization!"

All three of us landed, everything went just fine. NASA installed magnets in their shoes. "Way to go, Neil!" exclaimed Sorby. "I wouldn't have the guts to talk so candidly or humorously with a GENERAL!"

"Well, Sorby, he is a civilian taxpayer." reminded Fairchild. "He's paying my salary, I guess he can speak to me as an equal. But these MAJORS wouldn't dare and that is only proper." The majors laughed.

"Your turn, Sorby." I declared. "The other two astronauts are now cycling through *Columbia's* airlock."

"Well, I guess we can't expect you to do everything around here, I gotta pull my own weight." The personal bags from Easton and Davenport arrived and were caught.

"Nah. Just let the cable reel pull your weight. You go take a flying leap! Take these cable hooks with you."

"Aye aye, Neil!"

Sorby took the two tethers out to the two Majors. They were hooked up and reeled in. Metrola shut the door to Bay Four and pressurized the chamber. Pidonita fired up the fusion reactor and we pulled away from *Columbia*. It was nice to have 6 feet per second squared acceleration again. After I took my helmet off and took a breath of air, I left the Bay and headed over to the Shuttle Bay. Metrola liked Ian but wanted me for the trip to Kazakhstan. I couldn't take the pressure suit off. Normal safety procedure is to wear a pressure suit in the Shuttle, in case of a loss of air. Soyuz 11 lost air while still above the atmosphere, three cosmonauts died.

Monoloa was coming with us in the Shuttle, she knew wearing pressure suits would impress the Russians with our safety consciousness.

Metrola greeted me on the way to the Shuttle Bay. "Are we having fun yet?" she asked with a big grin on her face.

"Yeah, it was fun. I must admit that. This suit is a bit claustrophobic but once you're doing something in it you forget about that. Nothing like being 180 miles from the nearest anything to cure claustrophobia."

"You did well. A kiss, please?"

"Sure." After we kissed Monoloa joined us, already in her pressure suit, and we went to the Bay.

Monoloa spoke in her nice familiar Atlantean. "Pido is bringing us around to Kazakhstan. At least we don't have to go into free fall to launch the Shuttle."

"Yeah. But we'll do free fall a few more times. Our Shuttle can barely lift eight *gunds* of payload off the Earth. We were almost that heavy in Algeria. No way we can bring up the heavy equipment we need for Operation Rainbow. Fortunately the Cro-Magnons have big rockets for heavy lift into orbit."

"But payload transfers will require free fall every time."

Chapter Thirty Five

As I exited Bay Number Four to join Metrola at the *Neanderthal Return's* Shuttle, Trviea, Helga, and Lucinda passed by me. They went into the Bay to greet the four United States Air Force officers. The four Americans in their NASA spacesuits had already removed their helmets as had all of the Creation women. Mary Ellen lifted her face shield, but was too busy with her camera to remove her helmet. Nesla Teslakian made the introduction. "General Fairchild, this is Captain Trviea Harsradich. Captain, this is General Morton Fairchild, head of the American Missile Crew."

"Pleased to meet you, Captain. On behalf of every nation on Earth, we thank you for your participation in Operation Rainbow."

"You're welcome. We only desire a successful completion of Operation Rainbow. This is Helga Trvlakian,"

"We've met." Helga gave Morton a two handed handshake.

"and this is Lchnsda Renuxler."

"Thank you for your kindness when I was healing from my injury." Lucinda also shook hands with Morton. The language specialists went through introductions with the Majors.

Captain Harsradich continued. "I have asked Helga and Lchnsda to help you settle in and to instruct you on the things you need to know for your stay on the *Neanderthal Return*. You'll have to excuse me, I have to oversee the launch of our Shuttle. It's going down to Kazakhstan to pick up the Russian Bomb Crew. Then we rendezvous with *Mir* to pick up equipment that was brought up last week on a Proton rocket. Then we rendezvous with the new International Space Station for another load of stuff. Then we go dancing around the Planet picking up the payloads now being launched out of French Guiana, China, Japan, Russia's Amur Oblast and a sea launch platform in the Pacific Ocean."

"Captain, we walk in what seems like a light gravity." commented Major Davenport.

"We're under acceleration. The fusion reactor provides propulsion without expending reaction mass."

"Unlimited delta vee." he said in awe. He decided it would be impolite to inquire as to exactly how.

"The ship is this large to house the fusion reactor and the paraboloid reflection surface. We're not immune to the effects of radiation, so we need shielding. Mass, lots of it. Our spacecraft engineers didn't worry about shaving off every *coilon*. The minimum thickness of the aluminum hull of this part of the ship, where we live, is three *tig-its*. The windows are six *tig-its* thick and darken in the presence of a very bright light. This protects our eyes and it protects us from solar flares and other sources of radiation. Well, anyway, as proud of this ship as we are, I gotta go! Helga, Lchnsda, they're all yours." Trviea left the Bay.

"These are little pamphlets we've prepared to introduce you to the *Neanderthal Return*." announced Helga as she and Lucinda handed out booklets with the title *Welcome to the Neanderthal Return* written in English.

Beneath the title on the cover page is written "A physical description of the ship with living, housekeeping, working, safety, and emergency procedures translated for the English speaking passenger. Included is a brief introduction to the Atlantean language with emphasis on safety and emergency related commands and warnings, Base Twelve Creation numerals, and Creation weights and measures."

"Thank you." said each Air Force officer upon receipt of a copy.

"We want you to read and study these pamphlets. It's one thing for us to leisurely coast around Earth with a few Cro-Magnon guests on board. But Operation Rainbow will be a hazardous mission. We want everyone on this ship to know all safety and emergency procedures and the Atlantean phrases for emergency warnings and commands. Uh, can you hear me with those black and white caps on your heads?"

"Yes, yes! We can." The General took his cap off and motioned his Majors to take theirs off. "We call these Snoopy caps. They are officially called communication carriers."

"I see. We also have headsets we wear when we're on duty, like right now." Helga pointed to the tiny microphone hung out in front of her mouth. "Lucy, could you please turn around so we can show our guests our headsets."

Lucinda smiled and turned her head. "Because I'm bald you can see how the headset fits on."

"One thing I have to warn you about Lucinda, she does not consider her baldness to be a problem."

"If it was, I'd wear a wig."

"Which would float away during free fall." Both women giggled. "We all think she's a beautiful woman. For that matter, so does Henry Turnipseed."

Lucinda's face and cranium turned bright red for a moment. "A lot of Cro-Magnon men think I'm beautiful."

"You see how the padded bar of the headset is wrapped around Lucinda's beautiful ear with a speaker as small as a hearing aid tucked in the ear hole. This rear bar wraps around the back of this beautiful head and is secured to the other ear to keep it from falling off. Contrviea's Machine Shop is making up a bunch of these to fit your Cro-Magnon heads. This wire leads down between our breasts underneath our clothes, to this little control panel mounted on our waistbelts. There's also a little control button up here by the ear, just like your Secret Service communicators. When we put on a pressure suit for going out into space, we just pull the wire apart here," she uncoupled the wire at a junction a few inches below her throat, "and then plug into the suit. We don't wear a big fabric Snoopy cap."

"The first safety procedure you'll participate in will be Free Fall." announced Lucinda. "That means weightlessness or microgravity. We'll be picking up payloads lofted into orbit from Earth over the next few days. Each payload will be in a free fall orbit. To collect it, we have to match its orbit. That means we have to be in free fall. Whoever is pilot, Pidonita Hmlakian now, sometimes Sabar Duradich, sometimes Metrola Mornuxler, or Nesla Teslakian, or even Captain Harsradich,"

"We can all pilot the ship in an emergency, but we have a rotation of women who take turns in the pilot's seat." informed Helga.

"Whoever is piloting the ship will start to cycle down the fusion reactor." Lucinda continued her lecture. "She'll use the public address system to announce Free Fall in two *linits*. A *linit* is fifty seconds, that is all explained in your books. The Atlantean words for Free Fall in two *linits*, '*Bly jore aw ti linits!*' will be shouted by the pilot through the public address system. You will also hear it through your headset, as you will all such general safety and emergency warnings and commands. It's just like what you have on your Space Shuttle. You use the two *linit* warning time to tie everything down. If you're eating, you cover your food and put caps on your liquids. If you're in the shower bath, you shut it off and step out to towel dry. You operate a vacuum cleaner to suck up water droplets. We've put partitions around the shower baths to protect your privacy while nude. We understand your customs and feelings about nudity."

"What are your feelings about nudity?" asked a smiling Major Roslyn Easton to the accompaniment of gentle laughter.

"We were all women. No men. It was kind of like,"

"A women's locker room." finished Roslyn.

"Yes, I suppose you could say that. Now that we have men on board, we certainly have a different environment." Lucinda smiled sheepishly. "Free Fall is not too serious, you're already familiar with it. But what you have to be aware of is the commence acceleration call. In Atlantean it is '*Jore put*'. It's not too sudden, but you grab a hold of something or get your feet between you and the floor when you hear '*Jore put.*'"

"A more serious situation is the strap down command." admonished Helga. "This is called in an emergency or a drill. We'll be having Strap Down Drills. When you hear the words 'Strap Down!' shouted in Atlantean, '*Tix jord*!' you do what Lchnsda is doing."

"You head over to one of these cavities in the wall. Notice the new placards in English and Russian next to the writing in Atlantean. It reads 'Strap Down Station'. You climb on to this bunk bed." Lucinda demonstrated. "You place your feet into these foot restraints like this. You draw this harness made of straps, what you call webbing, across your body and snap into place. Your hands are free and you can easily unbuckle. The straps go across your thighs, hips, and chest. Not your waist, it's soft tissue, no bones. You adjust to fit snug without restricting your breathing. You bring this helmet down over your head, the strap stretches to fit. We have done this with Neil and the Science and Humanities people, so we know it works for Cro-Magnons. Attached to the helmet are a number of mechanical restraints. You can still turn your head, but not as easily. The purpose is to keep your head from snapping around, breaking your neck."

"What situation would call for a *Tix jord* procedure?" asked General Fairchild.

"You learn our language fast, General. Knowing those two words could save your life. Or at least keep your body from being splattered all over the place. Much easier to take to Medical that way. Situation would be like when we bomb the comet. If our pilot, most likely Pidonita for the Bomb Run, determines that we may be hit by a large object, she'll scream '*Tix jord*!' As you are aware, your physicists make good guesses as to how our propulsion operates. To avoid a collision, our pilot can realign the spin on the protons so the fusion core zips in a different direction during each pulse. If we're not strapped down, we'll be slammed into that wall. If she decides upon an emergency rapid acceleration, being strapped down protects your body from its own weight at 5 gees. This bed is designed for this purpose. Once you're in here strapped down like I am, you'll see a button labeled 'Oxygen' in Atlantean, English, and Russian. You can push this button and this face mask pops down, just like on your airplanes. Put this across your face, you are now getting pure oxygen. You can strap the mask on, you can work the fingers behind your neck even with the restraint helmet on."

"Several reasons for the oxygen mask." announced Helga. "If there is a loss of pressure, the pure oxygen will displace nitrogen out of your blood. Helps prevent bends. If there's low pressure or something wrong with the air, the oxygen mask should pop down automatically. If this happens, PUT IT ON! Should the pressure drop below eight *dollons*, or four psi, this shield, made of a plastic glass a lot like your Plexiglas, comes down to seal you in."

"We use a clear material to prevent claustrophobia and for other safety reasons." Lucinda continued the lecture. "You can push a control button, labeled in the three languages, to close the cover." Lucinda demonstrated and the shield came down, sealing Lucinda into the strap down enclosure.

Helga continued. "The capsule is designed to maintain an internal pressure of about 24 *dollons* per square *tig-it*, twelve psi. There are digital displays in front of Lchnsda's face that tell her the pressure, carbon dioxide, and oxygen levels inside and outside the capsule. Another reason to study Creation numbers and units of measure. Let's say the problem is that we have hard vacuum in this part of the ship. But we have people in these capsules. Can't expect 'em to stay there forever. So you put on pressure suits, like these NASA suits, and come over here to fetch Lchnsda. Follow these instructions on the wall, in Atlantean, English, and Russian. Turn these handles, and you can pull the entire capsule out of the wall and carry her to safety. It may take two or three people to carry her, even in free fall or low acceleration. The mass of this capsule with Lchnsda in it is about 400 pounds." Helga reset the handle locking the capsule in the wall.

"Much better than our rescue balls." commented Major Davenport.

"She has a window she can see out." noted Helga. "Being stuck in a dark yard diameter ball unable to see anything can do strange things to your mind. Like cause you to open the bag while in vacuum. Not good. In one of these capsules, at least you can see what's going on and you have these gauges to read."

Lucinda resumed the lecture. "Let's say there's pressure in this part of the ship. Enough to keep your blood from boiling, a few psi. But the air is not breathable. Say you have a reason to get out of the capsule: an evacuation order, a fire you must go and fight, or an injured person who must be helped. You pop this helmet off. You remove these straps. You open this panel above you. Inside is an oxygen bottle. It's not heavy, it's made of a composite material like your Kevlar. You unhook the tube to your face mask from here and attach to here. You turn this valve, now you're getting oxygen from the bottle. You remove the bottle to carry it with you. To leave the capsule you can open the shield by pushing the button you use to close it. Now you can get out of the capsule." Lucinda did so and stood breathing oxygen from the bottle. "As you can see, the bottle comes with a belt you can loop around your waist like this. Now your hands are free, you can fight fires or carry injured people to safety." She then removed the facemask and closed the bottle. As she removed the belt from her waist, she continued, "You'll find these bottles mounted on walls and at work stations everywhere on this ship, we take pains to check and maintain them. They are now labeled 'Oxygen' in the three languages. You'll also find fire extinguishers and medical emergency kits mounted everywhere and labeled in the three languages. If you open one of these kits, an emergency signal will automatically be sent to Medical, the Pilothouse, and to Captain Harsradich. They'll know exactly where you are. Remove a fire extinguisher from its mount and the fire alarm sounds. Please don't do this unless there actually is a fire. We disable the automatic signal for checking and maintenance and for drills, but we normally keep this circuit intact."

She replaced the oxygen equipment and restored the capsule to ready status. Helga wrapped up the session. "I want to thank you people for your patience. Here you are listening to our lesson while still in these pressure suits."

"We don't mind. This is important stuff. Thank you." reassured General Fairchild.

"You're welcome. We'll now show you to your rooms and give you a chance to get out of these suits and relax. Do study these pamphlets, please."

"This is the *Neanderthal Return* Shuttle, Monoloa Mrvlakian, calling the air traffic control for Leninsk, Kazakhstan and the Baikonur Cosmodrome." Monoloa spoke in Russian.

"This is Leninsk-Baikonur Air Traffic Control, we copy *Neanderthal Return* Shuttle." came the answer in Russian. "We can also speak English."

I laughed. "We copy that, Leninsk-Baikonur, this is Neil Peace. Do we have permission to enter Kazakh airspace?"

"Yes you do, N.R. Shuttle. You are also cleared for entry into the city of Leninsk and the

Baikonur Cosmodrome. Our people want to give you three a tour of the Cosmodrome and to brief you on the Energiya payloads." The ATC man switched to Russian language. "Monoloa, have you been here before?"

"Yes. I was treated like visiting royalty. It was fun. Thank you all for your hospitality. The Energiya, is it capable of lifting 150,000 kilograms to orbit?"

"With six Energomash strap-on rockets, yes. 200,000 kilos with eight strap-ons, but that would require a top mounted payload, we haven't done that yet. In the configuration we are using today, six strap on rockets, its capability is 150,000 kilos. We have two Energiyas sitting on two pads, several kilometers apart, so the launch of one does not endanger the other. The one advantage of Kazakhstan, plenty of land." He switched back to English. "Metrola Mornuxler, are you piloting the N.R. Shuttle?"

"*Da*. I am. We're now at about 350,000 feet, 100 *versty*, above Kazakhstan. We can see the Aral Sea, the Syr Darya River, and the highway. We can see Leninsk and the Cosmodrome. We're ready to come down." Metrola brought us to a stop above Leninsk. We felt gravity, not acceleration, 31.1 feet per second squared at this altitude.

"N.R. Shuttle, you have clearance to land at Leninsk Airport. We'll help guide you to the apron. Welcome to Kazakhstan."

"On our way." Metrola pitched us over and we fell. I read off the altitude readings every 10,000 feet until we were down close, then it was every thousand feet. The air traffic controllers guided us to our assigned landing zone. As we came within a few thousand feet, I noticed what looked like American C-5 transports. Military cargo planes the size of 747's. Metrola brought us to a nice soft landing on the apron. "Please allow us a few minutes to get used to Earth gravity, out of our pressure suits and to make ourselves presentable." she told our hosts.

"No problem." confirmed the radio voice. Working with Americans gave them the habit of using American idioms.

We climbed out of our suits and combed our hair using a mirror. We smoothed down each other's clothing. Monoloa spoke into a microphone in Russian. "We are coming out now."

We opened the door to the Shuttle and extended the ramp to the pavement. In mid-April, Kazakhstan was making its transition from stormy winter to hot summer weather. It was a pleasant 70 degrees and the Sun was shining. As we stepped out into the Sun we were greeted by a brass band and soldiers in dress uniforms rolling out a red carpet. The white, blue, and red flag of Russia and the blue flag of Kazakhstan flew over the site. School children lined up behind a rope cheered us waving Russian, Kazakh, American, and Atlantean flags. I recognized the dress uniforms of U.S. Air Force and Army officers. Those WERE C-5's parked on the flight line.

Metrola shut and locked the door behind us. A small hole next to the door is big enough for a finger to fit in. The lock computer has fingerprints of the crew stored in its memory.

We walked down the ramp and traveled the length of the red carpet as the band played festive martial music. We greeted and shook hands with the President of Kazakhstan, President Korsakov, officials in charge of the Cosmodrome, other officials, U.S. Air Force officers, and finally we greeted the Bomb Crew.

Anatoly Donovon. Yes, the old man was scheduled to don a pressure suit and ride up with us to the *Neanderthal Return*. He looked as healthy as a horse, grinned, and had a twinkle in his eye. He wore a Soviet flag pin on the lapel of his suit jacket. Yes, there were the mass starvations, purges and other horrible things that happened during the time of Stalin. But Anatoly is justifiably proud of what his nation accomplished under that flag. He was a part of that. Maria Romanov, a pretty blonde woman who looked to be in her forties. Her hair and cheekbones reminded me of the old grainy photographs of Princess Anastasia and her sisters.

Svetlana Lebed, a matronly brunette with gray streaks in her hair. Mikhail Dostoevski, who looks like the stereotype of the engineer. White shirt, tie, thick glasses, short hair.

We all shook hands in greeting. "Anatoly Donovon," I addressed him. I knew he knew English. "You are a true Hero of the Soviet Union. I'm sure these children would be thrilled to meet you."

"Oh, they don't care about an old man like me. It's you cosmonauts that they're excited about. Particularly the Creation women. Everyone loves Monoloa, and then there's Metrola, the Hero of the Algerian Desert."

"Don't sell yourself short, Anatoly." advised Metrola. "We're all going up to the ship for this mission. These children, we cannot let them, uh, I'm sorry."

"It's all right, Metrola. We'll knock that comet into a different orbit, you'll see."

We stood at attention as the national anthems of Russia, Kazakhstan, and the United States were played. We faced the three flags and listened to the schoolchildren sing the words. The flag of Kazakhstan has a bright sunburst in the center above an outline of a bird with outstretched wings. Along the pole is a vertical column of calligraphy. I was touched when I listened to the children sing the *Star Spangled Banner* in English. There were some other Americans in addition to the military officers, mostly from NASA and the joint venture between Lockheed-Martin and Energomash. The U.S. flag over the Kazakh steppe and the singing of our anthem honored us and American participation in Operation Rainbow.

After the ceremonies, we went over to the children and shook their hands. Some were fair skinned, ethnic Russian and Ukrainian, and some were the darker Kazakhs and Uzbeks. All were beautiful. It was particularly moving to see the Neanderthal women meet the children.

As we left the apron to climb into a bus, Anatoly gently gave orders phrased in the form of requests. His eyes twinkled, he was lavish with praise and thank yous, and was always smiling. The people loved working for this man. President Korsakov put him in charge of the Russian participation in Operation Rainbow. He and the President of Kazakhstan ordered their people to give Mr. Donovon their full cooperation. "All right, ladies and gentlemen, let us please get on this bus for the ride out to one of the Energiya launch pads." Some of the U.S. Air Force officers joined us on the bus.

The bus took us out of the airport on a concrete road designed for heavy trucks. We crossed a set of railroad tracks and drove toward one of the pairs of incredibly tall truss frame towers that stood by each launch pad with its gray and white Energiya. Each of these towers had a horizontal wedge shaped truss assembly that pointed at the other tower from its top.

"Those 200 meter towers suspend a cable between them to collect unwanted electrical discharges." informed Anatoly, our tour guide.

Six strap on rockets were arranged around one side of the central booster. The central rocket body was 25 feet in diameter and 193 feet in height. A Payload Carrier, 22 feet in diameter and 125 feet long, was mounted on one side of the main rocket. It had its own rocket engine at its bottom, a kick stage for final insertion into orbit. A gantry extended from the launch tower to the Payload Carrier.

"Impressive piece of equipment, no?" shouted the grinning and enthusiastic Anatoly Donovon. "We were an ambitious bunch. We had a plan of using this booster to launch a Mars mission. Go see Face Mountain. I know, I know, you Creation girls are afraid of Face Mountain. No American participation, just ourselves. We could easily pay a visit to the Moon. Then the Soviet Union fell apart, went bankrupt. There was a time, Neil Peace, a time when you Americans and we Soviets dared to do great things. Nowadays, we are full of excuses as to why we can't, we won't, we shouldn't, we can't afford it and if we could aren't there better things to spend the money on? What do we spend the money on? Bureaucracy! Useless, interfering, paper shuffling, stifling, small brained bureaucracy! Damned lawyers and apparatchiks who waste everybody's time! Every government in history that didn't succumb to military defeat or revolution was destroyed by its own bureaucracy. It happened to us, you Americans act like you think it can't happen to you. That's one of the symptoms."

Anatoly got up and walked down the aisle as the bus drove 40 miles per hour. He sat down between Metrola and Monoloa. He put his arms around their shoulders. "These Creation women. No men. How many of them are there? Something like 55 million? Out of that, one nation, Atlantis, Atlantis built a, are you ready for this," he paused, "a starship." He said the word with reverence and awe.

"That's right. Atlantis built the starship." confirmed Metrola.

"And how many Atlanteans are there? Probably as many people as living here in Kazakhstan. All women, no men. And they built a 900 meter starship and crossed the gulf of space. 41 trillion kilometers. Imagine Kazakhstan, by itself, building a starship and exploring the Universe. It could, you know, if it had the incentive. All these women needed was incentive. The incentive of the maternal instinct combined with the sex drive. Works every time!"

We laughed at Anatoly's comments, there was nothing he said that we did not agree with. The women accepted and returned the affectionate embrace of the old bomb engineer. "You ladies are so strong, so muscular, so beautiful. With your teeth and powerful jaws, so dangerous! To be young again. Maybe your Doctor Chumkun or Doctor Lamakian, maybe they can make it happen for me? You are twice as old as I, yet less than one third of my age, you did that too! Gave yourselves the TIME to build the starship and explore the Universe."

The bus arrived at the base of the launch tower. Anatoly got up to lead us off the bus. He stood by the driver and motioned the rest of us to file off in front of him. When we all stood in the warm sunshine, he came off to join us. "We're going to ride the elevator up the tower to that gantry." He pointed to the gantry that led to the Payload Pod. "We need to discuss what we have installed in the Payload Carrier."

We walked over and entered a door at the base of a huge gray tower. The scale of the place reminded me of my days at the Boeing Everett Plant. The rocket stood on a pad that itself was about 30 feet thick. The tower looked to be about 250 feet tall. Unlike the Western Washington that I was used to, there are no mountains visible on this Kazakhstan horizon.

We rode the elevator inside the tower and got off at the level of the payload gantry. Anatoly directed us out on to the gantry. We walked single file until we were packed in the gray gantry house that opened on the side toward the Payload Carrier.

Anatoly spoke. "Because of the joint venture between Lockheed-Martin and Energomash, Centaur boosters are already here at the Cosmodrome. They're 10 feet in diameter, two side by side require at least 20 feet, allow a few inches between them. We had an immediate engineering problem that caused us to put engineers on 16 hour shifts and fly in American structural engineers and pay them $100 an hour in hard currency. The Payload Carrier has a maximum diameter of 6.7 meters, which is 22 feet. That's plenty for two Centaurs side by side. But the allowable payload diameter was 5.5 meters, 18 feet, two feet short of what we needed. With sleep deprived engineers and overworked Kazakh machinists, we redesigned part of the Payload Carrier to accept two Centaur rockets side by side. This allowed us to place three Centaur rockets with their Halloween bomb in Penetration Vehicle warheads already attached into the Payload Carrier. Two side by side as you can see, another one above. The Centaur fuel is liquid hydrogen and liquid oxygen, just like the American Space Shuttle main engines and the large central booster of the Energiya. We need a yes or no answer from you Creation women. Do you have or can you produce these liquid fuels? We are talking about very cold temperatures."

Metrola is more of an engineer than Monoloa, she handled this one. "We can supply these fuels, we store water in huge bladders wrapped around the fusion reactor. The reactor burns hydrogen in nuclear fusion, the water supplies this fuel. When we accelerate the water in our cyclotrons, it becomes plasma, splitting into oxygen and hydrogen. We draw off the oxygen and send the hydrogen into the reactor. The reactor supplies all of the energy we need and then some. We can cool the oxygen and hydrogen gas until they're liquids and store the fluids in tanks. How much are we talking about?"

"I can answer that Metrola." General McCleary of the U.S. Air Force offered. "The Centaur carries 380 cubic feet of liquid oxygen and 760 cubic feet of liquid hydrogen. That is 30,400 pounds of fuel for each rocket. But the Centaur is not a permanent storage facility for cryogenic fluids. Launch procedure is to transport the rocket empty to the launch pad and fuel it from the launch tower. When it is fully fueled, start the countdown and light her up. After the *Challenger* explosion, we rejected the idea of hauling a Centaur in the Shuttle bay loaded with fuel. These Centaurs here in the Energiya Payload Carrier are empty of fuel, they each weigh about 5,000 pounds. Since we're planning on carrying five of the big Russian nuclear bombs with us on Operation Rainbow, we need to be able to fuel five of these Centaur rockets from the *Neanderthal Return*. That will be a total of 152,000 pounds of liquid hydrogen and liquid oxygen, or about that many pounds or pints of water if you can split the water with energy from your fusion reactor."

"How many cubic feet are we talking about?" Metrola was in deep mental concentration, thinking through the problem.

"Oh, 380 times five, 1900 cubic feet of liquid oxygen, twice that many of liquid hydrogen, 3800 cubic feet."

"Oh yeah, we can do that. When we draw off the oxygen while fueling the reactor, we store it in huge tanks as the liquid. Each tank is five dozen *potes*, 60 feet, long, twelve *potes* or feet in diameter. Three tanks are full, over 18,000 cubic feet of liquid oxygen. We store it because we breathe it and on a spaceship, you can never have too much oxygen. We have a 12 by 60 *pote* tank dedicated for liquid hydrogen, but never had reason to store any large quantity of it. But in a few days we can fill it with liquid hydrogen by running the spare cyclotrons."

"Can you spare some of your liquid oxygen?" asked Svetlana Lebed, who had Anatoly translate to English.

"Sure, want some?"

"For *Mir*. They're always repairing things and running low on stuff like oxygen."

"Sure. We can send over a one *hekt shlopon* tank. That's 144 *shlopons*."

"Is a *shlopon* like a cylindrical foot?"

"It is the volume of a cylinder one *pote* long and one *pote* in diameter. The *pote* is our foot, it is .986 American foot." Anatoly and Monoloa translated Metrola's answer.

The Russians held their hands a foot apart and pantomimed a cylinder of that dimension. "144 of these, that should be more than enough," concluded Anatoly, "if we can adapt a hose to fit our tanks. We would thank you very much for such a gift."

"You're welcome. We can adapt the hose. This Payload Carrier is way too big to bring into Bay Number Four." observed Metrola.

"Yes, we can open the Carrier in orbit." responded Anatoly. "Then you can collect the Centaurs one by one. Each Centaur and warhead package is ten feet in diameter and 44 feet 9 inches long, should fit through a 36 by 72 *pote* door."

"But it is a huge amount of mass to handle in one package. With the center of mass near the bomb."

"*Da.* The Penetration Vehicle is made of uranium 238, 5 centimeters thick, built like a pressure vessel. Each end is round, it looks like a giant hotdog. At the forward end is a cone of Inconel alloy to penetrate into the comet, hopefully down the hole made by the American missile. It alone weighs about 20,000 kilograms. Three of them and we are talking 60,000 kilos. Plus the weight of the Centaur boosters, 2300 kilos each for a total of 6900 kilos. 67,000 kilograms for the three Centaur missile packages, plus about a thousand kilos for the mounting brackets. That leaves 82,000 kilograms of lift capacity and plenty of cubic meters to put it in. Which is why we have the American Air Force here. General McCleary?"

"Thank you, Mr. Donovon. As you already know, the Aries missile package has a mass of about 24,000 pounds, which is 10,900 kilos for our Russian friends. Each package is four feet by four feet by 25 feet. Plenty of volume inside this Payload Pod. The limiting factor is the weight. We had enough left over capacity to fit in seven Aries missiles. Since there are only two Halloween Bombs in Penetration Vehicles mounted on Centaur rockets in the other Energiya booster, along with a spare Centaur, we have nine Aries missiles over there. That is why we have the C-5's parked at Leninsk-Baikonur Airport."

Metrola asked, "These Aries missile packages, they have the eyebolts?"

"Yes, of course."

"Good, we can draw them in, no problem there." Metrola worked the problems in her head. "But how are we to attach our cables and hooks to the Centaur missiles?"

Anatoly fielded that one. "Oh, yes. Sorry, Metrola. You see those big bracket rings around the Centaurs and another restraining each warhead? If you look closely, you can see the eyebolts. We know you like to use eyebolts. After we open the Payload Carrier in orbit, you can hook up your cables, and separate each missile from the others by removing the one inch diameter quick disconnect pins, and haul it into your Weapons Bay."

Metrola added: "We can bring in the Aries missiles by the method used before. But we need better control of this huge Centaur-Halloween Bomb package. We could attach cables from our Shuttle and pull in the opposite direction from our ship. That'll lock it into place, the cables from the ship will then bring it in, slowly, *tig-it*s per *prelate*, and GENTLY bring it to a rest inside the Bay. Will require a lot of people in suits out in the vacuum. Now can we store five of these and a spare Centaur in the Bay? Ten feet diameter, 45 feet long, about three dozen and nine *pote*s. Oh yes! Of course we can store them. The Aries missiles? They're small enough we can take some out of the Bay and store 'em in the hallways if necessary. We can leave pathways to bring them all out to the three dozen by six dozen *pote* door and out into space. Contrviea, Nesla, and Neil," she pointed to me, "have discussed inventing a spring loaded mechanism to push the Aries missile out of Number Four Bay into space. When it's at a safe distance, the Minuteman I rocket can be ignited and off it goes. Yes! We can do it."

"So it looks like we've got a plan!" exulted Anatoly. "Of course, we'll bring our pressure suits with us. My three colleagues have been through the Yuri Gagarin Cosmonaut School. Svetlana Lebed here spent a few months on *Mir* and performed three spacewalks. That's how she knew to ask for liquid oxygen."

"Excellent!"

I had a question. "I understand why we're bringing up as many missiles and nuclear warheads as we can for this mission. We may have to bomb the comet several times to get it to miss Earth. Nothing like this has ever been done before, it's better to have more nukes than we need than not enough. A 100 kiloton bomb in a B61-12 vehicle might be just the thing for a quarter mile chunk that breaks off the main comet and winds up on a trajectory to hit Earth. With that in mind, I was wondering if you could not strap on another two of these side rockets to each Energiya and bring it up to its full capacity? Put the Payload Carrier up on top, you did have a design effort for that configuration. That way we can pack in that many more Aries missiles."

Anatoly responded. "That's not a bad idea and we've thought of it. Can the American Air Force bring in more Aries missiles on C-5's?"

"Sure," answered General McCleary, "we can bring some more."

"The problem is, we've never launched the Energiya in that configuration." admitted Anatoly. "We've done it with the side mounted Payload Carrier and with the side mounted *Buran* Shuttle. We need the high yield bombs to accomplish this mission. We lose two or three if either Energiya has an accident during the launch sequence. So we will go with what we know. Side mounted Carrier and six strap on rockets works. The survival of our civilization is at stake. We have two Aries missiles brought up on *Columbia* and installed on *Neanderthal Return*. Sixteen here in Baikonur to go up on the Energiyas. Two more on *Endeavour* rolling out to the launch pad right now. Two more being installed on *Discovery* in the Vehicle Assembly Building. Total of 22 Aries missiles. Hopefully, that is enough. If we can move the main part of the comet, Earth will survive whatever pieces still hit. Even if they are as big as a quarter mile. There is a plan being worked out now to hit those pieces with missiles launched from Earth after we have completed our mission or died trying. The American Shuttles can keep flying and we have some Protons left in the inventory. Unfortunately, we have only these two launch ready Energiyas, it'll take a while to build more."

"Thank you, Mr. Donovon." responded Monoloa. "Shall we get ready to ride up to the *Return*?"

"We could do that, but you're welcome to stay to watch the launch of the first Energiya. It's a heck of a show, better than the American Shuttles, even better than the Apollo launches. Then we can ride your Shuttle up and prepare to bring in these payloads for our mission."

Monoloa looked at me and I nodded my head. "Sure, we could do that."

At the Baikonur Cosmodrome, we were invited to sit in the spectator viewing area reserved for VIP's and members of the cosmonauts' families. The Bomb Crew sat with their families. In the case of Anatoly Donovon, his grandchildren and great grandchildren. Some of them were already tearful and frightened at the prospect of their loved ones going on this mission, as they savored these last hours together.

We heard the countdown and cheered when the bright white flames roared out of the base of the rocket. Smoke glowing white, yellow, orange and red engulfed one of the 200 meter lightning rod towers as the Energiya lifted off and cleared the launch pad tower. The Energomash strap on boosters burn liquid oxygen and kerosene providing the bright white glow of burning carbon. The rocket performed flawlessly and delivered its payload to orbit.

After the launch, we went back to the apron where our Shuttle was parked. We were garlanded with flowers by our hosts. Metrola discretely placed her finger in the hole to be read by the lock computer. She opened the door to the Shuttle. Several boxes of fresh citrus fruit, melons, spices, and vegetables grown in Kazakhstan were delivered to take with us. 300 kilograms of beef, mutton, and horsemeat, the finest cuts, from Kazakhstan ranches was also delivered, they knew the girls upstairs loved big animal meat and missed having it. Traditional Kazakh spicy horsemeat sausages were included. A Russian Orthodox Priest blessed the craft. We all bowed our heads as he lead a prayer. When the muezzin called the prayer, the Muslims at this airport, in Leninsk and the Syr Darya valley prayed for our success and safe return, *Inshallah*, God willing.

We stood at the top of the ramp and waited as the Bomb Crew, garlanded with flowers, had one last hug and kiss with their families. We heard the crying, the soft words of love and hope and reassurance. We did not need to know Russian to understand. The Bomb Crew broke away and put on their pressure suits. They came up the ramp carrying their bags of personal belongings. The were proud, eager, happy, gung ho, can do, and impatient to get started. As we looked back upon the now genuinely frightened faces of the spouses and children, we all said a silent prayer for our success and safe return.

Chapter Thirty Six

It had been hectic. Five free fall drills in 24 hours as the *Neanderthal Return* picked up that many payloads from rockets coming up from that many spaceports around the Earth. The Japanese mission controllers at Uchinoura and the Chinese mission controllers at Xichang were not offended by Monoloa's absence. They knew English. While they would have appreciated the participation of the Angel of the South Gate who speaks their languages, they knew her presence at Baikonur was vital. Without the large yield Russian bombs, there is no Operation Rainbow.

In Bay Number Four, the growing quantity of equipment, tools, spare parts, and repair items was moved to the rear, and through the airlock into the corridors. The Air Force officers helped move the Aries missiles into those hallways to clear as much space as possible for bringing in the Centaur rockets and their warheads. One of the missile packages was opened so I could take measurements and make drawings for the purpose of designing our missile "crossbow", as we called it. I was all over it with rulers, micrometers, and tape measure. Creation women and Science and Humanities people put in long hours in Contrviea's Machine Shop filling every order as it came in. We not only had to work with *tig-its* split into eighths and sixteenths as well as into twelfths, one forty fourths, and *keetig-its*, we also had to work with our inches, split both fractionally and decimally, and get this, millimeters! Everything had to be converted to *tig-it* measure and Base Twelve numbers. We pounded our hand held calculators.

Every functional and safety related part and system was inspected and where necessary, repaired or replaced. False alarms sounded when exhausted women forgot to disable them before inspecting the emergency medical kits and fire extinguishers. The spare cyclotrons were fired up to make the large quantity of liquid hydrogen needed for the Centaurs from the lakeful of water stored on the ship. Liquid hydrogen and oxygen lines were routed to the outside of Bay Number Four. The plan is to hang a Centaur rocket outside the door in space and fuel it there. We rigged up a fueling gantry, taking up much of our engineering and Machine Shop time. I performed more engineering in a day than I did in years at Boeing. The Science and Humanities people proved invaluable in all of the electrical and mechanical work that needed to be done. They knew how to splice wires and troubleshoot problems; that is what they did for the cable channel.

On top of all this, Helga, Lucinda, and Monoloa ran us Earthlings through safety and emergency drills. We were drilled together with the Russians and some of the Creation women to get us used to working with each other under emergency conditions. Free fall drills didn't have to be faked, and us Earthlings participated in recovering payloads from orbit in our pressure suits.

In their spare time, what spare time? Our Russian friends read their Russian language *Welcome to the Neanderthal Return* pamphlets.

General Fairchild met with Anatoly, Trviea, and Helga. "We all look TIRED!" exclaimed Anatoly.

"True, we haven't been getting enough sleep." agreed Trviea. "Plenty of time for that on our ride out to the comet. And we WILL get enough sleep then, that's an order. It'll take 20 days to get out there and slow down enough to maneuver around it. We'll go through some more safety and emergency drills on the way, particularly strap down drills."

"We'll need to strap down if Pidonita needs to evade a piece of comet that comes after us."

"Yes, I know," protested the Air Force general, "that's all explained in the pamphlet."

"And we'll need to be strapped down if we are HIT by a piece of comet." reminded Helga.

"Yes. We're doing excellent," praised Morton, "Operation Rainbow is proceeding nominally."

Helga laughed. "Nominally? What's 'nominal' about an Operation where by necessity, we have to make it up as we go along?"

"I see your point, but things are going according to the plan we are making up as we go along. Uh, we need to discuss the issue of fraternization."

Fraternization? It hasn't been a problem for the women, in fact, it has been a blessing! Anatoly chuckled. "Oh oh! Here comes the Morality Police! These damn Americans have been having so much trouble with adultery, sex harassment and gays in their military. We won't even talk about President Clinton!"

"Please don't talk about Clinton. Anatoly, it's a matter of discipline." admonished Morton Fairchild. "The whole world depends on our completing this mission. We must work together without being distracted by problems from sex. I'm not judging you women from Creation. I just want you to understand that Air Force regulations ban homosexual activity in our officers."

"I know that." confirmed Trviea. "That's why I've quietly ordered Major Easton off limits. Our women will not in any way suggest to her any such activity. They are also under orders not to make Cro-Magnon women uncomfortable by public displays of affection. We know Mary Ellen's strictly heterosexual. We're not aware of any bisexual or homosexual orientation among the other Cro-Magnon women. So we don't think it's a problem."

"Are you sure it isn't a problem?"

Helga laughed. "General, it's possible for a Cro-Magnon woman to visit with a Neanderthal woman in the privacy of her quarters without us knowing about it. We can make rules about sex, but as long as people are discreet, we cannot enforce them."

"And I've learned not to try." admitted Trviea. "I only deal with sexual issues if it becomes a problem. You Earth military types try to maintain unit cohesion and cooperation by having a chain of command, rules that everyone must follow, and orders. We also try to maintain cohesion and cooperation. But for us that requires we trust each other."

"Let me show you something, General." Helga leaned over and put her teeth around Trviea's throat.

The General misinterpreted what he was seeing. "You're giving her a hickey right in front of me? At least you could be discreet about it, not during a meeting!"

Helga pulled away as both women broke up laughing. When Trviea calmed down, "That wasn't an act of sex you were witnessing. She put her teeth around my windpipe. Surely you've been briefed on us? On what Lchnsda did to that terrorist on the Olympic Peninsula? I had to trust Helga with my LIFE! Just now. She could have ripped my windpipe out! Look at us, General! We're as strong as your football players. We have the teeth and jaws of lionesses. It's just the way we grow. We're 47 scorpions in an aluminum bottle. We have to trust each other or we will kill each other. It's that simple. If the comfort and warmth of skin to skin contact is what it takes to maintain that trust, then so be it. I do not enforce abstinence orders because I CANNOT enforce abstinence orders."

"That's what she tried to do when Neil first came on board." informed Helga. "We have a keen sense of smell. Right now my nose is aware of the presence of two men in this room. We have not had any men at all for about 150 of your Earth years. Then Neil is brought on board and we can smell a man for the first time in such a long time. Trviea ordered us to not make love with him. He was angry with being kidnapped so there was no opportunity to violate Trviea's order. But we could smell him."

"So while I'm back in command of this ship," started Trviea, "I'm not going to jeopardize my command and this mission by trying to enforce any more stupid orders like that. I have suggested that there be no gay sex with Major Easton, but if Major Easton and her partner are discreet, I would not try to enforce such an order. You might be wise to wait until this mission is over and you are both on the ground before doing anything about it. That way your discipline problems are not MY discipline problems."

"Fortunately there's no chance Major Easton will violate the military rules against adultery and homosexuality. She's married to a civilian named Ronald Easton."

"That's wonderful! Nobody will approach a married person. Are there other married persons in your Missile Crew?"

"I'm married." declared General Fairchild. "Majors Davenport and McKenna are single."

"Excellent, we'll let everyone know, that way you'll not have any pressure and your two men will become popular."

The General smiled. "Uh, no. All three of my Majors are under strict orders against any such fraternization with the Russians, the civilian Earthlings, and the Creation Neanderthals for the duration of Operation Rainbow. We want their minds on the mission, not on Neanderthal pussy."

"Well now that is a disappointment." admitted Trviea. She chuckled. "I'll suggest that no one tries to tempt them, but if they do, I'll consider it your problem, not mine." The Americans dealt with, she turned to the Russians. "So Anatoly, you're in charge of the Russian Bomb Crew. What's your policy on this?"

Anatoly's eyes twinkled as usual. He's had the time of his life since the start of Operation Rainbow. All of his adult life, he had to worry about the possibility that his engineering effort could result in the deaths of millions and the destruction of civilization. It was not a big worry, he put it in the back of his mind. The western approach to Russia is a vast low plain with nothing interrupting it but rivers. Hostile armies crossed those rivers into Russia numerous times. Napoleon. Kaiser Wilhelm. Hitler. Each time, millions of Russians were killed. Before that, there were the Vikings, Tatars and Mongols. More recently China on one side and Western Europe, led by the power of the United States, on the other side. The big bombs were needed to deter any more aggression. But there was the nagging doubt that the very existence of them presented the risk of unimaginable destruction.

Anatoly, like most bomb engineers, lived with these thoughts in the back of his mind. Since it came to pass that his life's work was the only thing available to deflect a comet and save the world from something even worse than a nuclear war; he has been giddy with pride, relief, and redemption. And now he is surrounded by beautiful women of an exotic Race. What more can any man ask for? Well, there is one thing.

"What is my policy on this? Svetlana Lebed went through a divorce a year ago, it's final. My other two colleagues are married. Monoloa, Metrola, and Neil watched them say good bye to their spouses and children before leaving Leninsk. So if you have a taboo against adultery, I guess the married ones are off limits."

"Don't worry, Anatoly, you can trust us. Their spouses can trust us."

"Because you have rules against adultery?" asked General Fairchild.

"No." answered Helga curtly. "It's what we're trying to tell you. We HAVE to trust each other. Just like I have to trust Trviea to not kill me when I offer her my throat, we have to trust you when we allow you to place NUCLEAR BOMBS on board our ship. Want to commit suicide in spectacular fashion? Here's your chance! Or maybe someone sends a detonation signal up from Earth. We're trusting you to not do that. We're trusting the Russians to not detonate one of their big bombs."

"In the case of adultery," continued Trviea, "we went through the Virus Holocaust. The sorrow of those times is unimagina- na- ble. I'm sorry." Her voice broke and there was a look of consternation on her face.

Helga comforted Trviea with a hand on her shoulder. "It was a very painful time for all of us. We don't want to ever inflict any kind of pain on anyone. We know that adultery can inflict that kind of pain. As long as we know which Cro-Magnons are married, there will be no problem."

Trviea recovered. "No abstinence order is necessary. You can trust us. Are you married, Anatoly?"

"My wife, my Valentina, whom I loved dearly, went to Heaven fifteen years ago. But I am available. I guess. All of these beautiful women. Is there any possibility that Askelion or Meddi can give me any Youth Serum?"

Everyone in the room broke up with laughter. "I don't know about that, Anatoly!" shouted Morton. "If they give you too much, you'll be alive for the next 400 years! I'm not sure Russia can survive 500 years of Anatoly Donovon!"

"If Russia can survive Lenin and Stalin, it can survive a few hundred years of me! I have lived a full and wonderful life. I am blessed with wonderful children, grand children, and great grand children. If I die today, I will go to the Lord and thank Him for everything. But the Lord has seen fit to put me on a ship, unmarried, well at least widowed, with beautiful women of an exotic Race. All I want is a dash of that Youth Serum, and I'll be a happy man."

"We do need your brain," considered Trviea, "we cannot afford to let a blood clot blow it up. You're the engineer who designed these bombs. Maybe I'll direct Askelion to give you just a touch of Youth Serum."

"Thank you, thank you very much, Captain Harsradich."

Monoloa and I helped Svetlana Lebed into her Russian cosmonaut pressure suit. I knew only a few words in Russian, she knew only a few English phrases. Communication was by hand signals. Monoloa would translate, her English wasn't quite up to fluent, but she was an attentive student in my classes before and since her trip to Kazakhstan and Russia. A set of Atlantean gas jets and a helium bottle were installed in the backpack making the Russian suit bulkier. Inch wide red stripes run the outsides of her legs, arms, and around the backpack. The shoulder patch is the white, blue, and red flag of post-communist Russia. But on the chest was a faded patch of the hammer and sickle surrounded by wheat ears pointing to a red star at the top.

Mary Ellen Martin was already in her pressure suit filming us as we got into ours. Finally, Metrola, Monoloa, myself, Svetlana, Major McKenna, and Ian Miller were ready to go into the Shuttle. Pidonita's voice rang out. *"Bly jore aw ti linits!"*

"Free fall in two *linits*." Metrola translated. "Lets get strapped into the Shuttle." We went into the Shuttle Bay and entered the Shuttle. The second door was now unstowed and ready. When it is closed, it forms a three by five foot airlock with the outer door. Big enough for two astronauts in space suits. We checked to make sure the cable reels were properly installed. We went in and strapped down for the flight. Ian took his position next to Metrola, I was going out into the vacuum with Svetlana, Roy McKenna, Mary Ellen, and Monoloa.

Metrola came in last, she performed a last *linit* walk around inspection of the craft. She closed the outer door and took the pilot's seat. *"Bly jore."* announced Pidonita. We suddenly felt light in our seats.

"Shuttle is closed and ready." announced Metrola.

"Nonsuited personnel clear the Shuttle Bay." ordered Nesla, in control of the Shuttle Bay.

The Shuttle Bay was brought to vacuum, the door to space opened, and after the checklist, the Metrola launched the Shuttle. Metrola brought us around to the side of the first Energiya Payload Carrier opposite the main ship.

"All right, EVA crew, let's get started." ordered Metrola. "Let us test the airlock and our suits." We ran through the checklists on our suits and then we tested the airlock for function. Everything checked out, and we so reported. Then Metrola ordered, "Time to start cycling through the airlock. Svet, Neil, are you ready?"

"We're ready." we both answered.

"All right, please put your helmets on and get into the airlock."

We put our helmets on and sealed them, checking the seal. "My seal is fine." Svetlana has learned that much English in the last few hours.

"Mine is fine too." I confirmed. "Insuit pressure is one eight *dollons*, outsuit pressure is one eight *dollons*. Carbon dioxide and oxygen readings are fine. But as I'm breathing near pure oxygen from my suit tank, will start to get high if I don't get into lower pressure. We're now in the airlock, closing the inboard door."

"Inboard door is now sealed, you may depressurize, Neil."

I turned a handle. Reported my pressure readings. "Outsuit pressure is now zero eight *dollons*, insuit pressure is still one seven, reducing slowly to let the nitrogen out of my blood. How's your insuit pressure, Svetlana?"

Svetlana hesitated and Monoloa translated my question into Russian. Then Svetlana answered in English. "Pressure inside my suit is fine, 0.77 kilograms per square centimeter."

"Copy that, Svetlana." I turned the pressure valve the rest of the way. "Insuit pressure one six or seven, reducing slowly, outsuit pressure zero."

"My insuit pressure fine, now 0.68 kilos per square centimeter, will fall to about 0.35." confirmed Svetlana. Then she said something in Russian while I opened the door to the outside. Monoloa broke up laughing.

"Mono, what did she say?" I asked plaintively.

"Svet said that while she doesn't mind being in a very small space with you, these pressure suits take all the fun out of it!"

I laughed as I stepped out into space, found a tether line to a cable reel built into the hull of the Shuttle and snapped it on to one of my waistbelt rings. "Then tell Svet to step out here and enjoy the view. Ask her if she's doing anything later when we're done."

Svet stepped out and attached herself to a tether next to me. I closed the door to the airlock. She and Monoloa spoke some more Russian to their mutual laughter. Below, the Earth was covered with white fluffy clouds, I could not see any coastline or mountains to recognize. I did not even know which side of the Equator we were on. "Svet says that after we have brought the payloads into the Bay, she will try to seduce a rich American man so she can marry him and live in the United States."

As Monoloa and Major McKenna cycled through the airlock I wondered, "What's the big attraction of the United States?"

"Oh, it's this wonderful country with jobs, opportunity, wealth, freedom, and everything anyone can want." translated Monoloa.

"Tell her about the crime, the homeless, lying politicians, voters who choose to believe 'em. Consider President Clinton. We Americans knew damn well what kind of guy he was. But the sins he got in trouble for are so minor compared to the general willingness of all of our politicians and judges to violate our Constitution and rape the English language it's written in. We just couldn't see punishing him for lying about sex when we weren't even looking at the far worse things he himself and everyone else in our government have been doing. There's the judicial system run amok, juries that'll convict you on flimsy evidence but will set you free if you're actually guilty and can hire Johnny Cochrane, taxes and bureaucracy gone insane, and the occasional ammonium nitrate and fuel oil bomb leveling a city block. Not to mention the Avengers of Yahweh. It's getting so you can't take a nice drive down 101 to Olympia without getting killed."

"Most of the Avengers are in jail now. So they're not a problem anymore."

"Only because the she-male who shot Lucinda copped a plea and turned state's evidence."

"Why would a man make himself look like a woman? Other than as a disguise to evade the law?"

"Don't know. Never wanted to look like a woman. On top of all that, we speak English, use this funny measuring system, and get upset with our government for this, that, and everything else."

Monoloa told Svetlana all of that. She and Roy came outside and waited for Mary Ellen to come out with her camera. Svet spoke some more Russian. Monoloa translated for me. "That's what Pravda used to say! Everything Pravda said the opposite turned out to be true. Pravda means 'truth' and you couldn't expect to find any in a Communist government newspaper. So we Russians assume that America is a wonderful country because Pravda used to describe how terrible you were." Svet was not entirely serious, her tongue was in her cheek.

Mary Ellen came out of the airlock chuckling. "Mono, tell Svet that most of us are decent people, we're a decent nation, but there are problems and dangers. We're a little bit of everything. Sometimes we're bewildered by our social problems, but then every nation has that experience. We try our best, but we don't always know the answers. So we muddle through while enjoying life as much as we can."

Major McKenna chipped in. "Mary Ellen is right. Before you commit to immigration, you might want to visit the U.S. on a tourist visa and see if it's a place you can fall in love with. If not, then maybe God's telling you Russia needs you."

As we set Mary Ellen on a tether high above us, close to the emergency parachute pod, Monoloa ended this conversation. "Actually, Svet was kidding. She is a patriotic Russian and would never seriously consider immigration. But a little affair with an American, that's another story."

"We'll keep that in mind. Mary Ellen, are you filming us?"

"Yes I am, the perfect camera angle. Thank you."

"This is *Neanderthal Return* calling Zvezdny Gorodok." we heard Pidonita's voice.

"This is Star City, we copy *Neanderthal Return*." The Russian mission controller responded in English. Star City is English for Zvezdny Gorodok.

"This is Trviea Harsradich, Captain of the *Neanderthal Return*. Everyone is in position to recover the first Energiya Payload. Is this authorized by Russia?"

"Yes, Captain Harsradich. *Neanderthal Return* is authorized to bring on board Russian owned equipment from both Energiya payloads."

"Thank you, Star City, we copy. This is *Neanderthal Return* calling Houston."

"This is Houston, we copy. We confirm that NASA has purchased and taken delivery of the six Centaur rockets in the Energiya payloads from Lockheed-Martin and Energomash. You are authorized for acquisition of American owned equipment from the Energiya payloads."

"Thank you, Houston. Ladies and gentlemen, commence Payload Acquisition."

"This is Wlmsda Gtslakian in control of Bay Number Four. Russian cosmonauts, please open the Payload Carrier."

Monoloa repeated the request in Russian. Out of Bay Number Four leaped Maria Romanov and Mikhail Dostoevski. Metrola brought the Shuttle close and Svetlana kicked off and maneuvered her way over using her helium jets. We watched and Mary Ellen filmed as the cosmonauts deftly removed the 22 foot diameter nose cone and the 20 by 110 foot cover to the Payload Carrier. They maneuvered these parts around below the Carrier toward the Earth. We listened to the Russian language chatter and then we heard Monoloa's quick translation into Atlantean. "Pidonita, where is our current location relative to Earth?"

"We are crossing Brazil. The nose cone and the cover should reenter the atmosphere over the Atlantic Ocean between South America and Africa if you fire the retro rockets now."

Monoloa translated this into Russian. They triggered the retro rockets on the nose cone and the cover plate. These two huge parts blew away below and behind us. The cosmonauts drew themselves back to the ships on their tethers by operating the cable reels. Wlmsda Gtslakian then spoke in English. "First, we recover the Aries missiles. Go get 'em."

Sorby Mishlakian and Major Davenport leaped out of the Bay with their cables and hooks. They pulled quick disconnect pins to separate each missile from the rest of the payload. Metrola brought us close again, and I maneuvered over to place a tether hook on one of the eyebolts. Major McKenna hooked a tether on the other eyebolt. Working together, Metrola, Wlmsda, and Pidonita used cable reel tension and orbital maneuvering, both ships projected magnetic fields to repel against the Earth's field, to lift the missile crate slowly out of the Payload Carrier and then bring it into the Bay of the *Neanderthal Return*. With the Shuttle providing the opposing force through cable tension, there was no need to deploy the catch net. We repeated this procedure with each of the seven Aries missiles. The astronauts in the cosmic loading dock rotated the duty, General Fairchild participated in one of the missile recoveries, the Russians in some of the others. Then Metrola announced, "That is the last Aries missile, now we go for the big ones."

I heard Wlmsda Gtslakian's voice. "We're ready for the big rockets, Metrola."

"EVA crew. Grab your hand holds, please. Maneuvering to within two dozen *potes* of the payload assembly, as usual. You know what to do when we get there." We didn't have a big runway with which to sprint to a flying leap. We just kick off and maneuver with our helium jets.

The three Centaur missiles in the Payload Carrier loomed large in front of us. "Neil, please hook up the eyebolts to the lone one."

"Will do." I kicked off the side of the Shuttle carrying three tether lines. Metrola fed me line by operating the cable reels to keep them slack. I had some tension on my line. I maneuvered to an eyebolt on the bracket wrapped around the bomb. My tethers were color coded. I put the violet tether on the bomb bracket. I maneuvered away from the 44,000 pound warhead down the cone to the first bracket around the Centaur. I placed a hook, of the right color, to each eyebolt; they were about eight feet apart, about one quarter the way around the curve of the rocket. The center of mass of the whole package should be right in the middle of the pattern made by the three cables. I checked my cable to make sure I wasn't entangled. I returned to the side of the Shuttle by using the cable reel to draw myself in. "All done." Metrola kept the three cables to the rocket assembly slack to avoid affecting the orbit of the mass.

Sorby and Marla Syferkrip leaped from the Weapons Bay of the main ship and attached tether cables to eyebolts on their side of the rocket. "All done here." they told us. The *Neanderthal Return* tethers were also being kept slack, Wlmsda deftly operating the cable reels. Her tethers were hooked to four eyebolts with three forming the same pattern around the center of mass and one on the second bracket toward the base of the Centaur.

"Your turn, Svet and Major McKenna." announced Metrola. "This is where you earn your paychecks."

No kidding. Svetlana and Roy gently and carefully maneuvered themselves down to where the missile was attached to the Payload Carrier. Pidonita, Wlmsda and Metrola were on full alert at their controls. Monoloa provided rapid translation from Svetlana's Russian to both English and Atlantean. We heard Roy's voice first. "I am now at Pin Number One. Removing Pin Number One."

Roy went over the warhead to the other side of the Payload Carrier. He grasped a standard one inch diameter quick disconnect pin. The pins came from American military stores and were delivered by C-5 to Baikonur along with the Aries missiles. He wrapped his fingers around the handle of the pin and pressed the button on the end. A set of balls in the other end of the six inch long pin were pulled in and Roy slipped the pin out of the clevis formed by three one inch think aluminum mounting eyes. The pin was tethered by a two foot long wire rope to the side of one of the rocket brackets. He stowed the pin in a pair of aluminum eyes provided for that purpose. "Pin One is disconnected."

At the same time Roy was removing his pin, Svetlana did likewise for Pin Number Two. She had gone around the gimbaled nozzles at the base of the rocket and pulled the pin on that side and stowed it away. "Pin Two is disconnected."

Now they maneuvered around to Pins Three and Four. Each spacewalker maneuvered around to the pins on the side toward the Shuttle. The pins were deliberately offset by twelve inches to avoid forming a hinge that allows the missile to rotate freely. "Removing Pin Number Three." announced Roy.

"Removing Pin Number Four." announced Svetlana in English. As soon as the missile is free, the astronauts have to back away fast. If the two separated masses, one 49,000 pounds and the other 138,000 pounds, come back together, the spacewalkers can be crushed. Weightless is not massless.

"Pin Number Three removed and stowed." Roy pulled the pin and stowed it quickly. "Pulling back NOW!"

"Pin Number Four removed and stowed." Svetlana did likewise. "Pulling back NOW!"

Both astronauts got out of there in a hurry. Their lines were not tangled and they brought themselves quickly to the side of the Shuttle. Metrola's voice warned us. "Good job people. Now grab a hold of the Shuttle while I feed out a *hekt* of *potes* of line and back away." Metrola called each of our names and we verified we were secure on the side of the Shuttle.

We heard the cable reel motors whirl to life. It was a funny sound. Most of the action is silent because vacuum does not transmit sound. We talk to each other on our radios. But sound travels through our cable tethers and through metal, plastic, and fabric and across handhold to hand. So I could hear the cable reels through my hands as Metrola fed out line and backed off to a distance of 142 feet or 144 *potes*.

"Wlmsda, Pidonita, Shuttle is in position and ready." Metrola spoke in Atlantean. "All three cables are hooked up properly and the payload connecting pins are removed. We need to draw the missile straight up to clear the clevis brackets."

"We copy." both Pidonita and Wlmsda affirmed.

Pidonita took over. She piloted the entire *Neanderthal Return*. Wlmsda controlled the cable reels in Bay Number Four. Metrola controlled both the Shuttle and the Shuttle's cable reels. "All right ladies, on the count of three."

Metrola turned to Ian. "Ian, watch very closely and talk to me if you see something. These three controls are for the cable reels. You know how to operate them. The digital readouts are for cable tensions in *dollons* of force in Base Twelve numbers. You know how to read them. The cables are much stronger than that but let's keep the tension below one *kecht dollons* at all times. We're not in a hurry, we keep the relative speed of this heavy mass to a minimum."

"Got it. 120 megatons of yield, 49,000 pounds. Right!"

Pidonita counted to three in Atlantean and we watched the lines grow tight. The vee formed by the two ships, the cables, and the missile was very shallow. The missile slowly separated from the Payload Carrier. "Missile is clear, separation ten feet." I observed. The Centaur rocket is 10 feet by 30 feet, I used that as the scale.

"Thank you, Neil," called out Metrola, "we'll slacken the lines and let the missile build more distance as it assumes its new orbit."

The lines went slack again and the missile moved steadily away from the Payload Carrier. A tiny delta vee and they separate. We matched the new orbit of the missile. "Separation distance is now thirty feet."

"Thank you, Neil." responded Pidonita. "Now we can commence drawing it into the Bay." All eight lines tightened up.

Metrola warned us. "Okay spacewalkers, use the handholds to go around to the rear of the Shuttle. I know this is a fascinating show, but in case a cable snaps you are safer on the other side."

"We copy, Metrola." We all moved from handhold to handhold to the backside of the Shuttle.

"Mary Ellen, you can film from behind the parachute pod, it'll offer you some protection in case a cable snaps."

"Thank you, Metrola. Will do that."

The missile slowly approached the Bay at only 6 inches per second or so. Air supply might be an issue for the Air Force and Russian spacewalkers, but the Creation spacewalkers in the Bay had their air lines as part of their umbilicals. Monoloa and I breathed pure oxygen at 4 psi. We had plenty of oxygen, but if we ran low there were oxygen ports around the outside of the Shuttle we could tap into to recharge our oxygen bottles. I kept an eye on my digital readouts, all indicated normal operation, I was in no danger.

We watched from the side of the Shuttle ready to leap to avoid a snapped cable. The missile was held tightly between the two ships. The cable reels drawing in the missile were located all around the perimeter of the open door of the Bay. It was obvious that these women have done this many times before. After seven minutes, the missile slowly entered the Bay. The people in the Bay took control of it, gently slowed it to a halt, rotated it, and lashed it down in the rear of the Bay. "First Centaur Missile with Russian Blockbuster warhead is secure." General Fairchild triumphantly announced.

Metrola drew in all of the cables after they were unhooked from the missile. "All right people, we get to do this again. Grab a hold, we are going back to the Payload Carrier."

It only took another hour, though it seemed longer. We got the three rockets and warheads stowed in the Bay. The women inside the Bay put up catch nets to protect inventory from the second and third missiles as they came in.

When we returned to the Shuttle Bay, we were tired but happy. Captain Harsradich, Anatoly Donovon, and General Fairchild greeted us as we came off the Shuttle. The General was still in his NASA pressure suit and Snoopy cap, but he had his helmet off. Trviea kissed me. Then she spoke to all of us. "You did well, all of you. You too, General. I have to admire a senior officer willing to put on a pressure suit and do his share of the grunt work. In four hours we get to do this again for the other Energiya payload. I order you all to go to your rooms and get some sleep.

I mean sleep! No making love, no reading, no electronic entertainment, eat something if you must, but SLEEP!"

"That's an ORDER, Major McKenna." affirmed General Fairchild.

"Yes, SIR!"

We jumped at his shout. "No seducing Neil, Svetlana," advised Anatoly in Russian. He, Monoloa, and Svetlana laughed. "Get your rest. We need you in four hours to do this again."

"A half hour before we rendezvous with the second Payload," continued Trviea, "we'll sound the alarms to your rooms to wake you up and get you ready. I know this is a deviation from your normal expectations of privacy, but this is an extremely important part of Operation Rainbow. After we get the missiles secured in the Bay, we can go back to a semi-normal routine. Get some rest, and we'll see you in three and a half hours."

As we climbed out of our suits, the adrenaline drained out of our systems. We worked hard for sixteen hours and none of us had been getting enough sleep. I barely made it into bed when I crashed.

It was not long enough before I got buzzed awake. I had grown accustomed to getting plenty of sleep and having a nice strong Neanderthal woman kiss me awake so she could smother me with her lust. Not this time. I was alone and the light was suddenly on, shining in my face. The sound of the alarm died away.

My body didn't want to move. It just didn't. I think I fell asleep with the light on. The door opened. "Neil, get up! Please. We've got work to do!"

"Metrola, you're a beautiful lady but you just don't look sexy in that pressure suit. It doesn't flatter your figure. Bursting in like that, you could've seen me naked."

"I've seen you naked. Right now I want to see you in your pressure suit. Maybe later, after we get all of the missiles and bombs on board, and get enough sleep, I can see you naked again." She winked provocatively.

Metrola helped me stand up. She handed me clean underclothes as I needed them while dressing. When I had on the pants, socks, and tunic appropriate for wearing under a pressure suit, Metrola gave me a nice kiss. "What was that for?"

"For doing such a wonderful job out in the vacuum, and for the wonderful job you will do bringing in the second Energiya payload. You make me look good."

"Flattery will get you everywhere. I don't know what them paleoanthropologists were thinking. You girls know how to flirt, how to give that come hither look, and how to seduce a man, be he Cro-Magnon or Neanderthal."

"They should know we can seduce Neanderthal men. We survived for 200,000 years in Ice Age Europe. But to assume we couldn't seduce Cro-Magnon men? You Cro-Magnon men crave sex so much, a female warthog could seduce you!"

Laughing didn't make it easier to put on a pressure suit with sore muscles. "You know something else our paleoanthropologists say? The cave paintings were all done by Cro-Magnons. The Neanderthals never did any."

"I wonder how they know? I can imagine a Neanderthal working on a cave painting and having his friends yell 'Hey stop that! That's flat face behavior!'" We giggled. "Mustafa Khedr showed me a cartoon. Two Neanderthal men are working diligently on a cave painting. A Cro-Magnon man is adjusting his tie using a mirror. One of the Neanderthals says to the other 'It always works out this way. We do all the work, HE gets all the credit!'"

We went out in the Shuttle. The Russian cosmonauts opened the Payload Carrier. Just like before, I placed the hooks, Svetlana Lebed and Roy McKenna pulled the quick disconnect pins, Mary Ellen filmed it, and Monoloa provided her fast translation service. The two Centaurs with the heavy warheads were pulled in, then we finished up with the spare Centaur. Nine more Aries missiles were added to the nine we already had in inventory.

And yet, there was plenty of room in Bay Number Four. It was two hundred feet deep, actually 204 *potes*. The Centaur missiles with their warheads were almost 50 feet long, the Aries missiles half that. The Centaur rocket is ten feet in diameter, we allowed 12 *potes* of room for each, stacked together like a six pack in the rear of the bay. Nesla, Contrviea, and I took measurements to design the structure to hang them out in space. The measurements helped us design the fueling gantry.

After we completed loading the second Energiya payload, Trviea told me, Metrola, and several other people to get plenty of sleep. We have not had adequate rest since before we went down to Kazakhstan to pick up the Russian Bomb Crew. Trviea rotated the girls around, all knew how to operate the air pumps, cable reels, and door to Bay Number Four. Metrola joined me in bed. Too tired to make love, we slept in each other's arms.

While we slept, *Endeavour* came up with two more Aries missiles and another box of equipment. NASA did something quite unusual. *Discovery* was already halfway to the launch pad on the Crawler-Transporter when *Endeavour* went up. NASA would have had *Atlantis* in the Vehicle Assembly Building getting loaded up with another pair of Aries missiles were it not for the shortage of launch ready Morton Thiokols. The pairs recovered from the ocean after the previous launches were still being cleaned up and the spare pair was not yet fueled. In a twelve foot diameter tube loaded with aluminum powder and ammonium perchlorate, the plastic binder has to be fully cured before it can be removed from the casting fixture. After bringing the *Discovery* payload on board, it was decided that we go with the 22 Aries missiles.

Chapter Thirty Seven

Contrviea Tiknika, Nesla Teslakian, and I had a 1/24 scale model set up in Conference Room One. Captain Harsradich, the four Air Force officers, the Russian Bomb Crew, and other people came to see the dog and pony show. Contrviea started off. "This is a model of the spring loaded launcher for the Aries missile. We use a pair of coil springs made of one *tig-it* diameter chrome vanadium steel, drawn and tempered for high strength and ductility. Each spring has a loop diameter of twelve *tig-its* and has one *hekt*, 144, loops with an at rest length of four dozen, 48, *potes*. Both springs are seated on one side of the aluminum pusher assembly. The other side of this pusher assembly bears on the casing of the missile and not on the gimbaled rocket nozzle. It is designed like aircraft structure to save weight and allow as much of the spring energy to transfer to the missile as possible."

I took over briefly. "As you know, this is the old Minuteman I upper stage and has since been used by NASA as the Aries sounding rocket. It is supported by its casing when it is vertical for launch."

Nesla then spoke. "At the rear of the launcher is the static seat of the two springs and the cable reel. A quarter *tig-it* wire rope is attached to the center of the pusher assembly. It leads back between the coil springs to the cable reel. An electric motor operates the cable reel to pull in the wire rope and compress the springs. The springs are compressed twelve and eight, or twenty *potes*." She pushed a toggle switch and the little model cable reel drew back the model pusher ten *tig-its*. "When the pusher slides over a trigger mechanism mounted on its guide rails, these two heavy retaining teeth insert into these holes in the pusher and secure it into place. The cable reel motor shuts off and releases the cable reel to roll freely."

Contrviea continued. "Around the outside is the structure supporting guide rails for the pusher and hemp cloth covered guide rollers for the missile. The entire upper half of the assembly opens up to allow placement of the missile." Nesla pushed another toggle switch and tiny hydraulic actuators opened the upper half of the guide rail and roller assembly. "Because the compression of a pair of high energy springs presents a safety consideration, we designed in hydraulic actuators to effect the opening and closing of this structure. No need for human hands to get too close. People in pressure suits can safely prepare the missile before putting it in the launcher. The door to space will be open when we do this. The missile is picked up, carried and placed in the launcher by these clamps mounted on a jig in the ceiling of the Bay." Contrviea demonstrated. "We use the I-beam rails already in the ceiling of the Bay. The clamps release the missile when it's in place in the launcher." She pushed a button to release the model clamps.

Nesla pressed the toggle switch the other way. "The top of the launcher guide rail assembly closes on the missile. A pair of spring loaded rollers close upon the nose cone of the missile to hold it in place against the pusher. They retreat when the main springs push the missile."

"That way," continued Contrviea, "we don't impact load the missile when we pull back the retaining teeth to release the springs." She pushed a button. The model retaining teeth pulled back releasing the springs. The model missile flew out of the end of the assembly into a pillow set up to catch it. The model pusher oscillated back and forth. The little cable reel motor turned on and pulled on the pusher, damping it to a stop.

Hand clapping and cheering. Then I spoke. "Let me give you the numbers in Base Ten and American units. The at rest length of the springs is 48 feet. The cable reel takes up a couple more feet and it retracts the pusher 20 feet. The Aries missile in its present configuration is 24 feet long. The guide rollers are necessarily that long past the neutral point of the springs. The total length of the assembly is therefore 75 feet. The springs are made of an alloy of steel that has a shear modulus, that's the G value, of about 15 million psi. The two springs together will have a k value of about 178 pounds-force per foot. Compressed to launch position, the springs will exert 3570 pounds of force on the base of the missile, or about 116,000 poundals. This force will reduce in a linear fashion to zero when the springs reach their neutral point. The Aries missile package has a mass of about 22,000 pounds. The launcher will accelerate it to about nine or ten feet per second, ejecting it out of the ship. At that speed it'll be a mile away in less than ten minutes. Then we can light the rocket and send it on its way. Any questions?"

"We're not going to load it with the Bay door closed?"

"No! It's possible the springs can suddenly let go. The B61-12 warhead consists of a ton of steel encasing the nuclear warhead. It's DESIGNED to penetrate dirt or ice. It could easily penetrate the door if launched by these springs. So we load it only when the door is open. When not in use, the spring will be in the at rest position with the pusher held in place by the retaining teeth. The retaining assembly can be moved back and forth. We pick the 20 foot mark because that is enough spring force to launch the missile without overstressing the spring steel in shear. We can move it a little further back if we want more launch speed in the missile."

"It looks good." commented General Fairchild. "We haven't time to give it the critical design review process and spend billions of taxpayer dollars developing it. Paying engineers to sit around fucking around and never make a fucking decision. And then to have bullshitting politicians interfere with the whole process who never understood engineering and don't care. Sorry, excuse my French. It seems we can never just design it and build it anymore. I say, let's just go with this and build it. It's a neat idea, get about ten feet per second delta vee before burning a single ounce of rocket fuel."

"I like it." commented Anatoly. "You Creation women have beaten the reaction mass limitation with your magnetic drive Shuttle and your fusion packet pulse propulsion. Without all of this Nikola Tesla type technology you're using, we've been limited to rockets. Look at the Centaurs and Aries missiles packed into a corner of your Bay Number Four. Then consider the size of the American Shuttles and Energiya rockets, the amount of fuel they burn, to boost that relatively small amount of payload into space. To us, a spring loaded launch device is perfect! Like the wooden leaf spring our ancestors invented to launch a small spear!" Bow and arrow. "Get the missile out the door and coasting to a safe distance for ignition. Light the Minuteman I and away it goes, into the comet. Just one thing: We need to have the Centaur fueled and ready to go when we spring launch the Aries."

"That's right. But fortunately, the Centaur has always been used as an upper stage. It can contain a full load of the liquid hydrogen and oxygen fuel for the few minutes it takes for the Aries missile to deliver its warhead to the comet. The fully fueled Centaur should be floating a safe distance from us by that time. We light it up and remote control it into the hole left by the Aries. This spring loaded Aries launcher can be operated while we're fueling a Centaur."

"Or when the Centaur is fueled and ready to be cast adrift. We'll have to hold it in place to avoid hitting it with the Aries. Then we jettison the Centaur."

"We set up this launcher on the left side of the Bay and aim it out through the left side of the door opening. The Centaur has to be hung out over the right side, where it gets loaded with fuel."

"The Centaur has to be hung on a rigid structure, so it does not swing over in front of the Aries missile at the wrong moment."

"We can do all of this." declared Captain Trviea. "If everyone is agreeable, lets get started and build the thing."

Helga and Andemona had returned in the Shuttle. They went shopping all over Earth for the finest foods that can be found. Because of the money pouring in from publishing companies and television studios in royalties, they were able to pay for everything. Even at that, people often made their attempted purchases into gifts. They came back loaded with pork, sausages, and beer from Germany. Wines, cheeses, and horsemeat from France. Spices and pasta from Italy. Pita from Greece. Kosher food from Israel and New York City. Minke whale meat from the Faeroes. Lobsters and clams from the Atlantic Provinces and New England. Gallons of the best ice cream and a ton of good old American beef. On another trip they got sausage and beef from Argentina. Mutton and lamb meat from the Falklands. Taro root and poi from the Pacific Islands. Seeds of many food plants not known on Planet Creation from New Zealand and Australia. Spices and spice plant seeds from Indonesia. Roast duck and fish from Vietnam. Bok choy from China and saki from Japan. The priority was for seafood and meat from big animals. These foods simply cannot be grown on a spaceship, even one as big as the *Neanderthal Return*. They also loaded up on the finest alcoholic beverages of all types. Helga, Monoloa, and Andemona made full use of their language skills.

If nothing else, we'll eat well on this mission.

Then Lucinda informed me it was our turn to go down to the surface. "I understand there is plenty of Pacific salmon and crab meat available for purchase." She grinned at the anticipation of such good seafood. She could just smell it and taste it. "Isn't Dungeness crab called that because some of it comes from Dungeness?"

"Yeah, that's true. And your boyfriend happens to live near there."

She blushed. "Boyfriend? What boyfriend?"

"Henry."

"Oh, him." She said coyly. "Yes, he lives on a ten acre farm several miles inland from Highway 101 near the Hood Canal. We also have some last minute equipment to pick up at the Bangor Base. They've given us clearance to land there, Metrola is getting ready to bring us down. You can come if you want. I want you to come." She kissed me.

"Sure, I'll come. Maybe Angela can bring the children so I can see them."

"That would be an excellent idea! Len Taylor's going to meet us at the Bangor Base, I told him to bring your car. He'll be coming in at the gate across from Poulsbo. You can tell your ex that. Then in the evening, Len is scheduled to meet Henry at the Cabo San Lucas restaurant in Port Townsend. I'm looking forward to trying Mexican food. But don't tell Henry we're coming, it's supposed to be a surprise."

I could tell Lucy was in love, or at least infatuation. "What ever happened to Chmlee?"

"Chmlee's still there. He'll always have a place in my heart. But now, he has a high forehead, a pointy chin and short black hair. In our religion, we believe that reincarnation is possible. It doesn't always happen, but it sometimes does."

"I don't know if he's a reincarnated Chmlee, but Henry's a good guy. We went to the same high school. Very smart, but a real cut up. He could crack a joke that would leave everyone laughing."

"Yes! Yes! He really cheered me up when I was in the hospital. You know how much a bullet wound HURTS when you can't stop laughing? Chmlee used to do that to me. You know, the differences between you Earth Cro-Magnons: the Native American, the white, the black, the Asian, are really superficial, not fundamental. You Americans have fewer problems when you realize that. Look at me, a bald Neanderthal woman from Atlantis falling for a full blooded

Puyallup-Nisqually man. That's the thing about love, or at least lust, it doesn't seem to care about little details like race or ethnic background."

"I'll try to get a hold of Angela and get her up to Poulsbo."

"Yes, I would like that. Metrola and the other girls are great, but we lack experience with Earth men. Angela might be able to help me pick out a dress and look my best for Henry. She might also give me some pointers."

"You realize she is divorced."

"Yes. But she got you." She winked. "She must have done something right."

"Thank you. Are we over the Western United States?"

"Yes, you can make the call."

Lucinda kissed me again and went to put on her pressure suit for the trip down. I typed the code to get into the U.S. West system, then I hit the area code, 253, and then Angela's phone number. "Hello."

"Hi, Angela. It's me."

"Neil! I never ceased to be amazed that you can call me from the spaceship! Aren't you about ready to go bomb the comet?"

"Yeah, we pretty much got everything we need on board. But there is some stuff we've got to pick up at the Bangor Base. We'll be there this afternoon. I was wondering if you can bring the kids up to the Poulsbo Gate, I would like to see them one more time."

"Yeah, sure. Poulsbo Gate?"

"You come up Highway 3 and take the Poulsbo Exit. Only instead of going to Poulsbo, you go the other way until you reach the Base."

"All right, I know where you're talking about. Yeah, I can pick the kids up from school and get to the Narrows Bridge before the traffic gets ridiculous. I should be able to get to the Gate by about 4:30. Will they know I'm coming?"

"We'll tell them. I'll be coming with Lucinda and Metrola. You'll like Metrola. Len Taylor will also come by. We're planning on going over to Port Townsend to meet Henry Turnipseed at the Cabo San Lucas."

"That's on Water Street! The tourist trap part of Port Townsend."

"Good, you know where it is. Say, can you help Lucinda?"

"Help her do what?"

"Help her get ready to meet Henry. She's acting like a teenager about him."

Angela laughed. "That's wonderful! Sure, I'll do what I can."

"Good. Don't breathe a word of this to Henry. It's a surprise. He thinks he's just meeting Len for an enchilada."

"Got it!" Angela became enthusiastic. "We'll be there!"

I put on my pressure suit and joined Lucinda and Metrola in the Shuttle. Just the three of us going down. I helped with the Air Traffic Control and the Base controllers. They directed us down to the parking lot of the PX. The Navy brought in some of the finest salmon, crab, and prawns caught in Northwest waters. Fresh river trout. Northwest wines. Cases of beer, Rainier, Olympia, Henry's, all of the major brands. All properly packed and refrigerated. Several boxes of spare parts from the Base stores. Machine shop tools and fine micrometers and calipers sized in Earth inches and millimeters. Taps and thread cutters in all of the National Course and National Fine thread sizes, pipe sizes, and Metric sizes. Contrviea told the folks on the ground she needed these to make parts that fit the Earth equipment now loaded in Bay Number Four. Finally, a box of Earth type medical equipment and supplies Dr. Cuc Nguyen needed to set up her practice as a ship's doctor. All she had was what we originally brought to Algeria.

An MP came over. "Neil, Len Taylor is at the Gate with your car."

"A sixties vintage Pontiac?"

"Yep, that's the one."

"Let him in."

Len arrived at the parking lot with my car. Lucinda ran over to him and greeted him with a bone crushing hug and a kiss. I walked over to my car. Hadn't seen it in a while. "Len, I hope you've been taking good care of my car."

"Neil, it's in great shape!"

I opened the hood. The radiator felt too warm to check the water level. Everything looked to be in order. Not too much black crud on stuff. The aluminum intake manifold and the four barrel carburetor were still shiny and pretty. The original equipment wasn't working right, so I bought the fancy stuff at a high performance parts store. I was amazed at how good the fuel mileage was on the freeway. The air cleaner looked a little darker now than when brand new. With a paper towel, I checked the engine oil. "Oil level is fine, it looks nice and black. Have you changed the oil at all, Len?"

"Uh, no."

"How many miles you put on it?"

"Not too many since I got my truck fixed."

"Uh-huh. You drove it some, then." I walked around to the driver's seat and looked at the odometer. "About 3,000 more miles than I remember. We'll need to change the oil and filter."

"We can get that in the PX." offered a Navy man.

"Good. Do you mind if we change the oil here in the parking lot?"

"You won't be the first one to do that."

"All right, I want 7 quarts of Pennzoil 10-40."

"Seven?"

"I kid you not. This 326 engine is the downsized version of the 389. There is plenty of room in the crankcase for motor oil. Since I rebuilt it, it's clean in there. With the PH-11 filter, it'll take that much oil in a change. Maybe while we are at it, we should change the points, this engine really acts up if you don't. And the spark plugs."

We took out a pair of jackstands I keep in the trunk. We got out my hydraulic jack.

Metrola watched with interest. "Why are you getting out that jack?"

"To lift the car up on to the jackstands so we can change the oil."

"You don't need a jack for that." She grinned and winked at Lucinda. "Len, are you ready on your side?"

Len stood on the other side of the car with a jackstand. I carried the other jackstand to the driver's side of the car. Len said, "Ready for what?"

Lucinda and Metrola squatted down in front of the car and firmly gripped the bumper. "Can we lift the car by the bumper like this?"

We laughed. A crowd gathered to watch. "Sure, if you're strong enough." Their arm muscles do look impressive.

They kept their backs straight and lifted my car with their leg strength. "Hurry! Place the jackstands, our arms will get tired."

I quickly set my jackstand under the welded joint in the frame right behind the front wheel. "Jackstand in place on my side."

Len did the same on his side of the car. "Jackstand in place over here."

"Okay, girls. You can lower the car," THUD! "slowly."

"Don't worry," assured Len, "no damage done, it's built rugged, not like these new cars." New cars as in built since 1980.

A Navy enlisted man offered me a cat litter box for use as an oil pan. It had been previously used for this purpose. "I know where I can take the used oil for recycling." he reassured me. "I love your girlfriends. Good looking and can pick up your car. Must be a lot of fun on a date."

"Thank you!" both women exclaimed.

"You're welcome. What size wrench you need for your oil plug?"

"11/16ths." I answered. He dug through his tool chest, he had a '65 Mustang. He handed me a foot long wrench with the ends sized for 11/16 inch hex heads. "Thank you. I'll have it back quickly."

"When you're done. Don't worry. We all appreciate you going after the comet."

"I'm going into the PX to get the oil and filter and stuff." Len went with another Navy person.

I slid the cat litter box underneath my engine. With the wrench and some paper towels, I laid down on my back and crawled on my shoulder blades under my car. I broke the oil plug loose with the wrench. I used my fingers to screw the plug out. It was still very warm to the touch. I pulled the plug away quickly and wrapped it up in a paper towel. The hot black fluid poured out of the engine into the box.

These Navy people are great! I was offered a grease gun! I greased the lower ball joints and all of the steering tie rod ends. I crawled out from under the car and handed the grease gun back to the guy who loaned it to me. "Thank you." Len arrived with 7 quarts of 10-40 oil, a PH-11 filter, spark plugs and points for a '66 Pontiac with a 326 cubic inch engine. "Yeah, might as well change the sparkers while we're at it."

I dug a 3/8 drive ratchet, a three inch extension bar, and a 13/16 spark plug socket out of the tool box that I keep in my trunk. I pulled off one of the spark plug wires and commenced removing the spark plug. "Is there anything I can do?" Metrola is an accomplished mechanic.

"Here, everything is right hand thread." She took control of the ratchet and worked the spark plug loose. Then she removed the ratchet and spun the sparker out of its hole. While she did this, I opened one of the new spark plug packages. I checked the gap with a spark gap tool. I showed the new plug to Metrola. "Make sure this little gasket ring is on the threads when you spin it in. Let me see the old plug." It was tan. Nothing unusual. "Looks good." I pulled the old plug out of the socket. I put the new plug in. "I have to check the gap to make sure it's 35 mils. Point oh three five inches. Careful when you put it in, it's easy to cross the thread. Just flip the switch on the ratchet to turn it the other way."

Metrola has done this sort of thing all of her long adult life. She expertly threaded the new sparker and used the wrench to turn it in as I gapped another new plug. "How much torque for the plug?"

"Get it all the way in, then just muscle it, not too tight. Yeah, that'll work. Make sure the electrical clip in the wire is on."

She slipped the wire back on and felt the snap. "We'll do these one at a time to avoid mixing up the wires."

"Good idea, Metrola." We worked together to change all of the plugs and the points. We transferred the wires one by one from the old distributor cap to the new cap and placed it on. We changed the oil filter, put the oil plug back in, and started pouring in a quart of clean oil. The two women lifted the car by the front bumper off the jackstands to the amusement of our spectators and helpers. Neanderthal women are strong! We removed the jackstands and they set the car down, gently this time. The radiator was now cool enough to check. The water level was fine. When five quarts of oil were in, we turned on the engine and checked the dwell. It was a perfect 30 degrees. Timing a perfect 6 degrees below top dead center. The engine drank two more quarts after we ran it and circulated the oil through the new filter. We checked the dipstick with each quart. We drove the car around a bit, then with the engine warm again and running, I checked the transmission fluid. Level fine. We cleaned ourselves up, didn't get too much black crud on us. We put on clean shirts in the Shuttle.

"Neil, your ex-wife's at the Gate."

"Send her in!"

Angela's minivan drove in and parked next to my car. Christa and Virgil ran out and screamed "Daddy!" I received two hugs, I picked them up and carried them around. I showed them the car. And introduced them to Metrola.

"You are very pretty." Virgil knew that charms just about any woman. "You are even prettier than you look on TV."

"When did you see me on TV?"

"When you were the Demon Woman who got your Shuttle out of the desert." His eyes opened wide. "THIS Shuttle!"

"Yes, that was an interesting experience. I couldn't have done it without your father. He thinks quick and keeps his head. But I'm not a Demon Woman."

"I know that! But it didn't hurt to let the desert bandits think you are!"

"I guess it didn't."

I looked over and saw Angela and Lucinda chatting away. They seemed to hit it off. Angela looked over to me. "Neil, we'll meet you at the Cabo San Lucas. Lucinda wants to get prettied up for Henry. Can you take the kids and bring 'em over?"

"Hmm. Me, Len, Metrola, two children. Five people will fit in the Pontiac. Sure! Go ahead!"

"Yay! Metrola can ride in the back with us!"

"Would you two like to see the inside of the Shuttle?"

"Yeah. Just don't kidnap us!" They laughed.

"We don't do that anymore."

While Metrola gave my children a tour of the spacecraft, Angela drove off with Lucinda. An MP came running up. "Did one of the Creation girls just ride off with your ex?"

"Yes, she did. Is that a problem?"

"Mr. Peace, we are under orders, coming from the President himself, to keep these women ALIVE!"

"Lucinda seems healthy enough to me. I'm sure she'll be all right. The Avengers of Yahweh are all in jail or in hiding."

"Maybe we've got 'em all. But then maybe there are others."

"Well, if we don't get this in the press, nobody will be looking for 'em."

"Listen up!" The MP got the attention of the people in the parking lot. "Those of you in the Navy, you are under orders not to take any action that endangers the life of any woman from Planet Creation. Talking to the press or to any radio or TV station about these women before they are back on their spaceship is a violation of this order. Is that understood?"

"YES SIR!" shouted the personnel enthusiastically. They had no love for the press or for the broadcasters. The MP quickly and quietly spoke into his little radio.

"Listen, Ms. Peace!" The gate guard was exasperated. "We're under orders, they come from the President himself, to keep this woman ALIVE."

"But sir, she wants one last night on the town before going to do battle with a comet. It's a risky proposition, because in order for the equipment to work, the *Neanderthal Return* has to stay within interactive two way radio contact with the nuclear warheads. They have to radar map the comet core. That means getting CLOSE. They don't like to get close to comets anyway, stuff boils off 'em. Then we propose to pump in a hundred megatons of heat energy? Besides, if we don't get her together with her Cro-Magnon boyfriend, she'll die of a broken heart."

Lucinda leaned over to allow the gate guard a better look at her. "I'm touched by your concern for my welfare and I thank you. But I'm an adult the same as you. I'm willing to risk my life if the cause is important, just like you. I have flown 25 trillion miles through the vacuum of space. Please allow me the freedom to travel 25 miles through the State of Washington. Let us have some space. Freedom is what America is about, and that means sometimes we have to be allowed to take our chances."

"I don't think Henry or Len will hurt her." affirmed Angela. "I've known them since I first met Neil. They helped her and Helga get away from the Avengers. Most people know what's at stake here, they'll look out for us and protect us."

"Well, I tell you what. Oh, here comes my commander."

A dignified older gentleman came over. He spoke with his subordinate for a minute. Then he came to Angela's window. "Ms. Peace, Mrs. Renuxler, Lieutenant Rosenthal."

"Pleased to meet you." Both women accepted his handshake.

"Situation is like this: Ms. Peace is a civilian, an American citizen. If she wants to leave the Base, is not breaking any law or wanted on any accusation of breaking the law, I have to let her go. She can be killed in a car wreck but I have to let her take her chances. Mrs. Renuxler is a foreigner. She is legally in the country and is not breaking any law. Normally, we have to let her go and take the same chances any other person takes. But I have these orders to keep her alive. But I understand your need for freedom. So I tell you what I'll do. I'll send an unmarked car. It won't attract attention like a Secret Service limo, it'll be discreet. They'll keep their distance and you can have your evening. If something happens, he'll be Johnny on the spot to help you."

"That sounds like a reasonable plan." thought Lucinda.

"Yeah, it does. But I don't like being followed by the fuzz."

"Just this evening, Ms. Peace, please. He won't ticket you for a few miles over the speed limit. Just don't try to run away from him."

Lucinda knew the address of the Poulsbo branch of the bank with the Creation account. She withdrew several hundred dollars. "Damn! Lucinda, you could buy me some clothes!"

"Why not? Let's go to the dress shop." They went to a fine women's clothing store in Poulsbo.

The people at the clothing shop made both women look beautiful and elegant. They gave each a makeover. Being from Creation, Lucinda was not used to wearing makeup. But she warmed up to the lipstick, eye shadow, and face powder. Some was used to soften the skin around the back and top of her head and keep it from shining. Her muscle build is a challenge, her breasts a size D, but the store's experts know how to fit women who are difficult to fit. They were careful around her bullet wound. Finally, Lucinda admired herself in the mirror. Red dress, red carnation on a red headband, long legs properly displayed in dark nylons. Red pumps with three inch heels on the feet of a five foot ten Lucinda. "How do I look? Will Henry like it?"

"Henry's not gay." declared Angela. "He will love it!" Angela was dressed to kill in royal blue. "It's after six. Reservations are at seven in Port Townsend. Let's go."

Lucinda paid for everything and they left for Port Townsend.

"Dad, do we hafta go to a fancy Mexican restaurant?" asked Christa plaintively.

"Yes, we do. We adults like to go out like that. But I'll tell you what. There is a

McDonald's and other places like that on the old Highway 3 route through Poulsbo. Maybe we can get a Happy Meal or a Kid's Meal. If we do that, can you behave for us when we go to the Cabo San Lucas?"

"Yeah, we can do that!" They like burgers and fries.

"Okay, climb into the car."

Metrola asked, "If we're going out to eat, why take the kids to a fast food place?"

"You're not used to children. I find that if I let them have a little something they like to eat, they behave much better. It's better if they are not hungry, bored, and cranky when in a nice place like the Cabo San Lucas."

"All right. Let us change quick in the Shuttle, then I'll lock it up. They'll let us come back and get it."

"Will they?"

"They want us to bomb the comet?" She grinned. We went into the Shuttle and quickly changed into nice clothes. She had a nice dress in there, I was amazed. I pulled on my dress slacks and Arrow shirt, I managed to buy some clothes in D.C. After changing, Metrola locked up the Shuttle and we went to the car.

"Keys, please." Len handed me the keys to my car. The engine fired up, it sounded wonderful. I drove us out the Gate and headed to a hamburger joint to get the children something.

Lieutenant Rosenthal spotted wavy brown hair in the back seat of the old Pontiac. "Uh, exactly WHERE is Metrola Mornuxler?"

"Uh, she's back at her Shuttle, isn't she?"

"I don't think so. Damn!"

We pulled out of the drive through lane of the restaurant, the children were happy with their hamburgers, fries, and little toys. They love sitting next to Metrola. A Poulsbo Police cruiser came down the opposite side of the street. His lights flashed on, he spun around, and pulled us over. He refused my driver's license. "Is Metrola Mornuxler in there?"

"Yes, officer, here I am."

"Are you all right?"

"I'm great! Is there a problem, officer?"

"The Navy guys are a little worried about you." The policeman chuckled. "It seems you gave 'em the slip. Pardon me for a moment." After a few minutes on his radio he came back over. "There is an unmarked car waiting for you at the intersection ahead. They will follow you at a discreet distance. Don't be alarmed and don't try to run away from them. Their main purpose in life right now is to keep Metrola alive. They know you're going to Port Townsend. Have a good evening, and please don't be angry with us for safeguarding your lives."

"Thanks, Officer. Have a good evening."

We drove off to the Hood Canal Bridge. We caught up with and passed Angela on the way. Len rolled down his window and yelled to her. "Angie! Lookin' GOOD! Neil, would you mind?"

"We're divorced, Len. What do I care? I have Metrola here." I winked at her. "She can keep me happy."

"Just don't take me for granted."

"I don't, Met, I don't."

Len turned back toward Angela. "Let us go on ahead. Then we'll have Henry sat down when you arrive!"

"Okay!"

I sped on ahead and led the way across the bridge. We took the Route 19 road directly to Port Townsend. We sat down with Henry in the restaurant. He was happy to see my children. Mums the word. Then Angela and Lucinda were led to our table. Henry stared with his mouth dropped. "Lucinda, WOW! Oh, excuse me, where are my manners." He stood up. We all stood up for the ladies.

Lucinda embraced him, he returned the hug. They kissed. Len observed, "She gave me a nice hug and kiss too. But it wasn't," pause "quite," pause "like," pause "that."

They broke apart and we sat down to dinner. We had a wonderful time, the food was excellent, even the children tried it. They behaved. We paid our bill and went for a walk down Water Street and along the waterfront. Henry and Lucinda lagged behind us about 50 feet, they held hands and would stop to steal a kiss. We went out on the ferry dock and watched the water for a while. We watched a ferry come in and then we left the dock. One child and then another rode on my shoulders. Metrola carried on her shoulders whichever child was not on mine. The time came for Angela to go home with the children.

"You're going on Operation Rainbow?"

"Yes, Angie, I am."

She took a deep breath. "I know this needs to be done. Just remember, if you move the comet, our children need a father. Be careful." We are divorced, but I let her embrace me for a second.

I gave each child one last long hug, it was like the scene at Leninsk. The children didn't seem as frightened as their mother, they knew I was coming back. Henry drove off with Lucinda in his truck. We booked two rooms in one of the Victorian buildings. Len partied in the bars most of the night before turning in. Metrola partied with me in our room.

The next morning, we drove back to the Bangor Base. They let us in to get to the Shuttle. Metrola unlocked it. Everything was there. I handed Len my car keys. "Hey Neil, good luck, buddy." He shook my hand, we gave each other a quick hug. "I'll take good care of your car, won't drive it too much. It'll be waiting for you." He didn't let it show, but I knew he was concerned that I might not come back.

Henry arrived, bringing Lucinda. She had the glow on her face that Angela had on the first morning of our honeymoon. I was happy for her and for Henry. They embraced and kissed one last time. We didn't rush them. We could see Henry fight back tears as Lucinda boarded the Shuttle. Men don't cry in public. He didn't get back into his truck to drive home until he could no longer see the Shuttle in the sky.

Chapter Thirty Eight

Captain Harsradich took the pilot's seat and increased the pulse frequency of the fusion reactor. The ship accelerated away from Earth at ten feet per second squared. About halfway there, the ship turned around and decelerated to match orbits with the comet. Our maximum speed, relative to the rest of the Solar System, was 1250 miles per second. The trip to the comet took 16 days.

The acceleration of the ship is shown on digital readouts posted everywhere. In addition to the Creation numerals stating the acceleration in *potes* per *prelate* squared, Helga, Lucinda, and Andemona added Earth numeral readouts. The shorthand 'FT/S²' was written in Roman alphabet. The shorthand 'M/C²' is Cyrillic alphabet for M/S².

After we left Earth orbit, I went to the Machine Shop to build the spring launcher. It had roller mills and a foundry in addition to the machine tools. We watched as the rollers drew chrome vanadium steel of their high shear modulus alloy into one *tig-it* diameter round bar. Glowing orange with heat, the round bar was pulled into a helix by an 11 1/2 *tig-it* diameter forming spindle. Each spring as formed was one *pote* in loop diameter, 144 loops with a 4 *tig-it* offset every loop, total length, 48 *potes*. For each spring we used a little more than 452 *potes* of round bar, 446 feet, plus a few extra feet for the ends. Each spring has a mass of about 1160 pounds.

Each large spring was allowed to cool and we machined the ends to fit into the spring cap on one end and the static base on the other end. Then Contrviea and her expert steel workers heat treated both springs at the same time to give them identical properties. Normalized, quenched, and tempered. All this inside a spaceship.

It took us several days to manufacture the parts of the missile launcher, and then we built it in Bay Number Four. At the acceleration of 10 feet per second squared, each 1160 pound spring had a weight of about 360 pounds. Several of us carried it through the corridors into Bay Number Four. Nice to have Neanderthal physical strength for this kind of work. Most of the equipment had been moved back into the Bay clearing the hallways.

We laid each spring down in front of the cable reel and static spring seat already mounted on the Bay floor, eighty feet from the door to space. We attached each spring to the static seat with an omega bracket and a 3/8 *tig-it* bolt through a hole drilled through the spring itself. One of the Aries missiles was already suspended in the moving fixture. "Fit test of the missile in the Missile Loader is a success, as you can see." announced a proud Nesla Teslakian.

"I see one of the mounting brackets is placed up close to the warhead, the second bracket is placed about six feet from the base."

"Center of mass. The warhead's pretty heavy, 3,000 pounds. The clamps don't put any squeezing force on the missile; they just wrap around enough of it to contain it. We use rubber to line the clamps where they bear on the rocket casing." Garden Room has rubber trees. "We use hydraulic actuators to open and close the clamps and to move the rocket up and down and sideways. Here, try this control panel." She handed me the box with two joysticks. "Don't push this button here," she pointed to the button with a hinged cover plate over it, "you'll open the clamps and drop the missile. This joystick moves it up and down. This one moves it forward and back and sideways."

I pushed the left joystick and the missile moved up. Pulled it the other way, and the missile moved down. With the other joystick, I moved it around the Bay. "This should work for loading each missile into the launcher. Are we going to leave it hanging here to fit test the pusher assembly?"

"Yes, I believe we will do that, is the pusher almost finished?"

"It should be." Lightweight, made with nonweldable aircraft structural aluminum. We machined a ring with a groove to fit the base of the rocket casing, 3 feet 8 inches in diameter. We took two square tubes and placed them six inches apart. Upon these are mounted the two spring caps, press formed out of 1/8 *tig-it* aluminum plate, 13 inches in diameter. Beyond the spring caps, the tubes are bent to go around the rocket nozzle and connect to the ring. Since we cannot weld this type of aluminum, we made folded brackets to allow attachment with steel fasteners, just like Boeing aircraft. We added crossbars for intercostal type stiffening, and slant bars to form a kind of peace symbol shaped truss on each side with the ring. We cut sections out of the ring to clear the rocket guide rollers as the springs push the missile forward. We lined the remaining sections of the ring with cloth to avoid scratching the rocket casing. In the gap between the spring caps is mounted the cable bracket. Sawed out of a tee, the wide flange is cut to form a rounded point, to which a shackle is fitted through a hole. Attached to the outside of the ring sections are slide brackets to fit the guide rails.

Over toward the right side of the Bay, movable 142 foot long I-beam rails were installed. They are designed to extend out of the Bay when the door is open and carry the Centaur missile out to be fueled and made ready for launch. When the missile is hung outside, two fueling gantries, one for liquid oxygen and one for liquid hydrogen, are extended out to fuel the Centaur. If we had to maneuver, the assembly was designed to carry the Centaur fully fueled at two gees of acceleration. To free the rocket, the I-beam rails are withdrawn and the entire ship is pulled away.

After each missile is launched, the U. S. Air Force controls its flight. The Russians control the Centaur warhead. They, the Science and Humanities people and Creation women were all over the Viewing Lounge installing the Earth equipment and wiring it into the *Neanderthal Return's* electrical and radio system. It was a mess over there with small parts, tools, and wires.

Several people walked in with the pusher assembly, above described. "Neil, Nesla," called Contrviea, "we're ready to fit test this pusher assembly to the missile."

"Good. Let's do it to it." I cheerfully suggested. I lowered the missile to about three feet off the floor. Contrviea and Major McKenna carefully guided the grooved ring sections around the nozzle and up against the casing. "Clears the nozzle," I observed.

"The grooves fit the casing perfectly." declared General Fairchild. "Good work people."

"Now we need to fit it on to the guide rails." announced Contrviea. She and Roy carried the assembly over to the end of the steel guide rails. Two simple half by two *tig-it* rectangle cross section bars at the sides, each welded to mounting bars at three foot intervals, a total of 60 feet in length. They fitted the guide brackets of the cap assembly on to these rails and slid the assembly to the ends of the springs. They picked up the springs and fastened them into the spring caps of the assembly.

"How about fit testing the missile to the rollers?" I asked. "If we have to do it now, we have to compress the spring first, and then load the missile. For safety reasons, we don't want to do that with the door closed."

"We've already done that, it fits in the rollers."

"Good. When we close the top half of the assembly, do the quick disconnect pins fit?"

"Yep, they sure do. I like your idea of reusing the one inch quick disconnects from the Energiya payload retaining equipment."

"Well, our hands are clear of the spring pusher and rocket clearance envelope, so we can safely lock the two halves together by hand. Maybe we should test this launcher with a dummy missile. Put a launch crew in pressure suits and open the door to space, load the dummy missile and launch it out the door."

"Just toss two dozen *gunds* of mass out the door?"

"Sure. It's in free fall once we've launched it. We can recover it with slings, good training exercise."

"But a little dangerous at three *hekt kepfats* per *prelate* relative to the rest of the Solar System."

"A tiny half inch asteroid would kill like a bullet. But that can happen anyway. Yet we perform lots of spacewalks without anybody getting killed."

"Of course you don't schedule any spacewalks during known meteor showers. But people have been on *Mir* and on the new Space Station during those meteor showers."

"We've been lucky *Mir* hasn't been hit by a meteor. A problem with space stations, the Shuttle can come down to avoid exposure to meteor showers. Might be worth the risk. If we don't fetch it, the dummy missile will fly right out of the Solar System if we launch it at our current speed."

"We don't need to test it with a dummy missile. We can just test the cable reel and measure the *dollons* of force in the spring with each *tig-it* of compression."

Later on, we tested the cable reel. It proved capable of compressing the springs. We measured the force at the 20 foot compression mark as four *gunds* one *hekt* eight dozen and two *dollons*, or about 3756 pounds, about what we calculated. The retaining teeth proved capable of holding the springs in place. They should, we designed them with a factor of safety of 24. Then we released the pusher with the cable reel at full tension. We let the pusher slowly move out to the at rest position. With grease painted on the guide rails, we knew this baby would work just fine.

After all of the launch and control equipment was installed and tested, we still found plenty to do. We continued the fire drills, emergency medical drills, strap down drills, and so on. Every Earthling besides me attended Atlantean language classes, with an introduction to Creation history, politics, geography, and religions. The instructors were Helga, Lucinda, Andemona, and Monoloa. Because I taught most of the Atlantean women English, Anatoly asked me to drill his three Russian colleagues in English. In return, everyone on the ship received Russian language instruction from the Bomb Crew, Monoloa, and General Fairchild, who is also fluent in Russian. He and his Majors trained hard with the Russian Bomb Crew simulating launch and detonation scenarios.

Drinks in our hands, a bunch of us relaxed in a small lounge room with a window to view space. We could see the Centauris constellation and the Neanderthals' home star. The Air Force general reminisced about his days as a key turner in the Minuteman Launch Control Facilities. "We each had a loaded pistol. If either one of us thinks the other had gone crazy, he was authorized to shoot him. It's amazing that we haven't had more homicides resulting from the two missilemen getting on each other's nerves. That's because our psychological testing weeded out the ones who might react that way."

"So the pistol business was really a way of testing the validity of your psychological testing?" Anatoly Donovon's twinkling eyes and perpetual grin laughed at the irony of him listening to the American frankly discussing the procedures by which he would destroy much of the Soviet

Union. He also knew that he might have been responsible for the murder of millions of Americans if certain events had transpired differently.

"Well, you could say that. The psychologists would have a lot of explaining to do if we had a wave of missilemen shooting each other in the Launch Control Facilities. But anyway, after performing all of the verifications of the launch orders, I think we would know if they were in response to a Soviet First Strike. Induced earthquakes. We spent a lot of time trying to imagine what that would be like, in the hole when bombs are detonating all over the Central Plains. Dirty little secret is that we would've been extremely reluctant to turn the keys if we didn't feel anything like that and the telephone informed us of a lack of actual nuclear detonations. Clue: a facility that no longer exists doesn't answer the phone."

Anatoly chuckled. He's heard these stories from the Strategic Rocket Forces people. "If they answer the phone, you know they hadn't been hit yet! 'Hey, Morton! Good to hear from you! It's nice to know you're still alive, shhhhhhhhhh. Oh shit!'"

We laughed at the Strangelovian humor. Morton was still chuckling when he continued. "We both decide the launch order is genuine. Then we have the duty to launch the missiles whether we want to or not. Although if either of us don't want to, we don't launch the missiles. But anyway, we feed in the launch code sent to us, telling each missile warhead which one of the 200 targets in its flight computer to attack. We knew that with some of the targeting plans the missiles would fly right over the Soviet Union and come down in China. Why hit Russia if you're not the nation with whom we're at war? North Korea would become toast in most of the targeting plans. Take any country that made itself a pain in the American ass and you can bet it was in our targeting plans. You would think Khaddafy of Saddam would be a little saner, knowing this. After feeding in the launch code, we approach the key slots on opposite sides of our underground room. We insert the keys, and on the count of three, we launch the missiles. The 200,000 pound lids fly to open the silos, and the rockets rise out to play their role in Armageddon. We watch the horizontal bars on the panel light up. Each stage in the launch procedure for each of our little group of ten silos, another horizontal bar would light up. The bottom bar is 'Missile Away'. Soon all ten of our monitors would have 'Missile Away' lit up. We could launch the entire wing of 150 or 200 silos, but we monitor our little group of ten."

"What did your procedures say when all of your missiles are away?" Trviea's morbid curiosity got the better of her.

"Well that's the funny thing about 'em. They said nothing. Absolutely nothing. I guess we would still be in the Air Force, but that's about it. If we somehow survived the nuclear war, then we were free to report for duty to whatever United States government still in existence, IF it were still in existence."

Trviea shook her head. Her fear of Cro-Magnons proved rational. "A Dinosaur Killer event triggered by the dinosaurs themselves. We go to all of the trouble to blast this comet and shift its orbit. Then a few years later you all commit mutual suicide."

"It's not as likely as it used to be. Some of the Crazy States, Libya, Iraq, Iran, North Korea, could conceivably toss a nuke and get burned in return. It wouldn't be like a Big Show put on by Russia and America. Still, it wouldn't be good. Just consider this, Trviea, the Face Mountain aliens might have planted the Virus to deliberately kill off your Species. This comet might have been put on this trajectory for the same deliberate reason. We built the means to do to ourselves what they intended to do to us. Because we did, we now have the means to save our Genus from extinction."

"I can see why the Face Mountain aliens would want to avoid sharing the Galaxy with us."

General Fairchild looked like he knew something. "Trying to guess alien intentions is an interesting experience."

"IS an interesting experience, General?" my suspicions were aroused.

"Hey, we saw your Blue Light in our sky, we had to brainstorm your possible intentions, and map out our responses to whatever you turned out to be!"

"I understand that, General. But spending a few years sitting in Minuteman launchers isn't the only reason you were selected for this mission. There are plenty of Air Force officers who've spent time in the hole. I've done some checking around before leaving Earth orbit. You've been involved in some extremely black projects. And I don't mean missile silos that everyone knows about. So General, answer me this: Just what was it that crashed near Roswell?"

"Test dummies dropped with parachutes. They were mistaken for aliens."

"That's funny, I thought it was a weather balloon."

"Well, there was a balloon that was used to detect the radioactive debris from any Soviet nuclear test that might've then occurred."

"Right. That's almost believable given the general level of common sense usually exhibited by our government. Launch a balloon in New Mexico to detect radioactivity from nuclear explosions in the Soviet Union. Heaven forbid that we might launch such balloons in Alaska which is so much closer to the Soviet Union! Why keep it secret? Radioactivity from nuclear explosions was not a secret! Of course we monitored for it! The thing that crashed in New Mexico was such a balloon? Bullshit!"

"Well, that's what it was."

"It wasn't one of us." confirmed Trviea.

"I believe Trviea, I don't believe you."

"Why do you believe Trviea?" asked Morton.

Fair question. "A foxy Neanderthal woman in the pilot's seat of a crashed spacecraft? No way in Hell would that not have leaked out. Even if she died in the crash. If she survived, the rancher would've taken her to the local hospital and it would've been out then! Nobody has connected Neanderthal women with Roswell. Your test dummies don't look like Neanderthal women either and they weren't being used in 1947. Those were several years later, every Roswell aficionado knows that. Why did the Army Air Force tell the Roswell newspaper that it was a flying disk? That gave us the Daily Record headline reading 'RAAF CAPTURES FLYING SAUCER'. Then they tell the Daily Record it's a weather balloon! No mention of test dummies or of any monitoring for radioactivity. What's so damn sensitive about a lousy weather balloon? Or any of that other stuff? The alien crashed at Roswell theory doesn't make sense, at least it didn't before these girls showed up, but neither does your weather balloon explanation. So what was it REALLY?"

"Even if I knew, I wouldn't be authorized to tell you."

"Well General, I guess we don't have to bomb the comet if you're going to withhold information from us." Captain Harsradich actually looked serious. I knew she wasn't, Anatoly knew she wasn't, but the General spent too much time in D.C. to catch on. I like Anatoly. He's smart, an engineer's engineer, and he's not full of shit.

"Trviea, you wouldn't dare blackmail me like that. How would you justify something so immoral as sentencing six billion human beings to die because I refused to reveal classified information?"

"Coming from a man who confessed to being quite willing to launch 200 missiles, each with three warheads, for a total of 600 nuclear bombs, to go off all at once; well, I don't believe you're in a position to question the morality of my actions." She smiled sardonically. "Look, if what crashed at Roswell was a balloon, or a secret Nazi aircraft you were test flying, or even a magnetic drive flying saucer of your design, if there were your own test dummies, then it's not my concern. But if what crashed at Roswell is NOT of Earth origin, then we from Creation have a right to know WHAT it is."

"General," I added, "she has a point. Consider the aliens who carved Face Mountain on Mars. They have a brain inside a skull, a spinal cord inside vertebrae. But this is the product of parallel evolution. They are not related to us, they are not as closely related to fish and dinosaurs as we are. Why did they carve Face Mountain? Perhaps to draw our attention. If we develop a dangerous level of technology, our natural human curiosity would cause us to send astronauts to Face Mountain. They might find an information repository that causes them to hang around long enough to get completely infected with the Cro-Magnon version of this engineered Virus. The astronauts bring it back. This Virus in its benign form infects the entire male population of Earth. Then it turns nasty. That's the Face Mountain people. Now who are these Gray guys, who are NOT the species that carved Face Mountain, and what do THEY want?"

"General. The Face Mountaineers, they played God. They took my ancestors and transplanted them from Europe to Creation. Then for reasons we do not know, my Race died out on Earth. You Cro-Magnons have been blaming yourselves for the extinction of the Neanderthal. Yet you haven't a lick of evidence for such guilt. Even if Cro-Magnons were responsible for the Neanderthal extinction, you are not at fault any more than a five year old German child could be blamed for the Nazi Holocaust. I don't believe that's what happened. Wars, yes. But also trade, communication, learning each other's languages, assistance for the unfortunate. We humans do that as well. I seriously doubt Stone Age people would ever perpetrate a genocide, even if they were capable, which they were not. A disease that Cro-Magnons are immune to, but deadly to Neanderthals, would be a good explanation for why there are no Neanderthals on Earth but over an *enbeeyon* of Cro-Magnons."

"We're natural allies, General. Us and the Neanderthals. These true aliens, they might well not have our best interests at heart. Earth and Creation had damn well better learn to work together. What is the truth about Roswell?"

Morton Fairchild took a deep breath. "It was a probe, piloted by a computer. No biological pilot. The language looked unfamiliar. But we thought that was just a clever code. We were big on codes and ciphers and encryptions right after World War II. Then we analyzed the fasteners. Nuts, bolts, screws, rivets. Not millimeters. Not inches. Shit! All of the threads were left handed. Everything on Earth except turnbuckles use right handed threads. I've noticed the right hand threads on all of your fasteners. Even a top secret Earth project would use standard parts. In all of these years, that is all we could ever figure out about it."

"Is this wreckage kept at Area 51?"

"No. That's a disinformation campaign. Ellis Air Force Base is where we test the new top secret stuff. No alien technology there. The Roswell Wreck is kept in a special building in Antarctica a little over 100 miles from McMurdo. Perpetually cold, great for preserving things. We've seen to it that everyone who stumbles on to this building never says anything about it."

"Thank you, General." Trviea was subdued. There is more to frighten her in this Galaxy than Cro-Magnons and comets.

Mustafa Khedr, Chuck Carter, and Sabar Duradich finally had a chance to look at the photographs from the building at Kilometer 206 on the Bawiti Highway. "So we're all agreed, that these two lines represent units of measure." Sabar concluded. "That one hundred of these 'feet' are exactly equal to sixty of these 'cubits', and that distance turns out to be the length of one arc second of the Earth's surface."

"That's what we were able to determine." affirmed Mustafa. "Easy enough to do. Then we started to consider a common ratio. Split the '*Zep Tepi* foot' into twelve '*Zep Tepi* inches', twenty of them are equal to the '*Zep Tepi* cubit'. But we cannot find any evidence that they actually did this. Split the 'foot' into three 'hands', five of them equals one 'cubit'. The 'foot' is precisely six tenths of the 'cubit'. Now what does that mean?"

"A start on deciphering this language perhaps. Did they call the shorter unit a 'foot'? Is their word for this unit the same as their word for the thing on the end of your leg? I think this here," Sabar pointed to a series of symbols, "is the word for this unit of length."

"Could be." considered Chuck. "*Pes* is Latin for foot, *pod* is Greek for foot. Both words refer to the end of the leg, and for the unit of measure. Foot is the name of the pre-Metric unit of length in all of Europe. But *chih* is not Chinese for the end of the leg, and *shaku* is Japanese for 'car garage'."

"In the Far East, it seems that they gave the unit a different name, or *chih* and *shaku* have completely different meanings now than they did in ancient times."

"There is something else about pre-Metric systems of measure around the Earth. The British-American pattern: 12 inches equals a foot, three feet a yard, two yards a fathom, is surprisingly common. It is the pattern of YOUR system of measure, which you developed 4 light years away! American football games are broadcast on Spanish language stations, they use the word *yarda* for the yard. But *vara* is the pre-Metric Spanish unit equal to three Spanish *pies*. Six *pies* was a *braza*, used for many things in addition to water depths. These were once common in Latin America. The Chinese had a unit equal to six *chihs*. The Japanese had a unit equal to six *shakus*, sometimes referred to as Japanese fathoms."

"It shouldn't be too surprising that human factors based systems of measure would exhibit a similarity. The ratios in body dimensions don't differ that much, and people would naturally want to round off to integral numbers."

"This foot-yard-fathom pattern isn't the only human factors based regime. The Ancient Egyptians, Babylonians, and Hebrews had a preference for cubits, spans, palms, and fingers. Russia was not the only place that used a seven foot unit of length. The Greeks and the Phoenicians split their foot into 16 fingers, while the cubit was split into 24 or 28 fingers depending on who you talked to. That created ratios between the foot and the cubit a little different than the six to ten ratio we see in these ancient engravings."

"We still don't know if these were called feet by the people who drew these gold sheets. The reason we're even bothering with this is the engraving of the comet that matches right up with the appearance of Wormwood on October 13, 10,495 B.C. We need to determine what these engravers knew about this comet. We need to try to find out about their mathematics. At least we seem to have a good definition of their units of measure, and from these units, evidence that they knew the circumference and diameter of Earth."

"Maybe, maybe not. This is very speculative." Mustafa is still reeling from how Egyptology will react to all of this unbridled speculation.

"Don't worry, Mustafa." reassured Chuck. He chuckled. "Millions of miles from Egypt, we are free to speculate without worrying about losing our jobs. I've been looking at this plate, 1FB-2. I believe that these are numbers and that this is a lesson in arithmetic."

Chapter Thirty Nine

I slowly opened my eyes. It was dark, I couldn't see anything. I was breathing through hair, feeling the warmth of her body next to mine. Her long muscular back was up against my belly, my arms trapped around her front. Did it matter which one? She seemed extremely content. And sound asleep. I went back to dreamland.

Next time I opened my eyes, a naked woman combed her blonde hair in the mirror. A soft light allowed me to see enough of her to remember who she was. Helga turned around and smiled. "Nice to see you're still alive."

"Nice to be alive." I've always liked the tall women, six feet, fathom girls. With brow ridges and muscles, Helga is nevertheless a babe.

"I believe today is the day you get to launch a missile."

"I believe you're right. But right now, I only want to install it in the silo."

She came over. "I cannot think of a better place for it."

An hour later, we gathered in Conference Room One. A large video screen showed the comet. The coma was a diffuse white fog that hid the core. Sabar Duradich used a pointer and operated the display controls. "This is how Wormwood looks on the outside. We are now moving in a wide orbit around it. It is now May 6 Earth time, the comet is now one *hekt*, two dozen and four and 8/12 *beeyon kepfats*; 832 million miles or 1.339 billion kilometers from the Sun. Considering the 93 million mile orbit of Earth and its position on April 12, it has about 755 million miles to travel before hitting Earth. The coma is spreading. Those molecules accelerated to escape velocity by heat encounter nothing but the vacuum of space. Out here the weak solar wind does not turn these loose molecules and ions and form the tail. Even at this distance, we are flying through the outer reaches of the coma."

"Wonderful place for a spaceship." commented Captain Harsradich.

"Lotsa low boiling point gasses," I said, "290 below Fahrenheit, 5.3 BTU's per hour per square foot from the Sun."

Sabar pressed some buttons. "Yeah. Slight greenhouse effect from the coma gasses reflecting low temp infrared. Now we're getting the radar images. Just like we thought, the core is about three dozen *kepfats* in diameter. 58 miles. It's a big one. It's also as heavy as we feared. Fairly round from its gravity, as we can see. There are a few quarter to half *kepfat* chunks in orbit around the main mass. Boiling fumes lift them up and they fall back into the main mass. There are smaller masses, on the order of about a *hekt pfats*, down to a dozen *pfats*, ranging out to about a *hekt* of *kepfats* from the surface of the main mass. We can detect *chmfat* sized particles out to two *hekt kepfats* from the main mass."

"Close to the 57 pounds per cubic foot density of cold water ice."

"Yes, at least 40 pounds per cubic foot. We'll need the megatons of the Soviet bombs to move it."

General Fairchild thought through the Creation units. *Fat* means reach, knowing that makes this system of measure easier to understand. A *chmfat*, full-reach, is six *potes*, the Creation fathom. "So we have to dodge fathom sized ice cubes as far as 288 *kepfats* from the surface of the main mass? Lovely. It's like launching through a God damn volcanic eruption. Smaller pieces than that can wreck the Aries missile. We anticipated this, there is a radar in the nose cone to detect and avoid these chunks. But still,"

"Not exactly a one hundred per cent chance of success." added Anatoly Donovon. "The

Sandia warhead should punch through these small chunks, but the Minuteman upper stage might be destroyed by such a collision."

"Hopefully, we don't bury the Sandia in one of the smaller chunks and burn it."

"If that happens, we'll have to launch a second Aries missile."

"That means we cannot let go of the Centaur at such a high speed toward the comet. No problem, plenty of delta vee available in the Centaur rocket."

"We'll have to hold on to the Centaur until we know the results of the Aries attack. The window of opportunity is not that long. First, we have to blow the hole in the side of the main mass near its rotational pole. Hot gasses then blow out of the hole. We'll have to wait for it to cool down enough to allow in the Soviet bomb in its Donovon Penetration Vehicle, before launching the Centaur. But soon after that, the hole will start to close from gravitation, falling in on itself."

"What's the acceleration due to gravity at the surface of this thing?"

"We used the density of water ice when we did the first calculations, 57 pounds per cubic foot, to get the ballpark figures we used. We calculated something on the order of 0.06 or 0.07 feet per second squared. Behavior of the orbiting chunks verifies that. Sounds pretty low, but it's gravity nevertheless. We'll have time to insert the Big Bomb."

"Hopefully, the explosion of the Aries warhead should clear out the chunky debris and give us a relatively clear path for the Centaur rocket."

"Perhaps. If it doesn't break loose additional chunks."

"Neil," Trviea addressed me. "I've decided I want you in a pressure suit in the Missile Bay when the launcher is loaded."

"I thought you wanted me by your side during the Bomb Run."

"I do. You now speak Atlantean almost better than me. Anatoly and Monoloa tell me how amazed they are with the amount of Russian you've learned in just the last few days."

"All I did was figure out the Cyrillic alphabet."

"That's a good start." admired Anatoly.

"But I also want the engineer who designed the missile launcher in there when we launch the Aries." suggested Trviea.

"Contrviea and Nesla helped me with the design and building of that."

"I know, they're on the Launch Crew too."

"It's too bad that no one in the American military, and none of the Russians will be handling these missiles and nuclear weapons during the Launch Phase." lamented General Fairchild.

"I'm an American." I reminded him. "Some of the Science and Humanities people assigned to the Launch Crew are American citizens. None of your Air Force Majors can be spared from the Viewing Lounge. All the Russians have to be there too."

"Yes, I know." the General conceded.

"Captain Harsradich," started Anatoly, "I must congratulate you on getting everyone organized for this."

"Yeah, thank you. Pido, Metrola, and Sabar are assigned to the Pilothouse for the Bomb Run."

"Yes, I am ready." confirmed Sabar. "Metrola will be ready to run for the Shuttle Bay if for some reason we need to launch the Shuttle. If Pidonita keels over from a heart attack or something, I call Medical and take over the controls. Cuc Nguyen, Askelion, and Meddi will be on full alert. Donald Colburn, Fred Graf, and Benjamin Roy Sumner will be on alert as their assistants, like paramedics or nurses. Now the subject of targeting. We have to look at the rotation of the main mass. It is slow, about 35 hours for one complete revolution, affected by the jetting of gasses."

She typed some keys. "Now you see the planetary plane, the ecliptic, superimposed upon the main body. The poles of rotation cross the plane at about three dozen *deems* or thirty degrees. Right now, this comet is on a course to hit the Earth's Northern Hemisphere. So we want to deflect it north. We need to target this pole of rotation, here." She pointed at the pole below the planetary plane.

"Yes, I agree that's the target we need to hit. Don't want the nuclear powered jet spinning around, canceling itself out."

"All right, everyone," addressed Trviea, "Let's get ready and into position for the Bomb Run. Neil, as soon as you have the Aries missile launched, and we're certain that we don't need to launch a second one, I want you to join me in the Viewing Lounge where I'll be on station with the Missile Flight Control and Bomb Detonation Crews. You can climb out of your pressure suit while standing with me. Helga, Lucinda, Andemona, Monoloa, good job with the language work, thank you. Every sign and label is now in Russian and English as well as Atlantean, everyone can read the emergency and safety stuff. You did a great job."

"Here, here! Thank you girls, let's give 'em a hand!" Everyone clapped their hands. The women smiled with a little embarrassment and blushing.

Captain Harsradich ended the meeting. "Good luck, everyone, let's get to it."

"Hello."

"Len, you're home."

"Hi, Henry. I just heard, your girlfriend and our buddy Neil are going on the Bomb Run about three hours from now."

"My sister and her family are here right now, we'll be watching the television. Why don't you come on over? We've got some food: pizza, hamburgers, and stuff."

"I'll bring some beer. Sure, I can come over."

"We'll see you."

Len Taylor drove his truck, not my car as he promised, into the Turnipseed yard, several cars already there. Sharon Marshall, Henry's sister, greeted him outside the front door. "Hi, Len, nice of you to come."

"Hi, Sharon, I come bearing beer, gift of the gods."

Sharon laughed. "At least the gift of the barley malt. I'm not sure I want Henry watching this. It's like Marilyn Lovell watching the Apollo 13 reentry on television."

"Not knowing whether she's a wife or a widow. At least your brother isn't married to Lucinda Renuxler."

"I know. He claims they're just friends. Right, just friends. That explains Lucinda blowing a wad in Poulsbo for clothes and the way she and Angela carried on. That Shuttle sat there overnight, while they were supposed to be getting ready for this mission. Genetic diversity, the Creation girls wanted Native American sperm. They got it."

"Maybe. But I think there's something more to it than that."

"Oh, I'm sure Lucinda likes Henry and it's not just a sex thing. Henry will pretend it's just a sex thing, and like all men, he don't mind. But I think he would love to marry Lucinda. I like her. I think it would be great to have her as a sister in law, a neat aunt for the kids. But where would they live? Here? Or on Planet Creation? We would miss him if he went to live on Lucinda's farm. Could we ask Lucinda to give up everything she has back home? Children? We don't know if they could have children."

"They could adopt."

"Yes, they could adopt. There is a shortage of qualified Native American adoptive parents. Henry would qualify, no problem if his wife's not a Native American. They could adopt several Native American children who need a home. That would be good."

"Just like you and your husband. He's white, you're Native American, and you adopted a Native American child."

"Yes, we did. But," she started whispering, "Melissa doesn't know she's adopted. She doesn't need to know. Her brother and sister don't need to know, as they're not adopted."

"Don't worry, your secret's safe with me." Len whispered. "But if she ever needs an organ transplant,"

"I know. But, Melissa only knows of us as her parents and that's the way it is." Sharon returned to speaking with a normal voice. "The other thing I'm concerned with, is what if it turns out that Henry and Lucinda can make a child together, the normal way? Mixed race children can have special problems in our society, though we've been lucky with our children. Imagine a child who is half Neanderthal?!"

"It would prove that we're the same species. That would be wonderful. Every high school football coach in the state will want the Turnipseeds to move into his district."

Sharon laughed. "And the kid could toss the shot put sixty, maybe seventy feet! Let's go in and watch some TV." They went in, Len's beer was put on ice and they settled down in front of the television. The satellite dish outside brought the signal in good, past the mountain ridges that surround the place. They were greeted by a pleasant voice speaking with a British accent, pronouncing all of the h's.

"This is Ian Miller of the Science and Humanities Channel, broadcasting from the *Neanderthal Return*. We are now at a distance of 783 million miles from Earth, much closer than that, less than 2,000 miles, from Comet Wormwood. At 186,282 miles per second, it takes this transmission one hour and ten minutes to travel from this ship to Earth. So while we are broadcasting live, it is not actually live when you receive it. Everything you see and hear on this broadcast happened over an hour ago, but this is the earliest you can know about it. I am standing in the Viewing Lounge, with huge bay windows that allow us to see out into space. It was here that the entire crew gathered to watch the nuclear explosions in the Russian Arctic where we tested the types of bombs being used on this mission. Now Captain Trviea Harsradich is settled in behind a console with video screens giving her views from all over the ship and from the comet. To her left is settled the American Missile Flight Control Crew led by General Morton Fairchild. To her right is the Russian Bomb Detonation Crew led by the veteran and formerly retired nuclear weapons engineer, Anatoly Donovon. There was a last minute change in personnel assignments. Captain Harsradich asked Neil Peace to put on a pressure suit and join the Missile Launch Crew in Bay Number Four, the Missile Bay. Mary Ellen Martin is there. Over to you, Mary Ellen."

"Thank you, Ian. Neil Peace was asked to join the Launch Crew because he invented the launcher for the Aries missiles. We are now watching them load the rocket,"

While Mary Ellen watched and reported to her Earth audience, Nesla Teslakian operated the controls for the Missile Loader. Wlmsda Hotlund operated the cable reel drawing the pusher back, and Marla Syferkrip opened the upper guide roller assembly. "Just another foot, er, *pote*, Wlmsda." I observed. "A little more," the retaining jaws closed and locked the pusher. "Perfect. What was the maximum tension reading of the cable?"

"Four, one, eight, two, *dollons*." answered Wlmsda.

"Good, glad to hear that. At least we're not getting a different reading every time. 3,756 pounds. Go ahead and release the cable reel and feed out a few feet of line, please." Wlmsda did so, and the spring retaining jaws held. I crouched down and looked at it closely. "Looks good. I'll get out of the way and you can go ahead, Nesla."

"Here comes the rocket." Nesla maneuvered the rocket over and above the open launcher and lowered it into place. She set it down on the lower guide rollers. Nesla used her missile loader to force the spring loaded guide roller all the way down. Then she translated the missile down the launcher to place the nozzle end into the pusher assembly. I crouched down and watched it closely.

"Nozzle is clearing the assembly. Looks like the casing is lining up with the grooves, just a couple more inches. There, perfect, the casing's in the groove."

Wlmsda went around to the opposite side and took a look. "It's in the groove on this side." she confirmed.

"I'm letting go of the missile, now." Nesla opened the cover on her control panel and pushed the button. The clamps opened and she raised and moved the Missile Loader out of the way. The missile now rested on the lower rollers, the spring loaded roller pushed the nose cone up three inches, leaving the missile slightly cocked.

"I'm closing the top over." announced Marla. At her command, hydraulic actuators closed the upper guide roller assembly over the top of the missile. Its spring loaded roller pressed on the nose cone and countered the force of the lower spring loaded roller. The two spring loaded rollers combined to press the rocket casing squarely into the grooves of the pusher.

"Let's put in the pins." Nesla installed two of the quick disconnect pins toward the open end of the launcher pointing out through the open door to space. I put one in and Wlmsda put one in. "Aries missile is locked and loaded."

Meanwhile, one of the Centaur missiles hung out in space on the extended I-beams. Two fueling gantries poured in thousands of gallons of liquid oxygen and liquid hydrogen. Liquid helium was used to keep the combustibles cold and liquid. Helium gas was used to stabilize the thin wall stainless steel monocoque structure. The gleaming Inconel nose cone of Anatoly's Big Bomb pointed straight out into space. The two four foot diameter rocket nozzles pointed back into the open Bay. Not a good time to light up those Pratt and Whitney rocket motors!

"Oxygen tank of the Centaur is now fully loaded." announced Contrviea. A few minutes later, she announced "Hydrogen tank is now fully loaded. We're ready to go."

"Second Aries ready in the Missile Loader." announced Nesla.

I then heard Pidonita's voice in my earphones. "We're approaching Missile Launch Point, Captain Trviea."

"We're ready in the Viewing Lounge." declared Trviea. "Proceed with Launch Maneuver, please."

"Proceeding. We will go into Free Fall and will rotate the ship. *Bly jore.*"

The floor of the Bay felt like it fell away from my feet. We watched the stars move past the open door as the ship rotated. The foggy coma of the comet appeared at the top and then filled our entire view out the door. Mary Ellen panned the scene and narrated for her Earth audience. She was cool, professional, networks around the Planet carried her transmission.

"They are staring into the belly of the beast." observed Sharon quietly, sipping her beer in contemplation.

Henry, Len, and Ken Marshall, Sharon's husband, were more vocal, like football fans. "Hey, that's Neil in that pressure suit!"

"No, I believe that's Nesla Teslakian. Wait, it's hard to tell who's in which suit."

"That's Neil! See his face, the S&H gal is pointing her camera into his face!"

"Yeah, that's Neil! Way to go, Neil! Like your missile launcher!"

Sharon watched her men slap each other on the back, cheer, swig beer, wolf down pizza, and carry on like they were watching a ball game. Men! Boys will be boys. The children sat on their laps enjoying the party.

While there was no acceleration, we were in free fall at several hundred feet per second heading toward the core of the comet. We stared straight into white fog, unable to see anything. I heard Pidonita's voice in my earphones. "Approaching Aries missile launch point. Missile launch on my command, please."

Marla, Nesla, and Wlmsda crouched behind the cable reel. A *tig-it* thick plate of clear plastic protected them from the cable in case it snaps. Wlmsda let out some cable to provide slack. We heard Pidonita's voice count down *prelates* in Atlantean. When Pido said "zero" Nesla triggered the retaining jaws, they opened suddenly. Wlmsda operated the cable reel feeding cable out to prevent it from slowing the springs down. It took four seconds for the springs to push the missile the 20 feet to the neutral point where the rocket casing separated from the pusher. The missile traveled out of the end of the launcher into space at ten feet per second.

"Aries missile away! Rocket is clear of the ship." Wlmsda drew the pusher back and locked it. We removed the pins and Marla opened the guide roller assembly in case we needed to launch the second missile.

I heard Pidonita's voice. "Now we'll turn and get out of Free Fall. *Jore put.*"

We felt one to two feet per second squared acceleration as we moved perpendicular to the path of the missile we just launched, getting us out of the way of the rocket exhaust. We then watched the comet fog rotate out of view. When the stars stopped moving, Pidonita fired up the fusion reactor to increase the acceleration to 42 feet per second squared. It was not that we were accelerating away from the comet, it was that Pido was STOPPING our free fall INTO the comet. The coma was lit up to an incredible blue by our light exhaust. The Centaur rocket then carried a full load of hydrogen and oxygen fuel and its 44,000 pound payload, its total mass was then about 79,000 pounds. At 42 feet per second squared, the 79,000 pound mass weighed upon the I-beams with over 103,000 pounds of force. While the I-beams sagged slightly, they held because we designed them for this load.

After about twenty seconds, Pidonita called out again. "*Bly jore.*" We went into free fall and the ship spun around to point us right at the comet. We no longer approached the fog. In the distance, we could barely see the tiny dark shape of the Aries missile we had launched. Then the solid rocket flame lit up the cometary cloud. That signaled us to close the glare shields over our faces.

In the Viewing Lounge, General Fairchild's crew directed the missile. "So far so good, right on course. The missile guidance is following the path we mapped out."

"We radar mapped everything down to a meter, yard, *treefat* size. It's the foot sized chunks we worry about. Missile radar is not reporting anything, closing in on comet core, range to target, the core south pole, one five zero miles. Radar detecting foot sized mass, guidance making course correction to avoid. Avoidance successful."

"Aries returning to original course. Range to target, one four zero miles. So far so good." The missile flew without incident for a few minutes, range to target being called out every ten miles.

"Range to target three zero miles, now guidance is correcting to miss an increasing number of sub-yard sized particles. Go baby, go baby! Atta boy! It deflected! It hit something!"

"It hit a small mass, a few inches across. Missile guidance is correcting, not damaged, rocket still functioning. Range to target now fifteen miles."

"Closing in on the target. Debris is at a maximum, just avoid hitting the big stuff. Hit something small again! Missile still functioning. Range to target one mile!"

"Dark goggles, everyone!" ordered Captain Harsradich.

The B61-12 warhead sank into the side of the main mass, not far from its rotational pole. The surface material was soft, fluffy, like angel food cake. But it quickly hardened to solid ice of water and other compounds. About 100 feet in, the 100 kiloton bomb detonated. We saw the flash. Through our dark goggles and glare shields, we could see the core of the comet. The white hot jet from the nuclear explosion looked incredibly tiny on the rough surfaced sphere.

"We have detonation! 100 feet inside the surface less than a quarter mile from the rotational pole. Bullseye!" Cheering and hand clapping.

There was cheering on Earth, too. "Good ol' American know how!" exulted the Turnipseed living room. People reacted this way everywhere around the world. They were cautiously happy, waiting for the Russian Big Bomb.

I heard Trviea's triumphant voice. "Neil, we don't need to launch the second Aries missile! The girls can put it away without you. I need you by my side! Will you come, please?"

"On my way." I went into the small airlock and closed the door behind me. While I pressurized the airlock I watched the Centaur rocket cast loose from the structure. The I-beams retracted. Pidonita backed the ship away from the Centaur. When it was far enough, it fell out of view as Pidonita started us on a gentle four foot per second squared acceleration to clear us out of the way.

I climbed out of the airlock and was greeted by Lucinda and Helga. "Here, let me take your helmet." They took my helmet, my gloves, quickly I was out of the pressure suit walking into the Viewing Lounge.

"Neil, have a seat next to me, please." invited Captain Trviea.

"Sure, how we doing?"

"We have the hole we need. Anatoly and Morton are waiting until they agree the time is right to fire the Centaur." The two Crew Leaders conferred. "They have it oriented. As you can feel, Pidonita isn't accelerating any faster than half a gee because we need to stay close until the Big Bomb Detonation. Then it's haul ass. Did I say that right?"

"Close enough. What's the kiloton estimate of the Aries bomb?"

"Pidonita and Sabar report that from the neutrino count and the distance at time of explosion, 101.3 kilotons of yield. The fireball traveled for about half of a *kepfat*, a little more than three quarters of a mile, into the comet. The hot fumes are blowing out in a jet, we placed the Centaur and ourselves out of its way. We're getting two inches per second delta vee on the entire main mass."

"Not enough."

"Not enough. We've got a nice hole, a couple *hekts* of *potes* wide, almost a mile deep. Perfect. The jet is blowing out the chunky stuff, clearing the way for the Centaur."

Morton suddenly gave his command. "Fire the Centaur, Major Easton. Burn for 360 seconds to put missile on course and give it inertial spin. Then we have a second burn to guide the warhead into the hole."

"Centaur firing. Thrust is 33,000 pounds force, initial acceleration is 13.4 feet per second squared. Beginning axial rotation. We're guiding it into the pathway cleared by the Aries. Honeywell Inertial Navigation Unit performing nominally."

Anatoly gave his order in Russian. "Arm the bomb, Maria."

"Bomb arming code sent. Receipt of code confirmed, bomb armed."

Major McKenna started the range counts every thirty seconds. "Range to target 802 miles. Velocity relative to target 411 feet per second."

After six minutes. "Coming up on initial engine cut-off. Engine cut-off in ten seconds." Pause. "Five, four, three, two, one, ECO! Engine is off. Missile is on course for the target hole. Range to target 600 miles. Velocity relative to target 5,965 feet per second. In car terms that is 4,067 miles per hour. A mile every 0.88 seconds. Centaur is spinning along its axis at one half turn per second." The two gimbaled nozzles can spin it as well as turn it.

General Fairchild declared, "We have 113 seconds of engine burn left in the Centaur. Restart when the range is 100 miles, guide it to the hole."

"Range to target hole 550 miles." The range was called out every fifty miles.

After seven minutes, "Coming up on engine restart, in 22 seconds, on mark! 22, 21, 20," Major Easton counted down the seconds.

"When the range is ten miles, cutoff engine and separate the rocket from the warhead." ordered General Fairchild.

"As soon as the rocket is jettisoned, send the detonation code and start the ten second count down." ordered Anatoly. "We are facing away from the comet so the dark goggles aren't necessary."

"Five, four, three, two, one, engine restart. Range to target 98 miles."

A few more range to target callouts, the rocket flew faster and faster. They wanted to bury the Russian bomb deep, it was designed by Anatoly Donovon as a large version of the B61 warhead, with uranium instead of steel to increase the yield even further. "Coming up on engine cutoff and rocket jettison. Five, four, three, two, one, ECO! Jettison!"

Maria Romanov immediately took over. "Detonation code sent, receipt confirmed! *Dyesat, dyevyat, vosyem, syem, shyest, pyat,*"

"Warhead in hole!"

"*chetirye, tri, dva, odin, nol?*"

"Do we confirm detonation?" asked Captain Harsradich.

"We should see the flash, the diffuse coma gasses that surround us even at this distance should reflect it."

"No detonation."

"Shit!"

"We'll have to inspect all of the Russian bombs to figure out what went -"

FLASH!!!!!!

"We have detonation!"

"Better late than never!"

"Pidonita, how many megatons?"

"From the neutrino count during the flash and our distance, in Earth terms, computer calculates 123.4 megatons of yield! Point of detonation a little over two *kepfats* inside the main mass, good jet exiting the hole! This comet is MOVING!"

Everybody whooped! Trviea screamed in my ear, kissed me and gave me a bone crushing hug. I too screamed for joy. Like a crowd when the home team wins the championship at the buzzer. Relief and joy and ecstasy reigned throughout the ship.

"They did it!" they screamed in the Turnipseed house. A simultaneous celebration all over the world.

Anatoly sang the *International* at the top of his lungs, quickly joined by the other Russians. Then we Americans sang *God Bless America*. We were suddenly very heavy. I looked up at the acceleration display, 48 feet per second squared. 1.5 gees.

Up in the Pilothouse, the celebration had already ended as the three women concentrated on their screens. "Look at that! A *kepfat* sized chunk has broken off near the hole."

"Taking a lot of the momentum of the explosion with it. Moving away from main mass at three *hekt potes* per *prelate.*"

About two minutes passed as they tracked it. "It is now nine *kepfat*s away from the main mass. The main mass is not accelerating as fast now, might not miss Earth as much as it should."

"That'll complicate the delta vee calculations. Might not even miss Earth! We will have to do this all over again. What's the story on that breakaway chunk?"

"It'll miss Earth all right. It EXPLODED!"

"How did that happen?"

"I don't know, but we have particles bigger than a *chmfat* coming at us at *kepfat*s per *prelate!*"

"It's not going to miss us, *TIX JORD!*"

That's the strap down order! Everyone stopped celebrating. Pidonita screamed again into the public address. "STRAP DOWN!" This time in English. Again in Russian.

"She's not kidding!" screamed Trviea. "This is no drill! Bomb Crew, Missile Crew! Your job is done, to the wall stations!"

Trviea rapidly assigned each person to a strap down station, each in a cavity in the walls around the Viewing Lounge. I strapped myself on to the little bed in my hole in the wall, strapped on the head restraint. I could see the instructions written in three languages, relieved that one of them was English. Good job, Helga and Lucinda! Trviea checked me. "Neil, good!" She then went around to all of the stations, making sure everyone was properly set. She looked on the edge of panic, but maintained control. Her face was white.

Then I heard Pidonita's terrified voice. "Emergency rapid acceleration." She said it slowly and carefully in Atlantean and repeated in English. Then she started counting down from six *prelates* in Atlantean.

Trviea's concern for other people left her with no time to strap herself down. With Pidonita counting down to an acceleration of over 5 gees, she laid herself down on the floor as flat as she could. She placed the occipital bun of her Neanderthal head on the floor and stared straight up. The thick knot of bone should protect her brain from the heavy gees, but she was going to have one nasty headache.

In the Pilothouse, Metrola, Sabar, and Pidonita were strapped into their stations, head restraints on to prevent broken necks. They had face masks on and breathed pure oxygen to get the nitrogen out of their blood. When Pido counted down to zero, she pushed a toggle that she had uncovered.

The million pound fusion core is normally accelerated 6 feet per second during each pulse. Restraint by the magnetic bottle provided thrust to the ship. For 1.5 gee acceleration of the 200 billion pound ship, the core pulsed 1.6 million times per second. Design limit for normal acceleration. For an emergency rapid acceleration, the pulse frequency is reduced to 1.07 million times per second and the compression is increased. More fusion accelerated the core 30 feet per second each pulse. This yielded 5 gees of acceleration. But the 25 times more heat energy created during each pulse is too much to be exhausted by light alone. A tiny hole opened in the magnetic bottle allowing extremely hot fusion material to vent taking billions of BTU's. The added thrust from this rocketing is actually minuscule compared to the thrust from the pulsing fusion core.

This emergency acceleration mode had only been tested once before.

Several hundred pounds of fusion material jetted into space every second as the ship's terrified pilot tried desperately to get out of the way of debris flying at miles per second.

On Earth, the now quiet Turnipseed house watched their television.

"We have lost video transmission from the *Neanderthal Return*." announced a quiet voice.

"This is Metrola Mornuxler." Her voice was labored, frightened. "I'm now strapped down in the Pilothouse." She spoke in English, her words telecast live.

"Translate two three six *deems*!" shouted Sabar in Atlantean.

"Translating!" confirmed Pidonita in her language. She redirected the thrust of the pulsing fusion core by a few degrees to steer the ship sideways. The plasma ball is located at the center of mass of the ship with a variable offset to allow for rapid steering.

"Avoidance successful!" announced Sabar. "That was a *hekt pote* mass."

Metrola continued in English for the benefit of her Earth audience. "We just evaded a piece of comet 142 feet across. Big enough to completely destroy this ship." Pidonita and Sabar continued their Atlantean chatter as Metrola spoke. "Here's what happened: After the explosion of the Russian bomb, a *kepfat* sized piece broke off the main mass. It exploded, probably frozen carbon dioxide flashing to gas from the heat. We're now under emergency acceleration of five gees to get away from icebergs of up to several hundred feet across flying at us at extremely high speeds. Hopefully we don't -"

"We have lost voice transmission from the *Neanderthal Return*. We're trying to pick up a signal, any signal from the ship. Still no transmission of any kind from the ship."

Chapter Forty

"Mr. President, we're analyzing the data right now. We're doing the best we can!"

"I understand that. But we need answers."

"That was a huge flash. Bigger than the bomb explosion, but that was masked by being inside the comet. Metrola told us they were trying to get away from debris, then they were hit. The flash we then saw was the breakdown of the fusion reactor."

They were silent for a moment.

"Can we find the ship or its remains in the debris?"

"We can try. Can't find anything with infrared with all the hot plasma floating around out there. We're listening for a signal from the ship. We have the Arecibo Dish and the JPL deep space radio assets listening for lower wattage transmissions."

"Nothing yet?"

"Nothing yet."

"Send a hailing message. Something like, '*Neanderthal Return*, this is Earth. Do you copy?'"

"Yeah, we'll send that."

"What about the cometary core? Is it now going to miss Earth?"

"We don't know. They did everything right. They reported that the Russian bomb in its uranium penetration vehicle had a yield of 123.4 megatons. It penetrated 2 and 2/12 *kepfats* inside the core body, that's about three and a half miles. It jetted out the hole prepared for it by the Aries missile. That should be enough to deflect the main core body into a twenty to 30,000 mile miss of our Planet. But there are the breakaway bodies. The data from the *Neanderthal Return* shows a one *kepfat*, or one and a half mile particle breaking off from the main core and flying away from it at, uh, several hundred feet per second."

"Taking some of the kinetic energy from the bomb with it."

"Well, uh, yes. Law of conservation of energy. The kinetic energy in the breakaway pieces subtracts from the kinetic energy added to the main mass by the bomb."

"Are any of the breakaway pieces a danger to Earth?"

"The radar images sent back to us from the ship before the explosions show a large number of particles, ranging in size from a yard to a mile floating around the main mass. These pieces would be lifted off the surface of the main mass by jetting gasses, and then fall back into it. These could present a threat to Earth in that they were not attached to the main mass when the Russian bomb gave it the jolt. The tenuous gravitational attraction might not be enough to bring all of these smaller masses along with the main mass and they would continue their previous orbits."

"Taking them into Earth. Most of the small stuff should burn up in the atmosphere."

"Up to about ten meters, uh, yards. Sorry. Above that, we might see some meteorites hit the ground. Meteor Crater in Arizona, three quarters of a mile across, was made by a chunk of iron 25 feet across. Or so we think."

"But what we're talking about is ice."

"Which presents a different kind of threat. What we believe to be an 80 foot piece of Comet Encke entered the atmosphere over Siberia and exploded in the Tunguska region in 1908. We can survive a few such hundred kiloton explosions,"

"Tunguska was a hundred kilotons?"

"Knocked down trees for quite a few miles, just like Mount St. Helens. We could survive a few like that, as long as they don't hit any populated areas. We might want to target such cometary fragments with nuclear warheads if they prove to be on a path to Earth. They could hit a city by pure chance. If nothing else, we make the fragments smaller, cause less damage."

"How big does a piece of comet have to be to cause real damage? The kind that's worth sending a missile with a nuclear warhead to prevent?"

"Depends on how many pieces we're dealing with. How many nuclear warheads can we launch?"

"We could launch a few from orbit after delivery with Space Shuttles, Energiya rockets, and the big new Titan boosters. But we don't even need those to deliver a few thousand nuclear warheads. The MX was designed to carry a ten warhead bus. Reduce its payload to a single one megaton nuclear bomb without the reentry vehicle, it can accelerate it past the Earth's escape velocity. We can place the bomb anywhere in the Solar System. We're loading 'em up right now in Wyoming. The SS-18 can similarly deliver an even bigger warhead anywhere in the Solar System. They're loading 'em up in their old silos. There's only so much capacity at Canaveral, Baikonur, and Vandenburg. Since we're cooperating in this effort, we don't even need the silos, just stand 'em up and launch 'em."

"We still have them? What about the Arms Control Treaties? What about all the Russian officers who came over to help us destroy missiles and the Americans who went there to help them destroy theirs?"

"You still believe in the Tooth Fairy? That's P.R. The world demanded disarmament, we gave 'em the illusion of disarmament. We just took the rockets out of the silos and trotted out a few for public demolition. The rest, including their nuclear warheads in various states of disassembly, are in storage somewhere. We've got currently idle factories that can replace 'em all in a few months. We've got reactors on standby ready to produce thousands of pounds of weapons grade plutonium should we ever need a fresh supply. You think we've been keeping ALIENS at Area 51? True, we no longer have a Cold War with the Russians, but we still have an interest in keeping the Chinese deterred from any land grab bigger than Hong Kong. Science fiction writers aren't the only folks who speculate about an alien race showing up in the sky, even aliens who turn out to be displaced humans like these Neanderthals. We've known about the possibility of comets and asteroids crashing to Earth since Jules Verne, nay, since John of Patmos wrote about it, Wormwood. Indeed, since the time of the Ancient Egyptians."

"Or the Ancient Atlanteans. They found Edgar Cayce's Hall of Records, if the chamber with the gold plates from north of the Sphinx is that. The Foot and the Cubit depicted are exact fractions of an arc second of the Earth's surface. The Three Neanderthal College Girls are beautiful! Fantastic artwork. They look just like the Creation women, right down to the Asian shaped eyes. The plate with Comet Wormwood as it looked during its last flyby of Earth on October 13, 10,495 B.C., incredible! The background stars, Sagittarius, account for proper motions, *Zep Tepi* time! All right, Mr. President, getting back to the subject, we and the Russians can reload every silo within a week."

The President chuckled. "Our plan is to lay megaton yield nuclear warheads in the approach path of that comet and blast every particle on a collision course with Earth. Then there's the order we just placed with Morton Thiokol. Take one of those big solid fuel boosters like we use on the Space Shuttle. Only don't attach a Shuttle to it and get rid of the parachute. Say we have a few old 10 megaton Titan warheads gathering dust somewhere. Put three of 'em in a bus. We could intercept the comet while it's still beyond the orbit of Mars. Or even a pair of 25 megaton single warheads the Russians once deployed on SS-18's."

"Damn! We didn't need the *Neanderthal Return*!"

"We needed it all right. The 58 mile main mass is too big. We had to have accurate placement of a very big Russian bomb while it was still WAY out there. We needed the Creation ship to do it. If it has been successfully deflected from hitting Earth, THEN we can bomb the smaller pieces with our existing resources."

"Good plan. Some of the break-off pieces are huge, up to a mile in size. A mile sized piece would release MILLIONS of megatons of energy when exploding upon reentry. Much bigger than Tunguska, even if smaller than Alvarez's six mile Dinosaur Killer. The Shoemaker-Levy pieces that hit Jupiter were about that size. A well placed megaton bomb would take care of a mile sized piece of comet. Hundred kiloton sized warheads can be accelerated out of Earth gravity by Minuteman III rockets, of which we have plenty. Those can be used to take care of fragments down to fifty feet."

"Thank you, keep working at it and call me when you have more information."

"It has been a little over thirty minutes since we lost the transmission from the *Neanderthal Return*. The two nuclear explosions should have moved the main mass of the comet into a 20,000 mile miss of the Earth. But at this time, there is no way of knowing that for sure. Breakaway pieces could still be a threat to Earth; one that's several miles across could cause damage of the magnitude of the Dinosaur Killer of 65 million years ago. If the *Neanderthal Return* is disabled or destroyed, then it would be up to us to decide what to do with any breakaway pieces that still threaten Earth."

"Any word on the ship?" asked Sharon Marshall as she came back into the room.

Henry Turnipseed did not answer. He watched the television, not paying attention to anything else. Len Taylor was outside tossing a ball with the children. That left her husband Ken to answer. "No. All of the scientists think the main mass has been moved to at least a 10,000 mile miss."

"That's wonderful. But we don't know about Lucinda and Neil and the rest of them."

"No. We haven't heard anything about them."

"We should say prayer for them." suggested Henry.

"That is a good idea, Henry. I'll call in the children."

After Len and the children were brought in, they sat together and bowed their heads. Henry spoke the prayer, "Our Father, who art in Heaven, hallowed be Thy Name. Thy Kingdom come, Thy Will be done, on Earth as it is in Heaven. We pray for the souls of the courageous people who ride the *Neanderthal Return* and have bombed the comet exactly as planned. We thank thee, Lord, for giving us these heroes, and we pray for their safe return. Amen."

Christa Peace looked plaintively up at her mother's face. "Daddy's not coming back, is he?"

"I don't know, Honey."

"They kidnapped him, and we thought he was dead. How many times will he die?"

Angela couldn't help a laugh. "Once, Honey. Only once. They kidnapped him, then he talked them into bringing him back. They didn't mean to hurt us. They were just desperate to have their own little children, just like we can. But now, they may have saved us all. Why don't we ask God to bring Daddy back one more time?"

"Okay. Dear God, my Daddy is my hero, I love him very much. Please bring him back, and Helga, and Lucinda, and General, uh,"

"Fairchild. General Fairchild."

"And General Fairchild, and the Russian scientists, and even that Trviea Harsradich who had Daddy kidnapped. Bring her back too, I forgive her, she did good today. Please bring them all back. Amen."

Here is what you do: You attach a heavy piece of steel, about a foot thick, to the outside of the NASA astronaut training centrifuge. On the outside of the steel, you tape on a quarter stick of dynamite. You climb inside and strap yourself down. Have it spin to where you are experiencing five gees. Are we having fun yet? Then set off the dynamite.

That is what it felt and sounded like to me. I was all strapped in, the accelerometer in front of me read six six *potes* per *prelate* squared. That is equivalent to 160 feet per second squared, five gees, and believe me, you are extremely heavy at that acceleration. I heard a bang. Then there was the loudest metallic THUD I have ever heard in my life. The shock wave propagated through the structure and slammed me in the back. The lights blinked off and it was dark. There was screaming and yelling. I heard Trviea shout an obscenity in Atlantean. I felt a sensation like spinning, there were more crashes and thuds, but without the shock slamming me in the back. Then I was weightless, floating against the straps restraining me.

The emergency lights turned on and I discovered that my digital readouts were still working. Acceleration: zero. Pressure: two one *dollons* per square *tig-it*. That's good. I did not hear the rushing of air. Oxygen, carbon dioxide, these levels were good. I turned my head with effort, straining against the straps holding my helmet. Probably kept my neck from breaking. Then I saw the poor Captain.

Trviea floated in midair all doubled up. I could see her back. Her right arm hung like it was broken. She held her left hand to her face, her left arm seemed to be good. She kicked out her left leg and pulled it back in, but her right leg did not move. I heard her grunt with pain when she did this. I noticed the floating drops of blood.

I decided that if we get hit again by something else, so be it! I took off the restraining helmet, undid my straps and climbed out of this hole. I called on my headset. "Medical, Medical! Can you read me?"

"This is Medical, Donald Colburn, I read you loud and clear, Neil."

"I'm over in the Viewing Lounge. Trviea Harsradich didn't get strapped down. She's hurt! I'm going over to her side, I see drops of blood floating and her right limbs look bent and stiff."

"We got strapped down in Medical. Some of our equipment is damaged, but we're all in good shape. We'll be on our way."

"Thanks, Don. Be advised that we're pulling a First Aid Kit or two off the wall."

"I hope so."

It's not easy negotiating a weightless environment if you're not used to it. But I managed to get over to Trviea. She yelped in pain as I turned her around as gently as I could to look at her. "Let me see your face, Trev. Please." She lowered her left hand so I could look. "You look like you've been in one helluva fist fight."

A grin tried to appear on her mangled lips. "You should see the other girl."

"I'm sure you did quite a number on her. Medical! Report! The source of the blood, ack! Sorry, got splattered by a drop of floating blood. The blood is coming from cuts and lacerations on her face, it's all torn and bloody there. Nasty cut on her left, excuse me, right brow ridge, blood pouring out of the nose, may be broken, both lips are cut. Let me see, please, Trviea. A fresh chip off of her upper right incisor. Wonder where that is floating? Careful, people, don't take a deep breath unless you can see the air is free of tooth chips." People emerged from the strap down stations and came over to look at Trviea. "The skin around her right eye is already puffing up blue and purple."

Then I remembered something. As a father's rights activist, I dealt with some of the men who lashed out in frustration at their wives. Because they did, we all get treated like shit by the courts and everyone. Which does nothing to reduce the frustration which leads to domestic violence. I once looked over the case file of a guy put away for second degree assault. The prosecutor presented the photographs and records from the hospital that treated his ex-wife. Yuck! Hit a person near the eye hard enough, the shock wave can propagate through the eyeball and shatter the eggshell thin bone of the socket behind the eye. The eye falls back into the head and the victim experiences double vision.

I looked at Trviea's eye to see if this was happening. "How many fingers am I holding up?"

"Two, what are you driving at, Neil?"

"You're not seeing two images of my hand?"

"No. I can barely open my right eye now."

"Good."

"Good?"

"Let's check your arm." I tried to move it.

"E!-E!-E!" she yelped. "Please don't do that!"

"What happened to your leg?"

"I banged my knee on something."

"You see what all you hit?"

"No. The lights were out and I couldn't see a thing. My face hit something because I didn't see it to put my hands in front of it. My whole right side slammed into the console or something. It all happened fast."

"It's all right, Trviea. Just take it easy, we'll get you taken care of." Somebody brought a Medical Kit. In it was a pair of scissors. I cut away the sleeve of her shirt to reveal her right forearm. "Medical. Report. Right forearm badly swollen, possible broken bone."

"Got it, Neil." It was Cuc Nguyen. "We're finally unstrapped and on our way."

"What's taking you so long?"

"Lots of things. We took quite a jolt, we have a lot of damaged equipment. Door was jammed, we had a hard time undoing some of the straps. It took everyone here three minutes to get me out of these straps!"

I chuckled. "Please come, Captain Trviea can use a physician's attention."

"On our way, Neil. So far, we haven't heard of anyone else being hurt, and we aren't getting any alarms from the use of the First Aid Kits except in your Viewing Lounge. We haven't any fire alarms, which is good."

"Glad to hear it."

Suddenly, Trviea remembered she was still Captain and her brain woke up from its daze. "Pidonita! Damage report, please. Condition of ship!" she yelled in Atlantean into her headset with her usual authority. The headset wasn't working. With her good hand she ripped the headset off and threw it. "Can somebody please bring me another headset?" Another headset was brought and she put it on while we cleaned the blood off her face and held a cloth to her nose. She tried again. "Pidonita, can you read me?"

"We read you loud and clear, Captain. How are you feeling?"

"Except for a broken arm, a banged up knee, eye swollen shut, tooth chipped off, blood pouring out of my face and excruciating pain, I'm fine. How's the ship?"

"Ship's just like you. It's fine as long as we ignore the damage." They both chuckled. "We are still alive as you can see. The fusion reactor is out, I cannot form a magnetic bottle. We were hit in the rear by a *chmfat* sized comet particle and a bunch of small *tig-it* sized particles. The *chmfat* particle knocked Magnetic Coil Assembly Number Seven off alignment, causing the magnetic bottle to break down. The entire plasma ball blew out into space as it is designed to do. That was the jolt we felt. Seven will have to be fixed before we can form a magnetic bottle."

"Damage to reactor cavity?"

"I don't know. We can realign the magnetic coil assembly and check the other ones but we will have to wait several days for the cavity surface to cool down if we need to repair it."

"So we are adrift in free fall. What does our present orbit look like?"

"Tilted with respect to the planetary plane, several *hekts* of years around the Mother Star, we will not get anywhere near the orbit of Jupiter, let alone Mars and Earth. We accelerated at six dozen and six *potes* per *prelate* squared. We still don't know for how long. Between twelve and two dozen *prelates*. Somewhere around nine *hekt potes* per *prelate* of delta vee from the emergency acceleration, plus some more delta vee from the previous two dozen *pote* acceleration. The intense heat protected the fusion reactor cavity from the comet fragments. I maneuvered to avoid a one *hekt pote* sized iceberg which would have killed us all but flew into the path of the *chmfat* particle."

Trviea sighed as Askelion, Cuc Nguyen, and Donald Colburn arrived to minister to her injuries. Ask took one look at Trviea's arm and announced, "We're taking you to Medical. Let's go, you can still command the ship with your headset while we take some X-rays of your knee, arm, and face."

"Yes, please treat my injuries, I appreciate that. But use a local anesthetic. I need to keep my brain clear."

"Sure, Trev. But as this ship's physician, I can do whatever I need to patch you back together. I can relieve you of command if you refuse medical treatment without justification. If I need to put you under, you need to designate someone to take command."

"Metrola, can you hear me?"

"Yes, Trviea?"

"Can you assume command if the physicians put me under to treat my injuries?"

"Sure."

"All right, stand by while I link you up with my headset." Trviea made the adjustments to allow Metrola to hear everything she hears. "Pido, you need to stay with the controls. How is our energy supply?"

"Steam cycle is still operating off the heat of the fusion cavity, slowing down, soon be unable to spin the main turbine. Ready to redirect to the smaller turbines. Batteries and fuel cells are fine, we have plenty of electricity for emergency conditions. The ship automatically put us on emergency lights, power is at emergency conservation level."

"How is the fission reactor looking?"

"It should be undamaged. It tested out fine before we left Earth orbit."

"How about the water bladders?"

"They should be intact, I'm not seeing any evidence of a flood or leaking."

"Thank you, Pido. Nesla Teslakian, can you hear me?" We were moving Trviea over to the sick bay, she continued while we carried her.

"Yes, I can hear you, I am unhurt."

"Organize a crew of reactor operators for the fission reactor. The Russians are bomb designers, they should know nuclear reactors. Contrviea, how is the Machine Shop?"

"We are cleaning up the mess, but all of the tools and machines work. We have the full amount of compressed air and we have the fuel cell, but we will need that fission reactor on line to sustain full production rate. I've already called the Machine Shop Crew in here, we are getting everything ready."

"Good job, Contrviea. Stand by to fill orders for replacement parts."

"Captain," I addressed her as I helped her into the Medical Department, "Have we made a transmission to Earth since the collision?"

"They need to know we're still alive. Pido, can we transmit to Earth?"

"I've tried, but I can't confirm that signal is sent. All we need are a few dozen *pote-dollons* per *prelate* of transmission power to be received by the JPL system." Each Creation unit of power is about 1.011 watts, or about three quarters of a foot-pound per second. "We'll need an Electrical Crew working on the transmitters. Those Science and Humanities Earthlings are handy with the wire crimpers."

Sorby Mishlakian arrived. "How's my mom? Oh wow! You really need to control your temper, some of these other girls can kick your butt."

"Sorb, I'll be all right. You strap down?"

"Of course I did. I do what you say, I'm too smart to do what you do. Why weren't you strapped down?" Sigh. "And she sometimes gets drunk too."

"I was being Captain, making sure everyone else was strapped down. I didn't have time to get strapped down. Pido only gave us a six *prelate* countdown. It really was an emergency rapid acceleration. We lost the plasma ball, the fusion reactor is down. Put together a spacewalking Crew, we need to inspect that damage."

"Askelion, will she need any of my blood?"

"You're both the same blood type, and you're mother and daughter. Captain, we'll take three *glups* of her blood in case we need it, then she can go outside to play."

"Sure," agreed the Captain, "but as soon as you're done giving blood, get some girls into pressure suits. Helga Trvlakian can disable and reset the collars on Wlmsda Hotlund and Bchsda Bentlakian."

Nesla and Monoloa led the Russian Bomb Crew into the fission reactor control station. Monoloa provided her translation service. "This fission reactor is designed to provide the most power for its weight and volume. The fuel is 11/12 enriched uranium, eleven *dollons* of U-235 for every *dollon* of U-238. It is the power supply for charging the plasma ball and starting the fusion reactor. We have used it once for that purpose. At one twenty-fourth capacity it is capable of meeting all of our heat and electricity needs when not charging the plasma ball. We've burned it for a total of 36 days since the initial installation."

Nesla placed Monoloa and her Russians at the operator stations and taught them how to read the gauges. The in flight training in Base Twelve numbers, Creation weights and measures, and Atlantean came in handy. When she had them settled in, she took her place at the Main Control Panel. "First, we check for damage to the reactor systems. Then we can turn on the water pumps to circulate the coolant through the core."

She switched on a fuel cell burning hydrogen and oxygen to provide power for the reactor's pumps and control systems. "There are fuel cells like this all over the ship, they are being turned on now. Everything of an emergency or backup nature is mounted to resist a minimum of 24 gees of acceleration. This fission reactor is designed to withstand a minimum of 36 gees of acceleration. We get hit that hard, we won't need it anyway. These video screens show us the images from a number of miniature cameras in and around the reactor. I'll activate the automatic inspection procedure. Watch the screens please, let me know if you spot any possible damage."

The cameras moved as programmed to allow visual inspection of the parts. "Everything is checking out," Monoloa announced, "reactor vessel, control rods, fuel rods, surge tank pressurizer, pumps, and steam generator."

"We have no leaks in the core vessel, none of the mounts look damaged." confirmed Svetlana Lebed.

"Thank you. All of the diagnostics look good." Nesla flipped another switch. "Now we are pumping the water to pressurize and circulate through the core."

"Flow rate gauge is at the first red line." announced Anatoly Donovon.

"Water pressure in the core is rising, now one nine zero zero. No leaks visible to our cameras." announced Mikhail Dostoevski.

Nesla checked her own gauges. "I confirm that, water is now flowing through the core at the proper initial rate. If a leak is detected, the system will automatically shut down. It is enough for 6 per *hekt* power, the level we'll run until it comes time to recharge the plasma ball. The water flow is automatically coupled to the power level of the reactor. Shout if you notice any warning lights or buzzers. No warning lights? Video cameras showing everything normal?"

"No warning lights, water flow good." confirmed Anatoly.

"Pressure is now two eight zero zero *dollons* per square *tig-it*." declared Mikhail. 2,488 psi. At this pressure water stays liquid up to 667 degrees Fahrenheit. "Holding steady."

"Steam generator and steam cycle in order." announced Maria Romanov.

"Core vessel good." confirmed Svetlana. The reactor is similar in some ways to pressurized water reactors used in the United States for power plants. The enrichment level of the fuel is like that of Navy reactors, not like the civilian power plants.

"I am now pulling the control rods to the one per *hekt* power position," announced Nesla, "watch the radiation level and heat gauges. Okay, control rods in position, reading power level at one per *hekt*. Please confirm."

"We confirm 1/144 power level." announced Anatoly.

"Water pressure holding at two eight zero zero." announced Mikhail. "Temperature is increasing, passing one *hekt deems*." Human body temperature.

"Confirm that, one *hekt* and six *deems*. Now I will increase power level to six per *hekt* of full capacity." As they watched the temperature of the core coolant rise, Nesla continued describing the power plant. "The core water transfers its heat to the steam cycle which converts one third of it to electricity. The heat from condensing the spent steam is used to warm the ship during the absence of the fusion reactor. We have available an ammonia cycle for converting one third of the spent steam heat to electricity. We can condense spent ammonia gas at a low temperature by radiating heat to cold space. We use this cycle when charging the plasma ball."

They waited patiently as the temperature rose. "Water pressure at two eight zero zero," announced Mikhail, "temperature is now eight *hekt deems*." 607 degrees Fahrenheit.

"Steam cycle coming on line," announced Maria, "we are now generating steam, there go the turbines, we've got power!"

Nesla turned on her headset. "Captain, this is Nesla, can you hear me?"

"I can still hear you, Nesla, but our physicians want to put me under, I'm turning it over to Metrola Mornuxler. She'll be our temporary Captain."

"Can Metrola hear me?"

"Yes I can."

"Reactor is on line at six per *hekt* power. Turbine is turning, we have electricity."

"That's good to hear, Nesla. Six per *hekt* should be more than we can use. Hold it at that level until we are ready to recharge the plasma ball." ordered Trviea. "Both bones in my forearm are broken and I have torn ligaments in my knee. My nose is busted, needs to be reset. The physicians will put me under for the next few hours while they work on me. Cuc Nguyen is looking down on me with the drugs in her hand. Metrola, it's yours. This is Captain Trviea Harsradich, signing off."

Ian Miller and Mary Ellen Martin were underneath the consoles in the Pilothouse with Marla Syferkrip and Wlmsda Gtslakian checking for loose wires and cables. "Find anything yet in the Switching Room?" asked Wlmsda into her headset.

Juanita Asturias, an American with the Science and Humanities Channel, responded. "Sorry, Wlmsda, can't find anything here. I felt the jolt too, but these transmitter cables are fine here."

"Thank you, Juanita." They kept looking.

"Hey what's this over here?" asked Juanita.

"It's a power relay box. It relays the power of the signal being fed to the transmitters. Signal goes in here, it exits out here with a 1728fold increase in power. It goes through a series of these to feed the Main Transmitter, the big one we've been using for long distance communication with Earth. The end relays in the series are huge and have their own cooling coils."

"Should this connector go in here like this?"

"Yes it should, how did that get loose? Hook it up."

"It's hooked."

"Captain Mornuxler! Try it, now!"

"Thank you, people. Testing, testing. Confirm! We just transmitted! Earth should pick us up!"

Henry was taking a nap, Sharon was washing dishes, her husband Ken was taking his turn watching the kids in the yard. That left Len to stay next to the television. "The main mass appears to be in an orbit that'll miss Earth by between 10,000 and 15,000 miles. But there are the breakaway pieces, some big enough for Dinosaur Killer effects, and many others of the Tunguska size to worry about." The television also announced that both Americans and Russians were reloading missile silos, this time with reduced payload weights so the warheads can be placed in an interception path of the cometary fragments. With a promise to break in when further news on the *Neanderthal Return* became available, the station returned to its regular programming. Len didn't watch the program, he looked through a magazine to pass the time.

Suddenly, "*Neanderthal Return* Special Report."

"Everyone! A Special Report on the ship! Wake Henry!"

People came back into the room.

"We have picked up what NASA believes to be a signal from the *Neanderthal Return*, listen carefully, here it goes:"

"Testing, testing. Confirm! We just transmitted! Earth should pick us up!"

"That's Metrola's voice!"

"You sure?"

"I ate dinner with her two and a half weeks ago. That's her! She's still alive!"

"Now we are receiving another transmission from deep space."

"This is the *Neanderthal Return* calling Earth, Metrola Mornuxler, Temporary Captain."

"Ship's still intact. Temporary Captain? What happened to Trviea?"

"We're all still alive, none of us were killed in the accident. But one person was injured. Captain Trviea Harsradich was not strapped down. She suffered a broken arm, dislocated knee, and a broken nose; she is in Medical being operated on. She appointed me as Temporary Captain while she is unconscious."

Shouts of relief in the Turnipseed house. Christa and Virgil Peace screamed for joy that their father is all right. The rest of the world likewise cheered as Metrola filled them in on all that has happened so far.

365

Chapter Forty One

Sorby Mishlakian led the EVA crew outside the ship. The spacewalkers crawled along the hull toward the rear. "How is everything looking out there, Sorby?" asked temporary Captain Mornuxler.

"Everything is looking fine," she responded cheerfully, "but we are still on the side of the ship away from the impact site. Pardon me, I'll change tethers." Having reached the end of her 284 foot wire cable tether, Sorby located a cable reel station, opened up the small panel, pulled out the end of the cable with its hook and little control panel and attached herself to it. She unhooked herself from the other cable, hit the button on its control panel, and sent it away. The other astronauts did likewise. "All right, I am good for another two *hekt potes*. That Sun sure looks small and dim out here. We have plenty of light for seeing, but it's like looking at a light bulb, it doesn't hurt the eyes to look at it. Coming around toward the rear, we can see Comet Wormwood."

"Please describe our handiwork."

"Looks like a giant fuzzball, as comets will this far out. The explosion site on the core appears to have cooled down considerably, I cannot see it. I see the vapor plume from the bomb explosions, sweeping around past us. It is faint, fainter than the Milky Way, the gasses have already dispersed widely. I see a number of mini-comets forming from the small pieces broken off the main core and thrown wide. These pieces absorbed a lot of heat from the bomb explosions, so a *chmfat* sized piece will make a much bigger fuzzball than it would otherwise at this distance from the Sun. Let me get a fix on the planetary plane, the Zodiac. Can't see what the Earthlings call Leo, it is on the other side of the ship from us. Okay, I can recognize Taurus, Gemini, Orion. Aries, Pisces, Sun. When I block its glare with my hand, I can see Mars. Earth and Moon blend into each other as seen from out here, can't pick out Venus. Jupiter is incredibly bright, I see it, and there's Saturn. All right, I can make out the planetary plane. We are coming around to the backside now. I can see a number of vapor plumes around Wormwood. Oh wow!"

"SEVERAL vapor plumes?"

"Yes, a number of breakaways, in all different directions. We need to take more radar scans of the core solids. The main mass may not have been pushed as far from the collision course with Earth as we wanted. Momentum transfer to the breakaway pieces. The closer that main mass passes by Earth, the greater the threat from the orbiting particles. We may want to use one or two of the Russian big bombs to push it further away, and then pick off the breakaway pieces with the Aries missiles."

"Thanks, Sorby. Can you see the damage on the outside of our ship?"

"Just like you said. The panels over Magnetic Coil Assembly Number Seven are cratered. Will have to remove them and walk them over to Bay Number Four for repairs. Doesn't look as bad as we thought, the snowball that hit us was probably not a full six *potes* across, more like four or five. Or it was lighter in mass. Bring up the remote viewing camera, ladies, let's take a look at the fusion reactor cavity."

They screwed together the *hekt pote* sections of nonmagnetic aluminum pole and extended it over the 800 foot wide fusion cavity. A joint allows the bar to be bent into the cavity. With the camera mounted on a swivel that can turn in all directions, we got our first look at the surfaces. "All right!" exclaimed Sorby. "Looking good! No damage to the surface that I can see. Zoom up close, check the rim, everything looking perfect. No melt damage, the plasma ball did not

367

touch the surface. Would have vaporized it. Let's look deep toward the bottom, the surface still looks good, the injection ports are good. Everything is still glowing hot, *kechts* of *deems*, but that is normal."

I watched the image on a screen inside the ship. The cavity surface was bright orange, almost yellow. They were speaking in Atlantean, plenty of laughter and jokes, relieved that the ship was in better shape than we thought. I had become fluent in their language and understood everything they said. "Sorby, I'm curious about something. Exactly what is this material that can withstand the intensity of a fusion reactor plasma ball? That surface doesn't look like a mirror. How were you reflecting the waste heat light out to space?"

"Neil, I must compliment you on your Atlantean. You are speaking it very well. That is classified information, you know we can't reveal this to you. You Cro-Magnons are going to have to develop it yourselves. That is why we talk in Atlantean for many of these repairs."

"The only thing I can think of is a sheet of plasma to reflect the intense light emitted by the plasma ball. This plasma sheet also blew out into space. That orange heat in the surface is the result of glow through, enough to run the steam cycle I heard Pidonita mention. We're running the fission reactor because this is cooling off."

"No comment."

"You are willing to risk your lives to save us from a comet impact of a magnitude similar to the Dinosaur Killer. But you also want to stall off the day we show up in your Solar System in our own starship."

"Yes, that is true. If Columbus found a high population American civilization with an aggressive military tradition, he would not want to share his sailing ship technology with them. He would want to give Europe as much time as possible to get ready for the arrival of the Aztec ships, if he believed them to be capable of conquering and colonizing Europe. It is like that for us. Our spaceship technology is advanced, but we are behind you on some other things. You could overwhelm us with your numbers if you could build starship like the *Neanderthal Return*. As it is, just observing us is giving your engineers many valuable clues as to how to proceed."

"I understand where you're are coming from, Sorby. But the Sixteenth Century Europeans and Native Americans did not have a cooperative effort like this Operation Rainbow. Conquering other tribes and exploiting people as slaves and peons was standard operating procedure then. For the Aztecs and the Africans as well as the Europeans. The ideas of American liberty that we have today are the result of our disgust and opposition to these ancient evils of human nature. So it is different today, I think we would not colonize and immigrate in large numbers to Creation without your permission and cooperation. We want to help you have children so your Race does not disappear from the Universe."

"Yes, I understand, but we still have to try to keep some of our technology secret, though we know that such an effort is futile."

I continued to listen to the chatter of the women as they unbolted the damaged panels over Magnetic Coil Seven. Lucinda and Helga prepared Bay Number Four to receive the damaged parts. There was singing, laughter, and joking, but no horseplay or carelessness. "Sorby, everyone's cheerful, in spite of the fact that we were almost killed."

"None of us would be here if we didn't love spaceflight. Pido got us out of the way of a big *hekt pote* mass, in fact, we can see it right now. We're happy to be alive. There is no atmosphere except comet fumes to obscure the *beeyons* of stars that surround us. This far from the Sun, the sky is dark. Stars that you call seventh and eighth magnitude can be seen with our large Neanderthal eyes, all laid out like a vast glittering carpet of jewels, teasing us from beyond our reach. It is the vastness of the Great Holy Spirit's," she paused, "of God's Creation, a

Creation beyond anything us mere people or even those who carved the mountain on Mars could ever build. You can see *tibeeyons* of *kepfats* in all directions. It is hard to describe, but it is like the sea. You are on the vast ocean topped by the vast sky. Only here, we are surrounded on both sides by the sky, no ocean cutting off half of our view. There is the floating in free fall, being able to move *gunds* with just a light touch. Something about this, Neil, makes it worth the hard work, the danger, the uncomfortable pressure suits, the smells that we sometimes have to endure, it makes it all worthwhile."

"Sorby," called out Wlmsda Hotlund, "we are ready to walk this first panel around."

"Lchndsa, is Bay Number Four open?"

"It's ready, we are opening the door now. We are sending three Earthlings in their Earthmade pressure suits into the Bay."

"Good, they can help us get this tied down."

"While your people are walking the panel around, I'll be inspecting the coil assembly." announced Bchsda Bentlakian. She and Wlmsda were still under penalty, with metal collars, but they're part of the crew. "Contrviea, can you hear me?"

"I hear you, Bchsda. We are ready."

"We'll need at least three radial bracket assemblies, please stand by as I get down into this with my titanium tools and call out the part numbers."

As Betty listed the parts General Fairchild led Major McKenna and Svetlana Lebed in pressure suits through the small airlock into the Bay. The fission reactor was up and running, so Nesla was able to spare the Russian with the most cosmonaut experience. A few months in *Mir* and you get good at repairing things in space. "Helga, we're now inside the Bay."

"You have a few *linits* while Sorby and her girls walk the panel around. You could inspect your missiles while waiting. We want to make sure that the nuclear bombs and the solid rocket fuel is secure."

"Good idea." General Fairchild switched to Russian. "Svetlana, please look at the big Russian bombs while we take a quick look at the Aries and Centaur rockets."

"Sure." she responded in her language. "The jolt should not have affected the bombs, they are designed to withstand massive forces, but the mounting brackets could be damaged."

"The guidance systems!" exclaimed Roy. "They are delicate,"

"I know," Morton responded in English, "but let's wait until we can pull off the inspection plates. All we can do now is look for obvious damage."

"Nothing appears to be misaligned." observed Svetlana in Russian. "Oh no, the warhead on Centaur Number Three is off center." She then lined herself up with each Centaur to gauge the alignment of the warhead. "They are all that way."

"When we get the ship patched up, we can work on these missiles. Contrviea has a set of tools in inches and millimeters brought up from Earth."

"Heads up, General," called out Lucinda, using an American idiom she picked up, "Sorby and her girls are now arriving with the panel."

The three Earthlings went out to the opening to meet the four women maneuvering the 36 by 24 *pote* panel with the very noticeable dent on one side. Torn brackets were visible along its edge. "Morton, Svetlana, Roy, can you each please get cables attached to this panel? We need a cable from the opposite side of the Bay, next to the Aries missile launcher."

"Sure, we need to clear the Centaur launching mechanism, plenty of room in the middle of the floor for the panel, boy is it bent out of shape!"

They handled the panel into the Bay and got it lashed down. "Now we go get the other one." directed Sorby. "There is a lot of work to do while Contrviea's people bang these panels back into shape. We can use Bay Number Two for the smaller parts and tools." Bay Two is closer to the rear of the ship. "And there are plenty of human sized airlocks to cycle through."

"Excellent, the ulna is set, the radius is set." Askelion double checked the laser alignment mechanism. It is a medical version of such mechanisms used for high precision machine shop work, repair of wrecked automobiles, surveying, tunneling, and building construction layout. "Now we apply the cast."

"That looked like it would have hurt." commented Fred Graf on their just completed task of setting and aligning the bones.

"That is why we put her under. We couldn't use a local because we also had to set the nose. Fortunately, the bone of the eggshell thin eye socket is intact, Trviea will only have a black eye for a week or so."

"Maybe not that long, we gave her a dose of Healing Factor along with the unit of her daughter's blood."

Aside from the Healing Factor and the laser alignment device, Cuc, Donald, Fred, and Ben saw few things different than what is found in an Earth hospital. Base Twelve numerals and Atlantean language, the absence of Metric units of measure, these are cultural differences, not technological. The procedures were mostly familiar: Sterilization to prevent infections. Anesthesia to prevent the patient from experiencing cruel pain and thrashing around. X-ray and ultrasound photographs to evaluate the injuries and plan the repair. Broken bones and torn cartilage set so that the natural healing process can knit them back together.

Askelion performed a subtle procedure to reduce the size of the bulge in the bone that results from the healing of a break. Then they wrapped it up in a cast just as is done on Earth. They repaired the ligaments in the knee with laser surgical techniques. Cuc Nguyen commented that this could help football players with knee injuries. They wrapped a cast around the knee to freeze the leg in the straight position while the ligaments reattach themselves.

Finally, the nose. Askelion and Meddi used laser surgery to repair the torn cartilage in such a manner that Trviea's nose will look exactly the same as it did before. The bone chip in the brow ridge was carefully set so that it would knit back into the rest of the bone exactly as it was before. Stitches were used to tie the torn skin back together, just like it is done on Earth. Laser surgery can be used to remove scar tissue when the major injuries have healed.

"We're all done with the surgery. Let's get her into Recovery and watch her. The anesthesia should start to wear off in half an hour."

Everyone on board was pressed into service. I spent some time in the Machine Shop making parts, then I was sent into a pressure suit to Bay Number Two, to Bay Number Four, to the inside access to the fusion reactor magnetic coils, specifically Assembly Number Seven. I helped with the alignment process. Unlike the Shuttle, the tolerances only needed to be 1/12 of a *tig-it*. While that sounds better than 1/144 of the *tig-it* required for the Shuttle magnetic drive, it is also a much larger assembly with a mass of many tons. Could not bring anything of iron into this region, the magnetic fields are powerful, even with the reactor off. Wherever there was a need for extra help, I was sent. I delivered parts and torch equipment to the spacewalkers at Bay Number Two, a much smaller Bay than the big Number Four. It looked just like acetylene torch equipment, only without the bottles, they were using hydrogen and oxygen supplied through hoses.

"Oxygen at two dozen and six *dollons* per square *tig-it*, hydrogen at five dozen." Betty adjusted her valves to these pressures, reading her gauges. Hydrogen at twice the pressure of the oxygen, supplying two hydrogen molecules for every oxygen molecule. "Sparking the torch, now." She ignited the flame with an electric spark. She adjusted the nozzle and went to work.

"Now I'll bend some of this twisted aluminum back into shape." A second torch was brought out, but it was still hours of tedious work for the spacewalkers working for about thirty minutes at a time and taking turns.

"Neil, would you please go over to Bay Number Four and help 'em bang the panels back into shape?"

"Sure, Metrola."

"While there, I would like you to inspect your Aries missile launcher. We've just managed to scan the comet with radar, we needed the fission reactor up and running to do that. The main mass will miss Earth in its present orbit, but only by about two *kecht kepfats*, less than six thousand of your miles. With the attraction of Earth's gravity, we could easily see a half mile sized particle enter the atmosphere and explode with Dinosaur Killer effect. It's good to have pushed the main mass into a miss, but there are the orbiting breakaway pieces. Computer calculations indicate possible breakup of main mass due to tidal force at that distance. Pieces as small as eighty feet can explode with kilotons like Tunguska. Not very many people will be killed if it is an unpopulated area like that. But over Beijing or London or New York,"

"I get the picture. We'll have to hit it again. You know, we might ask the Russians if they could lengthen the detonation countdown. I would like to be much further away next time."

"That's an idea, I'll take it up with Anatoly, he's a pretty reasonable man. An engineer, not a bureaucrat overly concerned with his authority. He likes to find an even better way to do something. No offense, but your Morton Fairchild,"

"I know. He doesn't like to change his mind. He's reluctant to listen to a contrary opinion, almost like it's a personal affront. Which it is not, of course. Too accustomed to giving orders and having his way. There are advantages to that, he makes decisions. Can't have everyone waiting for him to agonize over all of the disadvantages of going either way. Flexibility is for the planning stage. Us engineers love to brainstorm and argue with each other. But we can't have too much of that once the Bomb Run starts."

"He was pretty crisp with his orders for the burn sequence of the Centaur. Placed the bomb perfectly. Uh, before you go over, do you need a break?"

"No I'm fine, I'm on my way."

"Thank you, you're a sweetheart. I'm glad you have so much patience with being shifted around so much. I'm trying to avoid doing that with the other Earthlings, but everyone has moments when they need the extra hands. Nobody has been asleep since several hours before the Bomb Run. Everyone is fine now, but I'll soon have to order people off their assignments and into bed."

After I headed toward the main Bay, Metrola received a call from Medical. "Metrola, this is your Captain, I'm awake again."

"Good, someone who has slept recently. How are you feeling?"

"Numb. I have tingling in my knee, arm, and nose. I am slowly becoming aware of the pain. It'll hurt for a while. I can see through my eye, physicians say nothing too serious, it'll just be black for a while. The physicians won't let me out of Medical for now, they want to observe me. I'm feeling the sexual lust from the Healing Factor, no problem, I just have to be aware of it. A drug effect. I'm still goofy from the drugs, don't want to take a chance on making an improper suggestion to General Fairchild."

They chuckled. "He is a bit straight laced. Glad to hear you are all right. When do you want to assume command?"

"Let's wait a while. I'm just goofy. Goofy! Goofy! Goofy! Never command a ship while under the influence! This is your brain on drugs, any questions? Tee-hee! You can fill me in on the current situation."

As Metrola briefed Trviea, Sorby called in. "Metrola, I'm checking the oxygen tank we're feeding off. Wlmsda and Bchsda both complain of reduced supply pressure. They're doing a good job, we are almost ready to start putting things back together."

"Hi, kid!"

"Mom, you're out of surgery! You gonna live?"

"That's what the physicians say. You having fun outside?"

"I always have fun when I'm outside. Don't like these pressure suits, but you can't breathe vacuum. I've recharged my suit's oxygen tank three times already. So have the other girls out here. We will have to come in soon to change our urine bags and lithium hydroxide canisters. But that's not too urgent yet. I'm glad to hear you're all right. Next time you get yourself strapped down!"

"Yes, dear. The cast on my nose will remind me of that every *prelate*. My headset is wired in with Metrola's. We'll be co-Captains until I recover a little more from these drugs."

"You were talking about the oxygen tank feeding your torches?" asked Metrola.

"Yes. Here comes Wlmsda and Bchsda. Our old security police. They are good with the torches. Hrtinsla and Marla are also out here, they have the torches now. What are your torch pressures, Hortense?"

"I still cannot get any more than twelve and ten *dollons* of oxygen. I compensate by lowering the hydrogen pressure to three dozen and eight *dollons*. But I would like more fuel to generate more heat. Slows down my work."

"I hear you. I'll open up this panel over the oxygen tank to take a look." Sorby stood on the panel over the adjacent hydrogen tank and reached down to open the oxygen panel. The hoses were attached to small hydrants next to the large panels. The small hydrants were behind small doors latched open to allow placement of the hoses. The pipes went through the structure below to the tanks which were under three by four foot panels. For safety reasons, the two tanks are isolated in separate compartments. During the accident the wall between them separated and allowed hydrogen to diffuse in with oxygen. The fittings to both tanks were leaking slightly. The oxygen tank started leaking faster causing the low pressure in the line. The leaked oxygen forced its way into the hydrogen tank compartment and mixed with the hydrogen.

BOOM! We heard it all over the ship.

"Sorby!" screamed Wilma. "Tank's exploded! Sorby has been thrown!"

"Sorby's line snapped!" screamed Betty. "Sorby can you hear me?!" Betty ran and leaped off the side of the ship and grasped for the recoiling line. She missed.

Wilma leaped for the line, she grabbed it. All metal is elastic, when a wire rope snaps, it is first stretched. When it gives, it is spring loaded and immediately contracts and curves back on itself with the momentum. Wilma grabbed the line which went taut between her and Sorby. But the loose part of the line continued its recoil. She screamed when it hit her like a whip. She involuntarily let go. The warning sound screamed in her ears for two *prelates*. "My pressure suit is ripped open! I'm losing pressure fast! Zero six *dollons* and falling!" When on pure oxygen from the suit tank, the insuit pressure is normally held at zero ten *dollons* per square *tig-it*, about five psi. "Regulator open! Helmet pressure recovered to zero seven, but I'm at zero five *dollons* around my body. Helmet pressure falling again, zero six." A rapid depressurization triggers open the regulator valve to the oxygen, as it triggers the alarm. The oxygen blew rapidly into the helmet to keep the head alive. But it is impossible to isolate any part of a pressure suit with a hardworking human body inside. The oxygen blew down the suit and exited through the rip.

"I see the rip in Wilma's suit!" screamed Betty.

"Reel her in!" commanded both co-Captains.

Andemona Chmlakian was at a monitor station, she punched the emergency button corresponding to the cable reel to which Wilma was attached. Wilma's line suddenly went taut as the cable reel whirled to life. Around the cable slot two doors automatically opened to reveal a padded compartment sized to receive a suited astronaut. The cable reel was mounted behind the shell of the compartment to prevent it from injuring the astronaut further when she is slammed in at twelve *potes* per *prelate*.

Wilma flew toward the edge of the opening. Betty bumped Wilma with her body to redirect her flight. Wilma's ears and face hurt and she passed out from the loss of pressure. She slammed into the pads. The doors automatically closed and sealed her off from the vacuum of space. A light turned on so she could see and to keep her from panicking further. Then she woke to great pain and the sound of air hissing. She painfully opened her eyes. Her ears popped several times. Everything looked red. She tried to speak, but couldn't. Her pressure gauges indicated one ten *dollons*, about 11 psi, both insuit and outsuit. Oxygen per*hekt*age dropped as nitrogen-oxygen air blew in through the rip.

"Ohhh." she moaned softly. Everything hurt. She could taste her own blood dripping from her nose on to her lips. Some blood drops floated around inside her faceplate.

"Wlmsda! Wlmsda!" a voice called through her headset. "Just relax, you're still with us, we read your heartbeat, we're coming to get you."

A door adjacent to Wilma opened and in came Meddi Chumkun and a man? That Canadian, Donald Colburn. Donald gently removed the helmet exposing Wilma to the air. "Take it easy, girl." he gently urged.

This kind man spoke in English, she had been learning it, but she couldn't figure out what he said. "What about Sorby?" she asked in Atlantean. "Have to get Sorby."

"Everyone else is getting Sorby." answered Meddi in Atlantean. "Your job is to come to Medical and let us help you. That was a brave thing you did out there, you are a hero."

"I don't feel like a hero. I wear this collar because I have done bad things to other people. It happened so fast, I didn't have time to think."

"That is the way with heroes. It always happens too fast. But you slowed Sorby, that might have saved her life."

"Let's hope so. Let me say a prayer for Sorby."

"Sure, go ahead." Wlmsda mumbled a prayer as they carried her down the tunnel to the main inhabited part of the ship and on to Medical.

At the ship's hospital, they removed the rest of her pressure suit and laid her on a bed. Meddi, Donald, and Fred inspected the torn torso section of the suit. The rest of the Medical Crew had left for Sorby. "We have to take your shirt off to look at your back."

"Sure, do what you have to. Thank you." She winced with pain as they removed the shirt to reveal the welt. The skin wasn't torn, but it was badly bruised. That and the effects of very low pressure. They put her under and began to treat her injuries.

"Sorby! Sorby! Can you hear me?" Metrola and Trviea frantically called on the radio.

"You should be able to see her with this telescope." announced Betty, just as she set it up.

"Thank you, Bchsda. Yes, we can focus it on Sorby. She and her cable are doing a crazy dance around each other." Sorby's limp body spun and jerked in the vacuum as the cable coiled and recoiled back and forth. The arms looked like they moved a bit. "Sorby, can you hear me?"

We heard a muffled groan through the speakers. Sorby was dazed, then she woke up. "I can hear you. I'm not attached to the ship, cable flapping around, what happened?"

"Some hydrogen and oxygen leaking from somewhere got mixed up and exploded."

"Oh."

"You were right on top of it."

"Yeah. Let me try to get this cable under control." She tried to coil the cable while using her muscle strength to damp the energy in the cable.

"Has your suit warning warble gone off?"

"Uh, no. I don't think so. My insuit pressure is zero ten, what it's supposed to be. I've got plenty of oxygen. Uh, my carbon dioxide is up to three *kechters*. Four." The warning sounded.

"We heard the warning here, Sorby. What's the story on your lithium hydroxide scrubbers? You said something about changing them just before the explosion."

"I had some time left on them. Switching over to emergency scrubber. Oh no. Cable flopping, my arm hurts, I cannot seem to make the switch. Uh, I believe that is smashed, I cannot route my air through the emergency scrubber. I can breathe off the oxygen feed to try to keep the carbon dioxide out of my lungs." Her grammar and pronunciation suffered.

I had been called over after the explosion. Both co-Captains turned to me, I could see the fear on their faces. "Apollo 13." I said.

"Apollo 13 was a HUGE air pocket compared to a pressure suit." noted Metrola. "Her carbon dioxide level will shoot up fast if she's not getting it scrubbed from her air. We don't have time. Trviea, can you take full command while I haul a rescue crew in the Shuttle?"

"I'm still under the influence of anesthesia drugs. I'll have to take that into account and overcome it. That's my little girl out there, and everyone's friend. Please get the Shuttle ready. Ask, Cuc, and Ben Roy should come with you, leaving Meddi, Fred, and Donald to work on Wlmsda and be ready on ship. Pido! Can you isolate Coil Assembly Seven and project a magnetic field for the Shuttle to work off?"

"I think so. I'm extremely tired."

"Sabar," asked Captain Trviea, "can you take over the pilot's seat?"

"Sure, Coil Seven is already isolated. Pidonita can stand by, she, we, all will be needing sleep. We'll need the fission reactor up to full power to project the magnetic fields."

"Nesla,"

"Pulling control rods all the way! Increasing to full power. Bringing ammonia cycle on line. Anatoly, Mikhail, please watch the gauges!"

"We have to get everyone cleared from the fusion cavity, cyclotrons, and coil compartments before firing up the coils." reminded Sabar.

"Everyone!" ordered Trviea. "Clear the fusion coils! Metrola will take the Shuttle to fetch Sorby. I'm resuming full command. Clear the fusion coils! Repeat, clear the fusion coils! Sorby, we're coming for you!"

"Good. I've managed to stabilize my carbon dioxide at one three *kechters*. If I can keep it there, I think I have enough oxygen to last two hours and two dozen *linits*."

"We won't leave you out there that long."

"Actually, I don't mind. It's incredibly pretty out here. When I stop wrestling with this cable, I can look at the Earth and Moon. Earth is a beautiful blue, even from out here. Its color dominates the white of the Moon. I see the *Neanderthal Return* in front of Comet Wormwood. I'll pull in and coil up this wire rope. Now it's wanting to wrap around me, tie me up. I'll have to rotate with it." She used her suit's attitude jets to spin her body with the cable. "Now I can pull in and coil this cable. I'll apologize to the Great Holy Spirit for my sins, just in case."

"Always a good idea anyway. But we'll get you. You know what to do when the Shuttle arrives. We are watching you with a telescope."

"Ahh, it's getting so a woman can't have any privacy." That made people laugh. "Another *linit* I can get this cable coiled, my body spins faster as I draw it in." Sorby finally got the full length of the cable coiled and fixed to her body. "Getting dizzy spinning around like this, I feel the centripetal forces and see the stars spinning past me. Better straighten myself out." She used her attitude jets to stop her rotation. "Ahhh! Much better!"

The Shuttle was launched. The three women who were outside working with Sorby and Wilma boarded through the double door airlock. "All right," announced Metrola. "As cheerful as Sorby appears to be," Sorby sang a lighthearted, humorous song in Atlantean. Her mother and the other women couldn't help themselves, they joined in. She performed a dance in the vacuum of space. She laughed, and we laughed. "We won't need the Medical staff. Sabar, are you ready with the magnetic field?"

"Firing up the coils, now. All but Assembly Seven. Getting full power from steam and ammonia cycle generators. I have selected the pure projection program, there will be no magnetic bottle in the reactor cavity. There is iron in Sorby's pressure suit and hemoglobin in her blood, the magnets in her shoes. So we'll try to slow her down from her velocity of two dozen *potes* per *prelate* away from the ship. She just passed one *kepfat* in distance from the ship. It has only been five *linits*." Four minutes and ten seconds. "All right, Metrola, you have magnetic field to work with."

"Thank you, Sabar. On our way. Only a *kepfat*, more than that now. That's not very far. You only have another *linit* to dance Sorby, sorry!"

"That is quite all right, Metrola. I'll just have to forgive you!" We chuckled. "I can see you coming. Tell Cuc and Askelion that I'm in perfect health. Except for this sore arm, uh, I think I sprained an ankle. Can still dance, no weight!"

"We'll have to examine you." admonished Askelion. "Ankle. Arm. Way you're acting, we'll have to add brain to the list."

Sorby chuckled. "Yeah. One day I went completely insane. Unfortunately, nobody noticed the difference! Oooh! Sabar, take it EASY! Those magnetic fields."

"Ah, come on Sorby." protested the mothership pilot. "You can't feel a thing. But we do have your velocity relative to the ship down to twelve and eight *potes* per *prelate*."

"You're right, I can't feel a thing. Shuttle's getting big! Metrola, please don't run into me!" That was followed by her sparkling laugh.

"Don't worry, I won't."

Suddenly, the warning signal went off in Sorby's helmet. "I'm losing pressure! Down to zero eight *dollons*! Regulator valve open. Venting air to space! Zero six *dollons*! I love you, Mother." We watched in horror as Sorby thrashed around trying to find the leak in her suit. She seemed to be trying to put her hands on the back of her helmet. "Zero four *dollons*." she wheezed.

"Don't bother matching speeds with her!" screamed Trviea. Sorby stopped thrashing. Her arms moved slowly in front of her to relaxed position. Her legs straightened and then bent slightly. "Catch her with the net!"

In the telescope image, we saw the small rockets extend the catch net out in front of the astronaut. The net caught her and the outer ropes wrapped around to envelop her. She was reeled to the side of the Shuttle. "Bchsda!" She was still in her pressure suit. "Get her!" ordered Metrola.

Betty went out through the airlock. She detached the net from the side of the Shuttle and pulled Sorby into the airlock. "Outer door secured, pulling repress valve NOW!" She turned the valve halfway, when the pressure gauge read twelve *dollons* per square *tig-it*, she turned it the rest of the way. "Airlock fully pressurized, opening door, bringing her in!"

Betty brought the limp astronaut into the Shuttle cabin. Hrtinsla pulled the helmet off. Ben Roy Sumner, a former paramedic with the Fire Department in Moose Jaw, Saskatchewan, placed his hand on Sorby's neck. "No pulse. No breath."

The pressure suit was pulled off fast. Cuc Nguyen began mouth to mouth. A defibrillator was applied by Askelion and Ben. They jolted her. They hand pumped her heart to attempt cardiopulmonary resuscitation. "Met, get us to the *Return*, fast."

We ran to the Shuttle Bay. As soon as air pressure was restored to the Bay, we went in. The Shuttle door opened. Askelion climbed out slowly, followed by Bchsda Bentlakian. Askelion Lamakian spoke softly with Captain Trviea Harsradich, just a few words.

We didn't have to be told. We knew.

Chapter Forty Two

Trviea started shaking. Askelion gave her a hug. She received a tearful hug from Betty. They went into the Shuttle. A few minutes later, they came out carrying Sorby on a stretcher. She was still in the tunic and pants she wore under her pressure suit. Trviea combed her daughter's hair, giving her as much dignity as possible in death. Sorby's face had been cleaned off, she looked serene, as if she was only asleep.

Trviea fought back tears and spoke through her headset to the ship. "Sorby Mishlakian is now with the Great Holy Spirit. I thank the Spirit for the wonderful gift of a daughter for me and a friend for all of us." She broke down.

Metrola was also devastated. But she managed to say, "I know we still have a ship to repair. We may have to hit the comet again. But for now I think we should stop repair work and have everyone take a twelve hour break. Get some sleep."

We carried Sorby to the Medical Department. Askelion and Meddi had the sad duty of placing her in a morgue that had never been used. Hrtinsla Pliklakian, who was working outside with Sorby when the explosion happened, went to the Garden Room. She cleaned up some of the mess. She picked flowers and made a very nice bouquet. She brought these flowers to the morgue and placed them by the crypt.

Trviea, Helga, Lucinda, Metrola, and Sabar came into Wlmsda Hotlund's hospital room. All had red eyes, emotionally numb, a state of false calm. Some managed to get sleep and were yawning. Wlmsda slept, Donald Colburn at her side keeping an eye on her.

"Donald, how is she doing?"

"She's doing fine. She was exposed to very low pressure. Her nosebleed is healing. There is damage to the airsacs in her lungs from the air being sucked out."

"The kind of damage that kept us from reviving Sorby?"

"Well, yeah. But Wilma was not exposed to low pressure for as long, and we don't think it got below one half pound per square inch. Sorby was exposed to hard vacuum. For a few seconds, but that's all it takes. There was a crack in the back of her helmet, probably from something hitting it. That crack held for most of the time she was out there. She was killed when it gave way and her oxygen tank emptied through the open regulator valve and then through the helmet crack."

"Yes we know that. We've spoken with Bchsda, Hrtinsla, and Marla. We would like to speak with Wlmsda."

"Nasty bruise across her back, but no broken bones. We've given her Healing Factor. Best thing for her now is sleep."

"She shall have it. Thank you, Donald. Please give us a call when she wakes up."

"Trviea," Donald addressed her softly, "Wilma is awake now."

They filed back into the room and stood at the side of Wilma's bed. "I am so sorry. So terribly sorry."

"Don't be. It's not your fault." It didn't help, Wilma broke down in tears. She wasn't told until she woke.

"We did not have any warning." declared Wilma after recovering her composure. "What happened to the detectors that warn us of an explosive mixture?"

"Did not work. We didn't know the extent of the damage from the collision. Electrical connections were ripped, barriers that prevented oxygen and fuels from mixing were torn. We have cleared these gasses from the entire rear of the ship. We will have to bring oxygen and hydrogen in bottles to finish the torch work around the coil assembly. We will have to inspect every fitting and electrical connection. All workers will have to carry warning units."

"I just wish I was able to hold on to Sorby's tether."

"I know, but no one could have held on the way that cable whipped you. Thank you for trying." Trviea bent down and kissed Wilma. She placed her finger to be read by the locking mechanism in Wilma's metal collar. The collar came undone. "We have talked it over and we have decided to release you from this. We have also released Bchsda. We will speak no more of the reason for this collar. Please rest and get well soon."

After the twelve hour rest period, Trviea directed the repair crews back to work. This time, every system containing oxygen and flammable gasses was thoroughly inspected. The hydrogen and oxygen that exploded were located fairly close to the impact site. Further away, the damage was considerably less, to everyone's relief. About half of the crew, including the Earthlings, were ordered to sleep. When they woke, they relieved the tired workers performing repairs. No one laughed and joked, the mood was subdued.

Pidonita and Metrola arrived at the Pilothouse. "Sabar, Captain Trviea, are you ready to be relieved?"

"We sure are." answered Trviea. "Sabar, you want to get some sleep?"

Sabar yawned. "Yes." They allowed themselves the first laugh since Sorby's death.

"Then get some sleep." Sabar left to take a shower and get some rest. Trviea continued. "Andemona Chmlakian is nearing the end of her shift at the fission reactor. Nesla is awake and will soon be ready to take over. At least three of the Russians are in the fission reactor control room at all times as they take turns sleeping."

"We know the fission reactor system tested good at full power."

"Yeah. Nesla and a full crew of Russians will bring it back to full power with the ammonia cycle on line. We are almost ready to recharge the fusion reactor. We will need a well rested pilot for that. You get some sleep, Pido?"

"Yeah. It wasn't easy at first, but I finally nodded off."

"You too, Metrola?"

"Yes, me too."

"Contrviea and a crew with Hrtinsla, Marla, and Wlmsda Gtslakian are bolting in the repaired panel sections right now. We are waiting for them to finish and clear the magnetic coils. Magnetic Coil Assembly Seven has been repaired and aligned."

"What's the situation with the comet?"

"There is nothing we can do about the comet until we are up and running. We need to get Sabar off pilot duty so she can concentrate on the comet and its breakaway pieces. When we can free Chuck Carter and Mustafa Khedr from the repair work, they can help her with the ancient Egyptian gold plates. Chuck thinks he has figured out the *Zep Tepi* arithmetic, number system, and units of length. Feet and cubits. He also thinks that they understood orbital mechanics from their eyeball astronomy. All three believe Comet Wormwood is depicted as it appeared the previous time it flew past Earth."

"I agree, we need to find out what the gold plate artists knew about Wormwood. But we have to deal with the comet as it is now."

"Yes. All right. Currently, the Wormwood main mass is in an orbit that will miss Earth by about two *kecht* and one *hekt kepfats,* calculation taking into account the pull of Earth's gravity.

It could shift a bit from the rocket effect of the boiling gasses. That is good, because it'll be deflected by Earth's gravity into an orbit outside the planetary plane. The problem arises from the breakaway pieces that orbit the main mass even without a tidal breakup. A tidal breakup could result in a huge number of *kepfat* sized pieces!"

"Some could be sucked away by Earth's gravity and slam into Earth."

"The sunlight shining on it will be six dozen times the intensity it is now when it crosses Earth orbit. That'll fluff up the surface and lift that many more breakaways. We'll have to move the main mass further away and let its gravity, weak as it is, draw away as much of the problem from Earth as possible. Then we can hit any breakaways that escape the gravity of the main mass and threaten Earth."

"This is Contrviea calling the Pilothouse."

"This is the Pilothouse, Captain Trviea here. Are you all done with the panels?"

"Yes we are. We are coming in now."

"Good. Thank you. Pidonita, the pilot seat's all yours."

"Thanks, Trev. Contrviea, are all of your girls inside yet?"

"Give us another *linit*, please." They waited about 50 seconds. "All right, we are all in the airlock cycling in."

"Thank you, Contrviea. Trviea, are the coils clear of personnel?"

"Yes, they are. You may fire the coils anytime."

"Nesla, this is Pidonita at the Pilothouse. How is the fission reactor?"

"Full power, Pido. Monoloa and all four Russians are at their stations. Ammonia cycle is on line."

"I confirm that. All right, here goes." She switched on the ship's public address. "Clear the magnetic coils. Two *linits* to firing the fusion reactor magnetic coils." She knew the coils were clear but the warning is a good safety precaution. "Firing all twelve magnetic coils, NOW. All twelve coils working. Forming magnetic bottles, NOW. Magnetic bottles have formed. Checking magnetic bottles. Fusion core magnetic bottle good. Shell magnetic bottle good. Plasma reflection sheet magnetic bottle good. Nucleus spin alignment field good. Pulse controls are good. Pulsing works. Momentum transfer field good. Control mechanisms good. Coolant steam flowing, coolant systems are good. Main Steam Cycle ready to receive energy. System is now ready for plasma injection. Water in cyclotrons is now plasma. Hydrogen oxygen separation good. Oxygen bleed off good, adjusting mixture. Mixture is good."

"Fission reactor good at full power. Fission reactor steam and ammonia cycles are both good, both producing maximum electricity."

"Thank you, Nesla. I confirm fission power availability. Now injecting hydrogen and oxygen plasma into core." Some but not all of the oxygen is bled off the water plasma before it is fed into the core. Oxygen in the plasma keeps continuous fusion from occurring and allows the pulsing phenomenon. "Injecting water plasma into the shell." Water, even as plasma, slows down the high speed neutrons generated by fusion. "Boron and cadmium plasma ready for injection." Boron 10 and cadmium 113 absorb neutrons, the Creation women have separated these isotopes from the natural ore. "Injecting boron and cadmium plasma into shell and reflection sheet." Reflection sheet forms a parabolic surface to direct most of the intense light emitted by the plasma ball to space. It absorbs what neutrons escape the plasma ball. Glow through energy heats the cavity surface. Coolant steam keeps the cavity surface from vaporizing and powers the main turbine. "Plasma ball forming. Boron and cadmium neutron shield forming around plasma ball. Plasma neutron shield good. Shell reaching minimum necessary thickness. Fusion core inside plasma ball forming. Fusion core good. Shell at minimum necessary thickness. Fusion core one *keetig-it* in diameter." A fusion core need not be big, protons are very small. "Commencing pulsing for unaligned fusion." For heat and electricity. Unaligned fusion does not provide momentum to thrust the ship. But the expansion against the restraining magnetic fields can be tapped for direct generation of electricity. It is analogous to a piston that compresses fuel-air mixture and receives the power stroke from the combustion. The fusion reactor is now helping to feed itself, augmenting the fission reactor power. The time necessary to inject the 18 million pounds of plasma to fully charge the plasma ball is thereby reduced from weeks to a few hours.

When fully charged, the six foot diameter fusion core contains over a million pounds of hydrogen and oxygen plasma. Its density is 160 pounds per pint or that many kilos per liter, or 5.5 to 6 pounds per cubic inch. Around the core is a shell of about one quarter that density with the outside diameter of 24 feet, containing another 17 million pounds of water plasma heavily loaded with boron and cadmium. When pulsed for aligned fusion the core propels the ship with an energy supply that can last over two dozen Creation years without being recharged. That is why helium spectral lines were seen, the women had been traveling for a while on ONE plasma charge. That plasma ball had plenty left when it blew out. The shell absorbs gamma rays, neutrons, and heat generated by the fusion core and retransmits that energy as light. High in the blue spectrum, including ultraviolet, but far less damaging to the rest of the ship and to us than the raw core energy.

Why so huge? Probably because they couldn't figure out how to make it smaller. Huge magnetic coils make for huge magnetic flux. Our fusion reactor experiments on Earth are too small to meet Lawson's criterion for deuterium and tritium, let alone for regular hydrogen.

We continued our repair work while Pidonita patiently monitored the charging of the fusion reactor. She announced every hour through the public address that everything is working as it should. Finally, "The plasma ball is now fully charged. All magnetic bottles are holding steady. Commencing aligned fusion now." We prepared for the resumption of acceleration. Nice to end the floating. "*Jore put!*" That fast. The floors came up on us and we had acceleration for the first time since the collision. We cheered and clapped our hands as we were back in business! Six feet per second squared acceleration. Nesla and her Russian crew shut down the fission reactor.

Captain Harsradich addressed the ship. "Ladies and gentlemen. We are up and running. Congratulations. There is still damage that needs to be repaired, the Garden Room, the long distance transmitters, some of the life support, we'll be busy for a while. We have moved the main mass of Comet Wormwood to an orbit where it'll miss Earth by two *kecht* and one *hekt kepfats*, 5800 miles or 9300 kilometers. But there is a problem with breakaway pieces and a possible tidal breakup of the main mass. We'll have to make another bomb run, maybe two bomb runs. Then we can pick off the smaller break off pieces as necessary with the Aries missiles. We must consider the ancient Egyptian gold plates that illustrate Comet Wormwood the previous time it visited the Inner Solar System. Neil Peace, Andemona Chmlakian, Contrviea Tiknika, Sabar Duradich, Chuck Carter, Mustafa Khedr, American Missile Crew, Russian Bomb Crew, and Monoloa Mrvlakian, get some sleep now. Please meet with me in Conference Room One in six hours."

Trviea went to the front of the conference room. She still had casts on her limbs and her nose. We noticed the improvement around her eye, the purple patches had faded. The stitches were gone from her lips and eyebrow. The Healing Factor worked miracles. "The repair of the *Neanderthal Return* is so far successful, we can repair most of the damage. Unfortunately, after we complete Operation Rainbow, we will have to remain in Earth orbit for about a year while we repair the thing that we shall call the Warp Drive. That is not what it is, we will not reveal to you how this technology works. We call it Warp Drive because that is the term you Earthlings are accustomed to using for faster than light drive."

"You do have faster than light drive!" exclaimed General Fairchild. "Why do you feel safe in revealing this much to us?"

"You already know we can travel faster than light. You don't believe we spent the last twenty or thirty years traveling here in what you call 'normal space'?"

"Why not? You're in desperate straits if there are no men and no way to have children. That is your explanation for an all female crew. Anatoly tells me his heartbeat and brain function are much better since Doctor Lamakian gave him what she said was a limited age stopping process. A process designed to keep him from having a stroke or heart attack during this mission. I agree with your reasons for doing this. Anatoly is free to pass on anytime AFTER we complete this mission. But right now we need the engineer who designed these big Soviet bombs. His descriptions of the treatment sound like genetic therapy. So I believe you when you claim that you have cheated death by shutting off the aging gene. Well, if you've got that accomplished, you can cross the four light years from Alpha Centauri without exceeding the speed of light. Our Earth physicists tell us NOTHING can exceed the speed of light. Impossible. So why should you be able to?"

"Good question." Trviea took a breath and thought for a moment. "For starters, travel from one star to another requires incredibly fast speeds. Or it simply isn't practical. Now we can, by maintaining a few feet per second squared acceleration for several weeks or so, achieve huge velocities relative to the rest of this Solar System. You witnessed this as we traveled out here to deal with Wormwood. The danger of this kind of speed is the possibility of collision with a particle, even a small one. A particle of one ounce, one *coilon*, even one gram can destroy this ship at such speeds. Punch a hole right through our three *tig-it* aluminum hull. Even a *treefat* or a *chmfat* thick hull. As a military man who has trained with guns and rifles, you know that a piece of lead just 22 hundredths of an inch in diameter, traveling at a few thousand feet per second, can kill you. Or at least punch an ugly hole in your body. Now imagine this ship hitting that same bullet, not at a few thousand FEET per second, but at a few thousand MILES per second. Kinetic energy of collision, one half mass times velocity SQUARED."

"No more ship."

"Exactly! Yet an alien race made it from a star in Leo to Mars and carved their face on a mountain. They transported my ancestors from Earth to Creation. We transported ourselves back to Earth. We did it by traveling faster than light. Sorry Albert Einstein, God does play dice with the Universe." Did Trviea give us a clue or is she trying to lead us astray? "Yet we do not annihilate ourselves by crashing into one of the *tibeeyons* of rocks and ice cubes that float between the stars. The bigger ones, larger than a few hundred feet across, are one thing, but what ought to impress you is that we manage to avoid hitting the inch sized particles."

"And you need to repair this Warp Drive?"

"It's a little out of adjustment. We can try heading to the Creation Solar System now, but we will most likely not wind up there. Where would we be? No way of telling. We would like to have it perfectly aligned. Then we can have some confidence that we will end up where we WANT to go."

"The more immediate problem is Comet Wormwood."

"Right, let's get back to the main subject. We don't want to be so close when we set off the next big Russian Bomb. Anatoly, is it possible that we can have a longer detonation countdown?"

"We can lengthen it out. We now know the burn sequence of the Centaur. Six minutes to get it started. Then seven minutes and 22 seconds of free fall, then another burn for a final course correction for another minute, and about ten seconds to enter the Aries hole. Total flight time, about 14 minutes 32 seconds. We could do it if we put in a different clock. Then we can send the detonation code and start the countdown when the Americans start the Centaur."

"Good. We can be much further away and going much faster with that much time after you send the signal. General Fairchild, can the entire Centaur flight be programmed now that we know the burn sequence? So we can take off when you send the signal?"

"Actually, we can. We had to make sure that the first one went in exactly right, we had to move the main mass away from its collision course with Earth at all costs."

"At all costs? We almost lost the ship. Wlmsda Hotlund is still recuperating in the hospital. My daughter is dead. And look at me."

"I know, Trviea. You have my condolences. But something like this killed the dinosaurs. There was nothing wrong with them, they were a successful life form. But they didn't have spaceships, rockets, and nuclear warheads. We do. We have a God given duty to do everything within our power to prevent this kind of tragedy. You came here because you need our help to have children and continue your Race. We also need to continue our Race. Both human Races need to work together to stop this thing, we need to help each other, even to the point of risking our lives. Sorby knew this, she accepted the risks. She died a hero, we will always love her and honor her."

"I know. Thank you. Well, right now, we still have to push that main mass some more. We create another hole with an Aries missile. Can we fit the Centaur with an infrared detector to allow it to follow the hot spot?"

"Make it a giant heat seeker? Sure, I don't see why not. Contrviea's people have the Metric and American inch threaded taps and drilling equipment brought up from the Bangor Base. Let's get to it."

"I agree, let's get to it."

The Giza Plateau is one of the world's special places. Every person visiting Egypt wants to see the Sphinx and the Pyramids which dominate the landscape around the south side of Cairo. If you are lucky enough to have a window seat on the south side of the plane, you can see the Giza monuments as you fly in and out of Cairo International Airport. Imagine the difficulties faced by the Egyptian Antiquities Organization in trying to keep an excavation secret!

But they've managed. There are the rumors, which people ignore absent an official announcement. It was the additional room just discovered, called the 'Map Room', a few feet beyond the 'Hall of Records' in the cliff immediately north of the Sphinx. At Kilometer 206 Charles Sheehy started the discussion. "These are the new artifacts from the 'Map Room'. You can see why we call it that."

"That's the Nile River all right, Nubia to the top, the Mediterranean Sea at the bottom, the Red Sea and the Gulf of Suez are right where they should be. But the Gulf of Suez is smaller than it is today. The whole coastline looks like the ocean is lower, like some of the continental shelf is exposed."

"It looks like the ocean is 20 meters lower than today."

"That might be consistent with 12,500 years ago, the end of the Ice Age. *Zep Tepi* time."

"Look at this, Giza is marked on this map. So is On, east of the River."

"That could be prehistoric Heliopolis. That is the location of modern Heliopolis. Look at how the Nile splits into two channels in the same place its splits today and has throughout historical times. More rain then, the lake in the Qattara Depression."

"Lake Qattara. The wadis are rivers, not the dry washes they are today. That's Egypt. Look at these other maps. We have the same 20 meter drop in ocean levels in all of them. Greece, Italy. Note how much smaller the Adriatic looks."

"Greece is interesting, Euboea part of the mainland, the Gulf of Corinth more like the Corinth River. Lesbos a peninsula of Asia Minor. The Black Sea appears to be as high as it is today, but draining through a river through the Sea of Marmara."

"You sure that is showing a river and not a strait?"

"Hard to tell."

"We haven't got the radiocarbon results yet, but with the other set of gold plates, the associated wood tested out to be 12,500 years old, the *Zep Tepi* age."

"Yeah. Look at this plate showing Britain and France. You're British, what do you think of this?"

"Yes. Right. On this gold map, the Isle of Wight is attached to the main part of England. The Thames stays a river all the way out to, uh, Southend is not on Sea. This north-south island east of the Thames Estuary is definitely Falls Head. Yes, what I'm seeing is consistent with a ten fathom drop. On the mainland, we can see the Rhine flowing as a single river through the Netherlands, picking up the Maas along the way. It appears to be following the Old Rhine channel, north of Rotterdam. Falls Head turned the Rhine north while turning the Thames south through the Strait of Dover. The two rivers did not meet. Further northeast, we see the Dutch and German coastline drawn outside the Frisian Islands."

"Look at these other maps, they knew about America!"

"The Bahamas are much bigger islands. Parts of the Grand Bahama Bank are exposed."

"That might explain the Bimini Road. If it was on dry land then, and there were people who would care to build it."

"We need modern charts with 20 meter or 10 fathom underwater contours to compare with these gold maps."

"Not every plate in this batch is a map. This is the plate! This is the one that blows everything to Hell."

"That is the Earth and Moon. There is Venus, Mercury, and the Sun. Over here, Mars, its orbit visibly wider in this direction. They knew that! And there is a comet, passing through Earth's orbit just ahead of Earth! All of this writing down here, looks like mathematical calculations."

"Thousands of years before Copernicus."

"We going to disclose this to the public?"

"Are you kidding? No! Of course not. But we need to disclose this to Sabar Duradich and Mustafa Khedr. Tight beam, coded transmission, per agreement."

"Fine, but what's to stop Chuck Carter from disclosing this? Typical American, he doesn't believe in keeping things secret."

"We'll just have to chance it. Sabar and Mustafa need the image of this plate. So Chuck discloses it to the public, let him. We need to get this comet taken care of."

"Wait! Let's discuss this. Their current President has been declassifying most of their secrets. Embarrassed OUR government a few times in the process. Not that the revelations surprised anyone. Chuck Carter is a fan of this policy. He would agree to keep something secret if there is a good reason, but doesn't think our good reasons are good reasons."

"He cannot understand how there can be ANY reason to keep an archeological discovery secret once the site has been secured from vandalism and theft. He believes photography and disclosure are the only sure fire means of preserving a find. The find can be destroyed, but published photographs live on."

"He believes people have a right to know what happened 12,500 years ago if something did indeed happen. What possible reason could there be for keeping what happened thousands of years ago secret?"

"That is the way he thinks. Never mind the riots that occur when 'blasphemous' stuff comes to the surface. Jordanians and Israelis were right to keep a tight lid on the Dead Sea Scrolls until they pieced them together properly and read them."

"Ancient writings that say the wrong thing can cause tremendous problems. What if we find an assertion in Ancient Egyptian or Hebrew that Moses wrote the Ten Commandments himself, he just made it all up, they didn't come from Allah? Or anything about Mohammed, Peace Be Upon Him. Think of the problems that would cause. To which a free speech loving American like Chuck Carter will say 'So what? People have a right to know and draw their own conclusions!'"

"Some of those damn Americans don't understand that we sometimes need to control information. We still have to send this image to the *Neanderthal Return*. Better to deal with the public disclosure that Carter will cause to happen, than to deal with a Dinosaur Killer impact."

"*Neanderthal Return*. It's too bad about Sorby Mishlakian."

"May she rest in peace. Allah bless her."

"Chuck, Mustafa, have you gentlemen a few minutes?"

"Sure, Sabar. We can always make a little time for you."

She smiled. "I'll bet. Got some questions concerning the development of technology. Take a glass tube. Add a quantity of mercury, the liquid metal. Mercury expands and contracts with temperature, and does so very consistently. Mark off lines on the glass tube, call them 'degrees', now you can put a numerical value on temperature. Very simple device. Quite elegant. Can be made by any society that has glass blowing and mercury smelting technology. Such as your Romans, some of whom were accomplished engineers. Invented lots of neat things, some far more complicated and difficult to make than a mercury thermometer."

"So why didn't anybody invent one before Gabriel Fahrenheit?"

"Exactly."

"I don't really know. Not everyone can be a Fahrenheit. Not every Fahrenheit has a receptive audience. Sometimes folks can be remarkably resistant to new ideas. Galileo was put under house arrest for suggesting that Copernicus was right."

"THAT's what I wanted to ask you. Copernicus deduced that Earth itself is a planet in orbit around the Sun, and that explains all of the observations of the visible planets, which also orbit the Sun. This is an observation available to any eyeball astronomer in any of your ancient societies. Yet NONE of them guessed the truth?"

"One did guess the truth. Aristarchos of Samos thought the Earth was a planet orbiting the Sun. But everyone else disagreed with him." commented Mustafa. "That the planets and the Sun are all in a plane is evident from the fact that they never wander from the Zodiac. The Zodiac was known throughout all ancient stargazing cultures. But we Cro-Magnons were just so attached to the idea that Earth was the center of the Universe, that we refused to grasp the fact that it orbits the Sun! Even though the evidence to prove it was right there in front of our faces!"

"Hey!" interjected Chuck. "Our prisons are full of people who claim they are the victims of juries who couldn't see a reasonable doubt if it bit 'em in the ass! That a few of 'em are right might explain why very intelligent people could miss something so obvious for centuries, even millennia."

"I see." concluded Sabar. "Our Egyptian friends found another cache of gold plates with illustrations."

"Marvelous."

"Come and look, please."

In my life I have: Completed a degree in mechanical engineering. Have years of experience at The Boeing Company. Been on this alien ship since last summer. I can now speak fluent Atlantean. I understand VQ over It and Mc over I. Shear flows and bending stresses. I know a 'kip' is 1,000 pounds. I can crunch the numbers of BTU's, add 460 to a Fahrenheit temperature to obtain it in absolute Rankine scale, and do the same thing with Metric units. So what fancy high tech engineering work have I been doing in restoring the Centaur missiles to usability?

Converting a bunch of millimeter and inch dimensions to Atlantean *tig-it* measure so the Machine Shop can replace damaged parts. Twelfths, 144ths and *keetig-its*.

Grumble. Grumble. Grumble. Now I know how Einstein felt about working in a patent office. "Nothing can go faster than light? So what! Get back to work, Albert, and quit wasting your time on that cosmic stuff! The faster you move, the faster the time goes. What do you mean that opposite is true? Albert, sometimes I don't understand you. Oh, so you say your mass increases with your speed? Why don't you try it and get this work done? Eat some strudel, that'll increase your mass! Mass increases with speed. That would explain why I can't seem to run this weight off."

The Russians replaced the clocks in their bombs. They lubricated the ancient final countdown mechanisms. Don't know for sure, but we could see how a dry and rusty mechanism can hang up and cause the delay we observed before the explosion. We reattached the big warheads to the Centaurs with new parts. The Centaur fuel tanks did not have any cracks or other damage. That's good news. We had to replace damaged bolts and nutplates. I explained the American National Fine and the International Standards Organization Metric thread series to Contrviea and her girls. The screws were a crazy mix of the two systems, but were aircraft quality Grade 9 in strength. We had some spare fasteners brought up from Earth.

At least I got to verify that the Aries missile launcher I helped design was undamaged and ready for use.

Fortunately, none of the Aries missiles were damaged. That figures. Minuteman I missiles were designed to be transported up the back roads of North Dakota and loaded in and out of silos. If that don't break 'em nothing will. They sat in the silos for years ready to launch. Temperature extremes? 120 above to 50 below. Nowadays, NASA uses these same boosters for sounding rockets. Send a payload up above the atmosphere for a few minutes to take a look at some temporary phenomenon. The plastic binder is still rubbery and not prone to cracks after all these years. The B61-12 warhead is designed to punch 100 feet into a wall of ice at thousands of miles per hour, then detonate. Nothing wrong with them!

Our Air Force people didn't let us watch when they checked the warheads. But they weren't security conscious about the guidance systems. The Honeywell systems in the Centaurs were already in Kazakhstan as part of the joint venture between Lockheed and Energomash! They helped the Russian Bomb Crew place the infrared sensors on the noses of their warheads.

The Centaur fueling gantries and launch assembly were repaired and thoroughly checked and double checked. No one wanted another hydrogen-oxygen explosion.

Then we were done. Ready for another Bomb Run. God help us. Mikhail Dostoevsky wrote on the Russian warhead we've selected for the next Bomb Run. He signed his name to the short message. "*Lyubim vyi*, Sorby Mishlakian." I read the Cyrillic letters out loud.

"*Da*, that is a correct pronunciation, sort of." Mikhail praised me, sort of.

"The *im* ending, that means 'we' in the verb." In the Russian classes, I learned to my horror, that verbs are conjugated in the Slavic languages as they are in the Latin. "*Vyi* means 'you'. But what does the verb *lyubim* mean?"

"It is present tense, not past tense. It means 'love'. The sentence means, 'We love you, Sorby Mishlakian.'"

I wrote, "I love you, Sorby. I miss you. I know you sit at the right hand of God. I thank Him for the short time that I have had the pleasure of knowing you. Loving you forever, Neil Armstrong Peace." Messages, poems, prayers, and signatures were soon written in three languages all over the rockets and warheads. News of what we were doing spread quietly and rapidly through the ship. Soon, everyone had a chance to sign his or her name and to write a poem or prayer. Some of us broke down and cried anew.

"She always loved to dance." Trviea told us. "She danced in my womb. All the time. Her legs were very strong." She winced to illustrate her baby kicking her hard. We laughed through our tears.

We love you, Sorby. We wish you were here.

Chapter Forty Three

Here we go again.

We met in Conference Room One. Sabar presented the latest radar images of the comet core using a pointer. "It is now May 10 Earth time, the comet is now one *hekt* two dozen and four point two *beeyon kepfats*, 829.4 million miles or 1.335 billion kilometers from the Sun. It has 750 million miles to travel before it passes Earth. This main mass is not likely to hit Earth. It has been deflected to an orbit where it will clear the Northern Hemisphere by two *kecht* and one *hekt kepfats*, which is about 5800 miles. It'll pass on the lag side of the North Pole. It's not likely to hit the Earth the next time around because the Planet's gravity will deflect its orbit by about one degree. It doesn't sound like much, but that's enough to get it off the ecliptic, the planetary plane."

"Actually above, uh, what latitude?" asked General Fairchild.

"60 degrees north. Or so." answered Sabar. "The flyby on the lag side will add some velocity to the comet, kicking it into an even longer orbit, maybe 20,000 years or more. It'll be at a slight tilt to the ecliptic, but enough to insure that it should miss the Earth by long distances on its subsequent orbits."

"So if all we had to worry about was the main mass, we're done! It's Miller Time! We can go home." exulted Major Roy McKenna. "But that's not the case."

"Unfortunately, we have to worry about the breakaway masses. I confirm the tidal force calculation. It'll be greater than the gravity holding it together. Anatoly, you're a Russian, how big do your scientists think the Tunguska meteor was?"

"You're talking about 1908? Our scientists estimate about 25 meters, or 80 feet. Still, it yielded kilotons in the explosion and flattened trees. Good thing it didn't come down over Beijing, it would have killed thousands, perhaps millions."

"Exactly." That was Sabar's point. "Our radar imaging of this comet is showing particles of three dozen *potes*, 36 feet, and bigger, ranging out from the core as far as three *hekt kepfats*. Particles that we pushed clear of the gravity of the main mass we also pushed from the collision course with Earth. We don't have to worry about them. We do have to worry about the orbital and suborbital particles, the ones the break off and fall back in. The heat input of our bombs, as impressive as that may be, is transient. The bulk of the BTU's that will boil this comet to form the coma and the tail will come from the Sun. The energy input will increase to 80 times what it is out here. The solar wind will soon blow the gasses and the small stuff to form the tail."

"The particles that threaten Earth are the ones that will be puffed off the main mass by boiling gasses during the approach and flyby." concluded Morton Fairchild. "And with a tidal breakup, all bets are off."

"A particle big enough to do major damage to Earth, even Dinosaur Killer damage, could float 5800 miles from the orbital centerline. It doesn't have to get that far to be sucked in by the Earth's gravity. There's no way we can predict such an event early enough to target the particle with a nuclear warhead."

"Earth's gravity will add 36,670 feet per second to the orbital velocity of 138,260 feet per second of any part of that comet that enters the atmosphere. Square 174,930 and multiply by half the mass. Figure 50 pounds per cubic foot. Divide by 10 to the 17th, that's megatons."

"That's why we have to move this thing further." declared Captain Harsradich.

"Yes, targeting." Sabar brought a close up of the rotating core to the screen. "The main mass is spinning at about the same rate as before, one revolution every 35 hours. But the poles of rotation are now almost perpendicular to the planetary plane. That's due to a slow precession caused by the bombs. So we punch our nukes right here, into this pole of rotation. We should push this entire mass three or four feet per second of delta vee, which translates into maybe a 30,000 to 50,000 mile miss of Earth. Then we can do this a third time. After that we pick off any breakaway pieces that by chance will be going toward Earth with the extra Aries missiles, and we're done."

"If we don't destroy the ship in the process." Trviea's concern. "So what's with the ancient Egyptian gold plate drawings? The *Zep Tepi* plates?"

Mustafa Khedr cleared his throat. "We at the Egyptian Antiquities Organization have conducted a number of secret excavations. We sometimes keep them secret until we have had a chance to secure the artifacts and evaluate them."

"So you've kept the gold plates from 10,500 B.C. under wraps?"

"Well, for starters, they are gold. 300 dollars per ounce. But the reason for secrecy is that we have not read the writing yet. We see illustrations of Neanderthals, of stars and comets, units of measure, and it all radiocarbon dates to 10,500 B.E.C. That is a long time before the Pharaohs and the Egyptian civilization. The writing is nothing like Ancient Egyptian or anything else we have compared it with. Not Indus Valley script, not Linear A, not anything."

"The mathematics appears to be using the number 120," added Chuck, "which is twelve times ten. Similar to the 'Great Hundred' of some medieval European cultures. A mixture of Base Ten and Base Twelve, we're still trying to figure it out. There appears to be astronomical calculations in terms of their Foot and their Cubit."

"What about the comet illustrated on that one plate?" asked Trviea.

"It's Wormwood all right." Sabar declared. "That's exactly as it looked when it passed Earth on October 13, 10,495 B.C. Same background stars. It passed through Earth's orbit 9 million miles ahead of Earth. A very slight deflection, about seven arc *prelates* or four arc seconds, due to Earth's gravity put it on this collision course we see now. Question is, did they know this back then, were they able to calculate orbits?"

"It's possible." declared Chuck. "Johannes Kepler derived his laws of orbital mechanics from very accurate measurements of planet locations taken by Tycho Brahe and himself before the invention of the telescope. Sir Isaac Newton derived his mechanics from Kepler's laws. An experiment by Henry Cavendish gave us an estimate of the Gravitational Constant. One does not need a telescope or technology to perform the mathematics."

"But computers allow you to perform the math quicker." said General Fairchild.

"Still, a society that will build huge astronomical monuments that can be used to take accurate measurements will have full time astronomers and mathematicians. It might even occur to them to perform a Cavendish experiment, with lead spheres and a torsion bar. It is thus possible for a pre-Egyptian civilization to develop Newtonian mathematics and calculate the orbit of a comet."

"What would be the consequence of calculating Wormwood's orbit? Of knowing the masses of the Earth, Moon, Sun, and the planets? The relationship between mass and gravity? Of knowing that the comet will smash into Earth 12,498 years in the future?"

"Almost every religion predicting the End of the World. A Doomsday. A Judgment Day. The End of the Fifth Sun. The Mayan Long Count Calendar first developed by the Olmecs that comes to an end on December 23, 2013. Not that far off from the April 12 this comet was on a course to crash into Earth before our intervention."

"This comet really is Wormwood."

"Sabar, your religion does not have a Doomsday or a Judgment Day?"

"Not in the sense that Earth religions do. We believe that there will always be a future, time will not end. What that future will be, is up to us. We will not be judged for our sins, we will be PUNISHED for our sins. That is why we apologize for them. The end of our future does not necessarily end anyone else's; it can be the consequence of our failure to act. We have never believed in a day when our whole world will come to an end regardless of what we do."

"Nothing like this comet, and the apparent calculations shown on the *Zep Tepi* Plates, have ever happened on Creation. The way your two Suns orbit undoubtedly swept up the comets that formed with your Solar System."

"We don't get as many comets as you do, that is true." confirmed Sabar. "But we still get the fall in from the Galaxy."

"Loose comets between the stars. But still no Judgment Day in your beliefs. But on Earth, we have widespread beliefs in a catastrophic End of the World. What do the new plates from the Map Room show?"

"The Map Room plates are newly discovered. Brought out in the last few days. Most of them show coastlines as they appeared when the ocean level was 60 to 70 feet below today. But one plate shows the Solar System. Sun, Mercury, Venus, Earth, Mars, and Jupiter, with orbits drawn to SCALE. The longitude of the perihelion of each ellipse, ACCURATE! For 10,500 B.C., Mercury! They saw what Copernicus saw. And the comet is shown passing 9 million miles in front of Earth."

"I see. Well, that doesn't change our plans for this next Bomb Run." Trviea concluded. "Let's get started."

I've been assigned to the Launch Crew again. With me at the Aries launcher are Nesla Teslakian and Marla Syferkrip, as before. We climbed into our pressure suits, this time checking and double checking all of the parts for flaws. It takes more courage to do this, knowing what can happen and how fast it can happen. "You have the fission reactor shut down cold, Nesla?"

"It should be. We have a way of scavenging fission products from the fuel rods when we run the reactor."

I laughed. "How you manage that? If you could share that technology with us, we could build safer fission power plants and simplify the waste problem."

"Each fuel assembly is a little more than two *tig-its* in diameter, two inches. Just inside the outer casing, we have a magnetic coil. It creates a miniature magnetic bottle to hold the uranium metal. When we pull the control rods, fission begins and the uranium heats up to a liquid metal. In your Fahrenheit scale that would be,"

"2070 degrees. It could exist as a molten metal anywhere from it's melting point to, I don't remember, we didn't build nuclear power plants at Boeing, but it's at least 3000 degrees Fahrenheit." Uranium boils at about 6900 Fahrenheit.

"The operating temperature of the uranium fuel is about 2500 on your Fahrenheit scale. At such temperatures, most fission products are gasses that boil out of the fuel. We vent these gasses out of the fuel assembly. Fission product is pretty hot when it's fresh out of the reactor, so we store it in a kind of heat exchanger that superheats the steam before it enters the turbine."

"All the while, the magnetic bottle contains the liquid uranium during fission. What if it breaks down during reactor operation?"

"We'd have quite a mess on our hands! But that doesn't happen. With most of the fission product scavenged out, we insert the control rods to effect cold shutdown. The uranium metal freezes up and we don't have a lot of fission product heat to deal with."

"What did you do with the fission product waste after shutdown?"

"Normally we keep it on board ship for a while before jettisoning it, but we decided to jettison it before this Bomb Run, one less thing to worry about."

"You JETTISONED the nuclear waste?"

"Shot it clean out of this Solar System, more than enough velocity to escape your Sun's gravity. It'll be an *enbeeyon* of years before it'll ever find its way into a solar system. By then there should be no radioactivity, all stable isotopes. Don't worry about it. The plumes from the two nuclear explosions on Comet Wormwood are loaded with fission products. They're out in space. You used to shoot off HUNDREDS of bombs on your PLANET, which insures that every *keecoilon* of fission product remains in your ecosystem. As you are not dead yet from ALL of this pollution on Earth, I'd say it's something you can survive better than a Dinosaur Killer."

"Just don't tell our hysterical anti-nukers."

She laughed. "All right, we won't."

Then Wlmsda Hotlund, helped by Don Colburn and Fred Graf, came hobbling down the hall. "You want to put on a pressure suit and help us out, Wilma?"

"Not today. I can still barely breathe. I don't hurt so bad, good drugs, maaaan." She had a marking pen. "Before we depressurize the Four Bay, I would like to add my signature to the rockets and warheads."

"Sure, Wlmsda." answered Helga Trvlakian, who had the duty of operating the Bay's pressure and door systems for this Bomb Run. "But please don't take too long. We have to get started in a few *linits*, get you back to Medical and let these handsome Medical men be on standby with our physicians."

"I understand, I won't take long, I know what I want to write."

Henry Turnipseed drove his minivan on to Len Taylor's farm and parked it next to Len's truck. My car was parked in the equipment barn next to Len's tractor. He climbed out of the minivan along with his sister and her family, and was greeted by his old friend.

"Hey! Melissa, Daniel, and Kimberly! How ya' doing kids!" Len hugged the children. "Thanks for coming, people."

"It was your turn to host the party, Len." reminded Sharon Marshall. As she, her husband, and her brother brought in the pop, beer, salads, and pizzas, she asked, "What's going on TV?"

"They're setting up to bomb the comet again."

"I wish they didn't have to"

"I know. But that main mass is so big breakoff pieces could be big enough for Dinosaur Killer effects. A piece as small as fifty feet in diameter that falls into our atmosphere can explode like an atomic bomb. No problem out over the ocean or a remote area, but we would not want that over Seattle and Tacoma."

"Understood." They brought the stuff into the kitchen and living room, the television set was on, a weather report.

"Len, how are Angela and the kids?"

"Talked with Angie just an hour ago. They can't come, too much to do at home. They were really frightened when the *Return* winked off after the detonation of the big Russian bomb."

"As we all were." Henry accepted his glass of beer and looked upon an edition of a Seattle newspaper. A full color portrait of a smiling Sorby Mishlakian, taken while she was in Washington, D.C., covered the top half of the front page. "That didn't help."

"Do you love Lucinda?" asked Sharon of her brother.

"I cannot really say. She is a very nice woman, one of the best there is. She was really broken up by what the judge in Port Townsend said to her before dismissing the case. When they kidnapped Neil, they kidnapped a father, hurting his children. We talked about this. What affected her all the more was that they've been treated so nice by everyone. Including Angela. All I could say to her was that we have done very well by this. One kidnapping and the kidnapped man was forgiving because he saw the relationship between our two Races to be far more important than himself. That's the Neil Peace we know and love. I told her that we Indians and whites did far worse things to each other upon first contact. In all too many sad cases. Can't change what has happened, what's important is what we do now and in the future." They were silent for a moment. "I wonder if they're overcompensating. For the act of kidnapping Neil, motivated by their needs and their fears, they're now desperate to prove themselves to us as heroes and our friends. That they're taking risks that are unnecessary?"

"I don't think so." offered Ken Marshall. "That comet absolutely positively had to be moved. A 58 mile ball of ice hits us and we're as dead as the dinosaurs. So they had to hang close and guide the Centaur rocket in, and let the Russians detonate with a ten second countdown. Anatoly Donovon and General Fairchild are very stable, very professional. They control the bombs, even if the Neanderthal women control the ship. They wouldn't allow any unnecessary risks. We know the women are safety conscious, they drilled the Earthlings hard in safety and emergency procedures. So I don't think the women were overcompensating. Lucinda might overcompensate, but Trviea's level headed."

"Trviea didn't get strapped down."

"But she made sure everyone else was. It's just that space travel is inherently dangerous. Nuclear bombs are inherently dangerous, and getting close to comets is inherently dangerous. What happened to Sorby was just one of those things."

"It was. To Sorby Mishlakian."

"To Sorby." They clinked their glasses and drank a toast to her.

"Hey, they've switched their coverage to the ship."

"This is Mary Ellen Martin of the Science and Humanities Channel on board the *Neanderthal Return*. As you can see, we're in Bay Number Four and pressure suits are the fashion of choice." She turned the camera on herself. "I'm wearing a pressure suit. We believe these pressure suits are safe, what happened to Sorby Mishlakian was the result of an explosion. Flying debris hit the back of her helmet and caused a crack. No one knew about the crack until it suddenly gave way and exposed Sorby to hard vacuum, killing her. That is the fundamental risk of space flight. Within one inch of my skin is a lethal environment of zero pressure that can destroy the airsacs in my lungs."

She paused to allow that to sink in. "It is the consensus that the main mass of the comet has not been moved far enough to prevent a major impact on Earth. The main mass will miss our Planet, but breakaway pieces can fall into our atmosphere and explode with megatons of force. So we are going to hit it again. As you can see, an Aries missile is being loaded into the launcher that Neil Peace helped design."

Wlmsda Hotlund is hurt, so I took over her duty of operating the cable reel, pulling back the pusher. "Another foot, Neil." Nesla Teslakian helped me while ready with the Missile Loader.

The retaining jaws closed and locked the pusher into place. "Four, one, eight, three *dollons*. Amazing there isn't more variation than that. Half a pound either way doesn't make any difference. Releasing cable reel, letting out a few feet of line. Nesla, you're on."

"Nesla Teslakian is now lowering the Aries missile into the launcher." Mary Ellen informed her audience. "Everyone on board this ship wrote their signatures on these missiles and warheads. You can see poems, and sentiments, and declarations of love and fond farewell to

Sorby Mishlakian, written in three languages and alphabets."

After we loaded the missile and locked the assembly over it, we waited for the fueling of the Centaur to be completed. It hung out in space on the I-beams as before, receiving the liquid hydrogen and liquid oxygen. Finally, Contrviea announced that the tanks were fully loaded, just as she did several days before. It was *deja vu* all over again.

Pidonita declared, "We're approaching Missile Launch Point, Captain Trviea."

"We're ready in the Viewing Lounge." Trviea responded. "Proceed with Launch Maneuver, please."

"Proceeding. We are going into Free Fall and rotating the ship. *Bly jore.*" We now know that what happens is the pilot stops pulsing the fusion core. It'll stay hot for quite a while. If necessary an unaligned fusion pulse once every few seconds can keep the core hot.

We floated as the comet spun into view, coasting without acceleration at several hundred feet per second toward the core of the comet. "Approaching Aries missile launch point. Neil, Nesla, launch on my command please."

"Yes, please count down in English." I requested.

She chuckled. "All right, I will." Nesla and Marla joined me behind the protective plate of clear plastic. I let out some more cable and let it slack. Nesla stood ready to trigger the retaining jaws. We heard Pido's countdown. "Six, five, four, three, two, one, zero."

Nesla opened the retaining jaws and I fed out cable to follow the springs as they pushed the missile. The missile left the bay at ten feet per second. "Aries missile away. Rocket is clear of the ship." I drew the pusher back and locked it. We removed the pins and Marla opened the guide roller assembly.

"Now we turn and get out of Free Fall." announced Pidonita. "We will be heavy for about two dozen and six *prelates. Jore put.*"

At first we felt two feet per second squared acceleration, dropping the Aries missile out of our view. Then we turned and Pidonita moved us at 42 feet per second squared. More than Earth, but not so much as to make us uncomfortable. We saw the blue of the propulsion reflect off the diffuse coma gasses. "*Bly jore.*" announced Pidonita. She spun us back around to look into the comet again. We saw the Aries missile ignite.

In the Viewing Lounge, General Fairchild's crew directed the missile. "Missile on course. Radar map showing considerably less debris, the chunks are swept around to the other side by our recent activities. Range to target, core south pole, one five zero miles."

The missile flew on without incident for 120 miles. "Radar detecting yard sized mass. Guidance making avoidance course. Avoidance successful. Returning to original course. Range to target two five miles. Radar detecting fathom sized mass, avoidance successful, returning to original course. Range to target two zero miles. Not like before, just fog this time. Avoided six inch mass, range to target one zero miles."

"Closing in on target. Debris finally showing up. Missile hit something! Rocket still functioning. Range to target less than mile!"

"Dark goggles, everyone!" ordered Captain Harsradich.

The B61-12 warhead slammed into the main mass. "We have detonation, point of detonation 96 feet from the rotational pole and about 100 feet inside the surface." We saw the flash through our goggles and glare shields. Another white hot jet blowing out of the core. "Bullseye!" This time we did not have any cheering or hand clapping.

Helga, operating the controls to Bay Number Four, called to me. "Neil, Trviea wants you to join her, just like last time. Lchnsda is standing by to undress you."

"Lucinda? Okay. Just don't tell Henry."

Beer blew out of Henry's mouth in a shower as he burst out laughing. "I thought Helga knew English better than that!"

"She does. She did that on purpose." argued Len.

"I'm glad to see they still have their sense of humor."

"Uh, Neil," interrupted Mary Ellen, "you remember the Apollo telecasts when you could hear the astronauts talk to Mission Control?"

I turned toward her and looked into her video camera. "Uh, yeah?"

"It's like that now. Everything you say is being transmitted back to Earth. Live."

"Are we being broadcast on TV?"

"We were last time."

"Uh, Henry, when Helga said that Lucinda was going to 'undress me', she meant help me out of this pressure suit. I have clothing under this. So don't worry. No big deal. Really."

"Knock it off, Neil!" Henry was dying of embarrassment. Len, Ken, and Sharon slapped him on the back and laughed at his predicament.

I knew Henry was going to get me back for this one. I had to make it up to him. "Actually, Henry Turnipseed is a good friend of mine from high school. Buy his book of poetry, you'll love it. *Musings of an All American Boy.* Now available in paperback."

"We haven't time for commercials, Neil!" Captain Trviea was trying to sound serious and demanding through her giggles. "Thanks for making us laugh. We needed that. We have the Centaur to cast off and ignite. Some distance to put between us and a 120 megaton bomb. Please come to the Viewing Lounge."

"On my way, Trviea."

Lucinda was polite and businesslike as she helped me out of the pressure suit. Then she put the suit aside and suddenly pinned me against the wall. Neanderthal physical strength. "How dare you and Helga EMBARRASS me like that?!"

"Uh, Lucy. We were just kidding. Trying to break up the tension. What are you going to do to Helga?"

"Nothing. She's bigger and stronger than me. It was funny, though." She grinned and quickly kissed my nose. "That darn Henry Turnipseed. Made me hungry for sex. Forgot how much I liked it. Well, no time. Trviea's waiting."

As we headed toward the Viewing Lounge, I put my hand on Lucinda and she quickly grabbed my wrist and forced my hand away. "Your Earth religions have a rule: 'Thou shalt not commit adultery'."

"You MARRIED Henry?"

"No. But I don't want to break up with him. Not yet. It has been a long time, I like having a man treat me the way he does. If it doesn't work out, then I guess I can loosen up and live a little. Ulp! Here we are."

"Glad you could make it." greeted Trviea. "Have a seat, please."

"How we doing?"

"Centaur missile is cast loose, we are slowly moving away from it while we clear the Bay. Excuse me." She activated the public address. "People in Bay Four. Remain in your pressure suits. Strap down in the pressure suits. In the event of hard vacuum, you can put your helmets back on and leave the strap down stations. You too, Mary Ellen. You can pull the straps over your suit; someone will show you where to stow the helmet. We need some people in pressure suits. The emergency oxygen bottle and face mask is not adequate for hard vacuum."

"She's real serious this time." commented Ken.

"Broken nose. Broken arm. Dead daughter. I'd be serious too."

"Medical?" inquired Trviea.

Askelion responded. "Yes, we are on standby. We will strap down on your command. We have Wlmsda all set." Wilma was strapped to a hospital bed in a specially designed cocoon that will isolate her from shock waves and keep her in breathable atmosphere.

"Thank you, Medical."

"Pilothouse, are you prepared?"

Sabar, Metrola, and Pidonita were at their stations. Pido responded, "We have oxygen masks fixed and we're purging our blood of nitrogen. We're ready."

"Thank you, Pilothouse. Are we at the maximum distance from the Centaur for launch communication?"

We were already accelerating at 24 feet per second squared. "We are approaching that distance."

"General Fairchild, Mr. Donovon, you may fire when ready."

Helga got the door to Bay Number Four closed and the Bay repressurized. She helped the Launch Crew and Mary Ellen Martin into the strap down stations. When they were all in, Helga put herself into a strap down station. Mary Ellen could hear a lot of voices softly apologizing to the Great Holy Spirit for their sins. She said the Lord's Prayer and asked Him for His Blessing and His Mercy.

"Maria," Anatoly gently addressed Mrs. Romanov, "arm the bomb, please." he ordered in Russian.

"Arming signal sent. Code received. Confirm. Bomb armed." Maria Romanov spoke in Russian.

"Well, Anatoly, is the green mowed and the hole ready?" asked General Fairchild in Russian.

"Your Aries groundskeeper has done his job. Let's go with the 9-iron."

"All right ladies and gentlemen, everyone be ready. Maria, start the countdown as soon as we get the firing sequence in the rocket started, and we confirm that guidance and both engines are functioning."

"I understand, Sir." Maria was ready to send the detonation code and the countdown, this time for 14 minutes and 20 seconds.

"Everyone except Viewing Lounge and Pilothouse Strap Down!" ordered Trviea Harsradich. She repeated in English and Atlantean. Ian Miller was with us with his video camera. He spoke into a microphone for the transmission to Earth.

Then General Fairchild gave his order. "Major Easton, fire the Centaur, commence the burn sequence."

"Centaur firing," confirmed Major Roslyn Easton, "both engines are nominal. Thrust is 33,000 pounds, initial acceleration 13.4 feet per second squared. Beginning axial spin. Inertial Navigation Unit performing nominally."

"Maria, go!" ordered Anatoly in Russian.

"Detonation signal sent, confirm signal received. 14 minutes 20 seconds, 19, 18, countdown started." Maria spoke in Russian. We understood, thanks to the language classes.

"Range to target 802 miles. Velocity relative to target, 410 feet per second."

"Pidonita," called Trviea, "codes are sent, Centaur on its way. Go to two gees if you can, please." She spoke in Atlantean.

"We'll get one and a half gees, anyway." We got heavy as Pidonita started pulling us away at 48 to 50 feet per second squared. I wondered how well that fusion reactor had been repaired.

Over the next six minutes the fusion reactor worked well and got us some distance. "Coming up on initial engine cut-off." announced Major Easton. "Five, four, three, two, one ECO!

Engine is off. Missile is on course for the target hole. Range to target 600 miles. Velocity relative to target 5,946 feet per second."

"Eight minutes 20 seconds to detonation." announced Maria Romanov in Russian.

We waited as Roslyn and Maria called out range to target and time to detonation.

"Range to target 111 miles. Coming up on engine restart. Ten, nine, eight," Roslyn counted, "three, two, one, we have engine restart. Both engines nominal, guidance is following infrared. Infrared device homing on Aries explosion site. Range to target 90 miles."

"55 seconds to detonation." Maria called out in Russian.

"Coming up on engine cut-off and rocket jettison. Five, four, three, two, one, ECO! Jettison!"

"*Dyesat, dyevyat, vosyem, syem, shyest, pyat,*"

"Warhead in hole!"

"*chetirye, tri, dva, odin,*"

FLASH!!!!!!

"We have detonation! No waiting this time. Way to go Russian Bomb Crew! Pidonita, how many megatons?" Some applause and cheering.

"We're getting that, uh, now! 121.6 megatons. Point of detonation nine twelfths *kepfat* inside main mass. Good jet exiting the hole. We are moving the comet again."

People on Earth couldn't help themselves. Many screamed for joy! We just might survive this pass of the Comet Wormwood!

Captain Harsradich took command. "All right everyone, we've done our job. To the strap down stations. We're much further away this time, but let's go just in case. That includes me. You too, Ian. Enough of the broadcast journalist work." Trviea grinned into the camera, showing off the healing injuries to her face. "Earth, we just might have successfully completed Operation Rainbow. To know for sure, we will have to evaluate the results after the explosion site on the comet cools back down. We may do this a third time for insurance. A hundred thousand mile miss should be far enough from Earth's gravity to keep it from pulling in the loose stuff. Then we could pick off any independent pieces we need to with the Aries missiles. So far, all of the Earth equipment is working like it should. Congratulations are in order for your scientists, engineers and shop workers who built this stuff. Please excuse us for a while. We have to strap down in case something happens."

Ian Miller resumed his telecast. "Thank you Captain Harsradich. As you can see, the Captain is checking to see if she needs to assign people to the strap down stations. Well, this is already planned, this time. The American and Russian crews are settling in. As you can see by the readout in three languages, we are accelerating at 48 feet per second squared, 14.6 meters, which is 1.5 gees. So we're struggling a bit against our weight. Oh, Trviea wants me in that one. I'll keep the camera going and continue to speak to you as I strap down."

"Neil," Trviea called to me from a few feet away. She hugged me with her good arm and kissed me. "I apologize to the Great Holy Spirit for kidnapping you and for all of my other sins. Please help me."

"Sure." I lifted her in. Not easy in this acceleration given her injuries. I pulled the straps over and snapped them into place. I helped put the helmet on to her head.

"Thanks for everything, Neil. Now strap down!"

After I strapped down, we suddenly lost acceleration. It fell below ten feet per second squared and continued dropping.

"Pidonita, what happened?"

"I don't know. Fusion pulses are happening, but a lot weaker. Don't want to lose another eleven *kecht* six *hekt gunds* of plasma." 18 million pounds. "Metrola! Sabar! Check the reactor! I'm keeping an eye on the comet and the debris. Some of that stuff has exploded. Everyone strapped down?"

"Everyone here in the Viewing Lounge is, including me."

"Glad to hear that Trviea."

"So what's happening?"

"We lost an electron feed in Coil Number Seven." answered Metrola.

"Good." Trviea felt relieved. Not a collision with a particle. "You sure?"

"Not yet. But that's what it looks like."

"It is the main electron feed to Coil Assembly Seven." confirmed Sabar Duradich. "That one we repaired. Do you confirm, Pidonita?"

"Yes, that is what my instruments indicate. The other coils compensated." If they did not, they would push the plasma ball into the side with the bad magnetic coil. Melt through everything and disable the ship. Possibly kill everyone on board. Instead, the other coils relaxed to keep the plasma ball centered. "Please see if you can reroute the electron flow. We can accelerate, less than a few *tig-its* per *prelate* squared. Want more than that with the explosion debris coming."

"Rerouting electron flow."

"We are getting more compression with each pulse." More compression results in more fusion, more momentum transfer to thrust the ship. "Coil Seven is working again. Acceleration is now increasing, but we will get no more than ten *potes* per *prelate* squared at maximum pulse frequency. Now acceleration is ten *potes*." 20 feet per second squared, less than one gee.

"Here comes the explosion debris!"

For the next few minutes, Pidonita dodged and weaved. She'd turn the alignment of the proton spin 90 to 180 degrees in less than a second. Loose objects flew and crashed everywhere. I was thrown against the straps in all directions. After what happened last time, this was nerve racking!

Up in the Pilothouse, the girls began to smile. "This isn't so bad this time. The particles are much further apart. The smaller ones are fizzing into nothing."

"Much easier to see, forming their own little comas as mini-comets. Not like bombing a rocky asteroid."

"Oh, that would be fun! Dodging pebbles and boulders. We are clearing the fast moving debris. All right, let's spin around and take a look at this comet with the radar. Everyone, you are released from Strap Down."

With relief and cheering, we climbed out of the strap down stations. I went over to Trviea. She managed to unhook herself from her straps with her good hand. She listened intently to her headset as I helped her out of the pod and stood her up. "We still have hot steam blowing out of the hole." she told me. "We should have moved that main mass into a 50,000 mile miss of Earth. We could send another Centaur with a Russian bomb into that hole right now! Save us an Aries. But we had better find out what went wrong with that electron feed in Coil Assembly Seven."

"How long does it take to find out how far we've pushed the main mass?"

"We'll have to track its movement for a few hours. While we are at that, we can inspect the electron feed. That's hairy. Don't want to dump the plasma ball. No fusion pulses, keep the gamma radiation down to tolerable. We have plenty of boron, cadmium, and water, so we can dump the plasma ball if necessary. Nesla, select a reactor crew and fire up the fission reactor. Wlmsda Gtslakian, select a crew to inspect Magnetic Coil Assembly. Contrviea, stand by in the Machine Shop, we may need parts for the electron feed in the Coil Assembly."

Chapter Forty Four

Wlmsda Gtslakian and her crew entered the Magnetic Coil Assembly. "It's like walking in a blast furnace."

"Not as cold as last time. The plasma ball is right out there, no fusion, but an awful lot of heat."

"That's why we're wearing these high temperature suits and padded gloves. Get that fan running. Air cooled by liquid nitrogen. Freeze your buns on one side, burn you to a crisp on the other. Let's start eyeball inspection. Pidonita said it was the main electron feed."

"Careful. Damn electrons can generate X-rays. Iron nuclei don't want to stay together what with the electrostatic force. Yet iron plasma circulating in these *treefat* diameter tubes is the secret to our success."

"The negative charged electrons circulating in the opposite direction is how we create iron plasma streams denser than iron itself. Everything looks fine here. What do you see?"

"I am looking at the relay connections. Everything is fine here."

"Power supply from the electrical system. Every cable connected, oh, I see it."

"What is it?"

"This nut backed off under vibration. Where did it go? Must have got tossed around during Pido's swerving. Cable came undone. Get me a four *tig-it* nut and lockwasher."

"Found the nut. A little banged up from Pido tossing us around. But the inside thread is good."

"Yeah, we can use this, ah thanks. The lockwasher. Get the cable on the post, good. Lockwasher on. Pretty warm, even through these padded gloves. The nut. Hmmm. The nut got cold, won't fit over the hot post." The silver post with gold plated threads for good contact is four *tig-its* in diameter at room temperature. But when it's hot, it's a little bigger than that.

"We'll blast it with some liquid nitrogen." Sssssss.

"Should be small enough now, hey, it fits! Spin it down. Six *tig-it* socket for the hex, compound torque wrench. Between five and six *hekt pote-dollons*, that should do it." The ordinary electrical wiring on the *Neanderthal Return* is copper and aluminum. The very high current connections use silver plated with gold. They mine an asteroid loaded with these minerals.

"That's what we found, Captain." reported Wlmsda through her headset.

Trviea sighed. Every mechanic knows about nuts loosening up and falling off. Happens in a rushed repair. "Glad to hear that's all it is. Torque it down proper, and check every other fastener in the coil assembly."

"Already on it. We should be done in an hour."

We were back in Conference Room One. Wlmsda Gtslakian gave her report on the malfunction in the Coil Assembly. "The nut backed off and this connection separated. That's when we lost the electron flow in the main feed. The other eleven coil assemblies automatically compensated to keep the plasma ball centered. The main feed keeps the iron plasma circuit fully compressed. This iron plasma circuit provides the magnetic field that align the protons at full compression in the fusion pulses. We lost compression and alignment, causing the loss of acceleration."

"How did we restore some of the acceleration?"

"We routed to the backup feeds, but the backup system was not designed to give us alignment at full compression. We now have everything repaired and this time properly tightened, we checked every fastener. The system tested fine, we are now running the fusion reactor with full compression and alignment."

"Thank you, Wlmsda." said Captain Harsradich. "Ship is back to normal. Sabar, please tell us about the comet."

Sabar put the radar images of the main mass on the screen. "It is still May 10, Earth time. The comet is still falling toward the Sun at eleven *kecht* three *hekt and* seven *dozen kepfats* per hour, or 31,500 miles per hour. It has only been a few hours, so we're still about one *hekt* two dozen and four *beeyon kepfats* or 829 million miles from the Sun. So much for where this comet is, the important question is where it is going. We've got a good efficient burn in the right location inside this core, right here." She pointed at the screen. "We verify a minimum delta vee of three *potes* per *prelate*, a little more than four feet per second. The new orbit of the main mass will pass Earth at a distance of at least twelve and seven *kecht kepfats* or 54,000 miles. That's a good distance. Tidal force at flyby much smaller, negligible. Most of the breakoff particles held by the gravity of the main mass will not be pulled away by Earth. But it is possible that a few particles larger than fifty feet could be pulled off by Earth's gravity and detonate with megatons after entering the atmosphere. Most of the particles that have been thrown clear of the main mass gravity will not hit Earth. There is a quarter *kepfat* particle that might pass close to Earth. We're keeping an eye on it."

"Thank you, Sabar. As she said, the main mass will miss by 54,000 miles. Breakoff pieces could still be a threat to Earth. The probability is much smaller than before, but the consequences of a piece breaking off within a day of closest approach and falling into the Earth's atmosphere are serious enough to consider further action. Still, every time we bomb the comet, we put the ship at risk. We have three of the large Russian warheads left, and four Centaur rockets. We have twenty Aries missiles with 100 kiloton warheads. We could use an Aries on the quarter *kepfat* chunk, should it prove necessary. Thoughts? Comments?"

"How far above the ecliptic plane will the main mass fly?"

"About forty to fifty thousand miles as it passes Earth."

"How far will breakoff pieces tend to float from the surface as this comet passes Earth?"

"No telling. The ices: carbon dioxide, methane, water, will be boiling from the solar heat. Solid chunks will be lifted off the main mass by this boiling action. It is a matter of how fast a chunk is lifted. The coma will be thousands of miles across, the tail millions of miles long. The Earth will actually pass through the coma. Gasses and ions, no problem. Solid particles will streak through the sky and burn up as long as they are small. It's possible that pieces larger than fifty feet will rise off the main mass far enough to be captured by the Earth's gravity and enter the Earth's atmosphere. Not likely, but possible. If so, there's no determining it soon enough that would allow anyone to hit it with a missile before entry into the atmosphere."

"If we hit the main mass again, and push it into an 80,000 to 100,000 mile miss, would it still be possible for a breakaway to hit Earth?"

"Possible, but very unlikely. Such a particle would have to leave the main mass over a million miles before closest approach to Earth. That would allow for tracking by Earth based systems and for targeting with a nuclear warhead."

"So it would be worth it to hit the main mass again. How about the quarter *kepfat* chunk you've mentioned?"

"The quarter *kepfat* chunk is in its own orbit, it'll form a small comet on its own. But its orbit is affected by the gravity of the main mass. We'll have to wait until we're done with the main mass before we can determine whether it presents a threat to Earth."

"We should be able to take care of it with an Aries missile."

"That depends on whether it's solid or fluffy. It's amazing how many BTU's it takes to vaporize one of these things, and how few BTU's are actually in a megaton. An Aries is only a tenth of a megaton. But we should be able to nudge it away from Earth with an Aries, if necessary."

"So, we have a plan." concluded Captain Harsradich. "One more go at the main mass. Then we determine if we need to hit the breakaway. This agreeable to everyone?" Heads nodded yes. Trviea needed the assent from those who controlled the bombs. "General Fairchild?"

"Yes, Captain Harsradich, I agree we should hit the main mass again."

"Mr. Donovon?"

"*Da*, Captain Harsradich, we Russians are ready."

"Then it's settled. We do it again, the same way we did it the second time."

The third attack on the main mass went perfectly. This time, there were no malfunctions. We launched the Aries, the warhead detonated with 102.3 kilotons about 80 feet from the rotational pole. The Centaur dropped its warhead into the hole and the Russian bomb yielded 122.6 megatons. We saw the flashes of the nuclear explosions, the people back on Earth thrilled to watch the films of the nuclear explosions we transmitted back. Pidonita deftly avoided the debris, we weren't hit by anything. As we climbed out of the strap down stations, Anatoly produced a small flask of vodka and passed it around.

"To our success!" he exulted. We each took a sip.

Trviea listened intently as Sabar described the results. "We have a good jet of steam from the heat of the nuclear explosions. The main mass fracture zones gave a little, but gravity pulled it back together. We should have good delta vee. Its orbit should miss the Earth by about, ohh, three dozen *kecht kepfats*."

"Yes!" screamed Trviea. "How about the quarter *kepfat* particle?"

"About a six dozen - six dozen chance of hitting Earth." That is a Base Twelve way of saying fifty-fifty. "But we could nudge it with an Aries missile and that'll take care of it. We could do this right away."

"All right. Neil, you come with me to Conference Room One. American Missile Crew, General Fairchild, bring your people to the conference room, please. Sabar says we should hit the quarter *kepfat* piece right away."

"Sure. Aries missile?"

"Yes. Sure, Anatoly, you can come." Anatoly grinned and laughed, everyone was feeling great. We all wanted to shout, but we were not quite done yet. "You know Anatoly, you really shouldn't be so sad and melancholy all the time. Lighten up. Laugh a little. Smile!"

"You're right!" He was trying to speak through his laughs. "I really should quit looking at the empty half of the glass. I'll try to smile more."

"Aries Launch Crew," called Trviea.

"Right here." Trviea heard Nesla and Marla Syferkrip respond through their headsets.

"Please stay in your pressure suits and come to the conference room. We're going to launch another Aries rocket."

In the conference room Sabar briefed us on the current situation. The new radar image of the main mass was on the screen. "It'll take a few more hours to be sure, but we have pushed it to at least a 100,000 mile miss of the Planet Earth."

We all clapped our hands, cheered. "Anatoly, Maria Romanov, Mikhail Dostoevsky, Svetlana, good job on the bombs. Congratulations, and thank you."

"We couldn't have done it without all of you. But we still have a problem with a 2,000 foot block of cometary ice."

Sabar brought the 2,000 foot block of ice on the screen. "Here's how it looks in visible light. It's already forming a coma, becoming a small comet in its own right. Now here is the radar image. It's oblong, not a sphere. Its longest dimension is almost a quarter *kepfat*. Would not want it hitting Earth. We hit it right here, the warhead can break it in half, and neither half will pass anywhere near Earth."

"Sounds like a plan, let's do it!"

We were ready to let go of the springs and send this Aries rocket out the door. We could see the quarter *kepfat* piece in the distance. Its coma was bright against the background of the more diffuse coma of the main comet. The missile was installed, the guide roller assembly locked shut. Nesla and Marla waited with me. This time the Centaurs were safely stowed, we were the only people in pressure suits in Bay Number Four. "Are you ready, Aries Launch Crew?" asked Pidonita.

"We're ready." we replied.

"Good. American Missile Flight Control Crew?"

"We're ready in the Viewing Lounge, Pido." confirmed General Fairchild.

"The Viewing Lounge is crowded." reported Captain Harsradich. "Except for our four American Air Force Officers, everyone here is a spectator. Everyone, you may proceed."

"Understood." confirmed Pidonita. "Thank you, Trviea. Coming up on Missile Launch Point. Neil, Nesla, launch on my command, please. I'll count down in English. Six, five, four, three, two, one, zero."

Nesla opened the retaining jaws and I fed out cable to follow the springs as they pushed the missile. The missile left the bay at ten feet per second. "Aries missile away. It is clear of the ship. I love this spring launcher! Nothing fancy and high tech, just works!"

For safety reasons, the door to space closed and Helga Trvlakian pressurized the Bay with air. "Pressure in the Bay, two zero *dollons*." she announced.

"Why don't you take your helmets off and come to the Viewing Lounge and watch the show?" invited Trviea.

"On our way."

We arrived at the Viewing Lounge and watched the Air Force direct the missile. "Range to target five miles. Missile is performing perfectly. Range to target one mile."

"Dark goggles."

We put on the goggles and saw the flash. "We have detonation. Point of detonation right in the middle, in the fat part of the mass. Look at this! It has fractured into three pieces! The pieces are separating at well over 40 feet per second! This thing is lighter than we thought! Fluffy!"

"Computing trajectories. None of the particles are going to hit Earth! The small one might hit the Moon."

"Moon's expendable! YEE-HAW!!!"

"We did it! Operation Rainbow has been completed!" Hugs and kisses and singing and dancing. We screamed and cheered.

People who were watching us on television ran out of their houses screaming and cheering and singing songs. Car horns honked as radio stations announced the news. It flashed across the scoreboards of soccer and baseball games all over the world. It would be many minutes before the games could resume.

On our ship, women broke out into spontaneous song, we heard the Atlantean words to a hundred songs in joyous female voices. There was laughter and there was crying, everyone was screaming.

Except Trviea Harsradich.

She smiled and she sang, and she clapped her hands. And tears poured down her face. I went over to her, put my arm around her and kissed her cheek. She put her good arm around me. "She's out there." I told her. "Right now. Surrounded by the great glittering carpet of stars. With no pressure suit to crimp her style, she sings and dances among the stars, nothing can make her happier than this success."

"I know."

Metrola Mornuxler spoke to us through the public address. "May I have your attention, please? May I have your attention, please?" We finally settled down enough to listen to her. "I would like to have a moment of silence and prayer for Sorby Mishlakian."

We were silent for a moment. Then we heard Metrola sing her prayer in Atlantean.

"We beseech thee Great Holy Spirit, Father of us all, on behalf of our good friend, Sorby Mishlakian. We forgive her of all of her sins, we apologize for all of our sins. We now consider her Innocent of all sin, all of her debts to us forgiven, all of our debts to her can never be paid. We thank thee Great Holy Spirit, for the time we have had with her, for this we are forever grateful. Our love for Sorby is as boundless as our gratitude to Thee. Our love for Sorby will never die. We only ask that you take care of her for us, until such time comes when we join her and you."

We heard them all join Metrola in her prayer. After it was over I asked Trviea quietly, "I thought Metrola was an Atheist?"

"It doesn't quite mean the same thing to us. Perhaps 'Atheist' is not the best translation for it. Metrola never denied the existence of God. But she was in grief for all of our men, including her father, brothers, and the man she wanted to marry. She was angry with the Spirit, for allowing the Virus to kill our men. Perhaps she is finally forgiving Him, making Peace, and thanking Him for all that we have. For me, I grieve for the men, but I have always thanked Him for giving me Sorby. Now, we are happy, with the Gift of this Opportunity. To work together, Neanderthals and Cro-Magnons, to stop a holocaust, to continue that marvelous experiment we call the Human Race. Pardon me for a *prelate*, please."

She broke away from me and took a central position in the room. She pushed a button on her headset. "Ladies and gentlemen. We have successfully completed Operation Rainbow. We have on board Kazakhstan beef and horsemeat sausages, German pork, Texas chili, Washington State salmon, shrimp from I forget where, it's Earth shrimp," laughter, "lobsters from New England and the Atlantic Provinces, sausages from Argentina, Germany, and Poland. The best wines of France, the best vodka from Russia, the best whiskey from Kentucky, the best tequila from Mexico. The best beer from Germany, Canada, and the United States."

The food started cooking, there was everything you could think of. I didn't remember what falafel was, but it tasted good and it came from Israel. Cuc Nguyen went into the Kitchen and they let her roast some ducks Vietnamese style. Wilma Hotlund felt better and joined us. We brought food up to the Pilothouse, Metrola was alone at the helm. She took us on a wide swing to get us far away from the comet and its debris, then planned to set a course for Earth. We brought her the 'virgin' versions of the drinks, she couldn't take alcohol when piloting the ship.

A few hours later, some of us relaxed while a group of girls performed a play by the great playwright, Arkelan Smenuxler. Mustafa Khedr studiously avoided alcohol and pork, he was the only sober person in the room. Anatoly Donovon was in heaven. His arms were wrapped around two pretty Neanderthal women, they love his perpetual good cheer. All he needed was a little more Youth Serum. Chuck Carter danced before leaving. He and a woman finally came back. Roy McKenna did Elvis. His *Hound Dog* was pretty good, his *Love Me Tender* wowed them. Where'd he go? Orders, shmorders. He is a single man, young and healthy. I suspect the General, puffing away on his victory cigars with a big shit eating grin, gave his Majors the go ahead.

The two actresses on the stage were dressed as men. Just like theater in Shakespeare's time when actors dressed as women to play the female roles. The two male characters argued and insulted each other. They pulled out swords and fought. One of them lost his sword, the other ran him through. The loser's wife came out on to the stage and wailed her anger and grief. The other swordsman left after telling her he was sorry but it was a matter of honor. Then the husband and wife declared their undying love as his life ebbed away. Mary Ellen wasn't bothered when the two actresses kissed. That's the arts for you.

We were interrupted by Metrola's voice on the public address. "Chuck Carter, Mustafa Khedr, and Sabar Duradich, please come to the Pilothouse. We're receiving a scrambled message from the Egyptian Antiquities Organization."

"Excuse me, Neil." Sabar was on my right arm. Svetlana Lebed was on my left arm. She whispered an improper suggestion in my ear. We both needed sleep anyway so we accompanied each other to bed.

Sabar, Chuck, and Mustafa arrived at the Pilothouse. "How are the three of you feeling?"

Chuck yawned. Sabar staggered. Mustafa spoke. "They need sleep. They're drunk. I'm sober, an advantage of following the Prophet."

"Yeah. Well Mustafa, you look like you've eaten too much, and you need some sleep. Excuse me for a moment, please." She spoke into her headset. "Medical, this is Metrola, at the Pilothouse, are you there?"

"Meddi Chumkun, here. What's up, Met?"

"Sabar and Chuck need magic pills."

"A Cro-Magnon. The magic pills work on Cro-Magnons. Is it really necessary?"

"We need a sober astronomer and two sober archeologists to figure out this new transmission from Egyptian Antiquities. Mustafa hasn't been drinking because of his religion, but he needs sleep. Sabar and Chuck need both sleep and magic pills. Let's get the magic pills into them and then all three into bed for the next four hours."

"Understood, send them down here, we'll get them taken care of."

"Thank you, Meddi."

Several hours passed. Trviea had also gotten some sleep. She came up to the Pilothouse and asked Metrola how she was feeling. Met admitted she was getting tired. Trviea took a magic pill and offered to take over the helm. Her fingers sticking out of the cast were functional. They waited until Trviea's mind was clear. With Trviea at the controls, the three people called over for the Egyptian message came stumbling in.

"WhoooWEEE!" shouted Chuck Carter. "Them magic pills are something else!"

Sabar and Mustafa yawned. Sabar commented, "Metabolizes the alcohol in a hurry. But then you feel just blasted. Now I remember why you shouldn't drink to excess, oooooh."

Mustafa and Metrola chuckled. "I think we've celebrated a little too soon." announced Metrola.

"What do you mean?" asked Mustafa, quickly waking up.

"The Egyptians sent their message with the scrambler Marla Syferkrip designed. It has to do with the mathematics on the gold *Zep Tepi* plates. We've been busy lately, so the experts in Egypt have been working on these plates for us. They brought in mathematics folks to try to reconstruct the ancient arithmetic. They sounded alarmed about what they found out about the ancient folks who apparently saw Wormwood the last time it passed Earth in 10,495 B.C. Anyway, in English they told us not to come flying toward Earth just yet. The rest of it is in Arabic. Chuck, Mustafa, you're the two people on this ship who can speak Arabic. This message is meant for you."

"I see. Cuc can speak Arabic, but she's not an archeologist. Let's roll the tape."

Metrola turned on the machinery and the transmission came up on the screen. "I know him!" recognized Mustafa.

"This is Charles Sheehy, Egyptian Antiquities Organization, calling the *Neanderthal Return*." he announced in English. "We have been studying the gold plates found in the newly discovered chambers in the limestone cliff north of the Sphinx. We believe we have made significant progress in understanding the language and mathematics displayed on these plates. It is what they are telling us with respect to their recorded sighting of Comet Wormwood in Year 10,495 Before the Common Era that concerns us. We strongly suggest that you do not head for Earth just yet, there may be more work for you to do. We praise Allah for your successful deflection of Comet Wormwood and pray for your safe return. The information we have is so sensitive, we must communicate it in Arabic for Mustafa Khedr and Chuck Carter."

The scene in the tape went to the gold plates safely stored at Kilometer 206. The building had been turned into a large research lab with many technicians and scientists employed. Two gentlemen appeared on the screen next to the gold plates. The men spoke in Arabic. "I am Professor Abdul Hussein Ibrahim of the Math Department at Cairo University. With me is Professor Heinrich Moltke of the University of Heidelberg in Germany. We have worked very hard in analyzing the ancient arithmetic. Arithmetic is a strong claim, but we believe that is exactly what the *Zep Tepi* culture was using."

"First, allow me to give you a little background on the history of numbers and arithmetic." began Professor Moltke in Arabic. "The Base Ten Place Value system of Arabic numerals we use today came relatively late in our history. It originated with the Hindus of India in the centuries AFTER the life of Jesus Christ, and just before the life of Mohammed. The Persian and Arab people adapted these decimal numbers into their usage. The Arab conquests in the century after Mohammed brought these numbers across North Africa and into Spain, and into the Balkan Peninsula as far as Croatia and Romania. The Europeans resisted the teachings of the Prophet, preferring the teachings of Christ, but over the centuries of the Middle Ages, they came to adopt Western Arabic numerals and the arithmetic developed by Al Khwarizmi to take advantage of them."

"To comprehend how important arithmetic is in leading to the technological revolution that allowed Europe to take over the world, you must consider what mathematical computation involved before arithmetic. Before arithmetic, almost all math was performed with counting boards or the abacus. Which can be quite cumbersome. The arithmetic we teach children in primary schools today was a revolutionary development in the Late Middle Ages."

"Before Arabic numerals, with place value and the zero, most number systems were tally marks. The tally marks for ten, hundred, and so on were different in shape, but you wrote in the marks until they added up to your number."

"So even the simple act of writing down a number was complicated. This might explain why the Greeks had small steam engines as toys, but did not have a widespread use of steam technology. Without arithmetic, how could you perform a James Joule experiment to determine the mechanical equivalent of heat? Develop a set of steam tables? Then use them?"

"Still, the Romans ran an empire, which required the calculation of large numbers of numbers. The Egyptians built their Pyramids to extraordinary precision. Arithmetic would have made these feats easier. The question for us today, is, are we seeing arithmetic in these ancient plates? It doesn't have to be Base Ten to be arithmetic, the Creation Neanderthals invented a place value number system with zero in Base Twelve. They perform arithmetic with this number system."

"We believe that the *Zep Tepi* culture used a mixture of Base Ten and Base Twelve, Base One Twenty. That's right, ten times twelve, 120. We are calling this the Great Hundred System."

The math professors presented a chart with symbols taken from the gold plates. "The *Zep Tepis* had a symbol for each number. These are the symbols for the numbers zero through nine. They represented ten with a single symbol. Eleven was represented by ten and one symbols, twelve by ten and two symbols, and so on. Here are the single symbols for twenty, thirty, forty, all the way up to one hundred, it looks like a Base Ten number system. But one hundred is represented by this single symbol, and this symbol stands for one hundred and ten. We looked for a single symbol that represented one hundred and twenty, but could not find one. One twenty, it turns out, is represented by a one symbol followed by a zero symbol."

"Base 120. We thought we were looking at the number ten, but analysis of the arithmetic proved that it could only be 120. They divided their circle into 360 degrees, just as we do today. They wrote 360 as a three followed by a zero. A one followed by a sixty symbol represented 180, a half circle. The ninety symbol is the right angle."

"We have determined that in this system, a ten symbol followed by a zero is 1200. A ten followed by a one followed by a zero is 1320. A one followed by two zeros is 14400. The place value is in powers of 120. Within each place value location is used this set of symbols that represent the numbers from zero through 119."

"How did they divide each degree of angular measure? A degree of Earth's surface is sixty nautical miles, a rather large unit of distance. Like the nautical mile and the meter, we believe the *Zep Tepis* based their units of measure on a fraction of the Earth's surface. We see two lines illustrated on Plate 4AB-16. We call them the Foot and the Cubit, because we think they were units of measure. We easily determined that the Foot is 1/100 of an arc second of Earth's surface, and that the Cubit is 1/60 of that arc second. How do these units relate to the way the *Zep Tepis* divided the degree of arc?"

"We believe that they divided the degree into 120 parts. Each of these 120ths were divided into 120 parts, each of which was 1/14400 of a degree. That works out to one quarter of a second. Which is 15 Cubits or 25 Feet. Why such fractions? Because they match up with human factors. They believed that for any measuring system to be useful, it had to involve human factors, if they could match human factors up with fractions of the curve of the Earth's surface, all the better."

"That explains the number system and the units of length. More to the point, we have transmitted a considerable amount of data in writing that explains where we go from here in analyzing these ancient plates. It is all in Arabic language, you will have to translate to other languages. We believe we have similarly determined their reckoning of time, their weights, they understood the distinctions between mass, weight, and force, they knew Newtonian mechanics. They calculated the orbit of Comet Wormwood, they knew when it was coming back, they knew it could hit Earth. They also knew something else."

Metrola handed them a pile of printouts. "All of this writing is in Arabic. I can't read this. Only a little bit in English."

Sabar was waking up. "Let's get this stuff to Astronomy where we keep the other stuff. Cuc

Nguyen can help with the Arabic translation. Helga and Lchnsda were in Egypt, they met Charles Sheehy and he took them to the warehouse where they store these artifacts. Please call them up to Astronomy."

"We'll have them take magic pills, they too are drunk."

In the Astronomy lab, the six of them pored over the data. Chuck, Mustafa, and Cuc translated the Arabic and then confirmed the mathematical interpretations of the ancient data. "Here it is," declared Chuck.

"I see what you mean."

"On this illustration of Comet Wormwood on Plate 3BR-13. They knew the length of the year is 365 and a quarter days. In their numbers, a three, a five, that doesn't mean thirty five, it means 365. Then this slash, that was like a decimal point, dividing the fraction from the integer. A thirty symbol. 30/120 is a quarter, the same way 25 cents is a quarter dollar."

"We have to concur with the Egyptian archeologists and their special experts. The *Zep Tepis* knew how to calculate orbits and the masses of the Sun and each of the planets. They had invented arithmetic for their Base 120 numbers, no need for an abacus or a counting board. They knew about the Precession of the Equinoxes. They knew the length of the orbit of the comet they observed and predicted that it'll hit Earth after 12,498 years! But look at this! That is the number two! In this sentence and this sentence. In their language. Two comets! Exactly two years apart! With identical orbits!"

"There is another comet. The second comet looked exactly like the first, it came two years later, on October 13, 10,493 B.C. It crossed the Earth's orbit, nine million miles ahead of Earth. The Earth passed through the tail, five days later."

"We're jumping to conclusions, here." Sabar took out the photograph of the recently discovered plate from the Map Room. "This plate shows the Solar System as viewed from several hundred million miles above the Earth's North Pole on October 13, 10,495 B.C. Or was it October 13, 10,493? With a two year time difference, the Earth would be in the same place. But the Moon would be about three quarters the way around from where it was two years before. And Mercury, Venus, and Mars would all be in different places." She typed some keys on her computer. On the screen was her computer reconstruction of the Solar System, as seen from above the North Pole. "This is my reconstruction of the Solar System when Comet Wormwood passed Earth on October 13, 10,495 B.C. It crosses the Earth's orbit nine million miles in front of Earth. Just as it is shown on the *Zep Tepi* plate."

"But Mercury, Venus, and Mars are in different places in their orbits!"

"Let's move forward two years." On the computer screen, the comet swept around the Sun in its parabolic path while the planets orbited in their counterclockwise paths. Earth came around two full revolutions. The Moon made about 26 and 3/4 orbits.

"It matches the ancient plate!"

"The plate did not show Comet Wormwood! It shows a second comet in the same orbit, exactly two years removed!"

"That second comet will cross Earth's orbit on April 12, two years later than when Wormwood passes. Unless something happened to it in the last twelve millennia."

"What about Jupiter?"

"Well, I and everyone else accounted for Jupiter's gravity in calculating the first comet's orbit. But the problem is that while Jupiter gets over to the Cancer pie slice when First Wormwood crosses its orbit, it never gets closer than seven dozen *beeyon kepfats*. At that distance, there is a gravitational pull from Jupiter, but it's very tiny. Less than one *heker* or one percent of the pull from the Sun's gravity at these distances." Sabar thought of an example to illustrate what she was saying. "What happened on May 5, 2000?"

"Nothing much. Tides at the beach were probably an inch higher."

"Right. Almost all of the tidal force experienced by Earth is from the Sun and the Moon. High tides occur when the Sun and the Moon are in alignment, not so high tides when they form a right angle with Earth. Most of the force comes from the Moon because it's close."

"But Jupiter and Saturn, even though they're big, they're nothing compared to the gravitational pull of the Sun which is only 93 million miles away. These planets were lined up with the Sun and Earth, but they were on the other side of the Sun, much further away, and had a minuscule effect on the tides. That one inch is an exaggeration."

"No massive earthquakes or volcanic eruptions. None that weren't going to happen anyway."

"The South Pole didn't shift over to the Falklands, the Antarctic Ice Cap didn't collapse. A big disappointment to the Chicken Littles who wanted to believe the Great Planet Alignment of Cinco De Mayo was going to cause such terrible disasters. But no surprise to anyone who knows Newton's gravitation equation and has access to a reference book."

"But we had great radio weather that May, NOT!"

"For some reason, planetary alignments affect the amount of radio static coming from the Sun. But I take it that Jupiter won't get close enough to this second comet to have much affect on its orbit?"

Sabar brought us back to subject at hand. "Jupiter will pass in front of us when Second Wormwood passes our current location two years from now. 350 million miles or so. When Second Wormwood crosses Jupiter's orbit three years from now, Jupiter will be between the Sun and Virgo. 250 million miles or so. I account for Jupiter's gravity, but it certainly doesn't keep these comets from hitting Earth."

"Saturn?"

"Saturn won't get to Leo in time to intercept this second comet, just as it did not intercept the first comet. Uranus and Neptune are clear on the other side of the Solar System toward Capricorn."

"So how did these planets interact with these comets in the *Zep Tepi* time?"

"Neither of the four big outer planets were in any position to affect these comets then. In 10,495 to 10,493 B.C. Jupiter orbited from Libra to Sagittarius. It made it to Capricorn when Second Wormwood crossed its orbit on the way out toward Cancer. Saturn was then orbiting in front of Pisces and Aries. Uranus was in Aries, Neptune in Pisces."

"We have 18 Aries missiles left in our inventory, but only two Russian Blockbusters and three Centaur rockets. We better go find this second comet. NOW!"

Chapter Forty Five

"NASA has confirmed that the *Neanderthal Return* is flying even deeper into space. But neither NASA, the ship, the President nor anyone will explain why the ship is not heading back to Earth now that it has completed its mission."

Captain Trviea Harsradich made a coded transmission to the Egyptian Antiquities Organization. "Dear sirs, we thank you very much for sharing the results of your archeology. This information has proven useful and relevant, we're looking for a comet that, if it exists, is presently too far from the Sun to form a visible coma. We are heading for the spot where it should be. If it's there we will find it. But EVERY Earthling on board the *Neanderthal Return* is advising me that it's imperative that you call a press conference and publicly disclose the discovery of the Hall of Records and the Map Room in the cliff north of the Sphinx. Disclose everything! There is no need to keep the public in the dark, and we object to being obliged to participate in this coverup. It's going to leak out anyway. We don't need another Roswell, Area 51, or Kennedy assassination. The public has a right to know about the possibility of a Second Wormwood."

Charles Sheehy was in an emergency conference with his own President and several other presidents. "Almost every religion on Earth predicts a Doomsday or Judgment Day. We already have numerous religious extremists condemning the deflection of Comet Wormwood as thwarting the Will of God. The anti-nuclear folks are going ballistic over the use of nuclear explosives in space. Imagine the riots that will follow the disclosure of the Gold Plates!"

"Charles, we know about the problems caused by religious extremists and other unreasonable people. But we all know that if the Angel Gabriel is destined to judge us all, there is nothing any human, Neanderthal or Cro-Magnon, can do to prevent it. The deflection of Comet Wormwood or the Second Wormwood is not an attempt to prevent the Judgment of Allah."

"It is not our primary interest to save the Egyptology community from the embarrassment caused by the *Zep Tepi* artifacts. It is proof that the Atlantis described by Plato did in fact exist!"

"It is EVIDENCE of Atlantis," objected Charles, "not PROOF. We still haven't studied this find enough for public disclosure."

"I'm sorry Charles. But we have to disclose this and let the chips fall where they may. The public knows about Afenor Cave in Algeria. The GIS has not done anything to the archeological sites. That one attack was aimed at the army troops. The Stinger missiles fired at the Neanderthal Shuttle were based on their policy of attacking foreigners who happen to be in their country. In fact, they pledge to preserve the sites should they win their war with the government. If the public can digest the discovery of a Neanderthal man who lived as late as the Fourth Dynasty of Egypt, they can handle illustrations of Neanderthal men and women that were made 8,000 years earlier. Were the *Zep Tepis* Neanderthals?"

"We don't believe they were Neanderthals, they were anatomically modern humans, Cro-Magnons, if you will. They undoubtedly had seen Neanderthals, they drew pictures of them. We may have had an interracial community, Neanderthals living with the *Zep Tepis*. We know nothing of the relationship between the Races in the *Zep Tepi* community. But I don't think the world is yet ready for the existence of such a highly advanced culture thousands of years before the Pharaohs."

"Oh, I think they can handle it. After all, the Black Studies folks have been teaching about the Pharaonic Egyptians who flew around the Pyramids in hang gliders."

Charles Sheehy laughed. "I wish I could make such a claim, but there is absolutely, positively no evidence that the Ancient Egyptians flew in hang gliders!"

"I know why," declared Charles' bodyguard, Anwar. "It was King Thutmose V. What? You've never heard of Thutmose V?" Charles smiled, he's heard this one before. "Well, they were embarrassed by him. Like they were of Akhenaton. That's why he don't show up on the king lists. You see, he built a hang glider. Three sticks of wood joined by a steel bracket, over which was stretched canvas. Thutmose would jump off a Pyramid in his hang glider and fly around. Not the most dignified behavior in a Pharaoh. But he's Pharaoh, what can you do? Well, one day, instead of flying AROUND the Pyramids, he flew right INTO the Pyramids. Couldn't even mummify him, his body was too badly broken up! So they cremated him and got rid of all of the evidence!"

Charles busted up laughing. "All right, Presidents. If the world can laugh at such folderol, I guess we can disclose the *Zep Tepi* artifacts."

At an average acceleration of six feet per second squared, with allowances for maneuvering, it was a 15 day trip out to where the hypothesized Second Wormwood would be. Sabar Duradich made her calculations on the assumption that the Second Wormwood was in the exact same orbit as the First Wormwood, but precisely two years behind. The pilots headed us out there, Sabar used all of the resources of the ship in her attempt to locate it.

I visited her in Astronomy. "How's it coming, Sabar?"

"Oh, hi Neil. So far, nothing."

"Maybe there's nothing to find. The *Zep Tepis* could have seen a second comet that's in an entirely different orbit."

"Let's hope so. But the more we decipher their language, us on this ship, and all of the ancient language experts on Earth, now that the find is disclosed to the public, the more we learn that they insisted that the second comet is in the same orbit as the first. If that is so, then right now we should find it at a location one *hekt* ten dozen six and 8/12 *beeyon kepfats* or 1.304 billion miles from the Sun."

"Shouldn't it be getting enough energy from the Sun to fuzz out? At least a little bit?"

"Wormwood has an impressive coma, at least when viewed up close. According to your astronomy community, 800 million miles from the Sun is just about the outer limit of where they first see comets. Most of them are much smaller than Wormwood, they're not discovered until they are well within 600 million miles. If this second comet has a fifty mile core, we should be able to see its coma. It would still be receiving five twelfths, actually two fifths, of the energy per square foot from the Sun as Wormwood was when we dealt with it."

"About two BTU's per hour per square foot. That should fuzz out some of the hydrogen and carbon dioxide and other low boiling point gasses."

"It should. The *Zep Tepis* describe both comets as impressive sights in the sky. But at a nine million mile closest approach, the core could be as small as a mile and be impressive."

"The big heavy comets are spherical, from their gravity. But the smaller ones could be oblong, potato shaped. Halley is 10 miles in its longest dimension, 5 miles in its shortest. And very low density, fluffy."

"Halley is in a short orbit, 76 years. It's named for the fellow who first figured that out. It has visited the Inner Solar System over a hundred times. With the Wormwood orbit type comets, where they are on only their second or third visit to the warmth of the Sun, we're more likely to see solid iceball, not fluffy. But even a solid iceball doesn't necessarily have the low boiling point gasses to give me a nice fuzzy coma to look at. Still seeing nothing."

The four language girls, Lucinda, Helga, Andemona, and Monoloa, and the two archeologists, Chuck Carter and Mustafa Khedr, had taken over Conference Room One. The photos of the Gold Plates, papers covered with scribbling, charts and graphs littered the room. Every hour they received a new transmission from the Egyptian Antiquities Organization with the latest research, theories, translations, calculations, and outright guesses by the anthropologists, archeologists, mathematicians, engineers and other experts working on the wealth of material left by the *Zep Tepis*. Included was a smattering of non-expert opinion from science fiction writers, talk radio hosts, psychics, clerics, witches, charlatans, and ordinary citizens. Most of it was garbage, but it can be entertaining. The public was enthusiastic about the *Zep Tepis*. Did they build the Bimini Road? Are they the Atlantis written about by Plato? Was one of them Quetzalcoatl? The Kennewick Man? The non-expert stuff was included because sometimes a non-expert makes a good guess or says something that sparks an idea. Non-experts don't suffer from institutional blindness.

I was in the Garden Room helping Hrtinsla Pliklakian. There were still repairs that had to be made, and the plants still had to be cared for. We picked some fresh fruits and vegetables and carried them over to the Kitchen. Hrtinsla picked a bouquet of beautiful flowers and tied them together like the best of florists. Lilies, roses, irises, and a few species that I did not recognize. Not every plant was a for food or fiber, some are there for their flowers. All of the plants perform the valuable function of cleaning the carbon dioxide out of the air. "Neil, could you please take these over to Sorby? The flowers there are a day old, we like to keep them fresh. Just take this basket and use it to bring the old flowers and leaves and stuff back here."

"Sure."

"Thank you."

The morgue is located adjacent to the Medical Department. Flowers, cards, momentos, handwritten poems and prayers surrounded the drawer in which Sorby's frozen body was stored. There were several photographs of Sorby Mishlakian: as a little girl; as a winner in a track meet, in a spacesuit when she was first approved as an astronaut; and on a fishing boat proudly displaying a salmon she caught. Standing next to her on the boat is her mom, both smiling and laughing.

The room is a quiet contemplative place, with beautiful geometric decorations illuminated by soft lights. As I went in, I noticed a silent Trviea Harsradich sitting there. "It's okay, Neil. Please don't go. You brought the flowers. Here, I'll help you." She helped me remove the old flowers and place the new bouquet. "Don't take this bunch, the Russians placed it there, see the Cyrillic letters? It has an even number of flowers. In their culture, an even number of flowers is a funeral arrangement. An odd number of flowers is what they prepare for a friendship offering. They presented this even number arrangement for Sorby, and presented me this odd number bouquet for friendship. Can you sit next to me for a while?"

"Sure. Let me check your face. Your eye is looking good, I see the physicians have removed the stitches and the nose cast. Your nose doesn't look any different!"

"Askelion prides herself on the quality of her surgery. Tells me I still have to be careful of the nose and brow ridge. A little more time for my knee and my arm. Please let me kiss you, I want to test my lips."

"Sure." I let her kiss me, being very careful of the healing nose.

"How was that?"

"It was a kiss, very nice, thank you. How about another one?"

She smiled and kissed me again. "That's all you get. I want to heal more before we do more.

You know I never kissed Sorby's father? Demoan Mishlakian was a decent man, a regular guy. Oh, he was not perfect, he liked to have fun, but he was one of the *beeyons* of ordinary people who made Atlantis work. He was like you, a regular guy caught up in extraordinary circumstances, doing the best he can. Imprisoned in quarantine, he nevertheless was able to give almost four *kechts* of us daughters before the Virus turned and took him. The Virus was vicious to all of the boys in the womb, and to their mothers. Demoan was informed of this, he died of a broken heart as much as of the Virus. If I have any regrets, it is not being able to bring Sorby to him, to allow him to see our newborn daughter through the glass." She took a breath. "That would have made him happy."

"We'll help you have more children."

"I know you will. 22 chromosomes from a Neanderthal egg put into a Cro-Magnon sperm with only its Y chromosome. Have it fertilize another Neanderthal egg. Implant into a womb, perhaps mine. Crazy plan. Don't know if it will work. Don't know if we can make a healthy baby with good old fashioned sex. Would not be a Neanderthal child, would be a hybrid. But that would be wonderful. Worth a try, both methods. After all, we don't grow old, we did stop the aging process. Anything is possible, if the Holy Spirit wills it. But we can never replace Sorby, she was special."

"She had a love of life."

"You see that picture of us with her fish? That was taken just before we came on this ship. We all drove out to Sindlinkian, a fishing village six dozen and five *kepfats* down the coast from Cair Atlaston. We chartered fishing vessels, it was our last party on Creation before taking off for Earth. Heading out to sea, Sorby climbed on to the front of the boat, hanging on tight as we dropped through the two *chmfat* waves, catching the saltwater spray in her face. I went up to warn her off and wound up having as much fun as she was. We were cruising through the waves at about seven *kepfats* per hour, the water splashing us both. That's why we're wet in the photo. What's neat about that fishing trip, was that before we were brought together to train for the *Neanderthal Return* mission, we had not seen each other for years. We had been living our separate lives, though both of us often went into space. I would command spacecraft, Sorby would work as a mechanic going out in pressure suits to repair everything that you could imagine malfunctioning." A sad smile. "At least we got know each other again."

Fifteen days had passed, it was now May 26 Earth time. The ship was slowed back down to match velocities with what the *Zep Tepi* plates seem to predict to be the Second Wormwood. Sabar turned to me with a wan smile. "There is absolutely nothing there. If there is a second comet in this orbit, a few thousand miles this way, or a few thousand miles that way, it ain't gonna hit Earth. Not this time around. Cannot find it anywhere that would make it a threat to Earth."

I grinned. "Then we're done! We can head for Earth! Repair your ship to allow your return to Creation with this precious cargo of sperm."

"And any Cro-Magnons who volunteer to come. It will take a year or so to fully repair the ship to where we can feel safe in making the return trip. Perhaps we could try a test pregnancy. The child would still be very young when we arrive at Creation, so he could be raised fully immersed in our culture, to become an Atlantean." She grinned. "We couldn't have him Thinking Metric and in Base Ten numbers."

"You don't mind the wild goose chase?"

"No. Part of the reason for space exploration is exploration. It is science, we collect data every *kepfat* we travel through the cosmos."

"Why don't we go to the conference room and tell the *Zep Tepi* experts what we didn't find?"

"Yeah, let's go, but first, why don't we celebrate our good fortune and Earth's good fortune." We celebrated.

When we arrived at Conference Room One we found Chuck, Andemona, and Mustafa crowded around one table with one photograph of a particular Gold Plate. "Hello people!" greeted Sabar cheerfully.

"Hello, did you find the Second Wormwood?"

"No! It's not there. It's just not there!"

"That doesn't surprise us. The Second Wormwood, according to these ancient documents, is in a long period orbit. The same 12,498 year period. The same eccentricity, the same semimajor axis length. Same distance to perihelion, and the same distance to aphelion. But, there is one difference. There is about a five degree difference in the orientation of the cometary orbit. It'll hit Earth, not two years after the Wormwood that we deflected, but two years and five DAYS after. On April 17. The Second Wormwood is 114 million miles that way." Chuck pointed with his outstretched arm and forefinger.

"Hold it, hold everything!" exclaimed Sabar. "Over fourteen days ago, a fortnight, we were all convinced that this Second Comet was in the SAME orbit as Wormwood?"

"Well, yes, but,"

"And because of this belief, based on some artifacts left by people at the end of the Earth Ice Age, written in a language we still have not entirely figured out how to read, we have spent the past fortnight traveling 3.8 billion furlongs? And it was all for nothing because we misread these ancient gold documents?"

"I understand your frustration but,"

"But what? We cannot go bouncing all over the outer edges of this Solar System looking for something that may or may not exist! We're basing all this on the writings of a people whose mathematics and astronomical observations were apparently ahead of their time. Maybe they were just wrong! Maybe they made a mistake. How do we know if they tested their hypothesis? If they could have? Or maybe they got locked into a dogmatic system of belief that didn't allow for new ideas or dissent? We today have computers and instruments and an understanding of the world around us that our grandfathers only dreamed of, indeed, could not even imagine, and yet WE make mistakes. So if WE can make mistakes, why couldn't the *Zep Tepis*?"

"It is possible that the *Zep Tepis* made errors in their arithmetic and their assumptions, theories, and models. But before committing them to permanent gold records, we believe they double checked their arithmetic. We haven't yet found a math error in any of their calculations."

"I would say an error of five degrees of angle translating into 114 million miles when it comes to the current location of the Second Wormwood would qualify as a significant mathematical error!"

"Sabar, the error is ours, not theirs."

"I don't doubt that. I've heard that there are still people who think the Giza Pyramids were designed in something like an inch."

"Which was proven wrong by Sir William Flinders Petrie." remembered Mustafa Khedr.

"Inch?" I asked. "What's this about the Pyramids being built in inches? Boeing airplanes are built in inches, that I know for a fact. But I thought the Pyramids were built in cubits. What's this inch theory?"

"The Astronomer Royal of Scotland," Mustafa began his answer, "Charles Piazzi Smyth, and his fellows believed the Pyramids were built by the Israelites during their time in Egypt. He came up with a theory of the Pyramid Inch, which was inspired by the Metric System, of all things."

"An inch theory inspired by the Metric System." Sabar was sarcastic. "Knowing Cro-Magnons, that doesn't surprise me."

Mustafa chuckled. "To invent the Metric System, the French decided upon a decimal fraction of some dimension of the Earth's surface as a basic unit. They knew that one ten millionth of the distance between the North Pole and the equator along a line of longitude was just about three of their French feet, which were longer than the English feet we still use. An *aune*, a French yard. They hired astronomical surveyors to make a new measurement of one degree of latitude, multiply by 90 and divide by 10 million, and came up with a length of their new Meter, just a little longer than the *aune*. Then they froze the definition of the Meter so that now the distance between the North Pole and the equator is about 10,002,290 meters. But for most practical purposes a meter is one ten millionth of that distance."

"What Piazzi Smyth hypothesized," added Chuck Carter, "was that the Ancient Egyptians used as a unit of measurement one ten millionth of the distance between the North Pole and the CENTER of the Earth, and then subdivided that into 25 inches. The distance from the North Pole to the Equator along the CURVE of the surface of the Planet is about 393.7 million inches. The distance between the North Pole and the center in a straight line is about 250.27 million inches. That made for a 'Mystical Cubit' of a little over 25 modern British-American inches and the 'Pyramid Inch' that was a hair longer than the modern inch."

"Flinders Petrie came to Egypt with the purpose of proving the Pyramid Inch theory and wound up disproving it." Mustafa was finishing the example. "The Egyptians did not invent the inch, the Romans did, when they divided the foot into 12 parts. Turns out that the Pyramids were built in terms of the Royal Cubit equivalent to 20.6 modern inches. Most Egyptologists today believe this Royal Cubit is the unit by which the Pyramids were designed. There is nothing wrong with proposing a theory as Piazzi Smyth did, as long as we're willing to give up the theory when it fails the test of hard evidence. That's what we're doing with these Gold Plates. We hypothesized that they indicated the existence of a second comet in the same orbit as Wormwood exactly two years later. We tested the theory with further study of these Plates and by coming out here and looking for the comet. The theory was a failure, not the experiment, the experiment was a success!"

"Sabar, you told me you didn't mind the wild goose chase." I reminded her. "Just now."

"All right. The second comet is not where we thought it was. But we took quite a hit when we bombed Wormwood the first time. We need to get back into orbit around Earth for repairs. Let's call Trviea in here."

"Good idea, we've got some decisions to make. Let's get Anatoly and Morton too." We used the ship intercom system to call them over. "Look, Sabar, please come over here." She went over to the table and looked at where Mustafa pointed. "You recognize the 'six' symbol?"

"Yes, followed by the 'ten' symbol. In this context we have six 120's plus ten, which adds up to 730, the number of days in two Earth years. So?"

"In this context, there's no indication of the quarter day in Earth's orbit around the Sun. We think they had leap years in their calendar, they may even have the further correction that we see between the Julian and Gregorian calendars."

"In this context, we are just seeing the number of days in two non-leap years."

"Exactly. Then you see this writing that comes after it. You know how in our languages that have alphabets, languages such as your Atlantean, Arabic, English, Russian, and such, the numbers have words that are spelled out." On a piece of paper, Mustafa wrote the number 5. "That's our number five in the Western Arabic that most of the Earth uses. And this is the number five as we write it in the Eastern Arabic nations, and this is how you write it in your

Atlantean numbers." Then he wrote the four Roman letters that spell the English word five. "And this is how 'five' is written out in English."

"I see. Do you know if the *Zep Tepis* did the same kind of thing?"

"We think so. That's why we missed it. If we didn't know how to read Atlantean, but knew the Creation numerals and the Base Twelve system, we would read the numerals but miss the number words where they're spelled out. Look closely, please. The word written out after the 730 number."

"I see it."

"That probably means 'days'. Everywhere we find it in these plates, it seems to mean that, the context looks consistent with it meaning 'days'."

"That could be the word for 'days'. But I thought there are over 500 different symbols in this writing?"

"Well, there are. Some of these symbols look like they are combined into single words, some of them could be words themselves, and some of them could be like alphabet letters, standing for individual sounds out of which we make words."

Trviea, Anatoly, and Morton arrived. "Hello people," greeted Trviea cheerfully, her leg cast was replaced with a tape wrapped around her knee. She could now bend her leg a little bit. Her eye was no longer discolored, her face looked normal. "What's all this about? Sabar, you find any comet?"

"No, Trviea, there is no second comet in the same orbit as Wormwood, at least not two years behind Wormwood."

"I see."

"Turns out the *Zep Tepis* didn't say that the second comet was in the same orbit with Wormwood. The second comet's orbit is in oriented five degrees over." Mustafa explained the above to the three new people. "That's why we think this word is the number five written out. We see this same word used at least 69 times throughout these plates. The context seems consistent with it being a number word. The phrase that it is in is repeated several times, but sometimes with the symbol for five. And look at this Arithmetic Instruction Plate. We see the number words in the text and the number symbols in the equations, almost like it was made to instruct children in a school. We didn't catch the relationship between number symbols and number words before."

"It could indicate that the Second Wormwood crosses the Earth's orbit five days LESS than two years later."

"Yes it could, but we think it is most likely two years PLUS five days."

"Well, this second comet, if it exists, should be almost two dozen *beeyon kepfats* from us. Much closer than it is to Earth telescopes." Trviea was thinking. She spoke slowly, choosing her words carefully. "Sabar, why don't we go up to Astronomy and take a search for this comet in this new theoretical location. If it doesn't have a coma, we can compare images of the sky taken an hour apart and look for the spot that moves." An orbiting comet moves relative to the background stars.

We all crowded into Astronomy, Sabar focused the ship's telescopes on the spot the comet would be in if the two year plus five day theory is correct. "All right, got the telescope oriented. Metrola's in the Pilothouse, she's holding the ship in constant attitude. Oh my!"

We saw the telescope image displayed on a large screen. "Fuzz spot!"

"The *Zep Tepis* knew their orbital mechanics!"

"Let's make sure we aren't looking at a nebula or a galaxy."

"Checking." Sabar asked her computer to check the portion of the sky for the presence of any known nebulae or galaxies in its Astronomical Database. "Nothing. It appears to be a comet."

Captain Harsradich called to the Pilothouse on her headset. "Metrola, are you getting the telescope image up there?"

"Yes, I am. Looks like a comet."

"Let's close to about one *beeyon kepfats* of this object. Sabar, track it, study it, collect data on it, if nothing else the scientists on Earth would like this information. If this comet is not on a collision course with Earth, no need to get closer than that. But in case it is,"

"We'll keep the Missile and Bomb Crews ready." assured General Fairchild.

"We'll inspect the rockets and warheads and make sure they're ready." promised Anatoly.

"This is a little comet!" It was now June 3.

"Potato shaped, three miles long, a mile in diameter, rounded ends, the whole thing's all lumpy and bumpy. Still big enough to be a Dinosaur Killer if it hits Earth."

"Got some hydrogen, cyanogen, carbon dioxide, that stuff is fuzzing out. Not a lot of boiling, we are 1.3 billion miles from the Sun. 330 below zero Fahrenheit."

"But look at the rotation of the main mass! End over end. One revolution every nine hours. The centripetal acceleration on the ends is almost equal to the local gravity, how is this thing holding together? We try to shove it with an Aries, it could baseball bat that warhead off to left field to detonate with little effect."

"That's why we need to time the detonation, we can also guide the rocket to sink the warhead into the ice by having it hit at a 90 degree angle."

"The B61 should sink into the ice, but that surface is pretty hard. Maybe we can fire two Aries missiles. The first one can soften up the surface with heat, the second one can sink the warhead in to generate some delta vee."

"But we don't want the delta vee absorbed into changing the rotation rate. We want it all translational. Move it, not spin it."

"Wait a minute! Why not break it in half? Convert that spin to momentum as it flies apart. We don't care which direction, as long as every piece is flying away at several feet per second or more, it'll miss Earth!"

"But will it miss US?"

"Gentlemen, ladies!" interrupted Captain Trviea Harsradich. "We don't have to do any of this if this core will miss Earth in its present orbit. Sabar, is it on a course to hit Earth or is it not?"

"It is possible that it will hit Earth on its present course. Wormwood is a huge mass, the jetting of its fumes does not significantly affect its orbit. That is why we had to hit it with six nuclear bombs, three of them the high yield Russian Blockbusters. But a little core like this one could be more easily pushed by its own boiling gasses. It's like a ship being affected by waves. An ocean ship of a *beeyon gunds* will ride steady but a little dinghy will be tossed around. So probabilities enter into calculating its orbit. Let's put it up on this screen." On the screen Sabar put an image of Earth. "The 11/12 cone of probable orbits envelopes the Earth."

"By 11/12," asked General Fairchild, "you mean that there is an 11/12 probability that the Second Wormwood comet core will orbit inside this round pathway you show passing around Earth. With Earth inside it."

"Yes." answered Sabar. "But this probability model is based on assumptions and guesses as to the nature of this comet and how it will react to the warming by the Sun. As you can see, there is a substantial chance that it will hit Earth. Which is what the *Zep Tepis* apparently knew from their observations and mathematical calculations."

"That is an unacceptable risk given the level of destruction that can result." declared the

General. "As small as this core is, at about three years and eleven months before it passes Earth's orbit, we should be able to send this out past the Moon with a single Aries shot. We have 18 Aries missiles left, we can push this baby out of the way with two or three of them. Then we can fly back to First Wormwood and use the remaining Russian bombs to push it even further away from Earth. Then use our remaining Aries missiles to pick off any breakaways that have even a remote chance of hitting Earth."

"Breakaways?" asked Anatoly Donovon. "I wonder if this particle is a breakaway from the main Wormwood mass?"

"Hard to say. Orbital mechanics could put a breakaway into an orbit this far away, while still having the same period due to similar velocities." Sabar Duradich was deep in thought. We were quiet, letting her think. "Two comets, each on a collision course with Earth, 735 days apart. Long odds for this to occur naturally. Comets and asteroids have hit Earth, the Dinosaur Killer. But this, it's almost as if the Face Mountain carvers deliberately set these comets on these orbits."

"Could they have done that?"

"They dragged Planet Creation into its present orbit. We have no idea how they did it, but we're certain they did it."

"I just don't get it. They experimented with us, and therefore learned how to create a replacement planet to relocate themselves as their home star billows up into red giant. I have no problem with that. But then why place booby traps to kill us off? What did we do to them?"

"Maybe they engineered and planted the Virus. Maybe they set these comets on this course, and the *Zep Tepis* were able to figure that out. But we don't know this for a fact. Maybe they knew we had the potential for space travel and didn't want to share the Galaxy with us. Or maybe the Virus was not intentional, it was an accident, and these comets are accidents of nature. Those who play God work in mysterious ways. Anyway, we've got to move this mass into a different orbit."

"Yes, but please safeguard this ship, this one is rich in low boiling point gasses, great for explosions resulting from the heat of a nuclear bomb." Trviea's injuries and grief were not allowing her to forget this consideration.

"We can circle around above the rotational pole, so if this mass flies apart we won't be in the way."

"But then we are exposed to the jet from the bomb explosion. At least with Wormwood, we didn't have to worry about the mass itself flying apart because of the extent of its gravity. We were free to just cruise around to the side to avoid getting hit."

"And we got hit anyway. With this one, we can get hit no matter where we are."

"I have an idea." Having ideas is one of my bad habits. Gets me into more trouble than just about anything else.

"We're listening, Neil."

"Instead of using a rocket to deliver a bomb, why not PLANT the bomb, and set the timer for 24 hours or something like that, and get the Hell out of there."

"Uh, we, uh, we would have to LAND on the side of this thing to do that."

"But we can. Yes, there's stuff boiling off of it, but it's nothing like the Wormwood main mass. We had to use rockets to deliver the bombs to the main mass because of the fumes and chunks boiling off it. It was 470 million miles closer to the Sun than this mass here. I think that the surface is solid enough that we can set down on it, drill a hole, and plant the bomb. We can use the Shuttle to take the bomb over."

"Why not take an entire Aries missile over? I know it's heavier than the rated carrying capacity of the Shuttle, but we're not going down to Earth. With microgravity conditions, we can strap the rocket on to the outside of the Shuttle and carry it to this rotational pole," she pointed to the computer enhanced image of the Second Wormwood, "right here."

"You mean like we could bury that warhead in the ice and stand the rocket straight up? When it lights up, it could drive the warhead deeper into the ice, the B61 is intended for this purpose."

"We could build a kind of cage to hold it straight up, anchored to the comet with long titanium stakes pounded into the ice."

"Why not use one of our big bombs?" suggested Anatoly. "We could attach it to the front of the Aries rocket and let the Aries rocket drill it into the comet ice."

"We could fabricate a heavy steel point to protect the Russian bomb and to facilitate the penetration into the cometary ice. The point could be made with a long taper and a sharp point. This streamlining would allow the rocket to drill the bomb even deeper into the comet core."

"To make a hole, why not build a large steel spear?" There I go again, another idea. An engineer can get into a lot of trouble this way.

"What?"

"Look, the Russian bomb in its Penetration Vehicle is about three feet in diameter."

"One meter," confirmed Anatoly, "four and a half meters long."

"Right, three feet four inches. The Aries rocket is three feet eight inches in diameter. That is how wide the hole needs to be. Now anyone who has played or worked with snow and ice knows that the easiest way to punch a hole in it is with a steel spike. An ice pick. So we fabricate a four foot diameter steel spike, make it about 30 or 40 feet long, and throw it like a spear."

"We could carry it with the Shuttle and let go of it while traveling at several *kecht potes* per *prelate* toward the target. Then we pull away like a dive bomber. Uh, can we generate the magnetic field? That's a lotta power."

"Sure we can. We can tap the momentum restraint. Less propulsion, but a lot more magnetic field to project. We can let more heat through the plasma reflector for the Main Steam Cycle, more electricity. We can run the fission reactor at full power."

"Excellent. Attach an inertial guidance from one of the Aries rockets and some attitude adjustment rockets to keep it pointed in the right direction."

"Don't need the inertial guidance, just let go of it right. It might punch all the way through the comet core, which is only a mile across at the rotation pole. If we throw this steel spear hard enough, a solid steel cylinder should penetrate very deep into the comet. Might as well plant the 120 megaton Russian bomb in the center of this thing. So if the steel spear can penetrate a half mile, or more, then it is just a matter of dropping the 44,000 pound mass of the bomb down that hole. There is some gravity, not much, but some, we could use it to center the bomb. Set that ticker for a nice long count and we can be back on the ship and a cool *beeyon kepfats* away when it lights off."

"Blasting it in two parts, the kinetic energy of the spin, which is substantial, plus the force of the blast, there is no way that any piece of this comet will get anywhere near Earth four years from now! Any particle that is not sufficiently accelerated out of this orbit to miss Earth will be vaporized by the heat of the bomb."

The *Neanderthal Return* is an immense ship. When the call for scrap metal went out, Contrviea Tiknika and her crew easily gathered up a *hekt* of *gunds* of iron and some aluminum, copper, and titanium.

We made our missile out of the 133,000 pounds of scrap steel, machine shop chips, and the Machine Shop's supply of bar, ingot, and pipe stock. In the foundry, we cast a bullet shaped slug of steel four *potes* in diameter and six *potes* long. A solid cylinder of steel four *potes* in diameter and six *potes* long was cast and then induction welded to the leading bullet while the iron was still red hot. These two forward sections massed 65,000 pounds. We cast eight tubes of steel that were each six *potes* long, four *potes* in outside diameter with a three *tig-it* wall thickness. These we assembled to each other and to the forward solid section by induction welding while red hot.

The result was a front heavy 133,000 pound missile that was almost four feet in diameter and sixty feet long. We quenched this for two reasons, to case harden it and to get it cooled down. We jacketed the forward surface with a shiny half *tig-it* layer of titanium to give it strength for high speed impact with cold comet ice. As a final touch, holes three *tig-its* in diameter were drilled to facilitate the clamps carrying it on the side of the Shuttle. We fabricated this in one day.

Chapter Forty Six

Helga Trvlakian kissed me. "Good luck, Neil."

We were in the Shuttle Bay, she just helped me into a pressure suit, I carried the helmet under my arm. "The only thing I'm worried about is the cyanogen. Pretty nasty. Kills you in a hurry."

"No worse than loss of pressure. The heater unit in your suit should boil off any non-water ice that sticks, extra heat in your feet. That should take care of the cyanogen. We increased the sensitivity of the cyanogen detectors in your suit and in the Shuttle airlock. We've also installed cyanogen scrubbers in the Shuttle and its airlock. If cyanogen is detected in the airlock as you come in, you will hear the warning and the cyanogen scrubber will automatically turn on. And keep your nose tuned to the almond smell."

"Great, I get to smell almonds and listen to that warble before passing out from a lethal dose. Can those scrubbers clean the cyanogen out of the air faster than my body can absorb it?"

"Breathe directly from your oxygen supply if you smell almonds. That'll help keep the cyanogen out of your system. Thank you for your idea of planting the bomb. Allows us to be far away when it detonates. We don't risk the ship."

"But we do risk the Shuttle and those of us who step out on the surface of the comet."

"Just think, this has never been done before." We looked at each other. "At least as far as we know." She smiled. "Be careful, please." She was serious. She kissed me again.

I went on board the Shuttle. On one side was mounted two giant hydraulic actuated clamps. The Machine Shop has a plentiful supply of structural aluminum and titanium alloys, and parts such as hydraulic rams, clamps, and bolts of all sizes. I strapped down next to a pressure suited Metrola Mornuxler at the control panel. Just the two of us this time. "Neil, are you ready for another adventure in this Shuttle?"

"No. But we're not gonna wait for me to get ready, are we?"

"Nope." She checked to make sure the Shuttle door was secure. Then she called out to Helga, standing by with her headset. "Shuttle crew is on board and secured. Shuttle door is locked and secure."

"Read you, Metrola." responded Helga. "Everyone, clear the Shuttle Bay." The three women in the Shuttle Bay left and secured the airlock. Helga went up to the Bay control room. She pumped the air out of the Bay and opened the door to space. They went through the checklist and Metrola pushed the button. We left the Shuttle Bay and went around to Bay Number Four.

We heard Pidonita call out *Jore put!* We needed Free Fall to maneuver the 133,000 pound mass. Main Steam Cycle at full throttle, fission reactor at full power, both its steam and ammonia cycles producing electricity. Metrola hovered at about 50 feet from the opening to the Bay. Six Neanderthal women used their physical strength to gently, GENTLY, push the 60 foot length of steel toward us.

"Steel missile is now exiting the Bay at one *tig-it* per *prelate*." announced Nesla Teslakian, working in the Bay.

"Thank you, Nesla." I responded. "I will now test the clamps. Closing clamps, now."

"I see the clamps close, Neil."

"Thank you. Now I open them." I pushed the button.

"The clamps open quickly. The cables and reels should halt the steel dart at about two dozen *potes* outside the Bay."

"Thank you, Nesla. Metrola, you watching that?"

"Yes, I am." The cables were hooked around the deadweight missile at both ends, large diameter wire ropes at the heavy end. We waited six minutes as the wire ropes brought the slowly drifting missile to a halt.

"All right, Neil, we will now approach it. I'll say 'feet' instead of '*potes*' and use Base Ten. We are now 40 feet from the steel missile. 30 feet. 20 feet. 10 feet. 5 feet, almost there."

"We're there." I looked at four video screens, one for each arm of the clamp. We put little cameras on each one, just like the Canadian Arm on the Space Shuttle. "Okay, I can line up the forward arm. Metrola, rotate down, please, got the other forward, uhhh, got it. The forward clamps are hooked, bring me around to line up the rear clamps. Oh excellent, Got it! Steel missile secure on the clamps. Locking for flight, locked!"

"We see it, Neil." confirmed Nesla. "Now we're removing the cables."

Four girls jumped out slowly and arrived at the ends of the inert steel. The other two stood by in reserve, ready to jump out or operate cable reels as necessary. "Rear of the steel dart free of the cables." called out Andemona Chmlakian as she tossed the cables back into the Bay.

The other three worked to free the heavy front end. They had to work around the clamps, they were located over the center of mass of the thing. The tail extended out behind us. Finally, "Front end free of the ropes." announced Nesla and she drew herself back into the Bay. "Good luck, Shuttle."

"Good luck." Anatoly Donovon and Svetlana Lebed were in Russian pressure suits, standing by their bomb. It was now detached from the Centaur rocket and contained in a wire rope basket. Its wire rope was wrapped in a huge cable reel. There was some other equipment next to them.

We moved away from the *Neanderthal Return*. "Shuttle Pilot ready to commence Deadweight Missile Run." announced Metrola.

"We read you, Shuttle Pilot." responded Trviea.

"Bombardier ready for Deadweight Missile Run." I announced.

"We read you, Bombardier. Good luck. Please commence Deadweight Missile Run."

Metrola took us away from the ship. "Pidonita, please extend your magnetic fields to the max."

"Extending." Pidonita Hmlakian directed the powerful magnetic fields in a cone toward the Shuttle.

"Woooa!" exclaimed Metrola. "Thank you, Pido. Love doing this strapped to a *hekt gund* chunk of steel. We could do this with our cyclotron shut off and just use the magnetism of this big steel bar."

"We do need to guide and aim the dart."

"Yes, yes, I know. There it is, the target." Out the window in front of us we saw the diffuse coma. The core was invisible to the naked eye.

"Not much outgassing."

"No. Let me turn on the telescope and the targeting computer." A video screen showed the core. It seemed to hold still even though it was completing one full turn every nine hours. Take a potato, pound a nail through the middle at its waist. Spin it around the nail and you model this comet. It was three miles in length, the outer ends were moving at about one mile per hour. On the screen the targeting computer placed a crosshairs right on the rotational pole in the waist of the spinning potato, as Metrola operated her controls. "We are approaching the Initial Point. There, the computer will take over. When you get the countdown for release of the missile, you just release it when indicated. Then I'll pull us away, we'll experience five gees. We'll be approaching the comet at one *kecht potes* per *prelate*. That's about 2500 feet per second."

"The whole thing is about 5,300 feet across where we're aiming it. Punch right through to the other side, in only a few seconds. Met, how's the radar map of the comet? How we doing on breakaway chunks?"

"Not many, mostly off the ends, where centripetal acceleration is almost equal to its gravity, and at that, none of them are bigger than a foot across or flying at more than a foot per second relative to the main mass."

"That's good. But WE are moving at 2500 feet per second relative to that main mass. I'd rather not hit an ice cube at this speed."

"Don't worry, I've got them all tracked, we'll pass well outside their paths after we release the steel. Approaching Initial Point." She flipped a toggle switch. "Now the computer is piloting the ship. It's tied into a computer on the *Return*, Pido is following us to keep us within her magnetic fields." She leaned back and relaxed, looking at me. "We have a few *linits*, er, minutes. Funny how those two words rhyme."

After a few minutes we approached the Release Point. "Get ready Neil." warned Metrola. The core of the comet became visible in the thin fog. Half a mile per second gets FAST when you get within 20 miles of a one by three mile comet core. "I set the computer to give you the countdown in seconds and English."

"That's good. Coming up on ten second countdown." We became weightless, in free fall for the missile release.

"Doing great, Neil." Trviea's voice assured me. "I understand this is being broadcast on Earth."

"Hello, Earth. Let me say 'hi' to my kids. Hi Christa. Hi Virgil. Here we go. Ten, nine, eight," Metrola was ready with her hands on the controls, watching me and the missile release. "Four, three, two, one, zero. Missile is released." The hydraulic actuators pulled the clamp pegs out of the three inch holes. Metrola gently backed us away from the long chunk of steel. "Missile away."

"Pulling us out of dive!" Metrola rotating us at five gees away from our fall into the comet core. We did not see our steel needle hit the comet.

But on the *Neanderthal Return*, they watched the video screens displaying the telescope image. The tiny looking steel needle flashed into the view of the icy potato. It disappeared into the comet core as fast as you could blink your eye. "Bullseye!" We heard their voices through our headsets as Metrola tortured me with five gees of centripetal force. "Good work, Metrola and Neil!" They were cheering and clapping on the ship while I was barely able to breathe. I gained about 800 pounds of weight in a hurry.

"How, much longer, Met?" I begged.

"Just a few more *prelates*" she wheezed as we sailed out of the coma of the comet.

"Did the steel dart come out the other side?" asked Trviea.

"Cannot tell." Metrola brought us around to look. "No, cannot find it on the other side, cannot find the exit hole."

"Please look at the impact site." requested Trviea. Lucinda operated the zoom lens on the telescope camera. "Nice hole! Look at all of the ice all broken up, cracks everywhere. Some loose stuff floating around, hydrogen and methane blowing out of the hole and from the cracks."

"Definitely a solid iceball. If it were fluffy, the steel dart would have punched through to the other side. Like a tunnel drilled through solid granite. It'll still be there a year from now. Just a lot of rocks and debris around there. Surface all broken up around the hole."

"And some cyanogen gas. LOVELY!" Trviea called to Bay Number Four. "Anatoly, you still feel good about planting your bomb in the hole in the comet?"

"You only live once!" he cheerfully answered.

"Stand by, Metrola will bring the Shuttle over. That right, Metrola?"

"That's right. We're out of the heavy gees, bit of a headache, but that should go away. Neil Peace, he did great!" Applause.

"Yeah, I guess so." I just pushed a button. Geez.

We came back around to the mother ship. Metrola parked us 50 feet outside the opening to Bay Four. The four Russians were ready in their pressure suits. The six women we saw before were there, and two of the American Air Force Majors, Roy McKenna and Wilbur Davenport. The clamps we used to carry the deadweight missile were removed and the clamp controls were sent out through the airlock.

Then the bomb was brought out very slowly and lashed to the outside of the Shuttle where we carried the big steel dart. After lashing this all important 44,000 pound mass, the cable reel carrying a half mile of three eighths *tig-it* wire rope was lashed to the side. Finally, 71 foot long titanium anchoring spikes. Looking at the pictures of the hole, I wasn't sure six dozen *potes* was long enough.

Then the personnel came in through the airlock, three at a time. The four Russians, Majors McKenna and Davenport, and the six women in the Bay. One of them was Monoloa Mrvlakian. Good for the languages. They brought in their equipment, tools, and sledgehammers. 24 *dollons* or 12 1/2 pounds of steel on the end of each sledge. No problem for Neanderthal physical strength. Everything and everyone was strapped down and secured.

"Shuttle secure, all passengers strapped down." announced Metrola.

"We verify that your cargo is secure." responded Trviea. "Please proceed with Bomb Placement. Beware of almond smell."

Metrola pulled us away from the *Return*. Now the fun part.

We headed out to the comet, this time at a much slower speed. After a half hour trip, Metrola brought us down to hover a hundred feet above the hole. "Here we are," announced Metrola, "commence Bomb Placement."

I looked out the window at the scene. "Me and my big mouth. Is there cyanogen out there?"

"A little bit," conceded Metrola, "but it's mostly hydrogen, methane, and carbon dioxide, at extremely low pressures. *Beecoilons* per square *tig-it*, basically hard vacuum."

"That ice sure is broken up. Uh, there's a spot that doesn't look so bad."

"Yeah," agreed Anatoly, "we'll anchor the cable reel there, about 20 meters, uh 70 feet from the hole."

We climbed out of the Shuttle, three at a time, all our pressure suit functions worked. In the distance, the sky was dark with a thin white fog. But we could see each other in the Shuttle's lights almost as clearly as in the hard vacuum of space. The first thing we did was to unhook the cable reel. It had a mass of 1800 pounds. In low gravity, a large mass can be maneuvered by gently pushing it and letting it glide to where you send it. You just don't want to be caught between large masses, you can get crushed. The cable played out as the reel drifted to the ice. We went after it. "Let's get this turned around, set it, good. You sure this iceball has gravity? This cable reel keeps bouncing like it's weightless."

"Yeah, bring down the *treefat* spike!"

Monoloa brought down a three foot long titanium spike and a sledgehammer. "Here," she said as she handed me the spike, "stab this through one of the mounting holes of the cable reel." I complied as she put special spiked boot coverings on her feet. We each had extra two inch thick boot coverings to protect our feet from the minus 330 Fahrenheit comet ice. The spike attachments were also insulated to keep the metal spikes from drawing our heat into the ice. She planted her feet firmly in the ice and with two swings of the 12 pound sledge sank the *treefat* spike all the way down. "Cable reel fixed. Now we need three of the twelve *chmfat* spikes."

Astronauts up above gently lowered one of the long spikes. I grabbed the point and stabbed it through a mounting hole of the cable reel. Major McKenna did the same with a second long spike, and I went around with the third. All four mounting holes of the cable reel now had spikes through them into the ice, one of them down firmly. A special six foot long spike with a mounting plate built in was thrown down like a spear. Monoloa asked me to "Stab that in at an angle, over here, toward the large cable reel. Thank you. Stand back please." She anchored herself with her foot spikes and sledgehammered it in. Two feet of the spike were still above the ground. She handed me her sledgehammer. "Hold this, please."

She took a small cable reel off of her belt and bolted it to the spike. She hooked the end of the cable to a D-ring on her belt, I could see the little control panel where she could reach it. Then she took her spike boot coverings off of her boots and handed them to me. "Please put these on and anchor yourself where you can hold my spike and reel. Warn me if it starts to come out. My sledgehammer, please."

I handed it to her. "Everything looks fine, so far." I assured her. Roy McKenna was similarly planted and helping Nesla Teslakian. Monoloa and Nesla each jumped up carrying sledgehammers. When they reached the top ends of the 71 foot spikes, their cables drew taut. "Hold my cable, please." each asked us. Roy and myself each had special pads built into our gloves that allowed us to hold personnel cables without damage. Each woman above swung her sledgehammer on to the top of a spike.

"What's keeping these spikes from buckling?" I asked. Ever have a nail bend to the side when you are pounding it? More likely to happen if it's 70 feet long. The titanium spike was only a *tig-it* in diameter. I thought about radius of gyration.

"We don't hit it too hard when we're up here." was the only reply. I noticed that the spikes only went in a foot or so with each hammer blow. When there were twenty feet to go, the women swung harder. The spikes would drop three or four feet if the material below was soft, but sometimes less than a foot if it was solid water ice.

"It seems that the material below has a lot of variance." I observed.

"So I've noticed. Any more good news?"

"Yeah, your anchor spike wants to come out."

"Keep holding it. That's why you're down there." Soon there were only a few feet of spike left to pound. "Thanks, Neil. Please give me your shoe anchors."

"Sure. Uh! I'm stuck in the ice."

"That's the idea." she chuckled. "Let me help you." She helped me out of the straps restraining my boots and we dug the spikes out of the ice. Much of the ice is methane, carbon dioxide and other such gasses. It therefore boils into these gasses without a liquid stage upon exposure to the heat of our pressure suits and activities. Since there is little gravity to hold it to the comet and nothing but space above, these gasses blow away for hundreds of miles. The pressure stays very low, millionths of a pound per square inch. The surface ice became a little softer and lighter because of this sublimation.

Monoloa and Nesla each put on the spike anchor shoes and sledgehammered the two long spikes the rest of the way in, securing the cable reel to the side of the comet. Nesla immediately handed her spike shoes off to Roy and jumped up with her sledgehammer to pound in the third long spike. Monoloa and I used a long pry bar to lift the short spike out to make room for the fourth long spike. We grabbed the point of the fourth long spike and stabbed it in through the mounting hole.

We repeated the earlier procedure, the *treefat* spike being delivered back to the Shuttle when

Monoloa jumped up to the top of the long spike. When all four long spikes were down, we announced, "Cable reel secured to the comet."

"Well done, ladies and gentlemen." praised Metrola. "Wish I was out there, fresh air, exercise,"

"Yeah, right. Sore muscles." objected Nesla to Metrola's chiding. "Cyanogen gas in the environment, micropressure."

"Of course, of course. Come back up for a well earned rest."

We went back up to the Shuttle. I heard some Russian language chatter. "What did Maria say?" I asked after hearing Mrs. Romanov's voice.

"The bomb is now armed." answered Anatoly.

"That's nice. Adds new meaning to the phrase, 'Be gone in a flash.'" Laughter.

Mikhail Dostoevski jumped to the ground next to the cable reel. "Hey Nesla, the digital readout is in Earth numerals, it reads 128." he remarked in English.

"Yeah, I reset it to read in Base Ten, your numerals."

"Is it in meters?"

"No, I didn't reset that, it's still in *potes*."

"Well now, wire rope stretches under tension, and there are other variables,"

"It's not accurate to within the difference between a *pote* and an American foot."

"I can manage, I'm used to meters, that's all."

"Now you know how we Americans feel when asked to do something in meters."

"*Da*. We used feet and inches before Lenin. And I've analyzed American and British stuff, I can handle it."

"Mikhail, are you ready?" asked Nesla.

"*Da*."

"Monoloa, please explain the procedure in his language, we don't want to get it wrong."

"Sure." Monoloa spoke in Russian. "The wire rope is 2600 feet long. We'll send the bomb down at three feet per second. At that speed, it'll take a little more than 14 minutes. But it might hit some ice and snow along the way, we are counting on the fact that there is some gravity on this iceball to keep it moving as long as it is on this side of the center of mass. So it could take longer. Maybe an hour. When it passes 2500 feet, if it passes 2500 feet, we want you to gently slow it to a halt. That'll place the bomb right in the center of this comet, and with 120 megatons of yield, blow it completely apart, nothing from it will hit Earth."

"But," interrupted Anatoly in Russian, "we don't know how far the steel dart went. It did not come out the other side, it is still lodged in the comet. We put a magnetic iron detector on the front of the bomb, the indicator is on the cable reel."

"I see it."

"It'll tell you if you are getting near the steel dart. Stop the fall of the bomb within 100 feet of the steel, just don't let it hit the steel. We don't want to mess up the bomb."

"Is the bomb ready for launch?" asked Metrola, still piloting the Shuttle.

"It's in position, the wire rope is clear, we just have to set the timer."

"Set the timer, please."

Maria Romanov typed codes into a device that looked like a laptop computer. Then we heard her speak in Russian. Anatoly translated for us. "Bomb is armed and the timer is now set for 24 hours. That should be enough time for us to plant it and get out of here."

"Everyone who's outside, please unhook from the Shuttle, get back away, at least a *hekt potes*, 150 feet, or 50 meters." We unhooked our tether cables from the Shuttle and free floated a

426

safe distance away as Metrola ordered. "Is everyone clear of the Shuttle, nothing in the way of the bomb cable?"

We all answered yes.

"Mikhail, please let out 300 feet of cable."

"*Da*, I'm doing it." Mikhail pushed a lever and fed out the requested length of cable.

"All right, here goes my Bomb Placement maneuver." Metrola brought the Shuttle to a height of 250 feet. A nose cap held the bomb against a retainer flap. Metrola started downward, the nose cap turned flat against the Shuttle hull releasing the front of the bomb. At 100 feet, Metrola abruptly stopped her ship, the bomb flew off the rear flap which then slapped against the side of the Shuttle and locked. The bomb flew freely at about three feet per second away from the Shuttle, which backed off to the side. The wire rope followed it.

I read the Atlantean writing on the side of the bomb: "She dances forever, on the glittering carpet of stars, we'll never forget her, Sweet Sorby." The bomb went straight into the ragged hole.

"Nice shooting, Metrola!" I shouted.

"Thank you."

I heard Anatoly instruct Mikhail in Russian. "Just feed out the line as necessary to keep it slack until you reach 2500 feet or detect the steel missile."

"All right, everyone," called out Metrola, "Start coming in through the airlock, three at a time. Make CERTAIN you are free of cyanogen on the outside of your suits before opening the inside door. I'm not protected."

We cycled in as Mikhail fed out cable below. For the safety consideration of the cyanogen present in the cometary material, everything that has been exposed to the cometary ice is strapped to the outside of the ship. Bringing a solid chunk of comet ice loaded with cyanogen into the cabin of the Shuttle could kill us all. We inspected each other and knocked off all specks of ice and snow we could see, hoping the heat of our suits boiled off the poison leaving water ice. Fortunately, the cyanogen warning only sounded twice, and the scrubbing procedures eliminated the problem. Heat, at about room temperature, boils cyanogen ice, Some air can be exhausted out of the Shuttle, carrying with it the cyanogen, the rest pumped through a scrubber, until it is absorbed and rendered inert.

As we cycled in, three of us still waiting our turn, Mikhail called up. "The steel dart is only 1650 feet down." he declared in Russian.

"Okay, bring the bomb to a halt, just short of the steel dart." instructed Monoloa.

"Already done. The bomb is 1.6 meters from the end of the deadweight missile." The iron detector was Russian equipment. "Cable reel is locked, at 1645 feet."

"Thank you, Mikhail, jump on up, clean the ice off yourself, and we'll cycle you in, be careful of cyanogen. Almond smell."

Finally, "All right! Everyone is on board, Shuttle is secure." exulted Metrola. "This is Shuttle calling *Neanderthal Return*."

"We read you, Metrola." responded Trviea. "You all done?"

"We have planted the bomb, the timer is set to go off in 23 hours and about 44 minutes. It is hanging about eleven *hekt* and five dozen *potes* inside the comet, the steel missile is just in front of it."

"There goes our scrap iron and steel supply. I was hoping to recover the steel."

"We can always smelt an asteroid."

"Or purchase more steel at Earth, bring it up with the Shuttle, seven or eight *gunds* at a time. Come on out of there."

"We may have some cyanogen ice on the hull."

"Bathe yourself in the light exhaust, you know the drill."

Metrola made an ugly face. "Eeeee. All right, don't want to endanger anybody with a cubic *tig-it* of cyanogen ice. We are on our way."

"Met, I understand the need to boil off any cyanogen ice before landing in the Shuttle Bay." I admitted.

"But,"

"But, I want to know, is bathing in the intense light exhaust of the fusion reactor the only way?"

"It's the quickest way, and we want to be as far away as possible when that Russian bomb goes off. We have to get cleaned off and then in the Shuttle Bay fast. We don't have a magnetic planet like Earth nearby. As long as Pidonita has to project magnetic fields for our benefit, she can't put the full momentum of each pulse into propulsion."

"But you made a face and went 'Eeee' when Captain Trviea ordered us to bathe in the light exhaust."

"We'll shield the windows, so we won't be blinded. We'll be at an angle so we won't be exposed line of sight with the plasma ball, we'll just receive reflected light. We will rotate slowly in the light until the hull achieves a temperature of three *hekt deems*." About 240 Fahrenheit. "Then we hold at that temperature for a dozen *linits*. Boils off the cyanogen ice completely."

"But this maneuver is not completely safe."

Metrola was annoyed. "Like everything else in space flight, we make a mistake or have an accident, we die. So what else is new?"

"Uh, Metrola, what would be the risk of just landing in the Shuttle Bay?" came a nervous voice in back.

"We brought up all of the equipment we didn't need to leave behind. Some of it was dug into the comet ice. We've bumped into some of the loose solids, no problem, we didn't hit them too hard. But like throwing a snowball into a wall, some of it sticks. Say one twelfth of it is cyanogen. We bring that into the Shuttle Bay. Pressurize with air at room temperature. We'll fill the Shuttle Bay with poison gas. Cyanogen. No thank you, we'll take our chances with the light exhaust."

"Bathing in the light would tend to kill any bacteria or other organisms living in the comet ice."

"It would. We've never found any such life forms in comet ice. Nothing we know about can survive a few thousand years near Absolute Zero. But that's a good point, thank you."

After a half hour, we heard Pidonita's voice. "Metrola, we see you are in position to commence Cyanogen Boil Off Maneuver."

"We are. We are securing for the Boil Off." Shutters closed over all of the windows, voices gasped. Claustrophobia time.

Trviea give us a pep talk. "I understand you're frightened. Nothing wrong with that, to not be scared is to be insane or suicidal. But if it makes you feel better, Pido is our best pilot for the *Return*. Met is our best pilot for the Shuttle. We'll be seeing you in a half hour."

The Shuttle was silent except the voices of Metrola and Pidonita. We seemed to rotate slowly, we only had our inner ears to tell us that. People held hands, a few prayed. Soft whispers and low voices. Chuckles at a joke told to break the tension. It began to get warm. The hull gets much warmer during descent to Earth, but that descent is over very quickly. When the entire hull is heated to a uniform temperature, the interior will eventually assume that temperature. That is how an oven works.

"We're done with the heating." announced Metrola. "We're now pulling away from the light exhaust. That wasn't so bad, was it?" She smiled, to everyone's relief.

"All right, pulling around to Shuttle Bay." Metrola opened the window shutters, and we felt much better. "We should cool off fairly quickly, infrared to deep space. Is Shuttle Bay ready for us?"

Helga answered. "Shuttle Bay is ready, the door is open, come on in, Metrola. Neil, you did great! I'm proud of you!"

"Thanks, Helga."

"You're still pretty warm on the outside. I'll spray you with some water after I pressurize the Bay."

Metrola brought us into the Bay and Helga closed the door behind us. "Shuttle secure in the Bay." she announced.

"Air coming into Bay." announced Helga. "Pidonita, get us out of here!"

"Glad to," responded Pidonita, "commencing twelve and three *potes* per *prelate* squared acceleration." Almost one gee.

"Full pressure in the Bay." said Helga. "Wait a *linit*, got to spray you down." Water sprayed all over the hull. "There is no cyanogen or other poison gasses in the Shuttle Bay, you are free to disembark."

We cheered as we opened the door and climbed out. We were getting out of the pressure suits as Helga came into the Bay. She greeted me with a hug and a generous kiss. A host of other women came in to help us. General Fairchild and Captain Harsradich arrived. "Congratulations, people!" exclaimed Trviea. "The bomb is planted deeper and more accurately than we could have hoped with the rockets. Blow that thing clean in half and boil quite a bit of it! Because of the rotation, the two halves will pull away from each other at five dozen *potes* per *prelate*, plus the push from the bomb. *Hekts* of *potes* per *prelate*. Small pieces will go real fast. What's left in the center, where the bomb detonates, will be nothing. That nothing is what will crash into Earth. Everything else will be up to a *beeyon kepfats* from Earth! You did good, all of you! Get showers, get food and drink, get some sleep, make some love!"

We laughed and cheered at that one! Trviea blushed and grinned.

Trviea finished her speech. "We'll get you up in time to watch the explosion."

Chapter Forty Seven

We were in the crowded Viewing Lounge watching the comet where we planted the bomb. "Another half hour to go." Askelion Lamakian cheerfully declared.

"About that treatment you gave us after the Shuttle mission,"

"A precaution, in case you were exposed to radiation."

"Yeah. So how do you repair damage due to radiation exposure? We have a serious health concern because we can't repair the damage done to DNA by gamma radiation."

"Oh, we just place a special set of enzymes, hmmm, I don't know if 'enzyme' is the word that accurately describes it. Well, what it does is that it compares the DNA of a lot of cells and determines what it was originally when you were born. Then it systematically goes through your body and repairs all of your damaged chromosomes, mitochondrial DNA, and so on."

"And because the DNA is the blueprint by which the body is designed, the healing process works much better. Uh, isn't this a part of your Fountain of Youth?"

Askelion smiled. "You will probably live about thirty to forty years longer than your natural life span. You don't mind that, do you?"

"Oh no! Not at all. As long as I don't get cancer or some other side effect."

"Cancer is the one thing you're less likely to get. That's a genetic damage disease, and you've been given a treatment that repairs genetic damage. Many of the afflictions we suffer as adults are either genetic damage or aging process effects. Cancer, heart disease, the brain afflictions you call Alzheimer's and Parkinson's, arthritis, these are functions of the aging process. So you will not experience these types of afflictions as soon as you would've without the treatment."

"What about having children? If we have children, we want healthy children."

"Gamete genes are also repaired."

"But isn't part of the aging process genetically commanded?"

"There are genes that command aging: gray hair, wrinkly skin, and other effects. The treatment you received did not shut off these genes. If it did, then you could live for hundreds of years the way we do."

"Is Cuc Nguyen figuring some of this out?"

"I'm afraid she is. We might have to take her back to Creation. Not that we mind, we can always use another physician. We're vulnerable to acute diseases. We recover better because our Youth Treatment, but we can't recover from a bug that kills us. So we'd be happy to bring home an experienced bug chaser."

"Are there special problems you women have because of your long life? You look great, you're physically strong, incredibly healthy, but some of your body cells don't split to replace damaged or dead cells."

"Uh, well, there are a few things where we have to be careful. The death of brain cells can be a problem. But we have a brain damage treatment. We regress a few cells around the injured part of the brain to what they were like when the person was a fetus in the womb. Then they can split to replace lost cells and repair the damage. Have to be careful, we can easily create an adult child. But as the new brain tissue matures and connects up with the rest of the brain, we can have an incredible amount of learning. Master five new languages or the physics of a fusion reactor. But we don't do this with an uninjured person. A very slow aging process can take place with brain and other tissue, such as muscle."

"You have no shortage of muscle."

She chuckled. "No, we don't. Fortunately muscle cells heal up extremely well from injuries. With the aging process shut off, both cartilage and muscle, and everything else, heal incredibly well, even without the Healing Factor."

"Are you gonna let Cuc go back to Earth?"

"If she really wants to, we'll have to let her go, regardless of her agreement to come to Creation if she figures out how we stop the aging process. Atlantis has one thing in common with America, a concern for the rights of the individual. We're not in the business of denying people their freedom. Wherever she goes, I would not be surprised if four hundred years from now Cuc is just as smooth skinned and beautiful and strong and black haired as she is today."

Trviea Harsradich came up to us. "Hey you two, it's almost time. Just a few more *linits*."

"How far are we from the comet?"

"A safe distance. Quarter *beeyon kepfats*. 1.2 million miles."

We watched for the explosion. Not sure that at this distance even a 120 megaton explosion would be easily visible to us. But we had plenty of screens displaying the giant potato. "Trev, I see the cast has been taken off your arm." I observed.

"Yeah, let me test it." She smiled and reached around my back and squeezed my shoulders with her great strength.

"I'd say that your arm is plenty strong enough. Ouch! Please don't hurt me!" She relaxed her grip but still held me, like a girlfriend. I responded by holding her around the waist. "Are you doing this because you genuinely like me or is it the Healing Factor?"

She giggled. "Both. But I'm also happy that everything is going well. I only wish my daughter was here." She looked guilty for being happy about things when in mourning for her daughter. A tear flowed. "I'm sorry."

"It's okay. Sorby wouldn't want us to stop flying in space and preventing comets from hitting Earth."

"I know that, life goes on. But sometimes I just feel empty. No emotion at all."

The Russians were seated at their bomb control equipment, the center of attention. "Maria," called Anatoly Donovon, "how's the clock running?"

Maria Romanov checked her digital timer. "Coming up on one minute to detonation."

Anatoly switched to English. "One minute, everyone!"

We settled in, and then Maria performed her ten second countdown. "*chetirye, tri, dva, odin, nol*?"

"No detonation?"

"Not yet."

"Didn't this happen with the first Russian bomb?"

"Yeah, but that bomb exploded. I thought we fixed that. The last two Russian bombs exploded on time."

"This bomb might explode yet." warned Anatoly. "It's dangerous to get close."

"So what do we do?"

"We can wait an hour, or we can talk to the bomb."

"Huh? It's buried inside 1600 feet of comet ice."

"But it still has the antenna routed out through the uranium casing. That was how we were able to send the arming code from here, and then the detonation codes, as we did with the rocket delivered bombs. I'm sorry we neglected to tell you this, but we attached this antenna to the wire rope basket." Anatoly was proud of himself, a good engineer. "Three eighths *tig-it* wire rope conducts electricity as well as any metal. Comes right up out of the hole to the cable reel. The device we attached that let Mikhail place the bomb within two meters of the end of the steel dart received the signal from the probe through the rope. Likewise we have an antenna that takes signal from the bomb through this same wire rope. Signal can go both ways. We can talk to the bomb."

"We are not on the same side of the comet as the cable reel. After we recovered the Shuttle, we flew over the comet and came over this way. We are off in a direction toward the First Wormwood so Sabar can keep an eye on it and its breakaway pieces." Trviea looked annoyed. "Anatoly, why didn't you tell me about this?"

"Uh, I thought we told Contrviea or, uh," Anatoly's humorous side took over. "My dear sweet Trviea, I am sorry. I apologize. We should have told you that we had a communications link with the bomb." Anatoly clasped his hands together and made such an exaggerated look of contrition that we broke up laughing.

Blushing, and trying to stifle her laughter, Trviea walked up to Anatoly, put her hands on his shoulders, kissed him on the nose and said, "Apology accepted. You nut! Now go talk to your bomb and find out why it didn't explode."

"Antenna's on the other side of a mile of comet ice."

"Oh yes. We have to go around to where we can reach the antenna on the cable reel. Anatoly, you didn't think you'd need to communicate with the bomb."

"It should have exploded. It might yet. Let's not get too close to it while we swing around."

"Pidonita," called Trviea.

"Right here, Trev."

"Oh. Who's in the Pilothouse?" asked Trviea through her headset.

"Me, Nesla Teslakian!"

"Nesla, have you been paying attention to what's going on?"

"I've heard everything. We've got to go around to where the Russians can communicate with their bomb."

"But don't get too close to the comet, it could go off anytime."

"Understood. A travel distance of least five or six *hekt kecht kepfats*. Take three or four hours to get there. Still want to maintain a three *hekt kecht kepfat* distance from the comet?"

"I don't like being that close to it." declared Trviea. "Anatoly, is this distance too far from that antenna?"

"What's that in kilometers?"

"Uh, 1.2 million miles, uh, 2 million klicks." I responded.

"Divide by 300,000, six or seven seconds each way for the signal." Anatoly thought for a moment. "As long as we have line of sight, we can do it at 2 million kilometers."

"Very well." concluded Trviea. "Nesla, take us there, drive in a circle, if the bomb detonates, then our problem is solved."

We waited four hours, Nesla drove us at 30 feet per second squared to bring us around, while maintaining a safe distance. We came to within 100,000 miles to shorten the time for the signal to travel between ship and bomb. The effects of these explosions are not limited by a planet's gravity and atmosphere. Out here, where there is little gravity and the vacuum of space, when things fly apart, they just keep on going. It is not a matter of being a safe distance away, it's a matter of dodging the solid chunks when they come. The farther we are from the comet, the greater the distance BETWEEN the chunks, the more time we have to react to them, the more time for the small stuff to boil into nothing.

Waiting. No explosion. It could happen anytime, but doesn't.

"Anatoly, try signaling the bomb again, please." asked Captain Harsradich.

"Nesla, are we within line of sight of the cable reel?" Anatoly asked in English through his headset.

"Almost there. It will be a few more minutes. In your terms, we're about 154,000 kilometers away. I'll tell you when we're there."

"Thank you, Nesla."

We waited for another three minutes. "We should be in line of sight, Anatoly." announced Nesla. "You can try it now."

"Thanks, Nesla. Let's do it, people."

Mikhail Dostoevsky sent a coded signal and waited two seconds for a response. "Nothing, yet." A few more minutes as Nesla brought us further above the cable reel's horizon. Mikhail tried again. "Getting telemetry from the bomb!" he announced in Russian.

"Good." exclaimed Anatoly. "What have we got?"

"Sending the interrogatories now. Hmm. This is interesting. The countdown stopped at 2 hours 48 minutes and 24 seconds."

"Try and get it restarted."

"Well, yeah, we just have to figure out why it stopped. Maria, what did you do when you set the timer?"

"I set the timer. Started it at 24 hours."

"Yeah, well it stopped. Why would it stop?"

"I wonder if it's the magnetic field from the 60,300 kilogram steel dart?"

"*Nyet*! It can't be that."

"Can we operate the cable reel from here?"

"To pull the bomb away from the steel? What good would that do?"

"Lower the strength of the magnetic field around the bomb. The timer is a robust kind of mechanical clock movement. The spring, gears, and the escapement are all made of steel. We felt that for long term readiness in a highly radioactive environment, half the hydrogen in the lithium hydride is tritium, such a mechanical clock would be the most reliable. All of the timers we brought for use in these bombs are this way. These steel parts could be affected by magnetic fields."

"They could be affected by lack of lubrication. More likely that. Or it just ran out of energy, thought we had enough clock energy for a 24 hour countdown. Can we operate the cable reel by a radio signal? It's Atlantean technology. Anatoly, could you ask the Atlantean women if they could operate the cable reel by remote control?" Mikhail didn't feel he knew enough Atlantean or English to ask a technical question and receive an answer. This kind of communication has to be precise.

Anatoly asked the Creation women. "The cable reel is powered by an electric motor and a battery." responded Contrviea, who built it. "There is no control mechanism other than the hand control. Somebody has to push the handle. There's no servomechanism that can be operated by radio."

"No remote control of the cable reel." muttered Mikhail after Anatoly translated Contrviea's answer. "We're going to blow it up, why get fancy? How are you doing, Maria?"

"I've sent the countdown signal five times. It won't respond. It keeps telling me that the clock is stuck."

"Can we disarm the bomb so we can approach it safely?"

"I don't know. I can try. But first, I could try to fire the bomb. When the timer counts down to zero, it throws a switch and an electric signal fires the high explosive detonators. There is a firing code we can send to bypass the timer and detonate the bomb."

"Hold on a moment." advised Anatoly in Russian. Then he spoke in English. "Trviea, Nesla. Maria wants to bypass the timer. We can send a signal to directly detonate the bomb."

"Push a button and it goes boom?" asked Trviea.

"Exactly."

"How close do we need to be to detonate on direct command?"

"This should be close enough. The closer we are, the easier it is to detonate the bomb."

"The farther we are, the SAFER it is to detonate the bomb. With more power in the signal, we can be further away. Marla Syferkrip, Wlmsda Gtslakian?"

"We're here, Trviea."

"Please go to the Switching Room and route the Russian equipment to the Main Transmitter. So much for talking to Earth. Ian Miller?"

"Pardon me," he said to his television audience, "Captain Harsradich wants a few words."

It was after school. Even though it was sunny outside, the Peace children were glued to the television set watching the Science and Humanities Channel for glimpses of their father. "Mommy! They're gonna try to set the bomb off with a radio signal!"

Angela Peace came into the room. "Timer failed." she observed. "Trviea's face is looking a lot better."

Trviea spoke into the camera and into living rooms. "Science and Humanities viewers, I'm sorry but we need the Main Transmitter. We want to be as far as possible from the bomb when Maria Romanov sends the detonation signal. That means we must transmit the signal with as much power as possible."

"Not only will we need the Transmitter for the signal, we need to POINT the Transmitter toward the comet, not toward Earth."

"That's right, Ian. Thanks for understanding. We'll transmit the films of the explosion later. If we succeed in setting it off." Trviea spoke into her headset. "Marla, Wlmsda, you ready to switch the Transmitter?"

"Yes we are."

"Switch in twelve *prelates*."

"This is Ian Miller, on board the *Neanderthal Return*, signing off."

"Well children, I guess this is a good time to come to the dinner table." directed Angela as she switched off the set. "Wash your hands."

Pidonita Hmlakian arrived at the Pilothouse. "You want to take over the controls?" asked Nesla.

"No, you're doing fine. Trev just wants me up here in case you suddenly pass out from a stroke or something." she smiled and winked at Nesla. Strokes almost never happen to Creation Neanderthals who have their aging gene shut off. "You're not tired or anything?"

"No, I'm fine."

"Ship is yours. Trev wants us to go straight above the cable reel on the surface, at a distance of three *hekt kecht kepfats*, about how far we were on the other side."

"Yes, I know. It'll be another two hours or so. Why don't you take a nap? If I get tired, we'll need you rested."

"All right Maria, we are in position. Fire when ready!"

"It'll take about seven seconds for the signal to reach the bomb, another seven seconds for us to see the explosion." Anatoly translated it into English, Monoloa translated it into Atlantean. Then Maria pushed the button and began the countdown. *"Chetir na dzat, tri na dzat,"* We all took our positions as Maria counted down. *"chetirye, tri, dva, odin, nol."* Disappointment marked her tone of voice.

"Still no detonation. What's the bomb telling you?"

"Signal not understood. It is coded, so that only a Russian, one of us, can detonate it. But also it could be that when I started the timer, it shut down that circuit, so that even a coded transmission will not be received. I'll try again." She pushed the button a second time. "*Chetir na dzat, tri na dzat,*" we waited for the signal to cross the 1.2 million miles of space and then for the flash, if any, to travel that same distance back toward us. "*chetirye, tri, dva, odin, nol. Nyet.*"

"Not working." Anatoly sighed. He switched to English. "Metrola, how much of a magnetic field were you using when you carried the steel dart with the Shuttle?"

"Uh, enough for us to accelerate at five gees after we let go of the thing. Since there is no magnetic planet like Earth or Creation nearby, we rode on projected magnetic fields from this ship. The strength of the magnetic field, uh flux, around the steel dart was probably many teslas, I don't know the conversion ratios between our magnetic units and yours."

"But it was quite strong. Sometimes a piece of iron will become a magnet when exposed to a strong flux. This might be what happened here. It might be what's causing the mechanical timer in the bomb to stick. But then, just shaking the bomb might unstick it. Maybe we can hit the comet core with an Aries. What do you think, Morton?"

General Fairchild thought for a minute. "We could sink a B61 warhead into it and send shock waves through the whole thing. Might do more than loosen up the timer. Right now, we can send the Shuttle to the cable reel and Mikhail can pull the bomb up out of there to where we can inspect and maybe repair it. But if we hit it with a 100 kiloton explosion, then we might not be able to monitor the timer and know whether or not the big bomb was going to go off. We would have no choice but to try to move it or break it up with a bombardment of Aries missiles and the last Russian bomb delivered by Centaur rocket. The whole time we are doing this, the Russian bomb that is in there now can go off without warning."

"And destroy us because we're too close." concluded Anatoly Donovon.

General Fairchild switched to Russian. "Maria, can you disarm the bomb so that it can be approached safely?"

"I'll try that. Sending the signal now. We'll know in fourteen seconds whether it confirms disarming."

They waited. "*Nyet.* Bomb won't disarm. Sorry."

Anatoly and Morton told everyone else in English the situation. And we all stood around thinking about it. "I guess there's nothing to do but pull the bomb up out of there with the cable reel." I concluded.

"The clock is stuck at two hours and 48 minutes?" asked Metrola, who would pilot the Shuttle again.

"And 24 seconds. If it starts ticking again, we would have time to get away."

"But because the *Return* has to be close enough to provide the Shuttle with magnetic field, we might not be as far away as we would want when it runs down to zero."

"Two hours and 48 minutes to get outta there, get back into the Shuttle Bay, and then have Pido or Nesla take us all away. I don't like it. What if we're down at the cable reel fussing with it and the timer starts ticking again?"

"Then we'll just have to either schedule a light exhaust bath to get rid of cyanogen ice or risk taking it into the Shuttle Bay and cleaning it out there."

"I used to like almonds." Metrola wasn't liking this at all. "Tell the Kitchen if they roast any almonds, I'll scream!"

Captain Harsradich used her headset to give the order to the Kitchen. "Keep the almonds put away, just like last time. Possible cyanogen exposure with the Shuttle, we need to keep the air clear of almond smell."

The Science and Humanities Channel announced that they were receiving the transmission from the *Neanderthal Return* again. "The situation is as follows:" explained Ian Miller. "The 120 megaton Russian nuclear bomb did not detonate. It is still inside the comet core, hanging at the end of 1600 feet of wire rope. They cannot remote control the cable reel to bring it away from the steel dart. They think the steel dart is now a 133,000 pound magnet only a few feet away from the bomb. It could be interfering with the timer in the bomb, which is an old fashioned mechanical clock mechanism made with steel parts. A strong magnetic field could keep the escapement from working. The timer is stuck at 2 hours 48 minutes and 24 seconds. We'll switch over to Mary Ellen Martin in the Shuttle Bay."

"Thank you, Ian. As you can see, the Shuttle is ready for another launch, the Bay is clear of any cyanogen ice or gas from the last time the Shuttle traveled to the surface of the comet. I detect no almond smell here. There is one Russian bomb remaining in Bay Number Four, detached from the Centaur rocket and ready to be loaded on to the side of the Shuttle. If it is needed, the Shuttle will come back from the comet to pick it up from Bay Four. The Shuttle has on its side all of the mounting equipment for carrying the bomb, cable reel and other equipment as needed for this mission. It'll be piloted by Metrola Mornuxler as usual; she'll be carrying six passengers, the four Russians, Monoloa Mrvlakian, and Neil Peace. Here they come in their pressure suits and carrying their equipment, to board the Shuttle."

Angela was exasperated that I was exposing myself to danger again. "Neil, you idiot! You don't have to be a hero! If they need your advice as an engineer, you can give it from the mother ship!"

"Mom! Dad's not an idiot."

"Sorry, first rule of divorce: Don't bad mouth the other parent in front of the children."

"Yeah, if you do, we'll tell."

"Oh, you'll rat on me, huh? If he gets himself killed, you won't have to do that. It's not that big a comet, not like the other one. Why couldn't they just blast away at it with Aries missiles? Your father comes up with these crazy ideas, all the time."

"Yeah. Like when we were stuck in the desert, before the divorce." Virgil giggled. "Remember that, Mom?"

"Yeah, I remember. That damn Pontiac of his broke down in the middle of nowhere. Had to use old US10, one car every three days, not including ours. Couldn't stay on I-90, noooo, had to take 10."

"But he found the water, told us how to look for it."

"That water was full of bugs!"

"That's how we knew it wasn't poisonous. We could have drank it if we had to. It worked just fine in the radiator!"

"Yeah it did. Good thing that engine block didn't crack. But them machine shop guys say they almost never see a cracked Pontiac block, at least from the sixties. That's your father, muddles through everything. Never plans ahead, just makes it up as he goes along. Car breaks down, he just pops the hood and says all seven words plus a few more I didn't think of, don't you children say any of them. Gets the car going again, just like Metrola getting her flying saucer flying again in Algeria." Angela shook her head. We had our good times, but she found my 'don't worry, we'll always think of something' approach just a little hard to take.

"Now they're taking that same flying saucer to the comet. Hope they fixed it good!" The children thought this was all a lark, they didn't seem to realize that their father could get KILLED out there.

"Just hope that bomb don't detonate while they're playing with it."

Mikhail Dostoevsky, Maria Romanov, and Svetlana Lebed jumped down to the cable reel. Monoloa and myself, we remained on station by the Shuttle. Anatoly and Metrola were inside. I heard their Russian language chatter, which Monoloa cheerfully translated for me.

"Anatoly, what's the bomb timer at again?"

"2 hours 48 minutes and 24 seconds and holding."

"Like a countdown to a space launch. We hold at 2 hours, and"

"Cable reel is at 1645 feet, just like you left it, Mikhail." Svetlana checked the magnetic iron detector. "Bomb is 2.4 meters from the end of the steel dart. Let me check something," she punched a few buttons on the device, "just as we thought. The steel dart acquired some magnetism, it is a giant magnet. Flux at the bomb is 200 gauss."

"That would result in steel parts experiencing a few dynes of force." concluded Anatoly. "Might not be so much as to keep the timer from ticking for 21 hours, but it could cause it to stick. All right Mikhail, bring the bomb up slowly."

Mikhail unlocked the cable reel and gently pulled the lever. "Cable reel pulling in the line at two inches per *prelate*."

"Per *prelate*?"

"It's in Atlantean, I can at least read the numbers, it's two *tig-its* per *prelate*, according to this dial. The Base Ten cable length readout is scrolling at about that speed."

"Bomb is moving," announced Svetlana, "It is now 3.2 meters from the end of the steel dart, magnetic flux has dropped to 195 gauss."

After a few minutes of hearing cable length, proximity to steel dart, and flux callouts, Mikhail announced, "Cable length is now 1615 feet."

"Bomb is now twelve meters from steel dart, flux is to 100 gauss."

"The timer has restarted!" shouted Anatoly in Russian. Metrola repeated in English.

"Let's get outta here! Mikhail, stop and lock the cable reel!"

"Cable reel locked at 1613 feet!"

"Bomb is still rising, 13.1 meters from end of steel dart, flux 95 gauss!"

"There is some gravity on this iceball, the bomb will stop rising and fall back to the maximum length of the cable, it's not going very fast, two *tig-its* per *prelate* won't take it too far, get in here!"

The three Russians jumped up to where we were. "Hold it people!" shouted Monoloa. We each had brushes. "Let's get the comet ice off your feet. We don't want to poison the Shuttle cabin with cyanogen ice." We tried brushing the comet ice off the boot insulation coverings. We gave up and removed the boot coverings and tossed them. We didn't panic and work too fast, we still had 2 hours and 46 minutes.

"All right, Metrola, they're ready to cycle in."

"Two at a time, people." she ordered.

The two Russian women went in first. As air blew into the airlock, the cyanogen warning sounded. As hot air was blown into the airlock and then fanned through a scrubber, "Mikhail, let me work some more on your legs, I see a small chunk of comet ice, about a centimeter." Monoloa brushed Mikhail some more while I inspected the rest of his suit. This particular comet is loaded with cyanogen, as much as 10% of the ice is cyanogen. It hasn't visited the Inner Solar System enough times to get it boiled off.

The all clear sounded in the airlock, the women were allowed in. Metrola commented, "you don't smell like almonds. All right, who's next?"

"We'll send Mikhail in." Mikhail went in, this time the warning did not sound, we cleaned him off better. But the hot air was blown through the scrubbers just in case.

I tossed my brush, it had specks of comet ice in it. "Let's toss these brushes, Mono."

"Good idea." She threw her brush away.

As soon as we were in the airlock, we were not weightless. Metrola wasn't waiting. "We're on our way. No cyanogen warning. Pressurizing. Monoloa pulled the handle the rest of the way and we were at two dozen *dollons* per square *tig-it*. We went into the cabin and took our helmets off.

"Strap down you two." ordered Metrola.

As we flew up out of the coma toward the ship Anatoly let out a curse in Russian. "The bomb's timer slipped a cog! It is now at 2 hours 15 minutes!"

"If this happens again, we don't have 2 hours 15 minutes."

"That's right."

"We're going to two gees for a few *linits*." Announced Metrola as she accelerated us out of the coma. "Pido has taken over the Pilothouse. Nothing wrong with Nesla, she has done well. But for this, we put in Miss Number One Pilot."

"It slipped again, now it's at 2 hours 4 minutes and 35 seconds, 34 seconds."

"What the Spirit is happening Anatoly?"

"It seems to be slipping every few minutes, not on a regular basis, malfunctions are like that. In a mechanical escapement, the lever pulls back and allows the gear to rotate one tooth, the lever is then sprung back to catch the next tooth. It oscillates back and forth quite regularly, keeping good time as long as the mainspring can supply a steady force."

"But if the lever sticks open, the gears can spin."

"Allowing a lot of time to run off the clock all at once. I suspect the lever was stuck closed until we lifted it away from the 60,300 kilo steel magnet we created."

"Why is this lever sticking open?"

"I don't know, we didn't get a chance to take it apart and look at it. It could be anything, maybe a burr on the metal that didn't get machined off or a broken spring, or something that got bent out of shape. It slipped again, now one hour 55 minutes."

"Anatoly, is it possible that the escapement could slip all the way to zero at once?"

"We see a big flash, that's what happened."

"Best news I've heard all day. Pido! We haven't time, the bomb timer is slipping, now it's one hour and, how many minutes?"

"54 minutes, Met."

"54 minutes. It keeps slipping, so we don't know how long we have until it explodes! We have to come into the Shuttle Bay without bathing in the light exhaust!"

"Got that, Metrola. Helga, can you hear me?"

"I'm here at the Shuttle Bay controls, Pido. I heard. We're not going to pressurize the Bay until we are certain we don't have cyanogen ice on the hull of the Shuttle. We can launch the Shuttle again to bathe it if we detect cyanogen after all of this is all over. Shuttle, this is Helga Trvlakian, can you hear me?"

"I hear you, Helga." responded Metrola.

"We're not going to pressurize the Shuttle Bay when we recover you. I'm just going to lock you down and close the Bay door. Then Pido will run for our lives."

Captain Harsradich called up to the Pilothouse. "Pido, Nesla, I think we should order Strap Down."

"I think you are right. I think Nesla, Helga, and me, we can strap down on our chairs at our stations. The Shuttle Crew is strapped down inside the Shuttle and can ride out this storm in the Bay. If we can get them in there in time. Everyone else, including you, should strap down in the personnel pods."

"I agree. Helga,"

"I already have my ankles secured." confirmed Helga. "Pulling the torso and shoulder straps. My head and hands are free but they have to be."

"We're doing the same in the Pilothouse." assured Nesla.

"All right. Be careful, girls. *TIX JORD!* STRAP DOWN!" shouted Trviea.

Pidonita repeated the order in both Atlantean and English. As before, Captain Harsradich checked to make sure everyone was strapping down in the pods. But this time, she made sure she got herself in one.

"The bomb clock slipped again! We now have one hour 23 minutes."

"That's what I like about you, Anatoly, you're always so upbeat and cheerful." Met could not resist a little sarcasm.

"I don't feel so upbeat right now. All my life I designed doomsday machines that could bring about the end of the world. Now used to prevent the end of the world, my doomsday machine might bring an end to me."

"Annie boy, we're all destined to go on to the Next World. Great Holy Spirit, I apologize for my sins. Neil, I apologize for piloting this Shuttle when we kidnapped you."

"I've forgiven you for that a long time ago. Since then, it's been a pleasure flying with you."

"Thank you, Neil, you're sweet. Before we go to the Next World, let's say we get in the Shuttle Bay?"

"Metrola!" shouted Pidonita, "You better slow down, you're going to fly right past us!"

"Might not be a bad idea, get us away from the comet."

"But if we lose our projected magnetic field, you're in free fall, you cannot pull yourself back to us. You are dead when your air and electricity run out. You cannot get anywhere by pulling on the distant Sun's very thin magnetic field."

"I know, five gees the other way." she wheezed as we felt the incredible weight.

After another minute, "Metrola, you are now matching speeds with us, distance three *kepfats*."

"Yes, we are. Feels good to be out of the heavy gees. Closing to within two *kepfats*. Rock steady, Pido, rock steady, now two *kepfats*." We came closer. "One *kepfat*, Helga, you ready?"

"Ready, Met. Door's open, just come on in."

"We're coming! Three quarter *kepfat*. Half *kepfat*. Quarter *kepfat*, I can see the door to the Shuttle Bay open." We slowed down after getting within a quarter *kepfat*. "Shuttle flight computer linked with *Return* flight computer, keep it steady, Pido."

The Shuttle came into the Bay. "Steady, easy, looking good, Met."

"Thanks, Helga."

"Shuttle in the Bay. Shuttle coming to a rest. CAPTURED. Shuttle is locked, closing door. Almost closed. Closed, door is locked and secured, pressure seal is secured. Pido, let's get outta here!"

"On our way!" Pidonita brought the fusion reactor to maximum pulse frequency, accelerating us at one and a half gees.

Then Anatoly shouted in alarm. "The timer is slipping again! Fifty minutes, 45 minutes! It's just scrolling!"

"Emergency rapid acceleration in six *prelates*. Six, five, four,"

"It caught again, 35 minutes and 23 seconds, 22, 21,"

"ERA canceled. Anatoly, don't scare me like that!" Pido was not happy.

"Sorry, Pidonita. There it goes again!"

"Emergency rapid acceleration, right now!"

As Pido accelerated us at five gees, we heard complete silence, and saw,

FLASH!!!!!!

Chapter Forty Eight

"Emergency rapid acceleration mode working fine," announced Nesla's labored voice, "exhausting three *hekt dollons* per *prelate*."

"That's good to hear, Ness. We can keep this up for half an hour; we lose acceleration as the fusion core shrinks. Russian bomb yield, 126.2 megatons. Comet core is blasted in half, the two main parts are separating at about three *hekt potes* per *prelate*. Not going anywhere near Earth, no way!"

A Science and Humanities camera in the Pilothouse transmitted the image and words of Pidonita and Nesla to Earth through the static generated by the bomb explosion. In the White House the President and his advisors watched intently.

"Look at the actuators on their metal sleeves!"

"And on their helmets. They're getting power assist for operating under heavy gees."

"But how?" asked the President.

"Probably from pressure sensors next to the skin. Pidonita exerts muscle force inside that metal sleeve, pressure sensor sends the signal to a microprocessor of some sort, which controls the actuators to move the sleeve in the direction she wants her arm to go. Same thing on the helmet. That way they can move with speed while under heavy gees."

"Do we have anything like that for our fighter pilots?"

"We have defense contractors working on something like this for flight suits. The medical and wheelchair industry are way ahead on this sort of thing. Allowing handicapped persons to walk. Sensors placed near muscles that are still working can allow a crippled person to operate mechanical legs."

"The Creation girls adapted this technology to help a pilot work under heavy gees."

"Interesting. How are we coming on the translation of their Atlantean speech?"

"Nesla told Pido that the emergency acceleration mode is working, exhausting three gross *dollons* per Creation second. Pido said that they can do this for half an hour, their fusion core is shrinking."

"They're compressing the core to get more fusion with each pulse, more momentum to accelerate the ship. But the power increase is the square of the thrust increase. They're rocketing out, uh," he punched his calculator, "326 pounds per second of plasma at fusion temperatures."

"Providing some additional thrust but mainly to exhaust the heat, it's more than the plasma reflector can handle."

"They can do this for a half hour?" asked the President.

"Go through 587,000 pounds of their million pound core. Hopefully they won't need it that long to evade the debris from this explosion. Pido also said they blew the comet clean in half! Each half is flying away from the other at three times 144 Creation feet per their 'second', uh," punching his calculator, "613 Earth feet per second! Ten million miles at closest pass! Above and below the planetary plane!"

"Those are the main pieces, what about the smaller pieces?"

"Oh they're moving even faster, up to a hundred miles per second, what these two pilots are trying to get away from. This Second Wormwood will not hit Earth at all!"

They whooped and they shouted! "We did it! No, they did it! Thank God for Stalin, Khruschev, and their big megatonnage Cold War bombs! Doomsday machines preventing Doomsday!"

While they celebrated in the White House, they were not so happy in the Pilothouse. "Nesla, help me! The first wave of comet debris is coming!"

"It's the small stuff! What do Earthlings say? Don't sweat the small stuff!"

"This small stuff is coming at us at *kepfats* per *prelate*!"

"Particle coming in! Translate two five zero *deems* to avoid!"

"Two five zero *deems*, translating!"

"It missed us! Another particle! Zero four six *deems*!"

"Translating! Zero four six! Here comes a bunch of them!"

"Missed us! All right, Pido! Rotate nine dozen *deems*," 90 degrees, "and translate at one eleven zero as fast as we can!"

"Rotating, quarter circle! Translating, one eleven zero, they're getting close!"

THUMP! We all heard it. The sound waves passed through the locking mechanism into the Shuttle. But the lights didn't blink, we didn't feel any shock. Still heavy gees.

"Pido, Nesla?" inquired Captain Harsradich.

"We had an impact, Trviea." confirmed Pidonita. "Well away from the fusion reactor, magnetic coils not affected. Fusion core is shrinking. Four and a half gees, but still running."

"You strapped down, Trev?" asked Nesla.

"Yes!"

"Good. Here comes another particle! Rotate nine dozen *deems*, the other way, translate zero two six."

"Rotating! Translating, zero two six."

"Missed us. Still stuff coming, but well away from us."

"We're in good shape now. Going make to normal mode. Will recharge the core, need to add two *hekt gunds* of fresh plasma. Shell intact, boron and cadmium providing maximum protection. Acceleration down to one gee, normal mode."

"Keep strapped down, we may have to move sideways. We're a good distance, moving at a good speed."

A few minutes later the accelerometers read 6 feet per second squared. "End Strap Down. Now recharging with fresh plasma. Will take an hour."

"Are we still in danger?" asked Trviea.

"We're always in danger, it's space. *Tig-it* and *pote* sized stuff is boiling off to nothing before reaching us, the *treefat* and *chmfat* sized particles are blowing past us. Bigger stuff moves slower, we can track it, none of the big particles are coming at us." The pilots switched to English and spoke into the camera. "Earth, we destroyed the comet with your Russian bomb. And we get to live too." The television watchers cheered. The White House. Henry Turnipseed and Len Taylor, Angela Peace and my children.

People cheered their relief as they climbed out of the strap down stations. We were still in the Shuttle. "Helga?" Metrola called.

Helga Trvlakian undid her straps and helmet. "I don't think you have any comet ice on you, but we can let you back outside to bathe in the light exhaust. Then you can inspect the impact site and report on the damage. Nesla, Pido, may we open the Shuttle Bay door to let them out?"

"Sure, go ahead. We can project enough magnetic field as long as they don't get too far."

The door to space opened and Metrola pushed us out. "We have heaters in the Shuttle Bay to boil off any comet ice you brought in." informed Helga. "That should cut down the roasted almond smell."

"Thanks, Helga. We are now outside the ship, Pido, are you projecting magnetic fields?"

"Yes."

"Moving around to the back, oh my!"

We saw what was left of the comet. The coma was lit up by the heat of the blast. We could see the bright glowing portions of what had been the potato shaped core moving apart and fuming with intense jets of gas. The center where the bomb was seemed empty. "None of that is going to hit Earth." announced Anatoly Donovon. "Whooooweee!" he screamed.

We all cheered. Metrola cried. Tears streamed down her face. "We actually did it! Operation Rainbow is a complete success! I just wish Sorby was here to see it."

"Sorby is here to see it." asserted Anatoly Donovon. "I know she is. Along with Andrei Sakharov. Those Americans on the Manhattan Project who invented the plutonium core design that Klaus Fuchs stole for us. They all made this possible. Along with Tesla and Edison, Einstein, the Curies, Faraday, Newton, Joule and Watt, Gabby Fahrenheit, all the way back to Archimedes. And their Creation counterparts. Even Imhotep, the architect of the Pyramids."

"Speaking of Egyptians, shouldn't we give a big round of applause to Mustafa Khedr and his Egyptian Antiquities Organization? And to the *Zep Tepis* who left us their warning that informed us of this second comet?"

"Yes indeed! Mustafa, Chuck Carter, Sabar! Thank you! Well done! Well done!" Metrola flew us around the back side of the ship. "We can see where the particle hit us. I see a crater in the outer hull, six *potes* in diameter, two *hekt potes* from the fusion reactor cavity. No problem, we can fix it in Earth orbit."

"That's good to hear!" exulted a relieved and triumphant Captain Trviea Harsradich. "Get the comet ice boiled off, then come on in, we can have another party!"

"This time for real!"

"Let's hope so!"

"We're in position." announced Metrola. "Ladies and gentlemen, it's claustrophobia time!" She closed the shutters to the windows and we bathed in the light exhaust to boil off any possible cyanogen ice.

When we came back to the Shuttle Bay, Helga announced, "No cyanogen detected in the Bay. Come on in folks, join the party. Somebody brought me a beer. Rainier, twelve fluid ounces, 355 milliliter. I thought you passed a Weights and Measures law. How come you still have Metric equivalents on your bottles?"

"Force of habit." I told her. "They are starting to disappear from the labels of stuff sold in the United States. I hope you aren't drinking it yet, we're still coming in."

"Don't worry, we'll have you cycled in before I open it."

We landed in the Shuttle Bay and locked into place. Helga closed the door and blew air into the Shuttle Bay until it was at 24 *dollons* per square *tig-it*. "No cyanogen folks! Feel free to come on out!"

We climbed out of the Shuttle. Greeted as before by the top brass. "Neil Peace, well done! Perhaps June 5 will be a holiday!" General Fairchild gave me a strong military man to man handshake and handed me a beer.

"Thank you, General, you're welcome!"

"You can join my Air Force anytime!"

"It's MY Air Force too. I'm an American citizen and I pay taxes. But to join, I would have to be a civilian employee. Engineer. Make me an offer, I might think about it. Just don't hand half my paycheck to the Support Enforcement bitches."

"Hey, we feds are now enforcing the Peonage Law. Officially started June 1. The father's rights folks screamed that the law should have been enforced since it was first passed in 1867, they didn't wait, and neither did some of the grand juries. Tearing new assholes in a lot of state court judges and a few federal ones. All because our President needed YOUR cooperation in this Operation Rainbow."

"Hey, General, I love my children. Forget all the deadbeat dad hate speech spewed against us. I might push the Peonage Law a little to secure the President's help in getting those bullshit charges against Helga and Lucinda dropped. But no way am I gonna hold the entire Planet Earth hostage and take even the tiniest risk of not getting these girls' cooperation for Operation Rainbow."

The General chuckled. "Oh, NOW you tell us! I still think it's great. I swore an oath to protect and defend the Constitution against all enemies, foreign and domestic. And I see what the judges do with it, I wonder why I bother."

"Because you're American and you love our country same as I."

"Yeah, I do. I held a key in my hand, duty bound to turn it if the call ever came. All because I believed the readiness to turn that key was the one thing that guaranteed our survival. The Russians were motivated by the same thing. We can't let a bunch politicians and judges violating their oaths of office stop us from defending our land. Which we have done with Operation Rainbow and by making friends with these marvelous Neanderthal women. Neil, if you want a civilian job with the Air Force, I'll see if I can fix you up with a good challenging engineering assignment. As far as any support garnishments on the paycheck, or with you getting custody of your children, Hell, I have no idea how that will turn out."

"Thank you General. Let's say we get out of this Shuttle Bay, I want out of this pressure suit, get some good food, and maybe even a good woman of an exotic Race."

"I'll join you with everything but the woman part, I'm happily married. Let's go party!"

As we headed back toward First Wormwood, we met in Conference Room One. "Breakaway Particle Number 17," continued Sabar Duradich, "or Twelve and Five, about four *hekt potes* across, will pass closer to Earth than any other of the particles larger than three dozen *potes*. It might, possibly, uh, get within 100,000 miles of Earth as it passes. Same distance as the main mass. More likely Number 17 will pass at 150,000 miles, maybe 200,000 miles."

"Halfway to the Moon." General Fairchild was thinking. "We could still hit it with an Aries missile to eliminate any chance of it hitting Earth."

"And possibly send a fragment into the Earth's atmosphere. As long as it's small no problem. But if the fragment is larger than a few feet across,"

"Tunguska. Well, if Number 17 changes course, we could always send an SS-18 or a Peacekeeper with a single warhead to take care of it. Same as we could with new breakaways off the main mass that rise high enough to be captured by Earth's gravity, we should have enough warning from our radar surveillance."

"Looks like we have Wormwood pretty much under control." announced Captain Harsradich. "We have 18 Aries missiles, three Centaur rockets, and one Russian superbomb in our inventory. Now that we have completed Operation Rainbow, what are we to do with these, uh, assets?"

"I take it you Creation women don't want these nuclear weapons?"

"Uh, no. This is a scientific and diplomatic mission. We come in peace. We didn't want to reveal our existence to you, but having done so, we're not interested in any violence whatsoever. We simply don't need nuclear bombs on this ship if we don't have a comet or asteroid to deflect. Back in the Creation Solar System, we have plenty of nuclear bombs and laser cannons for our defense. Let's see, our Shuttle has a lift capacity of eight *gunds* for going down to Earth and coming back up. That's, uh, 7,250 pounds or 3,290 kilograms. We could take a B61-12 warhead, maybe two, down to Earth with each flight of it and return the warheads to American inventory."

"That would work. Our Space Shuttles can take about 30,000 pounds back down to Earth."

"Not 60,000 pounds?"

"Our Space Shuttles can LIFT 60,000 pounds to orbit, but coming back down, it's a different story. But we could haul up to ten B61's with each load back down to Edwards Air Force Base to repatriate these weapons. We're amazed that it turned out we didn't need so many for this mission."

"Don't worry about that, General, we had no way of knowing how many Aries missiles we would need. With two flights of the American Shuttles, we can repatriate the American bombs. How about the American rockets?"

"We have plenty of solid fuel boosters, old Minuteman missiles. We can make more. NASA has no shortage of sounding rockets. But for our space exploration, rockets ABOVE the atmosphere could be most useful. Perhaps we can park the American rockets next to the new International Space Station we're building."

"The Centaurs as well as the Aries boosters?"

"Sure. We'll think of a way to fuel the Centaurs if we find a use for them."

"That takes care of the American rockets. So Anatoly, what do we do with the one Russian bomb?"

"That's a good question, Trviea." responded Anatoly Donovon. "Whoa boy! We never made much use of *Buran*. Couldn't carry 20,000 kilos back to Kazakhstan with it anyway. I take it 44,000 pounds is a bit much for an American Shuttle?"

"Sure is." responded Fairchild. "Going down. Perhaps you could pull the old Halloween bomb core out of the Uranium Penetration Vehicle and we can take it down in separate loads?"

"If you don't mind spilling a bunch of lithium tritide. That Hydrogen Three is pretty hot. The uranium casing actually protects us from the radioactivity inside. I don't like the idea of taking it apart on this ship. It's certainly too big for our little Soyuz reentry vehicles. Without *Buran*, we Russians can't bring large masses down through the atmosphere to Earth. That's where the Americans got us beat. But not even the American Shuttle can bring twenty Metric tons to Earth. I'm sorry, Trviea, I don't know what to do with the bomb." Anatoly was stumped.

We sat around thinking. "Push the main mass one more time?" I suggested.

"From a 100,000 mile miss to a 150,000 mile miss. Wouldn't buy us much, Neil. Slightly reduce the possibility of a breakaway hitting Earth."

"Get rid of the bomb. And what's so wrong with a slight reduction in the probability of a Tunguska event or worse? And would it be so slight?"

"Well that possibility is slight to begin with. We can cut it in half, but half of very little is very little."

"Be some risk to this ship." pointed out Captain Harsradich. "We could just keep the bomb, even take it back to Creation if we cannot figure a way of getting back down to the ground in Russia. Why don't we leave it on the Moon until the Russians develop their space program to the point of being able to take it back home?"

"Because it then belongs to whomever can retrieve it. Not good. Everybody's now trying to duplicate that Shuttle of yours, because it's such a jump start to a space program. Without depending on big expensive rockets, a Libya or an Iran can go into space with a magnetic drive ship, even go to the Moon. Even a private terrorist organization. Your Shuttle is not a heavy lifter. But once the technology is figured out, we can build heavy lifters. Libya and Iran can build heavy lifters if they can build magnetic drive."

"Leaving it on the Moon or any such place unguarded, is out. We don't need to take it back to Creation, we have plenty of bombs there, though we have never seen the need to make them

120 megatons. We have already survived four 120 megaton explosions, we seemed to have worked out the procedure as we did with the second and third attacks on the main mass. Now Anatoly, you and your Crew check and double check your bomb timer. We don't want any more problems like we had with Second Wormwood. Let us plan for a final push of the main mass further away from Earth."

We returned to the neighborhood of First Wormwood after traveling for sixteen days. In Conference Room One, Sabar briefed us with the latest information of the 58 mile comet core. "It is now June 21, Earth time. The Wormwood main mass is now one *hekt* twelve and nine and 9/12 *beeyon kepfats*, 798.5 million miles or 1.285 billion kilometers from the Sun. In its present orbit, it'll pass Earth at a distance of 102,000 miles at closest approach, above the North Pole, on the lag side. Slight chance that a breakaway piece will come off the main mass and be captured by Earth gravity. We can reduce this chance further with another push by the last Russian bomb."

"Risk to the ship?"

"Same as the other two times we did it with the longer countdown, 14 minutes and 20 seconds. Anatoly, have you figured out why your 24 hour clock hung up while in Second Wormwood?"

Anatoly Donovon addressed the issue. "We used the 24 hour mechanical clock for the Second Wormwood bomb. For the First Wormwood shots, we used this 30 minute mechanical clock for Bombs Two and Three." He held up the clock to display it. "The first bomb, we used the very simple and reliable ten second clock."

"Reliable? I remember the ten second clock hanging up for a few seconds."

"I have no explanation for that. But both 30 minute clocks set for 14 minutes 20 seconds worked just fine. We performed some experiments with the assistance of Nesla Teslakian and Contrviea Tiknika on this 30 minute unit and on the 24 hour clock. These clocks are made of steel parts and we proved that their performance is affected by intense magnetic fields. They hung up in five of our tests, the escapement spun to zero in two others. That's what happened with the Second Wormwood bomb. We're convinced that the presence of the 60.3 Metric ton steel dart was what caused the problem. That steel picked up magnetism from the Shuttle and the projected fields from the main ship. We determined that intense magnetic fields were present near the bomb when we went down to the comet surface and operated the cable reel. Now with this shot to be delivered by the Centaur, there will be no such intense magnetic fields at any time during the 14 minute 20 second countdown. The *Return* will be backed off at a good distance, not projecting magnetic fields, the clock should work and the bomb explode, just like the other times." Anatoly's facial expression begged us to believe him, to have confidence in his engineering and analysis.

We sat around thinking. "The other alternative," General Fairchild finally said, "is to drop it into the Sun. Can't leave the bomb laying around somewhere intact, and can't bring it back down to Earth, it's too heavy. We can explode it, that's one way of safely disposing a surplus bomb. Might as well push the comet even further away from Earth, get some good out of the fifth Russian bomb. We can use up one of the Aries missiles, one less B61 bomb to worry about. Are you willing to risk the ship Trviea? We could just drop the bomb into Jupiter and explode it there. Jupiter's gravity and atmosphere will keep the effect of the explosion from reaching out to bite us as can happen in the lack of gravity."

"Shooting off a bomb in Jupiter's atmosphere seems such a waste. Not fair to any life forms that may exist in the Jovian clouds."

"Jupiter recovered from Shoemaker-Levy."

"That was a natural disaster, nothing we could do about it. We don't need to cause such a thing. If we use the bomb to push Wormwood, we risk the ship, but we get reduced risk to Earth in the tradeoff. As Captain, I'm willing to make the tradeoff if the other Creation women are willing."

"I think we'll make the tradeoff." confirmed Sabar. "So we need to look at targeting." She put the radar image of the main mass up on the screen. "It is spinning, 35 hours for each rotation. We haven't done anything to affect this basic rotation rate; our bombs have been hitting near the rotation pole. The problem is that the rotation pole slowly, very slowly, precesses around. Right now, the pole of rotation is almost parallel to the planetary plane. This main mass is in an orbit that passes over the Earth's Northern Hemisphere on the lag side." She moved two balls with her hands to illustrate the motion. "Earth's going this way, here comes the comet this way. We punch a hole with the Aries missile at this rotation pole, then plant the last Russian bomb, we'll move the comet's orbit even farther on the lag side of Earth when it passes."

"Lag side is good, because with Earth moving away, it's less likely to pull a breakaway into its atmosphere with its gravity. Uh, Sabar, how are we for obstacles to a missile flight?"

"Comet Wormwood has had a month to return to normal. The transient heat input from the bombs has exhausted out to space with the boiling gasses. Most of the heat it now experiences is from the Sun, the solar wind is beginning to have an effect on the coma, blowing the ions and gas molecules to the rear. Chunks of comet ice are now present around the core in the same manner they were when we came in for the first attack."

"Tricky. We'll need to have a second Aries on standby. The first one could easily blast a suborbital chunk and not punch a hole in the main mass."

"In so doing, it could clear the way for the second Aries and let it in."

Wlmsda Hotlund was healed from her injuries. She was on the original Aries Missile Launch Crew. "Welcome back, Wilma!" I cheerfully greeted her as we climbed into our pressure suits.

"Glad to be back. Still a little short of breath, a few mysterious aches and pains. But I'm feeling much better, have been able to exercise. Practice our martial arts. You know I'm a trained soldier?"

"Yeah, I know. Best bodyguard I could hope for. Let's go launch a rocket!"

Wilma did her job perfectly and we launched the Aries missile. Pidonita brought our fall into the comet to a halt and rotated us around so we can launch the Centaur, fully fueled and carrying the last Russian bomb. Nesla had a second Aries missile ready in the Missile Loader. We had the missile launcher open and ready to receive the second Aries missile. We were in free fall looking into the bright white foggy coma of the comet. We saw the tiny black sliver of the Aries missile suddenly light up.

In the Viewing Lounge, General Fairchild's crew directed the missile. "So far, so good, right on course. Missile guidance is following the path we mapped out."

"Missile radar is not reporting anything, closing in on comet core, range to target one five zero miles." We waited as the missile flew. "Range to target, one two zero miles. Radar detected yard sized mass, thought we mapped 'em all, that size and bigger. Guidance making course correction to avoid, avoidance successful."

"Aries returning to original course. Range to target, one zero zero miles. So far, so good." The missile flew without incident for a few minutes, range to target being called out every ten miles.

"Range to target three zero miles. More yard sized particles. It hit something! Something BIG!"

"Warhead separated from rocket, tumbling in free fall!"

"Goggles! Shields!" ordered Captain Harsradich in English, she repeated in Atlantean. We heard her in our headsets and pulled the flash shields down across our faces. We saw the white glow of the shredded solid fuel rocket burning in the distance. Then,

FLASH!

"Detonation one six miles short of the target! Fireball will slam into the side of the main mass!"

"Aries Missile Launch Crew," Trviea addressed us, "please load the second Aries missile."

"Already doing it, Trviea." declared Nesla. We loaded the missile, closed the upper guide rollers and locked it with the quick disconnect pins. "Missile locked and loaded!"

"Good, *jore put*!" warned Pidonita. "The bomb didn't explode inside the main mass like it should. Getting out of the way of some stuff flying at us! Love doing this with a fully loaded Centaur hanging out the door. How's the Centaur?"

"Centaur's fine! Just don't accelerate past the safe load point."

"I'm watching it! *Tix jord*! Strap down!"

People inside the air pocket of the ship ran to the strap down pods and strapped in. In the Viewing Lounge, with no missile in flight and the one B61 bomb having detonated, Trviea directed everyone and herself into the strap down pods. In Bay Number Four, we ran to the strap down stations and pulled the straps over our pressure suits. We watched the fully fueled Centaur hanging out the open door in the vacuum.

Sabar Duradich and Metrola Mornuxler were in the Pilothouse with Pidonita. "Here comes the particles from the bomb explosion! Translate three *kepfats* at one ten zero *deems*, they should miss us."

"Thanks, Sabar. Translating one ten zero *deems*. 144 *potes* per *prelate*." After two *linits* and 36 *prelates*, Pidonita halted the translation and continued forward acceleration at about one and a half gees. From my strap down station, I looked up nervously at the suspended Centaur with its load of liquid hydrogen and oxygen. I remembered that NASA decided after the *Challenger* explosion that it was not going to haul fueled Centaurs in the Space Shuttles. The Centaurs were lifted from Kazakhstan empty because we could fuel them here. Now those safety reasons haunted me.

Whoosh! "Comet particle flew past the Centaur!" a bunch of us screamed into our headsets, in English and Atlantean.

"Did it hit it?" screamed Trviea's frightened voice.

"No! I don't think so! It looked about six inches, fuming pretty good. Only saw it for a second!" I screamed this information.

"Thank you, Neil." responded the Captain. "Pilothouse! Did we get any impacts? We didn't hear any thumps."

"I don't think so." responded Metrola. "We seem to be riding out the storm. The yield of the American bomb is 96.3 kilotons. The fireball flew into the side of the comet and reflected off. Loose particles got accelerated out of the coma by the reflected fireball. They got heated up. Sabar,"

"Yes. Many of the loose particles were boiled into nothing. We maneuvered to avoid the ones we could see, in radar and visible light. Not easy with a nuclear explosion going on. Apparently a small particle, half a *pote* according to Neil, came pretty close but missed."

Then we heard Pidonita. "We are backing off the acceleration, to about six *potes* per *prelate* squared. Let's give that Centaur holding structure a break. If nothing else, the bomb cleared the path to the target site on the main mass surface. The surface is hot, seven *hekt deems*, or 530 Fahrenheit. It's cooling, we should be able to hit it with another B61 warhead. End of strap down, we'll head back to the Aries Missile launch point."

Pidonita gently brought us around. In the Viewing Lounge, Captain Harsradich and the American Missile and Russian Bomb Crews resumed their stations. "Sabar, targeting information, please." requested Trviea.

"Bringing radar image of the coma and core up on the screens now, you should see it there." In Bay Number Four, standing by our missiles, we listened and waited. Mary Ellen Martin filmed with her camera, we knew this was transmitted to Earth for television audiences. "Got the image up. All right, as you can see, the first Aries warhead cleared most of the particles out of the way, should be smooth sailing. The surface of the main mass in the target area has cooled to four *hekt deems*, or 320 Fahrenheit. Cool enough for your warhead, Morton, or do you want to wait a bit longer?"

General Fairchild answered instantly. "It's cool enough. As soon as we feed in the new flight path from your new radar data, we'll be ready to launch. Are you ready in Bay Four, Neil?"

"Yes, we're ready."

"How's the Centaur missile looking?"

Marla Syferkrip went over to the Centaur missile. It was still covered with our signatures and expressions of love for Sorby Mishlakian. "I can only inspect it visually, from inside a pressure suit helmet. I don't see any sign of leaking or structural damage. I don't think the weight of the bomb bent any of the rocket structure. Everything in the Centaur Fueling and Launch System looks undamaged."

Morton looked at the video pictures of the Centaur assembly from several different cameras. He could see the front of the missile with the Russian warhead. "Anatoly, what do you think?"

Anatoly Donovon looked at the video screen. "Maria, what is the bomb telling you?" he asked in Russian.

Maria Romanov responded in her language, "Everything is fine. We can start the 14 minute 20 second countdown, or I can command detonate. I can arm it, it will receive our codes. Diagnostics check out."

Anatoly switched back to English. "We think the bomb is fine, Morton. How does your rocket guidance look?"

Roy McKenna answered that question. "Guidance systems of both missiles are in fine shape, will receive our commands and codes."

"Then it's a go. Neil Peace, launch the Aries missile when Pido places us at the Launch Point and gives you the countdown."

After this rather eventful start, everything went according to plan. We launched the second Aries missile. Pidonita brought us back around to the Centaur Launch Point. General Fairchild's crew lit up the old Minuteman upper stage and it sent the warhead to a perfect bullseye within a few feet of the rotation pole. It detonated inside the comet ice and we didn't have to make another escape. We gently let go of the Centaur with the last Russian bomb and removed ourselves to a nice safe distance from which the American and Russian crews could send it on its 14 minute 20 second flight and countdown into the hole left by the Aries warhead. The old Soviet bomb let go with 120.4 megatons a little more than one mile inside the hole and pushed the main mass into a 150,000 mile miss of the Earth on the lag side of the North Pole.

After this we had two new breakaways, between 100 and 200 feet across, that were in orbits that will take them to within 20,000 miles of Earth. Each had a small, but real chance of hitting the Planet, and were big enough to explode with megatons upon entry into the atmosphere at 119,000 miles per hour. We dispatched them with Aries missiles. We used another Aries to push Breakaway Particle 17 further away from any collision course with Earth.

After backing away to a distance of about 600,000 miles from Comet Wormwood, Metrola and a crew of engineers went out in the Shuttle to inspect for damage. It was more extensive than we had thought. The fusion reactor was in no danger, thank God, but it was time to take our battered ship to Earth orbit.

Chapter Forty Nine

Cuc Nguyen asked Lucinda Renuxler and Helga Trvlakian how they were feeling. "I don't feel any different." each responded.

"You will soon." assured the Cro-Magnon physician. "Restarting the menstrual cycle will lead to some changes. The bleeding is the easy part to deal with. Water weight gain is a little more difficult, I notice it because I'm as skinny as a rail. It's the weird feelings that are the hardest to adjust to. All part of being a woman. Just like being a teenager again."

"It has been a long time. I remember menstrual cycles. All the pain and pleasure of being female. But if we want children, first we must produce eggs. How do you Cro-Magnon girls deal with it?"

Cuc smiled. "We just deal with it. Most of us. The PMS is overhyped. Yes, there's a little anxiety, and men joke about how it's the wrong time of the month when they run into a difficult woman. But difficult women are that way all month long. Their husbands wonder why it lasts all month, month after month. Shouldn't they get a break from it each month?" She giggled. "Pleasant, cheerful women just smile their way through it, even if they are uncomfortable for a few days. If they are married or have a boyfriend, they know it's unfair to punish him for something that's not his fault. So they don't. Guys have special health problems all their own, like prostate gland problems, that I thank God I never have to worry about for myself. And you know the neat thing about men?"

"What's the neat thing about men?"

"They never expect you to 'understand' when they have a man type health problem. They just deal with it. If you stay with him and see him through such a thing, he'll love you all the more for it. Most men are wonderful, if you just give them the chance."

"We know. Meeting them is the best part of this entire trip. We sure have a good bunch on board this ship. I love every one of them."

We left Comet Wormwood on June 21. Our average acceleration was six feet per second squared, slower than the ten feet per second squared on the first trip out. There was no hurry and we wanted to take it easy with the ship after the battering. It took us longer, with Earth orbiting away from us at 66,600 miles per hour. In June and July Earth is on the side of the Sun toward Sagittarius, and we were coming in from Leo. Earth saw our bright blue propulsion light in the evening sky after we turned around on July 1.

Like all true heroes, we were embarrassed by the attention. In a way, it was like fixing a car or building a dam. Just a lot of analyzing, planning, to make use of the available tools, and hard work, with a bit of danger. The comets did not bear us ill will, they were just inanimate objects that we had to deal with. Job well done, but a job nevertheless. At least it was for us.

And while we were happy to have successfully completed the mission, we still felt the grief for a happy soul who always enjoyed life.

Cuc, Mustafa, and Chuck spent their time teaching Sabar Arabic and Ancient Egyptian. She was also fascinated with ancient astronomy and astrology on Earth. Not that astrology is anything other than entertainment, but astrologers made observations. There was a time when astronomers prepared astrology charts for paying customers. Tycho Brahe, Kepler, and Galileo prepared such charts. The hostility many modern astronomers have for astrology is the product of funding. Kepler had bills to pay. If his patrons wanted an astrology chart, he prepared them an astrology chart.

We had a lot of fun and partying on the way.

We arrived at Earth on July 12.

"That is a great idea you had, Neil!" exclaimed Metrola as we climbed into pressure suits for the trip down to Moscow.

"Which idea is that, Met?"

"Having us deliver the Russians to a private reception with their families, before going over to the Olympic Stadium for the big celebration."

"Seemed logical to me. We come down to Star City. The place is closed to the public. The Russians know how to keep out paparazzi. Our four Heroes of the Commonwealth of Independent States may hug and kiss their spouses, children, and grandchildren without it being broadcast to the world. The Shuttle will be safe there as it was in Leninsk and Bangor. Sensors on the ship will immediately warn of any tampering or attempt to remove an inspection plate. I'm glad you replaced the fingerprint lock with an optical scanner device. Your prints could have been lifted off something you touched. Also, we'll deliver the six *gunds* or so of Russian equipment straight to Star City and allow them to meet their security concerns."

"Plus the stuff we delivered to *Mir*. Anatoly is sending the 3,000 pounds of equipment he deemed nonsensitive down on the American Shuttles along with the unused B61 warheads."

"To be delivered back to Russia by United Parcel Service! What is the world coming to?"

The Russians arrived in their pressure suits, carrying their bags of personal belongings for the trip to Star City, on the outskirts of Moscow. Captain Trviea Harsradich arrived in a pressure suit, she was invited down by the Russians. And finally, Monoloa Mrvlakian, so indispensable with her language skills. "Looks like everybody's here." announced Trviea, who verified by counting heads. "Shuttle check out, Metrola?"

"It checks out fine, Captain." affirmed Metrola Mornuxler.

"Good." Trviea spoke into her headset and announced to the ship's public address. "We're ready to take the Russian Bomb Crew down to Star City and Moscow. Helga Trvlakian will be temporary Captain in my absence. Our English language skills should facilitate the transfer of the unused American bombs to the American Shuttles. To the American Missile Crew and all of the other Americans: it has been a pleasure flying with you. If you choose to ride the American Shuttles down, then we'll see you soon on the ground in the United States. Helga, take care."

"Thank you Captain, will do." Helga also spoke through the public address. "All right everyone, we are going to launch the Shuttle, then we'll rendezvous with the Shuttle *Endeavour* for the first transfer."

We arrived at Star City and the Russians greeted their families out of view of cameras. We unloaded the Russian equipment and employees of the space center placed it in a truck. Anatoly Donovon broke away from his great grandchildren long enough to come back on the Shuttle to verify that every piece of Russian equipment was accounted for, none left on the Creation spaceship. President Korsakov and the other Presidents of the members of the Commonwealth of Independent States were there to greet us. They held back and allowed us to complete the unloading and allowed their heroes to hug and kiss their families.

Svetlana Lebed hugged her grown children and greeted a new granddaughter born since she left Kazakhstan with us for Operation Rainbow. Her ex-husband, who came with their grown children, stood back, as befitting a man who is no longer married to the nuclear engineer. But Svetlana would have none of that kind of protocol. She went over to him and gave him the kind of bone crusher hug the Neanderthal women are known for and a passionate kiss. We witnessed similar greetings with the families of the still married Mikhail Dostoevsky and Maria Romanov. Maria's husband is a dead ringer for Peter the Great. An actor, he played the Czar in documentary films. Mikhail's wife ran to him and it was twenty minutes before she let him go.

We were garlanded with flowers and handed large bouquets. We held our bouquets in our left hands to leave the right hands free for handshakes. We each had about three or four leis around our necks. Each of the Presidents shook hands with each of us, telling us welcome to Russia and thank you for a job well done.

President Korsakov greeted Trviea. "Captain Harsradich, it is an honor. Welcome to Planet Earth."

"Thank you, the honor's mine, President Korsakov. You may call me Trviea."

"And you may call me Boris. In a few minutes, we will take all of you to the stadium where we held the Moscow Olympics of 1980. There will be a huge crowd and we will give you the heroes' welcome you deserve. I understand that most of you think of this as a job, a task, probably not as difficult as tasks others have successfully performed. And you know that it was possible only because of all of the scientists and engineers and craftsmen who developed technology of all kinds on both of our Planets. You accomplished this with the efforts of thousands of people around the world who put this Operation together. Your ship was built by thousands, uh, *kechts*, of women back on Creation. You can justly feel embarrassed as we honor you for your accomplishments."

"If you allow me to make a speech to the crowd, I'll credit all of those people."

"I'm sure you will, Trviea. But Trviea, you prevented Doomsday. And if you look at our most ancient stories, myths, religious beliefs, it was a Doomsday we Earth humans have known was coming for over 12,000 years. So please forgive people for thinking of you as a goddess. Not a demon goddess, but an Angel From Heaven. Angels From Heaven who came in our hour of need. May I ask you a personal, delicate question?"

"It's about my daughter, Sorby Mishlakian? Sure, go ahead, I will not be offended."

"Everywhere on Earth, people have been signing condolence books, burning candles, and sending flowers, all in the memory of your brave and wonderfully happy daughter."

"I know, the people who handle our affairs on Earth received thousands of bouquets of flowers. They tell me it's like when Princess Diana died."

"It's a lot like that. You have my sincere condolences."

"Thank you."

"Our program for the ceremonies today include a Moment Of Silence in honor of your daughter. If you do not wish this to happen, then we'll not do it."

"No, uh, go ahead, do it. A Moment Of Silence, that will be fine. I understand that, uh, that, uh, such ceremonies are not for the, uh, dead, but, uh, for the living. To allow them to grieve and to honor, to remember, to, uh, work through their feelings. It has been very hard for me, as you can understand. But I will not deny the people of Earth that." A few tears flowed from her eyes, but she kept her composure. "I thank you for whatever comfort and love you can offer me."

"You are welcome. We will have the Moment of Silence. If you wish, you may inter Sorby in the Kremlin Wall. You may lay her to rest in any cemetery in Russia. But we will not be offended in any way if you choose a cemetery in another country."

"Thank you, Boris. You are very kind. A funeral! We could take Sorby back to Creation and bury her there. Her body is extremely well preserved in our morgue. But it is not our way to keep our loved ones that way. The worst thing about the Virus, we had to abandon our traditions. We cremated our men in huge piles. In an effort to kill an infection we could not understand, we could not comprehend. Sorby will have a proper Atlantean funeral. We have to select her final resting place, that's all."

"We offer whatever assistance in that you require. Come Trviea, it is time to ride our Zil limousines to the Olympic Stadium."

"Thank you, let's go."

Metrola locked up the empty Shuttle and we rode the limousines to Olympic Stadium.

A few days later, Trviea Harsradich and several Creation women were in a NASA hanger at Cape Canaveral. NASA engineers and high ranking NASA officials were there discussing the helmet that Sorby wore when she died. "Such a tiny hole." observed Brian Winthrop, commander of Space Shuttles.

"Yes." confirmed Contrviea Tiknika. "Something, a piece of debris from the explosion, hit the helmet hard, back here. This hard material cracked, but the inner layers of soft fluid plastic resin should have kept the hole covered. But it apparently was too thin or brittle. Probably gouged out by something. It held for several *linits*, then gave way. The air rushed out and Sorby lost all of her air and oxygen."

"Pressure fell to zero before your Shuttle could get to her and that was that." The meeting had gone on for over an hour, as the space agency made sure it understood everything that could be understood about the accident.

Trviea looked apparently calm. Looking around, she saw some tools hanging from a rack. Wrenches, screwdrivers, vice grips, bolt cutters, that sort of thing. One of the tools was a sledgehammer with a three foot handle. "May I have the helmet, please?" Trviea firmly grasped her daughter's helmet. She took it out to the middle of the concrete floor and set it down. She walked forcefully over to the tool rack, selected the sledgehammer and returned to the helmet.

With a loud grunt, she swung the sledgehammer as hard as she could down on the helmet. She swung it three more times, each time with a loud scream. Each time, she hit one of the larger pieces of the helmet. The pieces were strewn over the floor. The fragments of glass held together by the resin core, much like a car's windshield that has been smashed.

Crying, Trviea placed the heavy steel end of the hammer on the floor and let go of the handle, letting it fall to the floor away from her. She sobbed uncontrollably, completely broken down. The other Creation women rushed to comfort her.

The NASA people stood around. Uncomfortable. Not knowing what to do. Helga Trvlakian spoke with them quietly. "Please sweep up the remains of the helmet. Do not put it in the silo with the *Challenger* remains. It is garbage. Dispose of it as you dispose garbage. Mix it in with the rest of the garbage. Let not one fragment of this helmet be a souvenir to be kept and sold for collections, to be displayed in museums. Let it vanish from existence."

Later, janitors swept up the helmet fragments and disposed them in the garbage. No amount of money could bribe them into violating Helga's instruction.

The Funeral Director was alone with Askelion Lamakian. They spoke quietly. "As a mortician, there are some delicate things I need to know."

"The condition of the body?"

"Yes. The condition of the body."

"Sorby was exposed to hard vacuum. Many of her small blood vessels burst. There was bleeding out of her eyes and nose. It was the bleeding in her lungs that made it impossible to revive her. Most of the air sacs burst and blood filled them. Cuc Nguyen tried mouth to mouth but there was no way. Nor could we get the heart beating again. All we could do was wipe her face clean and comb her hair. Pardon me. I know I should be tough as a physician. But I'm not accustomed to losing patients. And Sorby was more than a patient."

"It's all right."

They waited a few seconds while Askelion took a deep breath. "We carried her to the morgue. On our ship it's a high tech device. After the body is placed in the unit and closed away, we bathe the body with intense radiation, the type you call X-rays or gamma rays. Every bacteria, virus, and other such parasite is killed. Then the body is flash frozen. She can be preserved this way for as long as she remains in the morgue. When we can bring her down to a planet surface for burial, we let her thaw. She should stay fresh for the several days we can let her lie in state. It is our tradition that we lay the deceased on a platform, three by seven feet. We surround her with fresh flowers, people may view the body. There are handles for the pallbearers, white ropes to allow the pallbearers to gently lower her into the grave. We place the dirt right on top of her, there is no lid like you have with a coffin. Then, in her time, at her pace, she will become one with the surrounding earth."

"Thank you, Askelion. I know this is hard for you, you have my condolences."

Wlmsda Hotlund stood at attention, a soldier in full battle dress. Combat boots, lightweight body armor made from a material similar to Kevlar. Upon her helmet was a circle of flowers. In her right hand was the barrel of an Atlantis Five Zero Rifle. The butt of the weapon stood on the ground, the shiny titanium bayonet as high as her head. With a clip of 36 rounds, each bullet 5/12 of a *tig-it* in diameter, it could be set to single shot, semi-automatic, and full automatic operation. No one will say whether the rounds in her clip were blanks or for real.

Everyone understood the ceremonial purpose of her standing guard at the feet of the body of Sorby Mishlakian. Sorby was in the shirt and pants she wore under her pressure suit. She was a spacewoman, a spacewoman she will always be. Her eyes were closed, her face beautiful and serene, hair combed, she laid in perfect rest, surrounded by flowers. Trviea Harsradich performed her traditional parental duty of watching over her child on her Final Kepfat. She sat in a chair next to the head of her daughter. A circle of flowers adorned Trviea's hair. She wore a long white dress, tied at the waist with a blood red belt.

The police set up a metal detection station. People passed through, when declared free of weapons, they were allowed in to view the body. Many carried bouquets of flowers, which they laid at the base of the table upon which Sorby's platform sat. The flowers piled high. They offered their condolences to Trviea, who graciously accepted them.

"We are live, outside the chapel in which Sorby Mishlakian lies in state, awaiting the funeral scheduled for noon tomorrow. With me is Rhonda, who just a few minutes ago viewed the body. Rhonda, please tell us what it was like in there."

"After coming through the metal detector, we went into the chapel room. There were three condolence books available for us to sign. I wrote a simple thank you to the Creation women for introducing themselves to us, for sharing with us some of their language, history and culture, for deflecting the comets from their collision course with Earth, and for the brief time we had to know Sorby. There were signatures, poems, and many such thank you notes. Then I went over to the table. Flowers were stacked four feet high, I didn't bring any, but that was certainly all right. Sorby is a beautiful woman, she looked like she could wake up anytime. Her mother looked extremely tired. Trviea sat in her chair, her eyes would close. She quietly mumbled 'Thank you.' to each and every one of us. I saw the tall blond woman, Helga Trvlakian I believe she was, come up to Trviea. Helga leaned down close to Trviea and spoke quietly in their language. Trviea said something and Helga walked off. A moment later, Helga returned with a sandwich and a cup of water, which Trviea ate. A little self-consciously perhaps, with all of us there, but she had to stay by her daughter's side."

"How did Helga look?"

"Helga wore the same kind of white dress, long, down to her ankles, tied at the waist with the same kind of red belt. She had a circle of flowers in her hair as they all do. They look beautiful in those dresses. They really do. Wlmsda, I don't know, in full battle dress holding that huge rifle! The other one, they call her Betty, is also dressed like a soldier and carrying a huge rifle with a shiny bayonet. Each hour, the one off duty comes in to relieve the one on duty. They each have the circle of flowers on her helmet. I understand the ceremonial purpose of the fully armed soldier standing watch over the deceased, but it was a little intimidating to see her hold that rifle. But as long as everyone was quiet and well behaved, there were no problems."

"Thank you, Rhonda."

It was the next morning, we were in the reception room getting ready for the funeral. Leonard Taylor and Henry Turnipseed looked elegant in their dark suits and ties. I was dressed the same, waiting for Angela to arrive with our children. The Creation women were all wearing long white dresses tied at the waist with red belts. A circle of flowers adorned each head. Lucinda found a way to fix a circle of flowers to her head. Each woman took the time to tell me and the other people how much she appreciated us for coming. Cuc Nguyen, Mary Ellen Martin, and Svetlana Lebed elected to wear long white dresses tied at the waist with red belts and circles of flowers in their hair. The other Cro-Magnon women who rode with us on Operation Rainbow wore black, as befitting Earth custom. The four Americans who formed the Missile Crew were in full dress uniforms, proudly representing the United States Air Force. Anatoly Donovon and Mikhail Dostoevsky wore dark suits with ties.

Outside the church a long line of men and women in military dress uniforms stood at attention. They were from all of the branches of the American armed forces and from over 90 nations around the world. Each man and each woman held a rifle and twenty one blanks.

Finally, Angela arrived. She and Christa were dressed in black, Virgil wore a dark suit and tie. They were on their best behavior. But when they saw me, they ran. "Daddy!" I received Christa in my left arm and Virgil in my right arm. I hugged them and lifted them up in the air.

"You both are a lot bigger than the last time!"

"The last time was only a few months ago, in Port Townsend."

"I know, but you seem heavier." I let them down.

Angela came forward. "I know we're divorced, but if Svetlana and her ex can,"

"Sure, why not?" We held each other for what seemed like the longest time. I let her kiss me.

"This doesn't mean we're getting back together."

"No, of course not. Angie, you look great."

"Lost ten pounds, working out. I'm no Neanderthal, but I have a little more muscle."

"I noticed that. What have you been doing with yourself lately?"

"Working at Boeing, they're teaching me CATIA."

"Great! I'm glad to hear that. Any love life?" I was teasing her.

"Been going out with Len." Len grimaced, he wasn't sure he wanted me to know.

"Glad to hear that. Hate to see either of you lonely. Len, how's my car?"

"Car's fine. It's in the barn, out of the rain, haven't been driving it much, just once a week for a few miles, like you said."

"That's good, Len. You realize the whole reason I went on Operation Rainbow was to keep my car from being ruined." We managed some chuckles. "You've got my car, my wife, say, have you been taking care of my children too?"

"Noooo, no, no. They are welcome to visit, but I don't 'take care' of them."

Angie whispered in my ear. "Neil, we need to talk, in private, with the children."

"Sure, let's go outside, away from the crowd."

We went outside in the warm morning sunshine of late July and Angela expressed her concern. "I'm not sure the children are ready to attend a funeral."

"It will be emotional." I admitted. "Christa, Virgil, if you don't want to attend the funeral, you don't have to."

"Sorby gave her life repairing the ship so you could come back home." said Virgil, speaking with a wisdom beyond his years. "She helped make sure you could complete the mission and come home. I guess we can attend her funeral. Can we, Christa?"

"Sure, we can do that." Christa did not look so sure.

"Well," I said, "if you attend the service, you will have to be on your best behavior. Can't fidget all over the place. It will be very sad, there will be crying. The women will give speeches and prayers in Atlantean language. So you will not know what they are saying, but you will feel it. Are you sure you want to do this?"

"Yes, we're sure. We'll behave." They both said it.

The time came. We went into the church. We were seated right behind the Creation women, a sea of white dresses and flowers in front of us. Next to my family, Len and Henry sat. Lucinda stopped for a moment with Henry. They kissed, and she went up to the podium. The overtly Christian symbols of the church, the crosses and the images of Jesus, were tastefully covered up. Lucinda stood at the podium, where the preacher normally addresses the congregation. On the altar in front of her was laid Sorby on her platform, surrounded by flowers. On each side of Sorby stood Wilma and Betty, in their military battle uniforms, holding their rifles. Trviea was seated directly behind her daughter. Candles burned. The Creation women occupied the front several rows. The Cro-Magnons who have been aboard the *Neanderthal Return* and their families and friends were seated with us in the next few rows behind them. Mohammed and Labna Abbas and their children were there, I don't know how the Algerians made it, but I was glad to see them. The rest of the church was taken up by dignitaries, NASA astronauts and Russian cosmonauts, high ranking officials in the world's space agencies and the nuclear weapons agencies of Russia and the United States. Presidents and Prime Ministers from around the world were there.

A television camera was set up to show the podium and Sorby to the viewing audience.

Lucinda Renuxler began in English. "People of the Planet Earth, women of the Planet Creation. Welcome. We are gathered here, to bid farewell to a wonderful person, whom we love very dearly. The people of Earth sympathize with us in our loss, and we appreciate this sympathy. To the people of Earth, Sorby Mishlakian is a brave hero who gave her life so that we all shall live. To the people of Earth, Sorby is the tragic victim of an accident, a malfunction. Such has been happening ever since humans of either Planet have endeavored to explore their surroundings and achieve discovery and technology."

Lucinda paused. "To us, Sorby is a hero, and a victim, but she is much, much more. It is hard to explain to Earthlings, but I'll do my best. Anybody who has gotten to know us Neanderthals from Creation, will have noticed that there is a streak of melancholy in our souls. This melancholy is from the time when a terrible disease took our men from us. And while we love life and enjoy it as much as possible, we sing songs, we tell stories, we hunt and fish, we fly in airplanes and in space, the emotional scars from that terrible time are still there. But Sorby was born after the last man died. She was his daughter, as were her many sisters. The daughters of Demoan Mishlakian are special to us. We knew them as babies and little girls. We raised them. And we delighted in their love of life, and happiness of spirit. They are truly a wonderful gift from the Great Holy Spirit, whom you Earthlings may refer to as Allah or as God. Having been born after the end of our holocaust, they lack the melancholy that we suffer. They are Innocent of the Grief. For this we love them, the way we love our children."

Lucinda went on. "Sorby delighted in the freshness of the air after a rainstorm. In the feel of the wind and the sound it made through the trees. The crashing of waves upon the beach. She loved the exertion of athletic competition and the thrill of riding a galloping horse. She loved the roar of an engine. She loved to figure out what was wrong with something and out how to fix it. She loved to tell jokes, to dance, and to sing songs. She loved the feel of the ocean salt spray in her face. She loved to fish and she loved to hunt. She loved to work in a machine shop. The smell of fresh cut wood, the aroma of burning iron. And," pause, "she loved space flight. She loved to dance in the vacuum, surrounded by the stars, laid out like a glittering carpet of jewels, teasing her from beyond her reach. The song that she sang, was the song we used to sing to her when she was a little girl, all those many years ago. It was a song about all of these things."

Lucinda paused for a moment. Then she and all of the Creation women sang that song in Atlantean. It was a happy song, for all of their grief, Sorby lay in front of them, they wanted to make her happy, one last time. I don't believe they finished the song. They all broke down and cried openly. We all did. The two soldiers from Atlantis placed their rifles on the floor so they could grieve.

After a few minutes, we regained our composure and wiped the tears from our faces. Lucinda came down from the podium and took her seat with the other women. Metrola Mornuxler went up to the podium in her place. "Thank you, Lchnsda Renuxler. People of the Planet Earth, people of the Planet Creation, my name is Metrola Mornuxler. For the last 148 Earth years, I was what you might call an agnostic, an atheist. I could not believe that the Great Holy Spirit could allow a Virus, a little strand of DNA, only doing what it needed to do to survive, to take from us all of our men. My father, my brothers, my sister's husband and their little boy, and my fiancé. Men whom I loved dearly. Either I did not believe that the Great Holy Spirit existed, or that I could not forgive Him."

She paused to let that sink in. "But since then, in fact only recently, I have come to realize that He is there, that He loves me as He loves every human being, and that He has given me and all other human beings some profound gifts. First He gave us dedicated woman physicians who made some marvelous medical discoveries. If a Cro-Magnon version of the Virus should appear on Earth, we know exactly how to fight it and we can prevent the kind of holocaust that happened to us. We can map a section of the Virus' DNA. Find a sequence that is typical of this species of virus, and not found in any other. Then we make a kind of enzyme that will match up with this viral DNA sequence, and TEAR it apart! But the enzyme has no effect on any other DNA sequence. So it does not damage our own human DNA, in our mitochondria or our cell nucleus. And it does not affect other species of virus. The reason we are so healthy is that we kill every type of virus that plague our bodies. Perhaps we could whip up an enzyme that matches up with a typical DNA sequence of your HIV, the AIDS virus. The Great Holy Spirit, He gave us this. He gave us the Mishlakian girls, including Sorby. He gave us the women who developed all manner of modern technology, so we can hear radio and television signals from Earth. He gave us the medical treatment by which we have extended our lives. Sorby herself lived twice as long as most of our ancestors before the Virus. He gave us each other, He gave us our natural resources, and He gave us Earth and all of the people who live on Earth. He gave us the Galaxy, there for us to explore. He gave us the brains we needed to figure all of these things out. And He gave me, Metrola Mornuxler, abilities that until this past year, I did not know I had."

Metrola paused and took a deep breath. "I learned something with these comets that I have never before realized. Yes, the Great Holy Spirit put these comets on a collision course with Earth, just as He left the Virus to infect our men on Creation. But Anatoly Donovon pointed something out while we were on our Shuttle viewing the destruction of the Second Wormwood comet." She looked at Anatoly, seated two rows behind us, "Thank you, Anatoly. The Great Holy Spirit gave us Imhotep, who built the Pyramids of Egypt. He gave us Archimedes, Gabriel Fahrenheit, Johannes Kepler, Sir Isaac Newton, James Joule and James Watt, Benjamin Franklin, Albert Einstein, Marie Curie and her husband Pierre, and all of the engineers, scientists, inventors, crackpots, dreamers, charlatans, magicians, witches and warlocks, people who stood around trying to figure out how to build something or do something, on both of our Planets, the people who made our modern technology possible. I looked at the destroyed comet, I realized that not only did the Great Holy Spirit give us disasters, He gave us the means to deal with them. Yes, He gave us uranium and lithium and hydrogen, out of which we can make nuclear bombs, which happened to be, in this instance, the thing we needed to get the job done. But far more important, He gave us each a brain. He gave us our intelligence, our love, and our love of life, which Sorby had so much of. Thank you, Sorby Mishlakian, and thank you, Great Holy Spirit, for giving us Sorby. Please take good care of her until such time comes when we join her."

Metrola came down from the podium and took her seat.

Helga Trvlakian went to the podium. "I will now give our traditional prayers and lead the singing of hymns in our Atlantean language." For the next half hour the women said prayers in Atlantean language, including the traditional Prayer for the Dead. The hymns were sad and moving, but also powerful and full of hope.

And then the service in the church was over. The women of Creation stood up and took their positions. Eight pallbearers took up position around Sorby's platform, four on each side. They lifted the platform and placed the wooden handles on their shoulders. Trviea watched carefully. The pallbearers walked Sorby away from the altar and paused when they were out in the open floor. Trviea followed and took her position immediately behind her daughter. The other Creation women lined up in twos before and aft, about the same number before as aft. Trviea formed her own rank, two women immediately behind her. Wlmsda Hotlund took her rifle and walked to the front of the procession. Bchsda Bentlakian with her rifle went to the rear.

Quietly, with only the sound of their footsteps, the procession walked toward the door. As Betty passed our row, we stood up, filed out of the pew and took our position in the procession. Row by row, the people took their position in the procession and followed us out the door into the sunshine. The procession walked slowly in front of the rank of soldiers from around the world. We halted before the dress uniforms. Wilma and Betty left the procession and stood with the rank of soldiers, in the middle of the line. They each removed the clip from her rifle, and replaced it with a clip that contained 21 blanks. When they were ready, an officer gave them the command. Every soldier lifted his or her rifle, pointed it straight out, aiming for the sky, and fired. A single volley. They repeated this 20 more times, for a 21 gun salute. Our ears rang when they were done.

Wilma and Betty replaced the empty clips from their rifles with the original clips. They resumed their places in the procession. We walked slowly to the cemetery. The cameras did not follow us. Wilma led us to the open grave and walked around it. The two files of women split and walked around each side of the grave. The pallbearers centered Sorby over the grave and halted. Trviea stood in position at her daughter's feet. The women behind her went to one side of the grave, we went to the other side. They began singing in Atlantean.

As the sad and beautiful melody of breaking female voices wafted into the air, each pallbearer lifted the handle off her shoulders. She found the coil of white rope tied to the handle.

She tossed the coil behind her shoulders. Then she grasped the rope, suspending the platform from the ropes. Hand over hand, they slowly lowered the platform toward the grave.

Up in the Pilothouse of the *Neanderthal Return*, Pidonita Hmlakian wore a long white dress tied at the waist with a red belt. She had a circle of flowers in her hair. She was the only person on board the ship. Tears flowing from her eyes, she sang the same song. She operated the controls.

A bright blue light suddenly shown in the sky. It streaked across the sky toward us, as it passed the zenith, as Sorby passed the level of the ground, one of the women released a single white dove. The blue light streaked toward the north, seeming to disappear in the distance. When the platform reached the bottom of the grave, Sorby having traveled her final fathom, each pall bearer held the end of her white rope in front of her at arm's length over the grave, and released it. The pallbearers backed away from the grave.

Then one by one, each pallbearer removed the circle of flowers from her head. She approached the edge, held her flowers at arm's length, and dropped them into the grave. Then one by one, each of the other Creation women approached the grave, removed the flowers from her head, held them out at arm's length, and dropped them into the grave. Then Betty removed the clip from her rifle. She set the rifle down in front of her by the edge of the grave. She removed the flowers from her helmet, held them out at arm's length, and dropped them into the grave. After Betty replaced the clip in her rifle and resumed her position standing at attention, Wilma did the same.

Finally, Trviea stood at the side of the grave. She quietly removed the flowers from her hair, held them out at arm's length, and dropped them on to her daughter.

One by one, in her turn, each woman took a shovel and deposited dirt upon their dearly departed. When the last woman, Trviea, had done so, she handed the shovel to the gravedigger and allowed him to complete the task. A large and beautiful monument of stone, with inscriptions in Russian, English, and Atlantean, was ready to be put in place to mark the final resting place of Sorby Mishlakian.

In the three languages it read: "She dances in the sky, surrounded by the stars, a vast glittering carpet of jewels, no longer beyond her reach."

I was proud of my children, they behaved well.

We filed out of the cemetery.

Chapter Fifty

"Askelion Lamakian and Meddi Chumkun are renting a former abortion clinic in Kent, Washington. Behind heavy security, a fence like Fort Knox and a guarded gate, they perform research aimed at getting either Lucinda Renuxler or Helga Trvlakian pregnant with a boy whose Y chromosome comes from a Cro-Magnon, but the other 45 come from his Neanderthal mothers. Lucinda spends her evenings with her boyfriend, Henry Turnipseed. The rest of the women visit nations around Earth on goodwill tours, but most of their time is spent on the inspection, maintenance, and repair of their ship, the *Neanderthal Return*. Contrviea Tiknika, in charge of this effort, estimates that it will be at least one Earth year before they're ready to use their top secret 'Warp Drive' to return to Creation."

"How's it going, Askelion?"

"Still haven't successfully separated the twelve and ten non Y chromosomes from one of these tiny sperm cells." She exhaled a long breath.

"We haven't had any human sperms to work with for nine dozen Creation years. There's bound to be differences between human sperm and the chimpanzee and bonobo sperms we practiced with on Creation."

"I know. But we successfully created a bonobo boy with only the Y chromosome from his father, the rest of the chromosomes transplanted from a bonobo egg to the sperm. That sperm hit the other bonobo egg and we had a bonobo boy. Perfectly normal looking bonobo last time I saw him."

"Yes, he was healthy. But bonobos are not humans. And we weren't successful when we used the chimpanzee sperm and bonobo eggs, or when we used a bonobo sperm and chimpanzee eggs."

"Will we have the same problem with Cro-Magnon sperm and Neanderthal eggs?"

"I don't know. We seem to be similar. Only real difference other than shape of skull and jaw is muscle build. We are very similar in behavior. But many Cro-Magnons note how 'man-like' we are in taking charge of ourselves and going out to do 'guy stuff'."

"Let the Cro-Magnon women live without men for nine dozen years. They too would adopt a similar behavior pattern, taking care of themselves. They do that already. They just don't have the swagger and confidence we can project with our physical strength. Except the woman body-builders."

"The Cro-Magnon woman body-builders work extremely hard and take steroid hormones to achieve their muscle build. That much testosterone is bound to affect their personalities." They giggled.

"A few Cro-Magnon women naturally have a lot of muscle, and build it further with a strenuous lifestyle, there is variation in all species. Cro-Magnon women often seem content to let their men 'protect' them, while we were willing to protect ourselves. Other than that, not much difference, more cultural than anything else."

"But with bonobos and chimpanzees,"

"Bonobos! The original party animals! Straight, gay, they're happy either way! It is a complete surprise that Africa and Graciana aren't crawling with *beeyons* of bonobos the way they carry on!"

"Bonobos have a liberal attitude toward sex. In their eyes chimpanzees must strike them as a bunch of uptight prudes! Party poopers!"

"Bonobos walk on their hind legs more than chimpanzees."

"To show off their privates and willingness to get it on. That and they think they're lucies."

"I wonder if we should tell the Earthlings about the lucies of Planet Jayndye?"

"Ahhh, let 'em find out for themselves. Lchnsda is trying to get them to commit to recognizing our sovereignty over ALL of the planets, moons, asteroids and comets in orbit around BOTH of our Suns, like the American President suggested. Let them find out about a planet terraformed with Earth life forms orbiting our Second Sun, that might blow the whole Sovereignty Treaty works."

"A planet with a living population of lucies. I wonder how many planets terraformed with Earth life forms there are in this part of the Galaxy?"

"Don't know. Face Mountain aliens. Once they figured out how to do it, maybe they couldn't resist the urge to do it again and again. Playing God can be intoxicating like that."

"Yeah. They may have made the Virus as a safety valve; we had full sized brains when they transplanted us. The lucies are like chimpanzees or bonobos who happen to walk fully upright on their hind legs like we do. No need for a booby trap for them, they're still animals. They just look like humans, which is the weird thing about them. But us? Cro-Magnons and Neanderthals working together? What a scary thought!"

"There might be a terraformed planet with *Homo erectus* or *Homo ergaster* living on it. Could evolve full sized brains, happened twice before."

"With us and again with the Cro-Magnons. Sovereignty Treaty. We have a dangerous legal situation here. On Creation, all of our nations agree to claim joint sovereignty over our oceans and the planets, moons, and other objects within our Solar System. But the Earth nations claim a strip of ocean three nautical miles wide along their coasts and declare the rest of their ocean the 'high seas'. They also consider beyond the sovereignty of any nation their continent of Antarctica and their Moon and all of the heavenly bodies in their sky."

"Right, so the Face Mountain aliens can come into this Solar System and build facilities on the side of the Moon facing Earth and technically, they would not be violating Earth sovereignty. They could claim the Moon and say they could because Earth did not. They could similarly land on Antarctica and drop ships into the Earth ocean and legally, there would be nothing the American Navy or other navies could do about it until such aliens made war against a land mass."

"By then, it would be too late. Lchnsda needs to convince them to at least claim joint sovereignty over the part of their own Planet that is beyond their national sovereignty and over the moons and planets of their Solar System. If the Face Mountain people come back, we don't want them securing the resources of this Solar System for possible use against US."

"Maybe we'll have to teach the Earthlings how to build laser cannons."

"What do we do when the Earthlings find out about the lucies on Jayndye?"

"They might say something like, 'We'll let you have sovereignty over Creation, but with our population problems, why not let Jayndye be open for Cro-Magnon settlement?'"

"But Jayndye is for the lucies! We don't colonize it, we only have a few scientists there to study the lucies."

"Easy position for us to take, we can't have children. We can barely occupy Creation. What about Cro-Magnon immigration to Creation?"

"Men only would be quite acceptable. Satisfy our natural sex drive. Bring Cro-Magnon women along with the men, and we have the potential for children. We can see ourselves like the Native Hawaiians, a minority in our own land. That would be a hard sell back home. Another reason why this experiment is so vital. We have to be able to bear Neanderthal boys, even with Cro-Magnon Y chromosomes. Then we can feel safer with a limited number of Cro-Magnon women coming with their men."

"How about a true hybrid? Can we make a baby with a Cro-Magnon man?"

"Lchnsda is trying to get herself pregnant by Henry."

"An experiment she performs with great enthusiasm!" They giggled. "But if they have a child and prove that we are the same species, what then? Taking a Neanderthal boy back to Creation with only a single Cro-Magnon chromosome, the Y chromosome, that is one thing. But if the child has twelve and eleven Cro-Magnon chromosomes, his father has a powerful claim on him under OUR law as well as Earth law. As it should be."

"Take Henry home with us. As handsome as he is, he would be very popular. Drive Lchnsda nuts with jealousy."

"You think she is that attached to him? That she wouldn't share him with other women?"

"Before the Virus Holocaust, we had a strong taboo against adultery. Stronger than the Earth taboo. The Earthlings honor their Adultery Commandment in the breach. We could leave Lchnsda on Earth to marry Henry and raise their children together, if they are able to have any."

The telephone rang. "Helga, this is Askelion! We have a success! We removed every chromosome from the sperm cell except the Y."

"Whose sperm is it?"

"Neil's. We placed the twelve and ten chromosomes from Lchnsda's egg into the sperm. The sperm revived and healed. We sent it after your egg. The embryo now has four cells, the cells continue to split."

Silence for a moment. "Are you certain there is no damage to the chromosomes?"

"There is no damage to the chromosomes. The bonobo boy was perfectly healthy. Still was when we left the Creation Solar System."

"This is not a bonobo."

"I know. The embryo is developing normally, he needs your womb."

Lucinda put the tiny microphone to her mouth. "Lchnsda here."

"Lchnsda!" exclaimed Askelion. "Where are you?"

"I'm at a Chinese restaurant with Henry."

"Oh. We have successfully produced an embryo. Can you please come help us put it in Helga's womb?"

"Sure, I can come, it'll take us about three or four hours, maybe longer, to get there."

"From Port Townsend or Port Angeles?"

"No. Vancouver, British Columbia."

"What are you doing in Canada?"

"Eating kung pao beef with chop sticks. And drinking lots of water! Hooooowee! It's almost as bad as Cajun black catfish."

"How did you get across the border?"

"I will let Henry explain. You will have to switch to English." She handed the Atlantean communicator over to Henry.

"Hi, Askelion, it's Henry." He recognized Askelion's voice.

"Hi, Henry. So how did you get a Neanderthal into Canada?"

"You girls have a kind of visa or passport issued by whatever nation you visit when you come down. Lchnsda has an American passport specifying her as a citizen of Atlantis allowed to travel and reside within the United States until its expiration date."

"Yes, we all have that. I didn't know we could get into Canada with it."

"Well, apparently you can. We drove up I-5 to Blaine and across the border. There's no stopping on the American side when you go north. We were past the Peace Arch and across the line when we waited our turn at this toll booth like thing they have across the road. The border patrol woman asked the usual questions and I told her my name, I am American, and I live in Jefferson County, Washington. We intend to visit Vancouver this afternoon and evening and then return to the States. That would have been fine until she asked Lucinda the questions. 'Lucinda Renuxler' didn't faze her, there are lots of strange names in the world. Like Turnipseed. But when she told her that she was an Atlantean with a U.S. passport,"

"I take it that got her."

"The Canadian woman takes a good look past me and there's Lucinda smiling and holding out her passport. I pass her the passport and she's stammering. 'Neanderthal from Creation. Well, yes! I'm sure there's no reason you can't visit Canada. Canada wants nothing but peace and friendship with the nations of Creation. I'm surprised you haven't been invited up here for functions and parties and speeches and such. Why don't you park over there to clear the gate while I make a few phone calls.' So we park where they have you park to search your car for weapons and drugs and she's about three minutes on a phone. Finally she comes back and the passport's stamped. 'Enjoy your visit to Canada.' she says."

"So why a Chinese restaurant in Canada? There are plenty of such restaurants in Seattle, Tacoma, and the suburbs."

"Well, it's a little different up here. In Seattle, you go into a Chinese restaurant, a knife and fork is provided along with the chop sticks. Menu's in English, no Chinese characters. Half the people in the place are white. You know what I mean. I'm an Indian but folks don't know I'm Native American unless I tell 'em I'm Native American. But one thing I'm not, I'm not Asian. Anyway, your friend Don Colburn recommended this place in this neighborhood where Kingsway comes into 12th and Main and Broadway and such. It's just like he said. We're the only non-Chinese in the place and we're too macho to ask for a knife and fork."

"How do they treat you there?"

"So far, very nice. The other patrons are too busy enjoying the food and each other's company to pay us any mind. But for some reason Canadian whites don't go into these places. Except Don. When he goes into one of these places, he and his date are the only white people there. Same thing with Neil and Len. The waiter always seems to know they're Americans. Anyway, I'm accustomed to being the only Native American in the place, there are so few of us!" Henry chuckled.

"We don't want to rush you, enjoy your dinner. But when you are done, we'd appreciate it if you drive straight to Kent. Our little boy is becoming quite a collection of cells and he'll soon be looking for a place to implant. We have Helga's womb in the premenstrual state, we'll soon need your help."

"Sure, we're almost done, we'll be on our way in a few minutes."

After they left the restaurant and returned to their car, Henry drove around a few blocks trying to find his way out of there. "No friggin' left turns around here! Makes as much sense as putting kilometers on the road signs! Ahhh, forget 99."

"We could try 99A."

"Kingsway. Sure, if you don't mind stop lights every few blocks for miles and miles. A big long strip like Aurora Avenue. Ah, here we go. We'll ride 12th out to where it joins the TransCanada. That's a freeway. 80, 90, 100 klick per hour speed limits. Speed limit changes every few miles. It's got a neat bridge over the Fraser River."

"What's this Grandview business?"

"Oh, 12th jogs and hooks and becomes Grandview. But it pretty much goes straight east to the on ramp to the freeway."

"Straight east. TransCanada Highway. How do we get back to the States?"

"Take the Cloverdale Exit. The sign says that it goes to the U.S. border. Takes us straight to Blaine, there's a second border crossing 3/4 mile east of Peace Park. Top off the tank in Blaine, even with the exchange rate, the British Columbia price per liter translates into a higher per gallon price than in the State of Washington. Actually, that's not true anymore since the Canadian dollar fell so much in the exchange rate. Then it's on to I-5 and away we go."

They drove on to the TransCanada and Henry set the speedometer needle between 50 and 60 mph. "You weren't kidding when you said this is a neat bridge! 'Maximum 80 km/hr' That's fifty, right?"

"I'm watching my speed. Don't worry. You're an astronaut! Trillions of miles of space. And a little old bridge bothers you?"

"There's little gravity in space. There's plenty of gravity here. I'd say it's a couple *hekt potes* down to the water!"

"200 feet probably. Navigable waterway. That's how high a bridge must be built to not have a drawbridge. No worse than Tacoma Narrows or the Aurora Avenue Bridge. But I admit that those bridges don't have this long climb and curve. Is it just me or do these lanes seem narrower than American freeways? Probably some number of meters, not enough of 'em. A few more miles to the exit for the American border!"

They left the freeway for the 12 mile ride down Route 15 to Blaine. "96th Avenue. 88the Avenue. 80th."

"Yeah, every eight in the numbers is a mile. We're that many furlongs north of the border. This land was laid out before all these kilometers got put on the road signs. Zero Avenue is the street right on the border. If you live on Zero Avenue, you can look across the street to a playfield that's part of the American side of Peace Park. Your kids can go to the United States to play on the swing set as long as they're back in Canada in time for dinner!" Henry chuckled.

They arrived at the American border post. "You're Henry Turnipseed. Pleased to meet you. Is Lucinda Renuxler in there with you?"

"Yes, how'd you know?"

"Our Canadian friends called us on the ol' telephone and told us about you." He stamped Lucinda's passport and handed it back to her. "Have a nice evening."

They spent their remaining Canadian dollars at a Blaine gas station and then headed south on I-5. "Miles! Gallons! Cheaper gasoline! 70 mile per hour speed limit! It's great to be back in the good ol' USA!"

"Oh poor baby! Nowhere on this Planet are there any Base Twelve numerals. I'm used to *kepfats*! To me, three zero means three dozen, thirty six! Three dozen *kepfats* per hour, that's about our speed."

"Actually, with this higher speed limit, 70 translates into three dozen and seven *kepfats* per hour."

"You can perform that calculation but get all bent out of shape over a few kilometers in a nation that speaks English and the people don't really Think Metric? You want a culture shock? Try coming to Creation with us. At least we use feet and inches, sorta. But everything else is quite a bit different."

"The biggest difference is the few *beeyons* of women who haven't seen a man in nine dozen Creation years." Henry entertained his date with an exaggerated look of lust. "Okay, Lucinda,

I'll come to Creation with you. I might have to eat an awful lot of fresh vegetables to stay alive, but,"

"But what?" Lucinda grinned. "I'll be telling them all, 'He's with ME! Hands off! Do not touch!' Remember Henry, you Cro-Magnons joke about people biting your head off, but we Neanderthals can DO it!"

They laughed their way down the freeway.

Captain Trviea Harsradich stepped out of the Shuttle in clothing designed for extremely cold temperatures. She glanced up at her home star in the clear Antarctic sky. Several of her companions stepped out of the Shuttle and walked with her across the thin layer of snow on top of the ice. The building is hidden in a little valley formed by steep mountainous ridges of rock sticking up through the ice. No lights shined outside the facility.

General Morton Fairchild greeted them at the door of the heavily insulated concrete building. "Howdy, girls. As you can see, no one will be able to find this building unless they know exactly where to look."

"It didn't show up in infrared. Your McMurdo Sound and the Russian Vostok stations show up like sore thumbs in infrared." The Creation women are adept at American idioms. "Do you leave this building unheated?"

"That's part of the preservation as well as the security. Notice the special snow roof we built over the structure. The three feet of snow further masks this facility from both infrared and from visual observation by airplane or satellite. But today, we have had the heater on. It's 40 degrees Fahrenheit inside. Warm enough for our purposes."

"A lot warmer than out here." She spoke through the scarf across her face. "Why couldn't we do this during the Southern Summer?"

"Security. People would see your Shuttle come down and wonder why you come to Antarctica. To HERE! Draw unwanted people to this site. During the Southern Winter, everyone in Antarctica pretty much stays indoors. Except for the NASA U-2 surveying the ozone hole, they don't spend a lot of time scanning the sky, even when it's clear like this. They're not looking for magnetic drive flying saucers. We don't have military style radar because the Antarctic Treaties prohibit military weapons here and nobody has any reason to invade or attack the place."

"YOU'RE here. You are military, this facility,"

"Is different. This is Top Secret."

"Do the other nations know?"

"The scientists don't know, they'd blab it to the world. And be indignant and self righteous about it. But the top people with the Russians, Argentines, British, Norwegians, New Zealanders and such know about this facility and what's in it. This is not a violation of the Antarctic Treaties because they secretly okay it."

Trviea sighed through her scarf. "Why don't you just disclose this place and what's in it to the public? They know about US! They know we were transplanted by the true aliens who carved Face Mountain."

"That's because you flashed your damn blue light in Morse Code!"

Trviea laughed. "We did that because Neil Peace was pissed off at the Gray Aliens and us for all this sneaking around. So he told us to be very public about our presence. You had an alien spaceship in your sky, that chose to communicate in some of your languages, and there was no denying it."

"Trviea, you kept your presence secret while you ascertained the situation on Earth. Surely you understand the need to keep some things secret. Like your ship's 'warp drive'."

468

"You've got some smart engineers on this Planet. Neil Peace, for one. We wonder how long it'll stay secret. What's secret maybe the fact that you've already figured it out! Your American people can understand some secrecy. Technical details of some of your weapon systems because you don't want to be wide open to attack, or if you are, you don't want it known. If you're caught in a war, I can see why details of your deployment and your battle plans should be classified. It's not our concern, at least officially, but you have a big problem between the American government and the American people. They think you keep way too many things secret, things they have a right to know! They don't like being lied to, they don't like the ridiculous denial games, and they don't trust you. I don't blame them. We trusted you because we HAD to. Earth is our ancestral home Planet too. But sometimes you, by that I mean your government, you make it difficult to trust you. My advice, it is advice only, fully disclose this to the public as you will now disclose it to me."

"Trviea, I understand where you're coming from. As a starship captain, you have the need and the right to know about this Roswell Wreck. But we've been telling everyone this is a weather balloon since 1947! Whoever thought up that ridiculous parachute test dummy story exhibited the IQ of room temperature in Celsius. Damn!"

He focused his eyes into the optical scanner and thereby unlocked the door. He led them into the relatively warm 40 degrees. Metrola Mornuxler removed her scarf and pulled back her parka hood. She inspected all around the wreckage. "I see the controls to a magnetic drive unit, like our Shuttle. Where's the cyclotron?"

"We couldn't find it. It's like it was jettisoned. Might have fallen into the Gulf of Mexico."

"That's possible. This metal is shredded as if the cyclotron was blown out. Have you tried to date this aluminum? Determine when it was last molten, when it was rolled, formed, and machined?"

"It's alien aluminum, the isotope mix doesn't match up with Earth aluminum. We've never been able to date it."

"This didn't cross the distance between the stars by itself. Have you ever found any evidence of the mother ship?"

"Other than Face Mountain, no."

"Could've been in orbit around this Solar System for *beeyons* of years. Doesn't look like Face Mountain technology. We know some things about Face Mountain weights and measures. Have you tried to analyze this dimensionally to determine the units of length it was designed in?"

"We have. We have several proposed systems of measure that would fit it. Like the Stonehenge 'yard' derived from careful measurements of the monument. It was easier to do this with the Egyptian Pyramids and the Greek Temples, they were built to tighter tolerances and have lots of nice straight lines. You probably looked down on American land patterns and determined the mile as our unit of land measure, subdivided into furlongs. But it's a tricky thing to do if you don't know anything about the system of measure a thing was built in."

While he spoke, Metrola opened her little satchel and removed a ruler. General Fairchild saw that it was not marked in inches, *tig-its,* or centimeters. "This ruler is marked in what we think the Face Mountain units of measure were. Their number system was either Base Eight or Base Sixteen, we don't know which. Might've been both. Have you any of the fasteners from this craft?"

"This drawer over here. In these plastic bags are fasteners that actually came from the craft. In this other drawer, are replicas we made in a machine shop, to a tolerance of a ten thousandth of an inch. They were the first things we analyzed. All left handed threads, not right handed like we use. Not British Whitworth, not American style National Fine or National Course. Not pipe threads of any known pipe thread series. Not any of the Metric thread series that we know about. These threads don't line up with either inches or Metric units. Nor do they line up with any known pre-Metric units of measure. That's when we concluded that either an Earth shop went to the expense of not using readily available standard fasteners, or we are dealing with an alien ship."

Metrola held a replica bolt to her alien ruler. "This doesn't line up with these units either. Let me check the other replicas. Hmm. Have you made four or five inch long round bars cut with these threads continuously?"

"Yes. We did. Here."

Metrola checked all of the replica fasteners against her ruler. Then she checked some of the actual fasteners. "Probably not Face Mountain technology. Another mystery. We'll need to take samples of this ship so we can analyze it ourselves. We want to make sure that this isn't one of your 'dog and pony shows'."

Morton laughed. "Damn expensive dog and pony show. Everybody thinks this ship's at Area 51! This isn't an Earth created artifact. The isotope mixes of the aluminum, titanium, iron, and copper are all wrong for this probe to come from Earth ores. As far as the computer that drove this ship? It seems the silicon was melted by a self destruct device. AFTER the crash! Age? Anywhere from a thousand to a billion years. Beyond that, there isn't anything more I can tell you. We didn't develop any of our late Twentieth Century technology by analyzing this ship. Go ahead, take samples. You may take some replica fasteners, please leave the originals, we can make more replicas."

I held Helga's hand. Angela held her other hand. She was on her back on the table. Askelion, Meddi, Lucinda, and Dr. Osterman, an obstetrician and gynecologist, were busy on the other side of the shroud that obscured our view of Helga below the waist. Henry sat in a chair behind us. We all watched the inside of Helga's womb lit up on the video screen. It has been a few hours.

"Our little boy is not in a hurry."

"Give him time." counseled Dr. Osterman. "I've done this very thing before, with frozen embryos. How are you doing Helga?"

"I'm doing fine. Back's a little sore, legs' cold, been here an awful long time now. I would like you to get that thing out of my,"

We chuckled. "Yes, I know." responded the American physician in his best bedside manner voice. "But we need to see the little guy implant. You're a brave lass, keep it up a little longer."

"I know. But I much prefer the other way of getting pregnant. Don't you, Angie?"

Angela smiled and blushed. "It has a lot to recommend it. That wasn't the problem with our marriage."

"Now wait a minute, you said,"

"We were both angry. I was just saying that to hurt you. But it wasn't true. I'm sorry, Neil."

"Apology accepted." We had more important things to worry about. "Let's not get into a big fight in front of Helga when she's doing this."

"Ah, come on," pleaded Helga, "I don't mind a little entertainment." She grinned.

"Well, you're just gonna have to be disappointed." admonished Angie. "Look! I think Hmlee's found a spot he likes!"

"That's an excellent spot for a child to implant." assured Dr. Osterman.

"Yes, it is." agreed Meddi Chumkun.

"His name is Hmlee?"

"Hmlee Peace Renuxler Trvlakian." announced Helga. We watched the screen as Hmlee slowly buried himself in the lush tissues of the uterine wall. "Hmlee, for my brother. Peace for his father who contributed the sperm and the Y chromosome. Renuxler for the woman from whose egg a whole bunch of other chromosomes came. And for her husband, Chmlee, he was a good man, I remember him. You know what Lchnsda's maiden name is? Henry?"

"Pitsney." answered Henry. "She was Lchnsda Pitsney."

"I like the sound of Renuxler better." admitted Lucinda.

"And Trvlakian because now that you guys have done the easy part, I get to do the hard work for the next nine months."

After another half hour, the physicians studied close up shots of Hmlee very carefully. "He's implanted. Helga, you are officially pregnant."

We clapped our hands and cheered. "Now that I'm officially pregnant, will you PLEASE get that camera thing out of me and give Hmlee some privacy!" Askelion complied with her request.

Grinning, Helga leaped off the table and stood tall on the floor, not caring who was seeing her underalls. Henry looked away. Angie tossed her a pair of clean panties and she stepped into them and pulled them up. After getting her skirt on she gave us hugs all around. "It's safe now, Henry. I'm decent, you may turn around. Thanks, Henry. For being here."

"I didn't do anything."

"Just what we needed! You brought Lchnsda safely here, thanks for being a good autopilot."

"Autopilot?"

"You pilot the automobile, that makes you an autopilot!" We laughed at her deliberate fracturing of the English language while Helga gave Henry a big hug.

Then the Atlantean women stood in a circle holding hands. They asked us to join in, and while we held hands they said a prayer in Atlantean thanking the Great Holy Spirit for the wonderful gift of Hmlee Peace Renuxler Trvlakian.

Chapter Fifty One

The Avengers of Yahweh were finally brought to trial. Judge Meredith denied a defense motion for a change of venue. The jury selection was over in a week and Assistant United States Attorney Shirley Barton began presenting her case for the prosecution.

Jefferson County Deputy Sheriff Mike Carlson and other police and military officers described what they found at the scene of the wrecked Secret Service car. The prosecution entered into evidence the horrifying photographs of the carnage taken at the scene. After the crime scene was secured, the FBI forensic scientists came in and collected evidence for the lab. This was entered into evidence. They withstood cross examination as to their evidence gathering and chain of custody procedures. Coroners testified and the autopsies were entered into evidence.

Deputy Carlson testified about finding two defendants, Jack Plotkin and Frank Binford, handcuffed to the tree, the injuries he observed in them and the statements they made. These statements were entered into evidence over the objections of Stanley Babcock, the lawyer representing these two defendants. Carlson was thoroughly cross examined by Babcock. Paramedics and physicians described the defendants' injuries. X-ray photographs and hospital records were entered into evidence.

Len Taylor and Henry Turnipseed each gave their testimony. Their rifles and the bullets test fired from them were entered into evidence. None of the bullets recovered from the bodies of the Secret Service agents came from their rifles.

Helga and Lucinda waited their turn looking around the elegant United States Courthouse built into what was once Tacoma's Union Station. An assistant prosecutor found Helga and brought her down the hallway. Lucinda wished her good luck. Helga went into the courtroom.

"Miss Trvlakian," called the Judge, "please come forward and approach the bench." Helga walked up the center aisle of the crowded courtroom, the pews filled with families of the Secret Service agents and the press.

Some of the widows said "Thank you, Helga, God Bless you." as she passed them.

As she walked between the lawyer's tables, Shirley Barton helped her find the spot. The jury watched her with poker faces, the defendants showed no emotion. The Judge instructed her to "Please state your name for the record."

"Helga Trvlakian."

"Miss Trvlakian, are you a citizen of Atlantis, a nation on the Planet Creation in the Alpha Centauri System?"

"Yes, I am, your Honor."

"Are you a member of the crew of the ship known as the *Neanderthal Return*?"

"Yes, I am, your Honor."

"First of all, I want to thank you for introducing yourselves to us, letting we who live on Planet Earth know of your existence, and for all of your efforts at establishing a peaceful relationship between our two Planets. And I thank you for your participation in Operation Rainbow and for preventing a disaster beyond imagination. It has been established by the District Court for the District of Columbia that Neanderthal people from Planet Creation are persons for all purposes under the law. I find that there is no reason for this court to find differently. Therefore you are competent to give testimony in this case. However, there is the Agreement Between the United States of America and the *Neanderthal Return*. Under this

Agreement, you are immune from subpoena by any court in this nation. That means you cannot be ordered or compelled to appear and testify. Are you here on your own free will?"

"Yes, I am, your Honor. There is nothing in the Agreement that prohibits me from voluntarily appearing as a witness in a court case."

"Indeed there is not. But for your testimony to be admissible as evidence, you have to voluntarily waive your diplomatic immunity as to the crime of perjury during the time you give testimony. Perjury is the crime of knowingly making a false statement as to material fact while under oath. That means you knew the statement to be false, when you made it, while under oath. The court does not have any reason to believe that you would deliberately lie while giving testimony, but you must be legally liable for perjury prosecution when you give such testimony for it to be admitted. Perjury in a federal court is a felony punishable by up to five years in prison and a fine of up to $250,000. Do you, Helga Trvlakian, voluntarily waive your diplomatic immunity under the Agreement to prosecution for perjury, for testimony you give in this trial, the waiver limited to testimony you give in this trial, and do you promise to be available for both prosecution and defense to give testimony for the duration of this trial?"

"Yes, your Honor. I voluntarily waive my diplomatic immunity under the Agreement Between the United States and the *Neanderthal Return* to prosecution for perjury, for testimony I give in this trial, the waiver limited to testimony I give in this trial. I promise to make myself available for both prosecution and defense to give testimony for the duration of this trial. Uh, your Honor, I respectfully request that I be allowed to swear an oath in Atlantean language that the testimony that I shall give in this trial be under penalty of perjury under Atlantean law, and that I promise to be responsible to the Great Holy Spirit for my testimony. Hrtinlsa Pliklakian was not a witness to the events relevant to this trial, she was in the Garden Room tending to our food plants. She is present in this courtroom, in the front row."

"Yes, I was informed of this by Ms. Barton. Does the defense object?"

"No, your Honor, we have no objection."

"Miss Pliklakian, please step forward and administer the oath under your nation's law."

Hrtinsla came forward and stood facing Helga in front of the bench. She turned briefly toward the Judge. "Thank you, your Honor."

Then she faced Helga and they grasped all four hands while Hrtinsla spoke in Atlantean. "Helga Trvlakian, do you swear that the testimony you give in this trial be the truth to the best of your knowledge, and will you be responsible to the Great Holy Spirit for this testimony?"

"I swear." Helga declared in Atlantean.

The two women let go of each other's hands and turned toward Judge Meredith. "She is now sworn under our laws, your Honor." announced Hrtinsla.

"Thank you, Miss Pliklakian, you may return to your seat. Now Miss Trvlakian, for United States law, do you swear to tell the truth, the whole truth, and nothing but the truth?"

"I swear."

"Please have a seat in the witness' stand."

Shirley Barton gently walked Helga through the limousine trip from Port Townsend to the roadblock set up by the highway construction worker. Then, "Miss Trvlakian, did the highway construction worker give a name to the Secret Service agent driving the car?"

"Yes, he did."

"What was the name?"

"I am not sure I heard the last name correctly, but the first name was definitely 'Allen'. The last name was either 'Case' or 'Pace', it rhymes with that."

"Did you get a good look at this construction worker?"

"Yes, I did. I was seated on the left side of the back seat of the limousine, he came over to the driver to speak with him. We were there for about fifteen minutes when the driver tried to verify the roadblock. He yelled at us for a while about injustices in the American court system, particularly the court in Jefferson County and the denial of constitutional rights. I was able to see his face clearly and his entire body. I remember him very well."

"Could you recognize him if you saw him again?"

"Oh, yes, I could recognize him."

"Is the construction worker in this room?"

"Yes, he is."

"Please point to him." Helga fully extended her arm and pointed. "Let the record show that the witness pointed to the defendant Aaron Krueger."

Helga relived the entire horrible experience and pointed her finger at Frank Binford and Jack Plotkin as the two men found by the first aid kit in the forest. She described their conversation, between the two Creation women and the two Avengers, the seizure of ammunition for the rifles, and the flight into the forest.

After three days of testimony, Helga was released from the stand and Lucinda gave testimony for three days, after the above described formalities. She described the same things that Helga had. She identified Aaron Krueger as the 'Allen Case' and pointed her finger at him. She described from her point of view the rock hitting her head and her biting of Binford's wrist. She pointed her finger at Frank Binford and Jack Plotkin.

After Helga and Lucinda testified, it was our turn, those of us who were on the *Neanderthal Return* responding to the crisis on the Olympic Peninsula. Trviea Harsradich, Pidonita Hmlakian, and myself each took the witness stand and gave brief testimony. There was not much for either of us to tell.

And then we were done, though Judge Meredith ordered us Americans to remain available for recall testimony. He made that a request to the Creation women, reminding them of their promise. At this juncture, the only defendants we could place at the scene of the crime were Binford, Plotkin, and Aaron Krueger, the phony construction worker. It was obvious they didn't put any of the bullets into the Secret Service agents.

When a Secret Service agent is killed in the line of duty, the government wants the killer, and wants him bad. Real bad. The killer of the first agent, Randle Packwood, was killed immediately by Len Taylor. Henry Turnipseed prevented Glenn Morton from being able to kill anyone. The feds thanked the two Jefferson County men.

The forensic evidence was tremendous and this time, the FBI did a brilliant job with it. They learned their lessons from the fiasco that the O.J. Simpson trial became and the subsequent scandals and uproars involving crime labs, including the FBI's. But such evidence is no good without names upon whom to serve the search warrants. Search warrants were needed to find the clothing, carpet, leather, and DNA samples with which to match up with the evidence gathered at the crime scene.

Michelle Smith, the former Michael Schmidt, helped plan the assault on the Olympic Peninsula. She purchased the bondage items at the Portland sex shop. But she was miles away waiting at the safe house where they planned to hold Helga and Lucinda. Of all the Avengers of Yahweh that the feds could then identify, she had the least to do with the murders in the forest.

And she could nail the ones who participated and got away.

The judge declared a recess upon the completion of our testimony. We weren't around the next morning when Michelle Smith and her attorney Larry Bookbinder arrived. Bookbinder had sent each of the Creation women a letter of apology. He intended no offense, he was just representing his client to the best of his ability. The Creation women told him that they understand the duties of an attorney, they accepted his apology on the condition that he bear no ill will toward the Neanderthal Race.

Michelle Smith dressed as a woman with long brunette hair and makeup appropriate for a court appearance. She was pretty enough to make heterosexual men uncomfortable, as they knew about her but still couldn't believe their eyes. She cost Binford and Plotkin the opportunity for a deal to turn state's evidence and earn lenient treatment. Smith's testimony lasted three weeks. The defense lawyers viciously attacked her credibility. Cross dressing to evade the law. Hormone treatments. Facial hair removal. The crimes Michael Schmidt allegedly committed, but no longer wanted by the State of Washington. While looking more and more feminine, she still helped the Avengers plan and execute their crimes. Now she turned state's evidence because she got herself into trouble for shooting a Neanderthal woman.

But she held to her testimony and the evidence obtained on the search warrants backed her up. She described how Aaron Krueger broke into Allen Case's house and stole his wallet the morning of the attack. Allen Case had a clean record and looked like Krueger. Thus, Krueger was ready if the agents wanted to check his driver's license. After diverting the car, Krueger went back to Case's house and returned the wallet, including the money that was in it. Case did not even know his wallet was missing. Along with the forensic evidence from the crime scene and the top notch lab work, every defendant was tied to the scene of the crime and five of the defendants were tied to the guns used to kill the agents.

The jury believed Michelle Smith.

Binford, Plotkin, and the former Jefferson County Deputy Prosecutor Bruce Elders were convicted of possession and use of machine guns, destruction of federal property, and the unlawful imprisonment and reckless endangerment of federal agents and persons under their protection. Krueger used false ID to aid and abet federal crimes. They were acquitted on the charges of aiding and abetting the murders of the federal agents. The jury found that Packwood's action surprised everyone.

The other five defendants were convicted of the above charges, and in addition to that, the jury found they fired their guns into the helpless Secret Service agents. They were sentenced to death. Judges who are squeamish about the death penalty are retiring, one by one. The new judges have to have a record of supporting the death penalty to win confirmation by the Senate. The convicted killers will each have their date with the needle and the juice.

Michelle Smith got off scot-free, and disappeared into the Federal Witness Protection Program.

Helga Trvlakian, Lucinda Renuxler, and Captain Trviea Harsradich attended a reception in the Chinese Room at the top of the Smith Tower in Seattle. The Creation women arranged to have a big screen television and a VCR brought up the elevator and set up in one of the corners. Two dozen diplomats from around the world were there to relax with wine and cheese. Graham Kelvin of Australia walked with Helga around the balcony looking at the city from four hundred feet up. The balcony is several feet wide and wrapped all the way around the Tower. From the very low railing, curving above and attached to the building is a latticework of steel bars to prevent falls and suicides. "How's the little boy, Helga?"

Helga smiled. "He's fine. One head, two arms, two legs, so far, so good!"

"You both came through that bloody trial! I'm surprised you put yourself through that in your condition."

"A woman can withstand pregnancy and childbirth. Your masculine concern and protectiveness is touching and I appreciate it. It was difficult, I'll admit that, but I can sit in front of killers and tell the jury the truth!"

"You did the right thing. But now those men will be executed. How do you feel about that?"

"Australia does not have a death penalty?"

"No, we don't. We believe it is wrong for the state to deliberately take a life. Few of the advanced industrialized nations have a death penalty. It has been abolished in Australia, Canada, and most of Europe. But the bloody Americans," he lowered his voice, has to be careful when he's on our soil, "they can be an ornery bunch of buggers."

"Graham, I respect your belief that the death penalty is wrong. We respect Australia and those other nations for not having one. You take this position for the very best of reasons. But good, decent men, who committed no crime, whose only sin was maybe taking their jobs too seriously, were murdered in cold blood. Only a few yards from me. They were helpless, handcuffed to trees."

She looked her Australian friend square in the eye to let him see that a Neanderthal can hate, not him but the persons of whom she speaks. "If the United States were to slowly torture these cold blooded killers to death, I would not object. As it is, I'll respect the Americans for executing their death sentences in a manner designed to avoid cruel and unusual punishment. On Creation, we haven't been able to have children, we've been unable to replace ourselves. So when we convict a woman of deliberate murder, where she was not acting in self defense, in defense of another, or in defense of her nation, and it is upheld on automatic appeal by a court that has investigative powers far beyond any Earth appellate court, we put her to death. If the murder does not happen in the first place, there is no death penalty. Guess what? We have exceedingly few murders during times of peace on Creation. Therefore, very few death sentences. Please forgive us for believing that the almost certain execution of a death sentence deters murder."

"We forgive you. Shall we speak of more pleasant things?" suggested Graham.

"Yes, I would like that. Is that our star on your nation's flag?"

Graham laughed. "No, I'm afraid not. That's the Confederation Star under the Union Jack. It's too close to the Southern Cross in our flag to be either Hadar or Rigil Kent. While your star will pass in front of Hadar in the next 10,000 years, it'll be well north of where we put the Confederation Star."

"Rigil Kent. Bundula. Toliman. Nan Mun, the South Gate. Alpha Centauri, all different names for our star. I don't suppose you Australians and New Zealanders are claiming sovereignty over the Southern Cross stars with your flags?"

"Ha-ha! Hardly! That would require an ambitious space program on our part! The great state of Mimosa! Only 420 light years away. Or perhaps Gamma Crucis, a mere 88 light years."

"If you go, feel free to stop by for a visit. We're on the way! But please respect our sovereignty. We would like a treaty."

"The biggest problem everyone has with your proposed Sovereignty Treaty, is that you won't tell us a bloody thing about the planets in your Solar System over which you claim sovereignty. Not even how many of 'em."

"The Sovereignty Treaty we propose is drawn along the lines originally proposed by the U.S. President. We're willing to recognize all nine planets, the moons in orbit around these planets, and all of the comets, asteroids, and other naturally occurring particles in orbit around your Sun out to a distance of two *hekt enbeeyon kepfats*, over two trillion miles, almost four trillion kilometers, from your Sun, as being within the sovereignty of the Earth nations. The division and distribution of such sovereignty among the Earth nations is a matter for the Earth nations to decide. We will promise not to involve ourselves in any such territorial disputes, only to recognize territorial agreements the Earth nations make. Your high seas, beyond the three mile limit, can still be the high seas for Earth people, but we will recognize that Earth belongs to the people of Earth. Not us. Not the Face Mountain aliens. Not to whatever race who sent the probe that crashed near Roswell. Same kind of status for the Moon and the planets of this Solar System. And we will, if able, assist in the defense of this sovereignty should an alien race come to invade and conquer. We only desire the same kind of recognition by Earth nations of our sovereignty over the planets and moons of our Solar System, including the planets in orbit around the Second Sun, out to our proposed territorial limit of two *hekt enbeeyon kepfats*."

"That two *hekt enbeeyon kepfats* includes Proxima Centauri and its planets."

"Proxima Centauri is in orbit around the common center of mass of our Solar System, we call it the Third Sun. It's a real flare monster! We dare not get anywhere near it, intense gamma radiation during the flares, our unwomanned probes get fried! We're not claiming sovereignty over any other star. Within a hundred Earth years, you will most likely be able to build a ship like the *Neanderthal Return*. Even if Hmlee is born healthy, and he will be, and we bring our precious cargo of sperm and volunteer Cro-Magnons back to Creation, we'll not have anywhere near your numbers for a long time. We can visit other stars, but we have not the numbers to settle any of their planets. You have those numbers. Let us have our Three Suns and their planets. You will be able to settle the Galaxy!"

"As an Australian, I must confess sympathy to the problems of a small population occupying a large territory." Graham chuckled. "Just a hop across the water is Indonesia. Couple hundred million people, few of whom are white, few are Christian, few speak English, exceedingly few, if any, speak Australian Aborigine language, and these millions of people tolerated a MEAN dictatorship before their economic collapse and current unrest. Our Aborigines know what it's like to be a minority in their own land. Henry Turnipseed can tell you about that, his language living on in a few place names. I can bloody well understand why you don't want your Three Suns overwhelmed by Base Ten Numbers and the Metric System!"

"We certainly don't want the Metric System imposed on us."

Graham chuckled. "I suppose those bloody centi, milli, and kilo prefixes don't work so good in Base Twelve."

"Yeah, in Base Twelve, eighty four is the number of centimeters in a meter." They giggled.

"But we feel that you have an unfair advantage over us. You have been able to survey all of our planets, and you have the benefit of everything we Earthlings have learned about our planets. But we do not have the similar knowledge of the planets orbiting your Three Suns. And you're asking us to commit to recognizing your sovereignty over these planets without letting us know what it is we are committing to."

"I know. I understand that. It's unreasonable to hide something and later spring a surprise. Creation orbits Alpha Centauri A at 118 million miles. We have a moon that is too small to hold an atmosphere, just like your Moon. There is a planet orbiting 62 million miles from our Second Sun, what you call Alpha Centauri B. We've always called this Planet Janedye. We were intrigued with it because we knew it receives about the same amount of light from the Second Sun as we receive from our main Sun. Janedye is very luminous, it is covered with oceans with white clouds in its sky. Exploring Janedye was a major goal of our space program."

"What did you find at Janedye?"

"It has been terraformed with Earth life forms, with some species that are now extinct on Earth, just like Creation. There is one species of extinct Earth life on Jayndye that we have decided you need to know about."

"What species is this?"

"Lucies."

"Lucies?"

"*Australopithicus aferensis.*"

"Ohh, Lucy! Like the Lucy skeleton! You have a living population of lucies on Janedye!"

"Captain Harsradich has some photographs of them and a computer disc full of data on them, what we know about them. Right here in the Chinese Room. Perhaps we can watch a videotape of Planet Janedye and its lucies?"

"That's what the VCR and television set is for! I'd love to see this film! I'm sure everyone else will."

The film was narrated in English by the crew of the *Neanderthal Return*, it described the planets of the Three Suns. No gas giants. Planet Lakian, the Good Man, orbits inside of Creation at about 80 million miles from the First Sun. A hot world with a nitrogen-oxygen atmosphere, the average surface temperature of its ocean is about 185 degrees Fahrenheit. The reflection of sunlight off its clouds keeps it from being even worse. Creation women established a few settlements on high plateaus near the poles. They seem to be safe from local bacteria and viruses evolved for hotter temperatures than their bodies. The Face Mountain aliens didn't use it because its geology indicates massive planetwide volcanic eruptions that boil its ocean to steam. Orbiting about 120 million miles from the Second Sun is Coilon, the Golden Planet. Its color is due to sand, with thin atmosphere and small diameter, it is very much like Mars. Each diplomat was handed a book and a compact disc which fits Earth computers, that described these planets in more detail.

The lucies dominated the conversation.

"They look just like little people! From the neck down! You think you could just go up to 'em and talk to 'em!"

"I thought that would be your favorite part of the film!" exclaimed Trviea. "You saw all those lucies walking around Smilivan."

"Yeah, we've never seen a picture of a black Neanderthal."

"She's a Gracian. Graciana has chimpanzees and bonobos, Gracian scientists know apes far better than us Atlanteans. Atlantis led the way in the space program. When we discovered the lucies on Jayndye, we recruited Gracian scientists to study them. Smilivan has been living with this troupe of lucies recording information about their behavior and survival strategies."

"Just like Jane Goodall and Dian Fossey."

"Just like them! They rotate the duty, we bring them back to Graciana so they can restore their sanity after half a Creation year in the field on Jayndye. What we know about the lucies is this: Their level of brain development, intelligence, culture, tool use, and so on, is about the same as can be observed with chimpanzees and bonobos. Their social and sexual behavior is about halfway between chimps and bonobos. They like sex but they're not promiscuous like bonobos."

"Or humans."

"Oh, you doth exaggerate. We Neanderthals and you Cro-Magnons aren't quite as wild and crazy as the bonobos. But neither do we live up to any high moral standard, any such standard we honor in the breach!" Laughter. "The lucies are like us in sexual behavior. They tend toward long relationships between each mating pair. Marriages, so to speak. But they also cheat on each other and get into fights because of it." Laughter!

"They cooperate to raise their children." declared Lucinda. "As we do. As the chimpanzees and bonobos do. But before we impress ourselves too much with their humanity, these are very much like chimpanzees who are adapted to living in the savanna and away from the trees."

"How do they handle predators?"

"They are predators. They hunt. They eat meat as well as fruits, nuts and vegetables."

"But how do they deal with lions and hyenas? Cheetahs?"

"The cats usually leave them alone, even lucies, lukes actually, lone males, who wander the savanna by themselves. Smilivan wrote of an encounter she witnessed between a troupe of lucies and a lion. A very unusual encounter, they usually know enough not to bother each other. A young male lion, just learning to hunt, stalked a lucy and her baby. Her luke came screaming at the top of his lungs swinging a heavy stick. He beat the lion over his head and chased him. The lucy held her baby in one arm and threw rocks at the lion with the other arm. The whole troupe joined in the chase. Smilivan was unable to measure the distance of the chase, but she believes that after perhaps a quarter *kepfat*, the lucies broke off the chase and let the lion get away. Chances are, the lion learned not to mess with lucies."

"So they're not like fearful rabbits when walking the savanna?"

"No. They pay attention to their surroundings, but their facial expressions are like ours, they own the place!"

"Did Smilivan film or photograph the encounter?"

"No, she didn't have her camera equipment with her. Which was a big disappointment to her, as you can imagine. She knows the lucies are no threat to her as long as she's no threat to them. If, however, they perceive her to be a threat, they could hurt her bad, even if she is a big strong Neanderthal with killer teeth and jaw muscles."

Lucinda whispered in Henry's ear. They were both grinning, very happy. "There is an announcement that I would like to make." declared Lucinda.

"What is that Lchnsda?" asked Helga, who already knew.

"Ladies and gentlemen," she held hands with Henry Turnipseed, "we are the same species. I am carrying Henry's child."

480

Chapter Fifty Two

Lucinda Renuxler and Helga Trvlakian came out from behind the curtains, basked in the applause, kissed the host, and sat down on the couch. Helga still did not show. "Yes," exulted Lucinda, "it feels great to be pregnant!"

"That's" started Helga, "what I keep telling myself!" Laughter. "Actually, I feel great. As soon as the morning sickness is over, I'm fine for the day."

"So, how's the little nipper?" asked the night time talk show host.

"Hmlee is looking good!" That was answered with applause.

"That is great news. Lucinda, are you really pregnant?"

"I am really pregnant."

"Yours is a full hybrid, half Neanderthal, half Native American, will he or she be a healthy baby, if you don't mind my asking?"

Lucinda took a deep breath. "It's too soon to tell. The child is only a few weeks old. But my baby has 23 chromosomes from Henry, a Cro-Magnon, and 23 chromosomes from me. We pray that he or she will be normal and healthy, with a mixture of features from both of our Races."

"How is everyone treating you?"

"Everyone has been wonderful!" exclaimed Helga. "We have obstetricians from hospitals in the State of Washington who are with us all the way. Our men, Leonard Taylor, Henry Turnipseed, the fellows who rode with us on our ship, and of course, Neil Peace, all have been very supportive. And the women, Neil's ex-wife, Angela, she's been there for us, Cuc Nguyen drops into town to check up on us. Our own physicians, Askelion and Meddi, have been given access to whole of the Earth's health care system. We thank you very much for it."

"And Henry's Tribe?"

"The Puyallup and Nisqually Tribal people have been great, just great! All of the Native Americans we hear from are so nice to us."

"You both are holding up very well. We also admire you for testifying in that trial, after Helga knew she was pregnant with a child who is so extremely important to your entire Planet."

"Thank you." said Helga, a little somberly. "We witnessed a terrible crime. We respect the need of the United States and any human society to enforce and obey its laws. We could identify only three of the defendants, the rest wore ski masks. But we told the truth, the whole truth, and nothing but the truth. We did our part."

"How do you feel about the defense attorneys?"

"The defense attorneys performed a necessary duty, we respect them for having done it. They were nice to us, we answered their questions to the best of our ability."

"They were much nicer to us," broke in Lucinda, "than they were to the Avenger of Yahweh who turned state's evidence and squealed on their clients."

"I can imagine. How do you feel about Michelle Smith?"

Sigh. "She shot me." Lucinda felt the spot under her left breast. "It still hurts a little, when I take a deep breath. She tried to kill me. How am I suppose to feel?"

"She got off scot-free, into the Federal Witness Protection Program."

Sigh. "We couldn't identify the men who murdered the Secret Service agents and got away alive. They hid their faces behind ski masks. I'm glad Michelle Smith gave the testimony that led to the search warrants and to their convictions. I cannot criticize the authorities for the decisions they made. But I would like to make a statement to Smith, if she is watching."

"Sure. Go right ahead."

Lucinda looked right into the camera. "Michelle Smith, I want you to know that you have caused a lot of people a lot of pain. You helped set up the attack in the forest that cost four families their beloved men. As one who lost a husband, a father and other men whom I loved, I can tell you that you put these families through pure Hell!" She pointed to where the bullet entered her chest. "And this really hurt! You will not pay a penalty under the law for your crimes. How you atone for your sins and get right with your God is a matter up to you, we can do nothing about it. But if there is something you want to say to me, I will meet with you and I will listen."

"Why don't we talk about more pleasant things?" suggested Helga. "We have two babies on the way!"

Michelle Smith did not attempt to set up a meeting with Lucinda Renuxler.

A Microsoft millionaire invited us on to his boat to take us to a college football game at Husky Stadium. We rode the large yacht in the morning sunshine. Our host and his wife were dressed in glorious University of Washington purple and gold. "How ya doing, girls?"

"Doing great." answered Lucinda cheerfully. She sat on the bench with Helga and Angela. Christa and Virgil ran around the boat excited about going to a big game. "While I don't mind wearing this purple sweater, this funny hat is just not my idea of dignity."

We laughed. The bill of the purple cap is decorated with a gray husky dog head. Us guys were sitting on the other side of the boat watching our women. Past the women we looked across the water of Lake Washington toward the Medina shore. Through a sparkling laugh, Helga asked "Why don't you let me try that on?"

Lucinda gave the Husky hat to Helga, who put it on. "The hat looks perfect on you, Helga! Fits your personality! You are such a perfect female dog!"

We laughed, we know Helga is not a bitch. Helga good naturedly pretended to punch Lucinda in the face for saying it. Touched her very softly. Grinning beneath the cap, Helga pointed at Lucinda's head. "Look at this!"

On one side of her head was purple and gold paint arranged in a pattern with the letters 'U of W'. On the other side, in red and gold, the letters 'USC'. "While some women cover a naturally bald head with a wig," I observed, "Lucinda considers it an opportunity to make a fashion statement. One that causes the rest of us to WISH she would cover it up with a wig!" Laughter.

We enjoyed the boat ride, a gentle 5 knots. We arrived at the dock and went into the game.

Gay people from San Francisco boarded a cruise ship they rented for the day. The revelers arrived at the quayside, many in elegant clothing. Armani suits. Long gowns. Some of the cross dressers were very obvious, some were not, they could pass as women. And some were women, from the day they were born.

"Welcome aboard the *Silver Girl,* friends! We are going out beyond the three mile limit, then we can pull the covers of the gaming tables, break out the booze, strike up the band, and have a party!"

The *Silver Girl* steamed under the Golden Gate Bridge and out into the open ocean. A high pressure system kept clouds away from the entire Pacific coast. Football games and weekend drives, picnics, and children in the parks, all enjoyed a warm, sunny fall day.

"What a gorgeous day!" exulted Captain Warren Hale through the public address system, as the Bridge and the Frisco skyline faded in the distance. "I'm straight, get used to it!" The partygoers laughed at his reversal of the classic gay rights rallying cry. "I love the sea! The glittering water, the salt spray, the dolphins leaping. We will have a high today of 70 degrees, winds coming out of the east at five miles per hour. There will be no storms today, the Weather Service tells us the high will remain in place until at least tomorrow morning. And now it's official! We are crossing the three mile limit!" A cheer rose up. "We are now on the high seas! We will cruise at about ten knots, moving deeper into international waters. In another hour, we will be more than twelve miles from the California coast. Then we will cruise parallel to the coast"

The covers were pulled off the gambling equipment and the party began in earnest. People in bathing suits dived into the pool, sunbathers lounged in the deck chairs, an aerobics instructor led her students through a routine, a band played rock music.

Later, in the ballroom, the band completed its repertoire with a rousing rendition of *Macho Man* that had everybody singing the words and dancing. A man in a lavender tuxedo came out on to the stage and took the microphone. "Macho, macho, man, I'm gonna be a macho man! Ladies and gentlemen, and everyone else, too!" Laughter. "How many genders are here today? Five? Six? I lost count. Doesn't matter anyway. Now we come to the event we all have been waiting for,"

"We have?" The drummer made the pratfall sound, a quick series of beats descending in pitch. Chuckles ran through the audience.

"Yes, we have been waiting for this event."

"Not me, I haven't been waiting for this event."

"Trust me, we have been waiting for it. All of us."

"Not me, man."

"Okay, everyone except you. Every party has a pooper." Laughter continued in the ballroom. "This is an event where we raise money for AIDS research and treatment. As you know, treatment with AZT and protease inhibitors is not cheap. So today we will have a Slave Auction. Now there is no intention of violating the 13th Amendment or anything. These women are volunteers, doing this for a good cause and having fun at the same time. If you treat your slave rougher than she wants to be treated or do something she doesn't want to do, she has the right to end the scene. But these girls just want to have FUH - UN! And it is just for the ride, everyone is free when we get back to San Francisco, where we deliver some money to pay for AIDS treatment! All right, are you ready?"

"YES!" answered the crowd.

"Mistress, please lead out the slaves!"

The Mistress, in a black leather dress, thigh high boots with seven inch stiletto heels, and gloves up to the biceps led five women by the collar, five leashes in her hand, out on to the stage. The band played a brassy introduction. The very shapely women wore flashy bright colored dresses, loud hosiery covering their legs and opera pumps on the feet. With beautifully done long hair, smiling through bright red lipstick, each slave woman slowly turned 360 degrees on the stage to let the audience get a good look at her and her chrome plated handcuffs. The appreciative crowd whooped, cheered, and made catcalls.

The lavender tuxedoed man addressed the crowd again. "Before we begin the bidding, there is something I have to tell you about these ladies. One of them, you see, really is a woman. As in two X chromosomes in every cell!" Laughter. "BUT!" Dramatic pause. "We won't tell you which one!"

The crowd went "Wooo! Hooo!" Whistles.

"You lesbians out there, Dykes on Bikes, I see you out there, you may bid on these slaves if you want, but I'm warning you, there is a four out of five chance of disappointment." Laughter!

"For the rest of you, just think of it as a potential *Crying Game* surprise in reverse!" More laughter.

The bidding began, the lavender man talking a mile a minute like he was selling livestock, and then "SOLD, for $3,500!" This is a high income crowd.

The second women went for $2,500. Each winning bid paid in cash, into a bucket labeled "AIDS RELIEF".

"Now, ladies and gentlemen, the beautiful five foot eleven inch blonde bomber with dark roots who goes by the classic sobriquet, Mary Elizabeth! Let us give a warm round of applause and a few rude catcalls as she performs another 360!" Mary Elizabeth slowly and gracefully turned on her spike heel opera pumps. She kept her balance perfectly, on a ship with its pitch and roll and her wrists cuffed behind the small of her back. "Look at the magnificent jugs on this lady! Those aren't falsies tucked in under her bra, she really is a Size D. But are they live or are they Memorex? Natural or silicone? And what is under the skirt? We don't know!" More cheers and whistles.

The bidding began in earnest. Mary Elizabeth was popular with the audience. Five or six wealthy gay men and two wealthy gay women put in bids. Finally a bidding war between two of the gay men, in Armani suits. "We have $5,000 even, do we have, $5,500! All right, $5,500 do, $6,000! Six grand! Do we have $6,500? Going once. $6,500! We have a bid for $6,500! Do we have seven grand? Going once, going twice, anybody? SOLD! To the gentleman for $6,500! Put it in the pot my man, and you may lead the gorgeous Mary Elizabeth away by the leash to do what, EVER!"

Mary Elizabeth grinned at the high price she brought. Even more, the guy was CUTE! And he seemed very nice, she hoped. "Mary Elizabeth, my name is Jonathan Cummings. I think you are a fine person to play this part for charity."

"Why thank you, Jonathan, you are so kind. I would shake your hand but,"

"Oh!" They laughed as he reached behind her and shook one of her cuffed hands.

"Would you like to kiss me?" Mary Elizabeth asked. Just checking under the hood. Is he really a gay or bisexual man? Or at least uninhibited?

He gave her a polite kiss on the cheek The leash led to a stiff leather collar that went from her collarbones to her jawbone, keeping her head nice and straight. With the leash in hand Jonathan suggested, "Why don't we go for a little walk? I'll take you to my room and show you my stamp collection." He winked.

"Love to!" Mary Elizabeth was happy. Jonathan was cute, gentlemanly, and no sign of the mean streak some of her dates have. Dates, or customers, a girl's gotta pay the rent. A little bondage is fine, but for verbal and physical abuse, she has to charge extra. And maybe not return the phone calls. At least Jonathan looks like he wants to play happy, not mean or cruel.

They arrived at Jonathan's quarters. "Oh it's HUGE!" exclaimed Mary Elizabeth.

"This is one of the first class rooms. Allow me to close the blinds, now we have a little privacy. Here, let's undo these cuffs. Mary Elizabeth, I must say, you are exquisite, perhaps you are the one who actually is a woman."

Mary Elizabeth gave him a sly smile. "Want to take a peek?"

"Not right now. Why don't you put on this leather harness, over your dress."

"Over my dress? Okay." This fellow wants to start slow, it is early, not get naked at first. Cool! The black patent leather straps went between, above and below her breasts, two inch wide straps over her shoulders, a thick waist belt almost like a corset, additional straps around her crotch, not too tight, around her thighs, calves and ankles. The straps cinched firm, little padlocks secured everything together. The straps held her legs together. The harness had four inch wide leather cuffs that locked around her elbows and wrists, securing her arms to her sides. "This is lovely, secure, but not uncomfortable. This leather feels good."

Her master gently pushed her backwards and she fell on the bed with a whoop followed by laughter. She laid on her back, hands locked to her hips, legs locked together, unable to move, except to roll around. "I should leave you there while I go play some blackjack. Gotta win back some of the money I spent on you." He was kidding.

"What if I gotta go pee?"

"It would not be the first time the ship's crew had to clean up a mess like that. You have to pee?"

"No, not right now."

"Good. Now we put this blindfold on. Roll you over. How do you feel now?"

"I'm laying on my belly and I can't see a thing. Other than that, I feel great. What are you doing with my fingers?"

"Oh, just taking your fingerprints."

"Why? Is this a cop scene?" She giggled. "Whatever you're arresting me for, I didn't do it, I swear, I didn't do it! You gotta believe me, man! I'm innocent, I tell ya. All right! All right! I admit it! I confess! It was me who killed Nicole Simpson and Ron Goldman. Not O.J." She broke into giggles as each of her fingers were pressed, first into the inkpad, and then on to the paper. "You do that very well, rolling each finger from one side to the other. You really are a cop. A gay cop! Not the first one I met!"

After getting the prints off all ten fingers, he wiped the ink off with a wet towel. "You'll have to excuse me for a minute, I gotta run these prints."

"Tee-hee! Yeah, go run those prints."

A moment later, she heard several sets of footsteps come into the room "I have a surprise for you, a couple of lady friends of mine have come to join us. You don't mind if I bring in two women? They really are women, since birth." A pair of very strong hands grabbed each shoulder. The two women, gently but firmly, lifted her off the bed and on to her feet.

"Lady friends? Must be woman bodybuilders. Cool! They are both very strong! I know you on the right, you're a woman, or a she-male, I felt your titty brush my arm."

"They're not bodybuilders. These women are naturally strong, always have been. Here, let me undo your blindfold so you can see them, Michelle Smith."

"Michelle Smith, uh, who's Michelle Smith? TROGS!!"

"I am Wlmsda Hotlund."

"And I am Bchsda Bentlakian. Oh, and uh, please don't call us trogs."

"I'm sorry about calling you that,"

"Don't worry about that, just don't let it happen again. You have a real big problem, Mary Elizabeth."

"Big problem. Definitely a big problem."

"Your fingerprints are identical to the fingerprints of the Michelle Smith who shot Lchnsda Renuxler, and then turned state's evidence and nailed her Avenger of Yahweh friends who killed the Secret Service men. And your fingerprints match up with the Michael Schmidt truck driver who robbed banks and a whole bunch of other stuff in the State of Washington before you started, uh, doing this, taking hormones and stuff."

"My breasts are natural, the product of two X chromosomes. Yours are truly a work of art. Tell me, did the Federal Witness Protection Program pay for breast implants? You look so much more developed than you did at the trial."

"And I like the nose job and the fuller lips. Collagen, was it? Color the hair blonde and nobody knows you're Michelle Smith. How'd you heal up so fast?"

"Probably got some Healing Factor, it has been a couple of months since the trial. That darn formula is now on the Internet, translated into a hundred different languages, quantities in English and Metric units."

"Even our units. Anybody with lab equipment can make some. So Michelle, you had this marvelous surgery. You're now all healed up and beautiful. Your fingerprints tell the tale."

Michelle Smith was no longer having fun. "This scene is over! I demand you release me now!"

"The scene is over. You are under arrest for the shooting and wounding of a citizen of Atlantis. We will take you up to our ship and there, you will stand trial under our laws for the crime you committed last March 17, Earth time."

"What about your Agreement with the Earth nations? You promised not to kidnap another Earth person!"

"Oh! We are outside United States territory. Beyond the three mile limit. Indeed, beyond twelve nautical miles. Therefore, the United States cannot protect you, well they can, they have an impressive Navy and Coast Guard, but I don't believe they are obligated to protect you if you step outside U.S. territory. Tell me, did the Justice Department promise to protect you if you step outside U.S. territory?"

Michelle stared coldly at the Neanderthal women. "Trog bitches!" she muttered. "You managed to stop the Doomsday that was coming because you showed up. Congratulations. But there are many ways an angry God can punish the wicked, and the Covenant With Noah's Descendants doesn't apply to the Daughters of the Men of Renown."

"I see. We can't help being descended from Hercules and Achilles, if that's who we are. If God is planning to destroy the Universe, we're not gonna stop it. In the meantime, we'll just deal with whatever comets, alien invaders, and other natural and human made phenomena that comes along requiring action."

"You're right about one thing, there are many ways God can punish the wicked."

"And while you have done things with and to your body that most of the rest of us would not, we didn't come here to pass moral judgment on any Cro-Magnon's sexual practices."

"But when you wound a Neanderthal woman in an attempt to kill her, we're one of the ways God can punish you. You voluntarily came on to this ship, knowing it was going outside the three mile limit. You voluntarily submitted to bondage for the purpose of playing sexual games. So here you are, nobody is kidnapping you from inside the borders of your country."

"Also, the Agreement has an obligation on the part of the Earth nations. Each Earth nation that is party to the Agreement with the *Neanderthal Return*, has promised to take every reasonable step to prevent harm coming to any Neanderthal from Creation during her visit here. As a citizen of the United States, you are normally entitled to the protections of this Agreement. But you violated this Agreement by harming a Neanderthal woman. Therefore, you cannot claim the protections of the Agreement you violated."

"With the permission of the Captain of this ship, we shall take Smith on to our Shuttle. I believe Metrola has it floating somewhere around here."

"Let's go. Hmm. We should loosen her ankles so she can walk."

"Nah. If we lift her by the shoulders like this, she don't hafta walk."

"Good idea. It's not too far, and she's not that heavy, about two *hekt dollons*."

"Piece of cake, as the Americans say."

With Jonathan leading the way, Wilma and Betty carried Michelle out into the sunshine and to the dance and exercise floor. A crowd of people gathered to watch, word spread fast. Under the open sky, Captain Hale, a U.S. Coast Guard officer, an FBI agent, a representative of the cruise line, and the wealthy gay men who put up the charter fee waited. A Coast Guard cutter cruised the water parallel to the *Silver Girl* at a distance of about 50 yards. Metrola Mornuxler held the Shuttle in the air where it was visible from the ship.

"How you doing, Michelle?" inquired the FBI man cheerfully.

Michelle held her tongue, fuming, trying to think of a way out of this.

"Is she Michelle Smith?" asked Captain Hale.

"She's Michelle, all right. That's our girl. Isn't she beautiful? Your tax dollars at work." He giggled.

"Why don't you call a press conference and tell everyone?" Michelle spat angrily. "I thought you were giving me a new identity and protecting me from harm! I'm immune to prosecution for all of those charges! Let me get to a phone and talk to Larry Bookbinder, this ought to be worth millions!"

"Larry Bookbinder? We're trying to reach him now. Seems he's on vacation. Likes to go fishing in Canada or Alaska, just before winter sets in. Problem is, we don't know exactly where in Canada or Alaska he's fishing. If that's what he's doing. Which we don't know. You know some of these busy lawyers. When they take a break, they don't want to be where a damn phone can ring! Their wives, too. They need to spend some quality time with their husbands, get some undivided attention. Mrs. Bookbinder likes to go fishing too, it's how she caught him. All those wonderful years ago." He grinned. How romantic.

"Well, you are obligated to protect me!"

"Yes, up to a point. If you drive 100 miles per hour, we'll come by your hospital bed and tell you that we can't protect you from your own stupidity. If you engage in a high risk lifestyle, we can't protect you from AIDS. We can't protect you from the consequences of weird sex. And believe it or not, we can't stop every skip tracer in the country from tracking you down, we can only make their job a little more challenging. Jonathan Cummings is one of the best."

"Actually, that's not my real name. It's one of the phony names I like to use, to keep you from recognizing me as a private dick." Deliberate pun, one private dick talking to another, a chick with a dick. "And being gay, I really am gay you know, I don't mind going after she-males. There aren't that many she-males, there really aren't. Lots of cross dressers, but very few who will actually grow their breasts beyond Size A. When Trviea Harsradich hired me, we had two possibilities to go on. Either you reversed several years of hormones and diet, and went back to looking like a man, or you went even further down the road toward gender reassignment. If you had done the former, well, it would have taken longer. I mean, most guys are guys. You can find the needle in the haystack because it is DIFFERENT. But a specific piece of hay?"

An extremely annoyed Michelle demanded of the FBI agent, "Are you going to stop this already? I'm in the Witness Protection Program. You have an obligation, you got the cutter, the trog women aren't going to challenge your guns if the Coast Guard intervenes. There's no extradition treaty with the trogs! You can't extradite me without an extradition treaty ratified by two thirds of the Senate!"

"We're not extraditing you. And if we were inside the three mile limit, I would be inclined to agree with you on the rest of it, and we would demand that you be released into our custody and we'd take you outta here. But we're outside U.S. territory, Michelle, and like I said, we can't protect you from your own stupidity. Like making it so easy for Cummings to track you down."

"Instead of making yourself a piece of hay, you made yourself a needle, a needle that glows in the dark!" taunted Jonathan, "Goes beep! Beep! Beep! From what I know of the treatments used for she-males, none of them affect your height. So I could eliminate the ones who are not five foot eleven. And as Mary Elizabeth, you made yourself real flashy! You had to show yourself off! You've been in every fetish club and gay bar in California!"

"Look at it from our point of view, Michelle," started the FBI man, "these Creation women could have offed you anytime in the last two weeks. That is how long they've known who you are and where you live. Lots of ways they could've done it without it looking like they did it. Just another unsolved murder. Broken neck, a shot from a cheap unregistered handgun, rope around the neck, a knife stab through a piece of paper used as a blood shield, a mysterious fall. An IRA retirement plan installed in your car. But they're not like that. Tell me, Wilma, uh, Betty, is she facing the death penalty?"

"Lchnsda didn't die. We'll probably sentence her to a few years in prison. Long enough to make her regret shooting another person."

"That seems reasonable. Will she have to go to Creation to serve her time?"

"I suppose. But we would be willing to have her serve her sentence in an Earth prison. Not in the United States, you made an agreement with her to get her testimony. But we could pay Canada or Mexico or somebody to hold her in one of their prisons."

Michelle was now more exasperated than angry. "Will you PLEASE honor our agreement?"

"Michelle, our Witness Protection Program contract specifically states that we are NOT obligated to protect you when you step outside U.S. territory. I'm surprised Bookbinder didn't emphasize that with you. Perhaps you could sue him for legal malpractice. We're fifteen miles off the coast! International waters. We'll protect you if you somehow manage to get back within three miles of the beach. But until then you're on your own. Good luck, Ms. Smith, thanks for the testimony."

"The United States does not object if we arrest Ms. Smith and take her to the *Neanderthal Return* for trial?"

"Nope. We're not obligated to."

"All right, Captain Hale, it's up to you. This passenger is on a ship under your command. If you refuse to allow us to take her away, we'll respect your authority as Captain of the *Silver Girl*."

"First let me confer with the gentlemen who are paying for this ride. What do you think, guys?"

"It's like Cunanan. We will not shield a gay man wanted for violent crimes. We're a responsible part of the community, at least in that way. And we don't care for Avengers of Yahweh and their agenda of hate. Our only concern is safety. If you believe that Metrola Mornuxler can bring her Shuttle down and pick up Michelle Smith without undue risk to the ship and the rest of us, go ahead."

"Very well. Your Shuttle operates by magnetic fields, powerful ones at that. This ship is a big hunk of steel. Does that present a problem for Metrola?"

"No. That actually makes it easier for her to control her Shuttle's movements. There will be some induction currents in your steel, but that won't warm it up more than a few degrees, uh, Fahrenheit. Shouldn't be too much of a problem for your copper wiring, your electrical circuits. If you have anything sensitive, you might want to shut it down."

"Good idea. EMP Drill! EMP Drill!"

"EMP Drill!" the command was relayed.

"I thought only military ships had EMP protection." wondered Michelle. "You some kind of,"

"The *Silver Girl* is an expensive ship." declared Captain Hale. "Of course we'll try to protect her if we think a nuclear bomb is going to go off. We'll take the same precaution with this Shuttle."

"Ship is secure for EMP!" Computers and nonessential electric circuits were turned off, the engine and rudder controls were isolated and protected.

"All right everyone!" Captain Hale was shouting through a bullhorn. "Get back away! Fifty feet from the dance floor! In all directions! Wilma, tell Metrola she may approach the dance floor for a landing."

Wlmsda handed her communicator to the Captain. "You may tell her yourself."

"Metrola Mornuxler, this is the Captain Warren Hale of the *Silver Girl*. Do you read me?"

"Loud and clear, Captain Hale! Permission to land on the deck?"

"Permission granted!"

"On my way!"

As Metrola carefully approached the dance floor, Michelle screamed obscenities. She suddenly shut up when Betty displayed a syringe in front of her face. "It's not that you have the right to remain silent, but if you don't, we'll jam this into your butt! It won't kill you, but when you wake up, you will have one nasty headache!"

"Our laws do not prohibit cruel and unusual punishment, so you be a good girl, uh, boy, uh, whatever the Hell you are!"

Metrola deployed the landing gear and landed gently on the deck of the *Silver Girl*. The door opened and the ramp came down. Wilma and Betty swiftly took their now terrified prisoner up the ramp into the Shuttle. They stepped out briefly, big triumphant grins on their faces. "Thank you! Everyone! You were terrific! Thank you, Captain Warren Hale!" They saluted him.

Captain Hale returned the salute. "You're welcome!"

"Jonathan! Did you get the money?" asked Betty.

"Yes, I did! I'm paid! In full! Thank you!"

"You're welcome! And thank you! You earned it! Great job! The AIDS relief charity? The winning bid for Michelle, that was our money! Spend it well! Make sure somebody who is sick is helped, that's all we ask!"

The gathered crowd broke into applause and cheering. The ramp retracted and the door closed. Metrola piloted her Shuttle straight up, past a thousand feet in a few seconds. The people could see the dark spot in the clear blue sky heading toward the rendezvous point. The *Neanderthal Return* has become a familiar sight.

"Captain Hale, so far this is turning into quite a cruise! We're gonna have to charter the *Silver Girl* again."

"Pass is complete! 39 yard gain to the Trojan 29! Husky first down!" Lucinda's communicator buzzed while the crowd cheered the yardage gain. The purple clad fans made more noise than a Sammy Hagar concert. The band broke into *Tequila!* Again. We weren't paying attention to Lucy, we were into the game. Helga was going with the flow, it was fun to see her happy, enjoying the game. Her belly was just beginning to bulge. I better watch myself. I could fall for her, like I did for Angela. Angie sat next to me, the children shifting around us, Len Taylor, Lucinda, and Henry Turnipseed. Virgil was on my lap, Christa on Henry's.

What the heck is Lucinda doing? Oh. She's trying to talk on her communicator. The Huskies broke the huddle. The crowd quieted down to let the home team quarterback call the signals. We don't have such consideration for the visiting team's quarterback.

"Yes! Yes! I can hear you now!" pleaded Lucinda in Atlantean. "It's the middle of the third quarter, the Huskies are down 21 to 17, but they have the ball and are driving. They just picked up 39 *treefats*, uh, yards. I keep saying *treefats*."

"Yeah, we see you on television." confirmed Trviea.

"You do?"

"The game is being broadcast. Those zoom lenses focused up close on your faces! We could see Helga with that crazy dog hat! And what did you do to your head!?"

"Oh! I didn't think we would be,"

"You should have worn a hat or a wig. If you paint your bald head like that, it will draw the zoom lenses like sharks to blood."

"Nice analogy. Draw play, went nowhere, uh, one *treefat*. Second down and nine. Everyone keeps yelling 'Tequila!' whenever the band plays that song. But I don't drink any, not while I'm pregnant."

"I thought I'd let you know, our old friend Michelle went on the cruise, quite voluntarily, knowing it was going outside the three mile limit. Jonathan did his job, we've got her! Americans aren't complaining, not the government, not the gay folks, not the *Silver Girl's* Captain. They just insisted we catch her when she's outside the country. Michelle's the only American who's complaining."

"Michelle Smith is in custody on the *Return*?"

"Yes! We have her! She's not going to get away with it!"

"Thank you."

Chapter Fifty Three

Michelle Smith used the mirror to comb her hair. The shiny metal collar replaced the leather one she wore earlier. As it did for Wilma, it monitored her blood pressure, heartbeat, breathing rate, muscle exertion, and the signal flow in her spinal cord. When she moved too fast and got too angry, it paralyzed her. Wasn't a lot of fun. A warning buzzer next to her skin sounded before the paralysis kicked in. She could not exert any strength, or experience any strong emotion. No sexual experience of any kind. She was provided with several changes of clothes, the hemp and flax linen stuff the Creation women wear most of the time. The room had basic needs. A small wash sink with a mirror. A toilet built into a closet. A table and seats, some snack food, a garbage pail for recyclables, and a bed for sleeping. The door was locked and she could not get out. No entertainment was available. Just an intercom with which she could call for help if she noticed a fire or needed medical attention.

A knock on the door. "Who is it?" she asked in English. She didn't know Atlantean.

"Sabar Duradich, may I come in?"

"I can't stop you."

"I've been assigned the task of representing you."

"Oh. You're my lawyer, I take it?"

"Only friend you got. Yes, I guess you could say I'm your lawyer."

"I thought Larry Bookbinder's my lawyer."

"Been trying to reach him. We've finally heard from the American State Department. They'll be wanting to speak with you. Please! We can't accomplish anything shouting through this door."

"Come in."

Sabar came in and offered her hand to shake. Michelle shook her hand without enthusiasm. "How are you doing?"

"I've been treated well, all things considered. They made me take a shower, didn't give me any privacy. It must have been quite a sight. Large breasts and male genitalia. What a combination! Then after I dried off, they gave me these clothes and took mine. When can I get my clothes back?"

"After they've been washed. You peed in them."

"Oh yeah. Now I remember. Being dragged up that ramp by those two goon women was like being dragged to the electric chair. I was frightened like that."

"You're not facing the death penalty." Sabar's voice was actually kind. "You won't be charged for any part of your responsibility for what happened in the State of Washington. You're only facing the charges arising out of the shooting of Lchnsda Renuxler. She didn't die."

"I'm glad she lived. I'm sorry I shot her." Sigh.

"Do you mean that, or are you only sorry because you got caught?"

"Truth be told, I don't know. You're supposed to be extinct, only you're not. You're not descended from Noah, but you didn't get wiped out by the Flood. Now I don't know what God has in mind for you. Or for me. So, what'll happen to me?"

"First thing I'm gonna do is move for dismissal on the grounds that as a United States citizen, you had the expectation of the well publicized part of the Agreement where we promised not to remove any person from the Earth against his or her will. While your government has told us they don't object to an exception for you if you voluntarily leave U.S. territory; you personally did not consent to that exception."

"What are the chances of that working?"

"Small, I'm afraid. There's a tradition on Creation that if a citizen of a contracting nation violates a treaty or agreement, then she cannot claim the protections of that same treaty or agreement. In other words, you abrogated the Agreement when you violated it."

"I see. I'm not an attorney, and I'm certainly not an expert in international law, but I always thought the Earth practice was that remedies for a violation of a treaty were governed by the treaty, or subject to negotiations. The treaty didn't disappear, that only happened if it was abrogated by one or both sides, sometimes when the contracting nations went to war. Our Senate ratified the Agreement for a period of one year with a 99-0 vote. That makes it a treaty."

"I see. There isn't anything in the Agreement as to remedies for violations by individual citizens. I could argue that because you are an Earthling, you cannot be rationally expected to view this Agreement in terms of how we dealt with treaty violations on Creation. We must consider how you may view it in terms of how Earthlings dealt with such violations."

Michelle's mood brightened. "Would they go for it?"

"It's a compelling argument. We need to get along with Earth nations and to respect Earth law when we're in this Solar System. How do you think we should deal with your violation of the Agreement?"

"I shot Lucinda Renuxler, no denying that. At the time I felt I had good reasons for it. Now I'm not so sure. But I recognize that what I did was a crime under the law. If my reasons were good, then I should be willing to pay the penalty for what I did. If my reasons were not good, then I deserve to pay the penalty."

"Sounds like you have spent some time thinking about it. How would you pay the penalty?"

"I made a deal with the federal prosecutors that allowed me to testify under a grant of immunity. I suppose we could somehow make a deal here."

"Lchnsda is the injured party. She would have to agree to any deal, we'll most likely respect her wishes."

"What would she accept?"

"Lchnsda is a decent, wonderful person. She believes if you harm another person, you should pay a penalty. That's why she cried at her trial in Port Townsend. She was immune under the Agreement, but she harmed Neil Peace and his children. We all did. Neil forgave us completely and helped us introduce ourselves to Earth. We are grateful for this. It worked out because we apologized to Neil and to the Great Holy Spirit for our sin. Neil knew that we weren't going to harm him again. That was the key. Not only must you apologize to Lchnsda, you must mean it, and she must know you will never hurt her or any of us again."

"She was worried that I might take another shot at her?"

"Oh yes! We had no way of knowing what you would look like, a man or a woman. You colored your hair and you had cosmetic surgery. She's carrying a child by a Cro-Magnon father. That's what your Avengers of Yahweh wanted most to prevent."

"The 'sons of God' mating with the daughters of men, to create the mighty men of renown. When we read that passage, we thought of the Neanderthal skeletons. The ancient Hebrew tale tells us of a time when there were two types of human. After the Flood, there is only one type of human. Lucinda, I mean, Lchnsda, did I say it right?"

"Not bad. You should practice it, she appreciates it when somebody takes the time to learn how to pronounce her name."

"Good idea. She's pregnant by Henry Turnipseed. By the old fashioned method, not all this crazy manipulation of chromosomes as you did for the fetus in Helga Trvlakian. The Hebrews were right, Neanderthals could mate with Cro-Magnons, and create heroes. Last time that happened, we had the Flood. This time, we had the comet appear, on a collision course with Earth. Right about the time Neanderthal women appear, and start making love with Cro-Magnon men."

"But this time, we took care of the comet. You Earthlings knew about the comet, it was observed and recorded by the *Zep Tepi* people, along with their calculations. You forgot the specific calculations, forgot that it was about a comet, but you did not forget that a doomsday was portended. If you believed our appearance could lead to a disaster, why did you think killing one of us would prevent it?"

"I didn't think it would prevent it. Not really. But I felt I had to do something."

"Hmm. We all come to a time when we have to do something. But it has to be the right thing, not the wrong. We have to know you will never again try to hurt one of us."

"That sounds reasonable."

"It does. But not easy. You have quite a record of crime. We show up and you help plan the attempted kidnapping."

"I didn't think we were going to kill Secret Service agents. Our plans were to seize Helga and Lucinda and hold them hostage. Our demands were to be that you leave our Solar System without any sperm or Cro-Magnon men, because we thought interbreeding would lead to disaster."

"We wouldn't have agreed to any such demands, even at the cost of their lives."

"I know. As to crime, I was involved in some gay bashing when I was young. Strange as it sounds, I became gay, or at least bisexual. I no longer hurt people for being gay. I took these hormones because I thought it would tone down my violent tendencies. It didn't. Fewer women go to prison for violent crimes, but some do. I guess I shall never again hurt anybody for being Neanderthal. Instead of disaster coming, disaster was prevented."

"I have an idea. You Earthlings feared and still fear the nuclear bomb as the potential source of a disaster. But along came us and the comets. We used the bombs to deal with the comets and prevent disaster. God gave us the uranium, the comets, and each other. He also gave us our brains which He expects us to use. We can use them for good or for evil, a decision we must make everyday. You make up your mind that you will use what God gave you for good, and never again for evil, apologize to Lchnsda and to your God for your sins, agree to pay a penalty for your crimes, and I'm sure we can work something out."

"Thank you, Sabar."

"I'll see you later. I'll try to get a hold of Bookbinder."

"Miss Smith, it's Meddi Chumkun."

"Come in."

"We have the results of the tests we ran on your blood. You were negative for HIV as recently as your appearance in the trial. But you have it now."

"You sure?"

"You haven't had it long. No antibodies as would show up in the tests Earth physicians use for HIV. Almost 150 Earth years ago, a Virus Holocaust wiped out our male population. We've been studying viruses since. Our tests for viruses are designed to check the DNA strand itself and identify the species. Sent a sample down to Cuc Nguyen at the Center for Disease Control in Atlanta. She verifies it's AIDS, HIV Strain Number One."

"The common strain." Sigh. "I thought I took reasonable precautions. But it's easy to slip and have direct flesh to flesh contact."

"You're not surprised you have the bug?"

"Afraid not. I just got to enjoying life a little too much. That virus treatment Metrola Mornuxler mentioned during the funeral?"

"We've been working on it since we came back from Operation Rainbow. We're almost done mapping the DNA sequence, a typical sequence for every known strain of the human immunodeficiency virus. We'll soon have a test sample of the enzyme designed specifically for HIV and no other virus. Would you consent to be injected with this enzyme as a test?"

"Experimental treatment. Is there any risk?"

"Biggest risk is that it won't work. You would not be risking any side effects."

"I know a lot of people who need that enzyme. Sure, I'll be your guinea pig and try the enzyme, whenever you are ready. I ask nothing in exchange."

"Good. We'll let you know when we have it ready."

"Sabar, it is Larry Bookbinder."

"Where's he calling from?"

"Concepcion, Chile."

"He wanted to get away from it all. This is Sabar Duradich. Is this Larry Bookbinder?"

"*Si*! Yes, it's me, Larry Bookbinder. You're the one assigned to represent Michelle?"

"Yes, I've been given that enviable task."

"Man, you ladies interrupted one wonderful fishing trip. We were high in the Andes, my wife and I, catching trout and salmon in the little streams that flow into the Rio Bio-Bio. This country is incredible in the Southern Spring! We watched your star in the sky, Alpha Centauri, everyone in Chile knows where it is. We had to come all the way into Concepcion to get to a phone capable of reaching the *Neanderthal Return*."

"I'm glad you and your wife had a good trip. Sorry about the interruption."

"Ahh, it comes with the territory. Any time a lawyer takes a vacation, there's always a client getting into trouble. As soon as we get back to the States, we're gonna file complaints in the U. S. District Courts protesting this business of letting our client be kidnapped when,"

"Larry,"

"when a Coast Guard cutter is sitting in the water fifty yards away! I don't give a rat's ass about the ship being a lousy fifteen miles off the coast,"

"Larry!"

"We had a deal! My client gave testimony for which certain people in the right wing fringe want to kill her, and they WILL kill her if they find her, the government promised to protect her. That FBI agent on the ship confirming she is Michelle,"

"Larry, the fingerprints matched up, the secret was already out!"

"THAT's a violation of our deal,"

"Larry!"

"And you promised not to kidnap any Earthling against his or her will!"

"Larry, our client violated the,"

"So I'll file suit in the courts to enforce these agreements!"

"Larry, PLEASE!"

"Oh. You want to get a word in edgewise. I'm sorry, I sometimes do that. Please. Go ahead."

Sabar took a deep breath. "Our client doesn't deny shooting Lchnsda. She admits it. There's no doubt about that, is there?"

"No, but,"

"No buts. Look. You can do whatever you want in the American courts. Problem is, our client is not in the United States, she's a prisoner on board an Atlantean ship. Atlantean law takes precedence here."

"We could sue you and enforce the judgment against your bank accounts."

"Yes, we sell our culture and language, and we use the money to meet our needs while in the Earth Solar System. But before we came here, we didn't have any Earth money, and after we leave for Creation, Earth money will be of no use to us."

"I take it that I'm not saying anything that would impress your makeshift court on your ship?"

"That's about right. So what we have to do is allow me to represent Michelle in dealing with our court, and for that I need your help."

"What kind of legal training do you have?"

"I once defended myself from a charge of a minor crime, what you call a misdemeanor."

"What did you do?"

"I didn't do it. A fact that worked to my advantage."

Larry chuckled. "Did you represent yourself?"

"Yes. I was accused of stealing astronomical equipment, telescopes and stuff. It's my passion. I proved that I had permission to borrow the equipment and that I intended to return it at an agreed to time."

"Good for you, but that's not quite the same as a law degree."

"I know. We have some good lawyers back on Creation. But when you have only 46 people on a space mission, you have to improvise. Michelle needs an advocate, our judge Contrviea Tiknika appointed me."

"So what are you gonna tell Contrviea?"

"I'll ask her to dismiss the case on the grounds that we agreed to not take an Earth person against her will. The prosecutor, Nesla Teslakian, will argue that because Michelle brought harm to Lchnsda, she violated the Agreement herself and therefore cannot claim its protection. I will argue that as an Earthling, our defendant cannot be rationally expected to look at the Agreement in terms of how Creation handled violations by individual citizens. She can only consider it by how Earth handled such violations."

"I see."

"That's where I need your help. I need you to provide me with information about how this is dealt with on Earth, particularly agreements and treaties involving the United States where the violators are American citizens."

"Yeah. Generally, when this sort of thing crops up, we either go by protocols within the Treaty or Agreement, or if there are none concerning violations, we enter into negotiations between the contracting nations to find a solution to the problem."

"That's what I needed to know. Please call your office and get your people working on it. Then I can ask Metrola Mornuxler to come pick you up in our Shuttle and bring you to the *Neanderthal Return* to appear in court with me."

"You would bring me to your ship?"

"You're a lawyer. Your client is facing criminal charges in our court. Put on your best suit and tie and bring your briefcase."

Larry laughed. "I'm afraid I'm not licensed to practice before an Atlantean court."

"Me neither. I think you call it *pro hac vice*. A temporary license to represent a client in one particular case."

Lucinda pulled the roast out of the oven. It was ready, smelled wonderful. An excellent dinner with corn on the cob and a salad of vegetables from Henry's farm. The Shuttle was parked in front of Henry's farmhouse. Henry poured a glass of Johannesburg Riesling for Metrola and another for himself. Lucinda had a sparkling cider, no alcohol when carrying the baby.

"Thanks for inviting me, Henry." said Metrola. "You know how we Atlantis women crave big animal meat. Is this beef? It smells wonderful but,"

"Roosevelt elk. Lucinda shot it. She handled that .35 caliber rifle beautifully."

"Red dot sights. Made it easy to take the elk at 200 *treefats*."

"*Treefats*!" Henry laughed. "Can't you call 'em yards?"

"Hey, at least I'm thinking Base Ten. It was a range of a *hekt* and four dozen *treefats*, or eight dozen *chmfats*. A little more than that, I believe."

"I keep forgetting you Creation women use fathoms on land. This *hekt* business is gross."

"Just for that, we should punish you by adopting the Metric System."

"No! Anything but that! You adopt the Metric System, I'll rat on you. It was on my license that we took the elk."

"Don't tell anyone I shot the elk, Metrola. You could get me into trouble."

"I won't tell anyone. Could get you arrested and tried in Elk Court."

"Yeah, the elks might not appreciate me shooting an elk."

"Hey, there are animal lovers on this Planet who can't handle the fact that we WOMEN go out and kill animals. For meat, furs, and leather. Come on! It's like Jean Auel's story about Neanderthals. From what I've seen, Ayla isn't the only Cro-Magnon woman to kill animals for food. So why can't Neanderthal women?"

"No reason. I did it. As long as there are enough Roosevelt elk to supply game for hunters without risking extinction of the species, then I don't see any problem with it."

"Some people don't like us buying minke whale meat from the Faeroes."

"Whale meat is the protein source for those people, it's how they survive. Hunting whales to extinction, that's a mistake. But allowing the whales to rebuild their population, then limited hunting to prevent overpopulation, that's not wrong. I'm surprised they're not selling sea lion meat in the supermarkets in Seattle! That would take care of the problem with the steelhead run."

Henry laughed. "That's like the day someone in Seattle found out that maybe the Muckleshoots have a treaty right to take sea lions. They asked them to come to the Ballard Locks and please exercise their treaty rights! So far, the Muckleshoots won't do it."

"Probably get hauled before Sea Lion Court."

"I thought a Sea Lion Quart is one fourth of a Sea Lion Gallon. So," Henry decided to change the subject, "what are you gonna do with Michelle? Take her back to Creation?"

"We don't want to take her to Creation." admitted Lucinda.

"Well," began Metrola, "we'd put her in jail for a few years, then let her out. Michelle might prove popular on Creation."

"How could she?"

"No men for nine dozen Creation years. We learned a whole new paradigm when it came to, uh, sexual pleasure. Before Lchnsda made love with you, she made love with me."

"Metrola, I really didn't want to know." Henry smiled, he already knew.

"Even so, after nine dozen years, a man is mighty hard to resist. Michelle is still a man under her skirt. All of that equipment still works."

"Miracle of modern medical science!" commented Henry as he rolled his eyes.

"On Creation, that's good enough for most ladies. Does the penis get hard? If so, many

Creation women would not care what the rest of him looks like."

Lucinda wore a silly grin and pinched Henry's cheek. "We ought to do the same thing to Henry. No facial hair to remove, full blooded Native American. Soften up the skin. Lots of estrogen hormones. Breast implants. Let this gorgeous black hair grow long. He could look like a regular Pocahontas!" The women laughed.

"A six foot three Pocahontas. I think I'll pass. I like looking like a man, I really do!" Henry was cracking up.

They had a marvelous time eating dinner and cracking jokes. After the dinner was cleaned up and the dishes put in the machine, Metrola asked, "Henry, you haven't been up to the ship, have you?"

"No, I'm afraid I haven't."

"We've got the Shuttle out front. Why don't you come up with us, I brought an extra pressure suit, made to fit you."

"Fit me?"

"Lucy told us about your size and weight. She'll need your support when she confronts Michelle."

"All right, I'll come."

"Thanks, Henry." Lucinda kissed him.

Betty Bentlakian stood guard at the door to Medical. "All right, Michelle," spoke Meddi kindly, "we now have the enzyme in you. In 24 hours, you should be clear of the HIV virus."

"Thank you. I know I don't deserve being helped by you, but thank you."

"Thank you, we'll find out if we have an AIDS treatment. When we head back to Creation, we have to have a way of knowing that everyone on this ship is absolutely clear of the AIDS virus. It's the one thing folks back home don't want us to bring."

"Can't say as I blame you, you've had enough problems with viruses."

"Indeed we have. We're done here, Bchsda, you may take Michelle back to her room. And please, let her take something back with her to read." Meddi handed Michelle a copy of *Welcome to the Neanderthal Return* in English. "If she's going to be on this ship, might as well have her familiar with our emergency and safety procedures."

"Yes, I've noticed all of the labels in English and Russian as well as Atlantean."

"Please read that through, Michelle. Until we decide how to work this out, we don't know how long you'll be on this ship."

Betty motioned Michelle into the hallway and they immediately ran into Lucinda, who had come by for a checkup. "Lchnsda, please move aside." requested Betty in Atlantean.

Lucinda quickly placed the barrel of a handgun to Michelle's ribs, just below her manufactured left breast. It was a heavy caliber Five Six, 11/24 *tig-it*. "Go ahead." challenged Michelle.

Lucinda quickly pulled the weapon away and holstered it. "I'm not you!"

"I'm not me, either. I haven't been myself lately."

"That's what happens when you try to be something you're not."

"Lchnsda, not now, please. Just let me take her back to her room."

"Sorry, Bchsda." Lucinda allowed Betty and her prisoner pass. She went into the Medical Department.

Meddi greeted Lucinda with mild disapproval. "A pregnant woman should try to lower the level of stress in her life."

"I know, Meddi. But this THING tried to kill me."

"She really is sorry she did it. Perhaps we can work something out."

Lucinda sat down and let out a long breath. She suddenly looked very tired. "Yeah, maybe we can. Hate can be a poison. Insidious, like a virus that gets into every part of your body and then kills you. Hate is a virus of the soul. Perhaps we could offer to return her to Earth if she waives the immunity she received for her testimony. And only some of the immunity, to prosecution for the crime of shooting me. Then the American court can sentence her to an appropriate amount of time in prison. That would satisfy me."

"We would have to involve the American authorities in such a deal. Right now, they seem happy to have her out of their hair. With the killers of the Secret Service agents processing their appeals, they can think of nine times nine ways Michelle could open her mouth and screw everything up for them. She could cheat them out of their death penalties."

"Michelle could make stuff up."

"Why not, her whole life is make believe. She would have to promise in writing not to do that so they could strip her of immunity for all of the other crimes she committed."

"That might cause her to honor her agreements. And they will have to protect her. Her testimony put five Avengers on death row."

"Her lawyer in the American courts is back in his District of Columbia law office researching international law for Sabar. We'll have the preliminary hearing, and then we can talk about a possible deal. As your physician, I do not want to see you going through the stress of a trial while carrying that baby. You and Helga are the first Neanderthal women to carry children since Trviea carried Sorby."

"We're near the Washington Monument with Brent Matlock of the State Department and Larry Bookbinder and his law clerk. The Shuttle from the *Neanderthal Return* will be landing in the grass near here in a few minutes. So Mr. Bookbinder, what's going to happen today?"

"The Shuttle will arrive in a few minutes, right about here. Lieutenant MacGregor and his troops will deploy in a defensive arc around the Shuttle, but they'll allow the Creation women to exit the Shuttle and perform a kind of a reenactment of the crime. My client will not be on the Shuttle, they don't want to bring her back inside American territory at this time. But they'll carry a video camera to record what happens and Michelle Smith will be watching in her room."

"Is it true that you're going to ride the Shuttle after the reenactment to appear before the Atlantis Court on the ship?"

"Yes." responded Brent Matlock. "We have an American citizen held prisoner on a foreign ship. I will go on board the ship to look after her welfare and make sure she's being treated well. The Agreement doesn't have any clause governing this situation, so the President has asked me to look into this and be available for negotiations. We don't have any problems with our relations with the *Neanderthal Return*, they are as friendly as ever."

"And I'll help Sabar Duradich represent our client before their Court. In this briefcase is information concerning how Earth nations, particularly the United States, has dealt with violations of treaties and agreements by their individual citizens. Sabar asked me to perform this research and accompany her to the Atlantis Court."

"Here they come now."

Metrola gently landed the Shuttle on the lawn, within the circle of soldiers. After a few minutes several women came out and walked over to Larry Bookbinder. "Are you Larry Bookbinder?"

"Yes, I am."

"I'm Sabar Duradich, pleased to meet you." They shook hands. "That your research on Earth international law?"

"Yes, we've been working very hard compiling it."

"Thank you." She greeted Brent Matlock and the other people in the little group.

Another woman offered her hands to shake. "Nesla Teslakian, I'm prosecuting Michelle Smith."

Larry shook her hands, "Pleased to meet you."

"Contrviea Tiknika, I'm the judge of the Atlantis Court. These other women are here to help us. This is Wlmsda Gtslakian with the camera."

"People up on the ship, including your client, can now see you on video screens." informed Wlmsda.

"Hi, Michelle." Larry waved into the camera.

"Would you each like to wear a headset?" They put a headset on Larry and another one on Brent Matlock.

"Hi Larry." Michelle's voice said into the ears of Larry and Brent.

"How are they treating you?" Larry and Brent both asked.

"Not bad. Food is healthy, tastes okay. It's boring, they have me locked in this room with nothing to do. This chrome collar shuts you down if you get out of hand. They have examined me in their Medical Department. They say I tested positive for HIV."

"Sorry to hear that. Are they sure?" Larry asked while Brent nodded his head.

"They have some kind of whiz bang test that can identify a virus before you start forming antibodies. Cuc Nguyen at CDC verifies it. I can't say they're wrong. During the last few months in San Francisco, I've had all kinds of sex with all kinds of genders. Now that I remember, some of these guys didn't use condoms and I didn't care. Anyway, they think they've sequenced the DNA of the AIDS virus and have injected me with their experimental enzyme."

"Did they do this against," demanded Brent, in his sudden concern.

"I consented. Who doesn't want to get rid of the AIDS virus if possible? Earth medicine sure hasn't got viruses figured out, especially HIV."

"What are they going to do today?"

"I guess they want to reenact the crime. I get to watch on this TV screen."

They walked across Constitution Avenue to where Michelle stood with her gun. They pulled photographs of the shooting out of a briefcase. Many were published in newspapers. Wlmsda filmed the group from the south side of Constitution while they tried to place Michelle's location on the north side of the Avenue. Behind them through the Ellipse could be seen the South Portico of the White House. The President stood in the Second Floor balcony and watched through binoculars.

"Am I in about the right place?" asked Nesla.

"I was about twenty feet to the east, toward the Capitol." informed Michelle.

"Michelle, you don't hafta," advised Larry.

"Larry, right now I'm immune to prosecution in American courts. Thank you. I may be immune in Atlantis Court, if Contrviea grants Sabar's motion."

"Trust me Larry, she's doing the right thing in terms of Atlantean law." informed Sabar. "All we're doing right now is getting a feel for the scene of the crime and what happened. There's no question of Michelle's guilt, we have dozens of photographs of Michelle lifting the gun and firing, and then being tackled and taken into custody by the Secret Service agents."

Nesla moved the twenty feet toward the Capitol. "This better?"

"Yes, I think that's about right." responded Sabar, studying a 15 by 25 inch blowup of a photograph of Michelle firing from the crowd. "Is it, Michelle?"

"Yes, that's about right. I didn't stand at the front of the crowd, I was one rank back. The rope was on the edge of the sidewalk, you can see how close you are to the floats passing by.

When you plan to shoot someone protected by the Secret Service, you don't want to stand right in front. You want one line of people in front of you to shield your body from the agents' view. Being five eleven, like Nesla, I was able to see very well. I smiled and waved to look like the other people and avoid attracting attention to myself."

The other Creation women stood in a line along the edge of the sidewalk, Nesla, the same height as Michelle, stood behind the line. "The people in front of me were women, about five three to five foot eight." Michelle continued. The women in front of Nesla crouched down to mimic the height. "When the float carrying your women passed by, I very quickly pulled out the pistol with my right hand, extended to full length between two of the heads, used my left hand to brace my right wrist, aimed at Lucinda, and fired. Faster than that Nesla, try again."

Nesla extended her thumb and forefinger to mimic a gun the way a child does. She stood behind the other women along the sidewalk and quickly extended her right hand between two heads, braced with her left hand and said "Bang!"

"Yeah, that's about how I did it."

"All right," said Contrviea in Atlantean, "I believe that is enough." She switched to English and spoke to Brent Matlock. "Thank you for letting us do this."

"You're welcome. We have a few of the ladies who actually stood here in front of and around Michelle when she shot Lucinda. Ladies, you may come over."

The group of witnesses came over and was greeted warmly by the Creation women. But they gave Larry Bookbinder a cold stare. "We've prepared signed and notarized affidavits describing what we saw and heard when Michelle Smith ruined our St. Paddy's day."

"Are they sworn?" asked Nesla.

"Yes, they are sworn, we certified them under penalty of perjury under the laws of the United States and the laws of Atlantis."

"Thank you, we'll take these statements and read them. If we have a trial, we may call you to testify. We might bring you up to the ship or set you up in front of a video link. Your names and phone numbers? We can call from the ship."

"That's all in there! Are you in communication with your ship?"

"Yes, we talk with these radios. Here, I'll show you my headset." Nesla removed her headset. "They can hear us in the *Neanderthal Return*. One of the people listening in is Michelle Smith."

"Michelle Smith!" she spat out the name with disgust. "Can you hear me?"

"Yes, I can." answered a tiny voice out of the earphones.

"My ears still ring. That gun was right smack next to my head! It hurt for days, it was weeks before the seashell sound disappeared. I'm an old lady, I can't heal so fast. Here are these beautiful women coming down to us to make peace. I know they kidnapped Neil Peace, but he's forgiven 'em. And you have to go and shoot Lucinda, after first helping the terrorists who killed those poor Secret Service men, all because of racial hatred! I'm proud to be an American but I'm embarrassed that you are!"

"What's your name, please?"

"My name is Darleen Shannon. I am also proud to be Irish. You ruined our holiday!"

"Darleen Shannon, I am sorry. I don't know what else I can say."

"You don't mean it! You think you can take advantage of the naive good intentions of these wonderful women. Make 'em think you're sorry, they might let you go!"

"Ms. Shannon, believe it or not, I believe I should spend some time in prison for my crimes."

Darleen was taken aback by that. "You SHOULD do time!"

Nesla put her headset back on. "Thank you, Darleen, thank you very much."

"All right, ladies and gentlemen," started Contrviea, "we've agreed to take Larry Bookbinder and Brent Matlock with us to the ship. Metrola is waiting for us, let's go on over and get suited up for the trip."

"We get suited up?" asked Larry, in his suit and tie.

"Safety precaution, in case there's a leak in the hull when we're above the atmosphere. Can't breathe vacuum."

Chapter Fifty Four

Inspections and repairs took place all over the ship. But the busy mechanics and craftswomen were not annoyed that Contrviea Tiknika and Nesla Teslakian took time off to deal with the person who shot Lucinda Renuxler. Contrviea wore her regular clothes, but there was no doubt she had been appointed judge by Captain Trviea Harsradich. She sat in front of Conference Room One reading the pleadings, in English and Atlantean, filed by Nesla, Sabar Duradich, and Larry Bookbinder.

The other Creation women also dressed casually. As they freely admit, neither Sabar, Nesla, nor Contrviea have attended law school. But they had plenty of time during their voyage to study the extensive library on Atlantean law in the computers. Larry Bookbinder and Brent Matlock felt out of place in their suits and ties. The other Earthling in the room, Henry Turnipseed, dressed casually and sat with Lucinda, they held hands.

Wlmsda Hotlund led Michelle Smith into the room and let her sit with her lawyers. She wore the clothes she wore on the *Silver Girl*, minus the leather accessories plus the metal collar. At least no makeup, thought Larry, this isn't the place for bright red lipstick. No five o'clock shadow, electrolysis. But a masculine hardness crept into her/his face. The clothes! Normally he advises his clients not to dress so loud when appearing in court. Well, can't do nothing about it now.

Sabar and Larry spoke quietly with their client. After a few minutes, Contrviea asked Sabar in Atlantean, "How much longer do you need?"

"About 12 *linits*." Ten minutes.

"All right, we'll get started in about that much time."

After the ten minutes, Contrviea asked, "Is everyone ready?" She repeated in English. Everyone answered yes. Contrviea began, "Because the defendant is an American who speaks English and doesn't know Atlantean, and because everyone else here can speak English, we'll conduct this hearing in English. Michelle Smith, you have been charged in this court with one count of assault with a deadly weapon against a citizen of Atlantis, causing said citizen grievous injury. Allow me to explain some of our Atlantean procedure. In a criminal case, we first have a hearing to determine if the charge can be heard by this court, is correctly filed in this court, and that there is sufficient evidence to indicate that you may have committed the crime. This is not an arraignment, you won't be entering a plea today. This court has jurisdiction because the victim is a citizen of Atlantis. But the crime occurred within the territory of a foreign nation, the United States of America, a nation on the Planet Earth. The defendant charged with this crime is a citizen of this foreign nation. Ordinarily, we allow the foreign nation the responsibility of prosecuting and punishing the offender under its laws. However, in a deal we're not a party to, this foreign nation granted immunity to prosecution to the defendant, allowing a crime against a citizen of Atlantis to go unpunished. The defendant was subsequently found outside the territory of the United States, where she was arrested. The counsel appointed to represent the defendant has filed a motion to dismiss the charge. Sabar, please tell this court why we should dismiss the charge against your client."

Sabar did not stand up, she spoke from the table. "We have entered into an Agreement with the United States of America, that we negotiated with their President, said Agreement ratified by their Senate per their Constitution for a one Earth year term. This one year term is still in progress and is subject to renewal by the United States Senate and by ourselves. In the terms of this Agreement, we promised that we would not remove any person from Earth against that person's will. The Agreement specifically uses the word 'Earth'. It is not limited to the territory of the United States, but extends to the entire Planet. We violated this Agreement by removing a United States citizen from Earth against her will. Therefore, Michelle Smith is not properly before this court. We respectfully request the charge be dismissed and this court order Miss Smith to be returned to the territory of the United States."

"Thank you, Sabar. Nesla, please tell this court why the defendant's motion should be denied."

Nesla spoke from her table, in English. "It is true that the Agreement Between the United States and the *Neanderthal Return* prohibits us from removing a person from Earth against that person's will. But the Agreement also requires the United States to take every reasonable precaution to protect members of the crew of our ship from harm when we are within U.S. territory. Under American law, an Agreement with a foreign nation, or representatives of a foreign nation such as we are, negotiated by their President and ratified by their Senate, is binding upon all citizens of the United States. Michelle Smith is a citizen of the United States, bound by the Agreement. By aiming a weapon at Lchnsda Renuxler, firing, and causing grievous injury to her, Miss Smith violated the Agreement. It is a well known rule of international law on Planet Creation that when a person so violates an Agreement, that person cannot subsequently claim the protection of the Agreement. Therefore, Miss Smith cannot claim the protection of this Agreement unless she is acquitted of the charge of assault with a deadly weapon against a citizen of Atlantis, such action which violates the Agreement. Miss Smith is properly before this court to answer this charge."

"Thank you, Nesla. Sabar, please tell this court about any flaws you claim with Nesla's argument."

"Nesla would be absolutely correct if the United States is a nation on Planet Creation. But the United States is on Planet Earth and we are in the Earth Solar System. Therefore, we must look upon this Agreement and the violation of this Agreement alleged against a citizen of the United States in light of how international law has worked on Earth. The rule that Nesla cites simply does not exist on Earth. Because of the haste with which the Agreement was worked out, with the United States and the other nations of Earth, it is very clear that the Earth nations consider this Agreement an extension of Earth international law to relations with a ship originating from a Planet other than Earth. It is not rational to expect either the United States or a citizen of the United States to consider this Agreement in terms of how international law is practiced on Creation. We must consider this Agreement in terms of how it is practiced on Earth."

"Thank you, Sabar. We have had ample opportunity to study Earth customs in the time since we've first built receivers capable of reconstructing sound and video out of Earth radio transmissions. But Earth lacked a similar knowledge of our laws and customs. If we desired to incorporate a Creation custom into our Agreement with the Earth nations, we could have proposed it in our negotiations. We did not. Therefore, I find that we cannot apply Creation international law customs to our Agreements with Earth nations while we are in the Earth Solar System. I find that we must follow Earth customs in the application of our Agreement with the United States. I find that Michelle Smith did not automatically lose her protection under the Agreement when she allegedly violated it. Before I rule further, I need more information on how Earth nations have handled violations of treaties and agreements on the part of their citizens. Sabar?"

"Thank you, Contrviea. I asked Larry Bookbinder to come on board our ship and appear at

504

this hearing, a request he graciously granted. He has been Michelle Smith's lawyer representing her before the American courts. He is knowledgeable in American law and Earth international law, particularly where it involves the United States."

"Larry Bookbinder," greeted Contrviea, "welcome aboard the *Neanderthal Return* and thank you for coming. We have two clauses of the Agreement between our two countries that are relevant to this case. We have agreed to not take any person from Earth against that person's will. The United States agreed to take all reasonable steps to prevent harm to any one of us, said Agreement binding on Michelle Smith. Larry, how do we deal with this situation in a way that complies with Earth international law?"

"It is the general Earth practice that when violations of a treaty or agreement between two nations occur, we first look to the agreement for any remedies it provides, and absent such remedies, it is subject to negotiations between the two nations. Here, we have an Agreement that is silent on how to deal with violations. So what we have to do is to enter into negotiations to solve the problem. We should strive for a deal that all parties can agree to. When a treaty breaks down, we often have wars. Our wars have been catastrophic in property damage, lives, and human suffering. We're reluctant to consider an Agreement null and void because of a violation. The deal would have to speak to Lchnsda's injury and her need for an apology and to feel safe from any further harm by Michelle. But it would also have to speak to Michelle's rights as an American. It would have to speak to the rights of Atlantis and the United States as sovereign nations. There would have to be some give and take. And overall, we have to consider the continuation of excellent relations between the United States and Atlantis to be our top priority."

"Thank you, Larry. I will not at this time dismiss the charge against Michelle Smith. What I will do is recess the court for the purpose of allowing the parties and the representatives of our two countries to enter into negotiations aimed at resolving the issues presented by this case. Court is now in recess, you may use this room to conduct negotiations." Contrviea put her decision into writing, in Atlantean and English. She printed copies and provided them to Nesla, Larry, Sabar, Michelle, Lucinda, and Brent Matlock. She left the room to deliver a copy of her decision to Captain Trviea Harsradich.

"Before we begin negotiations," announced Brent, "I need to make a call to Earth and discuss this with our President. Let's take a break and meet back here in an hour." Everyone agreed to that.

The President granted Brent Matlock plenipotentiary power to transact business as a diplomatic agent. He gave his agent instructions designed to safeguard American interests now and in the future. First instruction was that he was not to agree to any arrangement where an Atlantean court shall pass judgment on an American citizen for a crime committed on American soil. If the Atlanteans wish to recognize the Solar System as being within the sovereignty of the Earth nations, then this has to be part of the sovereignty they recognize. Nevertheless, our relations with this other Human Race must be secured on a friendly basis. Some kind of settlement that deals with the injury to Lucinda Renuxler is in order, and some way of assuring that no further violence against any Neanderthal shall be perpetrated by Michelle Smith would be desirable. No waiver of the immunity previously granted to Michelle Smith for her testimony shall be made without the express voluntary agreement by Miss Smith herself. Otherwise, our Justice Department will be unable to make the deals we sometimes have to make in the enforcement of our laws.

Brent took this tall order into Conference Room One at the scheduled time.

During the break, Michelle Smith went to Medical for a checkup. Meddi informed her of the results. "The HIV has been completely eliminated from your blood, urine, saliva, mucus, and other body fluids."

Michelle screamed for joy. "Yes! Thank you! Get the formula for this to Earth!"

"We're not done yet. It is in your tissue samples we still have a problem. The virus is still present in your cells. About one twelfth of what you had before."

Michelle sobered up. "That's not good enough."

"Not good enough. You will live, oh, about five years longer than you would have without this treatment. But you are still able to spread it to your sex partners. So continue to practice celibacy. Or safe sex, which is do whatever you want as long as you don't touch each other." They both chuckled. "In the meantime, we'll give you a second dose of this enzyme, after we reformulate it based on these results, it should wipe out the remaining viruses in your cells. Then you'll be free of it, and we can pronounce our experiment a success."

"Okay, Meddi. Let's go for it."

"Mr. President, it's Brent Matlock."

"Hi Brent. What's going on upstairs?"

"We have a tentative agreement. But the negotiating team minus Michelle Smith wants to meet with you."

"Sure, they can meet me in the Oval Office. Metrola can land the Shuttle on the South Lawn inside the fence and they can come in through the Portico."

"Thank you, Mr. President. We're on our way. Oh, and the physician, Meddi Chumkun, will be bringing a medical bag with syringes. It's the cure for AIDS, or so she says. Please ask the Secret Service to take it easy with her and her satchel. It's something she wants to show you."

The Shuttle landed and the group went in to meet with the President in the Oval Office. After they explained the Agreement they worked out for Michelle Smith, the President told them that it looked good. But he warned, "Don't you girls think for a minute that Michelle is sincere in her remorse, she's most likely putting on an act to manipulate you. She/he is a hardened criminal, experienced in the art of make believe."

"That thought has occurred to me, Mr. President." admitted Lucinda. "But we can try to turn her around. Most likely we won't. I cannot afford the stress of being angry with someone, even one who tried to kill me. In my belly is someone who is far more important to me."

"I understand." affirmed the President warmly.

"I'm the injured party here, and this deal is what I want. Michelle Smith has agreed to waive the immunity to her attack against me last St. Patrick's Day. That should be sufficient for a few years of jail time, which she is willing to do. Larry Bookbinder has agreed to a recommendation of about five years. By the end of such a sentence, we should be on our way home to Creation or already there. A few of us may stay behind to form an embassy with the Earth nations, and we'll have to take our chances when Michelle is released. But in the meantime, those of us who come down from our ship will have one less person to worry about. For that I'm willing to accept Michelle's apology, to tell her that I forgive her, and to wish her good luck."

"I notice that there are no signatures on this Agreement." noted the President.

Larry spoke for his client. "Michelle said that she wasn't signing this Agreement unless she saw your signature."

"I concurred with her decision on that." noted Sabar.

"I understand that. If you give us a few hours, we will review this Agreement with our Attorney General and our lawyers and experts, and verify that this Agreement is in accord with

American interests and law. All right. Meddi! I understand you have something far more pleasant than dealing with a criminal."

"Yes I do, Mr. President." The smiling physician placed her bag on the table. It is a large rectangular briefcase. She opened it to reveal five two *glup* jars of fluid and 144 syringes with several times that many spare needles. "Here are eight *glups* of a saline solution containing a concentration just shy of saturation level of our HIV virus destroying enzyme. Note how small the syringes are. The dose shall only be two twelfths of a *dollop* of the fluid, two milliliters. We were able to perfect this enzyme and the treatment regimen by using Michelle as a guinea pig. She volunteered and did not ask for anything in return. After the second treatment the virus is completely gone from her as far as we can tell, but I would recommend a checkup every month she is in your prison to make sure. We have another two *glups* of the test fluid we use for HIV. Note the bottle is clearly labeled in English. It takes only 144th of a *dollop*, a tenth of a milliliter, of this fluid on a test sample of blood or tissue to test for HIV. If it finds an HIV DNA molecule, it replicates that DNA chain until we have enough to allow positive identification of the virus. Don't inject THIS stuff into an AIDS patient, we don't want MORE viruses in the patient. This should allow detection long before the antibodies start to form. It's during this stage, when the infected person doesn't know he or she has the virus, that it gets spread. The idea is to immediately inject two twelfths of a *dollop* of the ENZYME solution into the person's veins and kill the virus before that person can spread it further."

"Put an end to the epidemic."

"Exactly, Mr. President. This enzyme kills the virus by matching up with its DNA chain and tearing it apart. It then looks for another virus DNA chain to tear apart. It will do this in the blood and in the cells, everywhere the virus is. One injection should be enough to clear a person with full blown AIDS of the virus within a few days."

"Are you sure? You needed a second shot to clear Michelle, and she was in the earliest stage of the disease, when she wouldn't even test positive under our tests. Cuc Nguyen has been keeping me up to date on this, I thought you were several weeks away from fully mapping the DNA chain."

"Then Michelle showed up and she tested positive. We used her infected blood to finish the development of this enzyme. We needed the second treatment to perfect the enzyme's ability to clear the virus from inside cells. Now we have the most lethal virus killer ever made. And yet, because it cannot match up with the DNA chain of anything but an HIV virus, it's safe and will not have the side effects we have with drugs. We might beat the evolutionary process by killing ALL of the viruses and leaving none to pass on whatever characteristics that allow 'em to survive the treatment. There is enough here for a rigorous testing regime to satisfy your FDA. These English language pamphlets explain it all and how to make more, how to make it in mass production. We strongly suggest you license every capable pharmaceutical company on Earth to make this enzyme and this test solution. Before your FDA approves this, you should use this on an emergency basis for those who are near death. Clearing their bodies of the virus might not save them, but it's their only chance. We have several hundred of these packages on the Shuttle. While you are reviewing the Agreement as to Michelle Smith, we will take those bags over to the United Nations' offices here in Washington and to every embassy we can visit. It's imperative we get this into the hands of the UN World Health Organization and into the health care system of every nation on this Planet. Our goal is to not let one more square be added to the Quilt."

The President picked up the phone. "Dr. Nguyen, yes. You already know all about this. Good. Meddi Chumkun just briefed me and delivered the package of enzyme. Yes. Eight *glups* of enzyme solution ready to inject, 144 syringes each two twelfths of a *dollop* in size. Two *glups* of the test solution. You already have the test solution in production. About 10 gallons already. Good. Okay. Dr. Nguyen, I'm putting you in charge of this, I'll cut an Executive Order requiring everyone in the federal health care and research system to cooperate with you in the fullest. That's the Medicare, the FDA, the CDC, the National Institutes of Health, the military hospitals, everything. Meddi has a couple hundred of these packages; she will now meet with the World Health Organization and with as many embassies in town as she can visit. All right. Thank you, Cuc, you are a hero to the world, get on it!" The President put the phone down. He motioned to a Secret Service man. "Fred, get a detail together and escort these women as they make their rounds. When they get back later today, we should have this Agreement ready to sign."

They were back in Conference Room One. Judge Contrviea Tiknika began the hearing as before, informally. "I have read the Agreement. It is in English and Atlantean, I find that the translations are accurate. It has the signatures of the President and the Attorney General of the United States and of Brent Matlock as Ambassador Plenipotentiary of the United States. It also has the signatures of Nesla Teslakian as the prosecutor in this court, Sabar Duradich and Larry Bookbinder as the defense counsel, Michelle Smith the defendant, Lchnsda Renuxler the injured party, and Trviea Harsradich as Captain of the *Neanderthal Return* and representative of Atlantis. It calls for the dismissal of this charge in this court. By her signature, Michelle Smith waives her immunity to prosecution in American court for the crime she committed against Lchnsda last March 17, Earth time, and agrees to plead guilty in American court to the crimes of assault with a deadly weapon and reckless endangerment with the enhancement of using a gun in a crime. Michelle Smith, did you sign this Agreement on your free will?"

"Yes I did, your Honor. I read the entire Agreement and I understand it fully."

Contrviea understood and respected the Earth custom of referring to a judge as "Your Honor."

"Are you aware that you are now liable for the crime you committed against Lchnsda Renuxler in American court and that you have agreed to plead guilty to that crime and accept the sentence to be handed down by the American judge?"

"Yes, your Honor. My attorney for American court has agreed to recommend a five year prison sentence. But I also understand that the American judge is not bound by this agreement, he could impose a different sentence. I will undergo evaluation for a pre-sentence report, as provided in American law. I agree to this, freely and without coercion."

"Are you aware that upon dismissal of this charge in this court that we are bound by this Agreement to return you to the United States at the cemetery and deliver you into the custody of the United States Marshals?"

"Yes, your Honor, I agree to this condition."

"All right. I will now read the paragraph that the President of the United States added at the end of the Agreement, and it has been faithfully and accurately translated into Atlantean. 'The President, on behalf of the United States, and on behalf of the Secret Service and the families of the men murdered in the line of duty, declare as follows: We understand that Michelle Smith has agreed to take responsibility for her crime against Lchnsda Renuxler in Washington, D.C. on March 17. We will enforce the sentence the United States District Court for the District of Columbia will impose upon her for this crime. However, we needed her testimony to bring to justice all those who committed the horrible crimes near the Hood Canal in the State of Washington last February. We thank her for this testimony. We thank her for her contribution to the development of the treatment that may end the AIDS plague on Earth. For these reasons, while we will ensure that she serves her sentence, she is still in the Witness Protection Program and we will take whatever steps necessary to protect her life from any person who may harm her for the testimony she has given in *United States v. Binford, Plotkin, et al.*' Does everyone agree to this condition?"

Everyone answered yes.

"Do you, Michelle Smith, understand and agree to this condition?"

"Yes, your Honor. I wish to remain alive for a while longer."

"Very well. I hereby dismiss this case and remand Michelle Smith to the custody of the United States Marshals as required by the Agreement. That concludes *Atlantis v. Smith*. Good luck, Miss Smith."

The Shuttle landed in the parking lot outside the cemetery. Mrs. Bookbinder waited in her car to pick up her husband and to offer a lift to Brent Matlock. Two United States Marshals stood next to the U.S. Marshal's Service car and waited. While the details of the transfer were not released to the public, a few reporters were there on a hunch. A police roadblock kept them back. After a few minutes to allow everyone to climb out of the precautionary pressure suits, the door opened and the ramp was extended. Captain Harsradich came out and greeted each Marshal with a two handed handshake. "This will only take a few minutes, and then we will hand her over to you."

"Sure. We've been briefed on what you want to do. Take your time, we'll be here."

"Thank you." Trviea went into the Shuttle and emerged with a large bouquet of fresh flowers. She was followed by Lucinda, Henry, Metrola Mornuxler, Helga Trvlakian, Andemona Chmlakian, Sabar, Larry Bookbinder, Brent Matlock, and Nesla. Each carried a bouquet of flowers. Larry's wife came out of her car to join them. She brought her own wreath of flowers and greeted her husband with a kiss. Then Wilma Hotlund and Betty Bentlakian emerged, escorting Michelle Smith, dressed in her own clothes. Each also carried a bouquet of flowers.

The group formed a procession and solemnly entered the cemetery.

They arrived at the well tended grave. The stone monument towered over the grave. A stone lid covered the grave, small rocks were placed along the edge by Jews as a gesture of respect. The group gathered around the grave. One by one, each placed his or her flowers upon the grave. Chiseled in the stone in three alphabets is the name Sorby Mishlakian. They held hands and formed a human chain around the grave. The women spoke softly in Atlantean, the Prayer for the Dead. Tears flowed from their eyes, except for Michelle. Then a soft sad song in Atlantean.

Lucinda went to Michelle and spoke softly. "Michelle, please read the inscription. The epitaph. It's in three languages, one of them is English. Out loud, please."

Michelle read it. "She dances in the sky," her voice broke, but she continued, "surrounded by the stars, a vast glittering carpet of jewels, no longer beyond her reach."

"That's what we are about. You didn't know what we were about, you thought it was something else, causing you to hurt me."

"This is what you are about, how?"

"Well, uh, someday, I will die. You will die. Everyone here will someday pass on and join the Great Holy Spirit. Or God. Doomsday. It could happen. There may be a time when the last of us dies. And we will be no more. It happened to my Race on Earth. We don't know how. We don't know why. We only know that it happened. And we know it can happen. To us. To your Race. And to mine. And if there is such a day, it will truly be a Judgment Day, and we will have been judged. You understand, Michelle?"

"I think so. It is possible that the last of us dies, and we will be no more."

"No more human laughter, no more human sorrow. Our languages, our songs, our prayers, our beliefs, our voices, all gone from the Universe. No more human love, no more human hate.

This can happen. But it doesn't have to. It is a matter of doing the right thing, not the wrong thing. A decision I have to make every day. A decision you have to make every day. A decision everyone of us must make. Sometimes we have to think about it to decide. Fortunately God gave us everything we need. To make the right decisions and to carry them out. It is not easy. It is not guaranteed. It is up to us. If not enough of us make the right decision, then we will disappear from the Universe, just as my Race disappeared from Earth. But if enough of us make the right decision, then our future is as limitless as the stars among which Sorby dances. And they will no longer be beyond our reach. The proof of this is in my belly. It is in Helga's belly. It is in the bellies of millions of women on Earth. And if the Great Holy Spirit allows, it will be in the bellies of *beeyons* of women on Creation. The entire Universe is waiting for us, we only need to do the right thing, not the wrong thing. That is what we're about. Do you understand?"

Tears now flowed from Michelle's hardened criminal eyes. She nodded her head. "I'm sorry I shot you, Lchnsda Renuxler." She pronounced her Atlantean name correctly.

"I accept your apology. Will you plead guilty in the United States Court?"

"Yes, I will, and I will serve my sentence."

"Then I forgive you, Michelle Smith."

They walked back out of the cemetery to the Marshal's car. A Marshal placed the cuff on Michelle's left wrist and brought it around her back. He brought the other wrist and placed the other cuff on it. Trviea let her fingerprint be read by the collar and released it. She carried the collar away. Michelle was actually relieved that she didn't have to worry about suddenly being paralyzed. Lucinda said one last thing to her. "Good luck, Michelle." Then she turned to Brent Matlock and asked him quietly, "You think we got through to her?"

"I doubt it, she was just playing her part. It's the leopard changing his spots."

"It was worth a try." Sigh.

Michelle stepped into the back seat. A Marshal guided her head into the car with his hand.

Chapter Fifty Five

Henry Turnipseed and Lucinda Renuxler were getting ready in their very fancy hotel room. "Henry! Put your hand on my belly."

Henry placed his hand. "He's kicking!" He giggled.

"Yeah, it kinda hurts. But isn't it wonderful?" She put her arms around him and kissed him passionately. "Now put on your best clothes."

"Best clothes. For a football game?"

"We're invited to a luxury box. The sort of thing that happens when some rich guy wants celebrities to hobnob with him. It's the Super Bowl."

"I'm no celebrity. I don't have that kind of vanity. As for the Super Bowl, I'd rather watch it on television or be out in the crowd in the sun."

"January sun. But in this part of the United States, January can be warm. The Senate renewed our Agreement for another year, so I get to stay here a little longer. But I have to be a diplomat. For my Race, and my Planet. And you have to be a diplomat too. You're the father of the first truly interracial child in perhaps 30,000 years." They kissed again.

"Speaking of race, at least the Redskins aren't playing."

"I'm just plum happy they don't name a team the Trogs or the Cavemen." They giggled. "So why aren't Norwegians and Icelanders upset with all of these teams named Vikings?"

"In most places where a college or high school names their team the Vikings, and in Minnesota where the professional football team goes by that name, people of Scandinavian descent are in control. By dent of numbers or wealth, many of the movers and shakers in such communities are, well, Vikings. It's a popular choice among the people of that ethnic background and most don't mind the cartoon image of a blonde Norwegian man wearing a horned helmet. But no way in Hell are people of my race in control in Washington, D.C., even if the occasional Ben Nighthorse Campbell gets elected. 'Redskins' is a racial insult. Folks from Bombay and Calcutta probably think we Native Americans are pretty presumptuous calling ourselves 'Indians'. That's what Columbus called us because he thought he was in Indonesia. The cartoon characters they use to depict us as mascots are not flattering. Chief Wahoo looks like he's been smoking a pipe that had something other than tobacco in it. I'm not going to be a sourpuss and ruin it for those people who are only interested in enjoying a football or baseball game, but I do appreciate it when some high school or college changes their mascot to something other than a Native American caricature."

"Yeah, they can change it to Spartans or Trojans and hope Greek and Turkish people don't take offense." More laughter. "I guess if they were to name a team the 'Cavemen', I would have to realize they aren't talking about technologically modern humans who travel in spaceships."

"Well, the whole business of team mascots and school colors is just silliness anyway. They were never intended to be serious."

"No, they are intended to be part of people having fun on a game day. Let us dress elegantly and have a good time in the luxury box. I'm amazed I can find such good dresses that not only fit me, but can be fit to my five month pregnancy. Do this for me, Henry. Come with me to the luxury box, please?"

"I love you, Lchnsda. If you want me to watch the Super Bowl in a luxury box with somebody who inherited too much money and has no idea what it's like to have to take orders to receive a paycheck, I'll do it for you."

"We all have to make sacrifices."

Henry put on his suit and tie. "Lchnsda, how are we going to raise this child?"

"We'll raise him, or her. We'll give this child all of our love as any good parent gives. We'll work something out."

"The something should be marriage. There's no law against a Neanderthal marrying a Native American. Our Supreme Court would never stand for it, not when Justice Clarence Thomas is loving Virginia while living in Virginia because of *Loving v. Virginia*."

Lucinda sighed. This isn't the first time Henry asked. And while he has Popped the Question, she has not been ready to give him an answer. "Where would we live?"

"Wherever we decide to live."

"I love you, Henry. You are young enough to believe that love can conquer all. That no matter what the difficulties, we can overcome them and work things out. But here is what we are looking at: If you come to Creation with me, you'll be separated from every person you know on Earth, except the Cro-Magnons who come with us. You may never see your sister and her family again. You'll be separated from the rest of the Puyallup Tribe. Until the next time a spaceship can fly back to Earth. Are you willing to do that? For me?"

"If that's what's necessary, yes."

She looked at him in the eyes. Concentrated very hard. "Yes. I believe you would. You do love me." She smiled nervously. "If we stay here on Earth, you would not have to give up all that. We need to leave a few women representing Creation interests here on Earth. To be ready when the response by the Creation nations to our proposed Sovereignty Treaty comes. Until we build faster spaceships, or find a carrier wave faster than radio or light, communication across the 25 trillion miles will be difficult and slow at best. I will be cut off from everyone I know on Creation except the few other women we leave behind for our diplomacy. At least until our child grows up, I will not see Cair Atlaston again, or drive the Shirelind Road. Speak Atlantean in a country where everyone speaks Atlantean, and reckons in Base Twelve numbers. And I wouldn't see my farm. It's a wonderful farm, Henry, you would love it. I had many a wonderful time there, with," she suddenly stopped. She couldn't say the name.

Henry stood up, walked over to another chair, and sat down. "It's all right, Lchnsda. I won't stand between you and Chmlee."

"It's not that." She grabbed a towel and buried her face in it to wipe away her tears. A sob broke, muffled by the towel.

Henry understood how he could hurt her very bad. He didn't want to. He came back over and put his hand on her shoulder. "You're afraid."

"I don't want to get hurt again."

"I know. But it comes with the territory. You have a husband, if you will have me, and you have a child. I face the same possibilities you do. I was afraid I lost you on St. Patrick's Day. And again after you detonated the first Russian bomb in Comet Wormwood. But we cannot allow that to stop ourselves from knowing love."

"I knew love. I loved Chmlee more than anything else, more than I thought possible. I still love him. I drank from the silver cup, as your rock musicians say. Then I watched him suffer, and I watched him die. It's a bitter draught. The Virus can survive an incredibly long time in a cyst, in a dry place somewhere. The type of enzyme we are using to cure every AIDS patient we can find, is what we used to wipe out that Virus wherever it could be found. Askelion and Meddi are convinced that the Virus that took our men cannot replicate with a Cro-Magnon Y chromosome. But what if it can? You come to Creation, it can kill you the same way it killed Chmlee."

"That's the chance I'm willing to take."

"I know. But is it the chance I'm willing to take? I'm not Innocent of the Grief. Maybe if you come to Creation, we can marry you to a Mishlakian girl. They did not experience what we experienced. You and she would be happy, and you would still be around to see our child and to help me raise it."

"You're talking nonsense, Lchnsda. It is you I love, and you love me. And that is that. If the Virus becomes a problem, then we'll go after it with our medical technology. Look at all of the people we have cured of AIDS. All the HIV positives who are now clear of the virus. It's still rampant in Africa, but we're sending in the enzyme as fast as we can produce it. Everywhere else, we've got that bug on the run! We have not added a single square to the Quilt! Earlier, we took care of a comet. Instead of Doomsday, we will have Flyby Day, where it'll fill the sky, but not enter the sky. Now quit worrying so much about things, put a smile on that face and let's go enjoy the game!"

"You are wonderful, Henry."

"We can discuss marriage later."

Third quarter. Score was 20-17. The team that was behind had the ball and was driving. Henry found that the rich man wasn't such a bad guy and he enjoyed watching the game with him. He glanced back to where Lucinda was sitting. "Helga! What's with her?"

Helga broke her attention away from the game. "Oh! She tranced out. It's not serious, Henry. Let me wake her up. It sometimes happens to us." Helga glowed in her sixth month of pregnancy. Sure there were times when she was uncomfortable, but Henry had never seen a woman so happy in pregnancy.

Henry checked Lucinda's belly with his hand. "Baby's asleep."

"Baby needs sleep." Helga took Henry by the wrist and placed his hand on her own belly. "See? Mine's asleep too. Hmlee's a happy baby! Go watch the game! Lucy's okay."

Henry smiled, reassured by Helga's positive attitude. He received a quick kiss on the nose and the smiling face signaled him to go back to watching the game. He went back to the window and took his seat. He and everyone yelled their disappointment. The receiver dropped the ball in the end zone.

Helga sat down next to Lucinda to watch her. Lucinda seemed to be mouthing words. "Chmlee!" At least her voice didn't sound.

Oh no! Helga stood in front of Lucinda to shield her from view. Helga bent down and kissed Lucinda on her brow ridges. She shook her. Lucinda's eyes popped open. "Helga, what're you doing?"

Helga bent down close and whispered. "Let's talk Atlantean."

"He was there," whispered Lucinda in Atlantean.

"Let's go where we can talk in private. Some of these Earthlings know Atlantean."

"I see what you mean. We signed that contract with Berlitz. The books that teach the Atlantean language sell extremely well. Let's find the lady's room."

Helga helped Lucinda up and they quietly walked to the women's bathroom. A quick glance around, they were the only women in the room. "I nodded off, didn't I?"

"You nodded off for a few minutes. Are you getting enough sleep?"

"Well, sometimes it is hard. But I think I get enough sleep. When our little one is asleep. Now I remember. I had a dream. Chmlee was there. He was happy to see me, and he was ecstatic to see me with child. He hugged me and he kissed me. Felt my belly and grinned with joy. Told me he knew about your pregnancy, and that made him as happy as he has ever been. Then he told me to not let him stand in the way of my happiness. He said 'If you love him, marry him! You have my blessing! It'll all work out if you do the right thing.' Then he faded away and I called to him. Then you kissed my brow ridges to wake me up."

"How do you feel about this dream?"

"I do not know if it really was Chmlee who came to me. Or just a creation of my sleeping brain. Whether Chmlee really told me to marry Henry and blessed it, or it was just what I wanted him to say. I don't know what to do."

"Lchnsda, did Henry propose marriage to you?"

"He has been after me to marry him since we first found out I am carrying his child. He's on this Promise Keeper thing. But if I don't marry him, he can't keep any promises. The real problem, I am the one who is afraid of a commitment."

Helga laughed. "We fly through almost two *tibeeyon kepfats* of hard vacuum, from one Solar System to another. We carry nuclear weapons from Earth, HUGE nuclear weapons, bigger than any bombs we have ever built on Creation, snuggle up nice and close to a three dozen *kepfat* COMET, and explode the bomb in the comet! And you are afraid of a marriage?"

They laughed. "Space flight and nuclear bombs and comets don't bother me. But love, marriage, sex, pregnancy, and having a child frighten me more than anything. Helga, thank you. I love Henry, he is wonderful. I carry his child. I'll marry him."

They hugged very tightly, and then went out to the luxury box, glowing with happiness.

Lucinda did not tell Henry her decision right away. She wanted to wait until a private moment. Which they didn't have. They watched the end of the game. They then appeared at several receptions and parties. Finally, a flight back to Seattle.

The next day, Lucinda obtained a reservation for a window table at a waterfront restaurant in Seattle. They had a lovely dinner of seafood, looking out over Elliot Bay. No wine, in respect for her pregnancy. They could see the line of 'mechanical dinosaurs' on the port to the south. Big orange container loading cranes. They watched the Washington State Ferries cruise in and out of Colman Dock. "You seem very content today." commented Henry.

"I am very content. Henry, if you'll have me, I'll be your wife."

Henry smiled. He kissed her hand, and reached into his pocket. "I have been carrying this for the past several weeks."

She opened the little box. The ring is beautiful, a gold band with a large diamond surrounded by a dozen smaller stones. The small stones were a mixture of rubies, sapphires, emeralds, and amethysts for a rainbow of bright colors. Henry placed it on her finger. After the meal, they walked along the waterfront sidewalk. Even while wearing coats for the winter temperature of about 40 degrees, they danced and pranced. The Viaduct towered above them on one side, the docks extended out into the harbor on the other side. Like little children, they skipped along, going out on each dock that was open and looking out on the water. They danced a waltz on the plaza at the Waterfront Park, even though there was no music. They would steal a kiss, and laugh, crack a joke, sing a song, Henry would toss a dollar to a homeless man and wish him a good evening.

On a lark, they bought round trip passenger walk-on tickets for the ferry to Bainbridge Island just to ride the ship on the water. This time, Lucinda did not have to worry about the security arrangements of the Secret Service, she and her fiancé could simply enjoy the ride as regular people. When a deckhand found out that they had just decided to get married, he passed the news to the Pilothouse. They were outside on the passenger deck level, on the leading end of the ship, enjoying the wind. The cars were parked below them, the water glistened all around, clouds covered the sky. The deckhand tapped their shoulders and directed their attention to the windows of the Pilothouse. Hands waved at them, and they waved back. The ship's horn blew, and the other passengers applauded.

After they came back off the ferry in Seattle, Henry drove them toward the house the Creation women rented in Kent. It was just a few blocks from the clinic building Askelion rented and not far from the hospital at the bottom of the hill in the Valley.

As they passed the hospital, Lucinda suddenly cried out in pain. "What is it, Honey?"

"I don't know! It's my belly! The baby!" She screamed and Henry violated half of the Motor Vehicle Code getting their car into the Emergency Entrance of the hospital. He parked by the curb and raced to the doors.

"Better get the gurney! It's Lucinda Renuxler! Neanderthal woman! Five months pregnant! Screaming in pain! I don't know what it is!" The hospital people grabbed a gurney and raced to the car.

As they loaded Lucinda on to the gurney she held out her hand. "Henry! Take this! You know how to use it. Get the ship!"

Henry took the radio and spoke to the ship. "Get Meddi in Medical! It's Lchnsda! Something's wrong! Yeah, it's me, Henry Turnipseed."

"I'm here, Henry." It was Meddi Chumkun. "Exactly what happened?"

"Everything was fine. We ate seafood on the Seattle waterfront. We rode the ferry after that, it has been several hours, it can't be the food. We were driving back to the house, as we passed the hospital, Lchnsda suddenly screamed in pain. She thinks it's the baby! We got her into the Emergency Entrance of the hospital."

"The hospital has a helicopter pad?"

"Yeah, I see it. It's on the ground, not on a rooftop. You should be able to land the Shuttle there."

"Okay, we're on our way. Nesla will pilot the Shuttle. We should be down in a few minutes. I'm calling Askelion at the house. Neil Peace is there, he should be able to drive Ask over. Please clear the Emergency Entrance so Ask can get in."

"Yeah, okay. Lucy's in the hospital, emergency personnel are working on her. I'll park the car, tell Neil to deliver Dr. Lamakian to the Emergency Entrance."

"Neil! Wake up, you gotta drive me to the hospital!"

I opened my eyes. My body didn't want to move. "What's going on?"

"Henry just delivered Lchndsa to the Emergency Entrance. She was screaming in pain, might be her baby!"

I flew out of bed and threw on my clothes. Pulled on a pair of slippers. Got the car keys. "All right, Ask, are you ready to go?"

"Yes."

"Let's go. Into the Pontiac!" My '66, in five minutes I delivered her to the Emergency Entrance. "Just go, Ask. I'll park the car." As I drove over the parking lot, I saw the Shuttle land on the helicopter pad. After parking, I ran to the Emergency Entrance. The Creation physicians went in ahead of me, I found Henry and Nesla standing around. "How's she doing, Henry?"

"I don't know. She agreed to marry me."

"All right! Congratulations."

"We had a wonderful dinner. We walked along the waterfront, even rode the ferry. It was a wonderful date. We were so happy. There was nothing wrong with her! What if we lose the baby?"

515

Henry doesn't cry easily. Not as a kid, not in high school, not in all the time I've known him. I saw the tears on his face. "Henry, let's just sit down and wait. We haven't lost the baby yet. We can say a prayer."

We sat down, we prayed. Then to try to take Henry's mind off the worst that can happen, we asked him about their plans. He told us that the wedding would combine Henry's Christian beliefs, some Puyallup-Nisqually tradition, and Lucinda's Atlantean culture. Lucinda was wanting to remain on Earth to represent Creation interests when the *Neanderthal Return* heads back to Creation. It would be a long time before she ever goes back home, but her aging process is stopped. Henry thought it would be nice to have that treatment for himself, but they would have to go to Creation and live there. It was a decision they would make later, but hadn't yet.

Hours passed. Angela arrived with Helga. "The children are home, I called in a sitter. How are you all doing?"

We filled her in on what had happened so far. We waited.

It was the darkest hours of the early morning. A light rain fell outside. Askelion came out to us. She crouched down between us. She held my hand with one of her hands, and held Henry's hand with her other. Angela put her arm around Henry's shoulders and Nesla put her arm around mine. Helga positioned herself behind us and put her arms around both of us men.

"We lost the baby. Lchnsda should be all right."

"It was like when there is an incompatibility of Rh factors between mother and child." reported Meddi Chumkun. "There are antigens in Cro-Magnon blood that are not present in Neanderthal blood. The child inherited these antigens from his father. Even though the fetal blood in the placenta is kept separate from the mother's blood in the uterine wall, the antigens flow across. Lchnsda's system then created antibodies to the Cro-Magnon antigens from her child. Good thing we didn't pour Cro-Magnon blood into Lchnsda when she was shot. Lchnsda's immunity defense system may have affected the child. Our age-stopping treatments increase our ability to create antibodies. We found deterioration throughout the placenta, possibly caused by the antibodies. When it broke from the uterine wall, we lost the child and Lchnsda screamed in pain. That is what we know."

"Could we suppress the production of antibodies in a Neanderthal mother to allow her to bear a child with a Cro-Magnon father?" asked Captain Trviea Harsradich.

"That is possible. But it would take a great deal of research, we have to identify the exact Cro-Magnon antigens that generate the immune response in a Neanderthal woman."

"How are Lchnsda and Henry now?"

"They were both emotionally devastated by the loss of their child. But they're bearing up, they still love each other. We reassured them it wasn't the seafood they ate. But I don't know if they will get married now. We cannot allow Lchnsda to chance another pregnancy until we get to the bottom of this. We have taken steps to shut down her menstrual process. Until then, we cannot allow her to make love, at least not vaginal intercourse, with a man. Which is tough, they kiss a lot to comfort each other."

"If carrying a child with Cro-Magnon antigens in its blood can cause a Neanderthal women to make these antibodies, what is the effect of sexual contact with a Cro-Magnon man? We all have been making love with the men we meet."

"I know. We tested Helga's blood, she has made a lot of love with the men, at least before we made her pregnant. No antibodies detected. Lchnsda blood is swimming with them. We took the risk, had to, of placing a videoscope in Helga's womb. Her child is extremely healthy, the placenta shows no signs of deterioration."

"The gene that creates the antigen in the Cro-Magnon blood is not located in the Y chromosome."

"Apparently not. We have the entire medical research community on Earth working on this. We need to identify the antigen that we are reacting to. We need to figure out a way of suppressing that reaction, or we could literally be allergic to sexual contact with Cro-Magnon men, or at least incapable of interbreeding with them. We need to determine if this antigen is present in the semen. We need to find out if contact with us is creating antibodies in the Cro-Magnon men. We don't dare transfuse blood across the Racial line. We need to perform a lot of research on all of this."

"Thank you, Meddi."

"Well, good news, ladies and gentlemen." Askelion was actually cheerful. The strain caused by the miscarriage took a toll on her. She often climbed into bed after a 16 hour day at the lab. Then she would wake up without enough sleep, grab a snack bar and go back to work. Every Neanderthal woman contributed samples of blood, urine, saliva, and tissue for analysis. Every Cro-Magnon who had been on board the *Neanderthal Return* has also contributed samples. And a set of samples came from a control group of Cro-Magnons who had not been in contact with the Neanderthal women.

"We can sure use some good news." commented Lucinda, whose spirits have recovered some in the last few weeks. "Although it certainly helps to see Helga so happy, healthy, and just HUGE!" We clapped our hands and cheered.

"Yeah, I was scared for a while there." affirmed Helga. "But I feel so much better now!" She proudly placed her hands on her now magnificent belly. "Oooooh! He kicks so good! I think he's practicing to play on Atlantis's World Cup Soccer Team. And that is Hmlee Trvlakian! Scoring the winning goal against Argentina!"

"So what's your good news, Ask?"

"The tests show that Lchnsda is the only one of us who developed antibodies to Cro-Magnon blood. The rest of us did not react that way to our physical contact with the Cro-Magnon men. And it appears that none of the Cro-Magnons have reacted to contact with Neanderthal women by developing antibodies."

"All right, so we can continue to make love!"

"Yes, that is correct." Cheering. Hand clapping. "But no blood transfusions. If we put a pint of Cro-Magnon blood into a Neanderthal, she'll develop antibodies to the Cro-Magnon antigen, and we don't know what the consequences will be. We don't want to perform that experiment. Nor will we take the chance of putting a unit of Neanderthal blood into a Cro-Magnon. So we'll need to keep separate blood supplies, clearly marked to avoid an accidental crossracial transfusion."

"Have we identified the antigen in the Cro-Magnon blood that your bodies react to by creating the antibody?"

"We have identified two candidate antigens. They are complicated organic chemical compounds that flow freely in the plasma. These compounds are present in every Cro-Magnon blood sample we have tested. They are not present in any Neanderthal blood sample. That alone makes them suspect, but it doesn't prove that either is the gremlin we're searching for. These compounds are not present in any of the semen samples, so we do not have a problem with sexual intercourse." Applause. "Nor are they present in saliva, so feel free to kiss. They are present in urine, the kidneys flushing the excess."

"Helga's looking great! What's her prognosis?"

"Her what? Oh! Yeah. Earth physicians use that word a lot. All this time I thought it was a piece of anatomy that you don't touch without her permission!" Laughter. "Helga is perfect. Hmlee is perfect. Bone structure is looking Neanderthal, though in a child, it's not as noticeable as in an adult. He's far enough along now that if there's an emergency, we can pull him and take care of him as a preemie. We're keeping Helga right around here. Where we can get her to the hospital stat. They let us keep a locker at their maternity ward for our equipment, including a supply of Neanderthal blood compatible with Helga. But of course, it's best we let the child stay in the womb the full term."

Later, I spoke with Lucinda and Henry. "So what are you guys going to do now?"

"We're waiting until it's time for the ship to head back to Creation." responded Lucinda. "They are almost ready now. If I choose to stay on Earth as a diplomat to represent Creation interests, we'll get married."

"If Lchnsda chooses to go and I choose to go with her, we'll get married." confirmed Henry.

"But if I go and he stays, we'll not burden each other with a legal bond of matrimony."

"Whatever you choose to do, I wish you both the best of luck."

"Thank you. And we wish you the best of luck too."

Contrviea Tiknika briefed Trviea Harsradich on the condition of the ship. "We are almost ready to head back to Creation. Repairs and upgrades are within a few days of completion."

"Excellent. We will need to schedule a few test flights around this Solar System. We will have to move at least three *hekt beeyon kepfats* from the Mother Star and the larger planets, Jupiter and Saturn, before we test the Translocation Module."

"The Earthlings will be observing us closely with their telescopes and radio antennas."

"Of course, they want to know how our *warp drive* works." They spoke in Atlantean, but used the English phrase, 'warp drive' as the euphemism for the Translocation Module. "Aligning that is the all important and extremely complicated part. The computer software that controls the Translocation Module is enough to blow Bill Gates' mind. Marla Syferkrip would eat those Microsoft code slammers for lunch. A mistake in her programming could put us in the center of one of these stars."

"Instant char broil. Well done in a hurry! Or we could come out near one of the Orion Belt stars. Long walk home."

"Long walk indeed. Look at all of the good will messages we have on file from Earth. More coming in every minute. From schoolchildren. From presidents and prime ministers, and from everyone in between. From all of the nations, in all of their languages. In voice and print. In song and poetry. They express their desire for peace with all of the nations of Creation, would like to meet Gracians. We even have such messages for the lucies on Janedye!"

They giggled. "When the lucies evolve brains big enough to understand speech, we'll pass these messages on to them. Every Earth nation is promising to respect our sovereignty over Planet Creation. They hedge a bit, but I think they will respect our sovereignty over Janedye and all of the planets of the Three Suns."

"They better! Unless the laser cannon defense system has fallen into disrepair. But I don't think there will ever be a problem, at least not from Earth. Look at all of the stories and songs they now tell of Operation Rainbow. An Epic effort, though it did not seem that way to us."

"It was dangerous, exploding nuclear bombs in comets. And they honor your daughter. And hope you can have another one."

"Yeah." Trviea smiled. "I would like that. Here is one from a schoolboy in New Zealand, 11 Earth years old!"

"Eight Creation years."

Trviea read it in English. "Good luck, peace and freedom for all of the women of Planet

Creation. Thank you for helping us move the comet! Do not weep for Sorby Mishlakian, for she sits at the right hand of God and gives us all of her blessings." Trviea's voice broke, but maintained composure. "She is the brightest angel in Heaven. As bright as Mother Teresa. May you have happiness, peace, prosperity, a *beeyon* of children and a *tibeeyon* of descendants. May both of our Planets work together in friendship and explore the Universe. May we all be friends forever."

"Here's one that says *Vaya con dios*. That's Spanish, I believe."

"Yes, Andemona told me that means 'Go with God'. Americans speak English, but they say it a lot. The Spanish speaking people also say it."

"You think this will help the women back home accept our contact with Earth?"

"They will have to. No more radio silence on the side of the Planet toward Earth. They know about us, now we can have radio and television stations broadcasting the way they do on Earth."

"Well, I reckon a couple of months of test driving, then we head on home for real."

A third woman came into the room. "Trviea, we have a call from Kent, Washington. It's about Helga."

"Trviea here. What's happening?"

"This is Askelion Lamakian. We have taken her to the hospital. She's in labor. Her cervix is dilated 5 centimeters, or two *tig-its*. Contractions every four minutes or five *linits*."

"Thank you, Askelion." It was April 17, the child was due. Trviea turned on the public address and announced to all of the women on board the *Neanderthal Return* and the Cro-Magnons hired to help with the overhaul. "Helga Trvlakian is in labor. The baby is due. Be prepared to come to the Viewing Lounge for an announcement."

"It has been ten hours now." commented Angela Peace. "I'm sure glad my deliveries didn't take that long."

"I'm glad too." I told my ex-wife.

"You should be. I was cursing your name with every contraction. But I forgave you when I held each of our children."

"I'm glad to hear that. Oh man! This is taking long. Lucinda, could there be a complication from your great age?"

"Possible. Helga is about 176 Earth years old, I am about 173. We stopped the aging process, but who knows what isn't quite like a twenty-five year old? But I think this is just a long labor. Don't worry about Helga. We women are tough! Aren't we, Angela?"

"We sure are." Angela grabbed my hair and pulled it gently. "I survived being married to THIS guy!"

We laughed. "I am impressed!" chuckled Lucinda. "Now I know you're tough!"

There was a crowd of us. Len Taylor, Henry Turnipseed, Lucinda Renuxler, myself. Police kept the hundreds of other people back, especially the paparazzi. Angela came with the children. After a few hours, she sent them home with the sitter.

We now had plenty of money between the two of us, it no longer mattered that the state's child support agency is torn to shreds by the enforcement of the Antipeonage Act ordered by the President. As for those less fortunate than us, many of the women found their former husbands far more willing to help out voluntarily. The unmarried ones were marrying the fathers of their children in record numbers. It is amazing what happened when we removed the specter of impossible support orders, abusive and arrogant family law commissioners and judges, license suspension, contempt proceedings, and financial ruin. Peonage really is a crime! Some fathers didn't come forward and take responsibility, and some of the mothers didn't want them to.

Couldn't do anything about these cases anyway. The Constitution. Not just the Supreme Law of the Land, but a damn good idea! We ought to try it more often!

The hours continued to pass. Angie sat on my lap and kissed me. "You realize we aren't suppose to do that anymore?" I reminded her.

"I know, but so what!" I gave up and put my arms around her waist and let her sit on me as we waited.

Then we were summoned to the recovery room.

"Everyone," called Captain Trviea Harsradich, "please wrap up what you are doing and come to the Viewing Lounge. There is an announcement." Her tone was flat, like a poker player.

Helga was extremely tired. But awake. She was in the wheelchair, and I pushed it. Angela, Lucinda, Len, and Henry walked with us, as did Askelion and Meddi. We went into a room that had a camera set up.

In the Viewing Lounge the women gathered. They held each other. Arms around waists and shoulders. The Cro-Magnons, of both genders, were there with them. Their attention was focused on several large video screens. Out the windows was the West Coast of the North American continent. Through the bands of clouds could be seen Vancouver Island and the British Columbia fjords, Puget Sound, the Columbia River and the volcanoes of the Cascade Mountains.

We wheeled Helga into view of the camera. From speakers we heard the gasps, the screams, the crying, the applause, the cheers, the prayers, and every intense emotion imaginable. Hmlee slept in Helga's arms, strong and beautiful, eight pounds two ounces, thick blonde hair on his tiny head, a head that is Neanderthal in shape, though we could barely tell. He opened his mouth and yawned.

Creation Numbers and Units of Measure

NUMBERS

The numerical system of Creation is Base Twelve. The zero is represented by a dot, similar to modern Arabic. One through eleven are represented by single symbols.

Their number twelve looks like our number ten, a vertical line for one followed by a zero dot. 144 is represented with a one followed by two zero dots and so on for powers of twelve. The table shows the Atlantean words for powers of twelve.

Our 18 is twelve and six. 23 is twelve and eleven. 24 is called a word analogous to twenty. One hundred and twenty is "tenty". One hundred and thirty two is "eleventy".

12^2	= 144	*Hekt*	Because their zero is represented by a dot, they use a wavy vertical line as a dozenal point. 1/144 is called a *heker*, 1/1728 is called a *kechter*.
12^3	= 1728	*Kecht*	
12^6	= 2,985,984	*Beeyon*	
12^9	= 5,159,780,352	*Enbeeyon*	
12^{12}	= 8,916,100,448,256	*Tibeeyon*	

ANGLES

Creation Neanderthals split the circle into 36 dozen, or 432 parts each called a *deem*. Each *deem* is split into 72 *linits*, each *linit* of angle divided into 72 *prelates*.

432 *deem*s = 360 degrees = one circle

1 *deem* = 72 *linit*s = 5184 *prelate*s = 5/6 degree = 50 minutes

1 *linit* = 72 *prelate*s = 25/36 minute = 41 2/3 seconds

1 *prelate* = 125/216 second

On Creation one *linit* of latitude is one half of a *kepfat*, see next page. The circumference of Creation is 15,552 *kepfats* or 25,040 miles, a little larger than Earth.

TIME

The Face Mountain aliens set the rotation of Planet Creation to match that of Earth. The Creation day is thus very close in length to the Earth day. The Creation Neanderthals divide their day into 24 hours. Their hour is divided into 72 *linits,* each *linit* divided into 72 *prelates*. It takes 497.5 days for Creation to complete one orbit of Alpha Centauri A. The Creation calendar years alternate between 497 and 498 days. Earth Year 2000 is about Creation Year 2585 in Base Twelve.

1 hour = 72 *linit*s = 5184 *prelate*s

1 *linit* = 72 *prelate*s = 5/6 minute = 50 seconds

1 *prelate* = 25/36 second

LENGTH AND LAND AREA

Living in moderate and warm climates for 50,000 years, Creation Neanderthals evolved longer arms and legs than their European ancestors. With body dimensions similar to ours, they came up with units of length similar to, but a little different, than units used in English speaking nations.

1 *keetig-it* = 1/1728 *tig-it* = 570.6 microinches = 14.49 microns

1 *tig-it* = 0.986 inch = 25.04 millimeters

12 *tig-its* = 1 *pote* = 0.986 foot = 11.83 inches = 30.05 centimeters

3 *potes* = 1 *treefat* = 0.986 yard = 35.5 inches = 90.16 centimeters

5 *potes* = 1 *pfat* = 4.93 feet = 59.16 inches = 150.2 centimeters

6 *potes* = 1 *chmfat* = 0.986 fathom = 71 inches = 180.3 centimeters

1728 *pfats* = 1 *kepfat* = 8,519 feet = 1.61 miles = 2,596.6 meters

Pote is Atlantean for foot. *Fat* is the Atlantean word for reach. *Tree* is Atlantean for half. *Chm* is Atlantean for full or whole. Full reach is both arms stretched out, a fathom. Half reach is a yard. *Pfat* means foot reach, a two step pace. A *kepfat* is a *kecht* of *pfats*.

For land measure Creation Neanderthals defined the *plowdat* as a unit of area that is 12 *pfats* wide and 144 *pfats* long.

1 *plowdat* = 0.964 acre = 0.39 hectare

LIQUID MEASURES

The *dollop* is the volume of a cylinder one *tig-it* in height and one *tig-it* in diameter. The *shlopon*, which is 1728 *dollops*, is the volume of a cylinder one *pote* in height and one *pote* in diameter. For this table, we use U. S. gallons, pints, and fluid ounces.

1 *dollop* = 0.417 fluid ounce = 12.34 milliliters

12 *dollop*s = 1 *glup* = 5.006 fluid ounces = 148 milliliters

12 *glup*s = 1 *jug* = 60.07 fluid ounces = 3.75 pints = 1.78 liters

12 *jug*s = 1 *shlopon* = 5.64 gallons = 45 pints = 21.3 liters

TEMPERATURE

After thermometers were invented on Creation, they set the triple point of water at 12 *deems*. They set 144 *deems* at the normal body temperature of a human being. They set Absolute Zero at -974 and 9/12 *deems*

12 *deems* = 0.01 Celsius = 32.018 Fahrenheit

144 *deems* = 37 Celsius = 98.6 Fahrenheit

-974.75 *deems* = -273.15 Celsius = -459.67 Fahrenheit

WEIGHT

The weight of a flat cylinder of pure gold of the standard isotope mix, in face centered cubic crystallization that is one *tig-it* in diameter and one twelfth of a *tig-it* in height is a *coilon*. Twelve of these is a *dollon*, because it is a *dollop* of gold. 1728 *dollons* is a *gund*. For this table we use Avoirdupois pounds and ounces, and the grain defined as 1/7000 pound.

1728 *beecoilons* = 1 *keecoilon*

1 *keecoilon* = 0.0004 ounce = 0.177 grains = 11.48 milligrams

1728 *keecoilons* = 1 *coilon* = 0.7 ounce = 306 grains = 19.8 grams

12 *coilons* = 1 *dollon* = 8.4 ounces = 0.525 pounds = 238 grams

1728 *dollons* = 1 *gund* = 906.77 pounds = 411.3 kilograms

GRAVITY

Gravity on Creation is about 15 and 9/12 *potes* per *prelate* squared. This is equal to about 32.2 feet per second squared or 9.815 meters per second squared. This is their standard gravity for the purpose of defining their *dollon* of force. One standard Creation gravity is about 1.00087 standard Earth gravity.

FORCE

The *dollyal* is the force that will accelerate one *dollon* of mass one *pote* per *prelate* per *prelate*. 15.75 *dollyals* is a *dollon* of force or weight. Because the difference in gravity is so slight, one *dollon* of force is 0.525 pounds of force or 2.34 newtons.

WORK, ENERGY, POWER

The *pote-dollon* is the unit of energy or work. It is defined the same as the Earth foot-pound. The *pote-dollon* per *prelate* is used for both electrical and mechanical power. The conversion ratios are:

1 *pote-dollon* = 0.518 foot-pound = 0.702 joule

1 *pote-dollon* per *prelate* = 0.746 foot-pounds per second = 1.011 watt

About the Author

The author has lived all of his life in the State of Washington. He is an engineer with experience in the aerospace industry. Having experienced the pain of divorce and the joy of fatherhood, he looks after his two sons as best as he can. They are doing great and their father is proud of them.

Printed in the United States
By Bookmasters